7.95

69 2-24-69

DATE DUE

MAR 15 1993	
OCT 2 0 1993	
FEB 7 1994	
APR 2 9 1999	

DEMCO, INC. 38-2931

THE COLLECTED SHORT STORIES OF

CONRAD AIKEN

THE COLLECTED SHORT STORIES OF
Conrad Aiken

PREFACE BY MARK SCHORER

THE WORLD PUBLISHING COMPANY

CLEVELAND AND NEW YORK

Published by The World Publishing Company

2231 West 110th Street, Cleveland 2, Ohio

Published simultaneously in Canada by

Nelson, Foster & Scott Ltd.

Library of Congress Catalog Card Number: 60-10537

3wp67

CONTENTS

PREFACE BY MARK SCHORER

Recently a letter appeared in one of the literary reviews that reminded its editors that we have in the United States at least one writer who may still appropriately be called a man of letters, and the name was Conrad Aiken. It is curious how, year after year for more than four decades now, general readers and editors alike have *had* to be reminded of that name, which does indeed support an achievement that, in its brilliant distinction and, more than that, in its scope, makes Conrad Aiken so much more than a writer alone. He has the range of the literary master: the beautiful bulk of his poetry in all its formal splendor and variety; literary essays of pioneering quality; one of the most extraordinary autobiographies in the language; four novels, at least two of which— *Great Circle* and *King Coffin*—must endure; a play; more than forty short stories.

If the entire work of Conrad Aiken demonstrates this mastery of a range possessed by few modern writers, the forty-one short stories that are here collected demonstrate a range of mood and method, within the scope of the single form, that is almost as surprising; yet all of them, like the whole body of his work, are stamped with the mark of his imagination, and could have been written by Conrad Aiken alone.

In that complex imagination, there is a prominent strain of rather bemused irony that, when he gives it free rein, produces stories that are essentially comic, even rather light-hearted, with a satiric edge that cuts into a human foible or a paradox of personality or a turn of fate's screw, cuts deftly, delicately, without either the ritual air of major surgery or the thrust of passionate involvement. Such stories are "No, No, Go Not to Lethe," "The Necktie," "West End," "O How She Laughed!" and a good many others. They seem to say, with an air of the literary shrug, "Well, there it is. What do you think? Odd, isn't it?" Or, "Queer, isn't it, although surely he had it coming?" Or, "Amusing?" Yet even in these stories there is usually another strain, a note struck off from the taut strings of the stretched nerves, something sharp, shrill or somber, sinister, or mockingly morbid, an echo out of psychic chaos. Think only, for example, of that quite alarming hero of "No, No, Go Not to Lethe," whose ambition it is to enfold and paralyze others in the coils of his observation of them without ever himself becoming in the least involved. It is a comic story, but the laughter seems to come eerily up from the bottom of a very deep and a very old well.

This is, of course, the note that characterizes the most splendid and the best known of Conrad Aiken's short stories, those stories in which he moves from the mundane into the mysterious, into hysteria, horror, hallucination, phobia, compulsion, dream, death, and, more often than not, back again into the mundane. The sudden penetration into the shadows of consciousness, a veil surprisingly pulled back and dropped again, something beyond our perception perceived in it, a mythical beast suddenly gazing curiously up at us from the shrubbery at the end of our own well-kept garden: these are the gestures that are made by stories like "Silent Snow, Secret Snow" and "Mr. Arcularis" and many another. But let us consider one of the stories that is less well known.

"Life Isn't a Short Story" ought to be among the first documents in the demonstration materials of all people who profess to "teach" the writing of fiction, and among the instructional materials of all people who wish to learn to do it. It is about a story writer who "had run out of ideas; he had used them all; he was feeling as empty as a bath-tub and as blue as an oyster." This drudge of the imagination is having his breakfast—sitting in the window of a white-tiled restaurant, staring rather vacantly out into a busy city street, suddenly catching sight of a woman who might, if she were plumper, serve as the physical model for the woman in a story he is thinking about: for he isn't, after all, it seems, quite empty.

The story. The seed of the story had been planted in his mind as, passing through the lounge of a theater, he overheard phrases of a greeting—*"as I live and breathe!"* and *"in the flesh!"* I am *alive* and *you are alive;* these phrases translated themselves in his mind, and that, alive and not alive, was, he saw, the difference between life and a short story, even as he thought of his character, Gladys, a plump, commonplace creature who cannot tolerate such clichés, so plump and commonplace, any more readily than she can tolerate her simple and unrefined husband. So, sitting in the restaurant window, he imagines the proper town for Gladys to live in (Fitchburg, Massachusetts, seems right), imagines her apartment, imagines her story, which is the story of her intolerable marriage. Meanwhile, a horse-drawn laundry wagon has pulled up in front of the window, and the story writer's eye rests on the dejected horse, beaten by rain, while the story, through all its grimy fatalities, grows in his presumably disengaged, vacantly staring mind. When it reaches its climax, we know not only that the whole, dreary life of the street outside, bleary and rain-soaked, has been assimilated into the atmosphere of the life of Gladys and her husband, but we know also, as the writer does *not* know, any more than Gladys knows, that her poor old drone of a husband is the horse that pulls the laundry wagon. With their identification, the story is finished. Then we follow the horse up the street. "What did he think about, as he plodded from one dirty restaurant to another, one hotel to another, carrying towels? Probably nothing at all; certainly no such sentimental thing as a green meadow, nor anything so ridiculous as a story about living and breathing. It was enough, even if one was a slave, to live and breathe. For life, after all, isn't a short story."

Life isn't a short story because life, that spavined hack, keeps going on its rounds and never meets a climax; but a short story is life because, no matter where it may go all through its middle, it begins in life and it ends there, and if we look twice, we will see that, through that extraordinary process of imaginative osmosis whereby the details of life are lifted up into the patterns of art, its middle, too, is in large part the street outside the real window. A story by Conrad Aiken, in the characteristically fine middle, seems to rear up on its hind legs and throw its head into white clouds and among patterned stars, or it seems to race down into abysses of peculiar horror and shrill alarm, but all the time, poor creature (and the poor creatures that make it up), it is out there in the street, stodgy in the rain.

At the same time, there was the awful commonplaceness of the two phrases, the cheapness of them, the vulgarity— they were as old as the hills, and as worn; æons of weather and æons of handshake lay upon them; one witnessed, in the mere hearing of them, innumerable surprised greetings, innumerable mutual congratulations on the mere fact of being still alive. The human race seemed to extend itself backwards through them, in time, as along a road— if one pursued the thought one came eventually to a vision of two small apes peering at each other round the cheeks of a cocoanut and making a startled noise that sounded like *"yoicks!"* Or else, one simply saw, in the void, one star passing another, with no vocal interchange at all, nothing but a mutual exacerbation of heat. . . . It was very puzzling.

Puzzling, indeed, since it all starts in the lounge of the Orpheum, with a couple of portly blondes, and then at once loops out into space and history and mystery and the perfect terror of human experience as it plods through its generic hysteria, most of the time not knowing where it is, whether in the rainy street or in the stifled scream, when it is always in fact in both.

This is a story by Conrad Aiken: a horror all wrapped in an actuality, a fantasy all rooted and real, all rooted in a real detail. "For the most part, this companion seemed to be nothing but a voice and a wing—an enormous jagged black wing, soft and drooping like a bat's; he had noticed veins in it." *He had noticed veins in it.* If one could define the rhetorical mystery of this sentence, of this juxtaposition of the mad anatomy and the graphic physiology, one would probably have defined the effect of Mr. Aiken's fiction.

Just as the structure of these stories characteristically develops in the effort of the material to assert a reality beyond or below its mundane shape, so their drama characteristically arises within an individual mind as it struggles to break over the edge of its own limitations. This whole considerable body of fiction, long and short, has, for this reason, a central core of formal as well as psychological concern, an implicit, primary unity that marks it over and over as the product of this imagination and no other, as the work of this author. In one story, at least, the implicit becomes the explicit. "Gehenna" has as its protagonist an urban Everyman ("Smith, or Jones, or Robinson, or whatever his name happened to be") who reflects at the outset, "How easily . . . our little world can go to pieces! And incidentally, of course, the great world . . ." and then contemplates the imminence in the materials of consciousness of that disorganization of reality that is madness. But is that disorganization any less real than the organization which it has dispelled?

In an instant it will be as if I had stepped through this bright cobweb of appearance on which I walk with such apparent security, and plunged into a chaos of my own; for that chaos will be as intimately and recognizably my own, with its Smith-like disorder, as the present world is my own, with its Smith-like order. Here will be all the appurtenances of my life, every like and dislike, every longing or revulsion, from the smallest to the greatest; all the umbrellas—so to speak—of my life, all the canceled postage stamps and burnt matches, the clipped fingernails, love letters, calendars, and sunrises; but all of them interchanged and become (by change) endowed with demonic power. At a step, I shall have fallen into a profound and perhaps termless Gehenna which will be everywhere nothing but Smith. Only to the name of Smith will the umbrella-winged demons of this chaos answer.

This possibility of the altered kaleidoscope of being and the further possibility of altering that kaleidoscope by an act of will fascinates Smith—or Jones or Robinson. "Perhaps I could achieve this gradually," he thinks, "and step by step, just as I pace to and fro across the four rugs from Persia which cover the floor; item by item I would tear down the majestic fiction which is at present myself and the world, and item by item build up another. Exactly as one can stare at a word until it become meaningless, I can begin to stare at the world." In his bathroom, he stares at a door-knob, and through a kind of self-hypnosis, he allows the process to get under way, only, at the last moment, through another effort of will, to rip himself out of this new prison that his consciousness is already building. He goes to bed and dreams of "a small glass aquarium, square, of the sort in which goldfish are kept."

I observe without surprise that there is water in one half of it but not in the other. And in spite of the fact that there is no partition, this water holds itself upright in its own half of the tank, leaving the other half empty. More curious than this, however, is the marine organism which lies at the bottom of the water. It looks, at first glance, like a loaf of bread. But when I lean down to examine it closely, I see that it is alive, that it is sentient, and that it is trying to move. One end of it lies very close to that point at which the water ends and the air begins; and now I realize that the poor thing is trying, and trying desperately, to get into the air. Moreover, I see that this advancing surface is as if sliced off and raw; it is horribly sensitive; and suddenly, appalled, I realize that the whole thing is simply—consciousness. It is trying to escape from the medium out of which it was created. If only it could manage this—! But I know that it never will; it has already reached, with its agonized sentience, as far as it can; it stretches itself forward, with minute and pathetic convulsions, but in vain; and suddenly I am so horrified at the notion of a consciousness which is pure suffering, that I wake up. . . . The clocks are striking two.

It is at this margin, at this edge, where, without barrier, the water of daily human experience stands against the wall of air that is outside it—it is at this margin that Conrad Aiken's fiction is written. (His extraordinary novels develop and amazingly sustain the central concern of the stories.) And thus his fiction asks its great questions: "Was the North Star hung at the world's masthead only in order that on a certain day in a certain year an ugly wallpaper should be glued to the walls of this room?" Human tragedy exists because of the suffering that must inhere in a consciousness that can ask the question at all. It persists, with life itself, because the clocks in the city do strike, and with their reverberations, draw the invisible circles around that consciousness, saving it for its order, yes, but in the very act of saving it, re-committing it to an area within which questions must go on being asked.

We have, I think, no other body of fiction like this—so centrally coherent, its very coherence derived from a contemplation of the intransigence of that incoherence that lies scattered on all sides of us, and above and below, and, worst of all, within. But also best of all. For rationality would be a poor and shriveled thing if it did not have all that other to nourish no less than to alarm it. As life would be if it did not have the basic resources that can make it into art.

THE COLLECTED SHORT STORIES OF

CONRAD AIKEN

Miss Rooker dreamed that she was on board the *Falcon* in Marblehead Harbor. Dr. Fish was uncorking a bottle of champagne, contorting his face grotesquely, his gray mustache pushed up so that it seemed to envelop his red nose. Dr. Harrington, tall and thin in his white flannels, stood beside the gramophone, singing with wide open mouth, his eyes comically upturned towards the low cabin ceiling; his white flannel arm was round Miss Paine's waist. As he sang he seemed to draw her tighter and tighter against his side, his face darkened, Miss Paine began to scream. The cork came out with a loud pop, froth poured onto the napkin. Miss Rooker held out her glass to be filled, and a great blob of champagne froth fell upon the front of her skirt. It was her white duck skirt which buttoned all the way down with large mother-of-pearl buttons. "Oh—Dr. Harrington!" she cried. Dr. Fish reached down a hand to wipe it away—she was transfixed with delight and horror when instead he unbuttoned one of the buttons, at the same time bringing his mustached face very close to hers and intensely smiling. She had no clothes on, and he was touching her knee. Dr. Harrington sang louder, Miss Paine screamed louder, the gramophone cawed and squealed, and now Dr. Fish was uncorking one bottle after another—pop! pop! pop! She sat in the stern of the tender, trailing one hand in the water of the dark harbor, as they rowed rapidly away from the yacht. Dr. Harrington, slightly drunk, was driving rather recklessly—from side to side of the Boulevard went the car, and Miss Rooker and Dr. Fish were tumbled together; he pinched her side. She would be late—they would be late—long after midnight. The sky was already growing light. Birds began singing. A sparrow, rather large, ridiculously large, opened his mouth wide and started shouting in through her window: "Bring! Bring! Bring! Bring! Bring! . . ." She woke at this. A sparrow was chirping noisily in the wild cherry tree outside her window. She was in Duxbury. It was a hot morning in summer. She was "on a case"—Mrs. Oldkirk. Mrs. Oldkirk would be waking and would want her glass of hot milk. Perhaps Mrs. Oldkirk had been calling? She listened. No. Nothing but the sparrows and the crickets. But it was time to get up. Why on earth should she be dreaming, after all this time, of Dr. Harrington and Dr. Fish? Five years ago. Possibly because Mr. Oldkirk reminded her of Dr. Fish. . . . Brushing her black hair before the mirror, and looking into her dark-pupiled brown eyes, she felt melancholy. She was looking very well—very pretty. She sang softly, so as not to disturb Mrs. Oldkirk in the next room: *"And when I told—them—how beautiful you were —they wouldn't be—lieve—me; they wouldn't be—lieve—me."* Delicious, a deep cold bath on a sultry morning like this; and today the bathing would be good, a high tide about twelve o'clock. Mr. Oldkirk and Miss Lavery would be going in. . . . Miss Lavery was Mrs. Oldkirk's cousin. . . . Well, it really was disgraceful, the way they behaved! Pretending to "keep house" for Mrs. Oldkirk! Did anybody else notice it? And Mr. Oldkirk was very nice-looking; she liked his sharp blue eyes, humorous. *"And—when—I—told—them—how beautiful you were——"*

Mrs. Oldkirk was already awake, her hands clasped under her braided hair, her bare white elbows tilted upward.

"Good morning, Miss Rooker," she said languidly.

"Good morning, Mrs. Oldkirk. Did you sleep well?"

"No, it was too hot . . . far too hot . . . even without a sheet. The ice melted in the lemonade. It was disgusting."

"Will you want your hot milk this morning?"

"Oh, yes—certainly. What time is it, Miss Rooker?"

"Just seven-thirty."

All the windows in the house were open, as Miss Rooker passed through the hall and down the stairs. The sea-wind sang softly through the screens, sea-smells and pine-smells, and the hot morning was like a cage full of birds. "Bring! Bring!" the sparrow had shouted—remarkable dream—and here she was, bringing, bringing hot milk on a hot morning, bringing hot milk to a lazy neurotic woman (rather pretty) who was no more an invalid than she was herself. Why did she want to stay in bed? Why did she want a nurse? A slave would have done as well—there wasn't the slightest occasion for medical knowledge. The massage, of course. But it was very queer. There was something wrong. And Miss Lavery and Mr. Oldkirk were always talking together till past midnight, talking, talking!

Hilda was lighting the fire in the kitchen range, her pale face saturated with sleep, her pale hair untidy. The green shades were still down over the windows, and the kitchen had the air of an aquarium, the oak floor scrubbed white as bone.

"Good morning, Hilda—how was the dance last night?"

"Lovely. . . . But oh, sweet hour, how sleepy I am!"

"You look it. You'll lose your beauty."

"Oh, go on!"

The fire began crackling in the range; small slow curls of blue smoke oozed out round the stove lids. Miss Rooker went to the ice-chest, took out the bottle of milk. Holding it by the neck, she returned upstairs. On the way she saw Mary setting the breakfast table; she, too, looked pale and sleepy, had been to the dance. *"And when I told—them—"* She poured the creamy milk into the aluminum saucepan and lit the alcohol lamp. Then she went to the window and watched the sea-gulls circling over the naked hot mud flats. Seals sat in rows. On the beach, fringed with eel-grass, near at hand, Mr. Oldkirk's green dory was pulled far up, and rested amid gray matted seaweed.

By the time she had given Mrs. Oldkirk her hot milk, bathed the patient's face and hands and wrists (beautiful wrists, languid and delicate) with cold water, and combed her hair, breakfast was half over. . . . Mr. Oldkirk, leaning forward on one elbow, was regarding Miss Lavery with a look humorous and intent. Iced grapefruit.

"Ah, here's Miss Rooker," said Mr. Oldkirk, glancing up at her quizzically, and pulling back her chair with outstretched hand. . . . "Good morning, Miss Rooker. Sit down. We have a problem for you to solve."

Miss Lavery was wearing her pale green satin morning gown. It was becoming to her—oh, quite disgustingly—set off, somehow her long, blue eyes, lazy and liquid, tilted up at the corners a little like a Chinaman's. But far too negligee. The idea of coming down to breakfast like that—with Mr. Oldkirk!

"I'm no good at riddles. Ask me an easy one."

"Oh, this is extremely simple," Mr. Oldkirk said, with just a hint of malice, "merely a question of observation—observation of one's self."

Miss Lavery thought this was very funny—she gave a snort of laughter, and stifled it behind her napkin. Really! thought Miss Rooker—when she leaned forward like that!—with that low, loose morning gown! Scandalous.

"You're good at observing, Miss Rooker—tell us, how long does a love affair last—a normal, you know, ordinary one, I mean?"

"Well, upon my soul!" cried Miss Rooker. "Is *that* what's worrying you?"

"Oh, yes, poor man, he's terribly worried about it." Miss Lavery snickered, eying Mr. Oldkirk with a gleaming mock derision. "He's been wrangling with me, all breakfast through, about it."

"Seriously, Miss Rooker"—he pretended to ignore Miss Lavery—"it's an important scientific question. And of course a charming young lady like you has had *some* experience of—er—the kind?"

Miss Rooker blushed. She was annoyed, she could not have said exactly why. She was annoyed with both of them: just slightly. Glancing at Mr. Oldkirk (yes, he certainly looked like Dr. Fish) she said shortly:

"You want to know too much."

Mr. Oldkirk opened his eyes. "Oh!" he said—then again, in a lower tone, "Oh." He frowned at his plate, breathed densely through his grayish mustache. . . . Then, to Miss Lavery, who had suddenly become rather frigid, and was looking at Miss Rooker just a little impudently:

"Any more coffee, Helen? . . ."

"Not a drop."

"Damn." He got up, slow and tall.

"Berty! You shouldn't swear before Miss Rooker." Miss Lavery's words tinkled as coldly and sharply as ice in a pitcher of lemonade. Hateful woman! Were they trying to make her feel like a servant?

"Oh, I'm quite used to it, Miss Lavery. Doctors, you know!"

Miss Lavery, leaning plump, bare elbows on the mahogany table, clasping long, white fingers lightly before her chin, examined Miss Rooker attentively. "Oh, yes, you're used to doctors, of course. They're very immoral, aren't they?"

Miss Rooker turned scarlet, gulped her coffee, while Miss Lavery just perceptibly smiled.

"How's the patient this morning?" Mr. Oldkirk turned around from the long window, where he had been looking out at the bay. "Any change?"

"No. She's the picture of health, as she *always* is." Miss Rooker was downright. "I think she ought to be up."

"That's not my opinion, Miss Rooker, nor the doctor's either."

"Well——"

"She's been ordered a long rest."

"A rest, do you call it! With—" Miss Rooker broke off, angry and helpless.

"With what?" Mr. Oldkirk's tone was inquisitively sharp.

"Oh, well," Miss Rooker sighed, "I don't understand these nervous cases; I suppose I don't. If *I* had *my* way, though, I'd have her up and out before you could say Jack Robinson."

Mr. Oldkirk was dry and decisive.

"That's your opinion, Miss Rooker. You would probably admit that Dr. Hedgley knows a little more about it than you do."

He sauntered out of the dining room, hands in pockets, lazy and powerful.

"Another slice of toast, Miss Rooker? . . ." Miss Lavery asked the question sweetly, touching with one finger the electric toaster. . . .

"No, thank you, Miss Lavery. Not any more."

II.   "Don't read, Miss Rooker, it's too hot, I can't listen. And I'm so tired of all those he saids and she saids and said he with a wicked smile! It's a tiresome story. Talk to me instead. And bring me a glass of lemonade."

Mrs. Oldkirk turned on her side and smiled lazily. Indolent gray eyes.

"It *is* hot."

"I suppose you enjoy nursing, Miss Rooker?"

"Oh, yes, it has its ups and downs. Like everything else."

"You get good pay, and massaging keeps your hands soft. You must see lots of interesting things, too."

"Very. You see some very queer things, sometimes. Queer cases. Living as one of the family, you know, in all sorts of out-of-the-way places——"

"I suppose *my* case seems queer to you." Mrs. Oldkirk's eyes were still and candid, profound.

"Well—it does—a little! . . ."

The two women looked at each other, smiling. The brass traveling clock struck eleven. Mary could be heard sweeping the floor in Miss Rooker's room: *swish, swish.*

"It's not so queer when you know about it." She turned her head away, somber.

"No, nothing is, I suppose. Things are only queer seen from the outside."

"Ah, you're unusually wise for a young girl, Miss Rooker! I daresay you've had lots of experience."

Miss Rooker blushed, flattered.

"Do you know a good deal about men?"

"Well—I don't know—it all depends what you mean."

Mrs. Oldkirk yawned, throwing her head back on the pillow. She folded her hands beneath her head, and smiled curiously at the ceiling.

"I mean what damned scoundrels they are . . . though I guess there are a *few* exceptions. . . . You'd better go for your swim, if you're going. . . . Bring me some hot milk at twelve-thirty. . . . No lunch. . . . And I think I'll sit on the balcony for an hour at three. You can ask them to join me there for tea. Iced tea."

"You'd better try a nap."

"Nap! Not much. Bring me that rotten book. I'll read a little."

Miss Rooker, going into her room for the towel, met Mary coming out: a dark sensual face. "Oh, you dancing girl!" she murmured, and Mary giggled. The hot sea-wind sang through the screen, salt-smelling. She threw the towel over her shoulder and stood for a moment at the window, melancholy, looking past the railed end of the balcony, and over the roof of the veranda. The cherries in the wild cherry tree were dark red and black, nearly ripe. The bay itself looked hot—the lazy small waves flashed hotly and brilliantly, a wide lazy glare of light all the way from the monument hill to the outer beach, of which the white dunes seemed positively to be burning up. Marblehead was better, the sea was colder there, rocks were better than all this horrible mud—the nights were cooler; and there was more life in the harbor. The good old *Falcon!* "Them was happy days"—that was what Dr. Fish was always saying. And Mr. Oldkirk was extraordinarily like him, the same lazy vigorous way of moving about, slow heavy limbs, a kind of slothful grace. She heard his voice. He and Miss Lavery were coming out, the screen door banged, they emerged bare-headed into the heat, going down the shell path to the bathhouse. "Hell infernal," he was saying, opening one hand under the sunlight as one might do to feel a rain—"which reminds me of the girl whose name was Helen Fernald . . . that's what you are: hell infernal." Miss Lavery opened her pongee parasol, and her words were lost under it. She was very graceful—provocatively graceful, and her gait had about it a light inviting freedom, something virginal and at the same time sensuous. She gave a sudden screech of laughter as they went round the corner of the bathhouse.

"It's not a nursing case at all," she thought, standing before her mirror—"they pay me to amuse her, that's all—or *she* pays me—which is it?" She leaned close to the mirror, regarding her white almost transparent-seeming temples, the full red mouth (she disliked her lower lip, which she had always thought too heavy—pendulous) and the really beautiful dark hair, parted, and turned away from her brow in heavy wings. *"And when I told them—"* Did Mr. Oldkirk like her eyes? That awful word— oh, really dreadful, but so true—Dr. Fish had used about her eyes! But Mr. Oldkirk seemed to like Chinese eyes better. . . . Ought she to stay—just being a kind of lady's maid like this? And it wasn't right. No; it wasn't decent. She would like to say so to their faces. "I think you'd better get another nurse at the end of the week, Mr. Oldkirk—I don't approve of the way things are going on here—no, I don't approve at all. Shameful, that's what it is!—you and Miss Lavery—" But what did she know about him and Miss Lavery? . . . A pang. Misery. They were just cousins. A filthy mind she had, imagining such things. She had heard them talking, talking on the veranda, they went out late at night in the green dory; once, three nights ago, she had thought she heard soft footsteps in the upstairs hall, and a murmur, a long sleepy murmur. . . . *"How beautiful you wer-r-r-r-r-re."*

The bathhouse was frightfully hot—like an oven. It smelt of salt wood and seaweed. She took her clothes off slowly, feeling sand on the boards under her feet. She could hear Miss Lavery moving in the next "cell," occasionally brushing her clothes against the partition or thumping an elbow. Helen Lavery. Probably about thirty—maybe twenty-eight. A social service worker, they said—she'd be a fine social service worker! Going round and pretending to be a fashionable lady. Sly, tricky, disgusting creature! . . . And that one-piece bathing suit—! She was too clever to miss any chance like that. Of course, she had a beautiful figure, though her legs were just a shade too heavy. And she used it for all it was worth.

Miss Lavery was already thigh-deep in the water (in the gap between two beds of eel-grass) wading, with a swaying slow grace, towards Mr. Oldkirk, who floated on his back with hardly more than his nose and mustache visible. She skimmed the water with swallow-swift hands, forward and back, as she plunged deeper. "Oo! delicious," she cried, and sank with a soft turmoil, beginning to swim. "Don't bump me," Mr. Oldkirk answered, blowing, "I'm taking a nap."

The sunlight beat like cymbals on the radiant beach. The green dory was almost too hot to touch, but Miss Rooker dragged and pushed it into the water, threw in the anchor, and shoved off. "Look out!" she sang, whacking a blade on the water.

"Hello! Where are you off to, Miss Rooker?" Mr. Oldkirk blew like a seal.

"Marblehead."

"Dangerous place for young ladies, Miss Rooker. Better not stay after dark!"

"Oh, Marblehead's an open book to me!" Miss Rooker was arch.

"Oh, it is, is it!" He gave a loud "Ha!" in the water, blowing bubbles. "Better take me, then!"

He took three vigorous strokes, reached up a black-haired hand to the gunwale, and hauling himself up, deliberately overturned the dory. Miss Rooker screamed, plunged sidelong past Mr. Oldkirk's head (saw him grinning) into the delicious cold shock of water. Down she went, and opening her eyes saw Mr. Oldkirk's green legs and blue body, wavering within reach—she took hold of his cold, hard knee, then flung her arms round his waist, hugged him ecstatically, pulled him under. They became, for a second, deliciously entangled under the water. The top of his head butted her knee, his hand slid across her hip. Then they separated, kicking each other, and rose, both sputtering.

"Trying—woof—to drown me?" he barked, shaking his head from side to side. "A nice trick!"

"*You* did it!" . . . Miss Rooker laughed, excited. She swam on her back, out of breath, looking at Mr. Oldkirk intensely. Had he guessed that there, under the water, she had touched him deliberately? There was something in his eyes—a small sharp gleam as of secret intimacy, a something admitted between them—or was it simply a question? . . . Averting his eyes, suddenly, he swam to the upturned dory, and began pushing it toward the shore. Miss Lavery, who could not swim well, stood in shallow water, up to her middle, breathlessly ducking up and down. She looked rather ridiculous.

"What *are* you children doing!" she cried, chattering. "I'm cold; I think I'll go in."

Mr. Oldkirk pushed, swimming, thrashing the water with powerful legs. "You ought to be"—he puffed—"damned glad"—he puffed—"to be cold on a day like this"—he puffed—"Helen!" Then he called: "Come on—Miss Rooker! Give me a hand. Too heavy."

She put her hands against one corner of the green bow. The dory moved slowly. It would be easy to touch his legs again—the thought pleased her, she laughed, and, letting her laughing mouth sink below the surface, blew a wild froth of bubbles. Their faces were very close to one another. Miss Lavery, standing and watching, lifted conscious elbows to tuck her hair under her bathing cap.

"You swim like a fish," said Mr. Oldkirk. "Must be a grand-daughter of Venus. Was it Venus who came up out of Duxbury Bay on a good-sized clamshell?"

Miss Rooker laughed, puzzled. Was he flattering, or being sarcastic? . . . What about Venus? . . . "No," she said. "Nothing like that. But, oh, how I do enjoy it!"

In shallow water they righted and emptied the dory, restored the oars. While Mr. Oldkirk, getting into the boat, began hauling himself out to the anchor, which had fallen in, Miss Rooker climbed the beach toward the bathhouse. Miss Lavery stood before the door, taking off her bathing cap. Her face was hard. She was shivering. She struck her cap against the door jamb, sharply, and gave a little malicious smile.

"I know why you did that!" she said. She stepped in and shut the door.

Miss Rooker stared at the door, furious. Her first impulse was to open the door and shout something savagely injurious. The vixen! the snake! . . . She went into her own room—hot as an oven—and dropped the bathing suit off. Miss Lavery had suspected something. . . . Well, let her suspect. . . . She dried herself slowly with the warm towel, enjoying the beauty of her cool body. Let her suspect! Good for her. . . . Ah, it *had* been delicious! . . . She would let Miss Lavery hear her singing. *"And— when—I—told—them—"* . . .

Five minutes later Miss Lavery banged her door and departed, and Miss Rooker smiled.

III.   Mrs. Oldkirk, languid and pretty in her pink crêpe-de-Chine dressing gown, leaned back in her wicker chair resting her head on the tiny pillow and closed her eyes. Her silver-embroidered slippers, with blue pom-poms, were crossed on the footstool. The magazine had fallen from her hand. "Oh, how heavenly," she murmured. "Nothing as heavenly as a scalp massage. . . . You're very skillful, Miss Rooker. You have the touch. . . . Not so much on the top, now—a little more at the sides, and down the neck. . . ."

Miss Rooker, standing behind the wicker chair, stared over her patient's head into the dressing-table mirror. Massage. Massage. It was insufferably hot. The breeze had dropped. She felt drowsy. Zeek—zeek—zeek—zeek—zeek sang the crickets in the hot grass under the afternoon sun. The long seething trill of a cicada died languidly away—in a tree, she supposed. She remembered seeing a locust attacked by a huge striped bee—or was it a wasp? They had fallen together to the ground, in the dry grass, and the heavy bee, on top, curving its tail malevolently, stung the gray-pleated upturned belly, the poor creature shrilling and spinning all the while. Then the bee—or wasp—had zoomed away, and the gray locust, color of ashes, spun on its back a little and lay still. . . . Down the smooth soft neck. A curved pressure over and behind the ears. What was the matter with Mrs. Oldkirk? Too young for change of life—no. Something mysterious. She was very pretty, in her soft lazy supercilious way, and had a queer rich indifferent-seeming personality. A loose screw somewhere—too bad. Or was it that she was—Mrs. Oldkirk yawned.

"I love to feel someone fooling about my head: the height of luxury. When I go to the hairdresser I feel like staying all day. I'd like to pay them to keep on for hours. Especially if it's a man! Something thrilling about having your hair done by a man. Don't you know? It tickles you all over."

Miss Rooker laughed, embarrassed. Singular remark! "Yes—" she answered slowly, as if with uncertainty. "I think I know what you mean."

"I'm sure you do—you haven't those naughty black eyes for nothing, Miss Rooker! Ha, ha!"

"Oh, well, I suppose I'm human." Miss Rooker snickered. *Were* her eyes "naughty"? She wanted to study them in the glass, but was afraid that Mrs. Oldkirk would be watching.

Zeek—zeek—zeek—zeek—sang the crickets. What were they doing, where were they now? Was Miss Lavery taking a nap? Were they out in the car? . . . Her arms were beginning to be tired.

"Tell me, Miss Rooker, as woman to woman—what do you think of men?" Mrs. Oldkirk opened her gray eyes, lazily smiling.

"Well—I like them very much, if that's what you mean."

"*I* suppose so! You're still young. How old are you, if you don't mind my asking?"

"Twenty-four."

"Ah, yes. Very young. Lucky girl. . . . But you wait fourteen years! *Then* see what you think of men."

"Do they seem so different?"

"They don't seem, my dear girl, they *are*. It's when you're young that they *seem*. Later on, you begin to understand them —you get their number. And then—oh, my God—you want to exterminate the whole race of them. The nasty things!"

Miss Rooker felt herself blushing.

"Oh, I'm sure they aren't as bad as all that!"

"Devil's advocate! Miss Rooker. . . . Don't try to defend them. . . . They're all rotten. . . . Oh, I don't mean that there isn't a dear old parson here and there, you know—but then you remember the words of the song—'Even staid old country preachers are engaging tango teachers.' You can't get away from it! . . . No, the man doesn't live that I'd trust with a lead nickel. . . . By which, however, I don't mean that I don't enjoy having my hair done by a man! Ha, ha!" . . . Mrs. Oldkirk gave a queer little laugh, flaccid and bitter. She looked at herself, with parted lips, in the mirror: a distant sort of scrutiny, slightly contemptuous. Then, relaxing, she added, "Take my advice— don't every marry. It's a snare and a delusion."

"Why, I should *love* to marry!"

"Oh, you would! . . . In that case all I can say is I hope you'll have better luck than *I* did. . . ."

Miss Rooker was silent, confused.

"Tell me, has Betty, my husband—been flirting with you?
Don't be afraid to be frank—it doesn't matter, you know!"

"Why, no—he hasn't."

"You probably wouldn't tell me if he had. But if he hasn't
yet, he will. . . . Give him time!"

"Good heavens! What a thing to say!"

"Do I shock you? . . . I know him like the alphabet! . . . Poor
old satyr."

"You seem to!"

"Ah, I do. . . . Absolutely no principles—not a principle.
There's only one thing in Berty I've never been able to understand; and that's his dislike of Miss Lavery. Ha, ha! That's
why I have Miss Lavery keep house for me."

Mrs. Oldkirk closed her eyes again, faintly smiling. To say
such things to her, a stranger! What was the matter with her?
Miss Rooker was appalled at the indiscretion. . . . And Mr.
Oldkirk and Miss Lavery going out in the dory at midnight,
and talking, talking, long after everyone else had gone to bed.
. . . And that footstep in the hall, and the long affectionate
murmur—surely Miss Lavery's voice? . . . It was all extraordinary. She had never been in such a queer place. She thought
of the incident in the water, and then of Miss Lavery banging
her rubber cap against the door, and saying, "I know why you
did that!" . . . Well, Mrs. Oldkirk could sneer at Berty all she
liked; but for *her* part——

"I think that's enough, thank you, Miss Rooker. . . . You
didn't forget about the iced tea, did you?"

"No."

"Do you know where Mr. Oldkirk and Miss Lavery are?"

"No—I think Miss Lavery's lying down."

"Well—three-thirty. . . . Would you mind picking up my
magazine? It's fallen down. . . ."

. . . Miss Rooker descended the shell path and sauntered
along the hot beach. She sank down on the dry bedded seaweed in the shadow of the bluff. The seaweed was still warm,
and smelt strongly of the sea . . . zeek—zeek—zeek—zeek. . . . So

her eyes were naughty, were they! Perhaps they had more effect than she knew. She smiled. Perhaps Mr. Oldkirk—her heart was beating violently, she opened her book, for a delicious moment the type swam beneath her eyes.

IV.   "Good night," said Miss Rooker. As she switched off the light and shut the door, the brass traveling clock began striking ten. She went down the stairs, carrying the tray. The lamp on the sitting-room table was lighted, a book was open, there was a smell of cigarette smoke, but nobody was there. The warm wind sang through the screens, fluttered the pages of the book. Where were they? She felt depressed. It was horrible—horrible! She wouldn't stand it—not another day. Not another hour. . . . "Mr. Oldkirk, I want to speak to you: I feel that I can't stay on here. . . ." Would he try to persuade her to stay? Ah! perhaps he wouldn't. . . . They were probably on the beach—not on the veranda, anyway, or she would hear them. She carried the tray into the kitchen, pushing open the swing door. Mary and Hilda were standing close together at one of the windows looking out into the night. Hilda was giggling. They were watching something, standing still and tense.

"He is—he is"—said Mary in a low excited voice—"he's kissing her. You can see their heads go together."

"Well, what do you know." Hilda's drawl was full of wonder. "Sweet hour! . . . I wouldn't mind it much myself."

"Look! Do you see?"

Miss Rooker let go of the swing door; it shut with a thump, and the two girls started. Hilda's face was scarlet, Mary was saturnine.

"Who's kissing who?" asked Miss Rooker, looking angrily from one to the other. Hilda, still blushing, and putting back a strand of pale hair from her moist forehead, answered, embarrassed:

"It's Mr. Oldkirk and Miss Lavery, miss."

"Oh! And do you think it's nice to be spying on them?"

toward him. He stopped, they faced each other, and there was a pause. He stood against the lighted doorway, huge and silhouetted.

"I wanted to speak to you"—his voice was embarrassed and gentle—"and I wanted to wait till Miss Lavery had gone to bed."

"Oh."

"Yes. . . . I wanted to apologize to you. It must have been very distressing for you."

"Oh, not at all, I assure you. . . . Not in the least." Her voice was a little faint—she put her hand against the edge of the table.

"I'm sure it was. Please forgive me. . . . Miss Lavery, you know—" He gave a queer uneasy laugh, as if there was something he wanted to say but couldn't. What was it—was it that Miss Lavery was the one—? She felt, suddenly, extraordinarily happy.

"I think I'd better leave tomorrow," she answered then, looking away. "I think it would be better."

"Nonsense, my dear Miss Rooker! Don't think of it. . . . Why should you?"

Her heart was beating so violently that she could hardly think. She heard him breathing heavily and quickly.

"Well," she said, "I think it would be better."

"Why? There's no earthly reason. . . . No." As she made no reply, he went on—"It won't happen again—I can promise you *that!*" He again laughed, but this time as if he were thinking of something else, thinking of something funny that was going to happen. . . . Was he laughing at Miss Lavery?

Miss Rooker, unsteady, took a step to pass him, but he put out his hand. It closed upon her wrist. With his other hand he took slow possession of hers. She drew back, but only a little.

"Please," she said.

"Please what?"

"Let me go."

"Only when you've given me a promise."

"What?"

"That you'll stay here—with *me.*"

"Oh—you know I can't!"

She was trembling, and was ashamed to know that his hands must feel her trembling.

"Promise!" he said. She looked up at him—his eyes were wide, dark, beautiful, full of intention.

"Very well, I promise."

"Good! Good girl. . . ." He did not let go of her hand and wrist. "I'll make it up to you. . . . Don't mind Miss Lavery!"

"You *are* dreadful!" She gave a laugh, her self-possession coming back to her.

"*Am* I?" He beamed. "Well, I am, sometimes! . . . But what about you?"

"Oh, I'm awful!" she answered. She drew away her hand, rather slowly, reluctantly. "Good night, then."

"Good night."

She turned on the landing to look down at him. He smiled, his humorous eyes twinkling, and she smiled in return. . . . Heavens! how extraordinary, how simply extraordinary, how perfectly extraordinary. . . . She stared at her reflection in the glass. "Naughty" eyes? No—they were beautiful. She had never looked so beautiful—never. . . . Perhaps he would knock at her door? She locked it. . . . She combed her hair, and as she did so, began humming, "*And—when—I—told—them—*" Then she remembered Mrs. Oldkirk in the next room, and stopped. Poor old thing! . . . She got into bed and lay still, smiling. The wind whispered in the screen, the crickets were singing louder than ever. They liked a hot night like this. Zeek—zeek. Mr. Oldkirk passed along the hall. . . . Ah, the nice tall man with nice eyes, the very, very nice man! . . .

THE LAST VISIT

Marie Schley sat in the Watertown car by the open grilled window. It was a sunny afternoon, the first Saturday in October. Clouds of dust swooped over Mount Auburn Street, flew into the car, made the passengers cough. On the Charles River, an eight-oared crew was rowing round the blue turn, crawling like a centipede; the voice of the coxswain could be heard, the blades flashed irregularly. A subdued many-throated clamor came raggedly across the flat fields from the Stadium, suddenly rose intense, on a higher note, then died slowly. A football game must be going on there. Yes—there were the usual kites flying, flashing high over the Stadium. How familiar it all was! It made her feel slightly sad, and yet, also, she could not conceal from herself that she was much freer to enjoy its beauty, to enjoy it merely as a spectacle, than had ever been possible for her in the past. . . . It was familiar; but now that she lived so far away and came so seldom, it was also remote. It had now an "atmosphere"—she said almost aloud—an atmosphere. It was no longer so dreadfully a part of her own being. It was true there had been a time—the first year that she was in Boston, when she was twelve—a time when "going to Watertown to see Grandmother" was a positive delight. Even

that, however, hadn't been so much a fondness for Grandmother as a delight in the queer musty old furniture, the anti-
macassars, the tussocks, the rosy conch-shells on the gray carpet
—of an extraordinary size, and used as door fenders—and above
all, Grandmother's passion for good food. The cherries, for
which Marie with a pail used to climb the tree, the "plain apple
pie," the coffee cake so richly crusted with spiced sugar (Grandmother always called it "kooken")—certainly these had been
very important items. Even then she had been on her guard,
reserved, with Grandmother—there had never been any question of an intimacy between them. Grandmother had always
been hard and childlike, all her life had had that peculiar in-
aptitude for intimacy and sympathy which accompanies the
child's lack of "consciousness." Visiting her during the school
holidays, later, Marie had gradually, as she grew older, seen this
hardness clearly enough. Grandmother's hardness—oh, it was
really almost a meanness—had called forth, or implanted, a
meanness in herself. It had often seemed to her that Grandmother was cruel. How much these cruelties—which were wholly
of a psychological sort—had been deliberate, or how much they
had been simply the natural effect, unconscious, of a hard, cal-
lous, defeated old woman on a young and shy and sensitive
one, she had never known. Nor had she ever known, to tell the
truth, whether if she herself had been less of an egoist, she
might not have discovered more sharply, in her Grandmother,
the shy and affectionate girl, with remarkably nice blue eyes,
who occasionally laughed there and then took flight. Later still,
when she was going to college, she had in a measure "escaped"
the antipathy, had been able to challenge it laughingly, and
had worked a decided and delightful change in her relations
with the old woman. Grandmother's "meanness," she had found,
could often be undermined by laughter; her sense of humor,
or at any rate, of the ridiculous, was delicious. She was the only
woman Marie knew who often, and literally, "laughed till she
cried." Marie, ever since her college days, had used this discovery skillfully—she had been "free" to make the discovery

and to use it, in some unaccountable way, just after her return from a trip to Europe. Was it simply that then at last she had forced Grandmother to accept her as "grown-up" and an equal? At all events it had led to a kindliness between them. Yes, they had had a few pleasant days together. If they had formerly hated one another, quarreled savagely,—ah, those frightful quarrels over nothing!—quarrels had passed. Grandmother had, growing older, grown gentler; she herself, feeling herself to be superior, had learned to tolerate the flashes of cruelty and meanness. And now it was all to be ended—Watertown was to be rolled away—the dusty ride along Mount Auburn Street was to become less familiar, forgotten—Grandmother was going to die. A month—two months—five——

Watertown was changing extraordinarily. Her sense of its sharp difference, its newness, was a kind of reproach; for it seemed to hint that Grandmother had been neglected. If she had come oftener—seen the new houses being built, new cellars being dug, new streets being surveyed—she would not, she felt sure, be now so struck by its complete alteration. How horribly suburban it was, with all its rows of cheap two-family houses! Loathsome—shoddy little stucco garages, forlorn little barberry hedges, rows of one-storied little shops, built of garish brick— all this evidence of pullulating vulgarity where, in her childhood, had been green fields, hill pastures with tumbled stone walls, wild cherries, and, in autumn, thickets starred with the candid blue stars of chicory. She remembered a walk with Uncle Tom from Harvard Square to Grandmother's, when she was twelve. What an adventure in the wilderness! The hills between Belmont and Watertown were covered with juniper and birch trees. Skirting Palfrey Hill, they had come into Watertown past the old graveyard. It had seemed like coming down from a morning's walk on the Himalayas. And what were all these changes for? . . . What did it lead to? . . . It seemed as if men were determined to trample and vulgarize every inch of the world. She remembered that seventeenth—or was it eighteenth-century, song in an old song book—"By the waters of Watertown we sat down and wept, yea, we wept when we remembered Boston." . . . Poor Grandmother! It was as well, perhaps, that she had so long been a prisoner to her stuffy little antimacassared room, with its albums of daguerreotypes—she would have hated this change. Ah, but would she—would she! It was not so certain. Grandmother was a born provincial, a village democrat—perhaps she would have liked this show of energy, in which there was no pretense, and nowhere any distinction. It would perhaps have pleased her to see that Watertown, so palpably, was growing. . . . The churches would thrive. The markets would improve. . . .

Marie got off at Palfrey Street, and began climbing the hill. The mysterious brook, which used to flow under the street, full of old rusted pots and lidless tin cans, was gone. She climbed slowly—ah, not so rapidly as when she used to run up Palfrey Hill before breakfast to look for wild flowers! Silver-rod used to grow on Palfrey Hill—the only place she had ever seen it. That was before Grandmother had moved away from the house on Mount Auburn Street, with the cherry tree and the pear tree, and the "owners" (with whom Grandmother perpetually quarreled and bickered) living in the other half of the house, "playing the piano till all hours, and carrying on something awful." Marie wondered what they had been like. Probably they were very nice cheerful people. One of the daughters was a Christian Science Healer; the son worked in a music store. To Marie there had always been something romantic about them, and she had never passed their door in the hall without wanting to knock and go in. Once, she *had* gone in; all that she remembered was a plaster bust of a god or goddess who seemed, on top of the piano, to be meditating. There had also been a dog, which Grandmother detested and always shook her apron at. "Phoo! get out, you dirty beast!" she would cry, an expression of extraordinary hatred in her face. . . . Marie laughed, thinking of this. . . . She passed the weeping birch—its leaves were touched with yellow. . . . Slightly out of breath she climbed the wooden steps and rang the bell.

II.   "Oh, it's you, Mrs. Schley! How do you do! You're quite a stranger! . . . I think Mrs. Vedder's asleep. But I'll go and see. I'm sure she'll be delighted to see you!"

Mrs. Ling was detestable; that she was fearfully overworked, managing this private hospital, and that she was herself slowly dying (having lost, in her last operation, "all her insides," as Grandmother put it) did not make her more likable. A sly white face, with sly black eyes; a meager soul. Marie, standing in the suburban little hall, looked at the pious engravings, the cheap rugs. Above the mantel, Christ was leaning down, much haloed, into the valley of the shadow of death, reaching an incredibly long arm to rescue a lost lamb; over the dark valley hung a dove with bright wings. A pot of ferns stood on a small high bamboo table near the piano; the piano was a florid affair of pale oak. Marie looked at the music—the "Holy City," "Alexander's Ragtime Band," "Cuddle Up a Little Closer," "The Rosary." Here, at any rate, the piano would not be played till all hours!

"No—your Grandmother's awake. Will you go up?"

"How *is* Grandmother?"

"Well—about the same. She's very plucky!"

In the sick-room, with its gloom of lowered blinds, Marie at first found it difficult to see. The nurse hovered by the front window, smiling. Grandmother, in the great bed, turned the small shrunken face on the pillow, turned the pathetic blue eyes of a child. The forlorn little braid of streaked hair! Marie stooped and kissed the sunken weak mouth.

"Hello, Grandmother!" she shouted, remembering that the old woman was deaf. "Are you glad to see me?"

Grandmother looked up in a bewildered, slightly frightened way, as if, oddly, she were peering up out of a depth.

"What did you say?" The voice was slow and faint.

"I said, are you glad to see me?"

"Oh yes, always glad to see you. I'm always glad to see you."

"How are you feeling?"

Grandmother very slowly and gently focused her blue eyes—her pupils were very wide—on Marie's face. She seemed to be trying to see. She moved her lips, and then said weakly:

"Very bad. I can't eat."

"You can't eat? Why's that?"

Marie drew the chair closer to the bedside, determined to be cheerful. Mrs. Vedder fumbled with her thin trembling hand at the patchwork quilt, fumbled aimlessly, her eyes resting exploringly on Marie's face. It was as if she were struggling, for speech, with a profound dark indifference.

"How's little Kate?" she quavered.

"Oh, Kate's fine! She gets all over the house, now, holding on to chairs and things. . . . When we take her to the beach in her little bathing suit she crawls right into the water as if it were her native element. You never saw such courage and energy!"

"I wish I could see her. . . . She ought to be walking, oughtn't she?"

"Oh, no—she's not backward at all!"

"No—I suppose not. I wish I could see her. Is her hair the same color? Her hair was such a beautiful color—something like yours when you were little, only not so red. . . . I suppose you can't bring her up to town."

"No, it's not very easy, you see."

Marie, looking through the side window, by the bed, watched a gray squirrel running along the maple bough.

"It's my teeth—I can't use my teeth—that's why I talk so badly. The dentist was here last week. He said my jaw had shrunk, and this set of teeth wouldn't fit any more."

"Oh! What a shame, Granny! But can't you have them altered?"

"I can't afford it. . . . They charge me so much here. . . . It's wicked what they charge here!"

Miss Thomas, the nurse, approached, holding a spoon and a medicine glass.

"Time for my little girl to take her medicine!" she said, dipping the teaspoon.

"What good does medicine do me?"

"Now you take it like a good girl—there! . . . That's right!"

Mrs. Vedder sank back exhausted, the blue-veined hands lying inert. After a moment her eyes filled with tears.

"Little Kate!" she wailed— "How I wish—" She began crying, weakly and uncontrollably. Miss Thomas wiped her cheeks for her, Marie drawing back.

"She cries a good deal," said Miss Thomas in a low voice. "She gets an idea, you know, and just thinks and thinks about it, and cries and cries. Especially little Kate! She's always wanting to see your little Kate. . . . Now, Grandmother! Stop crying! You don't want to spoil your granddaughter's visit, the first time she's been here in so long! Do you?"

"No! . . . I can't help it. . . ."

Marie began thinking of one Sunday in the Mount Auburn Street house, seventeen or eighteen years before. They were having an apple pie for dinner: a warm sunny day, she remembered the pear tree in blossom. "Your grandfather, whom you don't remember, always used to say, 'Well, there's nothing I like so much as *plain apple pie.*' How furious it made me! He said it because he knew it infuriated me." Grandmother snorted, in a rage. " 'Plain apple pie!' I said to him, 'there's nothing plain about it! What do you know about cooking? You think a plain apple pie can be just thrown together by anybody. I'd like to see how many women could make a pie like this!' . . . But," she added, "he went right on gabbling about plain apple pie, plain apple pie." Marie had laughed, and Grandmother, relenting, or shaking off the past, had suddenly laughed also. . . . On Sundays, Grandmother always played on the little parlor organ, the seven or eight hymn-tunes she knew, singing in a thin distressing voice. The organ had been sold when Grandmother was moved to the hospital. . . . Other things had been sold, too—Grandmother's possessions had become very few—three or four chairs, the horsehair sofa, a whatnot, laden with family photographs, a framed lithochrome of the Rialto brought from Venice, a scrollwork clock made by her favorite son, who had died young. Presently these too would be sold.

"She's lost her memory, during this last month or so," said Miss Thomas, smoothing the fold of sheet over the quilt edge. "And her interest, too. But she's wonderfully brave." Then, shouting, *"Aren't* you, Grandmother!"

Mrs. Vedder lay apathetic, her small withered face turned on one side, a hand under her cheek. Distance was in her eyes. She paid no attention, or had not heard. She looked at Marie and the nurse as if they had no meaning, or reality. What was she thinking, Marie wondered. A cornflower blue, her eyes were, and still so extraordinarily young and innocent. There was a long silence, during which the squirrel in the maple tree began scolding—Marie, looking down through the screened window under the lowered curtain, saw a black cat cross the lawn, pretending to be indifferent. He sat down, put back first one ear, then the other, looked up into the tree, blinking affectionate green eyes, then trudged away, disillusioned and weary. . . . She ought to have brought something for Grandmother. But then, she had hardly had time. In the subway, it was true, at that little shop—but just then the Watertown car had come grinding round the turn; she would have had to wait fifteen minutes for another. Besides, Grandmother always had more flowers than she could use—and what, except hothouse grapes, could she eat? . . .

"I meant to bring you some grapes, Granny, but I didn't have time," she said. Mrs. Vedder seemed to go on listening after the remark was finished, as if she still had it somewhere and was giving it, slowly and with difficulty, all her attention.

"Mr. Sill gave me those roses," she brought out at last. She did not turn toward them (they stood on the desk) but simply assumed that Marie must have seen them. "He was here yesterday. . . ."

"What's he doing now that he's left the church?"

"What? . . . I don't know. . . . Teaching, I think. . . . How's

Paul?" It always annoyed Marie when Grandmother inquired about her husband.

"Oh, he's all right."

"That's good." Grandmother sighed, and looked away at the viney wallpaper.

"I went to New York last week, Granny!"

"New York? Went to New York?"

"Yes—to see Alice. And a queer thing happened to me." There was no response in the blue eyes. "Do you hear me?"

"No."

"I say a queer thing happened to me in New York. . . . While I was staying with Alice I got a letter from Sarah Allbright— you remember Sarah Allbright? That little girl I used to play with in Chicago. I hadn't seen or heard from her since I was there—the last time I ever saw her was the day we played 'hookey' from school and ran off and got lost somewhere out by Winnetka. We got home about eleven o'clock at night. Well, in her letter she said she was in New York, for a visit, and wondered if I could come down from Fall River to see her! So I went to see her! Wasn't it exciting! She's huge—very fat. I think I'd have known her, though. She's married to a lawyer, and has three children, and paints pictures. It *was* interesting to hear all about all the Chicago people I knew."

Grandmother stared, immobile.

"Who did you say looked after little Kate?" she quavered.

"Paul's mother." Marie felt herself flushing. Did Grandmother intend . . . ? But the old face was merely tired and expressionless.

"What was the queer thing that happened to you in New York?"

Marie's heart contracted. She moistened her lips and repeated the story, conscious of Miss Thomas's attention. But Grandmother, she saw, did not listen, after the first word or two, did not understand, merely rested the faded blue eyes on Marie's, as if it was not the story she was so darkly struggling to understand, but Marie herself. What was it she wanted so? What was

it she was trying to see? Life? Her own life, embodied now in
Marie and little Kate? Was she trying, dimly, to touch something which eluded her grasp, to feel something which she
could not see? . . . She made no comment. But presently her
eyes again, slowly, filled with tears, became intolerably bright,
and suddenly she cried out, weeping:

"I can't die! I can't die! . . . I want to die and I can't!"

She cried almost soundlessly, the tears running down the
wrinkles of her cheeks. Miss Thomas held up one finger, sternly.

"Grandmother, shame on you! You promised me not to cry.
And now look at you—crying like this for nothing at all!"

"She's greatly changed," Marie murmured to the nurse. "It
seems to me that she's seriously worse. Don't you think—"

Miss Thomas shook her head.

"Oh, no! She's very strong still. I don't see why she shouldn't
live through the winter."

A little later, Marie, looking at her watch, said that she must
run to catch her train. She would barely have time. She kissed
the sunken mouth once more, patted the cool hand. Out of the
brimmed eyes death looked up consciously and clearly, but
Grandmother said only, "Goodbye, Marie!"

III.   Tom was walking up and down in the
little alley that led to the theater, looking into shop windows.
When he saw her, he came toward her, grinning in his one-
sided freckled way. She felt that she had never liked him so
much.

"On that corner—a rose, if you like," he said, without preliminaries, "or on this, a cup of coffee."

"Coffee! I've had an awful time."

"Awful? Was it? Why on earth do you go?"

"Partly because it gives me such a good alibi—everybody
thinks I'm spending the whole afternoon in Watertown."

Tom smiled at her gratefully. They went into the lunchroom.

"But it's horrible, somehow," Marie went on, after a moment, stirring the cup of coffee which had been brought to the mahogany counter. "She's dying. Really dying. She said a most dreadful thing! . . . And I lied cheerfully about the train, and came gayly away to meet—*you*—of whom not one of my family or friends ever heard! . . . Don't you think it's horrible?"

Tom stared at his coffee.

"It's the way things are," he said slowly.

Presently they walked down the sloping dark aisle of the vaudeville theater, looking for seats. "Here are two," said Tom. A blackface singer, on the stage, was singing coarsely. The blinding disc of spotlight, with its chromatic red edge, illuminated his bluish makeup, made his tongue an unnatural pink, sparkled the gold fillings in his wide teeth. *"Hot lips,"* he intoned, grinning, *"that are pips . . . and no more conscience than a snake has hips."* . . . Tom took her gloved hand, inserted his finger in the opening, and stroked her palm. A delicious feeling of weakness, dissolution, came over her. Life suddenly seemed to her extraordinarily complex, beautiful, and miserable. "By the waters of Watertown we sat down and wept, yea, we wept when we remembered Boston."

MR. ARCULARIS

Mr. Arcularis stood at the window of his room in the hospital and looked down at the street. There had been a light shower, which had patterned the sidewalks with large drops, but now again the sun was out, blue sky was showing here and there between the swift white clouds, a cold wind was blowing the poplar trees. An itinerant band had stopped before the building and was playing, with violin, harp, and flute, the finale of "Cavalleria Rusticana." Leaning against the window-sill—for he felt extraordinarily weak after his operation—Mr. Arcularis suddenly, listening to the wretched music, felt like crying. He rested the palm of one hand against a cold window-pane and stared down at the old man who was blowing the flute, and blinked his eyes. It seemed absurd that he should be so weak, so emotional, so like a child—and especially now that everything was over at last. In spite of all their predictions, in spite, too, of his own dreadful certainty that he was going to die, here he was, as fit as a fiddle—but what a fiddle it was, so out of tune!—with a long life before him. And to begin with, a voyage to England ordered by the doctor. What could be more delightful? Why should he feel sad about it and want to cry like a baby? In a few minutes Harry would arrive with his car to take him to the wharf; in an hour he would be on the sea, in two hours he would see the sunset behind him, where Boston had been, and his new life would be opening before him. It was many years since he had been abroad. June, the best of the year to come—England, France, the Rhine—how ridiculous that he should already be homesick!

There was a light footstep outside the door, a knock, the door opened, and Harry came in.

"Well, old man, I've come to get you. The old bus actually got here. Are you ready? Here, let me take your arm. You're tottering like an octogenarian!"

Mr. Arcularis submitted gratefully, laughing, and they made the journey slowly along the bleak corridor and down the stairs to the entrance hall. Miss Hoyle, his nurse, was there, and the Matron, and the charming little assistant with freckles who had helped to prepare him for the operation. Miss Hoyle put out her hand.

"Goodbye, Mr. Arcularis," she said, "and *bon voyage.*"

"Goodbye, Miss Hoyle, and thank you for everything. You were very kind to me. And I fear I was a nuisance."

The girl with the freckles, too, gave him her hand, smiling. She was very pretty, and it would have been easy to fall in love with her. She reminded him of someone. Who was it? He tried in vain to remember while he said goodbye to her and turned to the Matron.

"And not too many latitudes with the young ladies, Mr. Arcularis!" she was saying.

Mr. Arcularis was pleased, flattered, by all this attention to a middle-aged invalid, and felt a joke taking shape in his mind, and no sooner in his mind than on his tongue.

"Oh, no latitudes," he said, laughing. "I'll leave the latitudes to the ship!"

"Oh, come now," said the Matron, "we don't seem to have hurt him much, do we?"

"I think we'll have to operate on him again and *really* cure him," said Miss Hoyle.

He was going down the front steps, between the potted palmettos, and they all laughed and waved. The wind was cold, very cold for June, and he was glad he had put on his coat. He shivered.

"Damned cold for June!" he said. "Why should it be so cold?"

"East wind," Harry said, arranging the rug over his knees. "Sorry it's an open car, but I believe in fresh air and all that sort of thing. I'll drive slowly. We've got plenty of time."

They coasted gently down the long hill toward Beacon Street, but the road was badly surfaced, and despite Harry's care Mr. Arcularis felt his pain again. He found that he could alleviate it a little by leaning to the right, against the arm-rest, and not breathing too deeply. But how glorious to be out again! How strange and vivid the world looked! The trees had innumerable green fresh leaves—they were all blowing and shifting and turning and flashing in the wind; drops of rainwater fell downward sparkling; the robins were singing their absurd, delicious little four-noted songs; even the street cars looked unusually bright and beautiful, just as they used to look when he was a child and had wanted above all things to be a motorman. He found himself smiling foolishly at everything, foolishly and weakly, and wanted to say something about it to Harry. It was no use, though—he had no strength, and the mere finding of words would be almost more than he could manage. And even if he should succeed in saying it, he would then most likely burst into tears. He shook his head slowly from side to side.

"Ain't it grand?" he said.

"I'll bet it looks good," said Harry.

"Words fail me."

"You wait till you get out to sea. You'll have a swell time."

"Oh, swell! . . . I hope not. I hope it'll be calm."

"Tut tut."

When they passed the Harvard Club Mr. Arcularis made a slow and somewhat painful effort to turn in his seat and look at it. It might be the last chance to see it for a long time. Why this sentimental longing to stare at it, though? There it was, with the great flag blowing in the wind, the Harvard seal now concealed by the swift folds and now revealed, and there were the windows in the library, where he had spent so many delightful hours reading—Plato, and Kipling, and the Lord knows what—and the balconies from which for so many years he had watched the Marathon. Old Talbot might be in there now, sleeping with a book on his knee, hoping forlornly to be interrupted by anyone, for anything.

"Goodbye to the old club," he said.

"The bar will miss you," said Harry, smiling with friendly irony and looking straight ahead.

"But let there be no moaning," said Mr. Arcularis.

"What's *that* a quotation from?"

" 'The Odyssey.' "

In spite of the cold, he was glad of the wind on his face, for it helped to dissipate the feeling of vagueness and dizziness that came over him in a sickening wave from time to time. All of a sudden everything would begin to swim and dissolve, the houses would lean their heads together, he had to close his eyes, and there would be a curious and dreadful humming noise, which at regular intervals rose to a crescendo and then drawlingly subsided again. It was disconcerting. Perhaps he still had a trace of fever. When he got on the ship he would have a glass of whisky. . . . From one of these spells he opened his eyes and found that they were on the ferry, crossing to East Boston. It must have been the ferry's engines that he had heard. From another spell he woke to find himself on the wharf, the car at a standstill beside a pile of yellow packing cases.

"We're here because we're here because we're here," said **Harry.**

"Because we're here," added Mr. Arcularis.

He dozed in the car while Harry—and what a good friend

Harry was!—attended to all the details. He went and came with tickets and passports and baggage checks and porters. And at last he unwrapped Mr. Arcularis from the rugs and led him up the steep gangplank to the deck, and thence by devious windings to a small cold stateroom with a solitary porthole like the eye of a cyclops.

"Here you are," he said, "and now I've got to go. Did you hear the whistle?"

"No."

"Well, you're half asleep. It's sounded the all-ashore. Goodbye, old fellow, and take care of yourself. Bring me back a spray of edelweiss. And send me a picture postcard from the Absolute."

"Will you have it finite or infinite?"

"Oh, infinite. But with your signature on it. Now you'd better turn in for a while and have a nap. Cheerio!"

Mr. Arcularis took his hand and pressed it hard, and once more felt like crying. Absurd! Had he become a child again?

"Goodbye," he said.

He sat down in the little wicker chair, with his overcoat still on, closed his eyes, and listened to the humming of the air in the ventilator. Hurried footsteps ran up and down the corridor. The chair was not too comfortable, and his pain began to bother him again, so he moved, with his coat still on, to the narrow berth and fell asleep. When he woke up, it was dark, and the porthole had been partly opened. He groped for the switch and turned on the light. Then he rang for the steward.

"It's cold in here," he said. "Would you mind closing the port?"

The girl who sat opposite him at dinner was charming. Who was it she reminded him of? Why, of course, the girl at the hospital, the girl with the freckles. Her hair was beautiful, not quite red, not quite gold, nor had it been bobbed; arranged with a sort of graceful untidiness, it made him think of a Melozzo da Forli angel. Her face was freckled, she had a mouth which was both humorous and voluptuous. And she seemed to be alone.

He frowned at the bill of fare and ordered the thick soup.

"No hors d'oeuvres?" asked the steward.

"I think not," said Mr. Arcularis. "They might kill me."

The steward permitted himself to be amused and deposited the menu card on the table against the water bottle. His eyebrows were lifted. As he moved away, the girl followed him with her eyes and smiled.

"I'm afraid you shocked him," she said.

"Impossible," said Mr. Arcularis. "These stewards, they're dead souls. How could they be stewards otherwise? And they think they've seen and known everything. They suffer terribly from the *déjà vu*. Personally, I don't blame them."

"It must be a dreadful sort of life."

"It's because they're dead that they accept it."

"Do you think so?"

"I'm sure of it. I'm enough of a dead soul myself to know the signs!"

"Well, I don't know what you mean by that!"

"But nothing mysterious! I'm just out of hospital, after an operation. I was given up for dead. For six months I had given *myself* up for dead. If you've ever been seriously ill you know the feeling. You have a posthumous feeling—a mild, cynical tolerance for everything and everyone. What is there you haven't seen or done or understood? Nothing."

Mr. Arcularis waved his hands and smiled.

"I wish I could understand you," said the girl, "but I've never been ill in my life."

"Never?"

"Never."

"Good God!"

The torrent of the unexpressed and inexpressible paralyzed him and rendered him speechless. He stared at the girl, wondering who she was and then, realizing that he had perhaps stared too fixedly, averted his gaze, gave a little laugh, rolled a pill of

bread between his fingers. After a second or two he allowed
himself to look at her again and found her smiling.

"Never pay any attention to invalids," he said, "or they'll
drag you to the hospital."

She examined him critically, with her head tilted a little to
one side, but with friendliness.

"You don't *look* like an invalid," she said.

Mr. Arcularis thought her charming. His pain ceased to
bother him, the disagreeable humming disappeared, or rather,
it was dissociated from himself and became merely, as it should
be, the sound of the ship's engines, and he began to think the
voyage was going to be really delightful. The parson on his
right passed him the salt.

"I fear you will need this in your soup," he said.

"Thank you. Is it as bad as that?"

The steward, overhearing, was immediately apologetic and
solicitous. He explained that on the first day everything was at
sixes and sevens. The girl looked up at him and asked him a
question.

"Do you think we'll have a good voyage?" she said.

He was passing the hot rolls to the parson, removing the
napkins from them with a deprecatory finger.

"Well, madam, I don't like to be a Jeremiah, but——"

"Oh, come," said the parson, "I hope we have no Jeremiahs."

"What do you mean?" said the girl.

Mr. Arcularis ate his soup with gusto—it was nice and hot.

"Well, maybe I shouldn't say it, but there's a corpse on
board, going to Ireland; and I never yet knew a voyage with a
corpse on board that we didn't have bad weather."

"Why, steward, you're just superstitious! What nonsense!"

"That's a very ancient superstition," said Mr. Arcularis. "I've
heard it many times. Maybe it's true. Maybe we'll be wrecked.
And what does it matter, after all?" He was very bland.

"Then let's be wrecked," said the parson coldly.

Nevertheless, Mr. Arcularis felt a shudder go through him
on hearing the steward's remark. A corpse in the hold—a coffin?

Perhaps it was true. Perhaps some disaster would befall them. There might be fogs. There might be icebergs. He thought of all the wrecks of which he had read. There was the *Titanic*, which he had read about in the warm newspaper room at the Harvard Club—it had seemed dreadfully real, even there. That band, playing "Nearer My God to Thee" on the after-deck while the ship sank! It was one of the darkest of his memories. And the *Empress of Ireland*—all those poor people trapped in the smoking room, with only one door between them and life, and that door locked for the night by the deck steward, and the deck steward nowhere to be found! He shivered, feeling a draft, and turned to the parson.

"How do these strange delusions arise?" he said.

The parson looked at him searchingly, appraisingly—from chin to forehead, from forehead to chin—and Mr. Arcularis, feeling uncomfortable, straightened his tie.

"From nothing but fear," said the parson. "Nothing on earth but fear."

"How strange!" said the girl.

Mr. Arcularis again looked at her—she had lowered her face—and again tried to think of whom she reminded him. It wasn't only the little freckle-faced girl at the hospital—both of them had reminded him of someone else. Someone far back in his life: remote, beautiful, lovely. But he couldn't think. The meal came to an end, they all rose, the ship's orchestra played a feeble fox-trot, and Mr. Arcularis, once more alone, went to the bar to have his whisky. The room was stuffy, and the ship's engines were both audible and palpable. The humming and throbbing oppressed him, the rhythm seemed to be the rhythm of his own pain, and after a short time he found his way, with slow steps, holding on to the walls in his moments of weakness and dizziness, to his forlorn and white little room. The port had been—thank God!—closed for the night; it was cold enough anyway. The white and blue ribbons fluttered from the ventilator, the bottle and glasses clicked and clucked as the ship swayed gently to the long, slow motion of the sea. It was all very peculiar—it was all like something he had experienced somewhere before. What was it? Where was it? ... He untied his tie, looking at his face in the glass, and wondered, and from time to time put his hand to his side to hold in the pain. It wasn't at Portsmouth, in his childhood, nor at Salem, nor in the rose garden at his Aunt Julia's, nor in the schoolroom at Cambridge. It was something very queer, very intimate, very precious. The jackstones, the Sunday-school cards which he had loved when he was a child. ... He fell asleep.

The sense of time was already hopelessly confused. One hour was like another, the sea looked always the same, morning was indistinguishable from afternoon—and was it Tuesday or Wednesday? Mr. Arcularis was sitting in the smoking room, in his favorite corner, watching the parson teach Miss Dean to play chess. On the deck outside he could see the people passing and repassing in their restless round of the ship. The red jacket went by, then the black hat with the white feather, then the purple scarf, the brown tweed coat, the Bulgarian mustache, the monocle, the Scotch cap with fluttering ribbons, and in no time at all the red jacket again, dipping past the windows with its own peculiar rhythm, followed once more by the black hat and the purple scarf. How odd to reflect on the fixed little orbits of these things —as definite and profound, perhaps, as the orbits of the stars, and as important to God or the Absolute. There was a kind of tyranny in this fixedness, too—to think of it too much made one uncomfortable. He closed his eyes for a moment, to avoid seeing for the fortieth time the Bulgarian mustache and the pursuing monocle. The parson was explaining the movements of knights. Two forward and one to the side. Eight possible moves, always to the opposite color from that on which the piece stands. Two forward and one to the side: Miss Dean repeated the words several times with reflective emphasis. Here, too, was the terrifying fixed curve of the infinite, the creeping curve of logic which at last must become the final signpost at the edge of nothing. After that—the deluge. The great white light of annihilation.

The bright flash of death. . . . Was it merely the sea which made these abstractions so insistent, so intrusive? The mere notion of *orbit* had somehow become extraordinarily naked; and to rid himself of the discomfort and also to forget a little the pain which bothered his side whenever he sat down, he walked slowly and carefully into the writing room, and examined a pile of superannuated magazines and catalogues of travel. The bright colors amused him, the photographs of remote islands and mountains, savages in sampans or sarongs or both—it was all very far off and delightful, like something in a dream or a fever. But he found that he was too tired to read and was incapable of concentration. Dreams! Yes, that reminded him. That rather alarming business—sleep-walking!

Later in the evening—at what hour he didn't know—he was telling Miss Dean about it, as he had intended to do. They were sitting in deck chairs on the sheltered side. The sea was black, and there was a cold wind. He wished they had chosen to sit in the lounge.

Miss Dean was extremely pretty—no, beautiful. She looked at him, too, in a very strange and lovely way, with something of inquiry, something of sympathy, something of affection. It seemed as if, between the question and the answer, they had sat thus for a very long time, exchanging an unspoken secret, simply looking at each other quietly and kindly. Had an hour or two passed? And was it at all necessary to speak?

"No," she said, "I never have."

She breathed into the low words a note of interrogation and gave him a slow smile.

"That's the funny part of it. I never had either until last night. Never in my life. I hardly ever even dream. And it really rather frightens me."

"Tell me about it, Mr. Arcularis."

"I dreamed at first that I was walking, alone, in a wide plain covered with snow. It was growing dark, I was very cold, my feet were frozen and numb, and I was lost. I came then to a signpost —at first it seemed to me there was nothing on it. Nothing but ice. Just before it grew finally dark, however, I made out on it the one word 'Polaris.' "

"The Pole Star."

"Yes—and you see, I didn't myself know that. I looked it up only this morning. I suppose I must have seen it somewhere? And of course it rhymes with my name."

"Why, so it does!"

"Anyway, it gave me—in the dream—an awful feeling of despair, and the dream changed. This time, I dreamed I was standing *outside* my stateroom in the little dark corridor, or *cul-de-sac*, and trying to find the door-handle to let myself in. I was in my pajamas, and again I was very cold. And at this point I woke up. . . . The extraordinary thing is that's exactly where I was!"

"Good heavens. How strange!"

"Yes. And now the question is, *Where had I been?* I was frightened, when I came to—not unnaturally. For among other things I *did* have, quite definitely, the feeling that I *had been* somewhere. Somewhere where it was very cold. It doesn't sound very proper. Suppose I had been seen!"

"That might have been awkward," said Miss Dean.

"Awkward! It might indeed. It's very singular. I've never done such a thing before. It's this sort of thing that reminds one— rather wholesomely, perhaps, don't you think?"—and Mr. Arcularis gave a nervous little laugh—"how extraordinarily little we know about the workings of our own minds or souls. After all, what *do* we know?"

"Nothing—nothing—nothing—nothing," said Miss Dean slowly. "*Absolutely* nothing."

Their voices had dropped, and again they were silent; and again they looked at each other gently and sympathetically, as if for the exchange of something unspoken and perhaps unspeakable. Time ceased. The orbit—so it seemed to Mr. Arcularis— once more became pure, became absolute. And once more he found himself wondering who it was that Miss Dean—Clarice Dean—reminded him of. Long ago and far away. Like those pictures of the islands and mountains. The little freckle-faced girl at the hospital was merely, as it were, the stepping stone, the signpost, or, as in algebra, the "equals" sign. But what was it they both "equaled"? The jackstones came again into his mind and his Aunt Julia's rose garden—at sunset; but this was ridiculous. It couldn't be simply that they reminded him of his childhood! And yet why not?

They went into the lounge. The ship's orchestra, in the oval-shaped balcony among faded palms, was playing the finale of "Cavalleria Rusticana," playing it badly.

"Good God!" said Mr. Arcularis, "can't I ever escape from that damned sentimental tune? It's the last thing I heard in America, and the last thing I *want* to hear."

"But don't you like it?"

"As music? No! It moves me too much, but in the wrong way."

"What, exactly, do you mean?"

"Exactly? Nothing. When I heard it at the hospital—when was it?—it made me feel like crying. Three old Italians tootling it in the rain. I suppose, like most people, I'm afraid of my feelings."

"Are they so dangerous?"

"Now then, young woman! Are you pulling my leg?"

The stewards had rolled away the carpets, and the passengers were beginning to dance. Miss Dean accepted the invitation of a young officer, and Mr. Arcularis watched them with envy. Odd, that last exchange of remarks—very odd; in fact, everything was odd. Was it possible that they were falling in love? Was that what it was all about—all these concealed references and recollections? He had read of such things. But at his age! And with a girl of twenty-two! It was ridiculous.

After an amused look at his old friend Polaris from the open door on the sheltered side, he went to bed.

The rhythm of the ship's engines was positively a persecution. It gave one no rest, it followed one like the Hound of Heaven, it drove on, out into space and across the Milky Way and then back home by way of Betelgeuse. It was cold there, too. Mr. Arcularis, making the round trip by way of Betelgeuse and Polaris, sparkled with frost. He felt like a Christmas tree. Icicles on his fingers and icicles on his toes. He tinkled and spangled in the void, hallooed to the waste echoes, rounded the buoy on the verge of the Unknown, and tacked glitteringly homeward. The wind whistled. He was barefooted. Snowflakes and tinsel blew past him. Next time, by George, he would go farther still—for altogether it was rather a lark. Forward into the untrodden! as somebody said. Some intrepid explorer of his own backyard, probably, some middle-aged professor with an umbrella: those were the fellows for courage! But give us time, thought Mr. Arcularis, give us time, and we will bring back with us the night-rime of the Obsolute. Or was it Absolete? If only there weren't this perpetual throbbing, this iteration of sound, like a pain, these circles and repetitions of light—the feeling as of everything coiling inward to a center of misery. . . .

Suddenly it was dark, and he was lost. He was groping, he touched the cold, white, slippery woodwork with his fingernails, looking for an electric switch. The throbbing, of course, was the throbbing of the ship. But he was almost home—almost home. Another corner to round, a door to be opened, and there he would be. Safe and sound. Safe in his father's home.

It was at this point that he woke up: in the corridor that led to the dining saloon. Such pure terror, such horror, seized him as he had never known. His heart felt as if it would stop beating. His back was toward the dining saloon; apparently he had just come from it. He was in his pajamas. The corridor was dim, all but two lights having been turned out for the night, and—thank God!—deserted. Not a soul, not a sound. He was perhaps fifty yards from his room. With luck he could get to it unseen. Holding tremulously to the rail that ran along the wall, a brown, greasy rail, he began to creep his way forward. He felt very weak, very dizzy, and his thoughts refused to concentrate. Vaguely he remembered Miss Dean—Clarice—and the freckled girl, as if they were one and the same person. But he wasn't in the hospital, he was on the ship. Of course. How absurd. The Great Circle. Here we are, old fellow . . . steady round the corner . . . hold hard to your umbrella. . . .

In his room, with the door safely shut behind him, Mr. Arcularis broke into a cold sweat. He had no sooner got into his bunk, shivering, than he heard the night watchman pass.

"But where"—he thought, closing his eyes in agony—"have I been? . . ."

A dreadful idea had occurred to him.

"It's nothing serious—how could it be anything serious? Of course, it's nothing serious," said Mr. Arcularis.

"No, it's nothing serious," said the ship's doctor urbanely.

"I knew you'd think so. But just the same——"

"Such a condition is the result of worry," said the doctor. "Are you worried—do you mind telling me—about something? Just try to think."

"Worried?"

Mr. Arcularis knitted his brows. *Was* there something? Some little mosquito of a cloud disappearing into the southwest, the northeast? Some little gnat-song of despair? But no, that was all over. All over.

"Nothing," he said, "nothing whatever."

"It's very strange," said the doctor.

"Strange! I should say so. I've come to sea for a rest, not for a nightmare! What about a bromide?"

"Well, I can give you a bromide, Mr. Arcularis——"

"Then, please, if you don't mind, give me a bromide."

He carried the little phial hopefully to his stateroom, and took a dose at once. He could see the sun through his porthole. It looked northern and pale and small, like a little peppermint, which was only natural enough, for the latitude was changing with every hour. But why was it that doctors were all alike? And all, for that matter, like his father, or that other fellow at the hospital? Smythe, his name was. Doctor Smythe. A nice, dry little fellow, and they said he was a writer. Wrote poetry, or something like that. Poor fellow—disappointed. Like everybody else. Crouched in there, in his cabin, night after night, writing blank verse or something—all about the stars and flowers and love and death; ice and the sea and the infinite; time and tide—well, every man to his own taste.

"But it's nothing serious," said Mr. Arcularis, later, to the parson. "How could it be?"

"Why, of course not, my dear fellow," said the parson, patting his back. "How could it be?"

"I know it isn't and yet I worry about it."

"It would be ridiculous to think it serious," said the parson. Mr. Arcularis shivered; it was colder than ever. It was said that they were near icebergs. For a few hours in the morning there had been a fog, and the siren had blown—devastatingly—at three-minute intervals. Icebergs caused fog—he knew that.

"These things always come," said the parson, "from a sense of guilt. You feel guilty about something. I won't be so rude as to inquire what it is. But if you could rid yourself of the sense of guilt——"

And later still, when the sky was pink:

"But is it anything to worry about?" said Miss Dean. "Really?"

"No, I suppose not."

"Then don't worry. We aren't children any longer!"

"Aren't we? I wonder!"

They leaned, shoulders touching, on the deck-rail, and looked at the sea, which was multitudinously incarnadined. Mr. Arcularis scanned the horizon in vain for an iceberg.

"Anyway," he said, "the colder we are the less we feel!"

"I hope that's no reflection on *you*," said Miss Dean.

"Here . . . feel my hand," said Mr. Arcularis.

"Heaven knows, it's cold!"

"It's been to Polaris and back! No wonder."

"Poor thing, poor thing!"

"Warm it."

"May I?"

"You can."

"I'll try."

Laughing, she took his hand between both of hers, one palm under and one palm over, and began rubbing it briskly. The decks were deserted, no one was near them, everyone was dressing for dinner. The sea grew darker, the wind blew colder.

"I wish I could remember who you are," he said.

"And you—who are you?"

"Myself."

"Then perhaps *I* am yourself."

"Don't be metaphysical!"

"But I *am* metaphysical!"

She laughed, withdrew, pulled the light coat about her shoulders.

The bugle blew the summons for dinner—"The Roast Beef of Old England"—and they walked together along the darkening deck toward the door, from which a shaft of soft light fell across the deck-rail. As they stepped over the brass door-sill Mr. Arcularis felt the throb of the engines again; he put his hand quickly to his side.

"*Auf wiedersehen,*" he said. "*Tomorrow and tomorrow and tomorrow.*"

Mr. Arcularis was finding it impossible, absolutely impossible, to keep warm. A cold fog surrounded the ship, had done so, it seemed, for days. The sun had all but disappeared, the transition from day to night was almost unnoticeable. The ship, too, seemed scarcely to be moving—it was as if anchored among walls of ice and rime. Monstrous that, merely because it was June, and supposed, therefore, to be warm, the ship's authorities should consider it unnecessary to turn on the heat! By day, he wore his heavy coat and sat shivering in the corner of the smoking room. His teeth chattered, his hands were blue. By night, he heaped blankets on his bed, closed the porthole's black eye against the sea, and drew the yellow curtains across it, but in vain. Somehow, despite everything, the fog crept in, and the icy fingers touched his throat. The steward, questioned about it, merely said, "Icebergs." Of course—any fool knew that. But how long, in God's name, was it going to last? They surely ought to be past the

Grand Banks by this time! And surely it wasn't necessary to sail to England by way of Greenland and Iceland!

Miss Dean—Clarice—was sympathetic.

"It's simply because," she said, "your vitality has been lowered by your illness. You can't expect to be your normal self so soon after an operation! When *was* your operation, by the way?"

Mr. Arcularis considered. Strange—he couldn't be quite sure. It was all a little vague—his sense of time had disappeared.

"Heavens knows!" he said. "Centuries ago. When I was a tadpole and you were a fish. I should think it must have been at about the time of the Battle of Teutoburg Forest. Or perhaps when I was a Neanderthal man with a club!"

"Are you sure it wasn't farther back still?"

What did she mean by that?

"Not at all. Obviously, we've been on this damned ship for ages—for eras—for æons. And even on this ship, you must remember, I've had plenty of time, in my nocturnal wanderings, to go several times to Orion and back. I'm thinking, by the way, of going farther still. There's a nice little star off to the left, as you round Betelgeuse, which looks as if it might be right at the edge. The last outpost of the finite. I think I'll have a look at it and bring you back a frozen rime-feather."

"It would melt when you got it back."

"Oh, no, it wouldn't—not on *this* ship!"

Clarice laughed.

"I wish I could go with you," she said.

"If only you would! If only——"

He broke off his sentence and looked hard at her—how lovely she was, and how desirable! No such woman had ever before come into his life; there had been no one with whom he had at once felt so profound a sympathy and understanding. It was a miracle, simply—a miracle. No need to put his arm around her or to kiss her—delightful as such small vulgarities would be. He had only to look at her, and to feel, gazing into those extraordinary eyes, that she knew him, had always known him. It was as if, indeed, she might be his own soul.

But as he looked thus at her, reflecting, he noticed that she was frowning.

"What is it?" he said.

She shook her head, slowly.

"I don't know."

"Tell me."

"Nothing. It just occurred to me that perhaps you weren't looking quite so well."

Mr. Arcularis was startled. He straightened himself up.

"What nonsense! Of course, this pain bothers me—and I feel astonishingly weak——"

"It's more than that—much more than that. Something is worrying you horribly." She paused, and then with an air of challenging him, added, "Tell me, did you—"

Her eyes were suddenly asking him blazingly the question he had been afraid of. He flinched, caught his breath, looked away. But it was no use, as he knew; he would have to tell her. He had known all along that he would have to tell her.

"Clarice," he said—and his voice broke in spite of his effort to control it—"it's killing me, it's ghastly! Yes, I did."

His eyes filled with tears, he saw that her own had done so also. She put her hand on his arm.

"I knew," she said. "I knew. But tell me."

"It's happened twice again—*twice*—and each time I was farther away. The same dream of going round a star, the same terrible coldness and helplessness. That awful whistling curve. . . ." He shuddered.

"And when you woke up"—she spoke quietly—"where were you when you woke up? Don't be afraid!"

"The first time I was at the farther end of the dining saloon. I had my hand on the door that leads into the pantry."

"I see. Yes. And the next time?"

Mr. Arcularis wanted to close his eyes in terror—he felt as if he were going mad. His lips moved before he could speak, and when at last he did speak it was in a voice so low as to be almost a whisper.

"I was at the bottom of the stairway that leads down from the pantry to the hold, past the refrigerating plant. It was dark, and I was crawling on my hands and knees . . . *crawling on my hands and knees! . . .*"

"Oh!" she said, and again, "Oh!"

He began to tremble violently; he felt the hand on his arm trembling also. And then he watched a look of unmistakable horror come slowly into Clarice's eyes, and a look of understanding, as if she saw. . . . She tightened her hold on his arm.

"Do you think. . . ." she whispered.

They stared at each other.

"I know," he said. "And so do you. . . . Twice more—three times—and I'll be looking down into an empty. . . ."

It was then that they first embraced—then, at the edge of the infinite, at the last signpost of the finite. They clung together desperately, forlornly, weeping as they kissed each other, staring hard one moment and closing their eyes the next. Passionately, passionately, she kissed him, as if she were indeed trying to give him her warmth, her life.

"But what nonsense!" she cried, leaning back, and holding his face between her hands, her hands which were wet with his tears. "What nonsense! It can't be!"

"It is," said Mr. Arcularis slowly.

"But how do you know? . . . How do you know where the——"

For the first time Mr. Arcularis smiled.

"Don't be afraid, darling—you mean the coffin?"

"How could you know where it is?"

"I don't need to," said Mr. Arcularis. . . . "I'm already almost there."

Before they separated for the night, in the smoking room, they had several whisky cocktails.

"We must make it gay!" Mr. Arcularis said. "Above all, we must make it gay. Perhaps even now it will turn out to be nothing but a nightmare from which both of us will wake! And even at the worst, at my present rate of travel, I ought to need two more nights! It's a long way, still, to that little star."

The parson passed them at the door.

"What! turning in so soon?" he said. "I was hoping for a game of chess."

"Yes, both turning in. But tomorrow?"

"Tomorrow, then, Miss Dean! And good night!"

"Good night."

They walked once round the deck, then leaned on the railing and stared into the fog. It was thicker and whiter than ever. The ship was moving barely perceptibly, the rhythm of the engines was slower, more subdued and remote, and at regular intervals, mournfully, came the long reverberating cry of the foghorn. The sea was calm, and lapped only very tenderly against the side of the ship, the sound coming up to them clearly, however, because of the profound stillness.

" 'On such a night as this—' " quoted Mr. Arcularis grimly.

" 'On such a night as this——' "

Their voices hung suspended in the night, time ceased for them, for an eternal instant they were happy. When at last they parted it was by tacit agreement on a note of the ridiculous.

"Be a good boy and take your bromide!" she said.

"Yes, mother, I'll take my medicine!"

In his stateroom, he mixed himself a strong potion of bromide, a very strong one, and got into bed. He would have no trouble in falling asleep; he felt more tired, more supremely exhausted, than he had ever been in his life; nor had bed ever seemed so delicious. And that long, magnificent, delirious swoop of dizziness . . . the Great Circle . . . the swift pathway to Arcturus. . . .

It was all as before, but infinitely more rapid. Never had Mr. Arcularis achieved such phenomenal, such supernatural, speed. In no time at all he was beyond the moon, shot past the North Star as if it were standing still (which perhaps it was?), swooped in a long, bright curve round the Pleiades, shouted his frosty greetings to Betelgeuse, and was off to the little blue star which

pointed the way to the Unknown. Forward into the untrodden!
Courage, old man, and hold on to your umbrella! Have you got
your garters on? Mind your hat! In no time at all we'll be back
to Clarice with the frozen rime-feather, the time-feather, the
snowflake of the Absolute, the Obsolete. If only we don't wake
. . . if only we needn't wake . . . if only we don't wake in that—
in that—time and space . . . somewhere or nowhere . . . cold and
dark . . . "Cavalleria Rusticana" sobbing among the palms; if a
lonely . . . if only . . . the coffers of the poor—not coffers, not
coffers, not coffers, Oh, God, not coffers, but light, delight, supreme white and brightness, whirling lightness above all—and
freezing—freezing—freezing. . . .

At this point in the void the surgeon's last effort to save Mr.
Arcularis's life had failed. He stood back from the operating
table and made a tired gesture with a rubber-gloved hand.

"It's all over," he said. "As I expected."

He looked at Miss Hoyle, whose gaze was downward, at the
basin she held. There was a moment's stillness, a pause, a brief
flight of unexchanged comment, and then the ordered life of the
hospital was resumed.

THE BACHELOR SUPPER

"You've got to be well oiled," Kit had said. "If you're well oiled, it's all right. You come over to my place before it, and we'll shake up a couple of good potent cocktails, and then you won't mind it. . . . Good God, why do you take it so seriously? It's all in a lifetime!"

No doubt. So was everything, perhaps. But why did it have to be? Why was it a part of the social scheme of things? It seemed to be compulsory—everyone was agreed about that. They all did it. Loo had had one—so had Bill—Everett had got out of his only because he was in Cuba, and hadn't been able to come home in time for anything but the wedding itself. There seemed to be no escaping it. In fact, it seemed to be a sort of social appendage to the wedding, indispensable preliminary. And the cost! . . . He had been staggered. A party of twenty, many of whom he would just as soon not have invited, but who—as his mother had said—*had* to be asked.

And why indeed *did* he take it so seriously?

He asked himself the foolish question as he took a last look at his necktie and the parting in his hair. It seemed to be—it seemed to be—well, a kind of smirch on the whole thing. A deliberate sort of mud-slinging. What must the girls think of it?

What would Loo's wife think of it, if by any chance she could have known what had gone on at Loo's bachelor supper? or how it ended, and where? What had Evelyn thought, when she heard next day that Bill had been picked up in a gutter by a taxi-driver, minus most of his clothes? Of course, most of these girls nowadays were pretty "hard-boiled." But what would Gay think, if the same thing were to happen to *him*?

He winced at the idea, as if it had been something physical. He knew what she would think. He knew what he would think himself. The next meeting between them would be more painful than he could bear. She would be subdued, silent, hurt, forgiving; she would say nothing about it; neither would he; but there it would be, a kind of ominous shadow. They would be embarrassed and silent; they would talk about other things, but with a horrible sense of *not* talking about the thing that most mattered to them. . . . And it might well be that the delicate balance between them would never again be quite as fine as it had been before.

Perhaps there was something wrong with him. Perhaps, as Kit had kept saying, it was simply that he wasn't mature about it. What did it matter? Men and women were profoundly different about these things—much better to face this fact and make the most of it or the best of it. Was there no romanticism in men? none at all?—or at any rate in the average man? Or was it true that in men the romanticism could exist side by side with this extraordinary "something else"? This queer, bare, hideous *propagative* instinct, which of course must have a sort of "tribe" sanction?

Frowning, he went slowly down the stairs and out to his car, which he had left in the drive at the side of the house. Fortunately, nobody was about. Mother was playing bridge at the golf club, Father hadn't come home yet from town. He drove slowly down the Avenue, took an extra turn round the Square, for no particular reason, and then got out and went into the apartment house in which Kit lived.

Kit had the cocktails all ready. Bacardi, and lots of it.

"These will put you right," Kit said. He gave the frosted shaker an extra rattle, and poured the frothed and pinkish liquid into two green glasses. "Here's to everything, God included. Bottoms up. Here's to Gay and Tom and all the little Gays and Toms."

"Fortune."

Kit smacked his lips.

"Pretty good, if I do say so myself. Why in hell, Tom, do you have to get into such a funk about it? They're all good eggs, you know. They won't hurt you. It'll be a good party, if you take it right. Here, have another. There are three apiece."

Feeling the glow in his belly, Tom walked to the window and looked down at the street. A balloon man was passing, with his bobbing cluster of multicolored bubbles. A small fox terrier circled the balloon man rapidly and suspiciously, then sped westward with an air of urgent destiny. A lot of sparrows were chattering in a tree.

"I suppose," he said, without turning, "I'm a sentimentalist. And of course I'm also, as you know, unsocial. To begin with, I hate, really hate, the god-awful publicity of the wedding ceremony; it's practically like going to bed in the middle of Boston Common. Does it seem decent to you? It certainly doesn't to me. . . . And as for this damned bachelor supper—that's worse and more of it. Do you know what I suspect?"

Kit shook the cocktail shaker again, listening to the rattle of ice with his head amusedly on one side.

"No. Don't tell me you've gone paranoid under the strain, and suspect us all of some deep plot against you! . . . You take life too hard."

"You bet I do."

"Well, don't. . . . But tell me what you suspect."

They looked at each other, smiling. The light curtains blew inward from the window on a warm current of air, and the room seemed suddenly to fill with the voices of the sparrows. The sound was multitudinous, idiotic, like life itself. But how was one to say it? Or how was one to be sure that it wouldn't simply be laughed at?

He looked aside, feeling almost guilty at the doubt—guilty and helpless; as if the constellation of his thought were as incommunicable and unanalyzable as that absurd chorus of little voices; as if one were to try to present, atom by separate atom, an ocean, or the world. Would Kit, with two cocktails fuming in his brain, grasp this idea, or all that depended on it?

"Oh, I don't know," he murmured, with conscious inadequacy. And then, a feeling of obligation overcoming him, a fear of hurting Kit's feelings, "It's like this. . . . You know some of those African tribes have a peculiar marriage custom. You know what it is? . . ."

"I can't say I do."

"Every man-jack in the tribe lies with the bride—before the husband is allowed to have her. I daresay you've heard of it. What's the idea behind it? It's not very pretty. . . . A sort of communal business: as if the tribe were itself taking possession of the woman by defiling her; humbling the bridegroom and putting him in his place. It certainly ought to cure him of any fine romantic notions about love, and blast out of him any notion of exclusive proprietorship in his woman! Oughtn't it? Assuming that African tribes *have* any romantic notions! . . . Just imagine what the bridegroom must feel about it."

"I very much doubt if he feels a damned thing."

"Maybe not, if he's completely tribal-minded. But suppose he's a little bit of an individualist—and after all, it's exactly through such preliminary outcroppings of individualism that civilization has developed—and wants to indulge in his own unique reactions to the world or God or whatever you want to call it, in his own way, without any pawings and meddlings and bellowings from the herd. Suppose he has his own little vision of beauty, if you like, and doesn't want it spat upon by the village fathers. He has this little secret something-or-other in his heart or soul, and it's damned precious to him. What's he going to feel about it *then?*"

Kit frowned, holding the palm of his hand against the top of the shaker. He was standing in a characteristic attitude, with one foot crossed over the other. His face was flushed, and he looked puzzled.

"You're getting a little deep," he said. "And yet I see what you mean. Sure, I see what you mean. It would be kind of nasty. . . . Have another?"

Tom held out his glass; Kit smiled and poured.

"Nasty is the word. And that's what a bachelor supper is."

"Don't kid me!"

"No kidding. I mean it."

Kit began to laugh—as if on the assumption that the whole thing was perhaps a rather amusing extravaganza—but then apparently thought better of it. He put the cocktail shaker on the mantelpiece beside a gilt-porcelain snuff-box. Then he rubbed his hand across his forehead.

"I had a couple of these before you came," he said. "So I'm ahead of you. Life is damned funny."

"The hell you say."

"For God's sake, Tom, you don't mean you take all that seriously? Snap out of it. What the devil does it matter? Sometimes I really think you're psychopathic."

"Don't make me tired. I thought you were intelligent enough to understand it. Or sensitive enough to feel it. My mistake."

He moved to the table, to put down his glass, and felt his first step waver slightly. His second was firmer, and he felt that his wavering had been quite unobserved. Kit was in no state to observe. The curtains lifted inward again, undulating, and something in his mind lifted and undulated in the same fashion. It was April, and such things were suitable. It would have been a nice evening for a walk or drive with Gay. To Concord or Lexington. Past that little knoll where the peach trees were always first in bloom. . . . Odd, how difficult, not to say impossible, it had been to discuss all this with Kit. And it had been the same way with Gay. He had thought of telling her about it—his shrinking from the supper—his feeling of contamination in the very idea of it—he had even begun to choose the phrases for it; but then, all of a sudden, he had become tongue-tied. Even in the *talking* about it something precious would be lost. The whole affair was so delicately balanced, so emotionally precarious. . . .

"Look here," said Kit suddenly. "I'm not such a fool as you seem to think. Do you know what? I believe I understand this damned thing perfectly. Perfectly. Now you listen to me."

He came to the window beside Tom, and took Tom's arm, swaying a little and smiling affectionately. With two fingers he lifted the spectacles on the bridge of his nose, and settled them again, his blue eyes remaining fixed on Tom's.

"It's like this. But I think we need one more before I can say it. Shall we have one more? Yes, let's have one more."

He flourished the shaker perfunctorily, poured from it, and came back with the two glasses.

"Now listen," he said, wagging a finger. "It's very, very simple, and it's like this, and you being what you are, it's all for the best in the best of all possible or potential worlds. In the first place —pardon me if I seem a little confused—it's a very nice world, and it passes in the twinkling of an eye, and we're gone, and so it doesn't matter a hell of a lot, anyway. Here we are, all of a sudden, looking out of a window and listening to a couple of hundred sparrows—don't they make the damnedest row you ever heard in your life?—and then all of a sudden here we *aren't*. So I don't see any good reason for getting into a stew about it. You can't fool me—nobody looks after the sparrow when it falls. If it chooses to have a nervous breakdown over some wormy trifle, no-body is going to start a revolt of the angels for *that*, believe me; and nobody is going to be any the better or worse for it fifteen minutes later. And you may not know it, but you're a sparrow. You're a sentimental sparrow, my boy! You've got some fine notion of a romantic vision about love, and Gay, and God, and ideals, and I don't know what-all; you're in that kind of a pink emotional state when you can't, simply can't, look the facts in their dirty little faces. And that's where *we* come in, my boy. It's our job to wallop you where your ideals are tenderest. And why? Do you know why? . . ."

"I can't say I do!"

"Well then, I'll tell you. We're doing it to save you from discovering *too late* that you've been nourishing a beautiful cream-puff of an illusion. Along we come with the big stick, and belt you over the head for too much star-gazing; just in time to save you from falling into the ditch. . . . Selah. . . . Now doesn't that sound to you like common sense?"

"Not a bit. But go ahead."

"That's all . . . that's the whole story. All we do is tell you that Gay is a human being; that you're both of you just plain god-forsaken animals; and that the sooner you realize it, and begin living on *that* plane, the better chance you've got of not making a hash of your life. . . . It's very simple. I'm surprised I didn't think of it before. Just the same, I think I'm pretty intelligent!"

"Remarkably."

"With which"—Kit said, grinning—"I suppose we'd better get going. It's six-thirty already. I ordered two dozen cheap wine glasses, by the way—the sort you can smash without going bank-rupt. *That's* the part I always enjoy. Smashing the glasses. Now what do you suppose *that* symbol means? It looks kind of suspicious to me. If some fool analyst got hold of it——!"

He put his hat jauntily on the back of his head.

"Come on, idealist, and we'll join the tribe."

II.   The drive to the club had temporarily cleared Tom's head. But when Kit pushed him into the private dining room, which was hot, and full of cigarette smoke, and already crowded with the assembled guests, he suddenly felt giddy again. A shout went up, he was at once surrounded by a howling mob of backslappers, the singers of "Mademoiselle from Armentières" broke away from the piano and charged him *en masse*, a potted palm tree was upset, and for no reason at all he found himself laughing, as if the gayety of the irresponsible crowd had abruptly infected him. He was pushed into his place at the head of the table, corks began popping, Kit was making a speech standing on a chair, and the waiters, somewhat flustered, were hurrying from glass to glass with napkined bottles.

"Gentlemen," shouted Kit, "we are here assembled for a biological purpose! We are here assembled——"

"Sit down, sit down!"

"We are here assembled——"

"*Can* it!"

"The glasses are all filled!"

"Propose the toast!"

"Gentlemen, I am here assembled for that very purpose, if only you wouldn't interrupt me." He reached down for his glass. "Gentlemen, I propose a toast to the blushing bride! Everybody up."

The twenty men rose, simultaneously tilted the goblets of champagne, after holding them obliquely toward their host; for a fraction of a moment were silent as they drank; and then, with terrific yells, flung the empty glasses at the fireplace. For an instant, Tom couldn't remember whether he too was supposed to drink and smash his glass; then he did so, noticing that it hit the top of an andiron. The whole floor, before the fireplace, was covered with broken glass. Several goblets had gone wild—one had struck above the mantel, another had hit the piano, another had landed in a Morris chair, without breaking. And instantly, as if this wreckage were the signal for a fury of sound, there was a renewal of yells and singing. A waiter began sweeping up the glass, while others brought new glasss and more bottles. In no time at all, the oysters and soup were dispatched, claret succeeded champagne, and whisky succeeded claret; Roger Day was completely drunk, as usual, and crowned himself with a melon. Kit had left the room, looking very white; and the stories had begun. At first comparatively unobjectionable, they became rapidly more Rabelaisian; shouts of delight greeted them; the table was banged; at one particular sally Roger Day smashed a plate on the floor. A series of limericks were sung, each bawdier than the last. *"O Johnny come up to me—O Johnny come up to me——!"*

After an hour of this, and of steady drinking, Tom began to feel tired of laughing. He also began to feel a deep undercurrent of anger and hostility in his soul; he drank more Burgundy, half listened to the filthy stories, and then abruptly pushed his chair a little back from the table, toward a cool current of damp air which was coming from the open window behind him. What time was it? It was beginning to thunder—the thought of a cool thunderstorm was refreshing. If only he could sneak out—! The lights swam a little above him—he looked up, to see if he could detect them in the act of moving.

"Coffee, sir?"

"Thank you. Some coffee——"

The coffee cup seemed far away—he reached toward it uncertainly. "Mademoiselle from Armentières" was begun again, then "Down in the Lehigh Valley," then "Colombo." Then several songs were sung at once in different parts of the room—the party was becoming disorganized. He felt as if a valve had closed in his ears; everything was curiously muffled. These flushed faces and wide-open mouths had nothing to do with him. A few of the guests were leaving early. Good riddance.

"How are you, old man?"

It was Kit, still very pale, leaning over him unsteadily, his eyes bright.

"Rotten," he said. "I think it's rotten."

"Why don't you try the Roman feather? It's two doors down on the left."

"Go to hell."

"All right. Go to hell yourself!"

A flash of green light flickered over the ceiling, over the glasses, making everything seem artificial, and was followed by a terrific peal of thunder. A ragged chorus of cheers. There was a moment's silence, then the men began stumbling to their feet.

"That was thunder," said Kit. "*I* know thunder when I hear it!"

"Who's for a party, before it begins to rain?" said Roger Day. "I can call up Helen. Don't all speak at once. There's only room for six."

He staggered to the window and looked out intently, holding the curtains aside with his two hands.

"It's raining already," he said. Then he shouted, "Look! There's a fire! Say, kids, there's a fire over there! Let's go! What do you say!"

"Where? Let me see!"

There was a stampede to the window, followed by a terrific exodus into the hall. Everyone at once. Somebody was lying on the floor, moaning. Kit grabbed Tom by the arm and tried to pull him along.

"Come on," he said.

"No. Let me alone. Get out. I'm going by myself and I'm going alone."

"You're drunk."

"You're drunk yourself. Let go my arm, Kit!"

"Don't be a fool. *You* can't drive in that state! This'll give you a chance to get out of it. . . . Come on! Get up!"

Tom permitted himself to be pulled to his feet.

"You're a bunch of lousy dirty little crabs," he said. "All of you."

"Shut up."

Kit dragged him along the hall, found his hat and jammed it on his head for him, and then pushed him out into the street.

"You wait here," he said. "Give me the key to the car."

He took the key and ran off into the darkness. The rain was beginning to quicken. Tom watched the huge drops falling on the circle of illuminated sidewalk under a lamp. They were as big as pansies. He leaned down to watch them. *Spat—spat—spat—* they fell; and one or two plopped on his hat. A car drove off, and then another, their headlights hollowing bright swarms of rain-drops out of the night. From the second car, a head was thrust forth and yelled, "Hurry up, Tom, you fool!"

"Go to hell!" he shouted back.

Let them all go to hell, the damned fools. He started to walk in the opposite direction from that which Kit had taken. There was another lightning flash. The rain began to fall harder. A good thing if he just walked away, and didn't go back. But where would he go? He couldn't go home like this—and there was nowhere else. What about the party at Helen's? He had heard all about Helen from Kit. A "telephone" place. Kit had been there several times; he liked Helen, also a girl from St. Louis who had been there, a married girl who came up to Boston now and then for a "holiday." . . . Or he might go to a movie, and sleep it off. Or the fire? . . . He looked up, and saw that the whole sky was red in the direction of the South Station, a wide glare against the clouds. . . . Kit suddenly seized him by the arm.

"Here! Where do you think you're going?"

"Let me go, you damned fool!"

"The devil I will. . . . You get into that car."

"Will you let me go?"

"No."

He felt Kit's hand closing hard about his wrist. Kit's face was thrust near to his own, white and intense. A giddy wave of hate suddenly overwhelmed him; he struck the white face hard with his open hand, hard as he could, and felt the light spectacles smash. Kit staggered backward, lifted both hands to his eyes, bent his head over in a curious way, and stood perfectly still. Tom took a step toward him.

"Kit!"

"What in God's name did you do that for!"

"Are you hurt? Let me see."

Kit removed his hands, slowly, detaching the broken spectacles, and lifted his face. Blood was streaming down his left cheek from a gash below the eye.

"My God, Kit, I'm sorry! Is your eye hurt?"

"No. . . . Just a little flesh cut, I think. . . . Does it look bad? Try a handkerchief on it."

They moved together into the ring of light under a street-lamp, and Tom began dabbing the wound with his handkerchief. Thank God—it wasn't as bad as he had thought.

"It's about half an inch," he said. "I don't think it's very deep.

You'd better hold the handkerchief against it. . . . Where's the car?"

They walked slowly to the car and got in, Tom taking the wheel. For a moment they sat still, listening to the rain on the roof. It was raining harder than ever, a steady drumming. Kit lay back and shut his eyes, still breathing rather quickly. Then he began to laugh.

"What damned fools we are," he said. "What idiots! Do you think you're sober enough to drive?"

Tom suddenly put his hand on Kit's shoulder.

"Kit, old man, I'm horribly sorry. . . . Do you know why it was?"

"Sure I know why it was!"

"Well—you're a good egg."

He began to laugh himself, a little hysterically, and then abruptly stopped, feeling that in another moment he would be crying.

"*That's* no good," he said, his voice breaking slightly. "Let's go! I'm going to spend the night on your sofa."

He touched the starter, switched on the windshield wiper, and the car began to move. . . . What an astonishing business—what an astonishing business. Thank God, it was finished. . . . And then he thought of Gay; and at once a queer deep feeling of exultation came over him, as if everything were again for the best, in the best of all possible worlds.

BOW DOWN, ISAAC!

I made my first visit to Hackley Falls when I was twelve years old. My mother had died in that year, and my widowed father could think of no better thing to do with me in the school holidays than to send me to visit my two maiden aunts, Julia and Jenny (his elder sisters), who still lived on the family farm, where he himself had been born; and it was here that he had met and married my mother. It was natural enough that he should send me to "Witch Elms"; and I confess that, after a childhood almost all of which had been spent in New York, I looked upon the adventure as a treat. My father impressed upon me that I should have to be helpful—I was given a clear understanding, in strictest New England fashion, of my duties. I was to get the mail twice a day, to fetch the kindling, to go to the village for groceries whenever requested by Aunt Julia or Aunt Jenny, to help old Jim with the livestock—which merely meant chivying the one cow to and from the pasture, or feeding the two pigs which lived in the barn cellar—and to keep my room tidy. If I was very good I might be allowed to drive the horse now and then. And I could help Jim pump the water up to the tank in the attic, which was done by hand.

All of these things I did and, surprisingly enough, didn't find them in the least like duties. I was happier than I'd ever been in my life. With a farm of two hundred acres to run over, with woods to explore, the Mill River to bathe in, and mountains to climb—and summer, too, just beginning—it may be assumed that I didn't find things very irksome. "Witch Elms" stood in the midst of a green valley-meadow, about a quarter of a mile from the river, which we could see from the front porch. The road crossed the river just there by means of an old-fashioned covered bridge, which was painted a raw scarlet; some of the planking was gone from its floor, and I used to love to lie on my belly and look down at the shallow brawling water, in which one could see every pebble and minnow.

Beyond the bridge rose Hateful Mountain, covered with sugar-maples, and along the flank of this the road climbed steeply eastward, eventually, after a mile or so, passing the white farmhouse (perched quite high on a spur of Hateful) which belonged to Captain Phippen, who was a distant connection of ours, and our only frequent visitor. He had been a sea captain, in the coastwise trade, and now lived with his son and daughter-in-law. He could almost invariably be seen on his porch with a powerful spyglass in his hand—he used to tell me that with that spyglass he knew everything that was done in the valley. He knew just which orchard Jim was picking, and how many bushels he got, and even pretended (with a twinkle in his eye) to know the size of the apples. He once told me that in summer, if the light was right, and the church windows were open in Hackley Falls, he could tell whether the Crazy Willards put ten cents or a nickel into the offertory box; but this I knew was apocryphal. I had looked many times through the spyglass myself, and knew that all one could see of the little white town of Hackley Falls was the church steeple, with a golden fish for a weather vane, and the little red cupola of the grammar school, with a black bell in it. Elms and maples completely hid the rest of the town; and in fact, from Captain Phippen's porch, as from our own, the only other human habitation which could be seen was the Crazy Willards', which stood halfway between our house and Hackley Falls—about a mile and a half westward and (looking from "Witch Elms") on the opposite side of the river. This was a low, square colonial farmhouse, which must at one time have been rather fine, but was now collapsing with neglect and old age, and black as pitch with rain-rot. Through Captain Phippen's glass one could make out easily enough the untrimmed trumpet-vine, which covered the western gable with scarlet blossom, and the foul cow-yard which adjoined the house on the east. One could also see the horns of the cattle over the unpainted fence. . . . But I am getting ahead of my story, for this sinister house is really my theme.

With a small boy's love of the abnormal—haunted houses, demon-murderers, crime, violence, and so on—it is not unnatural that the Willard farm should from the first have fascinated me. Nothing, for example, could have kindled my imagination about it more than the fact that I was from the outset warned against it. It was on my very first drive from Hackley Falls to "Witch Elms" that old Jim had first called my attention to the place—he pointed to it, sidelong, with his folded whip.

"See that?" And on my assenting, he added, "Keep away from there. That's the Crazy Willards'. Old Crazy Willard."

He chewed tobacco slowly, not turning his face toward the house. I looked at it, and it seemed then harmless enough.

"Who's Crazy Willard?" I asked.

"He's the very devil. The very devil himself in flesh! If you touched him with a wet finger, it would hiss."

This metaphor so impressed me at the time that I made no further inquiry. Too much had been presented to me all at once; and it was some days before I myself, one evening at milking time, when Jim was squirting the warm white froth into a resonant pail, his knees under Lemon's belly, again brought up the subject. I had passed the house daily—eying it across the little river, of course—but had only once seen any sign of life there. It had been a tall young woman, wearing a poke bonnet, who was rather fiercely raking the grass on the front lawn or yard and who, seeing me (I was taking home the mail), had turned for a moment, resting her hands on the rake handle, and shot at me a look of discomfiting intensity. I at once pretended that I was merely looking at the river.

"What does Old Crazy Willard look like?" I said. "And why is he crazy?"

Jim took so long to answer me that I thought he wasn't going to answer me at all. His rusty old bowler hat was tilted back on his forehead by Lemon's belly, and he chewed his cud of to-bacco. The tiny white threads of milk shot into the pail on al-ternate sides, *sping—spong—sping—spong,* and Lemon now and then tossed her head to shake off flies.

"Why is he crazy?" *Sping—spong—sping—spong.* "Well, I guess because the Lord meant him to be. Him and his wife, and Lydia, too."

"Who is Lydia?"

"Lydia? She's his daughter."

I reflected on this.

"But what does he look like?"

"Well, he's tall and white-haired and kind of stringy, and he has a lot of teeth."

"Does he do crazy things?"

"You leave your mind off him, Billy."

"Well, but does he?"

"He's crazy for religion. They all three are. They sing hymns, mornin', noon, and night."

"Oh."

"You listen when you go by—you'd think they was having conniption fits. And sometimes they are. . . . He's a powerful hand with a whip."

"A whip?"

My puzzled question fell unanswered, except by the singsong of the milk in the pail.

My aunts were as nice as they could be. I think they didn't know much about children—or small boys—and that I was a problem which very likely they discussed, sometimes, till late at night. What fantastic conclusions they reached, heaven only knows! They were very much alike—in fact, at first I couldn't tell them apart. They both wore spectacles and both had thin, white, kindly faces; they dressed in black, with lace over their shoulders, parted their hair severely in the middle, and had bright blue eyes. It was a day or two before I knew that Aunt Julia was the one who had gray hair and usually folded her hands as she talked. She was very gentle. Aunt Jenny was plumper, stuck out in front a little more, had a loud sudden laugh like a man and an aggressive sense of humor. Except to church on Sundays, when Betsy the mare was harnessed to the old closed carriage, and Jim wore a special coat, not quite so green with age as his other, and once a month to tea at the Minister's, and about as often to Captain Phippen's, they never went out. They lived in the house and garden, only occasionally going to the barn for an official inspection. Now and then, if there happened to be a "special sunset," they would take me with them to the upper orchard, from which one had a fine view right along the valley to the west, where one could see the notched mountains against the sun. But this was seldom; and they did it gravely, as if it were a kind of religious duty.

It was on such an occasion, as we stood by a fallen apple tree which, though half broken through at the ground, still continued annually to blossom and bear, and as we watched the sunset fading in the curves of the Mill River, that I first heard the Willards mentioned by my aunts. At that hour and in that light the Willard farm was unusually conspicuous. It stood very black and square and alone against the western light, and even at that distance it looked forlorn and deserted. From where we stood we could see also the little white footbridge which led across from it to the main road. And it was Aunt Julia who first noticed that someone was crossing the river.

"There he goes now," she said.

"Who?"

"Old Isaac. I wish he'd fall in and drown."

"He'd do well to drown in Mill River!"

I could just make out on the footbridge the figure of a man, who seemed to be carrying something in one hand.

"What's he carrying, Aunt Jenny?"

"Keg of hard cider, most likely."

"There'll be hymn-singing tonight, I guess."

"And more than that."

"What does he do?" I asked.

Aunt Jenny gave Aunt Julia a quick look, not meant for me.

"He beats time," she said. And then added, "With a razor strop."

"Jim said it was a whip."

"Well, I guess he isn't particular. It might even be a broom-stick. Anyway, you can hear it for miles around!" Aunt Jenny gave a quick laugh. "And then Lydia keeps out of sight for a while."

I wanted to ask questions, feeling that something queer was behind all this, but at that moment, as the best of the sunset was over, my aunts, picking up their long skirts, began to re-trace their steps toward the house, and nothing further was said. In fact, though the Crazy Willards were seldom far from my mind, and though I never went out without hoping, or half hoping, to meet Isaac, I made no further discoveries about them until several weeks later, when I had walked up to Captain Phippen's to take him a present of gingerbread from Aunt Julia. Long before I had climbed the hill (it was a very hot day) I could see him in his usual rocking chair, with his feet against the porch-rail and his spyglass at his eye. He watched me climb, and when I arrived at last he told me that he had been counting the sweat-drops on my forehead.

"You look hot," he said.

"I am!"

"Well, sit down on your hunkers and rest. Don't tell me your Aunt Julia is sending me more gingerbread! That woman will be the death of me."

I sat down and presently was allowed to look through the precious glass, and of course instantly turned it on the Willard farm.

"I'm looking at the Willard farm," I said.

"Well, I'd be careful, if I was you."

"I can see two great big seashells by the front door."

"If that's all you can see," he said, chuckling, "you're a lucky boy."

"Does old Isaac beat Lydia?"

"What made you think that?"

"Something Aunt Jenny said."

"Well, I dunno, I dunno, maybe he does."

"Is she bad?"

"Maybe she was. She ran away once with some young feller."

"Did she want to marry him?"

"Perhaps she did."

"And what happened then?"

"Old Isaac went and brought her back again. . . . You'll understand it when you're older."

"And did he beat her?"

"Yes, he beat her."

Captain Phippen's face had become grim.

"Your aunts happened to be driving by—I wouldn't be surprised if they didn't save her life! They went in with Jim and stopped him."

"Oh!"

"And now we'll talk about gingerbread."

Of course, I didn't dare ask my aunts about that scene, much as I burned with curiosity. The whole thing seemed to me such a queer mixture of things—the beatings and the hymn-singings and the drinking—that I couldn't in the least fathom it. As a result of a few hints to Jim, while driving Lemon to and from the hill pasture, or passing the Willards on our way to Hackley Falls for supplies (when the subject could be brought up quite naturally with a "There's the Willards', isn't it?") I added a new small item or two, but nothing of great importance. Apparently they were very poor and made only a bare living by selling milk and butter. Old Isaac was a tyrant. He made his wife and Lydia do all the work, while he himself got drunk night after night, slept it off in the morning, and read the Bible all afternoon. He had a violent temper, and at such times went purple in the face. Once he had gone into the post office, and accused the postmaster, Mr. Greene (who also ran the general store), of reading his mail. The fight which ensued was of epic splendor. Isaac had jumped over the counter and grabbed Greene by the throat. They had catapulted all over the store, knocking down boxes of shoes, upsetting glass cases full of cheap candy, wrapping themselves in ladies' muslin dresses, and finally had both rolled right through one of the front shop-windows. Mr. Greene had cut his right forearm so badly that it had to have seven stitches. Eye-witnesses said that Isaac's face was the color of an eggplant. For some strange reason, there had been no arrest; and later on Isaac had walked in one afternoon (when sober, I suppose) and publicly apologized and walked out again. It was still considered the best fight Hackley Falls had ever seen. Isaac, although fifteen years older than Mr. Greene, had had all the best of it—everybody had marveled at his strength. I never went into the store for the mail without hoping that Mr. Greene might, by some chance, have his right sleeve rolled up, so that I could see the scar, but he never did. I imagine he wasn't too proud of it.

Nevertheless, and not so long after my talk with Captain Phippen, it was thanks to Mr. Greene that I made the first of my only two actual visits to the Willard farm. I had walked down one afternoon to get a pound of coffee, and after I had got the tight fragrant paper bag under my arm and paid for it, Mr. Greene looked at me appraisingly over his glasses. He was holding a letter in his hand.

"Billy," he said, "I guess you'd be a good messenger. I'll give you ten cents to deliver this letter to Isaac Willard. What do you say?"

"Sure!"

"Are you going right back?"

"Sure!"

"All right."

He gave me the letter and the ten cents, and I started out almost at a run. It was too good to be true. I had seen at once, by the long blue stamp with a picture of a messenger boy on it, that it was a special-delivery letter—though heaven knows why old Isaac should be getting a special delivery. It came from Bennington, Vermont, and there was a name in the upper left-hand corner of it, but I can't remember what it was. Anyway, I was tremendously excited. What would be happening when I got there? Should I hear the whip or the razor strop going, or screams? It even occurred to me, naturally, that I might have to cut and run for it myself; it might be one of the days when the old man looked like an eggplant. And had Mr. Greene sent the letter by me because he was afraid to take it himself?

That was a disquieting thought and made me slow down my steps. It was quite possible. Nobody liked to go to the Willard farm, which was one of the reasons why their milk business had fallen away to almost nothing. As Jim had told me, if it weren't for everybody's feeling sorry for old Mrs. Willard and Lydia, nobody would have taken their dirty milk anyway. It was Mrs. Willard and Lydia who took the orders and delivered the milk (in an old blue wagon) and collected the bills. If it hadn't been for Mrs. Willard, Jim said, they'd all have starved to death.

The footbridge fascinated me. It consisted of two wide planks, laid over a series of rotten piles, with a handrail at either side. The water under it was very shallow and littered with every kind of débris. There were innumerable tin cans, bottles, fragments of rusted iron, quantities of broken glass—even an old muskrat trap, with a piece of rusted chain still attached, which I thought a little of salvaging. I stood there for several minutes, looking down into the water, and out of the corner of my eye glancing also at the house. There was no sign of life, not a sound. I could see the half-dozen cows up on the hill—a spur of Hateful—a half mile above me. All the windows were shuttered, except one on the ground floor, to the right of the door; and this, despite the hot weather, was closed. As I walked up the brick path I saw two humming-birds dart out of the trumpet-vine and whizz round the corner; and I caught the strong, rank smell from the cow-yard at the other end. I went up the four steps to the shabby porch and knocked at the door. Standing there, I could see into the cow-yard, which was paved with cobbles. Or rather, it *had* been paved at one time; now, one merely saw the cobbles here and there, amid dung and water. An old tub and pump stood at the far end, and beyond that the dilapidated shed.

I waited for several minutes without hearing anything and then, somewhat timidly, knocked again. The door withdrew itself swiftly from my knock, and a white-haired woman stood before me. She was tall, and had the blackest and fiercest eyes I have ever seen. She was rubbing one red fist against her blue-checked apron.

"Well!" she said, snappishly. And then, before I could muster speech, *"What* is it?"

I felt guilty, and stammered something about a letter for Mr. Willard, holding it out toward her half-heartedly.

At that, she merely said "Isaac!" in a sharp voice, and turned her back on me. As she walked away, I had a glimpse into the room. It was large, with a huge fireplace, but almost entirely bare. There were no rugs on the unpainted floor, which looked spotlessly clean, and the furniture consisted of three or four ordinary kitchen chairs and a kitchen table. Isaac I saw at once—he was sitting at the table with a book open before him. If he had heard his wife, he gave no sign of it. He continued to read as if nothing whatever had occurred. And while I waited for him to move, I saw another woman—Lydia, I supposed—at the other end of the table. Her head was down on the table, her arms outstretched, her hands clasped. I thought I saw her shoulders moving. Then Isaac rose, put his hand flat on the page for a moment, as if for a kind of emphasis, and came toward the door. He wore red rubber boots which swished as he walked, and his steps were heavy. His face—as I saw when he stood before me, or rather above me—was narrow and high and flushed, with the gray suspicious eyes set very close together. His mouth, turned downwards at the corners, was curiously arched over his big teeth, and the effect was a mixture of ferocity and weakness.

"Well?" he said.

"It's a letter for you," I said.

"Why didn't Mr. Greene bring it?"

"I don't know, sir. He asked me to bring it."

"Well, by Ephraim! . . ." He closed up his eyes to slits and glared. "Give it here. And don't you ever do his dirty work again."

He took hold of my shoulder so firmly with thumb and forefinger that it hurt me. "You hear?"

"Yes, sir!"

"And now, git!"

And with that he shut the door so quickly that I had to do a sort of skip to avoid having any feet caught against the jamb.

When my aunts and Jim heard of this expedition, they were unfeignedly horrified. I was told never to do such a thing again —never to go to the house, nor even on the Willard land. My Aunt Julia was especially alarmed. She seemed to feel that I had done well to escape with my life! Even Jim, I could see, was concerned; he shook his head and solemnly advised me to give old Isaac a wide berth.

"If you'd a' struck him on one of his bad days," he said, ruminating, "you might have got a hell of a licking, and a sermon thrown in. There was a kid in Hackley Falls got beaten black and blue once."

"Who was it?"

"Well, I don't remember."

"What had he done?"

"Well, I don't remember that either. But you keep away from there, Billy, and it won't do you no harm. That's what I say."

All of this not unnaturally only whetted more keenly my appetite for further adventure, and it wasn't long before I had discovered a new and thrilling pastime. Crossing the Mill River by the covered bridge, I would then turn westward, climb up what was called the Rock Pasture, one of those delightful New England hillsides of granite and cedar and juniper, and eventually come to the wood which covered the long spur of Hateful Mountain. This spur ran westward as far as Hackley Falls itself, roughly paralleling the river. It had occurred to me that if I were to scout through the edge of the woods, I should eventually come out at the upper end of Isaac's cow-pasture. And from there, taking cover behind the firs or birches or rocks, it would be easy to get a view of the Willard house, and from no very great distance.

What profit I expected to get from this, heaven knows! The first time I did it I took elaborate precautions—climbed high into the maple and chestnut grove, and then, when I began to approach Willard's farm, got down and crawled forward on my hands and knees. I crept through the fringe of white birches at the edge of the pasture and then found to my delight that I could make my way down the hill toward the house by crawling from rock to rock, at last taking up a position not more than three hundred yards from the back of the house. Here I had admirable shelter—a great granite boulder, covered with silvery lichens, beside which grew a cedar tree. There was a warm hollow of grass behind it and, looking between the rock and the tree, I could see perfectly without in the least being seen. Old Isaac's cows grazed peacefully round me, not at all disturbed; and I could look straight down into the cow-yard to which they would eventually be driven.

The house itself was shuttered, at the back, as in front. There were two doors—one leading down into the cow-yard, from the side, and another at the back, from which occasionally Mrs. Willard would come out to hang her washing on the clothesline, or she and Lydia together to work in the small vegetable garden. On such occasions they both wore old-fashioned calico bonnets. They worked grimly and in silence, hoeing and digging like men. At the end of the patch nearer to me, they were scarcely a hundred yards away, and I could hear the regular clink of their hoes on the pebbles, and once in a long while a remark—usually made by old Mrs. Willard and usually very brief and sharp. They never looked at each other when they spoke. When, now and then, they paused for a rest, they would stand with their hands on their hoes and gaze down toward the house. There seemed to me something ominous in the way they did this—they never looked anywhere else and they were always perfectly silent. It gave me the shivers. As for the old man, I wondered what he was doing. I never heard him singing, as he was supposed to do every afternoon, and very seldom saw him. Once in a long while he would come out of the house and lurch across the cow-yard to the shed—what he went for, I don't know —perhaps cider.

I made this expedition many times in my first three summers at Hackley Falls; and by degrees, as nothing spectacular ever happened, I was beginning to think myself a fool. Still, the rumors about the Willards grew in number and intensity—they were becoming almost legendary figures of heroic size—and it was easy enough, even for a boy, to see that all three of them were half crazy; one had only to watch the way they walked. Moreover, I had got into the *habit* of going to the Willard pasture—it was something to do. And in the fall there were the chestnut trees, the best of which were directly north of the field. I used to go there and club the trees and then carry my spoils down to my Tarpeian Rock, there to eat them at leisure while I kept an eye on the enemy.

I was clubbing my favorite tree one afternoon, in the third fall, when suddenly, from behind, a cold hand closed round my neck, and I felt myself being shaken. My heart fairly fell out of me when I looked up and saw that it was old Isaac who had hold of me. But to my astonishment—not that it by any means mitigated my terror—I saw that he was smiling, smiling in a horrible way which looked as if it might be meant to be playful or affectionate. He continued to hold me by the neck and to shake me gently.

"Whose tree is that?" he said.

"I don't know, sir."

"It's mine. So you know, now—don't you?"

"Yes, sir."

"Don't you never read the Bible?"

"Yes, sir."

"Ever learn the Ten Commandments?"

"Yes, sir."

Keeping his hold on my neck, he turned me round, so that I faced him directly for the first time. He had on a dirty corduroy coat with a red lining. He was still smiling, and I was more frightened than ever. It seemed to me that he was drunk.

"Well, what's the eighth?"

"I don't remember, sir."

He shook me playfully—but harshly—by the neck.

" 'Thou shalt not steal.' Say it."

"Thou shalt not steal."

"Who's your father?"

This question was shot at me so abruptly that I was confused. Did he mean—since we were talking of the Commandments— God? Or did he simply want to tell my father what I'd been doing?

"Mr. Walter Crapo, sir."

"Say! . . . I knew your mother. She was a godfearing woman. Now give me that there club."

I gave him the stick, which all this time I had been holding guiltily in my hand, and I trembled, thinking he was going to beat me with it. To my amazement, instead, he drew away, bent over backwards till the stick was touching the ground, all the while smiling at me with half-shut eyes (and I saw for the first time the thickness of his white eyebrows) and then with a whip of his long arm, let the club fly upward into the very top of the tall tree, where it went crashing among the thickest cluster of nuts. The burrs pattered heavily on the grass and sweetfern about us, and then the stick followed more slowly, rocking from branch to branch and sliding over the planes of nodding leaves. Old Isaac was delighted.

"That was good," he said, breathing heavily. "And I ain't done it for years, neither."

"Yes, sir."

"Now fill your cap, boy, and git home, and then you cut those nuts in two and butter them with cheese. That's Adamneve on a raft!"

"Yes, sir."

"And don't you go coming here any more like a thief! When you want my chestnuts, you come and ask for 'em."

Before I had time to say a word in reply, he turned and went plunging down the hillside. He had on his red rubber boots as usual, and his mane of white hair looked very bright in the sunlight. I watched him until he had entered his cow-yard, and the shed, and then, reappearing, had stumbled into the house. Then I gathered the chestnuts and went home.

But I said nothing to Aunt Julia and Aunt Jenny.

It was two years before I visited "Witch Elms" again, and when I did I found that startling changes had occurred. In the first place, Jim met me at the station with a spick-and-span brand-new Ford touring car. I could hardly believe my eyes. Were my aunts being modernized? To tell the truth, I was feeling this year rather grown up and superior, and had somewhat reluctantly consented to be sent once more to Hackley Falls. And as I see it now, the Ford was a very cunning piece of foresight on the part of my Aunts Jenny and Julia. Possibly my father had conferred with them. At all events, the sight of the Ford cheered me up at once. The summer wouldn't be so bad. And I felt still better when Jim told me that I was going to be taught to drive, after which I was to be the family chauffeur. I understood this further, when I saw that Jim himself was decidedly uncomfortable in the car. It was apparent that he missed his whip. He had also (I noticed with amusement) given up the old time-honored derby hat and substituted for it a tweed cap, in which he looked extraordinarily foolish. This too, I supposed, was a concession to modernity.

"Well, Jim," I said, "what's the news? I suppose the aunts are fine?"

"Well, yes, they been very well, Mr. Billy, they been very well this winter, except for Miss Jenny's gout, which troubled her some. But I reckon she'll be all right again, come hot weather."

"And Captain Phippen?"

"Yep—same as ever."

"I suppose he still sits there with that spyglass."

"Oh, sure! It's as good as a movie to him. Not much the old man misses with that glass!"

Jim drove very slowly, and it was some time before we passed the footbridge which led to the Willard farm. I turned and looked at the house, which was more incredibly dilapidated than ever. The shingles were beginning to curl with rot. A great poll of trumpet-vine had collapsed from the western gables and hung raggedly toward the ground, just as the wind had left it. The front fence of the cow-yard had fallen in, too, and lay where it had fallen. Otherwise, it was just as I remembered it, with all the windows shuttered except one. But there were no cows on the hillside at the back.

"Where are the cows?" I said.

"Didn't you hear?"

"Hear what?"

"Why, the old man, old Isaac, he had a stroke."

"A stroke? You mean he's dead?"

"Oh, no—no such luck. Just paralyzed. Paralyzed from the waist down."

"Good Lord. When did that happen?"

"Last year—year and a half ago. The judgment of God, too, that's what they say. He was beating Miss Lydia when he was struck down."

"You don't say!"

"Yep! He laid unconscious like a log for two weeks, and they thought he was all through. But then he come to. He would! Now he reads his Bible in a wheel-chair, and I guess, from what I hear, he gets what's coming to him from the women folks!"

"What do you mean, Jim?"

"Well, I guess it's *them* that beats *him* nowadays. Anyways, that's what young Hal Greene says. He said when he went there once he heard the old man screaming bloody murder. And serves him right! Hell will be too good for Isaac. Of all the mean sons of bees——"

I got no more out of Jim; but a week later, when for the first time I triumphantly drove the Ford up the hill to Captain Phippen's, I began to feel something very sinister and dangerous in the situation. Captain Phippen was surprisingly serious about it.

"You know what I think, Bill?" he said.

"What?"

"I think those scarecrows'll kill him. That's what I think. I think they'll kill him."

"Why?"

"They're crazy as bedbugs. To my mind, they should all have been locked up years ago. And Good Jumping Jupiter Almighty! look what the old devil has put them through! You couldn't blame them. . . . Not that I'm in love with the old man, any more than with those she-fiends either. But just the same it kind of gives you the shivers to think of him sitting there in a wheel-chair with his Bible, and those two harpies just itching to cut his throat! . . . Doesn't it?"

This was a new light on the situation.

"It does," I said.

"You bet it does!"

"Couldn't something be done?"

"Go and try it, my boy. Even Mr. Perkins, the minister, don't dare go near the place."

"Well, how do they live?"

"God knows. But they live, somehow."

I returned home with a new sense of disaster impending; but neither I, nor anybody else, could possibly have foreseen what shape it was to take, or how horrible it was to be.

It was difficult at "Witch Elms," however, to be for long concerned about remote possibilities of disaster; and as I settled down once more into the peaceful life with Aunt Julia and Aunt Jenny, I thought less and less about the Willards. To tell the truth, my boyish excitement about them had worn itself out. If indeed a tragedy was enacting itself in that forlorn old house, it no longer seemed to me of heroic proportions. My former terrors and wonder now seemed to me childish, and I drove past the house in the Ford twice a day with scarcely a glance at it. And, moreover, my aunts kept me busy. The car was a new toy, and they couldn't have enough of it. What with that and the new telephone, and the phonograph, the tempo of life had changed at the farm; and the days went like minutes. Hardly a day passed, in fact, that we didn't make a long expedition. My aunts had seldom been more than ten miles from Hackley Falls, and it was wildly exciting to them to be taken to Rutland, to Burlington, to Bellows Falls, or over the Mohawk Trail to Fitchburg. We even spent a night at Windsor, and I shall always remember with what girlish delight and flutter Aunt Jenny and Aunt Julia came down to dinner in the great gilt dining hall of the Green Mountain House. They were as pink as debutantes, and as coquettish, and they insisted on eating every item in an enormous table-d'hôte dinner. I even think they would have danced with me if I had suggested it—though Aunt Julia's scorn of "these modern so-called dances" was outspoken.

Meanwhile, Hackley Falls was having a new excitement of its own. A revival had come to town—something the town had never had before. I first heard of it from Mr. Greene at the post office; he was surprised I hadn't known. It had been there for three days already, and the whole countryside was wild about it. Farmers and their families were driving in from miles around.

There were mourners' benches and a sawdust trail and all the fixings, he said. And the Reverend something-or-other Boody, a Southerner, was a humdinger, a real old-fashioned artist in brimstone and hellfire. Fairly fried your liver in you, Mr. Greene said, and talked just like a nigger. . . . Mr. Perkins, the local minister (who got a salary of a thousand dollars a year) was furious. He had said something nasty about the Reverend Boody in his last Sunday's sermon. . . . But the Reverend Boody continued to take in money.

It was that same afternoon, when I was bringing the aunts back from a drive to Manchester, that I first saw it. It was a circular tent, of about the size used in county fairs, with a little peak at the top, and it had been pitched in a field on the Hammond farm at the western end of the town, half a mile out. At the far end of the field, which had been churned and trampled brown with feet and hoofs and wheels, was a motley assemblage of cars, wagons and buggies, and tethered horses. I wondered what Cross-eyed Hammond got for it. The tent itself was emblazoned, all the way round, with flamboyant posters. In scarlet flaming letters we were adjured to Hit the Sawdust Trail, to Come to Jesus, Repent, Repent, Seek Salvation in the Lord, Cling to Jesus, and so on. I stopped the car and invited the aunts to go in. We could hear the somewhat dismal sound of a hymn. But they declined, and I drove on, resolving to come back myself later.

The next day brought a typical northeast gale and rain. At such times the clouds seemed to come right down into the valley, like fog, and sensible people stayed indoors. My aunts had no desire to use the car, so I decided I would use it myself. I went for the mail in the forenoon and then drove out to the revival and, as I might have foreseen, found that the weather had been too much for most of Mr. Boody's audience. Only a half-dozen vehicles stood in the muddy field, and from the tent, though the wind was blowing toward me, I couldn't hear a sound. However, I got out and crossed the field and entered the tent through a flap-door. At first when I entered my entire attention was taken up by the tent itself, which seemed to be on the point of collapse. It rocked like a tree in a storm. I had no sooner got in and seen the sawdust trail before me than a violent gust almost lifted the whole structure. With a series of sharp reports like cannon-shots, the segments of canvas on the lee side bellied outward, and then, as the pressure relaxed, clapped inward again. The ropes creaked, a damp wind assailed me across the sawdust, and in the roof of the tent there was a continuous low whistling. And, uplifted against the elements, I could hear the shrill voice of the Reverend Boody.

"Who's a-goin' to discountenance the Lord?" he cried. And then after a moment he answered himself, *"No* one!"

And just as I sneaked into a bench at the back, the rest of the tiny audience stood up and chanted:

"Amen!"

I rose hastily and sat down when they did.

"Who's a-goin' to flout the King of Justice?" he cried—and I saw him now, a small, knock-kneed, plump fellow, with a frock coat and moist eyes. And again he answered himself sternly, *"No* one!" And again the small audience rose and sang, "Amen," drawling it out interminably. . . . *"Who's* a-goin' to fool the Lord of Hosts? . . . *No* one."

"A-a-a-a . . . me-n-n-n-n!"

I was just beginning to think that this business of standing up and sitting down might soon become a nuisance, when Mr. Boody launched himself into what seemed to be a kind of sermon. He walked to and fro on his little muslin-draped platform, with his pudgy hands clasped behind his back, and began shouting disjointed phrases.

"Abraham! Abraham and Isaac on the mountain! . . . And Abraham rose up early in the morning and saddled his ass and went unto the place of which God had told him!"

He paused, glowering at his audience, and it was in that moment that I saw, for the first time, the Willards, Mrs. Willard and Lydia. They were at the extreme left-hand end of the second row, all by themselves, so that I could see them in profile.

They were both in white, with black hats, and leaning intently forward. Their noses were exactly, preposterously, alike.

"And Abraham took the wood of the burnt offering and laid it upon Isaac his son; and he took the fire in his hand, and a *knife!* . . ."

A series of loud reports from the flapping canvas interrupted him, and with hand uplifted he waited for quiet. In that instant Lydia Willard turned round, and, by accident, looked straight at me. She had her mother's fierce black eyes, the same thin-lipped intensity and whiteness; but what most struck me about her face was its extraordinary smallness: it was almost a doll's face, or a monkey's, small, hard, and concentrated. It seemed to me there was nothing human in it whatever.

"And Abraham stretched forth his hand, and took the knife to *slay* his son. . . . My brothers and sisters in Christ"—Mr. Boody paused again for effect, and glared from one to another of his audience—"what does this mean for us? What does this grand story tell us? Two things . . . *two things!* . . . The first, that we must trust in God. His will is our will. The second—" Again he paused dramatically. And then suddenly, pointing a quivering finger directly at Mrs. Willard, who gave a start and then sat rigid, "What is the second? That we must be prepared to offer up to God in holy sacrifice even those things that are dearest to us. What He asks, we must give. If He asks us for our children, we must give them to Him. . . . Why, is God less dear to us than our children? Is His word less than our law? Do we understand Him? Do we dare . . . do we *dare* to say that we know what His purpose is? No!"

He was beginning to work himself up. He paced rapidly to and fro on his little wooden platform, now and then stopping for a moment to thump his fist on the deal table. But I thought I had had enough; and a little later, seizing the opportunity afforded by another shuddering series of explosions from the tent, I sneaked out to the car and drove home. It seemed to me a pretty poor show.

The wind blew all afternoon, with sudden squalls of hard

rain. At one time it was so dark that we had to light the lamp in the sitting room. Looking out of the front windows, we could at such moments see hardly farther than the red-covered bridge; Hateful Mountain had been engulfed in cloud. Then would come a sudden lifting of the flying rain, and a quick shaft of mild sunlight would show us the swollen river, brown with mud, rushing westward through the drenched valley. The dirt road was a solid sheet of water.

It was a little after five when the telephone rang. I heard Captain Phippen's voice.

"That you, Bill?"

"Yes."

"Hello, Bill? . . . There's something queer down at the Willards'."

His voice suddenly faded away.

"What's that?" I said.

"Can you hear me? . . . I say, there's something *queer* down at the Willard farm. Think you could come up here quick in your Ford, and fetch me?"

"Why, sure. . . . Sure, I'll be right up!"

Aunt Jenny put down her magazine and looked at me sharply.

"What's the Captain want?" she said.

"Oh, just company, I guess."

"Well, bring him back to supper—he owes us a visit. And tell him there's popovers."

"I will, Aunt Jenny."

I grabbed my hat and raincoat and ran to the barn for the car. It had almost stopped raining—there was a hole in the clouds overhead—but the northeast still looked black.

What on earth was happening?

I learned soon enough. Captain Phippen was waiting for me on his porch, in his oilskins. He had his spyglass in his hand.

"I didn't mean to scare you, Bill," he said, "but just take a look. It don't look right."

I ran up the wooden steps, took the glass from his hand, and directed it toward the Willard farm. I could see the house very clearly at that moment. A shaft of watery sunlight illuminated it brilliantly against the somber rain-colored country beyond. And it looked exactly as it always did. But when I swung the glass to the right, toward the cow-yard, what I saw amazed me. Above the fragment of board fence which still remained (where years before we used to watch the horns of cattle tossing) I could distinctly see the heads and shoulders of the two women. There was nothing so remarkable in that. What was remarkable was the way the heads and shoulders were behaving. They glided to and fro rapidly, now to the right and now to the left— and now and then it seemed to me that their arms were raised— but they always came back to the same spot. At this spot, the heads and shoulders would sometimes disappear entirely, only, the next instant, to leap high into the air again, exactly like puppets. It looked as if the two women were doing some idiotic sort of dance. In fact, it was so absurd that I laughed.

"It's damned funny!" I said.

Captain Phippen made no answer. He took the glass from me and leveled it westward.

"What do you say we go down there, Bill?" He put the brass telescope on the porch-rail.

"Sure, if you like!"

"All right."

"You think there's something wrong?"

"Yeap, I do. D'you see that chair on the porch?"

"No."

"Take another look."

I did so, and sure enough, on the little side-porch, next to the cow-yard, I could make out the wheel-chair, lying on its back, with its wheels in the air.

"That's queer," I said.

"And not so funny! . . . Let's go down there."

It took us about ten minutes to get to the Willard footbridge. The flooded river was almost up to the level of the bridge; and as we walked cautiously along the slippery planks, we could hear crazy shouts from the cow-yard. For the moment, we could see nothing, because of the low, straggling lilac-hedge which ran across the front corner of the yard. But when we had passed this barrier we stood still in sheer astonishment.

The two women had gone completely mad.

I'm sure they had seen us approaching; but if they had, they paid no attention to us. Round and round the cow-yard, which was half mud and half water, they were dancing in a grotesque, hobbling circle, like a pair of scarecrow bacchantes. They were so drenched with rain and mud, from head to foot, as to be hardly recognizable. Raising and flapping their arms, they shouted incessantly and incoherently something that sounded like *"Bow* down, Isaac! *Bow* down, Isaac!"; and as we ran forward we could see that the huddled object in the mud, which now and then they paused in their dance to kick, was old Isaac, but scarcely distinguishable from the filth in which he lay. The red rubber boots pointed mutely toward the river. It was when he saw these, I think, that Captain Phippen shouted something harshly at the two women; and, suddenly quieted, they drew a little way off from us and stared at us with the dull, curious surprise of animals. Without protest or comment, almost without interest (standing on a corner of the porch), they then watched us pick up the lifeless body and carry it, dripping, into the house. At first I thought Isaac was dead. It seemed incredible that such a shapeless thing—covered with water and mud and blood—could be alive. The sight of his face—no longer recognizably human—sickened me. But Captain Phippen, hardier than I, opened the soaked waistcoat and discovered that Isaac's heart was still beating. . . . I was only too glad to be sent for the doctor.

Two days later, nevertheless, old Isaac died, a sacrifice to the Lord. An embarrassed coroner and jury gave the cause of his death, officially, as "an apoplexy, induced by over-exertion." During this time, and for a few days after, Mrs. Willard and Lydia, who had both become suddenly very meek, were left unmolested; the town authorities were uncertain what to do with them. Was it a murder? Or, if not, what was it? . . . The State authorities were more decided. A week later we heard that Lydia and her mother had been "spirited" away, as the papers put it, to the asylum.

And on the same day the Reverend Mr. Boody left town very hurriedly. Mr. Perkins had again mentioned him (it seemed) in the pulpit of the Congregational Church. "As a direct result of the maunderings of this primitive and predacious fanatic . . ." said Mr. Perkins, among other things . . . !

But was it only that? I hold no brief for poor Mr. Boody; but it seemed to me that the affair wasn't quite so simple. Though it was true enough, apparently, that several people had seen the two women driving back from the revivalist meeting just before the tragedy, "as if hell possessed them." And even then (Mr. Greene said) "They were singing!"

A PAIR OF VIKINGS

The first I heard of it—and heard of them—was, of course, from the irrepressible Paul. Naturally. Nothing went on, in that little English country town, that Paul didn't at once know; and nothing he knew could remain for more than five minutes a secret. He was everywhere, with that long aristocratic nose of his, that hawk-bright and frost-blue stare—whether it was to make quick notes on his little pad for a sketch, or to make a sketch itself, or to take elaborately careful photographs of some obscure "subject" which was later to become, as he put it, an "idea." You would meet him anywhere, everywhere. Perched on a stile, miles from anywhere, in the middle of the marsh, you would find him waiting to get a very special and particular light on the reeds, meanwhile writing out, in his tiny needle-sharp handwriting, any number of color charts for proposed landscapes which read like poems, like Imagist poems. Once I discovered him astride an old wreck of a steamroller, which had been abandoned by a corner of the muddy little river. And once flat on his belly in the very middle of the path to the shipyards, taking, from that earthworm angle —angleworm?—a peculiar fore-shortened photograph of some up-ended, half-finished fence posts. In fact, he was into everything.

But people, too—he was just as excitable about people, just as curious about them, as about anything else. He was a "collector" of people, and especially the odd and queer ones, or the brilliant ones; and if his extraordinary studio was a perfect museum of oddments—shells, old bottles, misshapen stones, dead leaves, dead insects, broken dolls, whatever had taken his fancy, or struck him as suggestive—so his *salons* were full of the most surprising people imaginable. He didn't care where they came from or what they did, so long as they had character, or were handsome, or were amusing—those were the three tests. The social mixtures, at these semi-occasional *salons,* were simply indescribable—women with blue hair, yogis, dipsomaniac composers, circus dwarfs, countesses, mannequins, chorus girls—but it made no difference, they always seemed to have a good time, Paul saw to that; and of course Paul himself had the best time of all. Whether he was discussing the psychological implications of surrealism with a pale Belgian poet, or giving amusingly amorous advice about her make-up to a pretty, an extremely pretty, young society photographer, it was all the same to him. He enjoyed life immensely.

It was no surprise to me, therefore, when he came under my lighted window, late one summer evening, and told me, laughing excitedly, that he had something to show me.

"What is it?" I said.

"Come down and see."

When I had joined him in the cobbled street, and repeated my question, he asked one of his own—he asked if I knew that a fair had come to town. As a matter of fact, I did. Early that day I had seen the first of the brightly-striped tents and pavilions going up, and the gaudy gypsy wagons drawn up in a ring on the playing-salts, and the ditch being dug behind a canvas screen, for a latrine, and the fantastic red-and-gold horses of the merry-go-round emerging proudly from their dirty covers. It was the fair's annual visit to the town, for a week of penny gambling and loud music, but there was nothing so remarkable in that. And I said so.

"Ah—but have you seen it all—have you seen the Drome of Death?"

"The Drome of Death?"

"Yes—and my pair of vikings!"

"Vikings! A pair of vikings! What on earth are you talking about?"

"Then you *haven't* seen it all—not by any means. My dear fellow—the most beautiful pair of human beings you ever saw in your life! Come along, or we'll be too late."

We hurried along the High Street then, to the little cliff that overlooks the playing-salts, and there below us was all the glare and uproar of the fair—the crowds, the shouts, the strange squealing watery music of the merry-go-round, with its circling and nodding horses, the rows of painted swing-boats, with their tense and silent occupants clinging to the ropes as they darted up from light into shadow, and down into light again—it was all exactly as usual, exactly as it always was. Or so I was thinking, until I heard a sound that seemed to me unfamiliar. It sounded like a motor-bike being accelerated in bursts, each louder than the last—a crescendo of mechanical roars, and then a dying fall, and another crescendo of roars, and a third; and looking down from our parapet to see if I could find where it came from, I saw the Drome of Death for the first time, and then below it, in a dazzle of spotlight, standing on a little raised dais of bright red plush, with the two motor-bicycles beside them, the vikings.

Even at that distance, I could see that Paul must be right. There was something regal in the proud and careless stance of the two blue figures. They stood there above the crowd with a sort of indolent patrician contempt; you feel the same thing in a caged lion or tiger at the zoo. And when we had descended the steep stairway, which quartered down the face of the little cliff, and had pressed through the crowds of merry-makers round the gambling booths and coconut-shy, and came to the foot of the red plush dais, it was at once evident to me that not only had Paul not exaggerated, but that he was guilty of an under-statement. The boy and girl—for they seemed hardly more than that—were blindingly, angelically, beautiful. Angelically, because they were both so incredibly fair, so blond, so blue-eyed—but also because there was a fierce purity about them, something untamable, almost unchallengeable. Vikings, yes—Paul had hit the nail on the head, as usual. And the effect was further heightened—now that I looked again—by the fact that the girl, who was otherwise dressed exactly as the boy was, in a blue shirt open at the throat, and loosely fitting dark blue trousers, wore a snug little blue hat, which sat very close to her fair head, with bright silver wings at either side. The effect was really magical; for as she looked over our heads, undazzled by the brilliance of the spotlight in which she stood, it was as if she were already in swift motion, already positively flying. She was speed itself—she was an arrow. And her eyes were the bluest, and the fiercest, I have ever seen.

Meanwhile, the boy had raced the engine of his motor-bike three or four times with a shattering roar, the ticket seller announced through a little megaphone that the performance, the last of the evening, would begin, and people were climbing up the rickety stairs that led to the top of the great varnished cylinder which was called the Drome of Death. A perfect cat's cradle of wire stays tethered it to earth—I noticed that these, like the wall of the Drome itself, seemed to be brand new—a fact which subsequently, of course, was verified. The boy and girl wheeled their motor-bikes along the runway to a door in the Drome, which an assistant clamped fast behind them, Paul bought the two tickets, and we hurried up the stairs.

"Do you mean to say they're going to ride *round* in this mere barrel?" I said, as we seated ourselves, and looked down into the wooden interior. Viewed from the rim, it really looked like an enormous dice-cup. The two vikings stood beside their motor-bikes, wiping their hands.

"Of course. Nothing but centrifugal force—quite simple, really, I believe—they've been doing it for years in the States—but just the same it gives you quite a thrill. And those two *people*—my God, did you ever see anything like them? *Look* at that girl! *Look* at the way she stands there! Like a flame, my boy—she's like a flame. And he's really just as fine—they're married, I think."

"Married? Those children?"

"Well, she's wearing a ring—you'll see it when she comes up here."

"Comes up here?"

"Right to the top, almost up to the top—that's why they've got this guard-wire here. . . ."

The boy, his fair cool face turned upward, was saying:

"—you see how it is—the risks are thought to be too great, and therefore we are unable to obtain any insurance whatever. No life insurance company will take us—no matter what the premium. That is why I ask you to make any contribution you can, no matter how small—it simply goes into a separate fund which we keep in case of accident."

He stood there, looking up, calmly and as if appraisingly—one hand resting lightly on his hip—the girl was leaning idly, indifferently, against her motor-bike, not looking anywhere, and visibly bored—it was all quite extraordinary. A cultured voice, too, clear and firm—the accent that of a gentleman. Pennies, sixpences, a few shillings, fell spinning and rolling into the Drome—he said "thank you—thank you—" as he stooped unhurryingly, and with irreproachable dignity, to pick them up. The girl watched him, unmoving, for a second or two, and then began examining her fingernails.

She remained like that, too, exactly like that, at the center of the Drome, while he started his motor-bike, rode with increasing speed round and round the tilted floor at the bottom, and then suddenly was circling round the wall itself. The uproar was deafening. The pent-up racket of the motor-bike would have been quite enough by itself—but in addition the Drome began to creak terrifyingly under that swift rush of pressure and weight, and you could see it actually changing in shape as the rider flashed round the gleaming walls. Higher and higher he came, spiraling always nearer, until at last he was roaring past us within arm's reach of the top, the hot gust beating against our faces and gone and then back again, his fair hair blown back like a flag. And then he was dipping downward again: and had taken his hands off the handlebars; and his arms outspread, was circling as easily as a swallow. It was as beautiful, and looked just as easy, as that. It was pure flight.

I was just going to say something like this to Paul, and just thinking to myself that swallows alone, of all birds, seem to use flight for pure pleasure, when I happened to look at the girl. She had not moved. The proud face, under its silver wings, was turned slightly aside and downward, she again examined her fingernails, still leaning idly against her tilted machine, only once did she glance upward toward the moving figure above her; and then it was a glance not so much directed toward him as beyond him. Was she—as she appeared—so completely indifferent to him? Or was the whole behavior merely professional? It did not change when he dropped down, slowing, to the tilted floor, and came to a stop beside her—nor when he said something to her, in a low voice, either. Something very brief, only a word or two—he looking straight at her, she looking away—instructions, perhaps, or a word of advice. She simply continued to look away, as if through the walls, while he was announcing to us, in his polite and cultured voice, that he and his wife were the first in the world to ride two motor-bicycles simultaneously in the Drome of Death—adding, as a cautionary note, that it would be as well if the spectators would keep a little back of the guard-wire. And then, in another moment or two, the girl had mounted her machine, and was circling with greater and greater speed for her first strike onto the wall, and —flash!—she was already there, and the two bright wings were swiftly mounting toward us. It seemed to me that she had rushed the whole attack on the perpendicular wall much more rapidly than he had—or could I be mistaken? And that even now she was traveling faster. In next to no time she was whizzing round the very top, barely below the guard-wire, the beautiful viking face fixed in a sort of fierce serenity of speed, the loose blue collar blown back from the white throat; and then, below, the other machine had suddenly shot upwards; and in an indescribable uproar which seemed to be racking the walls to pieces the two flying figures circled and recircled, one above the other—the girl keeping rigidly at one level, the boy alternately dipping and soaring. One didn't know which of them to watch —the rapt face above, or the more brilliant performance of the boy below. But now, one *had* to watch him for once more he was sailing like a bird, with his hands off the handlebars, and now too he was taking something out of his pocket—it was a square of black silk, a black handkerchief, fluttering as fiercely as if it were flame in its attempt to escape from his hands, the two hands holding it up before his face. Yes—he was actually going to blindfold himself! The black square blew over his face, over his eyes, and was held stiffly there by the sheer speed at which he was moving, and now again, his arms outspread at either side, he swooped like a swallow round the shining Drome, easily, effortlessly, while the girl above, traveling a little more slowly, for the first time seemed to be watching him. . . .

But watching him with that same fierceness, still, that same air of remote and unbreakable pride—certainly without fear, either for herself or him. Almost angrily, in fact, or contemptuously; and as if impatient, too, for him to be done with it, to get it over with. You could feel her thinking—"Come on, come on, we've had enough of this now, you've shown off enough, let's get down off this wall and go home"—! But all the while, too, her own steel-like delight in the speed and danger, as if that gleaming perpendicular wall, for her, was something more precious than life itself.

It was coming to an end, however. The boy had whipped off the black handkerchief, had tucked it away quickly, was circling downward and slowing, the bursts of sound from the exhaust becoming irregular and intermittent—and now he was out on the floor again, and the girl, in her turn, was spiraling beautifully down the wall, slower and slower, the silver wings pointing downward, the fierce head held proudly back. In less than a minute, without any fuss, she had joined the boy in the center of the floor, they were stacking the motor-bikes for the night, and the people beside us were getting up to leave. Down below, the curved door in the wall of the Drome had been opened from outside, and the assistant had come in, bringing a wooden mallet. The girl went out first, without saying a word —the boy just pausing to say something to the assistant, then following. Our ten golden minutes were over.

"Well"—Paul said as we went down the narrow stairs—"was I right?"

"You were right. Words fail me. A pair of nonpareils. Why they're incredible! And how exactly like you to find them!"

He chuckled.

"Yes—it was a bit of luck."

"But tell me—why was there no applause?"

"Isn't that funny? There never *is* any. Not a scrap. You know —I fancy it's because people are really dazzled, really overcome— do you think it could be that—?"

"It may be—it may be. *I* certainly was . . . !"

Outside, the fair was closing up for the night. The merry-go-round had been darkened, lights here and there were being turned off, the last few stragglers were drifting across the littered playing-salts. Shadows moved on the curtained windows of the gypsy wagons and caravans—the fair-folk were going to bed. Beside the huge green lorry which was the power-plant, the night watchman sat in a wooden chair on the grass—he was reading a paper by the light of one naked bulb, stuck in the side of the lorry, and keeping an eye on his throbbing motors. Cables ran from the lorry across the grass to the merry-go-round, the Drome, the various wagons—we stepped over them carefully, deciding to walk home by way of the river.

The boy and girl were nowhere in sight.

ii.   Of course, we both saw them again, and not once but many times. How could we possibly keep away from them? We couldn't, and didn't. We became addicts, sitting through performance after performance—we took parties of friends—we went, in short, over and over again, returning willy-nilly to that delight as the drunkard returns to his bottle. Paul took along his camera, naturally, and got dozens of remarkable photographs—and how many sketches he made goodness knows. At the end, we knew those two lovely creatures absolutely by heart—as you usually know only those people you love. And all this time, right *to* the end, they both remained just exactly as superb and beautiful and inviolable as they had seemed at the beginning.

That is, as far as the *performance* was concerned. And in fact, the effect was actually heightened by what we found out about them—it added an element of the dramatic to know what we knew, and to know *why* they behaved as they did. How much more, too, if we could have known how it was destined to end, and how soon—! But that was impossible, of course, and nobody guessed it; and meanwhile it was quite enough for us to watch day after day the girl's savage and contemptuous indifference, and the angry pride which so enhanced her beauty, and counter to this, the boy's calm and cool and patient courage, the *quiet* courage of the one who knows that he can wait longest.

A start was made when Paul decided to ask them to Sunday tea, and did so, and they accepted. They were surprised, but they were also delighted. They came, and it was a huge success, and—as Margaret told me afterwards, for I was unable to go, much to my sorrow—they behaved beautifully, simply beautifully. Somehow, nobody had quite expected them to have much in the way of manners—an assumption which was quite unfounded, of course, and which collapsed instantly and startlingly when it came out, almost at once, that the boy was the son of a north-country vicar! A gentleman, in fact, and the girl a lady! Margaret was relieved; and Paul was amused; and everybody, as usual, had a good time. And lots of interesting things came out. They were both twenty-two, and had been married less than a year. The boy had spent a few months in New York

—it was there that he had learned his stunt-riding, while working as a mechanic for the Wall of Death at Coney Island, or
some such place. And he had decided that he would come back
to England and be the first to introduce it there. With the
money he came into from his mother on his twenty-first birth-
day, he bought the rights and plans for the first Drome of Death
in England, therefore, and had it built at Southampton—and
only a week before, at Southampton, he and his wife had given
their first performance. All the money had been spent—it was
a close thing—and they would be dependent on what they could
make, but they were confident. And so on.

It was noticeable—Margaret said—that it was he who did all
the talking. But a little nervously, and constantly turning to his
wife, as if half afraid of some shadowy criticism or disapproval.
The girl said practically nothing. She was perfectly self-possessed, and quite amiable, but she made it evident that she preferred to listen—now and then turning toward her husband,
Margaret thought, an expression that seemed perhaps just a
shade skeptical. Especially of his exploits—when he was telling
of his previous exploits. Not that he boasted at all—not in the
least. Apparently he had in fact been extremely modest about
it. But it was when he was telling of his winning the Isle of
Man trophy, and the race from Land's End to John o' Groats,
and a few other such things, that Margaret first noticed, as she
put it, what looked almost like a curl of the lip, and an angry
flash of light in the girl's eyes. It was odd, and a little disconcerting. And moreover, it seemed disconcerting to the boy.

But that was all, no further light was shed on it at the time,
and it was not till a few days before the fair left town, and took
the road for Folkstone, that the thing really came out.

And all through a package of cigarettes—and the fact that I
had to call at the jeweler's for my watch, which I had taken to
be cleaned. The jeweler's shop was at the end of the High
Street, just beside the cliff, and above the playing-salts; and
seeing the fair, and having nothing to do, I went down. Except

for one or two of the penny gambling stalls, the fair was not officially open in the morning, and therefore now it looked a little deserted. Nobody about—only a few children. But when I came to the Drome of Death, there, sitting on the edge of the red plush dais, dangling his blue-trousered legs, was the boy, all alone, and the minute he saw me his eyes lighted up with recognition, and he smiled.

"I imagine you've seen me before," I said.

"Many times. You're a friend of Mr. Nash, aren't you? I think he spoke of you."

I admitted this, and said that I was sorry I had been unable to come to the tea, and to meet his wife and himself, and I complimented him on the show, at which he was pleased, and then he asked me if I wouldn't sit down, and I did. But it was when I offered him a cigarette that he *really* showed his pleasure—he fairly beamed at me.

"You know"—he said—"I've been frantic for a cigarette—absolutely frantic. Ran out half an hour ago, and not a soul around the place, and myself alone here, so that I couldn't leave—nothing safe, you know, with these gypsies round—thanks!"

"You smoke a lot?"

"Afraid I do. I don't know, in this sort of business you need something to do in between-times, something to steady your nerves—you know what I mean? When you aren't riding. And in the morning, especially in the morning!"

"The morning?"

"It's a long wait in the morning—we were disappointed to find this town so small, you know, it means you can't have any morning performances—bad luck, too, just when we could do with some extra cash—and it's bad in this kind of business when you haven't got anything to do. You can't drink, not in this game—so there's nothing to do but smoke. I'm a chain smoker—so's the kid."

"The kid—?"

"My wife."

"Well, I suppose that's natural. I should think it *would* get on your nerves."

"Yes. You want to keep going. On the move all the time—that's the trouble with a little third-rate fair like this, they only hit the small towns, and there isn't enough in it. . . ."

He smiled, the blue eyes looking lightly at me, and then beyond me, as if to something in the future—something quite definitely bigger and better than this third-rate fair. But then he waved his cigarette toward the merry-go-round, and added—

"But it's all right, you know, and you've got to make a beginning somewhere, haven't you? So I suppose we were lucky, at that."

There was a pause, he blew the ash off the cigarette, and then after a moment I told him how much I admired the looks of the Drome—in which Nash, who was an artist, agreed with me. He was delighted with this.

"It *is* pretty, isn't it—?" he said. "Yes, it *is* pretty. A little shipyard at Southampton did the building, and they did a lovely job of it. Look at that woodwork—like a yacht, it is—everything of the finest! Much better built than the Yankee ones—much. You know, it's a tricky piece of work to do, too—there's got to be a lot of give and play in it, not too rigid—but not too slack either. Have you noticed when we go round there's a kind of ripple of the whole structure that goes with us—? Well, that has to be just right. We have to tune it up, keep it tuned, just like a fiddle. That's what the stays are for —we tighten 'em or loosen 'em—watch 'em all the time. And it'll get better as it ages a bit—got to weather, you know, like everything else. It's already improving—gets a little more supple."

We looked up together at the varnished woodwork of the Drome, the sunlight gleaming on its smooth brown flanks, he reached out his hand and touched one of the heavy wire stays —yes, it was true, it *did* remind one of a yacht—or even, yes, of a fiddle.

"Nash has taken some very good photos of it," I said.

"Has he?"

"Of you and your wife, too."

"Oh? I'd like to see them—I'd like to see them. He's quite an artist, isn't he?"

"Very fine. One of the best."

We smoked in silence for a minute, and then, to my great surprise, he said——

"And what do you *think* of my wife?"

"Your wife—? How do you mean?"

"I mean, in the show."

"Well, of course—I think she's wonderful."

"You do, eh?"

He was frowning at me, a little anxious, a little puzzled. I was uncertain where his questions were leading, so I merely repeated——

"Oh yes, we *all* do. And of course she's remarkably beautiful——"

"Yes—she is. . . . I say, would you mind if I cadged another fag——?"

I handed him the cigarettes, he lit one from the stub, and then, frowning again, he went on——

"You see, it's a problem."

"A problem?"

"Yes. This show business isn't so simple. Of course, she's good, I know that——"

"Oh, she is!"

"She's good, but there's more to it than that. You've got to think of the effect. On the people."

"How do you mean, exactly?"

He looked at me searchingly for a second, as if somehow weighing me personally in the light of what he was going to say next—a troubled look, too, and somehow a little pathetic.

"Well"—he said—"take yourself. Or Mr. Nash."

"Yes?"

"You come to our show, and, as you say, of course, you like my wife, and that's all right. But then, you see, there is this 'star' business. You see what I mean? There's always got to be a star. *One* of the performers has got to be outstanding—otherwise, you've got no climax."

"I see. Yes."

"You see?" He was visibly relieved at my agreement—he smiled, and went on a shade more confidently. "You've got to have that climax. People want a show to be built *up* to something. And that's what the kid won't see."

"No?"

"No. And that's what the trouble is. We can't both of us do the fancy stuff, can we? And what I say is, the audience wants to see the *man* do that, not the woman. Don't you think so?"

"Yes, I think perhaps you're right."

"Of course I'm right! But *she* won't see it—no, she won't see it."

He shook his head, gazing perplexedly down at his swinging feet, and the grass, where the stub of a cigarette was smoking, and repeated once more—

"She just won't see it. Mind you, *I* know she could do some of the things, *some* of them—she's got all the nerve in the world, anybody can see that—but that isn't the point. And then, besides, there's the risk. No woman is quite as good as a man—she's more liable to nerves, more liable to make a slip—and in this business there can't *be* any slips. Well, I tell her that, but it doesn't do any good. She's after me from morning to night, wanting this or that, just to try it once, or try it twice—you know how a woman is, and if you give in you're gone. . . ."

He looked at me quickly, and away—and I felt sorry for him.

"Well"—I said a little lamely—"I think you're perfectly right. The show, as it is, is as good as it could possibly be. Your wife, with her beauty, just adds the right touch—but if I were you *I* certainly wouldn't let her do anything else! Not me."

"You think that?"

"I do indeed."

"Well, I wish someone could persuade her—but when she gets an idea——!"

He laughed, frankly, boyishly, and affectionately too, as if he were thinking very precisely of his wife's beautiful stubbornness, and then he swung himself down to the ground, and I saw that his assistant, the mechanic, was approaching.

"Well," I said, "I expect you'll see us again later!"

"Right-o. And I say, will you tell Mr. Nash I'd like to see some of those photographs?"

"Yes—of course."

He was off then, with a quick nervous wave of the hand, and I had already turned away toward the cliff steps that led to the town when I heard him add——

"And please excuse me, will you? Got a little tuning to do!"—

I waved—he waved in answer—it was the last time we were to exchange greetings, though not by any means, the last time I was to see him. . . . That was to be a year later.

III.   A year later—yes. And almost to the day.

By that time, we had all but forgotten him, hadn't we—? and the beautiful girl who had been killed at Folkstone, while riding blindfold in a "novelty show"—so the newspaper phrased it—called the Drome of Death. We had read about it, only a few days after they had left us; and we had been inexpressibly shocked and saddened; and then the boy had written to Paul, and asked if he could have some of the photographs; and Paul had sent them. . . .

But a year later the same little fair came back, and with it again—much to our surprise—the Drome of Death. At first we thought it must be another—for it didn't look quite right, somehow, and it was certainly a great deal shabbier, as if it weren't properly kept up. Our doubts were resolved when we drew a little nearer.

There, on the faded plush dais, stood the boy—but himself too somehow faded and cheapened, and looking almost haggard—the beauty had gone out of him. Beside him was a girl, a little dark creature, dull-faced, dull-eyed. The same blue riding suits—but now, no silver wings. The boy was smoking a cigarette, and for a moment, when he saw us, he looked guilty. The recognition wavered, as it were, between us—and then he lifted his chin, proudly, turned his head, turned his eyes, and coldly, fiercely, dismissed us. . . .

And, with a pang, I knew that he was right.

The illuminated clock on the pavement before the brightly lighted lunchroom said five minutes to twelve. It was beginning to rain harder, a cold February rain, which threatened to turn to snow. Mixed with the black rain fell a few sodden snowflakes. The lunchroom was nearly empty. The after-theater crowd had come and gone, leaving behind it, on the wide arms of the armchairs, stained plates, empty bowls and cups with spoons in them, crumpled napkins flung on the floor, wet newspapers. Even in disorder it was colorful and picturesque; and it was warm. The bowls of fruit on marble counters, the salads and pies arrayed richly in glass cases gave an almost tropic air of luxury. O'Brien, a taxi-driver, who was finishing his bowl of cornflakes and cream and a cup of coffee, looked sleepily about him. He liked it—the warmth and color almost put him to sleep. He was so tired that he could hardly eat. A hard day; but profitable; he would be glad to get to bed. A steady succession of short runs from noon to six o'clock; and then, one of those freak fares, a man at the Touraine who wanted to go to Plymouth and back in the six hours before midnight. Judas! what a night. It had been an exhausting drive, pitch black, everything drowned in rain. The windshield wiper worked frantically, worked overtime. All that the headlights showed was a ghost-dance of rain, swirling, mixed with snow, and an unending inferno of puddles, rivers, and mud. His eyes ached. He wished to God he didn't have the drive to the garage ahead of him—a mile and a half. . . . However, after that it would take him less than fifteen minutes to hit the hay. . . . He shoved his ticket and the change over the cashier counter, turned up his collar, and went out. Twelve o'clock.

He had left his muddy taxi, flag down, in a deserted alley round the corner from the lunchroom. There was no time-limit there, the cops wouldn't bother him. Judas priest, what a rotten night! He stepped into an invisible puddle, cold water came through his shoes. Squelch, squelch. Hell's delight. He crawled stiffly into his seat and pushed the self-starter. Nga—nga—nga—nga—nga—it didn't start. Dead as a door-nail. Spark on—gas on—he pushed it again. Nga—nga—nga—nga—nga—nga nn! What the hell—cold probably. He primed it and was about to try once more when a girl, who must have come up from behind, made him jump by suddenly saying into his ear, "Hey, taxi!" Her hand was on his sleeve, and she laughed when she saw him jump. She seemed to be slightly drunk. Laughing, she showed, under the street lamp, several gold teeth. Her hat was sodden with rain, the fur piece round her neck was bedraggled, her wet pale face glistened.

"What the hell," said O'Brien and, disengaging his arm roughly, again pushed the self-starter. Nga—nga—nga! . . . No response. He heard his door slam, and, turning round, discovered that the girl had got in. He was furious. "Well, I'll be—" He banged on the glass and shouted, waving his arm. "Get out of there!" She didn't move. He could hear her laughing. "Jesus Christ!" he muttered. "What's the idea?" He sat, puzzled, for a moment; the problem seemed almost more than he could cope with, fantastic, horrible. It merely revealed to him his abysmal tiredness. He crawled out of his seat and opened the door. Rain struck his cheek, the door-handle was wet.

"Come on, Liz," he said. "Get out."

As she made no reply he put his head inside and stared at her. A smell of wet face-powder. She sat still in the far corner, smiling, showing a gold tooth.

"Come on!" he repeated. "You can't ride with me."

"I didn't say I wanted to ride with you, did I?"

O'Brien was taken aback.

"Well, what's the idea? Are you kidding me?"

She gave a peal of laughter, lifting up her feet from the floor in delight.

"Sure I'm kidding you," she giggled. "All I want is to sit down!"

"Oh, you do, now! You just want to sit down and have a nice little rest in popper's taxi!"

"*Sweet* popper!" she cooed. "Come on in and sit down. You're letting the draft in."

"You come on out before I drag you out!"

"Oo! Isn't he rough!"

"One—two—"

"If you touch me I'll scream, I swear to God I will! . . . Don't you dare! . . . Ow, you dirty dog, let go of my arm! Let go!" . . . She screamed, as if experimentally, her blue eyes uninterruptedly bright with amusement. He dropped her arm, astonished. Then, while he stared, silent, she added, taking off her wet hat and giving her bobbed yellow hair a shake, "You shouldn't be so rough, Charlie—that'll make a bruise on my arm. . . . And now that you've come in, for God's sake shut the door! It's cold."

"Are you drunk?" He sat down, as if merely temporarily, on the edge of the seat, wondering what to do.

"Sure, I'm drunk. You got to feel good *sometimes,* haven't you?"

"Well, you oughter be ashamed of yourself."

She slapped his cheek lightly, by way of administering an affectionate reproach. He seized her wrist and twisted it savagely. She screeched. Her face became hard and furious.

"Say, what the hell are you doing!" . . . She yanked her hand away, put her wrist to her mouth, and sucked it, absorbed, as if utterly forgetting him. In the silence he heard the rain pattering irregularly on the taxi roof. A shower of needles. He felt as if he were going to fall asleep, stared at her uncomprehending, shivered a little.

"Come on, kid," he said, altering his tone. "You know you can't stay here. I'm taking the boat round to the garage. I'm dog-tired and I want to hit the hay."

"Who's stopping you? *I'm* not stopping you!"

"Where do you live, then?"

She eyed him distrustfully, with a hard childlike guile.

"What do you want to know for? Bah, you make me sick."

"If it's on my way, I'll drop you there."

"Oh, you will, will you! Very kind of you, I'm sure. . . . Not a chance, Charlie, I'm wise!"

"What the hell are you talking about? . . . Come on, now, be a good kid and get out."

She looked at him, smiling. She leaned toward him, smelling of perfume, and smiled ingratiatingly, tilting her pale face a little to one side. She put her hand, with a very large wedding ring, on his knee, and gently squeezed it.

"Don't you like me, Charlie?" she chirruped.

He put his arm quickly around her waist—she was soaking wet—and picked her up bodily. She screamed. "Let me go, you devil! Let me go, or I'll break every damned window in your cab!" She struggled. As he tried to drag her toward the open door she struck his face, kicked in every direction, and finally had the brilliant idea of beating him over the eyes repeatedly with her wet velvet hat. Rain-water stung his eyes, blinded him. He dropped her on the seat again. Her fur piece had fallen off, and her dress, pulled up to her knees and twisted, showed a pale blue satin petticoat and gray silk legs, mud-splashed.

"Oo! How strong you are, Charlie. Regular caveman stunt. But don't try it again, let me tell you! or I'll smash your windows for you." She drew away into the corner of the seat again,

panting a little, and smiling apprehensively. Then she added,
"Oh, gee! look at my petticoat!" She giggled, and gave a flounce
to her skirt in an unsuccessful attempt to cover her legs. "You
don't mind looking at my legs, do you, Charlie! They're easy
to look at. . . . Say, my skirt's awful wet—I think I'll take it off
and hang it up to dry. . . ."

"What are you trying to do, get me pinched?" O'Brien pulled
the door shut and sat down. "You're a tough baby, all right!
. . ." He leaned back and for a second closed his eyes. With eyes
shut, he saw a long road swarming at him with sparkling puddles, rivers running, and a spotlight full of rain.

"Sure, I'm tough. I'm so tough, I spit brass! Ha, ha!" She was
immensely amused by this, and rocked back and forth, laughing, and looking at him with cunning blue eyes, sidelong.

"Well, you oughter be ashamed to say it, a young kid like
you! . . . And all boozed up like an old war horse. . . . Judas! . . .
Where'd you get it? Who gave it to you?"

"None of your damned business who gave it to me. I've been
given worse things, let me tell you! . . . It was a friend of mine
gave it to me." She was coarsely defiant.

"Well, he must be a crumby kind of friend, getting you all
tanked up like this on rotten whisky and then leaving you out
in the rain like an old cat! *Some* friend."

"When I ask for your opinion of my friends, you can give
it! . . ."

"Oh! Is that so!"

"Yes—that's so! . . . And my friend's a cop—you can put that
in your pipe and smoke it. You make me tired."

"A cop! . . . Tell it to the marines."

"A cop, I said! Do you understand English?"

"Now and then."

"Well, I guess this is one of the thens. . . . Say, Charlie, you
haven't got a cigarette, have you?" Wheedling, she slid her arm
under his and put her cheek against his shoulder. He looked
sleepily at her, unmoving. They remained thus for a moment,
hearing the rain on the sides and roof of the taxi—a delicate

irregular pricking of needlepoints. Now and then a snowflake, large and heavy, veered past one of the windows. . . . Recollecting himself, pulling himself back again from the verge of a dream, he fished out a cigarette for her and struck a match. Puff—puff. The match, flaring once, twice, showed clear blue eyes, pupils narrowed, under pale golden eyebrows delicately arched like the feelers of a moth. The white nose slightly cruel, rather fine.

"Thanks, Charlie. . . . Nice boy! . . . Snuggle up, let's be comfortable!" She gave a little wriggle, sliding her arm further under his. Her left hand, with its ring, fell upon his, which lay on his canvas coat, and bending her fingers she thrust them delicately, exploringly, up his sleeve. He did not move, merely swayed slightly.

"Sure, my friend's a cop." She went on, equably. . . . "Don't you believe me?"

"Oh, I'll swallow anything!" He smiled.

"But I didn't see him tonight. . . . I couldn't find him."

"You went looking for him?"

"All around—everywhere. Damned cold and wet, too! I'm soaked."

"What did you want him for?" He suddenly realized that his eyes had shut and that his chin had dropped onto his sheepskin collar. The rough touch startled him.

"I wanted some money. I'm strapped—absolutely not a thin dime tonight. . . . And the landlady took my key away this morning."

"Oh! she did, did she! You didn't pay the rent?"

"No, you poor simp! It was because the other lodgers complained." She tittered. "The old man in the next room to mine watched me like a hawk. I guess he thought—ha, ha!" . . . She blew a cloud of smoke. "I gave him the cold shoulder, you see, and last night when he found my friend was there with me— he went down to the kitchen with the glad news."

"Say, kid—you ought not to do it! You'll get into trouble."

"Mind your own business, Charlie!" . . . Her tone was friendly, but sharp. . . . "I'm no chicken."

"You said a mouthful, Queenie! . . . How old are you?"

"Seventeen."

"Seventeen—and an alley-cat! . . . Judas."

She slapped his face. He smiled stupidly, and she slapped it again.

"You shut up! You can't say things like that to me! . . . Not much."

She smoked, staring at him. She seemed to be examining him appraisingly, resting her blue eyes in turn on his mouth, his nose, his chin, eyes, canvas coat. Her eyes were close to his, dark-pupiled, her cheek still rested against his shoulder. He returned her gaze, somber and expressionless. He blinked repeatedly, the lids falling slowly, involuntarily, and his head at the same time nodding forward in jerks. With each nod and blink the road rushed at him, a soft interminable torrent, sparkling and seething. Each time, opening his eyes again to exclude the vision, he smiled at the girl's face, so startlingly near, smiled apologetically.

"What's your name, kid?"

"Flora, Flora des Neiges."

"Oh! You're a Canuck."

"Do I look it?"

"No—you don't."

"My mother was Scotch. That's where I get my yellow hair."

"I guess you got it out of a bottle."

"Like hell I did! That's fourteen carat. All gold to the roots." She shook it against his cheek, smiling, showing a sharp golden eye-tooth.

"Well—when did you come down here?"

"In October. I ran away. My pa's got a farm in Vermont. . . ."

He appeared not to be listening. He was looking out of the window, under the street lamp, watching the swirling of snow and rain—there was more snow, now. All of a sudden, turning, he said:

"Well, Flora, what's the idea? Where are you going to sleep tonight? . . ."

"Me? What's the matter with this?"

"Oh! And supposing some cop happens to come down here? That'd look pretty, wouldn't it! It'd sound nice to the judge, wouldn't it! . . . Yes, it would not!"

He was derisive, but at the same time profoundly inert, relaxed. The warmth of the girl's body was pleasant, and the clasp of her thumb and finger round his right wrist had a curious effect on him. He did not stir, did not feel like stirring. His money was safe enough. She couldn't get it without waking him. Supposing—supposing—he might give her a couple of dollars to go—but where would she go? Not to his own room. No . . . nor a hotel. She was too young-looking. . . . Supposing—supposing—what was it he was thinking of? Out into the country? Concord or Framingham? Brown rivers cut off his view, and he stared into a vast red-edged spotlight filled with rain. . . . The girl was saying:

"There won't be any cops here till five o'clock. We could go for a little drive in the parks before that. Out to Jamaica Pond or something like that. . . ."

"Sure. . . . Wake me at five! If you're waking, call me early!"

He would have to explain at the garage. A breakdown somewhere. Hanover Four Corners. . . .

". . . My friend, the one I ran away with I mean, worked in a drugstore in Cambridge, shaking sodas. He gave me the slip. I didn't care much, because he paid my fare down here, and that was the chief thing. Oh—he had a swell line of talk! Couldn't he sling the syllables! . . ."

"Those funny guys make me tired."

"Don't be such a gloom, Charlie! . . . Anybody'd think this was your dear mother's funeral."

"Ah—you make me tired." He gave a long shiver, shutting his eyes.

"Going to sleep, darling? Put your head down, there! That's right."

He rested his cheek against her head, felt her hand pass across his forehead. Hanover Four Corners was a queer procession of stilted sandwich-men. They stepped briskly, wheeled, waving their long stilts, their longer and longer stilts, their stilt scrapers, a babbling forest of stilt scrapers, very very tall, and high up among them, invisible were the small white faces which said *Hanover Four Corners, Hanovorners!*

The girl extinguished her cigarette on the window-sill and composed herself comfortably, keeping her arm locked into his and her hand on his wrist. For a moment she gazed, broodingly, straight ahead through the front windows, into the rain. Her lower lip drooped slightly, relaxed and sullen. Jesus! she thought. Jesus! . . . snow on the taxi roof like a wedding cake! . . . After a moment she too was asleep.

FIELD OF FLOWERS

Humming, he tied his striped black-and-green tie, pulling it from left to right between the flanges of soft white collar. Alack! his favorite tie, and it was beginning—unmistakably—to look worn and creased. He smoothed the firm knot with his thumb and finger, and stepped back from the dusty mirror to survey the effect from a greater distance, in a light not quite so trying. Hm, so-so. A little discolored, too. But then, if he wore his gray scarf rather closely about his throat—perhaps it might yet for a little while escape attention. . . . He stepped back to the dressing table and took up his brushes. Thank goodness—his hair was just in the right state, as always the day after a shampoo: not too fluffy, and on the other hand not too dull in color. Gwendolyn had commented on it. What lovely lights there are in it, she had cried, passing her small hand over it—my dear Tithonus, what lovely lights! Like copper and gold! Like copper and gold. . . . Tra-la-la-la—la-la—la-la. The sun was coming out, with a soft watery gleam on the rain-dark house-fronts opposite. It was going to be a nice day, for Gwendolyn's departure, after all; a gentle spring day in November. The sort of day when crocuses pop out of the ground singing like larks and larks glisten in the heavens like crocuses. The wet earth cracks and steams and the sudden army of grass brandishes its host of green spears. Tra-la-la-la—la-la. And the grackles creak like mad.

But now there was this deep, deep problem of the present for Gwendolyn: a problem (especially in view of his poverty, which Gwendolyn's unexpected visit had disastrously accelerated) almost insoluble. A book? No. Inadequate. Not sufficiently decorative. Not sumptuous enough. Nor quite the romantic and sentimental thing. But what, then? He descended the boarding-house stairs, humming and self-satisfied: these stairs down which he and Gwendolyn had crept stealthily not six hours ago. No mail this morning—damn. What's a morning without mail! It takes the bloom off the day—absolutely takes the bloom off it. High time, too, that he heard from the New York Music Company about the "Nocturne in Black and Ivory." Ah, that arpeggio passage, which Gwendolyn had likened to a fine rain seen through a late beam of golden sunlight! How nice she had been about that! Almost nice enough to make up for her—for her—well, for her general indifference to his music. Strange, that she hadn't liked his music better. And all these years of separation, too—one might have supposed that that alone would have made her a little more enthusiastic. The effect of nostalgia. Oughtn't her mere gladness at seeing him, and at being made love to by him, have made her like it a little better? Oughtn't it? . . . But then, she was such a self-centered little minx, so absorbed, so terribly absorbed, in her own funny dull little life, her husband, her country club out there in Akron, her funny dull little bridge-playing, horseback-riding friends, and her serious group of little Thinkers. . . . What else could one expect of a girl like that and a life like that?

"Let's see: four dollars. And a check in the wallet for ten more. He could afford a grapefruit this morning; with a withered maraschino cherry. And coffee and oatmeal. . . . Ot-*meeel!* bellowed the counter-man—that's two to come. . . . Good Lord—just to think that those two weekends with Gwendolyn had cost fifty dollars. Fifty! It was really staggering. And she hadn't made a single suggestion that she might help him out—not a hint; despite the fact that she was rolling, simply rolling, in money. There it was again—yes, there it was again. Funny. Maybe she just had that old-fashioned idea that the man always pays. Maybe she had been afraid—knowing that he was hard up—that an offer to help him might be embarrassing. Embarrassing! Hollow laughter. It was a kind of embarrassment that one could well afford. And there was he, with less than a hundred dollars to his name, trying to entertain her in the manner to which she had been accustomed! . . . Hell's delight.

But now this problem of the present. It had to be done; of that there was no question. It had to be done. And it had to be something really nice, something rather æsthetic; if possible, a symbol. But a symbol of what? . . . Ah! *That* was the question. Two weeks ago, or even five days ago, the answer might have been different—*would* have been different. For then—yes, as recently as that—he had thought he was in love with her. Fool! Jackass! Romantic jackanapes! Would he never get over this mad habit of running after will-of-the-wisps? . . . Yes, five days ago he had thought that a very nice Japanese print might be in order—a really *very* nice one—one of the sort, for example, with which he himself fell in love. Like the Hiroshige "Fox Fires" or "Monkey Bridge." Not too expensive—as the "Fox Fires" would be—but on the other hand not cheap. Anyway, a good print, chosen for love. . . .

But now? . . . He rose, extracted a paper drinking-cup from the tall glass tube of drinking-cups, filled it, and drank the cold waxy-tasting water. He replenished it and drank again. Something nice, and sanitary, about waxy-tasting water. . . . Now? . . . It was true—it might as well be admitted—that his feelings were obscure. Decidedly obscure. He buffeted through the swinging doors and out into the morning sunlight, his eyes a little dazzled by the brightness of the loud street. *Tra-la-la-la-la-la.* A heavenly day; he would walk across the Common, and perhaps for fifteen minutes sit on a bench and watch the people and the pigeons and the sparrows and the gray squirrels. Well,

it was still sufficiently true that she charmed him; true enough
to make the present genuine. It was still—wasn't it—a perfectly
spontaneous impulse. He still wanted to give her something
beautiful, and to give it to her tenderly. "I've brought a present for you"—he would say, with a slight smile, a smile quizzically tender, handing it to her—"I hope you'll like it." Silence:
they would look at each other with a long and delicious look,
half humorous and half loverlike; and she would then perhaps
bite her lip and look away—in that charming way she had—as
if she wanted him to see her profile. Her lovely profile. . . .
That was what he had planned; but now, all of a sudden——

He sank down upon the bench, which was slightly damp,
and beneath which (how filthy America is!) was a litter of pea-
nut shells. Nine o'clock: he had a full hour in which to get the
present and meet her at the station for the farewell. Plenty of
time. And the print shop was on the way to the station, too.
A diller a dollar a ten o'clock scholar. . . . If only the thing had
—if only it hadn't—if only—! He found a loose cigarette in his
side pocket, limp, with half its tobacco gone, and lighted it.
The cloud of gray smoke—delicious—undulated away from him
in a swooping belt on the sunshine, darted in swirls toward the
gravel path, and was lost. At the outset it had been perfectly
heavenly. That charming letter, in which she had accepted his
invitation to elope on a swan-boat on the pond in the Public
Gardens! "Dear Lohengrin"—she had said—"have your swans
ready . . . at six in the evening. . . ." And she had signed herself "Elsa." How awfully nice of her, and how exactly in the
right, the only, key! And then, when she had surprised him on
the little bridge, and had moaned at the discovery that there
were no longer any swan-boats, resting her two small hands in
comic despair on the bridge railing—how exquisite that had
been, and how young, how *young* she had looked, despite those
six enormous years. He had felt his old heart—his heart pre-
cociously old—positively blossoming inside him, positively
breaking open like a flame-colored tulip. Gwendolyn again!
The very same Gwendolyn, unaltered, no older, as buoyant as

ever, still carrying her proud little head as gracefully as a flower. . . . Life could offer few such moments as that. It had seemed the consummation of everything: the final and true crystallization of all that had gone before; the six years of separation, and her marriage, had simply vanished; and they had, as it were, resumed their walk across the Common, taking up the conversation precisely where it had been dropped. Ah—ah—ah —ah—he shook his head in a funny kind of misery, which was not exactly misery and nevertheless was not exactly anything else. Why could it not all have been like that? Why? She was as beautiful as ever, and she had strolled again into his heart as casually as she had strolled out of it, taking possession of it more completely than ever before; their delight with each other had been so instant and so frank; her wood-brown eyes had looked at him so warmly and kindly while she made comically disparaging remarks about her husband—"poor Mont"; and yet, and yet——

He flung the cigarette bitterly to the ground, and scraped it flat under the sole of his shoe. There were too many yets and buts in life; far too many. He had been prepared to fall in love —of course; but hadn't she, too? Was it fair to blame it all on Gwendolyn? And anyway, wasn't it better, after all, considering all the circumstances, that they hadn't? . . . Much better; much better. It was only one's disappointment that after a prelude so divinely seductive, so ethereal, celestially perfect, there should have been such a lamentable—well, drop. The first evening had been all that heart could have desired. It had been really beautiful. Sitting there, so far apart, so polite and even distant with each other, and nevertheless in so delicious a state of tension—just talking, talking, circumspectly maneuvering the conversation toward the forbidden topic; smoking innumerable cigarettes; and at last beginning, somewhat shyly and agitatedly, to enter upon the forbidden ground. . . . Ah—ah—ah—ah—he shook his head sadly again as he thought of that—it had been so very nice, so very nice. And then, when she had said that she must go, and he had summoned all his courage and kissed her—

heavens, how marvelous that had been! She had been surprised
—and yet not surprised, either; had drawn back for just the fraction of a minute; had drooped her small head for a second, as
if a little saddened and at the same time startled into a sense of
delighted wonder; and had then said, turning her face away from
him, and shutting her eyes, simply, "To think that it should be
you!". . . .

What, exactly, had she meant by that? . . . That she had long
been hoping for a lover, a real lover, and was now astonished
at the unhoped-for goodness of Providence in offering her *him?*
She had always, of course, somewhat assumed him to be a sort of
superior being—she was a good deal of an artist-worshiper. It
must have been that. That poor child—starved for love all these
six years with that absurd well-meaning little husband of hers;
starved for love and life. Partly her own fault, to be sure, for she
had deliberately married for money. But could one ask so much
of any human being? She had been touchingly loyal to her poor
Mont—but could one expect that sort of loyalty to go on forever? No—no—no— Impossible. All the poetry in her nature had
been stifled—sooner or later it would have had to break out; she
would inevitably have escaped from Akron as the butterfly from
the cocoon; and it was therefore only natural that she should
have thought, when circumstances brought her to Boston, of looking up *him*. . . . But why had she thought it necessary to be so
disingenuous about that? Why had she then—after the kiss—pretended so elaborately that this turn of affairs had come to her
as a total surprise, even as a shock? . . . Damn. It was precisely
then—it was just precisely at that point—just when she evaded
his hopeful questioning about that—it was precisely then that he
had begun to feel a—well, a something-or-other wrong. Couldn't
she, after all, be trusted? Was she not being honest with him?
Had there been—perhaps—others before him? . . . Curse it—as
if, after all, that could particularly matter! Nevertheless, it did
matter. Something indefinable, some ethereal and most volatile
fragrance, had then and there been irrevocably lost. Not to be
able to trust her! And in that sort of affair of subtle emotional

adjustment, unfortunately, there was no room for anything but the finest and completest honesty. She ought to have admitted, at once, with wide-open eyes, "Yes, I *did* think—I *did* hope—when I wrote to you—that our meeting might take some such heavenly turn as this. . . ."

But she hadn't. And at once a subtle barrier was—to him, at least—perceptible between them. She wasn't, to begin with, quite as—well, quite all that he had always thought she was. Evasive. Baffling. Possibly playing a sort of game with him. Certainly not anxious—as he was—to fall completely and honestly and whole-heartedly in love. No; she kept certain reserves, she turned her profile. And then, when she tried to keep up so long her pretense of loyalty to poor Mont—in the face of her so obviously having laid all her plans for this holiday—it had been impossible for him not to be irritated. He had lost his temper a little—had pointed out to her, somewhat tartly, her hypocrisy in this. Confound it—what a pity! And the whole fairy structure, all its elfin gossamer, had been wrecked; it had begun to appear that all she wanted was to commit an infidelity, to join the cynically laughing ranks of the unfaithful. Her friends had betrayed *their* husbands—they had told her all about it—why shouldn't she betray hers? And if she could manage to capture, as her partner, a promising young composer, wasn't that all the better? . . . It would make a nice story on the veranda of the country club, between dinner and a game of bridge. . . .

He rose to his feet, almost unconscious of rising, and stared down at the dust of the path, in which pigeons had left a delicate design of footprints. It was time to be moving. Time to be moving. He thrust his hands into his trouser pockets, and began to walk slowly. . . . Yes—that had reduced the whole thing to a mere—to a mere—*passade*. From the sublime to the obvious. He had resented it bitterly. Not, of course, that a *passade* wasn't enjoyable—especially with anyone so lovely as Gwendolyn. But to find, after all, after all these years, that just *that* was what Gwendolyn was like! To find that she didn't really love him at all, wasn't interested in love, wasn't even, very much, interested in *him!* . . . There it was again—that queer brooding indrawn self-ishness of hers. Her unwillingness, or perhaps it was inability, to meet him halfway, psychologically. An air of indifference had hung over her; an air of passivity; of remoteness and detachment. She had remained self-absorbed, her gaze averted during his caresses, as if his particular identity had not mattered to her in the slightest. A mere man; a mere convenience. What *he* needed, what *he* desired, were of no importance to her. And when some exclamation of his had given her at last a hint of this, and of the queer schism which had suddenly opened between them, she had been deeply surprised. It had been when they were standing before the snow-screen in the Museum. An appalling gulf had then appeared between them; and they had both felt miserable, helpless, and as if they had better separate. "If that's the way you feel"—she had said—"don't you think we had better not meet in the daytime at all—since we only somehow frustrate each other—and just meet at night instead? . . ." With what an agony they had then looked at each other! With what a bitter searching of eyes, and what passionate desire to cling with hands! Ah—ah—it had seemed almost unbearable. It had been their Gethsemane. And thereafter they had, as she suggested, met only at night.

Well! It had been too bad—and in consequence the whole thing had already begun to seem utterly unreal. It was already difficult to believe that they had actually been to Portland together—it was more as if he had gone there alone. What was there to remember about it? Nothing, except her amusing remarks about the frescoes in the dining room—then, for a moment, the scene had become real and exquisite. For the rest, it might never have been; the whole experience had gone over his soul as tracelessly as water. She had come and gone—she was already, to all intents, gone forever. Gone—gone—gone—gone. And in this sense, in view of this, it really seemed a shade anachronistic to be thinking of buying her a present. What for? Wouldn't it be, in the circumstances, almost ironic? Mightn't she be—even—offended? What nonsense! Of course not. No woman is ever offended by being given a sentimental present. She would perhaps cling to that trace of sentiment all the more happily because of her sense of the failure in the affair. For of course she did, she *did*, share with him that sad sense of having dismally failed.

He turned into the little shop, and climbed up the crooked old-fashioned stairs to the print room, and began turning over the big portfolios of Japanese prints. The Utamaros were far too expensive—and so were the Hokusais; but nevertheless he lingered over them for a little. What a lovely thing, this Utamaro of the three fisherwomen, with their pink-and-gray kirtles, and the wicker basket on the pale sand beside a starfish, and the twilight-pale water! Goodness—goodness—goodness. It was to enter into another world, to gaze at this—a world of serenity and perfection, of the lovely and the immortal. But twenty dollars! . . . He closed the portfolio and opened the next, which contained the Hiroshiges. Bad prints, most of them—the late uprights, and in garish dyes: too much aniline purple and poisonous green. And the occasional good ones—a few of the Tokaido road set— were costly. Fifteen—twenty-five—ten—seven—twelve—all beyond his means. There was one two-dollar print—but it was a rather commonplace and superficial fishing-boat affair, and much too bright. He turned again, and yet again, his eye seeking first the price-mark in the lower right-hand corner of each print; and then suddenly he was arrested by an upright Hiroshige landscape which was marked "one dollar." Heavens! Was it possible? Could it be possible? It was a print he had never seen before—entitled "Field of Flowers." And it was exquisite—it was like a poem—it was like a piece of music by Debussy. It was blue, and yet it was not blue—green, and yet not green—opalescent—a field of narcissus and daffodils in the spring, with a gray oak-tree arching over a winding path. Good Lord! Good gracious! His hand positively trembled as he held it. The ethereal evanescence with which that meadow faded into the distance, like a crepuscular sky in which one is only half-conscious of the stars! And those tiny butterfly ladies pausing under the tree for a talk, as if the wind, for just a moment, had let them rest there! . . . He stared and stared; and then, "I'll take this," he said to the waiting sales-man.

A find! . . . A veritable find! . . . He plunged out into the bright sunshine again, as if leaving behind him that enchanted field of flowers (though in fact he carried it under his arm, ten-derly), and blinked at the garish street. What an astonishing thing—a print like that for a dollar—for a single dollar! A Hiro-shige that positively sang in his heart, that flung open a gateway to the impossible, the inaccessible, the intangible, the impalpable azure of the soul! It was exactly the miracle he had hoped for. It was exactly the thing that met his needs. It was exactly—pre-cisely—ah! He paused in his step, faltered, inhibited by the bright intensity of his thought. For was it not true? Yes, it was true; it was exactly what the affair with Gwendolyn ought to have been, and hadn't been. . . .

He stood still at the curbstone, waiting for the stream of traffic to pass, and as he stood so, preoccupied, he felt a delicious and treacherous decision trembling, in his soul, on the brink of crys-tallization. To give away this print—to give it to Gwendolyn—wouldn't that be to give away the very thing, the precious and indefinable thing, the fragrance of his idealism, which Gwen-dolyn had not deserved? Wasn't it precisely this, after all, that he was entitled to keep? Wouldn't it be, in the upshot, the very finest of poetic justices that Gwendolyn should have missed this beauty, have failed to see it, and that he should himself preserve and guard it? . . . It was still only a quarter to ten. There would be time enough for him to take it back to his room, if then he should hurry to the station in a taxi. To do, or not to do. The stream of traffic came to an end; it was now possible to cross, but he did not cross. He turned back again, with a queer exultation in his heart, and hurried toward his room.

GEHENNA

How easily—reflected Smith, or Jones, or Robinson, or whatever his name happened to be—our little world can go to pieces! And incidentally, of course, the great world; for the great world is only ourselves writ large, is at best nothing but a projection of our own thought, and of our own order or disorder in thought. It was a moment's presumption that led a genius to write that genius and madness are near allied; proximity to madness is not a privilege of genius alone; it is the privilege and natural necessity of every consciousness, from the highest to the lowest; Smith and Robinson are as precariously hung in the void as Shakspeare himself. Do we not know that even the animals go mad? Have we not been informed that an ant, afflicted with a tumor of the brain, will walk in circles, bite his neighbors, and in every sense behave abnormally? His internal order, or habit, has been changed—and, *ipso facto*, the external order has been destroyed. By that little speck of accidental matter, unforeseeable, gods (perhaps) have been deposed, stars dislodged from their orbits, moons turned into alarm clocks. The fair page of the world, thus re-set, becomes a brilliant but meaningless jumble of typographical errors.

And thus—thought Smith, or Jones, or Robinson—it is with

me. At this very moment some little atom may have taken, in some tiny crossroad of my brain, the wrong turning. Some infinitesimal dead leaf may have lodged itself, in my thought's stream, against some infinitesimal twig; and the consequences may prove incalculable. On that dead leaf of matter or feeling or thought will depend the whole course of my life. In an instant it will be as if I had stepped through this bright cobweb of appearance on which I walk with such apparent security, and plunged into a chaos of my own; for that chaos will be as intimately and recognizably my own, with its Smith-like disorder, as the present world is my own, with its Smith-like order. Here will be all the appurtenances of my life, every like and dislike, every longing or revulsion, from the smallest to the greatest; all the umbrellas—so to speak—of my life, all the canceled postage stamps and burnt matches, the clipped fingernails, love letters, calendars, and sunrises; but all of them interchanged and become (by change) endowed with demonic power. At a step, I shall have fallen into a profound and perhaps termless Gehenna which will be everywhere nothing but Smith. Only to the name of Smith will the umbrella-winged demons of this chaos answer.

It is now—thought Smith, or Jones, or Robinson—past midnight, and this apartment house, with all its curious occupants, is asleep. The janitor has locked the outer door; the row of mother-of-pearl electric buttons (one for each occupant) is inert, for lack of inquiring fingers to complete their respective circuits; the brass letter-boxes yawn darkly for the absent postman; the elevator has settled down for the night on the fourth floor, to which it was brought by a late-comer at twelve-forty-three. Even the water in the innumerable pipes has gone to sleep, become stale and torpid. And here, in my room, I pace to and fro, thinking how easily I could change all this. Perhaps I would achieve this gradually, and step by step, just as I pace to and fro across the four rugs from Persia which cover the floor; item by item I would tear down the majestic fiction which is at present myself and the world, and item by item build up another. Exactly as one can stare at a word until it becomes meaningless, I can begin to stare at the world. What in heaven's name are these rugs? What in heaven's name are these walls, this floor, the books on my mantelpiece, the three worn wooden chairs, the pencils in a row on my red table? Arrangements of atoms? If so, then they are all perpetually in motion; the whole appearance is in reality a chaotic flux, a whirlwind of opposing forces; they and I are in one preposterous stream together, borne helplessly to an unknown destiny. I am myself perhaps only a momentary sparkle on the swift surface of this preposterous stream. My awareness is only an accident; and moreover my awareness is less truly myself than this stream which supports me, and out of which my sparkle of consciousness has for a moment been cast up. And how easy—once more—to slip back into the flux itself, into that deeper current, that primordial chaos, which is really I! My own Gehenna, now as always, awaits me there within, with all its horrors and all its magnificence.

Pausing at the window and looking forth at the row of snow-laden roofs opposite, above which hang the stars, I light one cigarette from another, and wave away the smoke with my hand. Let me also, with a mental gesture of waving (and what is thought but a gesture?), wave away this apartment house. At the mere notion, it has already begun to lose something of its reality. Was the North Star hung at the world's masthead only in order that on a certain day in a certain year an ugly wallpaper should be glued to the walls of this room? Is evolution only an evolution from the sublime to the ridiculous? This curious structure of bricks and wood, with its guts of lead and its nerves of copper, with its horizontal tiers of little caves, its stairs, its elevator, and the metal heart which sends warmth everywhere through metal arteries—why should it be as it is? Instantly, it becomes a horror. And its occupants, these other Smiths and Robinsons, lying asleep in dark little holes, with their hands hanging over the bed's edge, their eyes shut and their mouths open; so solemnly divesting themselves of their detachable skins, winding their watches, brushing their teeth, turning the handglass this way and that to see if their hair be thinner or the circles under their eyes be larger; these too become a horror. And how shameful that I have permitted them to cooperate with me in the erection of this fantastic fiction, how shameful that I should have submitted to this group-assumption of so much that cannot be assumed! Do these monsters dream, with their eyes shut and their mouths open, of the North Star hung aloft at our masthead; do they dare to reach out, with heroically destructive hand, toward that sparkle of consciousness, with intent to destroy? Do they ever for a moment think of looking down, through their own eyes in the handglass, to the glorious Gehenna which we are?

But suppose—as I pace to and fro on the Kerman rugs, and glance now at one picture on the wall and now at another— suppose that instead of a step-by-step approach to destruction I were to plunge into it all at once, like Empedocles into Ætna. Could I not, simply by an effort of will, go mad? Could I not, like a watchmaker, in a moment's exasperation, thrust a violent scissor-blade into the heart of the delicate mechanism? Not, of course, by anything so simple as a mere physical action; but rather, by an action of the mind on itself. Presumably, this would have to be an act of forgetting. I would have to forget who and what I am, why I am here, what this room is, these pictures, this floor on which I pace—why the room is square rather than spherical, why I am myself shaped as I am—and with these things, also, all sense of unity and continuity. Would this not be possible? Suppose, as I now begin to prepare myself for bed and sleep, I were to concentrate with particular ferocity of imagination on some one detail. For example, I have now shut myself in my bathroom, and as I brush my teeth I notice, reflected in the mirror, the knob of the door behind me. It is a brass knob, perfectly commonplace. On the top surface of it, a little to one side, the electric light is reflected as a small bead of brightness. Below it is the dark keyhole, and to one side of it the glass towel-rack on which hang two soiled towels. All these things seem suddenly absurd; but it is the doorknob on which I choose to exercise my imagination, for I already begin to foresee that it is in a fore-ordained sense the key to the whole situation. I stare at the knob, narrowing my eyes, at the same time aware of my own re-flection in the mirror, and of something in my expression which is already a curious mixture of insanity and fright. I have stopped brushing my teeth; I stare at the knob with my toothbrush in air; an extraordinary thrill of horror goes coldly and slowly up my spine and seems to burst, like a tiny cold little rocket, some-where at the base of my skull. For what I have now realized, acutely and profoundly, and with a mystic terror which is com-plete almost to the point of irremediable madness, is that this odd round little object of brass is my only remaining means of egress, not only from this room, but from this idea which is at present myself. I have come to the brink of chaos. Another slight-est step, and I am lost. If I continue to stare for another five seconds at the knob, further narrowing my eyes (and *ipso facto* narrowing my consciousness), I shall cease to know what the knob is for, and will at once, finding myself trapped, go mad with a kind of animal madness. I will dash myself against the walls, scream, fall exhausted; and falling, fall forever out of time and space into my own Gehenna.

Instead, I drop my gaze. I finish brushing my teeth. Not that I am really afraid to pursue the hallucination (if hallucination it truly is) but that I have a cunning notion of putting myself still further to the test. What I have now foreseen is that fearful moment when, before opening the door, I shall reach up my hand and extinguish the light. Again the cold little rocket bursts slowly in my skull, scattering its little seeds of death; the void whistles beneath me; I am absolutely alone in a world of which the only tenable principle is horror. I take a last look at myself in the mirror, calmly, detachedly, without any trace either of pity or amusement. There I am: with the scar on my forehead, the rusty gnarled eyebrows, the fine red spider-veining in my cheeks, and my two hands resting on the marble edge of the basin. Is my name Smith? But how preposterous. What on earth is a Smith? Would the Pole Star know me? Would the Pleiades take off their hats to me, or a jury of molecules pronounce me a unit?

In short, would the universe admit that it had produced me, or assume the slightest responsibility for me?

No, the question is no sooner asked than laughed at. It is obvious enough that these Smiths are an accident, a freak, an absurdity, a mere bad dream. Billions of years ago, in some minor interstellar clash, or some streamlike catalysis of unimaginable vapors, purposeless and terrible, there occurred a momentary conception of these funny little Smiths; the principle which created me is already dead; I am merely the posthumous life of that concept. In reality, I was dead before I was born. Belatedly, I see myself in the mirror, recognize my fatuity, have just time to laugh at myself, and am gone.

And so, I turn out the light. I am in pitch darkness. Not a single thing is visible. And suddenly, with an extraordinary sense of power and wisdom, I reach out an automatic and precisely directed hand, touch and turn the knob, and am released. Escaping one approach to Gehenna, I move at once unhesitatingly toward another; for now I stretch myself in bed, once again boldly extinguish a light, close my eyes, and begin to sink through slow turmoils of sound and sense to a dream. In this dream, I am standing before a small glass aquarium, square, of the sort in which goldfish are kept. I observe without surprise that there is water in one half of it but not in the other. And in spite of the fact that there is no partition, this water holds itself upright in its own half of the tank, leaving the other half empty. More curious than this, however, is the marine organism which lies at the bottom of the water. It looks, at first glance, like a loaf of bread. But when I lean down to examine it closely, I see that it is alive, that it is sentient, and that it is trying to move. One end of it lies very close to that point at which the water ends and the air begins; and now I realize that the poor thing is trying, and trying desperately, to get into the air. Moreover, I see that this advancing surface is as if sliced off and raw; it is horribly sensitive; and suddenly, appalled, I realize that the whole thing is simply —consciousness. It is trying to escape from the medium out of which it was created. If only it could manage this—! But I know that it never will; it has already reached, with its agonized sentience, as far as it can; it stretches itself forward, with minute and pathetic convulsions, but in vain; and suddenly I am so horrified at the notion of a consciousness which is pure suffering, that I wake up. . . . The clocks are striking two.

THE DISCIPLE

Four o'clock struck in the church tower he was passing—the wide bronze rings of sound fell over him mingled with a fine powdery snow. He looked at his watch —how absurd!—and found that the church was quite right. This seemed the last straw in his boredom, and as if instigated by it, he turned out of the quiet square, beginning to be patched with white under dim lamps, with here and there a black wheel-track showing, and moved listlessly toward the shopping district. "Why didn't I go?" he thought—without more than waving the vaguest of hands towards the imaginary destination or destiny. Then— "Middle age is a slow crucifixion." And then again, knocking snow from his coat, "I can't stand this damned solitude much longer." However, here were the shop windows, a long gaudily jeweled row of them, pouring their colored lights across the snowy pavement and illuminating brilliantly the hordes of fever-ishly gesticulating pedestrians, the prowling taxis, the furtively creeping beetle-like limousines, the wet sides of horses. He went slowly, like a heavy moth, from window to window. He pulled his mustache, he stared, stamped his feet, devoured with dry eyes all that he saw—opal necklaces, gold cigarette cases, umbrellas with carved ivory handles, embroideries of Chinese scarlet, opera glasses, microscopes—good God! what a strange collection. He felt as if he were somehow incrusting his soul with these things —he seemed to himself to be like one of those singular boxes, known to his childhood, covered all over hard, rough and corus- cating, with small sea-shells. Yes, exactly, and the box itself empty. Sea-shells—sea-shells. He thought of sea-shells with great pleas- ure, and then of the sea, the twilight valley floors of the sea, the strange soft trees that grow there, and himself as somehow a denizen—what precisely? A tortoise incrusted with barnacles, in- distinguishable from his bed of shells, immemorially old and white. Yes, something like that. . . .

"I should like," he said to the florid Jewish shopkeeper, "to look at some oddity in the way of a set of chessmen."

"An oddity?— Yes."

"A wedding gift, under peculiar circumstances. Something rather—" he waved a claw.

"—Rare?"

"—Old."

A Chinese set with dragons, a Hindu set with elephants, a Japanese set of carved cherry-wood, daimyos, priests. . . . No, these weren't quite the thing. The Jew looked at him intently under wrinkled lids like a parrot's. Was his tongue, also, as hard and dry and old as a parrot's? . . . The Jew hunched his shoul- ders almost up to his ears.

"Ah—I think I know what you want. But it can't be had."

"You mean——"

"You were thinking, no doubt, of the set of the 'Twelve Disciples'?"

Astonishing! He had never heard of the set of "Twelve Dis- ciples"; and yet there could be no question that it was what he was seeking.

"Exactly!"

"Ah! But it is lost. . . . And even if it were found, who could afford to buy it?"

"Oh! Afford! . . ."

"Ah—you are right—what does it matter?"

"And what is it like, this set of the Twelve Disciples?"

"Like? It is—but don't you know?"

The Jew, leaning on the glass case, peered at him, he thought, somewhat peculiarly.

"How should I? I've never even heard of it."

"But you said——!"

"Ah—forgive me—it is true that when you mentioned it—how shall I say—it seemed to me in some remote way—familiar. That was all."

"Ah. I see—I see! . . . You thought you remembered it. . . . And if you think, if you concentrate upon it—if you turn, in your mind, a sudden light upon it——"

"I beg your pardon——?"

"—You don't see it any more clearly?"

"Why, no—how should I?"

"Oh. . . . But the set really is quite ordinary—as carving. Nothing remarkable."

"Then why is it so valuable?"

"Perhaps because it is generally considered mythical."

"Mythical? . . . It doesn't, after all, exist? . . ."

"So some would say. As for me——"

"You believe in it?"

"I believe in it. . . . I have even, in dreams, seen it."

He found himself staring at the Jew, on this, as if at the revelation of some sort of obscure miracle. Yes, it appeared, the set of chessmen, in dreams; it came, in dreams, to this Jew. For a moment it seemed, in the oddest of ways, more tangible, it gave out a gleam and came nearer. Thirty-two pieces of ivory, close-clustered, one of them fallen over, and a candle lighting them. Had he dreamed this himself? It was vivid, and vivid was the hand he put out among them to right the fallen piece. But the fallen piece was stubborn, resisted, became massive. . . . He lifted his hand from the glass showcase, and stepped back. He had a sense of having resisted, barely resisted, and with an effort that left him trembling, a temptation not the less vast for having been incomprehensible. It was with a feeling of yielding to some obscure small issue of this temptation that he now said, with a conscious jocoseness that did not conceal excitement:

"And the piece that has fallen over—which piece is that?"

          II.   The effect of this remark was extraordinary. The tempo of the adventure—for adventure it unquestionably and profoundly was—instantly quickened. It was as if the stream on which they were being swept had not only broadened and taken on a dizzying speed, but had, as suddenly, dived underground through a phantasmagoric darkness. Specifically, he found himself looking at a Jew who had somehow changed—he was less the shopkeeper, less, even, the human being, and more—something else. What, exactly? More imposing? That, certainly; and also, singularly, more luminous—he gave out a light, and his eyes, looking down, seemed in the kindliest of manners to indicate that this light must also be a guidance. What it was that the Jew said he didn't catch. It was merely a short, vague exclamation, followed by a smile and a stare which were a little frightening in their suggestion of extraordinary intimacy. After that, it was as if every step taken was taken the more elaborately to insure for the ensuing talk the right seclusion and secrecy. The iron shutters outside the window were rattled harshly down and locked, the door was locked, the lights in the show window were switched off, leaving the heap of jewels, oddities, silks, and carvings in darkness. From outside in the night mingled with the subdued murmur of the street, came, even more subdued and tenuous, sounds of a bell, slowly struck, and as if blown down from a very great height. . . . When, having followed his host through a passage and up the stairs, an uplifted tall candle flinging cascades of banister shadows over the richly ornamented wall, he entered the room over the shop, it was with a vague sense of having come an incredible distance in space and time—the street seemed far away, remote seemed the snowy square where, surely only a quarter of an hour ago, the clock had struck four; remotest of all seemed his own poor lodgings where the fire probably needed replenishing. Had he not, even, come a long way from himself—was his name still Dace? . . .

"The piece that has fallen over!" said the Jew, and gave a short laugh. He had set the candle on the chimneypiece, where its light, duplicated in the dusty mirror, was sufficient to show a faded room crowded with odds and ends. "That's shrewd—that's shrewd. That goes, certainly, to the root of things. . . . So you knew, all the time!"

"Knew? . . ."

"You were merely drawing me out, leading me on! Well, well! That was clever."

Dace met the Jew's richly insinuating stare with bland and genial acquiescence.

"What makes you think I know?"

"My dear chap! . . . Are you joking? . . . Why, of course, it was your allusion to Judas."

"Oh, I see—my allusion to Judas. . . ."

"—The piece that has fallen over, as you so nicely put it!"

"Oh—that! . . . So that is Judas? . . . But I didn't, to tell the truth, know it at all. I knew nothing whatever!"

The Jew smiled at this with an excess of politeness, but the smile slowly faded.

"But—how extraordinary! . . . You really knew nothing?"

"As I say—nothing whatever."

"But how on earth, then, did you come to speak of the piece that has fallen over?"

They exchanged a long look over this question, as if (absurd! Dace found time to say to himself) it was, somehow, of tremendous import. But decidedly, it *was* of tremendous import. Whether the man were mad or not—and for the first moment Dace clearly formulated to himself that possibility—or whether he himself was on the verge of madness, did not seem particularly to matter. What was remarkable, or uncanny, was the way in which their sanity, or madness, brought them, in every consciousness, together. That singular vision of the chessmen—how explain it? His mental eye reverted to it, and he saw it now more sharply than ever. He saw the criss-crossing of shadows among the pieces, he saw deeply carved on the crown of the king nearest him the letters "I.N.R."—(and no doubt "I" was turned away from him); and there was Judas lying at the left-hand corner of the board, apparently on the point of rolling off. He put out his finger to it, tried to lift it—it was immovable, as if glued. But it *must* be moved! He felt the gathering within himself of a great wave of energy, all directed to a huge decuman crash against the implacable obstacle. . . . Then he removed his hand from the edge of the small taboret (which he had hardly noticed) and leaned back in his chair, once more with a sense of temptation undergone and partially resisted. But again, it was a yielding to some small faint beckoning, some fugitive far signal, that put the next words on his tongue.

"Well," he said, and he laughed a little uneasily, "I'm sure I can't explain it. But no sooner had you spoken of seeing the chessmen in dreams than I had, on the spot, a kind of waking dream myself. I've just had it again. I didn't see *all* the pieces plainly—but plain enough was the piece which you say is Judas, and plain enough was the inscription on the crown of one of the kings."

"You mean the letters——?"

"I. N. R. I."

"Ah, yes. Exactly. . . . Rex Judæorum. . . . How extraordinary!"

"To put it very mildly!"

"What? . . . Oh, I don't mean that."

"I beg your pardon, then—but what *do* you mean?"

The Jew regarded him searchingly; Dace felt himself being slowly fathomed and gave himself agreeably to the experience, with a sense that he must keep still, let the plummet go straight.

"I mean"—the Jew was deliberate—"that while you see so much, without assistance—oh, certainly, quite without assistance —you nevertheless don't see *all*."

"All?"

"Yes—that's what I find extraordinary. . . . When, downstairs in the shop, you suddenly asked me 'And the piece that has fallen over—what piece is that?'—how could I but assume that your identification was complete? . . . I—as you saw—accepted you. And now, you say, you didn't at all recognize the piece as Judas! Certainly, that is very peculiar. I must suppose, however, as all the circumstances urge, that you would, had you been given time, have named Judas yourself. Yes, undoubtedly that is the explanation."

The look which the Jew turned on Dace shone with the most perfect innocence and trust, and he replied to it with a grave nod. The logic was reasonable—was it not? Yet something in what the Jew said perplexed and escaped him; he went over it slowly, aware that somewhere, in this small plausible structure of words, was one word which was not so much a "block" as a "window"—it let through a light which was disquietingly suggestive of a space beyond space, of a depth which yawned beneath the solid, a world that was, as he was at last to phrase it, "other." He found this word quickly enough—it was "identification"—and looked hard through it. What on earth had he meant by it? . . . It was simply a depth, a gleam, and nothing more. Yet, for some reason, he decided not to challenge it—not, at any rate, immediately. Wouldn't it be more fruitful simply to wait before it exactly as one would wait before a lighted window, to find out at last what it was precisely that moved on the other side? Was it not also essential that he should in everything take his cue from the Jew?

It was therefore with a sense of the imperative necessity of delaying, of somehow gaining time, that he rose from his chair as if merely to look about him. The room to which he had been brought was extraordinary—a museum in microcosm. The candle, placed on the white marble mantel precariously between a tall much-figured clock and a Han horse, lighted the chamber only sufficiently to show its richness and its confusion. The only cleared space was that immediately before the fire, where the two chairs faced each other obliquely on the worn Persian carpet: for the rest, narrow lanes led hither and thither among a chaos of furniture and oddments which, in the gloom, had amazingly the air of a jungle. Chairs stood on tables, ivories and pictures balanced on chairs, shields, swords, and suits of chain mail hung on the walls with tapestries and Chinese paintings. Half a dozen clocks were ticking confusedly, only one of them visible. And dust was everywhere, thick, gritty dust, deposit of decades —on the mantel, the clock, the floor, the tables, here and there finger-marked. Even the mirror was dusty. And Dace, feeling the eyes of the Jew upon his back, and looking into the glass above the candle flame, to examine the shopkeeper at his leisure, was able to see of him, in the veiled gloom, only the dimmest of outlines. He turned and faced his interlocutor.

"You have some fine things here," he murmured. "That horse, for example."

The Jew was inert. It was as if he knew Dace to be evading him. He stared a moment, then dropped his eyes.

"Ah—that little Han horse."

He was not interested in the horse, that was clear; and did not intend talking of it. But as Dace again sank into his chair, sighing, the Jew leaned sharply toward him, and smiled. Dace was touched by something in this smile—it was singularly gentle and friendly, a little humble. Why was it, nevertheless, that it seemed so oddly belied by the eyes? For in the eyes, lidded like a parrot's, something disquieting flickered.

"You do not yet altogether trust me—do you!" said the Jew, still smiling.

Dace laughed outright, but not entirely with conviction. He was still trying, as it were, to gain time.

"Trust you? But why on earth shouldn't I? Is it any question—"

"Oh, not of business, no! Certainly not. . . . We are not concerned with business. . . . Isn't it really," he lowered his tone a little, "something very much more important?"

"Important?"

"Yes. Isn't it at bottom simply the question of our trusting— *completely* trusting—one another?"

Dace looked hard into the little eyes, which, in intensity of meaning, seemed to blaze.

"Oh, that!" he exclaimed gently. He directed his unseeing stare at the fire in an effort to conceal his confusion. Where, where on earth, he cried to himself, am I going? He felt slightly dizzy, but managed to affect a calm. Whether the shopkeeper was a madman or a prophet seemed for the present a wholly irrelevant question.

"That's of course taken for granted—isn't it?" he went on. And then added, for all the world as if the words were not so much his own as somehow *given* him, "What I mean is—isn't it sufficient guarantee of our mutual trust—or sympathy, at all events —that so far, for all the singularity of our intercourse, we so easily and with so little error, *follow* one another?" He was pleased with himself at this, and showed it by smiling a little more lightly than before, and also by relaxing slightly in his chair.

And the shopkeeper, too, was pleased. He again, in that curious way which Dace had noticed downstairs in the shop, seemed before his very eyes in the act of changing; it was as if he became more significant, as if all his colors became brighter and richer, as if a secret low light within had somehow been sharply turned up. The wrinkled lids lifted a little, and the face became luminous with words of which Dace felt that he could almost, in advance, see the shape.

"Ah," came the pleased murmur. "Exactly. That's a good deal better, isn't it? We begin to know where we are. And isn't it important that you should agree with me, since you use the word 'follow,' that *I follow you* quite as successfully as *you follow me?* I don't mean to urge or press you—no—no. But that, I think, if you will permit my saying so, is—er—a point——"

"Of cardinal importance? Yes—I believe it is. You mean—"

"I mean that, in all the experience we are sharing, or are about to share, you are contributing—quite without any assistance from me—as much as I. Or, to put it in another way, that you have been as free to accept as complete *my* identification as I have been to accept or reject yours. The responsibility is divided."

"Responsibility?"

The Jew's face clouded.

"Perhaps that's not the best word," he explained a little painfully. "There's of course no serious question of responsibility. Responsibility for what?" He laughed. "No. We can put that aside. . . . Though it might be as well, afterwards, to know that it had been said."

It was clear to Dace the Jew meant, by responsibility, responsibility for their mutual delusion. And surely there could be no harm in appearing to admit a share in the creation of it?

"Well—I'm quite ready to grant it, if you are—why not?"

Dace's friendly, and perhaps slightly paternal, grin was met by one as friendly. They remained so for a moment, smiling, smiling as over the exchange of something secret and precious. Then, firmly, Dace continued——

"But we've got rather far away, haven't we, from the set of the Twelve Disciples. What about that?"

"Ah, my dear fellow! Are you so determined to make a joke of it?"

"A joke? Why no."

"But surely you realize that it's just that that we've *been,* all this time, talking about!"

"Oh! Oh! I see."

"But my dear chap—*do* you see? . . ."

The shopkeeper's voice, on this, had become rather surprisingly loud and agitated. "*Do* you see! . . . Or have I been, after all, so hideously mistaken?"

"But how could you have been?"

"Ah, yes—how could I have been? It's ridiculous. . . . Tell me"—he went on slowly, as if he were feeling his way with the greatest of care. "When you think of this set, when you light it sharply for yourself—do you feel toward it, in any way, any sort of—impulse?"

Dace was startled. Impulse? Of course, he did. But was it wise, after all, to admit it? What was this singular shopkeeper up to? . . . The rapidity of events had confused him. But it was necessary, after all—it was even imperative—that in this other-world darkness some sort of outline should be made out, some purpose or design should be guessed. Certainly, it did not seem an extravagance to suppose that the Jew was mad; nor was it in any way an extravagance to perceive, as he was almost sure he perceived, a slow, methodical, careful effort on the Jew's part, to weave strongly the illusion, and to weave into it, as a vital part of it, both himself, and, what was more important, Dace. More obscure was the question whether the Jew was conscious of doing this. When he had so emphatically caviled over the point of their divided, their cooperative responsibility for the delusion —if it *was* a delusion—it had certainly appeared that he was, even if mad, aware of what he was doing. He had seemed quite consciously fearful lest Dace should suspect something. This odd something which he had so zealously guarded—was it, at bottom, nothing but a dim kind of hypnosis? But, if so, what was it for? . . . Dace looked hard into this tangle. It had no beginning and no end, and there was no point at which he might, with any clearness of view, start to unravel it. Most disquieting of all was his inability to distinguish, in his own mind, that part of this growing, glimmering, mutual delusion which might, quite genuinely, and quite, as the Jew had said, "without any assistance," be his own strange contribution. But was *any* of it his own? . . . To admit that was to admit either one of two possibilities, neither of them comforting. It was to admit either that he himself was on the border of a kind of madness, or else that he had suddenly, with a catastrophic crash, gone through some queer crust of the world into a dimension which he had not hitherto known to exist, but which was none the less grotesquely real. But surely this was absurd! The man must be mad. Mad, but with a madness of which some intrinsic and secret element was an extraordinary power to exert an influence. Could it be also that he, Dace, by some psychological freak, was in exactly the right state of mind to be easily influenced? *Was* he responsible? . . . His misgiving, however, was only momentary, and, hearing again, in that still, strange room, the ethereal far ringing of the half-hour bells of the church tower, in the world he had left outside, and in a sense so far behind, his feeling of adventure was once more

deepened and renewed. Strange, strange, he said to himself, and
found himself, for no reason, staring at his hands, which he had
lifted. Old hands; old and scarred. He stared at them, hard, as
if he desired to look into them, to discover there some curious
and embedded revelation. It embarrassed him, presently, to find
that the Jew was watching this action intently, and had lifted
his own hands into the same position. His answer was thus, in
a manner, startled out of him. Was the Jew, then, in the very
act of hypnotizing him? . . .

"Impulse?" he said. "I thought I had told you. Yes—I have an
impulse, a curious and very strong one. I think it must have
been because of that impulse that I've just found myself, as you
seem to have observed"—he laughed—"staring so idiotically at
my old hands. . . . Each time that I have clearly visualized this
set of chessmen, with its kings, and its fallen Judas, I have half-
surrendered to the most unaccountable impulse to *right* the
fallen piece. And each time, on coming to my senses, I've found
myself pressing, very hard, against—well, the showcase downstairs, the taboret, here. That, I suppose, is what you mean?"

The Jew nodded.

"Exactly. And now— But first let me repeat that you are—how
shall I put it—mentally quite free in this matter—isn't that true?"

"But, of course—how could it not be?" Dace, saying this, felt
a little disingenuous.

"Well. The interesting question then is—do you see any *reason*
for this impulse? . . . Don't let me hurry you—take your time.
Try, if you like, lighting the board for yourself once more. Observe, if you can, when you feel this impulse, whether it is connected with any profound feeling of *identification*—or shall we
say, rather, sympathy. . . . Perhaps I embarrass you. I'll turn my
back."

The Jew walked to the mantel, and resting one foot on the
brass fender, appeared to stare into the disintegrating coal fire.
Identification! That word again. It was important—it meant that
something, something very peculiar, was expected of him. Left
thus to himself, Dace felt that at last a definite turning point

had come, and felt also, quite clearly, that it was in his power to "go on" or not, just as he chose; not merely a power to refuse or acquiesce, but something much more singular—a power, if he liked, to acquiesce *creatively*. If the man was mad—and certainly the worn and shiny back, the high peaked shoulders, and comically bald head combined to produce an effect of decided queerness—his madness might be harmless, and was also, for Dace—and this struck him as remarkable—perfectly, potentially *transparent*. What Dace felt was indeed that if now he were to make the smallest effort (of a sort which he recognized brilliantly, but could scarcely analyze) he would not only be able to see the mechanism of the Jew as clearly as one sees the mechanism of a glass-cased clock, but also exactly what that mechanism, so driven and so eccentric, would demand of *himself*. Even this was not all. For was it not also true that, once he accepted this course, something of himself would have to be surrendered? . . . Would it not definitely involve his "descent," or "ascent," into that curious void, already glimpsed, of the "other" world? . . . Was he not quite clearly putting himself in the hands of this Jew? . . . Certainly the mere summoning up once more, before his mind's eye, of the chessboard, the peculiar set of chessmen, was absurdly easy—he could do it without any effort whatever. It was, in fact, already there—he had only to look at it. If there was something just the least disquieting in this fact—in the fact that he might almost say that his mind was, in a manner, *possessed*— he at once waved the suggestion away. He looked, then, once again at the visionary board. It was closer, more pressingly vivid and alive, than ever. He could certainly, if he liked, put his hand out and touch it—he could certainly put his hand among the pieces, past the White King (whose crown showed the letters I. N. R.) and lift the fallen Knight, which was Judas. This was what he desired to do—he put out his hand, and as he did so, realized for the first time how extraordinarily important this action was for him. The fallen piece, however, resisted him as before, resisted his thought, would not be otherwise conceived than as fallen. But it *must* be lifted! He strained at the shadow, concentrating against it a whole world of shadows. He bent his life against it. It could not be seized, it would not budge. It was as if he were—yes—trying to lift a part of himself—a symbol——

The revelation was sudden enough to shock him. He broke into a cold sweat, and barely mastered an impulse to spring to his feet. There was still time to "go back"—he seemed to see it, however, as a long way, and involving, also, a sort of cowardice. It was to go back into—hadn't he, in the snow-filled square, called it the slow crucifixion of middle age—boredom? This could hardly be worse; though he now knew, with a sense rather spacious and vast than precise, that it involved danger. Still, it was possible to go forward, with caution. He would keep *some* part of his wits about him—still free, and his own. He was a match, he felt, for—well, for that Jew. He needn't be influenced, beyond a certain point? . . .

He opened his eyes, which during his waking dream he had shut, and rose. The Jew turned about. For a moment the two men regarded each other in silence, a silence broken only by the small feverish ticking of invisible clocks. The shopkeeper, when at last he spoke, spoke in a tone which had become, for no apparent reason, sardonic and slightly tyrannous. He leaned back, with his elbows behind him on the white marble mantel.

"Well?" he said.

Dace was cool—he allowed himself a slightly ironic smile.

"You were quite right," he rang out. Then, measuring with the nicest accuracy the queer light in the other's eyes, he went on, with a considered leisureliness, which he perhaps intended to be provocative—"I do identify myself with one of the pieces on the board—as you so perspicaciously suggested. . . . I identify myself with Judas."

"I didn't suggest it"—cried the Jew. "I didn't suggest it! As God is my witness. . . . Don't think it!"

Dace was amazed by the violence of this outburst. He was amazed also by the change in the Jew's appearance. He stood rigid and tall, his fists clenched at his sides, his face white as the marble, his large mouth grotesquely opened in a fixed and tragic expression of suffering, like the mouth of the tragic mask. He was absurd—Dace had even a fleeting desire to "kick" him— but he was also portentous.

"I think you misunderstand me," Dace pursued, endeavoring to speak without agitation. "You merely suggested that I might, during this waking dream, experience some feeling of sympathy—am I not right? Well, I now tell you that is true. God knows how you guessed it!" He laughed apologetically. "And I improve on your suggestion, quite clearly, when I tell you that in this dream *Judas and I are one and the same person.* . . . Isn't it extraordinary!"

The Jew, at this, merely gasped. Then relaxing, and as if he had suddenly become faint, he sank into a chair, where he dropped his face into his hands and began absurdly rolling his great, dark curly head from side to side, as if in an ecstasy of pain. "Ah, my God," he breathed through his hands, without looking up. "Ah, my God, my God!"

Dace, if he was surprised by the spectacle, did not show it. He merely watched, with the absorbed amusement of a child, this uncontrolled and unexplained behavior, and smiled. The top of the Jew's head, with its bald spot ringed with curls, thus rolling heavily and serpentinely, with that sinuous unction peculiar to camels, simply struck him as funny.

III.   He was also, however, somewhat disgusted. And it was with some severity that he asked, after a moment:

"Are you feeling ill?"

The shopkeeper stopped rolling his head. His face remained hidden in his hands, nevertheless, and it was some time before he sat up, looking extraordinarily ravaged and pale, and with his large mouth still tragically relaxed. His voice, when at last he spoke, had changed, had become harsh, deep, tortured, uncertain—"Biblical"—Dace had time to say to himself.

"You persist in being flippant," the voice cried. "You have

no seriousness. You permit yourself merely to be amused by all this. And you have the impertinence to ask me if I am ill when. as you might see, I am simply overcome by compassion. My God! Don't you see that it is serious, that it is tragic—that we sound together the whole horror of the world?"

He glared at Dace with unexpected ferocity. Then, before Dace had time for anything but a turmoil of bewilderment, he sprang up, approached Dace's chair menacingly, leaned over him, pointed at him with a white thick finger on which he wore three rings.

"You are Judas, and you admit it. Don't pretend any longer that you don't fully realize it. The time for such foolery is past. You are Judas. You knew it before you came in here—you came in to tell me. You knew the countersign—you asked for the set of Twelve Disciples. Ah! I know everything. You tried to fool me, but you couldn't—I saw through your pretenses from the beginning—I knew you were coming today. And why shouldn't I? It's Easter Eve. You know as well as I do that we always meet on Easter Eve! . . ."

Dace sat as if hypnotized, his glassy eyes fixed on the thick withered eyelids of the Jew. He was frightened, and found it difficult to control his voice.

"Why, what do you mean?" he stammered.

"What do I mean! You ask me what do I mean! Ah, my God! Do I have to drag it all out of you like this? You have no honesty, no seriousness, no repentance? You are Judas. You were born in the Island of Kerioth. You murdered your father and married your mother. Pilate! Pilate! Do you hear? You kept books for Pilate. You cheated him. And then you went looking for Jesus, because you thought He could forgive you for incest. Ha! And you cheated Him too; you stole from Him. You kept back the moneys. Your passion came on you—you wanted gold and silver. You stole from the shepherds in the market place— you stole from the other Disciples. Finally, because your fingers itched, you sold Jesus. What's the good of denying it? I can see that you remember it—you knew it all the time. It's Easter Eve, and you've come back again. I knew you were coming—I know everything."

The Jew stepped back with a gesture of triumph, dropping his hand. He squared his high peaked shoulders as if in a paroxysm of righteousness. His coarse face was radiant—transfigured.

"Well," said Dace, in a small voice, but clearly, "suppose I *am* Judas—suppose I *do* admit it. Suppose I admit even that I knew it before I came here, and came here with the sole purpose of revealing myself to you. You know everything—so I suppose I'll have to grant you that I even knew that the set of the Twelve Disciples was the password—which, I take it, we're in the habit of exchanging, in this extraordinary fashion, every Easter Eve. *Is* this Easter Eve? I didn't know it. I suppose I'm allowed a respite from Hell on Easter Eve—is that it? . . . But, supposing that all this is true—what about it?"

"Ah," the Jew cried, "you're incorrigible. . . . Why do you always make it so—difficult for me! If only once, once, you would admit it all—tell me everything from your heart—help me to sound the horror of the world, instead of leaving me to sound it alone! Only once!" He sank into his chair, flung his head back, and regarded Dace pityingly as from an immense moral distance.

"Listen!" said Dace. "I want you to believe me when I tell you that I'm not trying to deceive you or make it hard for you. I'm honestly trying to tell you everything I know. If there are some things I don't know which you think I ought to know— well, it's because there's some barrier which I don't understand, some barrier. Do you see? . . . For example, I suppose I ought to know—since I've met you so often—who you are. But I don't! . . . Who are you?"

"I am Ahasver—the eternal Jew."

"Oh! You are—I see. And we meet every Easter Eve."

"Every Easter Eve."

"You are eternal—of course, I've heard of you. As for me, I suppose I'm just, for the moment, reincarnated."

"Reincarnated."

"That, I suppose, is why you can remember me, but I can't remember you."

"You *must* remember!"

"I don't. I remember nothing."

"Try! Think of last year."

"I don't remember last year."

"Salt Lake City! It was in Salt Lake City. Do you remember?"

"No, I've never been to Salt Lake City."

"You have—you were there last year. My shop was in Myrtle Street. We met outside it, just as six o'clock struck. You were smoking a pipe. When I asked you who you were, you said your name was O'Grady."

"Oh! Did I?"

"Yes. You said at first that you wanted to pawn something— your watch. You looked very different. You had a beard. Then, we were inside the shop, and the door was shut—"

"Ah! I asked for a peculiar set of chessmen!"

"You remember! You remember! . . . And the year before it was at Buenos Aires. . . . My shop was on the second floor, over a colonnade. I had a sign hanging outside—with my name on it, Juan Espera en Dios. . . . You were a little Portuguese Jew named Gomez—your skin was very yellow, you were suffering from the jaundice. Do you remember?"

"No—I've never been to Buenos Aires. Never."

"Ah, you shameless liar! . . . Liar! . . . You lie merely to make me suffer. Don't! Don't! And the year before that—"

"My dear fellow, do you remember them all?"

"Every one. It was on the Ponte Vecchio—my name was over the door, Butta Deus. A very small shop, with bracelets and fili-gree necklaces. Ah, you were very droll that time—and very shabby, poor. A poor tailor, you said your name was Fantini. You had no thumb on your left hand, and said it didn't inter-fere with your work—you showed me how flexible and cunning were your fingers. And ah, my God, how stubborn you were,

how you denied it! But you always deny it, you always torture
me. . . . It is my punishment."

The Jew covered his eyes with one hand and sank into an absorbed silence. He looked as if he were praying. Dace examined
him in astonishment—observed the tufts of grizzled hair in his
ears, the gray sparse whorls of beard under the edges of the jaw,
the greasy old-fashioned black stock under the lowered chin.
Three heavy gold rings were on the fourth finger, one of them
set with a coarse peach-agate. . . . Behind him in the tumbled
room somewhere a clock struck seven in a small sweet voice,
then another, nearer at hand, more briskly and loudly, then two
others, simultaneously, their voices, one brazen and one treble,
infelicitously mingling. Seven o'clock? But to Dace the world
semed timeless; and he felt extraordinarily, with a bright trans-
lucence, that made him bodiless, that he was existing separately,
at one and the same time, in Salt Lake City, Buenos Aires, Flor-
ence—and where else? He seemed to know himself perfectly as
O'Grady—he was tall and bearded, smoked a pipe, walked, in
the warm, clear dusk, into Myrtle Street, where, sure enough,
the Jew awaited him. But what was the Jew's name there? He
had forgotten to say. . . . Certainly, as Gomez he had had the
jaundice, as Fantini had lost his left thumb. Absurd! And this
ghostly multiple career extended back, troubled, passionate,
full of sinister echoes, for eighteen hundred and thirty-five
years. And the unchanging secret in him, through all this harle-
quinade, was Judas! These hands were the hands of Judas—the
hands of the parricide, the thief, the betrayer. . . . And what, in
all this amazing nightmare, so profoundly actual, did the Jew
want of him? Sympathy? An exchange of understanding? . . .
He tried to remember what it was that the Jew had done, what
offense it was that his eternal wanderings were a punishment
for. Perhaps if he closed his eyes it would come back to him.
For a moment he would submit a little, allow this extraordinary influence— Ah! It began to come back to him. It was something outrageous, something revolting—there was a crowd—Jesus

was passing, carrying something—and the shopkeeper—Ahasver
—what was it he did? He leaned forward out of the crowd and
spat at Jesus and said something—that was it. Something hateful.

"What was it you said?" Dace asked.

"On the Ponte Vecchio?"

"No—on Golgotha."

"Ah, I won't repeat it—every time you ask me to repeat it!
And you know as well as I do!"

"I know you said something—I don't know what you said."

The Jew leaped to his feet, his face flushed with fury. He
made a gesture of curved hands towards Dace's throat, as if he
would like to strangle him.

"Hypocrite! You sit there and pretend you know nothing—
you, my only friend! Well, I'll tell you what I did—I spat in His
face, that's what I did! Yes! I leaned over and spat right in His
face, and said in a loud ugly voice: 'Go on quicker!' And He
stopped and looked at me—ah, you can see Him stopping—and
answered—'I go; but thou shalt wait till My return!' . . . That's
what happened, Judas! . . . And you, where were you? On Oli-
vet, with an old bit of rope, the halter of an ass! But it did you
no good. No. You were merely doing what you'd have to do
over and over again. For you, too, were included in the words:
'There be some of those that stand here which shall in no wise
taste death till they see the Son of Man coming in His kingdom!' "

"We are friends, then," murmured Dace. "We are friends!"

"We are the oldest friends in the world. And yet you torture me."

"I don't mean to torture you. I am trying to understand."

"I forgive you, my friend—I forgive you." And suddenly the
Jew leaned down and touched, with his white soft hand, the
right hand of Dace, where it rested on the arm of the chair; a
touch fawning and horrible. There were tears in his eyes. He
patted Dace's hand twice, with a grotesque and repulsive tenderness, and smiled; then, straightening:

"No one else forgives us—why shouldn't we forgive each

other? God has forgotten us—He only remembers to forget us. Ah, my old friend, let us not forget each other! Let us remember each other all we can, and forgive each other with all our hearts. You see why it is that I want so horribly, so horribly, to have you remember me! To be an outcast, eternal, hated by God and man, unforgiven, loved by none—to be used by God for His own inscrutable purpose, yet punished for it forever! Perhaps God means that we shall be a comfort to each other. Perhaps He means in that way to reward us—to grant us, as recompense, the greatest, deepest, oldest friendship ever known by men."

"Yes," said Dace faintly, "why not? Why not? Perhaps He does."

"I am sure of it, my friend—Judas, I am sure of it! We have a bond, the greatest of bonds. Each of us committed a sin in its way unparalleled. No others have sounded the depths that we have sounded. At the very bottom of the world, most miserable Gehenna of Gehennas, we meet and embrace. Surely that is something! Yes, I believe it is a proof of the essential goodness and wisdom and mercifulness of God. I wrong Him by saying that He has forgotten us! He has not forgotten us. Isn't it perhaps truer to say that we are a part of God, the part of Him that is evil and that suffers? What a vision! What pride we can legitimately take in being ourselves! In us is concentrated the most intense suffering, the deepest darkness, the most unmitigated horror, of the world. . . . Let us share it, old friend—on this one day in the year when we meet, for these few uncertain hours in an infinity of torment, let us share our grief and pride, and open our hearts."

Dace was extraordinarily moved by this speech; but he could scarcely have said whether he was more impressed, or horrified, or amused. So this was where they were—at the bottom of the world, at the bottom of the bottomless pit. What a vision, indeed! And himself and this repulsive shopkeeper, sinister dual embodiment of the world's evil, embracing passionately in the blown smoke of Gehenna. Treachery kissing obscenity! Laughter would have been a relief to him, but he felt, with a peculiar anxiety, that the moment was not propitious. Wasn't there still, somewhere in all this, a danger? Something there was which the Jew had said which had alarmed him; but he could not now recall it. Decidedly he must keep his wits with him.

"Yes," he answered slowly, with averted eyes, "we are old friends, our sympathies ought to be of the profoundest. We are, as you say, in the same boat—if it isn't flippant to put it in so homely a fashion. We know each other, don't we?"

"Ah," said the Jew, "but do you know me as I know you? That is the question that curses me, that always curses me! You are so hesitant, so uncertain! You distress me so with your questions, and the blanks in your memory! If only we were *exactly* alike, and you remembered, each year, all that I remember!"

"It's a pity—it's a pity."

"A tragedy, rather! . . . For me a tragedy. . . . Yet I mustn't be selfish. That is the part assigned to me—to remember, to be the memory. I must remember your sorrows as well as my own. It is my privilege to remind you. Corfu, for example! Do you remember Corfu?"

"Corfu? No."

"Tonight in Corfu they are stoning you. Listen!" The Jew lifted a peremptory finger, commanding silence. Dace listened intently, as if he really expected to hear something; but nothing disturbed the sequestered hush of the room save the ticking of clocks, their own breathing, and the sinking of coals in the grate. Why on earth Corfu? An island in the Adriatic, was it?

"I hear nothing," he said.

"In Corfu, on every Easter Eve, they stone you. Every window is opened, and old crockery, stones, and sticks are flung violently into the streets. I can hear it. I can see the angry faces. I can hear the screams of hate and triumph. And ah, my God, I can feel the stones on my body, in my soul, wretched compassionate creature that I am. . . . Do you feel them? Do you hear them?"

"Nothing whatever—no."

The Jew seemed hurt, bewildered. He stared at the floor.

"No—you hear nothing, feel nothing. . . . I suppose God intended it so. . . . And yet it seems as if you ought to be prepared. A warning would be an act of mercy. To remember nothing, to experience the tragedy afresh each time! Horrible."

"A warning? What do you mean?"

The Jew fixed Dace's eyes intently. What strange light was it that tried there, through the smoke of confused emotions, to flash out? Compassion? Cunning? But the eyelids lowered, the Jew looked away. Then he said tonelessly:

"I mean for your hanging."

IV.   Dace, at this, felt that his heart had stopped beating altogether. His consciousness flew off like a vapor, he experienced, for a timeless instant, a perfect and horrible annihilation. Then his ears began ringing, his temples were hammered like cymbals, his arms violently trembled. The room came back to him, but smaller, more real and shabby in the candlelight; and the Jew before him, musing in his chair, seemed also unaccountably shabbier and smaller. He felt slightly sick.

"Oh," with hardly a tremor, "I'm to hang myself?"

"Ah, my dear friend!" wailed the Jew, "my dear friend!" He wrung his hands.

"But here—in this room?"

"It is better so—is it not? That's as it always is."

"Oh, it's always so, I see. . . . And O'Grady, what about O'Grady?"

"O'Grady? What do you mean?"

"He hanged himself, for you, in Salt Lake City?"

"Not for me—not for me! For God!"

"And Gomez—and the tailor, Fantini?"

"Yes—" the Jew whispered. "They, too. All of them. Every year. . . . My poor friend! I was afraid, afraid that you didn't remember. I've done my best for you. I've tried to—"

"Break the news gently? Yes! So you have. I thank you from the bottom of my heart."

The two men stared at each other. It was then Dace who went on.

"There's the trivial, purely practical matter of the rope," he said. "I suppose you have the rope."

"Yes. I'll get it for you. It's the same one."

"The halter of the ass?"

"Yes."

The Jew rose, sighing, took the candle, and went to a high cupboard in the front corner of the room by the shuttered window. The lifted candle, when the door had been flung back, lighted a tall crucifix within, the figure of Christ carved of a pallid greenish stone. Below it, on the cupboard floor, stood an earthen bowl. It occurred to Dace that the bowl might bear the stains of sacrifice. The Jew lifted from a hook a small coil of rope, closed the cupboard, and returned to Dace.

"There!" he said. "Take it."

Dace rose, but he did not take the rope. Instead he took up his hat from the taboret. At the Jew's look of astonished incredulity he laughed.

"No," he then said. "I shan't take it—I must be going. It's late."

"Going?" stammered the Jew. Then he cried out again, horribly, in his Biblical prophetic voice: "Going, without——"

"Certainly. Going without hanging myself. Do you seriously expect me to hang myself for you?"

He laughed again. Then, as the shopkeeper, angrily flushed, took a step forward, he took a step forward to meet him.

"Listen," he cried, "you're insane! insane! and you know it."

A look of desolation, of horror, relaxed the Jew's face—the jaw sagged, the large mouth opened. He sat down, still holding the rope.

"That's right—sit down. And don't you dare to move till I'm out of this house—do you hear? Sit still! Or I'll report you to the police."

He took the candle, and walked slowly to the door through the aisle of dusty furniture. At the door, a thought suddenly struck him. He set down the candle, took out a card, wrote on it, and put it on a table.

"Here's my name and address," he said. "Send me, in the morning, the set of the Twelve Disciples! . . . Goodbye!"

The shopkeeper, whom he could only dimly make out in the now almost unlighted jungle of bric-a-brac, made no answer. Dace turned, went down the stairs, put the candle on the floor, and let himself out.

v.   When three days had passed, without his having had any signal from the Jew, Dace determined to go and see him. The adventure, he thought, must be an anticlimax; but there were one or two possibilities about which he was curious. Was it not conceivable, for example, that the wretched man, in some obscure sort of religious ecstasy, might have done himself a violence? . . . It was in bright sunlight that he passed this time through the square and turned into the shopping district; not yet noon. Missing, for a fraction of a minute, the shop, which was small, he had a renewal of his excitement—it seemed to him not too incredible that the shop, and its singular proprietor, might never have existed at all. But here it was.

What startled him was that the Jew did not recognize him; not in the slightest. He had uttered no greeting, on entering, had merely looked at the shopkeeper, expecting that the result would be an exclamation. But the Jew simply looked up from his glass case, which was opened at the back, and where he seemed to be arranging a small plush tray of jades and corals—looked up with a mild, polite interest. And as Dace, surprised, stared at him, it was the Jew who was the first to speak.

"Good morning!" he said. His tone was friendly—not intimate, not obsequious. "Is there something I can show you?"

Dace looked very hard at those green eyes under their sleepy lids.

"I am looking, as a matter of fact, for something odd in the way of a set of chessmen."

The shopkeeper was suavely interested.

"Chessmen? Certainly. . . . Had you anything particular in mind?"

Dace's heart gave a leap. The Jew was putting away his jades, unconcerned.

"Well—what I should really like to get hold of is a set I've heard called the set of the Twelve Disciples. . . . Do you happen to know anything about it?"

The shopkeeper tapped his fingers idly on the glass.

"No, I can't say I do. Twelve Disciples! No. . . . Very curious. . . . Do you know where it was made?"

Dace leaned forward against the case.

"I don't; no. . . ." He stared at the shopkeeper, who was very close to him. "Tell me—haven't we met before?"

The Jew returned his stare perplexedly.

"I don't think so—have we? . . . I have a good memory for faces—bad for names. Still, I may be at fault!"

"I think you are—I think you are!" Dace said—and laughed. "You're wearing glasses today—you weren't before."

"Oh?" The Jew's smile was friendly, but vague.

"Yes. . . . Don't you remember taking me to your room upstairs? You showed me a crucifix in a cupboard."

"Did I?" The shopkeeper smiled, wagged his ugly head, shrugged his shoulders. "Ah, then I *am* at fault. I take so many people up there, you see, to look at things—you must forgive me!"

"Oh, I forgive you!"

They chuckled together, amicably. Then Dace bought a Chinese set of carved ivory and bade the Jew good morning.

IMPULSE

Michael Lowes hummed as he shaved, amused by the face he saw—the pallid, asymmetrical face, with the right eye so much higher than the left, and its eyebrow so peculiarly arched, like a "v" turned upside down. Perhaps this day wouldn't be as bad as the last. In fact, he knew it wouldn't be, and that was why he hummed. This was the bi-weekly day of escape, when he would stay out for the evening, and play bridge with Hurwitz, Bryant, and Smith. Should he tell Dora at the breakfast table? No, better not. Particularly in view of last night's row about unpaid bills. And there would be more of them, probably, beside his plate. The rent. The coal. The doctor who had attended to the children. Jeez, what a life. Maybe it was time to do a new jump. And Dora was beginning to get restless again——

But he hummed, thinking of the bridge game. Not that he liked Hurwitz or Bryant or Smith—cheap fellows, really—mere pick-up acquaintances. But what could you do about making friends, when you were always hopping about from one place to another, looking for a living, and fate always against you! They were all right enough. Good enough for a little escape, a little party—and Hurwitz always provided good alcohol. Dinner at the Greek's, and then to Smith's room—yes. He would wait till late in the afternoon, and then telephone to Dora as if it had all come up suddenly. Hello, Dora—is that you, old girl? Yes, this is Michael—Smith has asked me to drop in for a hand of bridge—you know—so I'll just have a little snack in town. Home by the last car as usual. Yes. . . . Gooo-bye! . . .

And it all went off perfectly, too. Dora was quiet, at breakfast, but not hostile. The pile of bills was there, to be sure, but nothing was said about them. And while Dora was busy getting the kids ready for school, he managed to slip out, pretending that he thought it was later than it really was. Pretty neat, that! He hummed again, as he waited for the train. Telooralooraloo. Let the bills wait, damn them! A man couldn't do everything at once, could he, when bad luck hounded him everywhere? And if he could just get a little night off, now and then, a rest and change, a little diversion, what was the harm in that?

At half-past four he rang up Dora and broke the news to her. He wouldn't be home till late.

"Are you sure you'll be home at all?" she said, coolly.

That was Dora's idea of a joke. But if he could have fore-seen——!

He met the others at the Greek restaurant, began with a couple of *araks,* which warmed him, then went on to red wine, bad olives, *pilaf,* and other obscure foods; and considerably later they all walked along Boylston Street to Smith's room. It was a cold night, the temperature below twenty, with a fine dry snow sifting the streets. But Smith's room was comfortably warm, he trotted out some gin and the Porto Rican cigars, showed them a new snapshot of Squiggles (his Revere Beach sweetheart), and then they settled down to a nice long cozy game of bridge.

It was during an intermission, when they all got up to stretch their legs and renew their drinks, that the talk started—Michael never could remember which one of them it was who had put in the first oar—about impulse. It might have been Hurwitz, who was in many ways the only intellectual one of the three, though hardly what you might call a highbrow. He had his queer curiosities, however, and the idea was just such as might occur to him. At any rate, it was he who developed the idea, and with gusto.

"Sure," he said, "anybody might do it. Have you got impulses? Of course, you got impulses. How many times you think —suppose I do that? And you don't do it, because you know damn well if you do it you'll get arrested. You meet a man you despise—you want to spit in his eye. You see a girl you'd like to kiss—you want to kiss her. Or maybe just to squeeze her arm when she stands beside you in the street car. You know what I mean."

"DO I know what you *mean!*" sighed Smith. "I'll tell the world. I'll tell the cock-eyed world! . . ."

"You would," said Bryant. "And so would I."

"It would be easy," said Hurwitz, "to give in to it. You know what I mean? So simple. Temptation is too close. That girl you see is too damn good-looking—she stands too near you—you just put out your hand it touches her arm—maybe her leg—why worry? And you think, maybe if she don't like it I can make believe I didn't mean it. . . ."

"Like these fellows that slash fur coats with razor blades," said Michael. "Just impulse, in the beginning, and only later a habit."

"Sure. . . . And like these fellows that cut off braids of hair with scissors. They just feel like it and do it. . . . Or stealing."

"Stealing?" said Bryant.

"Sure. Why, I often feel like it. . . . I see a nice little thing right in front of me on a counter—you know, a nice little knife, or necktie, or a box of candy—quick, you put it in your pocket, and then go to the other counter, or the soda fountain for a drink. What would be more human? We all want things. Why not take them? Why not do them? And civilization is only skin-deep. . . ."

"That's right. Skin-deep," said Bryant.

"But if you were caught, by God!" said Smith, opening his eyes wide.

"*Who's* talking about getting caught? . . . *Who's* talking about doing it? It isn't that we do it, it's only that we *want* to do it. Why, Christ, there's been times when I thought to hell with everything, I'll kiss that woman if it's the last thing I do."

"It might be," said Bryant.

Michael was astonished at this turn of the talk. He had often felt both these impulses. To know that this was a kind of universal human inclination came over him with something like relief.

"Of *course,* everybody has those feelings," he said smiling. "I have them myself. . . . But suppose you *did* yield to them?"

"Well, we don't," said Hurwitz.

"I know—but suppose you did?"

Hurwitz shrugged his fat shoulders, indifferently.

"Oh, well," he said, "it would be bad business."

"Jesus, yes," said Smith, shuffling the cards.

"Oy," said Bryant.

The game was resumed, the glasses were refilled, pipes were lit, watches were looked at. Michael had to think of the last car from Sullivan Square, at eleven-fifty. But also he could not stop thinking of this strange idea. It was amusing. It was fascinating. Here was everyone wanting to steal—toothbrushes, or books—or to caress some fascinating stranger of a female in a subway train—the impulse everywhere—why not be a Columbus of the moral world and really do it? . . . He remembered stealing a conch-shell from the drawing room of a neighbor when he was ten—it had been one of the thrills of his life. He had popped it into his sailor blouse and borne it away with perfect aplomb. When, later, suspicion had been cast upon him, he had smashed the shell in his back yard. And often, when he had been looking at Parker's collection of stamps—the early Americans——

The game interrupted his recollections, and presently it was time for the usual night-cap. Bryant drove them to Park Street. Michael was a trifle tight, but not enough to be unsteady on his feet. He waved a cheery hand at Bryant and Hurwitz and began to trudge through the snow to the subway entrance. The lights on the snow were very beautiful. The Park Street Church was ringing, with its queer, soft quarter-bells, the half-hour. Plenty of time. Plenty of time. Time enough for a visit to the drugstore, and a hot chocolate—he could see the warm lights of the windows falling on the snowed sidewalk. He zigzagged across the street and entered.

And at once he was seized with a conviction that his real reason for entering the drugstore was not to get a hot chocolate —not at all! He was going to steal something. He was going to put the impulse to the test, and see whether (*one*) he could manage it with sufficient skill, and (*two*) whether theft gave him any real satisfaction. The drugstore was crowded with people who had just come from the theatre next door. They pushed three deep round the soda fountain, and the cashier's cage. At the back of the store, in the toilet and prescription department, there were not so many, but nevertheless enough to give him a fair chance. All the clerks were busy. His hands were in the side pockets of his overcoat—they were deep wide pockets and would serve admirably. A quick gesture over a table or counter, the object dropped in——

Oddly enough, he was not in the least excited: perhaps that was because of the gin. On the contrary, he was intensely amused; not to say delighted. He was smiling, as he walked slowly along the right-hand side of the store toward the back; edging his way amongst the people, with first one shoulder forward and then the other, while with a critical and appraising eye he examined the wares piled on the counters and on the stands in the middle of the floor. There were some extremely attractive scent-sprays or atomizers—but the dangling bulbs might be troublesome. There were stacks of boxed letter-paper. A basket full of clothes-brushes. Green hot-water bottles. Percolators—too large, and out of the question. A tray of multicolored toothbrushes, bottles of cologne, fountain pens—and then he experienced love at first sight. There could be no question that he had found his chosen victim. He gazed, fascinated, at the delicious object—a *de luxe* safety-razor set, of heavy gold, in a snakeskin box which was lined with red plush. . . .

It wouldn't do, however, to stare at it too long—one of the clerks might notice. He observed quickly the exact position of the box—which was close to the edge of the glass counter—and prefigured with a quite precise mental picture the gesture with which he would simultaneously close it and remove it. Forefinger at the back—thumb in front—the box drawn forward and then slipped down toward the pocket—as he thought it out, the muscles in his forearm pleasurably contracted. He continued his slow progress round the store, past the prescription counter, past the candy counter; examined with some show of attention the display of cigarette lighters and blade sharpeners; and then, with a quick turn, went leisurely back to his victim. Everything was propitious. The whole section of counter was clear for the moment—there were neither customers nor clerks. He approached the counter, leaned over it as if to examine some little filigreed "compacts" at the back of the showcase, picking up one of them with his left hand, as he did so. He was thus leaning directly over the box; and it was the simplest thing in the world to clasp it as planned between thumb and forefinger of his other hand, to shut it softly, and to slide it downward to his pocket. It was over in an instant. He continued then for a moment to turn the compact case this way and that in the light, as if to see it sparkle. It sparkled very nicely. Then he put it back on the little pile of cases, turned, and approached the soda fountain—just as Hurwitz had suggested.

He was in the act of pressing forward in the crowd to ask for his hot chocolate when he felt a firm hand close round his elbow. He turned, and looked at a man in a slouch hat and dirty raincoat, with the collar turned up. The man was smiling in a very offensive way.

"I guess you thought that was pretty slick," he said in a low voice which nevertheless managed to convey the very essence of venom and hostility. "You come along with me, mister!"

Michael returned the smile amiably, but was a little frightened. His heart began to beat.

"I don't know what you're talking about," he said, still smiling.

"No, of course not!"

The man was walking toward the rear of the store, and was pulling Michael along with him, keeping a paralyzingly tight grip on his elbow. Michael was beginning to be angry, but also to be horrified. He thought of wrenching his arm free, but feared it would make a scene. Better not. He permitted himself to be urged ignominiously along the shop, through a gate in the rear counter, and into a small room at the back, where a clerk was measuring a yellow liquid into a bottle.

"Will you be so kind as to explain to me what this is all about?" he then said, with what frigidity of manner he could muster. But his voice shook a little. The man in the slouch hat paid no attention. He addressed the clerk instead, giving his head a quick backward jerk as he spoke.

"Get the manager in here," he said.

He smiled at Michael, with narrowed eyes, and Michael, hating him, but panic-stricken, smiled foolishly back at him.

"Now, look here—" he said.

But the manager had appeared, and the clerk; and events then happened with revolting and nauseating speed. Michael's hand was yanked violently from his pocket, the fatal snakeskin box was pulled out by the detective, and identified by the manager and the clerk. They both looked at Michael with a queer expression, in which astonishment, shame, and contempt were mixed with vague curiosity.

"Sure that's ours," said the manager, looking slowly at Michael.

"I saw him pinch it," said the detective. "What about it?" He again smiled offensively at Michael. "Anything to say?"

"It was all a joke," said Michael, his face feeling very hot and flushed. "I made a kind of bet with some friends. . . . I can prove it. I can call them up for you."

The three men looked at him in silence, all three of them just faintly smiling, as if incredulously.

"Sure you can," said the detective, urbanely. "You can prove it in court. . . . Now come along with me, mister."

Michael was astounded at this appalling turn of events, but his brain still worked. Perhaps if he were to put it to this fellow as man to man, when they got outside? As he was thinking this, he was firmly conducted through a back door into a dark alley at the rear of the store. It had stopped snowing. A cold wind was blowing. But the world, which had looked so beautiful fifteen minutes before, had now lost its charm. They walked together down the alley in six inches of powdery snow, the detective holding Michael's arm with affectionate firmness.

"No use calling the wagon," he said. "We'll walk. It ain't far."

They walked along Tremont Street. And Michael couldn't help, even then, thinking what an extraordinary thing this was! Here were all these good people passing them, and little knowing that he, Michael Lowes, was a thief, a thief by accident, on his way to jail. It seemed so absurd as hardly to be worth speaking of! And suppose they shouldn't believe him? This notion made him shiver. But it wasn't possible—no, it wasn't possible. As soon as he had told his story, and called up Hurwitz and Bryant and Smith, it would all be laughed off. Yes, laughed off.

He began telling the detective about it: how they had discussed such impulses over a game of bridge. Just a friendly game, and they had joked about it and then, just to see what would happen, he had done it. What was it that made his voice sound so insincere, so hollow? The detective neither slackened his pace nor turned his head. His business-like grimness was alarming. Michael felt that he was paying no attention at all; and, moreover, it occurred to him that this kind of lowbrow official might not even understand such a thing. . . . He decided to try the sentimental.

"And good Lord, man, there's my wife waiting for me——!"

"Oh, sure, and the kids too."

"Yes, and the kids!"

The detective gave a quick leer over the collar of his dirty raincoat.

"And no Santy Claus *this* year," he said.

Michael saw that it was hopeless. He was wasting his time.

"I can see it's no use talking to you," he said stiffly. "You're so used to dealing with criminals that you think all mankind is criminal, *ex post facto*."

"Sure."

Arrived at the station, and presented without decorum to the lieutenant at the desk, Michael tried again. Something in the faces of the lieutenant and the sergeant, as he told his story, made it at once apparent that there was going to be trouble. They obviously didn't believe him—not for a moment. But after consultation, they agreed to call up Bryant and Hurwitz and Smith, and to make inquiries. The sergeant went off to do this, while Michael sat on a wooden bench. Fifteen minutes passed, during which the clock ticked and the lieutenant wrote slowly in a book, using a blotter very frequently. A clerk had been dispatched, also, to look up Michael's record, if any. This gentleman came back first, and reported that there was nothing. The lieutenant scarcely looked up from his book, and went on writing. The first serious blow then fell. The sergeant, reporting, said that he hadn't been able to get Smith (of course—Michael thought—he's off somewhere with Squiggles) but had got Hurwitz and Bryant. Both of them denied that there had been any bet. They both seemed nervous, as far as he could make out over the phone. They said they didn't know Lowes well, were acquaintances of his, and made it clear that they didn't want to be mixed up in anything. Hurwitz had added that he knew Lowes was hard up.

At this, Michael jumped to his feet, feeling as if the blood would burst out of his face.

"The damned liars!" he shouted. "The bloody liars! By God——!"

"Take him away," said the lieutenant, lifting his eyebrows, and making a motion with his pen.

Michael lay awake all night in his cell, after talking for five minutes with Dora on the telephone. Something in Dora's cool voice had frightened him more than anything else.

And when Dora came to talk to him the next morning at nine o'clock, his alarm proved to be well-founded. Dora was cold, detached, deliberate. She was not at all what he had hoped she might be—sympathetic and helpful. She didn't volunteer to get a lawyer, or in fact to do anything—and when she listened quietly to his story, it seemed to him that she had the appearance of a person listening to a very improbable lie. Again, as he narrated the perfectly simple episode—the discussion of "impulse" at the bridge game, the drinks, and the absurd tipsy desire to try a harmless little experiment—again, as when he talked to the store detective, he heard his own voice becoming hollow and insincere. It was exactly as if he knew himself to be guilty. His throat grew dry, he began to falter, to lose his thread, to use the wrong words. When he stopped speaking, finally, Dora was silent.

"Well, say something!" he said angrily, after a moment. "Don't just stare at me! I'm not a criminal!"

"I'll get a lawyer for you," she answered. "but that's all I can do."

"Look here, Dora—you don't mean you——"

He looked at her incredulously. It wasn't possible that she really thought him a thief? And suddenly, as he looked at her, he realized how long it was since he had really known this woman. They had drifted apart. She was embittered, that was it—embittered by his non-success. All this time she had slowly been laying up a reserve of resentment. She had resented his inability to make money for the children, the little dishonesties they had had to commit in the matter of unpaid bills, the humiliations of duns, the too-frequent removals from town to town—she had more than once said to him, it was true, that because of all this she had never had any friends—and she had resented, he knew, his gay little parties with Hurwitz and Bryant and Smith, implying a little that they were an extravagance which was to say the least inconsiderate. Perhaps they *had* been. But was a man to have no indulgences? . . .

"Perhaps we had better not go into that," she said.

"Good Lord—you don't believe me!"

"I'll get the lawyer—though I don't know where the fees are to come from. Our bank account is down to seventy-seven dollars. The rent is due a week from today. You've got some salary coming, of course, but I don't want to touch my own savings, naturally, because the children and I may need them."

To be sure. Perfectly just. Women and children first. Michael thought these things bitterly, but refrained from saying them. He gazed at this queer cold little female with intense curiosity. It was simply extraordinary—simply astonishing. Here she was, seven years his wife, he thought he knew her inside and out, every quirk of her handwriting, inflection of voice; her passion for strawberries, her ridiculous way of singing; the brown moles on her shoulder, the extreme smallness of her feet and toes, her dislike of silk underwear. Her special voice at the telephone, too—that rather chilly abruptness, which had always surprised him, as if she might be a much harder woman than he thought her to be. And the queer sinuous cat-like rhythm with which she always combed her hair before the mirror at night, before going to bed—with her head tossing to one side, and one knee advanced to touch the chest of drawers. He knew all these things, which nobody else knew, and nevertheless, now, they amounted to nothing. The woman herself stood before him as opaque as a wall.

"Of course," he said, "you'd better keep your own savings." His voice was dull. "And you'll, of course, look up Hurwitz and the others? They'll appear, I'm sure, and it will be the most important evidence. In fact, *the* evidence."

"I'll ring them up, Michael," was all she said, and with that she turned quickly on her heel and went away. . . .

Michael felt doom closing in upon him; his wits went round in circles; he was in a constant sweat. It wasn't possible that he was going to be betrayed? It wasn't possible! He assured himself of this. He walked back and forth, rubbing his hands together, he kept pulling out his watch to see what time it was. Five minutes gone. Another five minutes gone. Damnation, if this lasted too long, this confounded business, he'd lose his job. If it got into the papers, he might lose it anyway. And suppose it was true that Hurwitz and Bryant had said what they said—maybe they were afraid of losing their jobs too. Maybe that was it! Good God. . . .

This suspicion was confirmed, when, hours later, the lawyer came to see him. He reported that Hurwitz, Bryant and Smith had all three refused flatly to be mixed up in the business. They were all afraid of the effects of the publicity. If subpenaed, they said, they would state that they had known Lowes only a short time, had thought him a little eccentric, and knew him to be hard up. Obviously—and the little lawyer picked his teeth with the point of his pencil—they could not be summoned. It would be fatal.

The Judge, not unnaturally perhaps, decided that there was a perfectly clear case. There couldn't be the shadow of a doubt that this man had deliberately stolen an article from the counter of So-and-so's drugstore. The prisoner had stubbornly maintained that it was the result of a kind of bet with some friends, but these friends had refused to give testimony in his behalf. Even his wife's testimony—that he had never done such a thing before—had seemed rather half-hearted; and she had admitted, moreover, that Lowes was unsteady, and that they were always living in a state of something like poverty. Prisoner, further, had once or twice jumped his rent and had left behind him in Somerville unpaid debts of considerable size. He was a college man, a man of exceptional education and origin, and ought to have known better. His general character might be good enough, but as against all this, here was a perfectly clear case of theft, and a perfectly clear motive. The prisoner was sentenced to three months in the house of correction.

By this time, Michael was in a state of complete stupor. He sat in the box and stared blankly at Dora who sat very quietly in the second row, as if she were a stranger. She was looking back at him, with her white face turned a little to one side, as if she too had never seen him before, and were wondering what sort of people criminals might be. Human? Sub-human? She lowered her eyes after a moment, and before she had looked up again, Michael had been touched on the arm and led stumbling out of the courtroom. He thought she would of course come to say goodbye to him, but even in this he was mistaken; she left without a word.

And when he did finally hear from her, after a week, it was in a very brief note.

"Michael," it said, "I'm sorry, but I can't bring up the children with a criminal for a father, so I'm taking proceedings for a divorce. This is the last straw. It was bad enough to have you always out of work and to have to slave night and day to keep bread in the children's mouths. But this is too much, to have disgrace into the bargain. As it is, we'll have to move right away, for the schoolchildren have sent Dolly and Mary home crying three times already. I'm sorry, and you know how fond I was of you at the beginning, but you've had your chance. You won't hear from me again. You've always been a good sport, and generous, and I hope you'll make this occasion no exception, and refrain from contesting the divorce. Goodbye—Dora."

Michael held the letter in his hands, unseeing, and tears came into his eyes. He dropped his face against the sheet of notepaper, and rubbed his forehead to and fro across it . . . Little Dolly! . . . Little Mary! . . . Of course. This was what life was. It was just as meaningless and ridiculous as this; a monstrous joke; a huge injustice. You couldn't trust anybody, not even your wife, not even your best friends. You went on a little lark, and they sent you to prison for it, and your friends lied about you, and your wife left you. . . .

Contest it? Should he contest the divorce? What was the use? There was the plain fact: that he had been convicted for stealing. No one had believed his story of doing it in fun, after a few drinks; the divorce court would be no exception. He dropped the letter to the floor and turned his heel on it, slowly and bitterly. Good riddance—good riddance! Let them all go to hell. He would show them. He would go west, when he came out—get rich, clear his name somehow. . . . But how?

He sat down on the edge of his bed and thought of Chicago. He thought of his childhood there, the Lake Shore Drive, Winnetka, the trip to Niagara Falls with his mother. He could hear the Falls now. He remembered the Fourth of July on the boat; the crowded examination room at college; the time he had broken his leg in baseball, when he was fourteen; and the stamp collection which he had lost at school. He remembered his mother always saying, "Michael, you *must* learn to be orderly"; and the little boy who had died of scarlet fever next door; and the pink conch-shell smashed in the back yard. His whole life seemed to be composed of such trivial and infinitely charming little episodes as these; and as he thought of them, affectionately and with wonder, he assured himself once more that he had really been a good man. And now, had it all come to an end? It had all come foolishly to an end.

THE ANNIVERSARY

Charles Cleghorn and his friend Jackson were playing billiards in the smoky billiard room in the basement of their club. They were both middle-aged, both bald, and neither of them played well. They walked a little heavily round the table, chalked their cues with unnecessary frequency, laughed a good deal at shots fantastically bad, and occasionally paused for passages of laconic conversation. It was Cleghorn who had suggested the game of billiards. He was fond of Jackson (a doctor) but knew from long experience that a whole evening in Jackson's company became fatiguing unless they "did something." Usually, when they arranged to dine together, they went afterwards to the Casino, which could always be relied upon for a vivid burlesque show. They both enjoyed a good burlesque show, one with plenty of legs, laughter, smut, and "snappy music," the sort of show in which the brilliantly blonde heroine comes out to the footlights dressed in the star-spangled banner—and dressed, as it turns out at the end of the cheap patriotic song, to which her gilded slippers have been beating time, *only* in the star-spangled banner. This sort of thing always pleased them; they nudged each other. Cleghorn, fiddling with the end of his grayish mustache, felt that he would like to know a girl like that. He entertained fleet-ing thoughts of meetings at stage-doors, taxi rides late at night, perhaps a champagne party in a secretly kept flat, or in a shabby hotel. The idea of the expense, however, always frightened him. Taxis, flats, champagne, little suppers at hotels—one couldn't indulge in these unless one were rich, or unmarried. Also, he had always been very respectable, and he was afraid of being seen. And also, he wasn't sure that he would know how to go about it. He suspected that Jackson knew a great deal—but Jackson never talked freely of his own adventures with women, had always assumed that Cleghorn was, in this regard, in-violably respectable. This understanding had existed between them for seventeen years, and had become sacred.

"I wonder if it's still snowing," said Cleghorn, sitting down for a moment with his cue between his knees.

"Sure, it's snowing. It's going to snow all night."

"I hope to God the cars are running. I'd hate to walk all the way from the Square in this."

"Good for you. . . . You don't get enough exercise anyway."

Jackson stooped beside the table, flushing, to get the cue-bridge. He arose with the bridge clutched in a plump pink hand, tight-skinned. He gave a puff, blowing out his cheeks. Cleghorn laughed.

"Well, I don't lose my wind when I stoop for a bridge, any-way," he said. "You're getting fat, Henry."

"Don't be personal."

"I know why it is, too." He gave a sly smile, which had the effect of pushing his gray mustache up toward his spectacles. Jackson, calm, absorbed, leveled his cue along the bridge and began aiming it at the white ball. Cleghorn knew that he was listening, and went on. "It's all this high living. All these little parties."

Jackson made his stroke sharply, and snorted, following the balls with an angry eye.

"What parties? . . . You don't know what you're talking about."

"Ha! don't I! . . . My detectives inform me, Henry, of your every gesture."

"Oh! they do, do they? A lot of good may it do them."

Cleghorn sighed, rose, walked heavily round the lighted table, peered closely and near-sightedly at each ball in turn.

"Ah! I wish to God I wasn't married," he said. "I'd show you some tricks, Henry!"

"You don't know what you're talking about. . . . Have a lemonade?"

Cleghorn gave a violent shot which made the cue-ball leap off the table. It crashed to the floor, and rolled to the wall.

"If I couldn't play billiards any better than that," Jackson continued evenly, "I'd sell out and keep pigs. I'd be ashamed of myself."

"Well, I'll bet you I can pick it up without losing my wind, anyway. And that's something."

He picked up the ball and dropped it with a little thump on the green baize. Then, by a tacit agreement they sat down, somewhat wearily, in two chairs by the wall, both holding their cues between their knees.

"Some women," said Jackson after a moment, "are damn fools."

"You surprise me, Henry. . . . Have a cigarette."

"No, thanks. . . . Yes. . . . A patient telephoned me this morning at ten o'clock, to say that she had started to have a hemorrhage, and what should she do. It's a childbirth case with a threat of abruptio. We've been expecting it to happen. I told her to get a taxi and run straight to the hospital—not to stop a minute. I telephoned to the hospital and had everything ready. Thomas was there. I was there myself in twenty minutes. And that woman took *three hours* to get to the hospital—*three hours!* As a result of which she's dying."

"What on earth made her do that?"

Jackson stared at the green lights over the billiard table.

"Oh, she wanted the proper clothes with her—did a regular packing up, as if she was going for a holiday at Palm Beach. . . .

Lots of them do that. . . . They've got to have their best Sunday-go-to-meeting nighties. . . . And there she is."

"Really dying?"

"I think so. A transfusion didn't help. I'm expecting a call any time tonight. Thomas is there."

Cleghorn felt depressed. Seeing people die was no joke. Supposing he had, at this hour, on such a night, to go slopping through a foot of snow and slush to a hospital, all to watch a foolish woman die? . . . All the same he envied Jackson. Jackson had more experience in a day than he himself had in a decade. All sorts of queer intimacies and insights. Intimacies with young women. The nurses, too, of course. The doctors weren't supposed to know the nurses. But then—! . . . Besides, was it any worse for Jackson to trot off to a hospital on a winter night than for himself to trot home, every night in the year, to Clara? . . .

"I wonder if it's still snowing," he said, morosely.

"Sure, it's snowing. Snowing like hell, probably. Thank God, I put the chains on my car this morning."

"Tomorrow's the fifteenth anniversary of my wedding."

"Go on!" . . . Jackson was surprised, goggled at Cleghorn with round protruding eyes, apoplectic.

"What does that make it—brass?" . . . Cleghorn was sardonic. "The twenty-fifth is silver."

"I don't know. It ought to be something pretty good after fifteen."

Jackson took a slow deep breath and, seeming to become absent-minded, stared at the floor, inclining his head against his cue, and rubbing his forehead against the cool polished wood. He moved his head softly from side to side, staring.

"Well," he said with a kind of abstracted gentleness, "I think that deserves a little drink." He turned and pressed a button in the wall. "A health drunk in near-beer never hurt anyone."

"Beer is thicker than water," Cleghorn replied, "but not much."

The two men sighed almost simultaneously and became silent. Cleghorn, leaning his head back on the chair, blew a tur-

bulent cloud of smoke toward the ceiling, propelling into it, at
the end, a rapid succession of small swimming rings. He watched
them admiringly. Wedding rings. Wedding rings of smoke.
Smoke, but horribly binding, just the same. What a simple solution if Clara had only, like this woman at the hospital—what
was it Henry called it? . . .

"I sometimes wonder why it was you never married, Henry."
His expression was a little malicious.

The boy brought their drinks on a tray, pulled the little table
near to them, and carried away their cues. Jackson lifted his
glass.

"I would have, Charlie, if I'd been as lucky as you. Here's
how—happy returns!"

"Well, I'd swap with you for nothing—for an old doughnut
and a pair of emasculated garters."

Jackson growled, frowning into his beer, where he seemed
to see something that annoyed him.

"You don't know what you're talking about. Swap? By God,
I'd swap, let me tell you."

"All right then—you go home to Clara tonight, and I'll take
your case at the hospital. Also the key to your secret flat." Cleghorn gave a peculiar self-conscious laugh. Over the rim of his
beer glass he eyed Jackson with an uneasy challenge.

"You make me tired when you talk like that. You ought to
know better. . . . What the devil do you mean by the key to my
secret flat?"

"Don't be so coy, Henry. The nice little flat where you entertain your chorus-girl friends. . . . Ah, I wish to God I wasn't
married! I'd show you some tricks."

"Phhhh! You make me sick. Chorus girls! What do you think
I am?"

"My detectives watch you night and day, Henry. You've been
seen putting your bald head out of your car window in the
alley behind the Casino. Lulu, the star-spangled queen, was
seen to leap in beside you, giving a loud parrot scream of delight, and scattering diamonds. At the oyster house, later, it was

observed that you devoured two dozen oysters and a hen lobster, while Lulu worshiped. . . . Introduce me to Lulu, Henry. I'd like to know her."

"Who the devil is Lulu? . . . You're crazy. . . ."

Cleghorn laughed, and then sighed.

"I like to talk through my hat," he said. "If I'm not crazy already I'd as lief be. . . . You can talk till all is blue about the sacred joys of married life, but I'm sick of it."

Jackson, at this, gave a quick startled look at Cleghorn, who was staring at the ceiling. He opened his lips as if to say something, but then, instead, lifted his glass, turned it meditatively around, and took a deep drink.

"Funny I haven't heard from the hospital," he murmured. He looked at his watch. "Nine o'clock."

There was a pause, during which the two men stared across the smoky room, watching three players who moved about a table at the other side, having a noisy game of cowboy pool. "Put the five in the corner pocket," one of them shouted. "Ah, he's got a glass eye and a wooden arm," said another. The shot was made, and all three shrieked with laughter, thumping the butts of their cues against the floor. "The boy has brains! The boy's clever!" . . .

"I think I'll get drunk tonight," said Cleghorn, reflectively smiling, and pushing his gray mustache up towards his spectacles. "At that place on Atlantic Avenue."

"Don't be a fool. That rot-gut whisky!"

"That's all right—it's got plenty of kick."

"It'll kick you over the fence into eternity one of these days."

"So much the better. . . . You think I'm joking, Henry, but I'm perfectly serious."

"Serious about what?"

"Married life. . . ."

"Are you still worrying about that?"

"Worrying? No. I've made up my mind, that's all."

"Oh."

"It's a queer thing, you know, how deep a disgust can go.

Right into the most vital and living part of your consciousness. . . . So that you hate the physical with a hatred—" He broke off, making a tense, spasmodic clawlike gesture with his hand. His eyes were opened rather wide. "If only we could get rid of the whole thing!"

Jackson goggled angrily at Cleghorn.

"What's eating you? . . . What do you say, shall we finish the game?"

He was still staring at Cleghorn when the page came into the room with a slip of paper in his hand. "Dr. Jackson!" he bawled, walking. "Dr. Jackson!"

"Here!" said Jackson, rising. "Good night, Charlie. . . . Take my advice and go home like a good boy. See you Tuesday." He rested his plump pink hand on Cleghorn's shoulder for a second, beamed, and walked briskly away.

For a few minutes, Cleghorn sat perfectly still, staring at the green-shaded lights and watching the tobacco smoke coil into them in lazy clouds. He felt miserably a sense of defeat. He had hoped to draw out Jackson, or at any rate to compel him to listen, and had for some reason felt a peculiar need for a heart-to-heart discussion. It had been useless to attempt it. With Jackson, the attempt was always useless. Jackson always growled and changed the subject, or became inarticulate, or pretended to misunderstand. . . . Good old Henry. . . . The three young men began arguing loudly at the table on the far side of the room, flourishing their cues. "Of course, I put it up—you were seventy-nine before and now you're eighty-four—what could be simpler? . . . Solid ivory!" . . . Cleghorn felt angry with them, rose, and walked heavily out of the room and up the stairs. He went and looked out from the reading-room window, lifting the shade, to see if it was still snowing. It was snowing hard. Long white diagonals flew in straight lines under the arc light at the corner. A horse-drawn newspaper wagon went by, the horse plodding slowly in deep snow, his head down, his hoofs not making a sound. A taxi stood opposite the club, with white-drifted roof and a blanket flung over the radiator. It had a dere-

lict look. "Escape!" it seemed to say—"Adventure! Mystery!"
. . . He recalled stories of men who had engaged cabs simply
saying to the driver, "If you know a good place, take me to it.
Here's a dollar. Here's five dollars. Here's a thousand dollars.
. . . Take me to the Queen of Sheba. Take me to the number
of numbers in the street of streets. 1770 Washington Street.
No. 2,876,452 Eternity Street. Minus seven Insanity Street. . . .
Anywhere you like." . . . Dropping the window shade, Cleghorn went to the coat room for his hat and coat. A young man
came in, stamping snow off his feet on the marble floor. "A
taxi," said Cleghorn to Peters, the doorman. "There's one at
the door now, sir." "Oh, is there? Thanks." . . . A large snowflake crashed coldly into his left ear. "Rowe's Wharf!" he
shouted to the driver, who as he inclined his face to listen
reached a hand to turn down the flag.

The taxi bumped softly through the snow, while Cleghorn
smoked a cigarette. Swarms of flakes flew past the windows.
The streets were almost deserted. They passed an electric snow-
plow moaning along the car tracks with slipping wheels. Delightful, to be running away like this—not a soul in the world
knew where he was. Old Henry, bungling stupidly off to the
hospital in Brookline to watch the death of Mrs. Feldeinsamkeit; Clara, reading a magazine before a fire of wet logs; Lulu,
the star-spangled queen coming down to the footlights, rubbing
one pink knee rhythmically, caressingly against the other, and
singing "Come on, take a chance, and we'll dance to that syncopated mellow-dee"; while he, in a taxi, smoking, escaped
through the wild, wild night, soundless and trackless. Was
Henry in love with Clara? Ha, ha! what an idea. Let him have
her, then. A good solution. . . . "Are you dying, Mrs. Feldeinsamkeit? . . ." "Dying, doctor, dying." . . . "Give me your
rings then, and your gold watch with the lock of hair in it,
and the twenty-dollar gold-piece which you wear round your
neck. Sign your name along the dotted line, or, if you cannot
see, make a cross. You hereby solemnly declare that you are
about to die; that you are already dead from the soles of your

feet to your breastbone; that you have no longer a heart, or any of the grosser appetites, or a digestive system; that you have only the signal beauty of your face and the waning light of your brain, and these, too, presently being dead, you will be dead forever. You give me your solemn oath that you will not again countenance existence in the flesh or in the spirit, in this world or in any other. In witness whereof you affix hereto your name, FELDEINSAMKEIT." . . . "I swear." . . . "Nurse, remove the pillow from beneath her head. Feldeinsamkeit is dead. Strip the sheet from this emaciated corpse. She died young. . . ." The funeral comes next. Died: Clara Feldeinsamkeit, of a loss of blood. The corpse, corrupt, is hermetically sealed to prevent botulism. The horses are lashed, they gallop, an endless procession of galloping black horses. Farewell, Feldeinsamkeit! Up the vast pyramid of eternity you go, the rain-maned horses silhouetted galloping against the sky, hoofs crashing against rock. Poise the coffin on the pinnacle—she is lost in the Feldewigkeit. . . . And Clara turns the page, sighing, looks at the clock, looks at her watch, and reads on. "Darling! Your violet eyes! Your eyes which are pools in which irises have been drowned! Speak to me! Tell me that it is not true, that it is only a hideous dream, a fearful nightmare! . . . Speak! . . . SPEAK! . . ." It was the bronzed young engineer who was thus imploring the heroine to speak. Ah—it was only too true. . . . Among the drowned irises something moved, it was there that the alligator had laid her eggs. The little alligators swarmed, grinning. . . . Bong, bong; half-past nine, and Clara, lifting her left leg off her right leg, and then the right leg onto the left leg, rustling, reads on. . . . And the star-spangled Lulu undulates in the purple and green light, undulates, oscillates, swaggles, singing, "The world goes round, to the sound, of a syncopated mellow-dee." . . .

Rowe's Wharf. The elevated was a fantastic structure of iron and snow. The taxi stood in the snow like a sinking ship—snowflakes swirled about it as Cleghorn fished out the dollar and a half for the driver. "Good night!" he shouted, and began plunging through drifts of slushy snow toward the brightly lighted

Bar, before the steamed windows of which he could see that the sidewalk had been partially cleared and strewn with wet sawdust. The word Bar on the left window had lost its white enamel R, and become a bleat. Bar—bar—black sheep, come and have a pull. Yes, sir, yes, sir, three barrels full.

At the long bar of polished wood, on which at regular intervals were small potted palm trees, a straggling line of men leaned or stood in the various stages of lifting up or putting down their glasses, their feet on the railing, hats pushed back on backs of heads. At the farther end he could see Tom, shaking something in a cocktail shaker. He was talking, and shaking as he talked, and making, as he always did, a ritual of it; the glittering shaker was moved not only back and forth, but rose and fell in graceful curves from white stomach to blue chin, from blue chin to white stomach, twinkling. Moving nearer, he heard the cold rattle of the ice in it. And he saw that Tom was talking to Jerry Zimmerman, a disreputable young lawyer.

"Hello, Tom and Jerry!" he said, slapping Jerry on the back.

"Well, if it isn't old Charlie-horse," cried Jerry. Cleghorn shook hands solemnly with Tom.

"How're they hanging, Tom?"

"Oh, up and down, up and down," said Tom with a grin. "How is it by you?"

"Dry," said Cleghorn. "Let me have one of those, Tom. Well seasoned."

"Seasoned is the word."

"Have one, Jerry?"

"Don't mind if I do."

Tom produced a small flask from his hip pocket, seasoned the ginger ale, and they drank. "To crime," said Jerry. "Happy days," said Cleghorn, and gave a loud smack over the emptied glass. . . . "Another?" Jerry's dishonest face twinkled. "A hundred more." said Cleghorn. . . . Tom produced the flask again, extracted the loose cork with his teeth, poured the ginger ale, poured the whisky, smiled wearily. "It's a great life if you don't weaken," he murmured. "Snowing still?"

"Snowing like hell. Snowing like the devil. And I'm a long, long way from home."

"It's the wrong way to tickle Mary," said Jerry, swaying against the bar.

"Hello! I believe Jerry's got a little slant on!"

"He'd oughter have," said Tom, "the amount he carries. A regular watering cart."

Jerry beamed, dishonestly affectionate, subtly oscillating. "You said it, Tom. Strong waters run deep."

"Well, I'll soon be with you," said Cleghorn. "Wait for me there. Have another?"

"Now don't you tempt me, Charlie."

"No, I wouldn't think of it. Make it two, Tom."

Ten minutes later, Cleghorn felt the blood swarm suddenly against his temples, something changed in his ears, and the whole hot smoky room seemed to be singing with a sound like telephone wires in a wind. He smiled at his glass.

"There's a wind blowing here," he said, "with furies in it."

"You don't say so," said Tom, wiping a glass. "There's a lot of them round this year. Good-sized ones, too."

"From Brookline, I don't doubt. There's a funeral there today."

Jerry hiccoughed, candidly. Then, smiling loosely:

"A funeral? Who's dead?"

"Clara. . . . Feldeinsamkeit."

"Oh? Hup. No friend of mine. Never even heard of her."

"She died at curfew. Of botulism. I had a vision of it when I was in the taxi."

"Acute or chronic?"

"Acute."

"I hope she had an easy passage. Must be a rough night on the Styx."

"She gave her oath she'd never live again. Swore on the telephone directory."

Jerry closed his narrow eyes, rubbed his forehead. "Something's wrong with me," he said. "I can't understand a word you're saying. What was that?"

"Acute bottleism," said Tom. "You've both got it."

"And the doctor was a brute," said Cleghorn. "Told the nurse to pull the pillow out from under her head! I distinctly heard him. And then they stripped the sheet off. . . . Still, there was nothing left of her anyway."

"No, there wouldn't be," said Tom. "Them furies" (he winked at Jerry) "eat out a man from the inside, like. There's nothing will stop them once they get a hold of you. And they're particularly bad this winter. I hear they come from New Jersey."

"It's mosquitoes," said Jerry, pawing a vague foot vainly at the rail.

"Nothing left but the head, which was shining, but dimming, if you see what I mean, like a lamp going out. The doctor said something to her about her waning brain. When it went out, they had the funeral."

"As quick as that!" said Tom, laconically.

Jerry got his foot onto the rail. "I'm damned if I like this conversation," he said, and put the bottom of his empty glass against his forehead.

"Thousands of black horses. Millions of black horses. All galloping. Up the edge of a pyramid. They poised her coffin on the pinnacle; Mrs. Feldeinsamkeit."

"Was she a friend of yours?" Tom wiped the counter, lifting the glasses. He refilled the glasses, and Jerry put down a dollar and a half. Cleghorn smiled, pushing up his gray mustache toward his spectacles. He wagged a mysterious finger, leaning forward on the bar. His hat was over his left ear.

"Ah! Now you're asking a question. The question of questions. . . . Where's Jerry?"

"Here," said Jerry, disembodied, in a voice which went round and round the room like a planet, whizzing and ringing.

"I thought you'd gone. . . . And I want you both to hear this; I want your advice."

"Good advice," murmured Tom, looking toward the other end of the room with a jaded eye, "is what I don't give nothing else except."

"This Feldeinsamkeit," pursued Cleghorn, confidingly, "is really my wife."

Tom looked surprised.

"What!" he said.

"But she's not dead. Not yet."

"Not yet! . . ." Jerry set his glass down rather hard. "What's the idea?"

"Feldeinsamkeit is just a name I chose for her."

"An affectionate little nickname," said Tom.

"A disguise. . . . It means I want to kill her."

"Oh, is *that* all! Why didn't you say so?"

"It's what I've been telling you all this time, only you're so slow. . . ."

Cleghorn became morose. He looked down at his wet feet, which he saw standing all by themselves in wet sawdust. He felt baffled. There was something locked, which he couldn't open. He moved his right foot over a dead match. The idea went up like a kite, swooping, with a long tail of jingling sleigh bells, and darted out of sight.

"Yes; I'm going to do it tonight. A bath of blood. The hateful body must be deposed. Down with the digestive organs!"

Jerry gave a sudden whoop of laughter, stared, and gave another whoop.

"A padded cell," he said, "and meals in paper saucers, through a little window. . . . Ha, ha!"

"Don't be an idiot," said Cleghorn. Then he shouted: "Don't be an idiot!"

He became absorbed in a strange weaving and unweaving network of sounds, sounds which seemed to be visible as little shivering evanescent cords. The knots gleamed and dissolved. Jink—jink went the cash register. A lot of words were all spoken at once. Tom and Jerry were talking to each other very far away. Tom looked at him, then back at Jerry, shaking his head.

"No!" said a voice. "I tell you—" said another. The front door opened, a draft came in, a man went out. Snow.

"I'll think I'll go out"—his own voice—"and stand on my head in the snow. Keep my hat."

He put his hat over his glass on the counter. Jerry took his arm.

"You stay here, Charlie. You're all right—I'll look after you."

"No!"

"Yes!"

Jerry was putting his hat back on his head, a little uncertainly. Cleghorn felt like crying.

"You're a good scout, Zimmerman, even if you *are* a crook."

"Sure I am. . . . You come along with me, now."

"I want to talk to Tom!" cried Cleghorn despairingly. "I want to tell him about Lulu, star-spangled queen!"

"Tom'll wait for us."

"Sure I'll wait for you." Tom grinned, rattling his knuckles on the counter. "You just walk round the block."

. . . Outside, he tried to get away from Jerry's arm and slipped in the half-melted snow. They both floundered. He took a series of deep drinks of cold air, and the snowflakes, touching his cheeks and forehead, made him feel intelligent. He threw back his head and laughed.

"Drunk as a fish! But I'm beginning to feel sober now. . . . I understand everything."

"This air'll do us both good."

"Lots of air tonight, like sherbet. Have a quart, Jerry. Eat it. . . . Was that a clock striking?"

"No—signal on a ferryboat."

"I thought it was midnight—the beginning of my anniversary."

"What anniversary?"

Jerry spoke absent-mindedly—he was looking for a cab. Not a cab in sight. He dragged Cleghorn along toward the South Station, where there would be sure to be one. Cleghorn slipped again and lunged violently against him, gasping. The snow was beginning to stop.

"Wedding," said Cleghorn. "Married life—take my advice—don't ever marry!"

"I'm married already."

"Well, then, you fool, don't marry again. . . . Where are we? On the Great White Way? Ha! I know. What we want to go to is No. 8,756,432 Infinity Street. Or minus seven Insanity Street. . . . One of those houses where cab drivers take you if you give them five dollars. . . . This isn't the way!"

"Don't be an ass, Charlie—come on!"

"Don't you call me an ass, you cheap shyster! . . . Where are we going?"

"If you don't shut up and behave yourself I'll leave you right here."

"Leave me, then! . . . Oh, God, how rotten I feel . . . like the bottom of a bird-cage."

They walked for several blocks in silence, plunging and slipping in the soft snow. Water dripped heavily from eaves, pitting the sodden white banks. Drops flashed slowly from rims of arc lamps. The ferries could be heard hooting in the harbor, and a train, casting brilliant lights on the snow, rattled along the elevated, rhythmically clanking.

"There's a cab," said Zimmerman. "Come on—make an effort. Farthest north."

They plunged across the wide square filled with brown slush. Cleghorn was half pushed, half lifted into the cab, and sank back on the seat. An effort, he thought, an effort. Zimmerman, outside, murmured something to the driver. Mumble, mumble. The driver took something out of his pocket and gave it to Zimmerman. . . . "Ta-ta!" shouted Zimmerman, but Cleghorn, staring, made no reply. Zimmerman vanished from the window, the dark world swirled, water swashed, and Cleghorn shut his eyes. Zimmerman had gone. Where? Into the Feldewigkeit. . . . Surprising. . . . Gone down like a ship in a fog. . . . Clara

Feldewigkeit, with violet eyes, bleeding to death, smiled while she read a magazine. She rustled and tinkled. "Why, Charlie! What *have* you—"

. . . He was suddenly aroused by the opening of the cab door. The driver was looking in at him.

"Here you are," he said—"Want to get out?"

Cleghorn stared. It was his own house. It was dark—Clara had gone to bed. He let himself in and stood in the hall—not a sound. Removing his wet shoes he went softly up the stairs, holding to the banisters. Clara's door was shut. He went into his own room, undressed in the dark, and went to bed. Midnight began to strike on Clara's clock. . . . No, it wasn't a bell —it was the ringing, the clashing of hoofs. A parade. A warm sunny day in spring. The escort came galloping first on black horses, their swords flashing. Then came a white horse. It was being ridden by a girl—but she was enclosed in a glass case which was strapped to the horse's back. Then he noticed that she was only a head and arms—she had no body. She wore an enormous wide-rimmed black hat, and her face was beautiful. Her arms were bare, and she held the reins in her hands. She looked neither to left nor right, the horse galloped, and she was gone. Farewell, Feldeinsamkeit!

HELLO, TIB

The quarrel had amounted to very little, to practically nothing, and yet it had cast its shadow over the evening. They had gone to bed without speaking and—more disturbing still—she did not get up to make his breakfast; and this although she knew he was going to town, and by the early train. He had had to forage in the dark kitchen by himself, attended only by Squidge, the cat; hunting among innumerable unlabeled cans for the coffee, spilling the sugar, and in general allowing himself the luxury of feeling pretty annoyed. A silly business, altogether—damned silly. And he mustn't let it spoil his day in town.

And what a day it was, what a day it was going to be! A lovely spring morning—yes, a perfect spring morning if there ever was one. Blue as a baby's eye. The apple blossoms just getting ready to pop, the song sparrows shouting in the lilac bushes, the robins—there seemed to be hundreds of them everywhere—saying over and over their loud and all-too-contented "Cheerio, cheerio, cherilee!"—or was it jubilee? Well, yes, perhaps it was jubilee. And why not indeed? The whole world seemed to be bursting with good will.

The little local train which would take him as far as Appledore came clanking and hissing round the bend, under the crazy footbridge, and he climbed aboard, deferring the reading of the morning paper till the longer run from Appledore to town. Besides, the marsh on a morning like this was too good to miss. Bathed in sunlight, the last of the night mist just curling away in the creeks and shadows, it looked wonderfully peaceful. Crows were quarreling over some shapeless white object in a ditch; a blue heron stood poised and arrowlike beside a pool, as still as his own image. What a morning, what a morning! And the little train rattling and clanking through it, as if only to keep the whole thing from being too precious, too lonely.

Well, it was a pity she hadn't got up and come down to see him off, for she would have enjoyed it. And it served her right. And all because he had said— What was it he had said? That he was more perceptive—yes, that was it, perceptive. Good heavens, the word perceptive had been like a red rag to a bull! Had that been so outrageous? To claim that women weren't by any means as perceptive as they were supposed to be, and that he himself was a devil of a lot more perceptive than most? Well, you never knew when you were going to injure a woman's vanity, and that was, of course, what he had done. It had been tactless. He ought to have shied off, changed the subject when he saw that she was upset about it. But then she had been so damned positive, so damned certain of herself, so conceited, in fact, about her perceptiveness, and so incredulous about his, that he became suddenly mad, and the fat was in the fire. Extraordinary how quickly a quarrel can blaze up out of nothing, absolutely nothing! One minute everybody perfectly serene and happy, in the best and most serene of all possible worlds, and then—bingo, one little word or look blows the whole thing to smithereens. And there you are, glaring at each other like a couple of starved hyenas. And in a state of smoldering fury, moreover, that seems unlikely ever to come to an end.

Just the same, he had been perfectly right—it was perfectly true. All nonsense, this notion that women had a sort of sixth sense, or a superhuman kind of clairvoyance. What rubbish!

True enough, of course, that a woman might understand a child—but did she always? Even that was debatable. And as for her understanding of other women, or men— No, most of the time she was just thinking about herself, thinking of her own feelings and, above all, of the impression she was making. She was only perceptive when it was somehow useful to her, that was it—and very seldom perceptive merely because she had to be. No.

He was pleased with his little analysis, and smiled out of the train window as they crossed the red-iron bridge. The tide was out; mud banks were showing, channeled and raw; a rowboat hung down the muddy slope at a steep angle, as if caught in the act of falling; and further down, by the bend of the river, the old dredger was at work. How peaceful, how eternal it all seemed! It would go on forever exactly like this, there was no doubt of it. Mud, sun, and tide, day after day, the bridge rotting, the marsh rotting, the old dredger rotting, and the sun calmly blazing down on everything—world without end. And a good thing, too. . . . The train was stopping. He got to his feet without thinking, and followed the others toward the platform of Appledore Station.

He walked the length of the platform and back, tapping the rolled newspaper against his knee, and looked at the early-morning people. Early-morning people—exactly! What was it that gave them so definitely an early-morning look? Not merely the somewhat orange-colored light of the early sun on their faces and hands—though no doubt that played a part in it. No, it was something in their half-sleepy, half-awake indifference, as if—though refreshed—they were not yet quite aware. The young married couple, sitting against the station wall on their up-turned suitcases, were leaning a little forward, faintly smiling to themselves, but not saying a thing. It was almost indecent to catch them like that—they were actually, at this very minute, in the act of waking up, and totally incapable of thinking of anything but their own delicious well-being. The tall man beyond them, standing with his paper held up before him, was only pretending to read. Every now and then he looked up over the edge of the paper, looked away over the living marsh, as if that tide of reality out there was much too strong for him, much too strong for anything so pallid as the printed word. But the three schoolgirls, with their strapped books and lunch-boxes—there was certainly nothing sleepy about them! They teased each other, giggled, became suddenly serious; started to play tag, and stopped as unpremeditatedly as they had begun; and then ran up the ramp to the raised platform at the end where freight cars were loaded, and ran down the smooth cement surface, screaming with delight. Energy—good heavens, what it was to have all that energy! He had to step aside quickly to avoid being run into by one of them, the smallest—the swung lunch-box slapped his hand, the blue eyes looked up at him abashed but laughing, and then abruptly all three were gone, vanished, round the corner of the station, but of course only to be back again in no time.

It was in that small interval, as he himself turned round, smiling, to walk back again, that the little cat appeared. Tail in air, she advanced serenely and happily along the platform, putting down one white paw in front of the other, and if she came tentatively, the reason for that was at once obvious: the little creature was so manifestly delighted, so simply delighted, with everything and everyone she saw that she really didn't know where to begin. So many wonderful people and things to investigate! You could positively see her feeling this, as she turned, first one way and then another. She had to go and rub her cheek against the delicious shoes and suitcases and ankles of the young married couple, making a lovely loop of her tail for their benefit, though they scarcely noticed her, truth to tell, so lost were they in their own world; and then she had to stroll back to a wooden box which lay on the platform, and sniff it daintily and distantly; and then rub her smile against one of its pointed corners. A kitten, rather than a cat—not half-grown—an ordinary, perfectly ordinary, gray-striped tabby with yellow eyes—

but, good gracious, there had never been a creature so bursting, absolutely bursting, with love and good will!

He watched her coming toward him in her slow and intermittent progress, drawn every which way by distractions. She rubbed her sides against the tall man's legs, she revisited the married couple, she went to the station door and looked in, meanwhile kneading her paws against the platform floor in ecstasy; she turned back, she turned forward—the little creature would obviously go anywhere, do anything, out of sheer love. He stooped and snapped his fingers, once, twice—and sure enough, she came at an eager trot, she came running, as if only too delighted to receive an express invitation, but nevertheless not in the least surprised. After all, that was what life was, wasn't it? . . . Love, nothing but love! She twined about his outstretched forefinger, butted his knuckles, rearing up like a little goat to do so, all the while keeping up a continuous purring, an absolute uproar—and then, of course, she saw the three little girls, and *they* had to be attended to. Away she went, once more at a trot, and once more she was a huge success. And what more natural?

"Hello, Tib!"

"Hello, Tib!"

"Hello, Tib!"

All three cried their greeting, all three began stroking her and patting her. For a moment cat and children became inextricable; and then the smallest girl, the one who had bumped into him, or almost, took it into her head to begin jumping over the little cat. To and fro she jumped, back and forth, the other girls laughing; and so close, too, that he thought of intervening. But no, she never quite struck the cat, and the cat, although a little surprised by so much violence, remained quite self-possessed, sat quite still, watching the strange antics with complete trust.

Complete trust—yes! Good heavens, yes! And suddenly he was looking at the little cat with fascination. For this, he now recognized, was one of those rare creatures who are so essentially innocent, and good, and loving, as to be totally defenseless. This little creature, with her tremendous love, was already doomed, by her own wonderful simplicity—that entire trustfulness was nothing but an embodied invitation to death. In a world dominated everywhere by violence and evil she could not possibly live, or not for very long, and wasn't it precisely this obvious impossibility that made her pathetic openness and innocence so bewitching?

And there was more to it than that, even. For as he turned and looked across the tracks toward the marsh—turning away, as a matter of fact, so that if the cat should be struck or hurt he would not see it—he became aware of the fact that he and the cat had now, together, constituted a unique and extraordinary relationship. The cat was innocence, or love, or both: the fundamentally innocent thing; and he himself, with his brilliant perception of the cat's nature and need, was knowledge, godlike knowledge, with all its latent powers for good or evil. For was he not the only person here, on this early-morning platform, who had really seen and loved this little cat, and foreseen her tragic destiny? The others had been perhaps for a moment amused, or touched, but they had seen nothing of all this; for them the cat was simply another cat. Perceptiveness! Good heavens, yes—this was a case in point, it was indeed *the* case. It was the fundamental instance of the all-embracing, all-cherishing, all-sustaining power of perceptiveness. In this sense, the little cat's life was in his hands. . . .

What an extraordinary thing! And how extraordinarily delightful!

He was still feeling pleased with the whole idea, and with himself, when the train came swiftly and silently toward the station. And turning then for a last look at the cat he saw that she had left the three little girls, and had gone up the sloping ramp of concrete at the end of the platform. There she sat, at the very edge of the raised platform, looking down at the tracks—not fifteen feet away from him—and then she began putting her white paws down the wall, preparing to jump, and just as the heat and shadow of the engine passed him, she jumped. Straight into the middle of the tracks, and the engine had gone over without touching her—but then he saw the agonized darting of the small body from side to side, seeking escape, the frightened back and head darting from side to side, and through an obstruction of wheel or truck the flash of an outstretched convulsive hind leg, white, and upside down; and then nothing. The train had stopped; the three little girls were clambering up the steep steps at one end, the married couple at another; the tall man had disappeared. No one had seen it but he—no one. It was as if nothing had happened.

But as he moved toward the steps *he* saw her again. The eyes closed, the meek upturned face meeker than ever, she lay quite still. And as he sat down in the train, trembling and sick, with all that dreadful action still horribly vivid before him, and as if *still* in action, he felt like a murderer. He alone knew that she was dead. He alone could have saved her.

She had lived, and died, for *him*.

SMITH AND JONES

Smith and Jones, as far as one could tell in the darkness, looked almost exactly alike. Their names might have been interchangeable. So might their clothes, which were apparently rather shabby, though, as they walked quickly and the night was cloudy, it was difficult to be sure. Both of them were extraordinarily articulate. They were walking along the muddy road that led away from a large city and they talked as they went.

"As far as I'm concerned," said Smith, "it's all over. No more women for me. There's nothing in it. It's a damned swindle. Walk right up, gentlemen, and make your bets! The hand is quicker than the eye. Where is the elusive little pea? Ha ha! Both ends against the middle."

He struck a match and lit his pipe; his large pale unshaven face started out of the night.

Jones grumbled to himself. Then turning his head slightly toward Smith, in a somewhat aggressive way, as if he were showing a fang, he began to laugh in a peculiar soft insolent manner.

"Jesus! One would think you were an adolescent. No more women! If there aren't it'll be because you're dead. You were born to be made a fool of by women. You'll buzz round the honey-pot all your days. You have no sense in these matters, you've never had the courage or the intelligence once and for all to *realize* a woman. Look! here's a parable for you. There are an infinite number of little white clouds stretching one after another across blue space, just like sweet little stepping stones. To each of them is tethered a different-colored child's balloon—I know that would rather badly fracture the spectrum, but never mind. And behold, our angel-child, beautiful and trustful, flies to the first little cloud-island, and seizes the first balloon, enraptured. It's pink. But then he sees the next island, and the next balloon, which is orange. So he lets the first one go, which sails away, and flies vigorously to the next little island. From there he catches sight of a different shade of pink—sublime! intoxicating! and again dashes across an abyss. . . . This lovely process goes on forever. It will never stop."

Smith splashed into a puddle and swore.

"Don't be so damned patronizing, with your little angel-child and toy balloons. I know what I'm talking about. Adolescent? Of course I am—who isn't? The point is, exactly, that I *have* at last realized a woman. That's more, I'll bet, than you've done—you, with your damned negativism!"

"Negativism!—how? But never mind that. Tell me about your woman."

"It must be experienced to be understood."

"Of course—so must death."

"What can I tell you then? You, who have always made it a principle to experience as little as possible! Your language doesn't, therefore, extend to the present subject. You are still crawling on your hands and knees, bumping into chairs, and mistaking your feet for a part of the floor, or your hands for a part of the ceiling. Stand up! Be a man! It's glorious."

"Was she blonde or brunette?"

"If you insist, she was a Negress tattooed with gold and silver. Instead of earrings, she wore brass alarm clocks in her ears, and for some unexplained reason she had an ivory thimble in her left nostril."

Jones laughed; there was a shade of annoyance in his laughter.

"I see. . . . I forgot to mention, by the way, that when the angel-child flew so vigorously from cloud to cloud his wings made a kind of whimpering sound. . . . But go on."

"No, she was neither blonde nor brunette, but, as you suggested, imaginary. She didn't really exist. I thought she did, of course—I had seen her several times quite clearly. She had a voice, hands, eyes, feet—in short, the usual equipment. In point of size she was colossal; in point of speed, totally incommensurable. She walked, like Fama, with her head knocking about among the stars. She stepped casually, with one step, from town to town, making with the swish of her skirts so violent a whirlwind that men everywhere were sucked out of houses."

"I recognize the lady. It was Helen of Troy."

"Not at all. Her name, as it happened, was Gleason."

Jones sighed. The two men walked rapidly for some time in silence. The moon, like a pale crab, pulled clouds over itself, buried itself in clouds with a sort of awkward precision, and a few drops of rain fell.

"Rain!" said Jones, putting up one hand.

"To put out the fires of conscience."

"Gleason? She must be—if your description is accurate—in the theatrical profession? A lady acrobat, a trapeze artist, or a Pullman portress?"

"Wrong again, Jones—if error were, as it ought to be, punishable by death, you'd be a corpse. . . . Suffice it to say that Gleason loved me. It was like being loved by a planet."

"Venus?"

"Mars. She crushed me, consumed me. Her love was a profounder and more fiery abyss than the inferno which Dante, in the same sense, explored. It took me days of circuitous descent, to get even within sight of the bottom; and then, as there were no ladders provided, I plunged headlong. I was at once ignited, and became a tiny luminous spark, which, on being cast forth to the upper world again on a fiery exhalation, became an undistinguished cinder."

"To think a person named Gleason could do all that!"

"Yes, it's a good deal, certainly. I feel disinclined for further explorations of the sort."

"Temporarily, you mean. . . . You disliked the adventure?"

"Oh, no—not altogether! Does one dislike life altogether? Do we hate this walk, this road, the rain, ourselves, the current of blood which, as we walk and talk, our hearts keep pumping and pumping? We like and dislike at the same time. It's like an organism with a malignant fetid cancer growing in it. Cut out the cancer, which has interlaced its treacherous fibers throughout every part, and you extinguish life. What's to be done? In birth, love, and death, in all acts of violence, all abrupt beginnings and abrupt cessations, one can detect the very essence of the business—there one sees, in all its ambiguous nakedness, the beautiful obscene."

Jones reflected; one could make out that his head was bowed. Smith walked beside him with happy alacrity. It began to rain harder, the trees dripped loudly, but the two men paid no attention.

"The beautiful obscene!" said Jones, suddenly lifting his head. "Certainly that's something to have learned *chez* Gleason! . . . It suggests a good deal. It's like this road—it's dark, but it certainly leads somewhere."

"Where?"

"That's what we'll discover. Is it centrifugal or centripetal? The road is the former, of course. It leads, as we know, away from civilization into the wilderness, the unknown. But that's no reason for supposing the same to be true of your diagnosis— is it? And yet I wonder."

He wondered visibly, holding his coat-collar about his throat with one hand, and showed a disposition to slacken his pace. But Smith goaded him.

"Look here, we've got to keep moving, you know."

"Yes, we've got to keep moving."

They walked for a mile in complete silence. The rain kept up a steady murmur among the leaves of trees, the vague heaving shoulders of which they could see at right and left, and they heard the tinkling of water in a ditch. Their shoes bubbled and squelched, but they seemed to be indifferent to matters so unimportant. However, from time to time they inclined their heads forward and allowed small reservoirs of rain to slide heavily off their felt hats. It was Jones, finally, who began talking again. After a preliminary mutter or two, and a hostile covert glance at his companion, he said:

"Like all very great discoveries, this discovery of yours affords opportunities for a new principle of behavior. You are not a particularly intelligent man, as I've often told you, and as you yourself admit; so you probably don't at all see the implications of your casual observation. As often occurs to you, in the course of your foolish, violent, undirected activity, you have accidentally bumped your head and seen a star. You would never think, however, of hitching your wagon to such a star—which is what I propose to do."

Smith glanced sharply at his companion, and then began laughing on a low meditative note which gradually became shrill and derisive; he even lifted one knee and slapped it. It was obviously a tremendous joke.

"Just like you, Jones! You're all brain to the soles of your feet. *What* do you propose to do?"

"Don't be a simpleton, or I'll begin by murdering you—instead of ending by doing so."

This peculiar remark was delivered, and received, with the utmost sobriety.

"Of course," said Smith. "You needn't dwell on that, as it's an unpleasant necessity which is fully recognized between us. It doesn't in the least matter whether the event is early or late, does it?"

"What I mean is, that if you are right, and the beautiful obscene is the essence of the business, then obviously one should pursue that course of life which would give one the maximum number of—what shall I say?—perfumed baths of that description. . . . You say that this essence is most clearly to be detected in the simpler violences. In love, birth, death, all abrupt cessations and beginnings. Very good. Then if one is to live completely, to realize life in the last shred of one's consciousness, to become properly incandescent, or *identical* with life, one must put oneself in contact with the strongest currents. One should love savagely, kill frequently, eat the raw, and even, I suppose, be born as often as possible."

"A good idea!"

"I propose to do all these things. It has long been tacitly understood that sooner or later I will murder you, so, as you tactfully suggest, I won't dwell on that. But I shall be glad to have Gleason's address . . . beforehand."

"Certainly; whenever you like. Telephone Main 220-W (I always liked that W) and ask for Mary."

"The question is: what's to be done about thought? . . . You see, this road of reflection is, after all, centripetal. It involves, inevitably a return to the center, an identification of one's self with the All, with the unconscious *primum mobile*. But thought, in its very nature, involves a separation of one's self from the—from the——"

"Unconscious?"

"From the unconscious. . . . We must be careful not to go astray at this point. One shouldn't begin by trying to *be* unconscious—not at all! One might as well be dead. What one should try to get rid of is consciousness of *self*. Isn't that it?"

Smith gave a short laugh, at the same time tilting his head to let the rain run off onto his feet. "Anything you say, professor. I trust you blindly. Anyway, I know that my pleasantest moments with Gleason were those in which I most completely lost my awareness of personality, of personal identity. Yes, it's beautiful and horrible, the way one loses, at such moments, everything but a feeling of animal force. . . . Analogously, one should never permit conversation at meals. And it was decidedly decadent of Cyrano to carry on an elaborate monologue in couplets while committing a murder—oh, decidedly. Quite the wrong thing! One's awareness, on such occasions, should be of nothing, nothing but murder—there should be no overlapping fringe which could busy itself with such boyisms as poetry or epigram. One should, in short, *be* a murder. . . . Do I interpret you correctly?"

Jones, at this, looked at Smith with a quick uneasiness. Smith appeared to be unconscious of this regard, and was as usual walking with jaunty alacrity. The way he threw out his feet was extremely provocative—the angle of his elbows was offensive. His whole bearing was a deliberate, a calculated insult.

"Quite correctly," said Jones sharply, keeping his eye on Smith.

"Here's a haystack," replied the latter, equably, but also a little sneeringly. "Shall we begin with arson? We can go on, by degrees, to murder."

"By all means."

The two men could be seen jumping the ditch, and laboriously climbing over a slippery stone wall. Several matches sputtered and went out, and then a little blaze lighted the outstretched hands and solemn intent faces of Jones and Smith. They drew out and spread the dry hay over the blaze, the flames fed eagerly, and the stone wall and the black trunk of an elm tree appeared to stagger toward them out of the darkness.

"I think that will do," observed Smith cheerfully.

They climbed back over the wall and resumed their walk. The rain had become a drizzle, and the moon, in a crack between the clouds, showed for a second the white of an eye. Behind them, the fire began to spout, and they observed that they were preceded, on the puddled road, by oblique drunken shadows. They walked rapidly.

"A mere bagatelle," Smith went on, after a time. "But there's a farm at the top of the hill, so we can, as it were, build more stately mansions. . . . Were you aware, at the moment of ignition, of a kind of co-awareness with the infinite?"

"Don't be frivolous."

"Personally, I found it a little disappointing. . . . I don't like these deliberate actions. Give me the spontaneous, every time. That's one thing I particularly like about Gleason. The dear thing hasn't the least idea what she's doing, or what she's going to do next. If she decided to kill you, you'd never know it, because you'd be dead. . . . Not at all like you, Jones. You've got a devil of a lot to unlearn!"

Jones reflected. He took off his hat and shook it. His air was profoundly philosophical.

"True. I have. I'll put off a decision about the farm till we get to it. I suppose, by the same token, you'd like me to give up my habit of strict meditation on the subject of *your* death?"

"Oh, just as you like about that!" . . . Smith laughed pleasantly. "I assure you it's not of the smallest consequence. . . . It occurs to me, by the way, somewhat irrelevantly, that in your philosophy of incandescent sensation one must allow a place for the merely horrible. I never, I swear, felt more brilliantly alive than when I saw, once, a Negro sitting in a cab with his throat cut. He unwound a bloody towel for the doctor, and I saw, in the chocolate color, three parallel red smiles—no, gills. It was amazing."

"A domestic scene? . . . *Crime passionnelle?*"

"No—a trifling misunderstanding in a barber shop. This chap started to take out a handkerchief; the other chap thought it was a revolver; and the razor was quicker than the handkerchief. . . . The safety razor ought to be abolished, don't you think?"

Jones, without answer, jumped the ditch and disappeared in the direction of the farm. Smith leaned against the wall, laughing softly to himself. After a while there were six little spurts of light one after another in the darkness, hinting each time at a nose and fingers, and then four more. Nothing further happened. The darkness remained self-possessed, and presently Jones reappeared, muttering.

"No use! It's too wet, and I couldn't find any kindling."

"Don't let that balk you, my dear Jones! Ring the doorbell

and ask for a little kerosene. Why not kill the old man, ravish his daughter, and then burn up the lot? It would be a good night's work."

"Damn you! You've done enough harm already."

There was something a little menacing in this, but Smith was unperturbed.

"What the devil do you mean?" he answered. "Intellectually I'm a child by comparison with you. I'm an adolescent."

"You know perfectly well what I mean—all this," and Jones gave a short ugly sweep of his arm toward the blazing haystack and, beyond that, the city. The moon came out, resting her perfect chin on a tawny cloud. The two men regarded each other strangely.

"Nonsense!" Smith then exclaimed. "Besides you'll have the satisfaction of killing me. That ought to compensate. And Gleason! think of Gleason! She'll be glad to see you. She'll revel in the details of my death."

"Will she?"

"Of course, she will. . . . She's a kind of sadist, or something of the sort. . . . How, by the way, do you propose to do it? We've never—come to think of it—had an understanding on that point. Would you mind telling me, or do you regard it as a sort of trade secret? . . . Just as you like!"

Jones seemed to be breathing a little quickly.

"No trouble at all—but I don't know! I shall simply, as you suggest, wait for an inspiration."

"How damned disquieting! Also, Jones, it's wholly out of character, and you'll have to forgive me if, for once, I refuse to believe you. What the deuce is this walk for, if not for your opportunity? You're bound to admit that I was most compliant. I accepted your suggestion without so much as a twitter—didn't I? Very unselfish of me, I think! . . . But, of course, it had to come."

The two men were walking, by tacit agreement, at opposite sides of the road; they had to raise their voices. Still, one would not have said that it was a quarrel.

"Oh yes, it had to come. It was clearly impossible that both of us should live!"

"Quite. . . . At the same time this affair is so exquisitely complex, and so dislocated, if I may put it so, into the world of the fourth dimension, that I'm bound to admit that while I recognize the necessity I don't quite grasp the cause. . . ."

"You're vulgar, Smith."

"Am I? . . . Ah, so that's it—I'm vulgar, I seize life by the forelock! . . . I go about fornicating, thieving, card-cheating and murdering, in my persistent, unreflective, low-grade sort of way, and it makes life insupportable for you. Here, now, is Gleason. How that must simply infuriate you! Three days in town, and I have a magnificent planetary love affair like that—burnt to a crisp! Ha ha! And you, all the while, drinking tea and reading Willard Gibbs. I must say it's damned funny."

Jones made no reply. His head was thrust forward—he seemed to be brooding. His heavy breathing was quite audible, and Smith, after an amused glance toward him, went on talking.

"Lots of lights suddenly occur to me—lights on this extraordinary, impenetrable subject—take down my words, Jones, this is my death-bed speech! . . . I spoke, didn't I, of the beautiful obscene, and of the inextricable manner in which the two qualities are everywhere bound up together? The beautiful and the obscene. The desirable and the disgusting. I also compared this state of things with an organism in which a cancer was growing —which one tries to excise. . . . Well, Jones, you're the beautiful and I'm the obscene; you're the desirable and I'm the disgusting; and in some rotten way we've got tangled up together. . . . You, being the healthy organism, insist on having the cancer removed. But remember: I warned you! If you do so, it's at your own peril. . . . However, it's silly to warn you, for of course you have no more control over the situation than I have, or Gleason has. The bloody conclusion lies there, and we walk soberly toward it. . . . Are you sorry?"

"No!"

"Well then, neither am I. Let's move a little faster! . . . Damn it all, I *would* like to see Gleason again! You were perfectly right about that. . . . Do you know what she said to me?"

Smith, at this point, suddenly stopped, as if to enjoy the recollection at leisure. He opened his mouth and stared before him, in the moonlight, with an odd bright fixity. Jones, with the scantiest turn of his head, plodded on, so that Smith had, perforce, to follow.

"She said she'd like to live with me—that she'd support me. By George! What do you think of that? . . . 'You're a dear boy,' she said, 'you fascinate me!' 'Fascinate!' That's the best thing I do. Don't I fascinate you, Jones? Look at my eyes! Don't I fascinate you? . . . Ha, ha! . . . Yes, I have the morals of a snake. I'm graceful, I'm all curves, there's nothing straight about me. Gleason got dizzy looking at me, her head swayed from side to side, her eyes were lost in a sort of mist, and then she fell clutching at me like a paralytic, and talking the wildest nonsense. Could you do that, Jones, do you think? . . . Never! It's all a joke to think of your going to see Gleason. And if you told her what had happened she'd kill you. Yes, you'd look like St. Sebastian when Gleason got through with you. . . . Say something! Don't be so damned glum. Anybody'd suppose it was *your* funeral."

"Oh, go on talking! I like the sound of your voice."

"And then to think of your pitiful attempt to set that barn on fire! Good Lord, with half a dozen matches. . . . That's what comes of studying symbolic logic and the rule of phase. . . . Really, I don't know what you'll do without me, Jones! You're like a child, and when I'm dead, who's going to show you, as the wit said, how to greet the obscene with a cheer? . . . However, I wouldn't bother about that rock if I were you—aren't you premature?"

This last observation sounded a little sharp.

Jones had certainly appeared to be stooping toward a small loose fragment of rock by the roadside, but he straightened up with smiling alacrity.

"My shoelace," he said, cynically. "It's loose. I think I'll re-tie it."

"Pray do! Why not?"

"Very well! If you don't mind waiting!"

Jones gave a little laugh. He stooped again, fumbled for a second at his shoe, then suddenly shot out a snakelike hand toward the rock. But Smith meanwhile had made a gleaming gesture which seemed to involve Jones's back.

"Ah!" said Jones, and slid softly forward into a puddle.

"Are you there?"

Smith's query was almost humorous. As it received no reply, and Jones lay motionless in his puddle, Smith took him by the coat-collar, dragged him to the edge of the ditch, and rolled him in. The moon poured a clear green light on this singular occurrence. It showed Smith examining his hands with care, and then wiping them repeatedly on the wet grass and rank jewel-weed. It showed him relighting his pipe—which had gone out during the rain—with infinite leisure. One would have said, at the moment, that he looked like a tramp. And, finally, it showed him turning back in the direction he had come from, and set-ting off cheerfully toward the city; alone, but with an amazing air, somehow, of having always been alone.

Five o'clock. He looked at his watch, hoping that it was later—late enough for dinner. That was characteristic. He was always hoping that it was later than it really was, hoping that an hour had gone, a day had gone. Other people were anxious about being too late—he was anxious about being too early. Supreme, everlasting, devastating boredom. His watch was a symbol of that, and now as he put it back in his pocket, cherishing its warm smoothness, he cursed the hour and a half that yawned like a chasm before his next "action." He walked wearily along the gravel path. Piles of leaves were burning, and the smoke came heavily over his face. Wet leaves; there had been a shower. He was irritatingly conscious of his stick, which kept entangling itself with his coat, and which was so light that it would not properly thrust against the gusty wind. Besides, it was too long, struck the ground too sharply, and was particularly annoying in a deserted street, where its rhythmic clack on the stones made him feel like screaming. In a moonlit street it became positively portentous, and it seemed to him that he was trying to balance a telegraph pole. It scraped now against an unforeseen rise in the path, and he drew it up under his arm, regaining a little of his composure. Then he stepped off the path onto the grass, swung the stick triumphantly, and thrust it into the ground, at every step, with delight. He impaled an empty match-box. He impaled a yellow leaf. He aimed it as if it were a gun at a robin, who took no notice, but, with suddenly lowered head, performed a little mechanical run and then stood still, listening for a worm. "Fly away south, old man! No worms here, unless you listen to my head." His face did not change expression—he was conscious that it didn't—but in imagination he heard himself laughing loudly.

That was exactly the problem, the problem that kept him awake late at night, that woke him up early, and that nevertheless made him long for sleep as he longed for nothing else—profound, profound nothingness and annihilation of sleep, complete and harmonious escape. Yes, that was the problem: to find and name this worm that gnawed at his brain. What on earth was this new obsession for—this horror of shaving? He had had it now for three days and three nights, and his nights it had made hideous; for his thoughts kept reverting to the new razor, and whenever he saw it, in his mind's eye, lying there on the shelf in all its bright sheerness, he felt a spastic contraction of the chest. He had lain awake for two hours, the first morning, wondering whether he would dare to shave with it. In a sinister way it had seemed to be connected, as with steel wires, to his jangled nerves, and gradually he had become convinced that as soon as he touched it some obscure impulse would turn the blade against his flesh. He had conquered his terror—had managed to shave, trembling a little, and noting with astonishment the pallor of his face, and the narrow intensity of his pupils. . . . Well, obviously, it was too late in the day for any mere timidity about shaving to develop! It was something deeper than that. Whatever the worm was, it had bored into the very center, and his brain was honey-combed with galleries—hollow enough to float—its specific gravity markedly impaired.

He sat down on a wet bench, and as he did so the sun came out and made a pale sparkling brightness of the grass. This was refreshing; it gave a change of scene. He was not exactly sure where it put him. He was barefooted, that was clear, and he was exquisitely conscious of the cool, dispersed wetness of the grass under his sensitive feet, and of the sharpness of twigs. Coarse, thick, ropy spider's webs glistened on the dingy box-hedge, and at the bottom of every silken funnel he could see a vigorous spider with curved claws. The smell of wet leaves was like early morning. Then there was some question of nasturtiums, matted snakily together by a heavy rain in the night—acrid; he liked the yellow ones best. . . . The warm smell of burning leaves came again over him, and the thought of the razor, with its sinister bracketing of edge and flesh. He began to compose a letter to Sara. Should he address her by her "pet" name—Sahara—the name originally suggested by the fact that she pronounced her name to rhyme with the desert? Too flippant at this crisis.

"My dear Sara: Why is it that you are made of flesh—why, indeed, if God, as it is reported, created you in His image, did He not dispense for once with the common straw and clay and dip His hands into the clear brightness of the ether? I cannot, no, I have made up my mind on the point, reconcile myself to the fact that your mouth, which I once in a vision saw as a flower without function, exists really for the taking in of food and of men; that you have an alimentary canal, liable at the most inopportune moments to utter its obscene borborygmi—or as Jake coarsely puts it, its bubbling of the gut—amid harmonies seemingly more ethereal; that you have kidneys, and liver, and ductless glands, all plying at all times their little secret juicy trades. It is no good retorting, as I hear you angrily retort (between mouthfuls of the best beef), that all this holds just as well of me. Of course. To be sure. Certainly. That's precisely why I should like to find in some hallowed corner of this dingy universe a creature of a beauty and texture more translucent—compounded, let us say, of air and fire. You will say that this is an unreasonable demand. But if it is really unreasonable why does it occur to me—is it only a disease of the flesh that enables flesh to conceive the finer-than-flesh? . . . At all events, my dear Sahara Desert, what I passionately want you to understand at this crisis in our lives, is that if I now take flight from you and recede rapidly into the blue obscure, weaving about myself a fine shroud of stellar air, it is not the individual but the generic you that I flee from, finding horrible. For this horror is ubiquitous—its yellow tooth is everywhere, in all women, in all men. I have fought against it for years. Yes, I recall its fangs in even my very first love affair, when years ago walking in a dark London square with a woman whose affection for me was a little too public and unrestrained (she suddenly tried to embrace me, murmuring, no, shouting, passionate phrases!) I observed a sign, happily emblazoned against the palings of a fence, 'Organs and street cries prohibited near here,' and read it aloud to her, with the fortunate result that she was dissolved into shrieks of laughter. . . . I do not know in the least why I should want to recite to you this oblique episode of my past. Perhaps only because it gives you a little of my background. But background is so important and so complicated! What use to give you a mere fragment like this? Isn't it equally important that I should tell you that I dislike intensely the odor of female perspiration; that I have an obscure passion for jungles, snake-infested thickets, and the sound of horns; that a dull pencil makes me miserable and inert, as if paralyzed, and that I find intolerable any business dealing with a stranger? . . . Even so, I make hardly the slightest of beginnings. I'm a sort of nexus of loathings. As I sit here in the park, with the sun just dipping his chin into a swift cloud and a few drops of rain beginning to fall among moist pebbles and dead leaves, it seems to me that I am really a vast net of unpleasant sensation, a net of boredom which enmeshes everything, and down the slack nerves of which run tremors of feeble disgust from the uttermost stars. What a paltry attempt at the poetic that is! I am ashamed of myself. What I mean, of course, is merely that my own nervous system is degraded—perhaps by too much sensation, and sensation too precise.

"Ah, Sahara, those precise sensations! Did you know that there has always been something peculiarly offensive to me in the line of the gums above your upper teeth? On chilly days,

too, I have noticed that the part of the chest which shows above
your blouse is very apt to be of a bluish hue which I find extraordinarily repulsive. And then, to pass from the physiological
to the psychological, how singularly you have misjudged, from
the very outset, the sort of stimulus with which to play upon
me! If only you had known how to be proud instead of humble,
reserved instead of placatory, mysterious instead of dumb! . . .
These are extraordinary things to be saying to a woman at the
very outset of 'love'; no doubt, you will be simply dumfounded.
'How is it possible?' I hear you asking. 'Did you not kiss me last
night? Surely there was no sham about that? You loved me then
—is it possible that love should evaporate so soon?' . . . Yes, I
loved you last night, that is true. When I left my own lodgings
and started off in the evening to see you I will not deny that I
did so with tremendous excitement, that I had taken the very
last care with my appearance, and that all the way, in the
car, my imagination, like an expert contrapuntalist, performed
the most amazing feats of virtuosity with the simple theme of
'you.' I saw you burning like a creature of light, alternately
fusing and paling with the pulse of fire. I trembled when I
thought of you. I could feel waves of psychic blindness go over
me periodically, and when at last I climbed the steps to your
house I felt as if my head and my body had been somehow separated. . . . But then, when I saw you, these feelings began rapidly
to change! I saw something a little coarse in you; I found you
to be stupid; the curve of your jaw seemed to me to be too
heavy. You manifested also a disposition to abuse those gestures
which I had at first found charming. How sick I became of your
trick of looking up at me from your pillow with silly admiration, just allowing me a glimpse of your small blue eyes between
the fingers of your hand! How I loathed you for the arch way
in which you kept turning your back. I responded to these
things as you expected, but you did not guess with what weari-
ness and anger.

"However, it was not at all my intention to say things that
might injure you—not at all, not at all. What I want intensely,

miserably, to make clear to you is that it is not in any real sense you that I thus shamefully betray and abandon, but humanity, the world, and, above all myself. In this particular case, I suppose I might say that the difficulty lies in the fact that when I came to you it was with the last failing spark of my wearied enthusiasm for love affairs. But it is really far more complicated than that—it is not fair to you or to me to let you suppose that I am merely a jaded Don Juan. Not so. My love affairs have been very few, very fugitive; and if now my love for you is as it were, stillborn, it is because at last my faith in beauty seems dead. . . . If you could realize, Sara, how much I *want* to love you! how infinitely healing it would be to me! But I am powerless in this, as I am in everything; I have no gusto for life; I am a mass of complex contradictory impulses that leave me in a mammering and at a stay. When I fall asleep at night it is with the hope that I may never wake. When I wake in the morning, it is with passionate resentment. I look ahead through the day in the faint hope that I may find the promise of one event that will be pleasant. If it happens that I am to dine in the evening with X, then I live through the tedium of the day, and all its exasperating trifles, in expectation of that one hour of pleasure—which, under so great a strain, usually turns out to be rather dull. . . .

"And then, finally, there are my obsessions, which I cannot explain. My latest is a horror of shaving! I cannot think of a razor, of a sharp edge of any sort, without a shudder which touches the very center of my vitality. When I take up my razor in the morning it is almost with a conviction that some obscure impulse will transmit itself to the blade, which will suddenly turn against my weak flesh. . . . By my troth, Nerissa, my little body is a-weary of this great world. . . ."

. . . What an admirable letter! How profoundly it would stir the chords of pity in Sara's heart! . . . But the pace of the rain was beginning to quicken, a continual patter came from the dead leaves, and he rose, buttoning his coat. Ten minutes to six. . . . If he walked through the park, slowly, and then by the long way through Essex Street, he would reach the station just in time to meet Sara for dinner. He began walking. Leaves blew along the path before him, came down in streams from the blown trees. Incredible melancholy. All that was needed was a dejected faun shivering in a hollow tree and trying to blow a melody from his rain-soaked reed. Everything was gray in the gray light. Large drops from the boughs of trees pattered on the rim of his hat, and the crook of his stick, becoming wet, rubbed irritatingly on the palm of his hand. Sodden leaves; sodden newspapers; sodden world.

To be or not to be: no, that wasn't the question at all, but whether or not to dine with Sara. To approach her through this silver jungle of rain, with all its bells; to weave himself like a shuttle through this vast and exquisite fabric of mercurial silver, finally coming upon Sara, in a green dress, waiting happily; to see for a flash the clear quality of her face in rain-light, and to hear the first full sound of her voice under an umbrella tense and murmurous with rain; to feel a drop of water on the back of his hand, and to hear her laugh—didn't all this, after all, offer a sort of beauty? . . . Yes, no question, it did. But it was only for the first instant. After that came the tedious necessity of finding a restaurant where they would be safe from the eyes of acquaintances, the necessity of talking and talking with Sara, of touching her foot under the table, of spending three desolating hours of the evening with her—she wouldn't let him off with less. Agonizing complications. Misery a thousand miles deep. If he did go to her, what should he say? . . . He would greet her wearily. She looked concerned—no, alarmed! "Henry! You're worried. What's the matter?" "Well, Sara—don't be shocked—but to tell the truth I was wondering, all the way here, whether or not to abandon you." . . . Would she cry—grow white? No—she looked far away, at nothing, compressed her lips. "I see." . . . That's what she'd say. "You see, Sahara, in a sense you've become for me, momentarily, a symbol of life itself. And if I speak of abandoning you, what I really mean is the abandonment of everything." He couldn't prevent a touch of *vox humana* getting into that last phrase—it was a shade too much like a sob, but then, anything was permissible when one was dealing with a woman. "I don't think I mean suicide"—this was said slowly and ponderingly; the "think" was, indeed, masterly! . . . But suppose she simply, with a flash of amusement, answered, "Why not?" . . . Heavens!

He turned the corner, and there was Sara just as he had foreseen, in the green dress, waiting serenely under her tinkling umbrella. She laughed frankly.

"Henry, you do look dejected!"

"Why shouldn't I? I'm thinking of committing suicide."

"Do!"

"But first I must have some dinner—I'm starving to death!"

"Very well—I'm hungry myself."

"And afterwards—I must kiss you."

"No!"

"Yes. Just behind your left ear."

"What an idea!"

"We'll take a taxi and do a whirl about the city among the rain and puddles."

"That sounds reasonable."

A sudden fury possessed him. He stood still.

"Don't be so damned reasonable! Only death is reasonable."

He saw Sara looking at him with fright, as if she saw something horrible in his face. What did she see? A sharp green-lit vision of him hanging from a gas fixture? . . . A torrent of grief seemed to be released within him, he felt a quickening sensation in his tear-ducts; and, tightly clasping Sara's forearm with his hand, he started walking again.

SILENT SNOW, SECRET SNOW

<hr>

Just why it should have happened, or why it should have happened just when it did, he could not, of course, possibly have said; nor perhaps would it even have occurred to him to ask. The thing was above all a secret, something to be preciously concealed from Mother and Father; and to that very fact it owed an enormous part of its deliciousness. It was like a peculiarly beautiful trinket to be carried unmentioned in one's trouser pocket—a rare stamp, an old coin, a few tiny gold links found trodden out of shape on the path in the park, a pebble of carnelian, a seashell distinguishable from all others by an unusual spot or stripe—and, as if it were any one of these, he carried around with him everywhere a warm and persistent and increasingly beautiful sense of possession. Nor was it only a sense of possession—it was also a sense of protection. It was as if, in some delightful way, his secret gave him a fortress, a wall behind which he could retreat into heavenly seclusion. This was almost the first thing he had noticed about it—apart from the oddness of the thing itself—and it was this that now again, for the fiftieth time, occurred to him, as he sat in the little schoolroom. It was the half-hour for geography. Miss Buell was revolving with one finger, slowly, a huge terrestrial globe which had been placed on her desk. The green and yellow continents passed and repassed, questions were asked and answered, and now the little girl in front of him, Deirdre, who had a funny little constellation of freckles on the back of her neck, exactly like the Big Dipper, was standing up and telling Miss Buell that the equator was the line that ran round the middle.

Miss Buell's face, which was old and grayish and kindly, with gray stiff curls beside the cheeks, and eyes that swam very brightly, like little minnows, behind thick glasses, wrinkled itself into a complication of amusements.

"Ah! I see. The earth is wearing a belt, or a sash. Or someone drew a line round it!"

"Oh no—not that—I mean——"

In the general laughter, he did not share, or only a very little. He was thinking about the Arctic and Antarctic regions, which of course, on the globe, were white. Miss Buell was now telling them about the tropics, the jungles, the steamy heat of equatorial swamps, where the birds and butterflies, and even the snakes, were like living jewels. As he listened to these things, he was already, with a pleasant sense of half-effort, putting his secret between himself and the words. Was it really an effort at all? For effort implied something voluntary, and perhaps even something one did not especially want; whereas this was distinctly pleasant, and came almost of its own accord. All he needed to do was to think of that morning, the first one, and then of all the others——

But it was all so absurdly simple! It had amounted to so little. It was nothing, just an idea—and just why it should have become so wonderful, so permanent, was a mystery—a very pleasant one, to be sure, but also, in an amusing way, foolish. However, without ceasing to listen to Miss Buell, who had now moved up to the north temperate zones, he deliberately invited his memory of the first morning. It was only a moment or two after he had waked up—or perhaps the moment itself. But was there, to be exact, an exact moment? Was one awake all at once? or was it gradual? Anyway, it was after he had stretched a lazy hand up toward the headrail, and yawned, and then relaxed again among his warm covers, all the more grateful on a December morning, that the thing had happened. Suddenly, for no reason, he had thought of the postman, he remembered the postman. Perhaps there was nothing so odd in that. After all, he heard the post-man almost every morning in his life—his heavy boots could be heard clumping round the corner at the top of the little cobbled hill-street, and then, progressively nearer, progressively louder, the double knock at each door, the crossings and re-crossings of the street, till finally the clumsy steps came stumbling across to the very door, and the tremendous knock came which shook the house itself.

(Miss Buell was saying, "Vast wheat-growing areas in North America and Siberia."

Deirdre had for the moment placed her left hand across the back of her neck.)

But on this particular morning, the first morning, as he lay there with his eyes closed, he had for some reason *waited* for the postman. He wanted to hear him come round the corner. And that was precisely the joke—he never did. He never came. He never had come—*round the corner*—again. For when at last the steps *were* heard, they had already, he was quite sure, come a little down the hill, to the first house; and even so, the steps were curiously different—they were softer, they had a new se-crecy about them, they were muffled and indistinct; and while the rhythm of them was the same, it now said a new thing—it said peace, it said remoteness, it said cold, it said sleep. And he had understood the situation at once—nothing could have seemed simpler—there had been snow in the night, such as all winter he had been longing for; and it was this which had ren-dered the postman's first footsteps inaudible, and the later ones faint. Of course! How lovely! And even now it must be snowing —it was going to be a snowy day—the long white ragged lines were drifting and sifting across the street, across the faces of the old houses, whispering and hushing, making little triangles of white in the corners between cobblestones, seething a little when the wind blew them over the ground to a drifted corner; and so it would be all day, getting deeper and deeper and silenter and silenter.

(Miss Buell was saying, "Land of perpetual snow.")

All this time, of course (while he lay in bed), he had kept his eyes closed, listening to the nearer progress of the postman, the muffled footsteps thumping and slipping on the snow-sheathed cobbles; and all the other sounds—the double knocks, a frosty far-off voice or two, a bell ringing thinly and softly as if under a sheet of ice—had the same slightly abstracted quality, as if removed by one degree from actuality—as if everything in the world had been insulated by snow. But when at last, pleased, he opened his eyes, and turned them toward the window, to see for himself this long-desired and now so clearly imagined miracle— what he saw instead was brilliant sunlight on a roof; and when, astonished, he jumped out of bed and stared down into the street, expecting to see the cobbles obliterated by the snow, he saw nothing but the bare bright cobbles themselves.

Queer, the effect this extraordinary surprise had had upon him—all the following morning he had kept with him a sense as of snow falling about him, a secret screen of new snow between himself and the world. If he had not dreamed such a thing—and how could he have dreamed it while awake?—how else could one explain it? In any case, the delusion had been so vivid as to affect his entire behavior. He could not now remember whether it was on the first or the second morning—or was it even the third?—that his mother had drawn attention to some oddness in his manner.

"But my darling"—she had said at the breakfast table—"what has come over you? You don't seem to be listening. . . ."

And how often that very thing had happened since!

(Miss Buell was now asking if anyone knew the difference between the North Pole and the Magnetic Pole. Deirdre was holding up her flickering brown hand, and he could see the four white dimples that marked the knuckles.)

Perhaps it hadn't been either the second or third morning—

or even the fourth or fifth. How could he be sure? How could he be sure just when the delicious *progress* had become clear? Just when it had really *begun?* The intervals weren't very precise. . . . All he now knew was, that at some point or other—perhaps the second day, perhaps the sixth—he had noticed that the presence of the snow was a little more insistent, the sound of it clearer; and, conversely, the sound of the postman's footsteps more indistinct. Not only could he not hear the steps come round the corner, he could not even hear them at the first house. It was below the first house that he heard them; and then, a few days later, it was below the second house that he heard them; and a few days later again, below the third. Gradually, gradually, the snow was becoming heavier, the sound of its seething louder, the cobblestones more and more muffled. When he found, each morning, on going to the window, after the ritual of listening, that the roofs and cobbles were as bare as ever, it made no difference. This was, after all, only what he had expected. It was even what pleased him, what rewarded him: the thing was his own, belonged to no one else. No one else knew about it, not even his mother and father. There, outside, were the bare cobbles; and here, inside, was the snow. Snow growing heavier each day, muffling the world, hiding the ugly, and deadening increasingly—above all—the steps of the postman.

"But, my darling"—she had said at the luncheon table—"what has come over you? You don't seem to listen when people speak to you. That's the third time I've asked you to pass your plate. . . ."

How was one to explain this to Mother? or to Father? There was, of course, nothing to be done about it: nothing. All one could do was to laugh embarrassedly, pretend to be a little ashamed, apologize, and take a sudden and somewhat disingenuous interest in what was being done or said. The cat had stayed out all night. He had a curious swelling on his left cheek ·—perhaps somebody had kicked him, or a stone had struck him. Mrs. Kempton was or was not coming to tea. The house was going to be housecleaned, or "turned out," on Wednesday in-

stead of Friday. A new lamp was provided for his evening work
—perhaps it was eyestrain which accounted for this new and so
peculiar vagueness of his—Mother was looking at him with
amusement as she said this, but with something else as well. A
new lamp? A new lamp. Yes, Mother, No, Mother, Yes, Mother.
School is going very well. The geometry is very easy. The history
is very dull. The geography is very interesting—particularly
when it takes one to the North Pole. Why the North Pole? Oh,
well, it would be fun to be an explorer. Another Peary or Scott
or Shackleton. And then abruptly he found his interest in the
talk at an end, stared at the pudding on his plate, listened,
waited, and began once more—ah, how heavenly, too, the first
beginnings—to hear or feel—for could he actually hear it?—the
silent snow, the secret snow.

(Miss Buell was telling them about the search for the Northwest Passage, about Hendrik Hudson, the *Half Moon*.)

This had been, indeed, the only distressing feature of the new
experience; the fact that it so increasingly had brought him into
a kind of mute misunderstanding, or even conflict, with his
father and mother. It was as if he were trying to lead a double
life. On the one hand, he had to be Paul Hasleman, and keep
up the appearance of being that person—dress, wash, and answer
intelligently when spoken to—; on the other, he had to explore
this new world which had been opened to him. Nor could there
be the slightest doubt—not the slightest—that the new world was
the profounder and more wonderful of the two. It was irresisti-
ble. It was miraculous. Its beauty was simply beyond anything—
beyond speech as beyond thought—utterly incommunicable. But
how then, between the two worlds, of which he was thus constantly aware, was he to keep a balance? One must get up, one
must go to breakfast, one must talk with Mother, go to school,
do one's lessons—and, in all this, try not to appear too much of
a fool. But if all the while one was also trying to extract the full
deliciousness of another and quite separate existence, one which
could not easily (if at all) be spoken of—how was one to manage?
How was one to explain? Would it be safe to explain? Would

it be absurd? Would it merely mean that he would get into some obscure kind of trouble?

These thoughts came and went, came and went, as softly and secretly as the snow; they were not precisely a disturbance, perhaps they were even a pleasure; he liked to have them; their presence was something almost palpable, something he could stroke with his hand, without closing his eyes, and without ceasing to see Miss Buell and the schoolroom and the globe and the freckles on Deirdre's neck; nevertheless he did in a sense cease to see, or to see the obvious external world, and substituted for this vision the vision of snow, the sound of snow, and the slow, almost soundless, approach of the postman. Yesterday, it had been only at the sixth house that the postman had become audible; the snow was much deeper now, it was falling more swiftly and heavily, the sound of its seething was more distinct, more soothing, more persistent. And this morning, it had been—as nearly as he could figure—just above the seventh house—perhaps only a step or two above; at most, he had heard two or three footsteps before the knock had sounded. . . . And with each such narrowing of the sphere, each nearer approach of the limit at which the postman was first audible, it was odd how sharply was increased the amount of illusion which had to be carried into the ordinary business of daily life. Each day, it was harder to get out of bed, to go to the window, to look out at the—as always—perfectly empty and snowless street. Each day it was more difficult to go through the perfunctory motions of greeting Mother and Father at breakfast, to reply to their questions, to put his books together and go to school. And at school, how extraordinarily hard to conduct with success simultaneously the public life and the life that was secret! There were times when he longed—positively ached—to tell everyone about it—to burst out with it—only to be checked almost at once by a far-off feeling as of some faint absurdity which was inherent in it—but *was* it absurd?—and more importantly by a sense of mysterious power in his very secrecy. Yes; it must be kept secret. That, more and more, became clear. At whatever cost to himself, whatever pain to others——

(Miss Buell looked straight at him, smiling, and said, "Perhaps we'll ask Paul. I'm sure Paul will come out of his daydream long enough to be able to tell us. Won't you, Paul?" He rose slowly from his chair, resting one hand on the brightly varnished desk, and deliberately stared through the snow toward the blackboard. It was an effort, but it was amusing to make it. "Yes," he said slowly, "it was what we now call the Hudson River. This he thought to be the Northwest Passage. He was disappointed." He sat down again, and as he did so Deirdre half turned in her chair and gave him a shy smile, of approval and admiration.)

At whatever pain to others.

This part of it was very puzzling, very puzzling. Mother was very nice, and so was Father. Yes, that was all true enough. He wanted to be nice to them, to tell them everything—and yet, was it really wrong of him to want to have a secret place of his own?

At bed-time, the night before, Mother had said, "If this goes on, my lad, we'll have to see a doctor, we will! We can't have our boy—" But what was it she had said? "Live in another world"? "Live so far away"? The word "far" had been in it, he was sure, and then Mother had taken up a magazine again and laughed a little, but with an expression which wasn't mirthful. He had felt sorry for her. . . .

The bell rang for dismissal. The sound came to him through long curved parallels of falling snow. He saw Deirdre rise, and had himself risen almost as soon—but not quite as soon—as she.

II.   On the walk homeward, which was timeless, it pleased him to see through the accompaniment, or counterpoint, of snow, the items of mere externality on his way. There were many kinds of brick in the sidewalks, and laid in many kinds of pattern. The garden walls, too, were various, some of wooden palings, some of plaster, some of stone. Twigs of bushes leaned over the walls: the little hard green winter-buds of lilac, on gray stems, sheathed and fat; other branches very thin and fine and black and desiccated. Dirty sparrows huddled in the bushes, as dull in color as dead fruit left in leafless trees. A single starling creaked on a weather vane. In the gutter, beside a drain, was a scrap of torn and dirty newspaper, caught in a little delta of filth; the word ECZEMA appeared in large capitals, and below it was a letter from Mrs. Amelia D. Cravath, 2100 Pine Street, Fort Worth, Texas, to the effect that after being a sufferer for years she had been cured by Caley's Ointment. In the little delta, beside the fan-shaped and deeply runneled continent of brown mud, were lost twigs, descended from their parent trees, dead matches, a rusty horse-chestnut burr, a small concentration of eggshell, a streak of yellow sawdust which had been wet and now was dry and congealed, a brown pebble, and a broken feather. Farther on was a cement sidewalk, ruled into geometrical parallelograms, with a brass inlay at one end commemorating the contractors who had laid it, and, halfway across, an irregular and random series of dog-tracks, immortalized in synthetic stone. He knew these well, and always stepped on them; to cover the little hollows with his own foot had always been a queer pleasure; today he did it once more, but perfunctorily and detachedly, all the while thinking of something else. That was a dog, a long time ago, who had made a mistake and walked on the cement while it was still wet. He had probably wagged his tail, but that hadn't been recorded. Now, Paul Hasleman, aged twelve, on his way home from school, crossed the same river, which in the meantime had frozen into rock. Homeward through the snow, the snow falling in bright sunshine. Homeward?

Then came the gateway with the two posts surmounted by egg-shaped stones which had been cunningly balanced on their ends, as if by Columbus, and mortared in the very act of balance; a source of perpetual wonder. On the brick wall just beyond, the letter H had been stenciled, presumably for some purpose. H? H.

The green hydrant, with a little green-painted chain attached to the brass screw-cap.

The elm tree, with the great gray wound in the bark, kidney-shaped, into which he always put his hand—to feel the cold but

living wood. The injury, he had been sure, was due to the gnaw-
ings of a tethered horse. But now it deserved only a passing palm,
a merely tolerant eye. There were more important things.
Miracles. Beyond the thoughts of trees, mere elms. Beyond the
thoughts of sidewalks, mere stone, mere brick, mere cement. Beyond the thoughts even of his own shoes, which trod these sidewalks obediently, bearing a burden—far above—of elaborate
mystery. He watched them. They were not very well polished;
he had neglected them, for a very good reason: they were one of
the many parts of the increasing difficulty of the daily return to
daily life, the morning struggle. To get up, having at last opened
one's eyes, to go to the window, and discover no snow, to wash,
to dress, to descend the curving stairs to breakfast——

At whatever pain to others, nevertheless, one must persevere
in severance, since the incommunicability of the experience demanded it. It was desirable, of course, to be kind to Mother and
Father, especially as they seemed to be worried, but it was also
desirable to be resolute. If they should decide—as appeared likely
—to consult the doctor, Doctor Howells, and have Paul inspected,
his heart listened to through a kind of dictaphone, his lungs, his
stomach—well, that was all right. He would go through with it.
He would give them answer for question, too—perhaps such an-
swers as they hadn't expected? No. That would never do. For
the secret world must, at all costs, be preserved.

The bird-house in the apple tree was empty—it was the wrong
time of year for wrens. The little round black door had lost its
pleasure. The wrens were enjoying other houses, other nests, re-
moter trees. But this too was a notion which he only vaguely and
grazingly entertained—as if, for the moment, he merely touched
an edge of it; there was something further on, which was already
assuming a sharper importance; something which already teased
at the corners of his eyes, teasing also at the corner of his mind.
It was funny to think that he so wanted this, so awaited it—and
yet found himself enjoying this momentary dalliance with the
bird-house, as if for a quite deliberate postponement and en-
hancement of the approaching pleasure. He was aware of his

delay, of his smiling and detached and now almost uncomprehending gaze at the little bird-house; he knew what he was going to look at next: it was his own little cobbled hill-street, his own house, the little river at the bottom of the hill, the grocer's shop with the cardboard man in the window—and now, thinking of all this, he turned his head, still smiling, and looking quickly right and left through the snow-laden sunlight.

And the mist of snow, as he had foreseen, was still on it—a ghost of snow falling in the bright sunlight, softly and steadily floating and turning and pausing, soundlessly meeting the snow that covered, as with a transparent mirage, the bare bright cobbles. He loved it—he stood still and loved it. Its beauty was paralyzing—beyond all words, all experience, all dream. No fairy story he had ever read could be compared with it—none had ever given him this extraordinary combination of ethereal loveliness with a something else, unnameable, which was just faintly and deliciously terrifying. What was this thing? As he thought of it, he looked upward toward his own bedroom window, which was open—and it was as if he looked straight into the room and saw himself lying half awake in his bed. There he was—at this very instant he was still perhaps actually there—more truly there than standing here at the edge of the cobbled hill-street, with one hand lifted to shade his eyes against the snow-sun. Had he indeed ever left his room, in all this time? since that very first morning? Was the whole progress still being enacted there, was it still the same morning, and himself not yet wholly awake? And even now, had the postman not yet come round the corner? . . .

This idea amused him, and automatically, as he thought of it, he turned his head and looked toward the top of the hill. There was, of course, nothing there—nothing and no one. The street was empty and quiet. And all the more because of its emptiness it occurred to him to count the houses—a thing which, oddly enough, he hadn't before thought of doing. Of course, he had known there weren't many—many, that is, on his own side of the street, which were the ones that figured in the postman's progress—but nevertheless it came as something of a shock to find that there were precisely *six,* above his own house—his own house was the seventh.

Six!

Astonished, he looked at his own house—looked at the door, on which was the number thirteen—and then realized that the whole thing was exactly and logically and absurdly what he ought to have known. Just the same, the realization gave him abruptly, and even a little frighteningly, a sense of hurry. He was being hurried—he was being rushed. For—he knit his brow—he couldn't be mistaken—it was just above the *seventh* house, his *own* house, that the postman had first been audible this very morning. But in that case—in that case—did it mean that tomorrow he would hear nothing? The knock he had heard must have been the knock of their own door. Did it mean—and this was an idea which gave him a really extraordinary feeling of surprise—that he would never hear the postman again?—that tomorrow morning the postman would already have passed the house, in a snow so deep as to render his footsteps completely inaudible? That he would have made his approach down the snow-filled street so soundlessly, so secretly, that he, Paul Hasleman, there lying in bed, would not have waked in time, or waking, would have heard nothing?

But how could that be? Unless even the knocker should be muffled in the snow—frozen tight, perhaps? . . . But in that case——

A vague feeling of disappointment came over him; a vague sadness as if he felt himself deprived of something which he had long looked forward to, something much prized. After all this, all this beautiful progress, the slow delicious advance of the postman through the silent and secret snow, the knock creeping closer each day, and the footsteps nearer, the audible compass of the world thus daily narrowed, narrowed, narrowed, as the snow soothingly and beautifully encroached and deepened, after all this, was he to be defrauded of the one thing he had so wanted —to be able to count, as it were, the last two or three solemn footsteps, as they finally approached his own door? Was it all going to happen, at the end, so suddenly? or indeed, had it already happened? with no slow and subtle gradations of menace, in which he could luxuriate?

He gazed upward again, toward his own window which flashed in the sun; and this time almost with a feeling that it would be better if he *were* still in bed, in that room; for in that case this must still be the first morning, and there would be six more mornings to come—or, for that matter, seven or eight or nine—how could he be sure?—or even more.

III.   After supper, the inquisition began. He stood before the doctor, under the lamp, and submitted silently to the usual thumpings and tappings.

"Now will you please say 'Ah!'?"

"Ah!"

"Now again, please, if you don't mind."

"Ah."

"Say it slowly, and hold it if you can——"

"Ah-h-h-h-h-h——"

"Good."

How silly all this was. As if it had anything to do with his throat! Or his heart, or lungs!

Relaxing his mouth, of which the corners, after all this absurd stretching, felt uncomfortable, he avoided the doctor's eyes, and stared toward the fireplace, past his mother's feet (in gray slippers) which projected from the green chair, and his father's feet (in brown slippers) which stood neatly side by side on the hearth rug.

"Hm. There is certainly nothing wrong there . . . ?"

He felt the doctor's eyes fixed upon him, and, as if merely to be polite, returned the look, but with a feeling of justifiable evasiveness.

"Now, young man, tell me—do you feel all right?"

"Yes, sir, quite all right."

"No headaches? no dizziness?"

"No, I don't think so."

"Let me see. Let's get a book, if you don't mind—yes, thank you, that will do splendidly—and now, Paul, if you'll just read it, holding it as you would normally hold it——"

He took the book and read:

"And another praise have I to tell for this the city our mother, the gift of a great god, a glory of the land most high; the might of horses, the might of young horses, the might of the sea. . . . For thou, son of Cronus, our lord Poseidon, hath throned herein this pride, since in these roads first thou didst show forth the curb that cures the rage of steeds. And the shapely oar, apt to men's hands, hath a wondrous speed on the brine, following the hundred-footed Nereids. . . . O land that art praised above all lands, now is it for thee to make those bright praises seen in deeds."

He stopped, tentatively, and lowered the heavy book.

"No—as I thought—there is certainly no superficial sign of eyestrain."

Silence thronged the room, and he was aware of the focused scrutiny of the three people who confronted him. . . .

"We could have his eyes examined—but I believe it is something else."

"What could it be?" That was his father's voice.

"It's only this curious absent-mindedness—" This was his mother's voice.

In the presence of the doctor, they both seemed irritatingly apologetic.

"I believe it is something else. Now Paul—I would like very much to ask you a question or two. You will answer them, won't you—you know I'm an old, old friend of yours, eh? That's right! . . ."

His back was thumped twice by the doctor's fat fist—then the doctor was grinning at him with false amiability, while with one fingernail he was scratching the top button of his waistcoat. Beyond the doctor's shoulder was the fire, the fingers of flame mak-

ing light prestidigitation against the sooty fireback, the soft sound
of their random flutter the only sound.

"I would like to know—is there anything that worries you?"

The doctor was again smiling, his eyelids low against the little
black pupils, in each of which was a tiny white bead of light.
Why answer him? why answer him at all? "At whatever pain to
others"—but it was all a nuisance, this necessity for resistance,
this necessity for attention; it was as if one had been stood up
on a brilliantly lighted stage, under a great round blaze of spotlight; as if one were merely a trained seal, or a performing dog,
or a fish, dipped out of an aquarium and held up by the tail. It
would serve them right if he were merely to bark or growl. And
meanwhile, to miss these last few precious hours, these hours of
which each minute was more beautiful than the last, more menacing—! He still looked, as if from a great distance, at the beads
of light in the doctor's eyes, at the fixed false smile, and then,
beyond, once more at his mother's slippers, his father's slippers,
the soft flutter of the fire. Even here, even amongst these hostile
presences, and in this arranged light, he could see the snow, he
could hear it—it was in the corners of the room, where the shadow
was deepest, under the sofa, behind the half-opened door which
led to the dining room. It was gentler here, softer, its seethe the
quietest of whispers, as if, in deference to a drawing room, it
had quite deliberately put on its "manners"; it kept itself out
of sight, obliterated itself, but distinctly with an air of saying,
"Ah, but just wait! Wait till we are alone together! Then I will
begin to tell you something new! Something white! something
cold! something sleepy! something of cease, and peace, and the
long bright curve of space! Tell them to go away. Banish them.
Refuse to speak. Leave them, go upstairs to your room, turn out
the light and get into bed—I will go with you, I will be waiting
for you, I will tell you a better story than Little Kay of the
Skates, or The Snow Ghost—I will surround your bed, I will
close the windows, pile a deep drift against the door, so that none
will ever again be able to enter. Speak to them! . . ." It seemed
as if the little hissing voice came from a slow white spiral of

falling flakes in the corner by the front window—but he could not be sure. He felt himself smiling, then, and said to the doctor, but without looking at him, looking beyond him still——

"Oh no, I think not——"

"But are you sure, my boy?"

His father's voice came softly and coldly then—the familiar voice of silken warning.

"You needn't answer at once, Paul—remember we're trying to help you—think it over and be quite sure, won't you?"

He felt himself smiling again, at the notion of being quite sure. What a joke! As if he weren't so sure that reassurance was no longer necessary, and all this cross-examination a ridiculous farce, a grotesque parody! What could they know about it? these gross intelligences, these humdrum minds so bound to the usual, the ordinary? Impossible to tell them about it! Why, even now, even now, with the proof so abundant, so formidable, so imminent, so appallingly present here in this very room, could they believe it?—could even his mother believe it? No—it was only too plain that if anything were said about it, the merest hint given, they would be incredulous—they would laugh—they would say "Absurd!"—think things about him which weren't true. . . .

"Why no, I'm not worried—why should I be?"

He looked then straight at the doctor's low-lidded eyes, looked from one of them to the other, from one bead of light to the other, and gave a little laugh.

The doctor seemed to be disconcerted by this. He drew back in his chair, resting a fat white hand on either knee. The smile faded slowly from his face.

"Well, Paul!" he said, and paused gravely, "I'm afraid you don't take this quite seriously enough. I think you perhaps don't quite realize—don't quite realize—" He took a deep quick breath and turned, as if helplessly, at a loss for words, to the others. But Mother and Father were both silent—no help was forthcoming.

"You must surely know, be aware, that you have not been quite yourself, of late? Don't you know that? . . ."

It was amusing to watch the doctor's renewed attempt at a smile, a queer disorganized look, as of confidential embarrassment.

"I feel all right, sir," he said, and again gave the little laugh.

"And we're trying to help you." The doctor's tone sharpened.

"Yes, sir, I know. But why? I'm all right. I'm just *thinking,* that's all."

His mother made a quick movement forward, resting a hand on the back of the doctor's chair.

"Thinking?" she said. "But my dear, about what?"

This was a direct challenge—and would have to be directly met. But before he met it, he looked again into the corner by the door, as if for reassurance. He smiled again at what he saw, at what he heard. The little spiral was still there, still softly whirling, like the ghost of a white kitten chasing the ghost of a white tail, and making as it did so the faintest of whispers. It was all right! If only he could remain firm, everything was going to be all right.

"Oh, about anything, about nothing—*you* know the way you do!"

"You mean—daydreaming?"

"Oh, no—thinking!"

"But thinking about *what?*"

"Anything."

He laughed a third time—but this time, happening to glance upward toward his mother's face, he was appalled at the effect his laughter seemed to have upon her. Her mouth had opened in an expression of horror. . . . This was too bad! Unfortunate! He had known it would cause pain, of course—but he hadn't expected it to be quite so bad as this. Perhaps—perhaps if he just gave them a tiny gleaming hint——?

"About the snow," he said.

"What on earth?" This was his father's voice. The brown slippers came a step nearer on the hearth-rug.

"But my dear, what do you mean?" This was his mother's voice.

The doctor merely stared.

"Just *snow*, that's all. I like to think about it."

"Tell us about it, my boy."

"But that's all it is. There's nothing to tell. *You* know what snow is?"

This he said almost angrily, for he felt that they were trying to corner him. He turned sideways so as no longer to face the doctor, and the better to see the inch of blackness between the window-sill and the lowered curtain—the cold inch of beckoning and delicious night. At once he felt better, more assured.

"Mother—can I go to bed, now, please? I've got a headache."

"But I thought you said——"

"It's just come. It's all these questions—! Can I, mother?"

"You can go as soon as the doctor has finished."

"Don't you think this thing ought to be gone into thoroughly, and *now?*" This was Father's voice. The brown slippers again came a step nearer, the voice was the well-known "punishment" voice, resonant and cruel.

"Oh, what's the use, Norman——"

Quite suddenly, everyone was silent. And without precisely facing them, nevertheless he was aware that all three of them were watching him with an extraordinary intensity—staring hard at him—as if he had done something monstrous, or was himself some kind of monster. He could hear the soft irregular flutter of the flames; the cluck-click-cluck-click of the clock; far and faint, two sudden spurts of laughter from the kitchen, as quickly cut off as begun; a murmur of water in the pipes; and then, the silence seemed to deepen, to spread out, to become world-long and world-wide, to become timeless and shapeless, and to center inevitably and rightly, with a slow and sleepy but enormous concentration of all power, on the beginning of a new sound. What this new sound was going to be, he knew perfectly well. It might begin with a hiss, but it would end with a roar—there was no time to lose—he must escape. It mustn't happen here——

Without another word, he turned and ran up the stairs.

IV.   Not a moment too soon. The darkness was coming in long white waves. A prolonged sibilance filled the night—a great seamless seethe of wild influence went abruptly across it—a cold low humming shook the windows. He shut the door and flung off his clothes in the dark. The bare black floor was like a little raft tossed in waves of snow, almost overwhelmed, washed under whitely, up again, smothered in curled billows of feather. The snow was laughing; it spoke from all sides at once; it pressed closer to him as he ran and jumped exulting into his bed.

"Listen to us!" it said. "Listen! We have come to tell you the story we told you about. You remember? Lie down. Shut your eyes, now—you will no longer see much—in this white darkness who could see, or want to see? We will take the place of everything. . . . Listen——"

A beautiful varying dance of snow began at the front of the room, came forward and then retreated, flattened out toward the floor, then rose fountain-like to the ceiling, swayed, recruited itself from a new stream of flakes which poured laughing in through the humming window, advanced again, lifted long white arms. It said peace, it said remoteness, it said cold—it said——

But then a gash of horrible light fell brutally across the room from the opening door—the snow drew back hissing—something alien had come into the room—something hostile. This thing rushed at him, clutched at him, shook him—and he was not merely horrified, he was filled with such a loathing as he had never known. What was this? this cruel disturbance? this act of anger and hate? It was as if he had to reach up a hand toward another world for any understanding of it—an effort of which he was only barely capable. But of that other world he still remembered just enough to know the exorcising words. They tore themselves from his other life suddenly——

"Mother! Mother! Go away! I hate you!"

And with that effort, everything was solved, everything became all right: the seamless hiss advanced once more, the long white wavering lines rose and fell like enormous whispering sea-waves, the whisper becoming louder, the laughter more numerous.

"Listen!" it said. "We'll tell you the last, the most beautiful and secret story—shut your eyes—it is a very small story—a story that gets smaller and smaller—it comes inward instead of opening like a flower—it is a flower becoming a seed—a little cold seed—do you hear? we are leaning closer to you——"

The hiss was now becoming a roar—the whole world was a vast moving screen of snow—but even now it said peace, it said remoteness, it said cold, it said sleep.

ROUND BY ROUND

The half-filled bottle stood at the right of the typewriter, and beside it the heavy tumbler; the green-shaded drop-light swung in the draft from the window over his head; he took a drink of whisky and typed in capitals ROUND ONE. He propped up his penciled notes of the fight against the calendar pad, then pulled it nearer, trying to make out his own shorthand. Romero led with left and followed with light right before going into clinch. He typed quickly with his two forefingers. The door of the alcove opened and Cush came in with his coat over his arm, his hat on the back of his head. He dropped the coat on top of his roll-top desk and went to the window.

"Well, and how was the fight of the century?" he said, as if to the office building across the alley, or as if to the fire escape. "Or was it in the bag like all the rest of them?"

"It was a peach, but I wasn't looking. Have a drink."

Cush brought a glass and poured himself a drink.

"These musical shows get my goat, they're all alike. Jesus, what the hell can you say about them? Sprightly and whimsical and fantastic. If you could only say the smut was only so-so, or

A No. 1 Gorgonzola. This one is a piece of cheese, but the chorus is pretty good."

"Was his honor the mayor there?"

"Sure he was—sitting right next to the censor. But he needn't have worried. This one won't be taken off. It wouldn't hurt a fly."

"How do you mean, fly?"

He continued to type, while Cush pulled the black oilcloth cover off his machine. Micky then drove a right to the ribs and left to face. Romero landed a left to face. Zabriski landed right to body. Zabriski drove right and left to body, which Romero cleverly blocked. At this point, he remembered, the man behind him said, "He won't last it out, he won't last ten rounds. Zabriski will kill him, he hasn't got the guts." Zabriski's fiancée, in the fourth row, was being photographed—she was sitting with her mother and two other janes. She looked drunk. This was before she had begun to yell at Zabriski—come on Patsy, come on Pat, give it to him.

"Well," said Cush, to his typewriter, "did Zabriski win it, or who?"

"There is a new champion, and it was a swell fight, science defeats slugging, but I didn't watch it. I was elsewhere."

"All right, I'll bite, where were you?"

"I was picking flowers."

"You mean Ann's given you the bum's rush again, or something. Who is it now?"

He didn't answer at once, he frowned over his notes. Cush turned the sheet of paper into his machine and began typing. Round even. ROUND TWO . . . Zabriski scored a light left to jaw before clinch. Romero reached the champion with two good rights to jaw. The man behind him was saying, say this fellow's good, this fellow is pretty good, watch him. Zabriski can't touch him, look at the way he ties him up. Oh, baby, and was that a sock.

"It isn't the same guy, it's two other fellows. If you know what I mean."

"Well for Christ's sake why don't you call it a day and give her the gate? Why didn't you marry one of those chorus floozies and have someone faithful?"

"Faithful! heh heh. Isn't that a laugh? That word isn't in the dictionary any more, I looked it up. Nowadays all you've got to do is be yourself, that's what the psychologists say, just be yourself. Ann's herself, all right—she's herself with everybody."

"Well, don't let it eat you, she isn't worth it."

Cush was typing quickly. The window shade began flapping in the draft, he got up and gave the cord a twitch so that the shade flew up to the top and wound itself silent with a series of ecstatic slaps against the casement. He leaned for a moment on the window-sill, and looked down into the squalid alley. Forty feet of midnight. Forty feet of emptiness surrounded by rusty fire escapes. But to jump down was no good, he didn't want to die, that wasn't the idea at all. What he wanted was Ann, all right—Ann standing here with her hands on the window-sill, seeing how desolate an alley could be at midnight.

II.   He sat down and took a drink, and turned the yellow copy-paper, and drew the penciled notes still closer. The writing was hard to make out, he had done it carelessly. Romero stepped into a right to the jaw and missed a hard right to the head. Both traded wallops at close quarters without damage. Romero landed a hard right to jaw but missed a left swing. Zabriski's right to body was blocked. Romero missed two hard rights to body. Romero's round. Four tough kids in the balcony began yelling and jumping up and down in their seats—what's the matter, are you yellow, Zabriski, say would you like a nice piece of steak, what's the matter are you afraid of him. And then there was that new buzzer which announced when it was ten seconds before the bell, and the urgent bell following almost immediately, and the two men springing out from their corners, and the seconds climbing swiftly over the ropes with the stools in their hands and the towels over their shoulders.

The enormous canopy hung over the ring, its forty lights looking like a vast brooch of opals, swirls of tobacco smoke ascended
toward the obscure ceiling, and the two great clocks looked
down at the fighters, counting the seconds with important
hands. How much had he missed by watching the clock, looking up over the heads of the two men, over their shoulders,
over the interlaced arms and struggling bodies, beyond the
naked shoulders reddened with repeated blows. A lot, probably. He had taken it down automatically, all except the ninth
and tenth rounds, when he had gone out for a glass of beer; and
those he had copied from Peters.

"Oncet in a while," Cush murmured, "oncet in a while, why
don't they give us a decent show oncet in a while."

"Next time we can swap assignments, I'll throw in Ann for
good measure. That is, if you can find her."

"Well, where is she?"

"Ask me another. She was supposed to be having dinner with
Mabel Innes, but when I called up Mabel, would you believe
it, Mabel didn't know anything about it."

"Looks like bad teamwork, boy."

"Yeah, I thought better of Mabel. She can usually think
pretty fast, but this time I caught her on the wrong foot. *If* you
know what I mean."

The four tough kids had begun yelling, say what will your
fiancée think of you now, go on back to Worcester, Zabriski,
would you like a hot dog. She had turned and shouted angrily
at them, shut up you coots, and then she began saying, over and
over, come on Pat, come on Patsy, give it to him, show him
what you can do, show the kike what you can do, go on in and
finish him, he can't take it, he can dish it out but he can't take
it. ROUND SIX.

He paused in his typing, and straightened his back, and
looked up at the dingy white-washed wall, on which hung a
small photograph of the James family—Henry and William sitting in garden chairs beside a wicker table, Alice standing behind them holding a sunshade, a cocker spaniel sprawled on

the path. The garden was an English garden, an apricot or perhaps a peach tree was crucified flat on the brick wall, and the three good faces looked forward at him with an extraordinary integrity. Integrity! Yes, that was it, it wasn't only the intelligence, the wisdom, it was the profound and simple honesty of all three faces—faces carved slowly out of serene honesty as if out of some sort of benign marble. A book lay on the table—too large for *The Wings of the Dove,* too small for *Varieties of Religious Experience.* What would it be? And what were they thinking, what were they remembering together, as they thus faced the camera, or the world, with such triune simplicity and kindness? They all seemed to be looking steadfastly at the truth.

He interrupted his meditations on the English garden, the peach tree, the three faces, by sitting forward again and dropping his hands at the side of the machine. Cush went out of the alcove with a sheet of yellow paper, holding it up and reading it as he pushed open the door. . . . Romero crossed a right to the jaw as Pat scored with a light left to face. The challenger neatly ducked Zabriski's right and left swings. Both landed light lefts to body. In a sharp mixup Romero outpunched the champion and forced him to break ground. Zabriski had a hard time finding his fighting range, the feathery-footed challenger weaving, bobbing, dancing around, making it impossible for the champion to score. . . . The man behind him was beginning to say, gee, what's the matter with Zabriski, come on Zabriski you're rotten, for Christ's sake keep that left up, keep up that left. Why, he's making a monkey out of you. . . . The four tough kids, ejected from their seats in the balcony, had reappeared on the floor at the back, they were standing up on their chairs and booing, everybody turned to look at them, and a cop began walking slowly down the aisle toward them. One of them had a dirty cross of sticking plaster on his forehead.

Cush came in again, with the sheet of paper still in his hand, and said——

"I don't know what it is, but whenever you really want something in this office you can't get it."

"Ain't that the truth. What is it now?"

"Nobody cares, my boy, nobody cares. They just don't take any interest. By the way, you aren't driving back I suppose, by any chance?"

"No, I'm walking."

"Walking! for the love of God."

III.   They both typed steadily for a while. Above the sound of the machines they could hear the shrill whine of the dynamo in the basement and a vague rumor from the press-room. Now and then a voice floated up from an open window in the alley. The fiancée had certainly been a hard-boiled jane, and no mistake—a genuine gum-chewing blonde, with a jewel in every hole. But she was game, she was loyal. The woman marching by the beaten man! Her voice rose to a scream. Come on, for God's sake Patsy, that left can't hurt you, go on in under that left, make him stop dancing and fight, mix it up with him. Lookit, his knees are getting weak, he's getting groggy. O come on and stand up to him you big boloney. . . . ROUND ELEVEN.

There was something merciless, something fascinating, something profoundly cruel, like the snake hypnotizing the sparrow, in the way Romero's long left kept flashing lightly to Zabriski's right eye, right cheek, jabbing the side of his head, pushing him off, stabbing again and again. The champion, at first mystified, and then annoyed, at last became angry—he tried to rush that grinning superiority, to break down that dancing guard, he pushed the challenger repeatedly to the ropes, trying desperately to get to close quarters, but always to find himself blocked. Above him would always be that eye, that curious half-amorous, half-derisive look, gleaming down at him with a kind of infinite understanding, an understanding faintly and humorously tinged with pity. The fiancée was becoming more and more silent—only now and then, but with flagging conviction, saying —come on now Patsy, come on now bozo, don't let him get away with it. But the murmur from the whole hall grew every moment louder, more excited, more electric—it was becoming obvious that there would be a new champion. If Romero could last, if he could continue to compel Zabriski to box, avoid a last-round knockout—ROUND THIRTEEN.

"I suppose you heard that Bill Coit was through!"

"Yeah. Yeah, I heard it. Too bad. But surprising it didn't happen before."

"And would have, believe me, if it hadn't of been for Mary. That's a game kid, and she deserved better. Right now she ought to be in Arizona or a sanitarium or something."

"Yes, I know."

"The demon rum."

. . . As they shook hands for the final round, Zabriski sent a hard right to Romero's head and sent lefts and rights to body. Romero swung himself off his feet when he aimed a right to Pat's head and dropped to the canvas. Romero made a great rally. While plainly tired, he stood toe to toe with the champion and slugged freely. Romero landed a stinging left jab to Pat's face, while Zabriski dropped a right and left on Romero's body. The champion fought madly, crowding Romero but missing badly. Romero drove home several good rights and lefts to the head to finish the round with a light lead. Romero's round.

The excitement of the decision, the unanimous decision, the whole audience standing on chairs, the ridiculous knock-kneed dance of Romero as he shook his two gloves together in the air high over his head, all this was much less impressive than Zabriski lying on the table to be rubbed down, just saying laconically I was overtrained, I knew two days ago I couldn't make the weight. Fifteen pounds was too much, now I know better.

He fell asleep under the hands of the rubber, while his fiancée was having a drink with the manager outside the door. Sure, she was saying, I know, you don't need to tell me, I wasn't born yesterday. You just watch him next time.

And, of course, yes, there would be a next time. He pulled

the yellow sheet out of the machine. Twelve o'clock. Cush had stood up and was putting his coat on.

"If you're going down, will you take this, Cush? I want to write a letter."

"Sure. Good night."

"Good night."

iv.   But it wasn't a letter exactly—he got up and began looking at the photograph of the James family once more. What he wanted to say to her was something about that —something about those people sitting there in a garden. If it were somehow possible to say that. To make her realize what that could mean.

"My dear, instead of writing you a letter, in the ordinary sense of the word, or instead of arguing with you further about this issue which has reared its scaly head between us, or telling you again for the thousandth time that I simply cannot bring myself to believe in this easy and casual habit of promiscuous flirtation, which you and so many other men and women eagerly defend, I am going to do something else. Perhaps this means that I've given up all hope of convincing you, perhaps it doesn't; it may even mean that I think any attempt to do so is now too late, since the gulf between us is already so immense that the wings of Father Imago himself seem too frail for such a voyage. Are you in fact not already lost to me? am I not lost to you? When we argue about it, no matter how amiably, we speak in turn, but neither of us listens, neither of us hears. It is no use my repeating again that I do not like to see you being kissed by every Tom, Dick, and Harry who claims that privilege on the ground of his friendship for us both; it is no use my saying that I experience a deep revulsion, a deep schism of the spirit, when I see you yield yourself, not unwillingly, to attentions even more sensuous than these, not only in my presence, but in the presence of other people as well. You will merely reply, wearily, that I am jealous, which I am; or that I am a prude, which I am not; you will say again, as you have so often said, that these things do not matter, that these little physical manifestations do not matter—as if one could ever for a minute separate the physical from the spiritual, as if the body were not just as much a part of the soul as the soul is a part of the body. If body and soul are indeed at all separable, which I doubt, then they are separable only in the sense that a pair of dancers is separable: as long as they dance, they are one; when they separate, the dance is over, something vital has come to an end. It is this disunion which seems to me evil, seems to me destructive. To love with the soul, but not with the body, is to love God, and that is perhaps a kind of death; to love with the body, but not the soul, is certainly a kind of death, for it starves the soul as swiftly as the other starves the body; only when we permit body and soul to love together do we really live. Before me as I write is a photograph of three people. What I really want to tell you about is these three people. I would like to tell you what they mean to me, what art-shape they made of their lives, what it might mean to you or to anybody to *realize* what they are as they sit there——"

He dropped his hands from the machine in a sudden despair. It was impossible, it was a kind of absurd day-dream, it was unreal, he ought to have known better. It could not be done, would never be done. It could not be said. You felt these things or you didn't. . . . Instead, they would quarrel, and then quarrel again, they would quarrel day after day and night after night, there would be no end to it forever.

THISTLEDOWN

The dandelion seed, when it blows, does not know where it is going: it will cross miles of meadow, sail over forests of pine, travel down mountain gorges, be caught for a day in a cobweb, and at last find its growing place in the least likely of spots. It will perhaps try to grow in an old shoe, or an empty tomato tin, or a crack in a wall. And, of course, it will have no memory of the poor plant, leagues away, from which it set out on its journey. There is a kind of pathos in this, and something beautiful also. And it is with just such an image that I always think of Coralyn, that gallantest of creatures, when I try to tell her story. There is, to be quite truthful, no story—at best, only the materials for a story. Life seldom arranges itself in an obvious pattern. It may surprise us—and often does—or it may shock us, or turn swiftly from melodrama to comedy, or from the humdrum to tragedy; but how few lives do we know in which there is any perceptible "form," any design of the sort that novelists employ! Coralyn's story is at best a chronicle—hardly even that. It is a series of episodes, an uneven progress in time; it is as aimless as the voyage of the dandelion thistle, and almost as purposeless. And as I look back on it, with its span of five or six years, I even wonder, sometimes, whether

Coralyn, any more than the thistledown, remembered where she had come from, or knew where she was going. This is an exaggeration, of course—that she did, now and then, remember, was attested by those strange despairs into which now and then she would suddenly pass. Abruptly, she would drop her gayety, her frivolity, her tomboyish violences and absurdities, and be plunged into a half-hour of despair and weeping with which I never in the least knew how to deal. Did she, at such moments, remember and foresee? Did she have some sudden foreknowledge of doom? She would never tell me. All that she would say to me, when I tried to comfort her, was the phrase (which always struck terror to my heart), "I'm afraid! I'm afraid."

What was it that she was afraid of? Was it life itself, perhaps? Not, certainly, in any obviouse sense. She was a brave girl, clear-eyed, clear-headed, straightforward (with some exceptions), and I never knew anyone who so consistently, even recklessly, took life with both hands. It may have been this, indeed, that she was afraid of; she may have guessed, sooner than we did, and more accurately, the dark forces that were at work in her and to what end they would bring her at last. For there was little or no self-deception in Coralyn. If now and then she flinched a little from telling us, or telling me, the truth about herself, I am sure she never flinched from facing the truth where it most, after all, matters—in her conscience and consciousness. When she had occasion to be dishonest, she knew it.

One of the earliest instances of this was at the very beginning. She had come to act as secretary to my wife, who was an authoress; Mabel had found her through a local employment agency. What Coralyn was doing in New Haven, where we then lived, we couldn't make out. She was vague about this, only telling us that she was a graduate of a Western university, that she came of an old Virginia family, that her relatives were, with one exception (a cousin), dead, and that she had come East simply because of a conviction that there were more opportunities, of a mildly literary sort, in New England. Heaven knows where she had got this idea, or why she should, of all places, have picked out New Haven. Possibly the presence of the university had something to do with it—I seem to remember that this is what we thought at the time. Anyway, we both liked her and believed her. She was charming, gentle, quiet, refined, never obtrusive, delightful to look at without being exactly pretty, and extremely intelligent. She was then, I think, about twenty-two. One had only to see her for a moment to realize that she was by no means the ordinary sort of secretary. She was always quite beautifully dressed, but without any flashiness, and struck me as singularly uncorrupted by those minor vulgarities of the moment which so many of her generation regarded as the sign manual of sophistication. If she rouged, one didn't guess it. In fact, the most pronounced impression she made, with her candid forehead and gray eyes and straight carriage, and a kind of touching simplicity of speech, was of an almost frightening unworldliness and innocence. I know now, of course, that this appearance was by no means entirely true—or true, at any rate, only to the role for which she had cast herself. And isn't this a very essential kind of truth? She was escaping from something of which, for various not very good reasons, she was ashamed; and she was molding herself, or trying to, very courageously, according to an ideal.

About all this she was, I am sure, quite explicit with herself. I imagine she said to herself: "Now Coralyn, you little fool, here is your chance! Let's have no sentimental nonsense about it. It won't help the Wassons to know things about you that they needn't know. It won't help you either. For the love of Pete, keep your mouth shut, be a lady, be refined, or learn to be, and take one clear step upward or forward to the sort of life you want to lead. Onward to literature and New York and, maybe, a good marriage! . . . And anyway there'll be good 'contacts.' " . . . And she played her part to perfection. Mabel—poor soul—always said she was the best secretary she ever had. Not only in the mere drudgery, either—for by degrees, as the two women came to know and like each other, Coralyn was more and more called upon to act also in a critical capacity. I myself was never much use at this. My wife was a writer of best-sellers

—historical romances and such—and my own tastes simply didn't happen to run in that direction; my passion for Trollope was Mabel's despair. But Coralyn, as by degrees she came out of her shell, or was invited out of it by Mabel, and as she was more and more permitted to step out of her position as employee and assume that of friend, became, as Mabel used often to say, invaluable. She was an excellent judge of "what the public wants," and with this, also, she was an uncommonly keen judge of detail, and of matters of style. When I came home from the office at the end of the day, as that first winter passed, it was increasingly often that I found Coralyn still in the drawing room with Mabel, discussing the latest novel over a cup of tea or a cocktail. From this, it was by the easiest of transitions that she became Mabel's most intimate friend; in so far as poor Mabel, who never had much genius for friendship, could be said to *have* an intimate friend. Coralyn was kept not only for tea, but for dinner. She was kept not only for dinner, but overnight. She stayed with us for week-ends, she sometimes ran the house for us when we went to New York, she filled in at bridge, she helped with the preparations for parties, and, in short, she ended by becoming, before many months were over, practically a member of the household. Which, as I see now, was exactly what she was after.

And this brings me to the first point, in the story, at which I myself became at all intimately involved with Coralyn; I will try to tell it as simply as possible. From the outset, I had been fearfully attracted to her. So much so, I recall, that at first I was almost studiously rude to her, out of a sort of instinctive fear. At the time, Mabel and I had been married ten years. We had no children, we had separate interests, and while we were as fond of each other as the average married pair, nevertheless we were no longer, naturally, wildly in love. Just the same I was, as I always was, extraordinarily fond of Mabel, had the very highest admiration for her, and wouldn't have hurt her for worlds. Nor had I ever had any great desire for extra-conjugal adventures, or to be any kind of Don Juan. All this came into my mind when Coralyn appeared; we had no sooner looked at each other than I experienced a dread. I knew that I attracted her; I knew that if I let her guess that I too was attracted there would be trouble; I wanted to see her, but also I wanted to avoid trouble, and to avoid hurting Mabel. Consequently, while I took great pains to tell Mabel that I thought Coralyn an admirable person, I was, as I say, very often deliberately rude to Coralyn herself. I made a point, from time to time, of quite obviously avoiding her. On several occasions when it happened that we were left alone in the house together I made palpably lying excuses and left her; I could see that she was distressed. If she tried to draw me into conversation *à deux,* I would answer her monosyllabically, or retreat to my study for a pretense of work; there to smoke cigarettes one after another and to wonder what would happen. . . . I might have guessed.

For it is plain enough now that my tactics were precisely the worst in the world. What could have been better calculated to attract the girl than this studied unapproachableness, this air of remoteness and superiority? Particularly when one recalls that she herself was drawn to me from the beginning, and also that she was at that very time struggling almost obsessedly to get away from her own sense of inferiority and obscurity. The result was that I became for her a symbol; I was the obstacle itself: for the time being, the goal itself; I was something to be overcome. I doubt whether she phrased this explicitly, or separated out the various elements of which the complex was composed. She only knew, instinctively, that she was there, in that queer house, simply to be near me, and in the hope of getting nearer still. Much later, years later, she told me that she had from the outset thought me the nicest man she had ever met, and the wisest—adding, to soften the blow, that she had also always thought me something of a fool. She didn't exactly want to fall in love with me—what she wanted was to *learn* from me, to make me a kind of father, or even (I don't know at which stage she thought of this) a father-lover. But the motive anyway was a desire for knowledge; she simply thought I could help her. . . . I often wonder whether I ever did.

II.   Certainly not at the first climax of our little affair, our absurd little affair. There was never anything more grotesque, more delicious, more ridiculous, more lovely, more pathetically or beautifully a failure. It was early in the spring that it came about. Suddenly, one day, my wife was invited by wire to give a lecture in Baltimore as substitute for another lecturer who had failed to appear. As it happened, we had just lost our two maids; a comic interlude into which I won't digress. Mabel was in a panic. Who was to look after things— the dog, the cat, the canary, not to mention poor Philip, her husband? It was then that Coralyn stepped forward; this was her cue for effective—oh, very effective—entrance. This was the chance for which she had been waiting, and for which she and I, for months past—she consciously and I unconsciously—had been elaborately preparing. It was not for nothing now that we had had so little to do with each other, had spoken together so little, had appeared even to avoid each other. More than once Mabel had reproached me for my indifference to Coralyn. She had, therefore, not an atom of a suspicion that she was about to be betrayed. She accepted Coralyn's offer with joy, took the first train out of New Haven, to be gone for three nights, and there, heaven help us, we were.

What happened was inevitable; if only because we had resisted it so long. We came together as naturally as leaf touches leaf or the grass bends to the wind. As soon as we sat down together at the dinner table, and looked at each other across the candles, we both knew it; our talk became a mere subterfuge; and when afterwards we went out to the garden, where it was growing dark, and she put out her hand to touch a lilac bud, it was really to me she put out her hand, and I took it. When I kissed her, she laughed into my mouth, and turned her face away, and then turned it back again. After that, everything was madness.

And the next day it was madder still, but in a different way. For the first time I knew Coralyn as she really was—a hoyden, a tomboy, the very wildest of creatures; her mouse-like demureness had merely been a surface. She assured me she was not in love with me—why should she be? She laughed at me for being a sentimental fool—I told her that I, for my part, was falling in love with her; which indeed I was. I sat on a tree stump in the garden, while she smoked a cigarette. I felt very wretched.

"You'll get over it, nice old Philip"—she ruffled my hair—"You ought to know better. Why drag in feelings and things? I was in love once myself, or thought I was, but now I think it's all the 'bunk.' You know what that means? Or are you too old-fashioned in New Haven."

"You're a demon, Coralyn."

"I'm a changeling. I have no heart."

"Some day you'll find it—maybe too late."

"Oh, don't for God's sake be sententious. . . . All the same I'm afraid! I'm afraid. . . ."

"What of?"

"Oh, ask me another. I don't know. I wish I did. Where do we go from here?"

It was then that she told me about Michael, her sweetheart. She had been engaged to him for two years. He was an ensign in the Navy. Finally she had decided that she really wasn't in love with him at all.

"But I thought I'd give the poor kid a square deal," she said, looking at me soberly, "so I came to Newport to meet him and tell him about it. I spent a week with him—just, you know—to make it easier for him."

"You mean you lived with him?"

"Sure. Why not? . . . Which is why you found me in New Haven."

"What *about* Michael."

She shrugged her young shoulders, arched her eyebrows, made

a light gesture as of dusting some infinitesimal object off her fingers.

"He was nice. . . . But why should we get married and ruin each other? . . . Oh, no! Oh, no! I'd outgrown him. Outclimbed him. And that was that."

"Well, well."

"Well, well . . . let's go for a ride."

We rode, we walked, we dined, we danced, we dropped in at a show of paintings (where I kissed her in a deserted room before a brilliant water-color by Dodge MacKnight), and all the while we talked feverishly, jokingly, uneasily, in a kind of attempt to find just what our odd relationship was going to be. She was very detached, very cynical, very passionate, but also very remote. I was—I am ashamed to say—eager; it was my first transgression, and I hoped it would be prolonged.

Coralyn made fun of me.

"Don't look at me like that when we're dancing. The cops'll pinch you."

"They'll think we're engaged."

"They'll think you're my sugar daddy! . . . I *love* this thing— what *is* this thing?"

And then there was Mabel. Would she mind, would she guess? Would she mind very much if she did guess?

"But there won't," said Coralyn, gently, murmuringly, "be very much *to mind,* will there?"

And as a matter of fact, there wasn't; Coralyn saw to that. She farced the whole thing. Divinely passionate one moment, she was a clown the next. If I may put it in the vernacular, she deliberately set out to raise hell with anything that might threaten to become a "grand passion." And she was singularly successful. In twenty-four hours she had, as she herself put it, spanked it out of me. I accused her of being heartless—I accused her of being everything. I was angry, I threatened her with a dire future, a future without home, without friends, without love—she laughed and threw a slipper at me. She told me that I ought to have been a Shakspearean actor. She suggested that my eyebrows ought to have been purple, that I needed a beard (at which point she imitated quite admirably the bleat of a goat), and then, abruptly kissing me, she said that she liked me best when I was slightly tight. (She had seen me tight just once.) I was not only defenseless—I actually found myself liking this new Coralyn, and this new friendship, better than the old. . . . By the time that Mabel came back, our new terms had been so well formulated that Mabel saw or suspected nothing. Our three lives went on just as before, until, some while later, Coralyn suddenly announced that she had a chance for a job in New York. She went, and for three months we heard not a word from her.

III.   What we then heard was the somewhat surprising news that Coralyn had gone into business for herself —she had opened a literary agency in partnership with a young Frenchman, a Greenwich Village Frenchman, named something-or-other Rivière. She solicited my wife's business, and Mabel politely refused, but asked her down for a week-end. To this Coralyn replied that she was too busy, but suggested that if we should happen to be in New York we should look her up; she had an apartment (as I recall it) in East 35th Street. As it happened, I was planning at that very moment to go to New York on business; and when, two weeks later, I took the train, I wired Coralyn to meet me, if she could, for lunch. I don't know quite what I expected would occur; but I do know that I thought our little affair would have a kind of recrudescence—as indeed, in a way, it did. When we met, amid the marble columns of the Hotel Belmont lobby, and sat down together on a gilt and red-plush sofa, I came under her spell as sharply and deliciously as before; and she too (as she told me later) felt not only a revival of her feeling for me, but a deepening also. As a matter of fact, it was at this moment that she began to make a sort of father of me, or father-confessor; though other feelings were mixed with this as well. As for me, I was again in love with her, but in a very curious and unanalyzable way. Did I feel sorry for her? Perhaps. At any rate, I noticed at the very outset a change in her, and one that disturbed me, made me a little unhappy. She was prettier, maturer, gentler, softer—but also—could I be mistaken?—in some indefinable way cheaper. Greenwich Village, or New York, had already left its mark on her.

"You've got on too much lipstick," I said.

"And observe the eyebrows—I've plucked them out."

"So I see. The exquisite eyebrows of the night-moth."

"And admire the snakeskin shoes, for God's sake! Aren't they the bee's moccasins?" She flourished a foot at me, a very smart foot, and prodded my ankle with her toe, laughing.

I admired her shoes, her frock, her hat, her gloves, taking the opportunity to pinch her little finger; and at once the same sort of delirium came over us that had so suddenly overwhelmed us at New Haven. But with a difference. For while we continued our light banter, at lunch, over a bad bottle of wine, I was continually aware, beneath it, of a deep melancholy, a note as of desperateness, even of tragedy. She was, I felt sure, unhappy, or bewildered—she made one think of a lost child. Even when she laughed—which as always she did a good deal—I seemed to detect an evasiveness in her, a fugitiveness, a flight from something; her eyes would explore mine and waver away; she would make a joke, only the next instant to catch her breath as if in tension. Her agency, she said, was flourishing. Her partner was a charmer—she had met him at a party.

"Are you in love with him?"

"Oh, no! You know my notions about love. It's a fake."

"But you *are* in love with somebody. I can see it."

"Have I got red wings on? Are my eyes like stars? Philip, you're a scream. Where's your purple beard?"

"I shaved it off. But you're unhappy."

"No. But I'm afraid! . . . Let's get a taxi."

Her apartment, it turned out, was sublet from Rivière, who had "taken a room in the Village." Some of his things were still

about—a raincoat, a couple of hats, a pipe rack hung with dirty
pipes, a violin case. She waved a hand at them.

"He's coming to get them—some day. Would you like to meet
him?"

"No. Why should I?"

"I'd like to know what you think of him. He wants to marry
me."

"The devil he does!"

"But I don't think—oh, I don't know."

I put my arms around her—she rested her hands on my breast
and kissed me, at first lightly, quickly, repeatedly, laughing a
little, and then, all of a sudden, with an extraordinary ecstasy
of surrender, murmuring softly into my mouth as she did so.

"You're nice, Philip."

"So are you, Coralyn. But you're unhappy."

"Yes."

"Tell me why."

"I will—but not now."

"Tell me."

"Don't be a nuisance."

She drew back from me, laughing, her hands still on my
breast, and I saw that tears were in her eyes.

"I'll tell you at breakfast," she said, "and in the meantime,
for God's sake, let's be happy!"

And we were, with such happiness, such ecstasy—perhaps the
sharper for that—as can come to two people who know, every
moment, beneath, around, above their happiness, the shadow
of tragedy. Perhaps the sense of time, the sense of doom, played
into our hands. At all events, everything conspired to make that
twenty-four hours the happiest we ever knew together. It
rained, and we walked in the rain all the way to the museum,
where we scandalized the other visitors (who were very few) by
making an absurdity of everything. Coralyn was at her best; at
her best and most tomboyish and most ridiculous. The Turners
reminded her of dishes on which poached eggs and strawberry

jam had been successively eaten; she whinnied before the El Grecos; and the Rodin sculptures, she pretended, made her sick, reminding her of the "sort of pale underdeveloped over-involved things you see in bottles in a medical school." She kissed me behind the model of the Parthenon, before Manet's parrot portrait, in the presence of a mummy, and—what was worse—in the presence also of a very solemn museum attendant, who had come unexpectedly from behind the plaster horse. She declared that I had gray hair, and that she was a disgrace to me; taking my handkerchief out of my pocket, as she said so, to blow her nose.

"You're an old fogey, Philip."

"I know it."

"You're a darling, Philip."

"Of course."

"I think you ought to wear sideburns and a stock, and carry a gray umbrella."

"Why not a bird-cage?"

"Or an organ and a monkey. Let me be your monkey, Philip."

And at once she imitated, startlingly, a monkey, grinning rabidly and searching for fleas under her armpits. She was per-fectly hideous; dowagers and art students stared; and I adored her, at the same time leading her quickly into another gallery.

After that we walked in the Park in the rain, admired the wet riders on their wet horses, admired the reservoir, the camels, the ducks and swans (I told her about the Italian immigrant, newly arrived, who though they were wild, and shot a brace for his supper), and proceeded down Sixth Avenue (my favorite street) to a French *table d'hôte* dinner. Everything was as delightful as could be. We dawdled over the bad cocktails, we dawdled again over the cognac and coffee, amused ourselves with the conversa-tions at the adjacent tables, all the while with a feeling that we were avoiding the issue. Coralyn was gay; she told me about the wild parties she had been to, in the Village, and of the freaks she had met. Epicenes of both sexes. Professional Bohemians, careful cultivators of the attic and the coal-hole. She assured me that I wouldn't at all like the sort of thing; I agreed with her. Once at a dance a well-known novelist had bitten her on the shoulder, just before he passed out in the middle of the floor. So-and-so, the publisher, had insisted on seeing her home—very affectionately—and had been sick in the cab. She had made a friend of a policeman, who had introduced her to a new speak-easy—a very nice one. She had gone with him there several times. And so on and so on. . . .

I might have guessed what was coming, of course, but I didn't; and in consequence, as I see now, I made things all the harder for her. What she wanted was sympathy, understanding, guidance; what I gave her, unwittingly, late that night, was a rather nasty little lecture. I had had a few drinks too many, and her unshakable flippancy had ended by irritating me. I told her once again that she had no soul, no heart, would be lost; and while I did indeed say these things without anger, I nevertheless said them seriously, and said them (what was worse) between kisses. How intolerably that must have hurt her! And what a fool she must have thought me. That she took it admirably is, in the circumstances, the highest praise I could give her. She merely covered my mouth with her hand, and said, "Wait," and then, with a curious air of abstraction and gentleness, ran her fingers through my hair, stopped the gesture as soon as it had begun, laughed, and fell asleep.

And at breakfast it all came out.

"Now," she said, "holding up this nice red apple in the healthy morning sunlight, and preparing to bite it, I'll tell you. I've been bad."

"Bad?"

"Bad! Very bad. New Haven wouldn't have any idea."

"You wouldn't kid me, would you?"

"I've had six affairs since I saw you last. And they've been a perfect scream."

"Coralyn!"

"Oh, don't for God's sake look pious! Have a prune."

"I don't like prunes. They look so senile."

"So do you."

"Well, tell me about it. I don't know whether to say I'm sorry or glad."

"Why be either? Ain't nature grand? I've had a good time."

"No, I don't think you have. I suppose Rivière is one of them!"

"Of course—don't be an ass. So was the policeman. So was the novelist. So was the publisher."

"Coralyn, you're a damned fool."

"Don't I know it? But I wanted to hear you say it."

She smiled across the small bare table at me, and as she smiled her eyes suddenly brightened with tears. Unblinking, still smiling, she let the tears fall. And without the slightest change in her voice she said:

"I'm afraid, Philip! I'm afraid. I really am."

We talked about it all morning. She said she couldn't understand it—it had just happened. She had been bored, lonely, wanted excitement, needed to feel that men were attracted to her, liked the attentions of men, especially literary men. As for the policeman—well, that was just a mad and slightly drunken experiment. What harm was there in it? She didn't regret it at all.

I began to feel slightly sick about the whole thing, and found myself replying to her in arid monosyllables. Then I was ashamed. I told her frankly that all this had somewhat changed my feelings about her; she smiled, and said she was sure it had. Then, assuring her repeatedly that I had no real moral objections to what she was doing, I begged her to believe, as I believed, that such a way of living would bring her to ruin. She would become spiritually bankrupt. The whole thing would become meaningless. She wasn't sure—she quarreled with me about the word spiritual. What was spiritual? I found, not unnaturally, that I wasn't any too sure of its meaning myself; so I shifted to more material grounds. What of her life, viewed as a whole? Suppose she wanted, later, to marry, etc., etc., and the man she wanted to marry. . . .

"Yes, darling Philip, you're so good but I know all that. That's in the first grade, you learn it when you learn genders and conjugations."

"So you do. But you learn other truths as well; and truth is truth."

"And west is left and east is right, and never the twain shall meet."

"Good Lord, Coralyn, you're hopeless. What's the use of talking to you?"

"None, I fear. I've simply got to go through with it. Ain't it awful?"

"No—it really isn't. Don't, whatever you think, think that!" (This was my one feeble moment of magnanimity.) "It will come out all right. But for heaven's sake don't be in such a rush to seize life with both hands—! You'll get them both burnt."

"I burned both hands before the fire of life: let that be on my little headstone."

More and more, as we bantered in this fashion, I had a feeling of entire helplessness. What on earth could I do? My time was growing short—I knew I must leave her at twelve, not to see her again for months—and this only added to my misery. What was going to happen to her now? She liked me, she liked to think that I respected, or even loved her; and now I had unmistakably given her the impression that I no longer did either. I walked up and down her shabby little sitting room, looking now and then angrily at Rivière's pipes and coats and things (what sort of chap was he, anyway?) and tried vainly to formulate some sort of plan. The only thing I could think of was to urge her to marry. But why, she countered, if it was her nature, as it seemed to be, to be frivolous, should she marry? For in that case she would make not one, but two, people unhappy. She hadn't yet encountered a man with whom she would want to live for more than a week. She thought men as a race were detestable, conceited, boring creatures, interesting only because they were so naively and disingenuously unscrupulous.

What answer was there to this? None. I looked at my watch,

and glared at Coralyn, and packed my things, frowning, and all she did was to offer me from time to time a marshmallow or an apple or a little present for Mabel. A present for Mabel! A singular moment for that, as Coralyn, confound her, damned well knew. And nevertheless, here was this extraordinary thing between us, this deep understanding which not even petulant badinage could effectually conceal. We were both of us unhappy, and we parted unhappy, and the only assurance I extracted from Coralyn was that she would really, and quite soon, come down to New Haven for a week-end. . . . Even to this, however, she added that she would probably bring a young man, a prospective bridegroom, for my "august inspection and approval." . . . And, laughing once more, she shut the door between us.

IV.　　As it turned out, it wasn't merely months before I saw Coralyn again—it was a year and a half. I wrote to her twice and got no answer. (I suggested that she reply to me at my office.) About seven months after the New York episode, a postcard came from Paris, addressed in her handwriting, with nothing on it but the word "So!", a cryptic utterance which I confess I never fathomed. What on earth did she mean by it? Mabel and I turned it over and over (it was a picture of the Eiffel Tower!) but came to no conclusion. Perhaps her business had taken her abroad? I thought of her French partner, and said nothing. Perhaps she was married? A holiday merely? In which case she was, of course, prosperous. . . .

All of which was to be solved for me when she did, eventually, turn up, but only after (and only very shortly after) another odd little episode had befallen me.

It began with a telephone call. A male voice asked me if I could dine with him—he was an old friend of Coralyn. He didn't want to see me in the office, in office hours—it was rather a private and delicate business—did I mind? My curiosity was aroused and I made an appointment for dinner with him.

It was Michael, of course. A nice chap, simple, straightforward,

fair-haired and blue-eyed—and by this time a full-fledged lieutenant. I liked him immediately, and I think he liked me. I told
him I had heard a good deal about him from Coralyn; he blushed.
He then apologized, somewhat hesitantly, for intruding on me
in this fashion, but, as he said, he got the impression from Coralyn that I cared a good deal for her, and as he did himself, always
had and always would, he had thought he would like to talk
to me.

What ensued was extraordinary. We both put our cards on the
table, quite without jealousy, and in an entire unanimity of devotion to Coralyn. He had guessed that Coralyn had had an affair
with me—though, as he added, he knew Coralyn well enough to
know there was nothing so remarkable in that. (An observation
which a little disconcerted me.) He spoke very gently and slowly
—in a quiet low-pitched voice, looking at me shyly and steadily—
and I couldn't help feeling all the while that he was the man
that Coralyn should have stuck to. Why hadn't she? Not enough
imagination in him? A little too Western? too young? . . . I
couldn't imagine, and meanwhile he was telling me that in the
last analysis it was because he felt sure I loved Coralyn (as who
couldn't) that he had come to me. I assured him that I did indeed love her—that she was a very charming and very talented
girl. And then, after a pause, he suddenly asked me if I knew
that she was going to the devil.

After that, the deluge. He had known a great deal more about
it than I did—not because she had seen him, or permitted him
to come to her, but simply because, in a sort of dog-like spirit of
devotion, he had made it his business to keep watch on her. I
don't know yet how he did it, but he did. Detectives, perhaps?
I don't suppose he could have afforded it; nor do I believe he
would have stooped to it. At all events, he knew. He had the
names at his fingers' ends: all the Toms, Dicks and Harrys. All
the addresses at which she had lived—and they were many. The
jobs she had had—ditto. One after another. The literary agency
had been a fiasco from the first, not a red cent in it, only a bluff,
and Rivière all the time supporting her. (With a pang I recog-

nized that at the time I had almost divined this.) The lampshade shop—did I know about the lampshade shop? Well, the lampshade shop (Christ! he said) had been endowed, *pro tem,* by some blankety-blank fairy of a newspaper art-critic. He had met him once at a party in Washington Square, and had with difficulty refrained from beating him up. He carried a gold-headed cane and had a purple handkerchief sticking out of his pocket. Did I know what he meant? I knew what he meant. Then there was the publisher, and the Socialist Messiah. . . .

We groaned together, we had several drinks together, we played pool; but what, I asked him, could we do about it? And he had no solution to offer, nor had I. He went on to tell me about her past. About this it turned out that she had, to put it mildly, prevaricated. She was not a graduate of a Western university—she had had one year at a small commercial college in St. Louis. Nor did she come of an old Virginia family—far from it. In fact, her people were perilously close (so he said) to what is called in the South "poor white trash." Moreover, her mother was still alive, very much and very dreadfully alive; she was, Michael said, chalking his cue, a terrible woman: vulgar, whining, aggressive, spiteful, and altogether a thorn in poor Coralyn's side. Coralyn had been good to her—had sent her money faithfully (she lived in South Carolina) on condition that she left Coralyn alone to make her own career without interference. No wonder Coralyn had pretended her relatives were dead; there was nothing, said Michael, which she so much dreaded as that some day her mother would turn up in the North and try to attach herself. She had continually threatened to do so. And if I had ever seen the object! . . . Christ, what a woman.

In the light of which, when Mabel and I discussed it later that night, we decided that we liked Coralyn more than ever. A typical case of a gallant creature trying to pull herself out of the mud by the roots, and on the whole succeeding. Who wouldn't, in the circumstances, have lied a little? Who wouldn't have tried to build a romance, given such a background, or, what was gallanter still, tried to live up to it? And the quite extraordinary

refinement and subtlety and wit which Coralyn, with no upbringing to speak of, had achieved! As for her sense of values, moral
values—naturally I didn't go into that with Mabel, and Mabel
knew nothing about it. I said not a word to her about Michael's
report that she was "going to the devil"; I merely put it that he
was worried because she seemed to have dropped him. . . .

And Mabel, poor soul, being a romantic herself, and having
into the bargain a novelist's imagination (of a sort), was at once
deeply stirred and wrote Coralyn a long sympathetic letter. It
was this that brought about Coralyn's final visit to New Haven.
An answer came from her, as usual from a new address in New
York (whereupon I wondered 'Who is it now?'), and a few weeks
later Coralyn herself appeared.

But not alone. Just as she had threatened, she brought along
with her a young hopeful; apologized for him gayly and breathlessly, saying that she had been simply unable—did we mind?—
to get rid of him; and that if we wanted to we could just send
him back to Bank Street, where he belonged. The young man,
whose name was Pope, effeminate, long-haired, pallidly sensuous
and dissipated-looking, stood by with offensive assurance while
she said all this, and obviously had no intention of going anywhere; just as obviously too, had been instructed by Coralyn to
stick it out. He stuck it out, we had to ask him to stay, and stay
he did. He was by way of being a budding novelist, whose bud
has since, thank God, been nipped; and immediately he was all
professional attention to Mabel, with an air of patronage which
infuriated me. Mabel didn't see through it at all.

As for Coralyn, she had begun to lose her looks. She was thinner, her face was older, she was quite shamelessly made up, she
was expensively and a little too brilliantly dressed, but as amusing as ever. Just the same, I was annoyed by the whole proceeding,
and didn't attempt to conceal it from her. During the afternoon
and dinner I said hardly a word to her, contriving (exactly as I
used to do in the very first stages of our acquaintance) to keep
out of her way on one or another thin pretext, and, of course,
with a quite conscious and deliberate intention of hurting her.

I succeeded. I even made a point, at dinner, of addressing all my remarks, much as I disliked doing so, to the young worm opposite me; and I did so, moreover, with an undisguised undercurrent of sarcasm.

The result of this was very painful, and I'm now ashamed of the whole episode, extremely so. For—a little after dinner—while Mabel and the worm were discussing the form of the novel in the garden, with the highest of high seriousness, their uplifted voices floating in through the open window mixed with the scent of sun-warmed phlox, Coralyn came quietly into my study. Her face was somber, soft, hurt—I had seen that expression before, and it always moved me. All the same, I was stubborn, and made no move to speak, merely looking at her with a hard detachment —as if, perhaps, she were merely a servant girl who had come to make an apology. She stood at a little distance from me, with her hands rather pathetically at her sides.

"Why are you so mean to me, Philip?" she said.

"You know perfectly well why."

"Because I brought Hugh down?"

"Of course. You ought to have asked us."

"There wasn't time. And I thought you wouldn't mind. If it was too casual, I'm sorry."

"Of course, it was too casual. You can't ignore people for two years and then do *this* sort of thing. . . . You know that as well as I do."

There was a pause, she didn't move, and then she said——

"It's really because you don't like him."

"My dear Coralyn——"

"Oh, for God's sake, don't say 'my dear Coralyn' like that—my darling Philip!"

She tried to smile at me; but I was still hard.

"I don't think it was very good manners, Coralyn."

"I know it wasn't. I've said I'm sorry. And I know in general, too, Philip, that you think I'm a disgrace and a scalawag—as I am. But for the love of Pete"—and her voice broke—"is life all *manners?* I thought we liked each other."

I went to the window and closed it. Mabel and the worm were at the far end of the garden.

"I know that."

"Well, then, for God's sake be human!"

"I'm all too human. I think it was outrageous, and I think your young—I think he's revolting."

She turned, at that, suddenly away from me, and I knew she was crying—crying, as she always did, with just the fall of a tear or two, and no sound. She removed the tears with a quick fingertip, and then turned back again to face me as calmly as before.

"Why don't you like him?" she said.

"I don't know. I just don't."

"You wouldn't be jealous, and kid me, would you?"

"Good God, what do you think I am? . . . Haven't you got any eyes or any taste? Why he's a sap, Coralyn, a perfect sap! A backbone of boiled vermicelli, the soul of a lascivious fish! The woods are full of such things. Greenwich Village woods especially. He's weak, he's conceited, he'll use you as a convenience and discard you when he's tired of you—but what's the use of saying all that? You know it as well as I do."

It seemed to me that she shivered a little, as she stood with her back to the empty fireplace.

"I know his appearance is against him—but he's really nice, when you know him."

"Perhaps he is"—I shrugged my shoulders—"but I assure you I don't *want* to know him."

"I think you're mean, Philip."

"What's mean about it?"

"It's the way you say it that's mean. . . . You know how much I wanted your opinion of him—and how much I wanted it to be favorable. I wouldn't have done such a thing with anyone else in the world, and you know that too. And really, *really*, Philip, I thought you'd like him."

She let fall another pair of tears, silently—I lighted a cigarette—the clock struck the half-hour—a planetary world of dust-motes danced in the blurred shaft of sunlight that came between the curtains at the window.

"You see," she said, "I'm in love with him."

"Dear Coralyn—I know you are.

"Do you think I ought to marry him?"

"Certainly not."

"He's younger than I am—but he's older than he looks."

"And no doubt very sophisticated! In fact, it sticks out all over him. It wouldn't surprise me to learn that he has a lobster in his pocket or a couple of perverted kinkajous."

She sat down slowly in a chair by the hearth, and then said——

"*That* wasn't necessary."

"No—I'm sorry. I'm sorry. . . . But you see——"

What had crossed my mind, suddenly, was all that background which poor honest Michael had sketched for me. Should I dive into that?

"You see," I said, "I know much more about you than you think I do. Michael has been here."

Her face hardened.

"Oh, has he!"

"Yes. . . . And to be perfectly frank, I wonder whether the time hasn't come for you to drop all this sort of nonsense en-tirely, once and for all. It's no good. As Michael said, and it won't hurt you to hear it, you're simply going to the devil. . . . Good God, Coralyn, can't you see it when you look into your mirror in the morning? I even know what you were doing in Paris." (This was a lie.)

She flushed, her lips parted, she looked as if she were again going to cry, but didn't, and after a pause during which she looked at me steadily and with an extraordinary sadness, she said——

"I know it, Philip—I know it, I know it—oh, my God, don't I know it! . . . What else for God's sake do I think about from morning to night? That's why I want to marry Hugh. Even sup-pose it turns out badly, it's at least a temporary anchorage—I can rest——"

"No, you couldn't. The only rest for you would be to clear out of New York, and this sort of life, for good and all. Marry Michael—that's the thing for you, if you want my honest opinion!"

She laughed at me quite frankly, for this, and with a sudden real gayety.

"Oh, Michael!" she said. "Poor old Michael. . . . Why, he wouldn't last a week. Why, he's too good. He's a lamb—much too much of a lamb. Good God, no."

"Well, then, dear Coralyn, I shrug my shoulders, as the saying is. I have no further suggestions to offer, except that you should reform——"

"—while there's still time, you mean."

"Yes!"

"Thanks. Keep the change."

"You're entirely welcome."

The conversation dropped; and before it could be resumed, Mabel and the worm came in from the garden, and we sat down to the inevitable game of bridge. I had no further private talk with Coralyn—she and her abominable little vermiform appendage went back to New York early the following morning. If I had only known it, it was the last time I ever had a decent talk with her. And how miserable it makes me now to realize that; to realize how little I did for her, how unkind I was, and how unsympathetic. If I had only tried a little harder—but what use is there in being sentimental about it? And as for the final episode in my relations with poor Coralyn—I can hardly bear to speak of it. It's quite the most revolting thing I ever did in my life.

v.   Before that was to happen, however, a great deal of water was to flow under bridges. To begin with, it became evident that Coralyn had practically dropped us—or to be more exact, had dropped *me*. It was clear enough too that I had hurt her feelings—had spoken too much of the truth—had seen into her a little too deeply. Anyway, we ceased to see her at all. We had a hasty note or two from her (as usual from new addresses) a postcard or two from holiday resorts—Atlantic City, Louisville, Hot Springs—and that was all. A year passed, and with it brought our own beginnings of tragedy. Mabel fell ill with consumption—at first it was not thought to be serious, and it was merely suggested, not urged, that she ought to go to the mountains. It was with the idea of making a virtue of necessity that we decided to spend a year in Europe, mostly in Switzerland —the first holiday we had had in a long time; and one from which poor Mabel was not destined to return. It was on the eve of our departure that we had really staggering news from Coralyn—the announcement of her marriage to Michael. A characteristically breathless and frivolous note from Coralyn, to which was added in a postscript, "You see, funny old Philip, I've taken your advice!" (A postscript, I may mention, which made Mabel look at me with some surprise—and perhaps with something of a surmise as well.) There was also for me, at my office, a letter from Michael. It was a typical seafaring man's letter—curt, inarticulate, honest; it conveyed the impression that Michael had practically forced Coralyn to marry him, and as a sort of last desperate measure for saving her. Something in it, between the lines—I don't now recall just what it was—made me think that things must have been pretty bad. It made one think of the animal rescue league, or something like that. Had she actually, finally, gone completely to the dogs? And would she now be successfully reclaimed? Or would she pull poor good Michael—that lamb—down to whatever it was that she herself had fallen to? What about that? . . .

We sent them a wedding present, and went to Davos. Into this part of my life, with its tragic ending, I won't digress—it has really nothing to do with the story of Coralyn. Let it be enough that at the end of just over a year I came back to America alone. And it was this time purely by chance that I encountered Coralyn—and again in the lobby of the Belmont, where I was staying.

She looked appalling—quite literally appalling. Her face was a ghastly white, except for its deliberate scarlets; she was shabbily overdressed; and there was a new furtive something in her bearing. She continually dropped her eyes, or turned them away, in the brief moment of talk we had, and punctuated her remarks with a short little laugh which sounded insincere and possibly hysterical. I asked her where Michael was—Oh, he had lost his job in the Navy, and they were living in a boarding house in Fourteenth Street, temporarily hard-up. On my asking whether I couldn't see them before I went back to New Haven, she was at first markedly evasive; and then, with obvious reluctance, asked me to drop in after dinner. It was only as we parted that she showed a flash of the Coralyn I knew—otherwise I might to all intents have been talking with a stranger.

"That was the very best of your clumsy fox-paws, poor old Philip!" she said. "You transcended yourself, that time."

"What on earth do you mean?"

"Marrying me to Michael, you goose!"

"*I* marrying you——"

"Yes, *you* marrying me—but in the wrong sense!" and with that she turned quickly and walked away.

And that evening—but perhaps the less said of it the better. I understood quickly enough why Coralyn had not wanted me to come. The boarding house was forlorn beyond words—dark, smelly, dirty, with rails missing from the banisters; the kind of thing you see in movies of the slums. And the little room into which I was shown at the back of the house was as dreary. Coralyn opened the door—she looked better in the meager gaslight, and in an old dress (one that I remembered) somewhat worn, but becoming. She indicated the sofa, with a vague gesture and a smile, and there I saw Michael, asleep.

"Michael is *hors de combat*," she said. "Looking for a job all day."

"I'm sorry."

"But sit down, do."

We sat down, but somehow had little to say. I became uneasily conscious of the fact that Michael was not so much asleep as drunk. Presently he half opened his eyes and stared at me.

"Oh, hello!" he said. "Glad to see you. Talk to Corry. Don't mind me—I'm a little tight! . . . Sleep it off. Glad to see you. . . ."

That was Michael's only entrance into the conversation. He fell genuinely asleep, and snored, while Coralyn and I made a pretense (extremely uneasy, in the circumstances) of keeping things up. She said they had lived in Chicago for a while; she thought a little of going back there. They had lived also in Buffalo, in Boston, and in Perth Amboy. Why Perth Amboy? I never discovered. She had had lots of adventures—she laughed, looking at me out of the corners of her eyes, to make sure that I got the furtive implication—and she still managed, in spite of everything— (and here she glanced at Michael)—to have a good time. She smoked a cigarette with a long holder, and I saw that her stockings were rolled below the knee. Presently, when Michael's snores had become louder, she said——

"I don't suppose you want to go out anywhere? . . . There's a nice little speakeasy just round the corner. . . ."

I declined this gambit; just why, I don't know. Somehow it offended me. She knew that I was offended. She herself looked hurt for a moment—with that extraordinary childlike appearance of softness and innocence which she was always capable of —and changed the subject. I asked, eventually, how Michael had lost his job—she gave her odd little laugh and said we had better not go into that. And then added, quietly, lowering her eyes and voice, while she touched delicately her cigarette ash into an ashtray, that she and Michael were agreed to get a divorce. . . .

"I've made a hash of it," she said.

"So I see. I'm sorry, Coralyn."

"Oh, I shall get along—I'll enjoy myself, don't worry, for God's sake. But it was a hell of a trick on poor Michael. Wasn't it, Michael?"

Michael made no answer.

"And a bad move for little Coralyn. But I'm hard-boiled now. You don't know the half of it! I could shock your heart out, Philip."

"I don't doubt it," I said bitterly. "You ought to be ashamed. Why don't you snap to?"

"Oh, *ideels—*" she said, snapping her fingers in the air—"I ain't got none no mo'. . . . Every woman for herself, from now on. And the devil take the blindest!"

I left, shortly after this—she saw me to the door.

"Come again"—was all she said—"when I'm single."

vi.   And it was, as a matter of fact, after she was again "single" that I did next talk to her—and for the last time—a year later—but it was also after the terrible episode which I have mentioned: my betrayal of Coralyn, the betrayal for which I am afraid she never forgave me—or should I say *will* never forgive me? I don't know. Nor do I really know altogether how it was that I came to do such a thing. It was simply one of those quick blind chemical reactions (or perhaps I should say psychological?) to which all of us yield, from time to time in our lives, without clearly realizing what we are doing. There is no doubt that I was angry with Coralyn—disappointed in her—perhaps even jealous. That last scene, in the boarding house, had distressed and poisoned me. I found it hard to forgive. Did I perhaps, actually, for a while, hate Coralyn? I think I did. I wanted to revenge myself. Just why, or for what—after all, she had done little enough to me—I find it difficult to say. I felt, certainly, that she had let me down. I felt too that she had behaved atrociously to poor Michael—she seemed to be absolutely without any moral sense in her treatment of him—it was clear enough that she had ruined his life. I had no doubt that in some way it was she who had lost him his job, and reduced him, poor fellow, to the wretched state in which I had seen him. And if, underneath all this, I was aware of a deep sympathy for Coralyn, it was certainly not uppermost when, during my talk with Tom Thaxter, my fiendish idea occurred to me.

Tom—whom I met, for the first time in several years, at a class reunion—had been one of my best friends at college. He was a notorious Don Juan. The list of his conquests would have made Casanova turn in his grave. He was bold, witty, ruthless—not ex-

actly handsome, but certainly impressive—with a fantastic imagination; and one of the most entertaining talkers I have ever
known. When one talked with him, one talked about women. It
was a foregone conclusion. In fact, it became a sort of class joke.
One simply slapped him on the back, when one met him, and
said, "Well, who's the latest?" And Tom would narrate the conquest of the latest, with something very like genius. He was famous for his bawdy after-dinner speeches. And especially famous
for one particular occasion, when, at a dinner in mixed company
(the wives being present), he rose, and began to tell us a story
which he had previously told to the men alone. The story was
a frightful one—instantly there was a panic. Whispered adjura-
tions to "sit down, Tom" and "shut up, Tom" were addressed
to him in vain. In vain were his coattails plucked. He grinned
and went on, while the rest of us cowered in our chairs. And when
the climax to the story arrived, he gave it an ending of entire
innocence, quite as funny as the other. Though, funny as it was,
I think the ladies never clearly understood why it was so extravagantly applauded.

And it was while Tom was telling me his latest, over a Tom
Collins, that my fiendish idea occurred to me. I would tell him
about Coralyn—describe her in the most glowing terms—make
her out to be the most skillful and witty and wary of adventur-
esses—and then bet him that he couldn't add her to his list. It
would serve her right. It was just exactly as she ought to be
treated. Do her good. And what was more, I would get an enormous satisfaction out of hearing from Tom, later, all the details
of the battle. It would have the effect for me of finally, once and
for all, putting Coralyn in her place. . . .

Tom, needless to say, was delighted; his eyes glowed. We made
a bet of ten dollars on it, I gave him her address, he promised
to let me know what happened, and off he went, smiling with
anticipation. As for myself, I then screwed the affair to its highest possible pitch by writing to Coralyn. I told her that I was
sending my friend Tom Thaxter to see her, and warned her,
facetiously, that he was "dangerous." I added that I thought him

the most attractive man I knew, rich, unmarried, and merciless. Fastidious, a difficult man to please, an even more difficult one to outwit. . . . She wrote no answer to my letter.

And what happened I heard from Tom two weeks later, when he spent a night with me in New Haven especially to tell me. They had had three or four terrific parties, one after another, at dances, speakeasies, in her apartment; as he put it, a stand-up knock-down fight. Hammer and tongs. The cagiest girl he had ever met. Amusing as the devil. The second night, when she had taken a few too many drinks, she weakened a little, in the taxi going back to her apartment at two in the morning, and there had been a pretty violent love scene. He had thought he was on the verge of victory. But no such luck; she slipped away from him at the door and locked him out, laughing.

"The little devil!" he murmured, reminiscently. "The little she-fiend!"

He shook his head, and continued. After that, it appeared, she had been warier. She made fun of him. When he tried to kiss her, she tickled him. She even suggested that he had been put up to the exploit by his nice friend Philip. (I winced.) But when he suggested that she should join him in Philadelphia for three days, she astonished him, all of a sudden, by saying that she *would*. And what is more, she did! She wired him at his hotel and arrived. But again she surprised him. She arrived with another girl —a girl whose name I've forgotten, and whom I'd never heard of—and they got three days of extremely expensive entertainment out of him—to be exact, she cost him two hundred dollars in parties—and all for nothing.

"Nothing?" I said.

"Not a thing. Not even a kiss."

"Well, I'm damned. A mere gold-digger."

"Gold-digger! . . . Wait till you hear the rest of it."

The rest was brief and to the point. On the last night, when he again tried to make love to her (and he said she was really looking quite beautiful) and when he proposed that she should come away with him somewhere, she again staggered him by saying that she would: on one condition. When he asked what the condition was, she said, "A thousand dollars."

The thing had floored him; he couldn't believe it. This wasn't at all (and he looked at me a little oddly) what I had led him to expect! He asked her if she meant it, and she replied that of course she did.

" 'Do you mean to say'—I said to her—'you just want *money?*' "

" 'That's what I said, kid—one grand!' "

And he had, of course, left it at that. That had made it—in every way—did I see?—out of the question. Impossible. It had simply ruined the whole thing. . . .

I acquiesced, there was a pause, and then he said——

"You know, I think she's in some sort of trouble. I may be wrong, but I think so. I even hinted as much to her, but she only laughed at me. Just the same—have you any idea what it might be?"

I assured him that I hadn't—cursing myself for a damned liar and cad—and after discussing the strange affair a little further, casually, we went to bed. But I lay awake a long while, wondering whether Tom wasn't right. . . . Why had she needed that thousand dollars? . . . Why?

vii.   I never saw Coralyn again. A few weeks later I spoke with her on the telephone, and tried in vain to make an appointment to see her—she laughed, she was vague, she said she was busy, she called me an old fool, and finally, in the middle of a long speech I was making, she hung up the receiver with an ironic "goodbye, old dear." I was so angry that I swore I'd never attempt to look her up again.

I did try, however, as might have been expected; but in vain. I found that she had disappeared; this was six months later. I spent an entire day in New York, a day of misery, tracing her from one address to another. At the last, in West 22nd Street, I drew a blank. The janitor said she had left two months before, owing rent, and had never sent for her things. There was some

mail for her, too—she had apparently not left a forwarding address at the district post office. Was I a friend of hers? Did I want
to see her things, or take them away? . . .

I went into a dusty storeroom in the cellar, with white-washed
walls, and under a dull gas-jet looked at the pathetic remnants. A
trunk full of worthless oddments. A few books—a copy of *Daniel
Deronda,* one of *What Maisie Knew,* a file of clippings from
newspapers (mostly culinary), a pair of Japanese slippers, a gray
tweed coat which I had seen many times before, and a box of
letters—there was little enough. I took the copy of *What Maisie
Knew,* and told the janitor to do what he liked with the other
things; I also took the letters, giving the janitor my address, in
case Coralyn should turn up; though somehow I felt sure she
wouldn't. Then, after paying Coralyn's rent—the first and last
time I ever paid Coralyn's rent—I took the letters home un-
opened, and locked them in my desk.

Five years have passed. Is Coralyn still alive? Is she dead? What
has become of her? . . . Almost against my will, I hope she is
alive, for I desperately want to see her again—why? Am I still in
love with her?—But at the bottom of my heart I hope, for her
sake, she is dead.

STATE OF MIND

In retreat. In full retreat. In disorderly retreat. In flight. In full flight. In disorderly flight.

He walked along the sidewalk with eyes downcast, meditating morosely. An unimportant rain pattered on his hat and shoulders, spotted his spectacles, touched here and there a cool spring on his cheeks or chin. He noticed, in a small puddle on the brick sidewalk, a rusty hairpin. Further on, he observed also a rusty buckle, lost from a galosh. Does one speak of a single galosh? Galosh and goulash. Another hairpin. Dead matches. Cigarette ends, yellow at one end and black at the other. And an empty match-box, with a picture of a ship. Some crumpled tinfoil.

One's mind was like this—a puddled sidewalk littered with such odds and ends. Or like this exposed cellar which he was now passing, whence the building had been removed: a chaos of rubbish, piles of mortar and dead bricks, plaster-covered beams, twisted pipes, a bed spring, a scarred radiator lying on its side, and at the bottom of all, a melancholy wreck of a furnace, its torn pipes gushing cold air. And the rain falling gently and impartially on it all.

What is the mind after a defeat? A battlefield covered with

the dead and dying. A field incarnadined with dying images, with dead affects, whence a few wounded percepts try to crawl away to secrecy through the red grass. Heavily defeat. In disorderly retreat. After the anguish, one must find peace. After the love, one must find forgetfulness. After the idea, one must find annihilation.

If love was not reciprocated; if one's love was not understood or valued; if one could not find a convincing expression or action of one's love; then one's being is an opened horror of cellar, whence the building has been razed. One's heart is a furnace with torn pipes, exposed to the hostile infinite, the unfamiliar rain. And thus, one dies. One becomes dead. An organization disorganized.

Mud was beginning to spatter the worn toes of his shoes. And he observed spatters of mud on the white stockings of women.

How could one project, in satisfactory form, this desire for annihilation?

Not in suicide, but in imagination?

A small boy in a blue sailor suit, with a knotted silk tie, and spots of mashed potato on the blouse—and a round sailor hat on the back of his head—himself that small boy—years and years and years before——

He stared in at the shop window in Liberty Street, the toy-shop window. There were battleships of cardboard, lead soldiers slotted in rows in a cardboard box, a toy combination bank of steel, a red and yellow tin monkey, with a red cap, who depended with prayerful paws from a cord, a pile of comic valentines, an air-rifle, a box of BB shot. But there was also, in the middle, a goldfish bowl, bright in the light, filled with crystal-clear water. It was otherwise empty—moveless, still, eternal. He read, slowly, a second time, then a third, the placard. Two water-snakes had inhabited this bowl. Of a sudden, obeying a simultaneous impulse, they had begun eating each other's tails. They had thus formed a ring, which, as they devoured, became smaller. Smaller and smaller this ring of snake had become—till at last, as each snake performed the final swallow, they had both abruptly vanished. They were gone. Gone into the infinite. And here, of course, was the bowl of water to prove it.

Yes, some such action as this would now be the perfect, the appropriate action. Some such image of annihilation, the giving of form to some such concept of flight from reality—this would be a divine relief.

A nest of sodden matches in the gutter as he stepped across.

Ghosts, for example. A ghost, or sequence of ghosts, reality with each progression becoming less real. Would this be an image for what it was that he desired?

Three men sitting apart in the compartment of an English train, an English train dawdling through sleepy sunlit country. Hop-fields with multitudes of upright poles; and geometrical designs of twine, laced and interlaced, like a cat's-cradle, for the vines. Oast-houses, cowled like nuns, with their air of brooding alertness, as if they expected something from the southwest. Cottages of orange-lichened tiles, and fields of sheep.

Time hung heavy; time hung palpably; the train stopped, gently panting, for a long while at a small station, where empty milk-cans were clanked on to the asphalt platform. Except for this sound, everything was profoundly still. One of the three passengers in the smoking compartment put down his *Daily Mirror* and looked out of the window. He smiled a little, to himself, as if pleased with some secret cleverness of his own; then glanced amusedly at each of his fellow passengers. The one opposite him was looking at an Ordnance Survey map. The other one, at the other side of the carriage, was staring out at the landscape.

"Now I suppose," said the smiling one, "you don't believe in ghosts?"

The man addressed in this surprising fashion lowered his map. He eyed his *vis-à-vis* suspiciously. The idea of a conversation seemed somewhat repugnant to him.

"Ghosts?" he said, raising his eyebrows rather superciliously.

"Yes, ghosts. You probably don't believe in them?"

"It all depends on what you mean by believing?"

The third man turned his head sharply, uneasily, toward the two talkers, and then as sharply away again. He appeared to be annoyed. The train gently, imperceptibly, began to move from the station. The black and white sign slid past—"Ham Street."

"There's an article in this paper about ghosts. The writer says that he has seen many ghosts—hundreds of them—and that they are never, in appearance, human. Mere wisps of fog. Or the usual sort of hobgoblin thing you read about in shilling shockers. He doesn't believe there is any such thing as a *human* ghost. . . . Do you agree with him?"

The man with the map merely grunted and allowed his moving eyes to follow the moving fields and cherry orchards. His interlocutor, baffled, gave a little laugh of annoyance. But he was not so easily to be put down.

"I see that you *don't* believe in ghosts," he said.

"I didn't say I didn't," said the other.

"Ah, but I can see that you don't. . . . And the joke is, you know, that *I* am a ghost."

He delivered this statement with widening bright eyes and an air of great triumph, smiling delightedly. But, though the third passenger, at the other side of the compartment, gave a distinct start, his chosen victim remained quite impassive.

"Oh, *are* you?" answered the latter. "You have discovered that, have you?"

"Discovered?"

The "ghost" seemed a shade nonplussed by this.

"Yes. I've been wondering, all the way from Ashford, whether you had yet discovered your unreality, or how soon you would."

"My dear chap!"

"For you see, as it happens, it was I who created you; I imagined you; you only exist in my imagination. And if I should stop imagining you—as I do now—you would simply cease to exist."

The ghost disappeared at once; and the man with the map

turned, smiling, to the other passenger, who had already sprung to his feet and was pulling the communication cord to stop the train.

"*You*, at any rate," he said, "will now believe in ghosts!"

This individual, badly frightened, did not look at his queer companion, did not answer, but, hurriedly opening the door, as the train came to a stop, jumped down to the flint road-bed. He saw the guard running toward him with a rolled green flag in his hand.

"Look here!" he said. "I can't ride in a compartment with ghosts!"

"Ghosts?" said the guard, peering into the compartment. His peer was a mere matter of form—the compartment was quite empty.

"Well, I'm damned! . . . There were two men there—and they're both gone. They *both* must have been ghosts."

He stared incredulously into the vacant compartment. The guard laughed scornfully.

"Why, that's a mere trifle," he said. "The whole thing is a ghost. The train, the passengers, the driver and myself—even the rails."

So saying, he waved his rolled green flag, and the whole thing vanished. The solitary passenger found himself alone in a rolling green meadow. There was no train—there was no track. Four sheep lay under an oak tree. The sun was shining—the thrushes were singing—everything was marvelously peaceful. And he was totally and appallingly alone. If only he himself could disappear, he thought, the ending would be perfect! And, as he thought it, he vanished. . . .

And so, only the bowl of water was left.

Himself in retreat, in full retreat, in disorderly retreat, from a world of memories altogether too painful.

STRANGE MOONLIGHT

It had been a tremendous week—
colossal. Its reverberations around him hardly yet slept—his
slightest motion or thought made a vast symphony of them, like
a breeze in a forest of bells. In the first place, he had filched a
volume of Poe's tales from his mother's bookcase, and had had
in consequence a delirious night in inferno. Down, down he
had gone with heavy clangs about him, coiling spouts of fire
licking dryly at an iron sky, and a strange companion, of pro-
tean shape and size, walking and talking beside him. For the
most part, this companion seemed to be nothing but a voice and
a wing—an enormous jagged black wing, soft and drooping like
a bat's; he had noticed veins in it. As for the voice, it had been
singularly gentle. If it was mysterious, that was no doubt because he himself was stupid. Certainly it had sounded placid
and reasonable, exactly, in fact, like his father's explaining a
problem in mathematics; but, though he had noticed the orderly and logical structure, and felt the inevitable approach toward a vast and beautiful or terrible conclusion, the nature and
meaning of the conclusion itself always escaped him. It was as
if, always, he had come just too late. When, for example, he had
come at last to the black wall that inclosed the infernal city, and

seen the arched gate, the voice had certainly said that if he hurried he would see, through the arch, a far, low landscape of
extraordinary wonder. He had hurried, but it had been in vain.
He had reached the gate, and for the tiniest fraction of an instant he had even glimpsed the wide green of fields and trees, a
winding blue ribbon of water, and a gleam of intense light
touching to brilliance some far object. But then, before he had
time to notice more than that every detail in this fairy landscape seemed to lead toward a single shining solution, a dazzling
significance, suddenly the infernal rain, streaked fire and rolling smoke, had swept it away. Then the voice had seemed to
become ironic. He had failed, and he felt like crying.

He had still, the next morning, felt that he might, if the opportunity offered, see that vision. It was always just round the
corner, just at the head of the stairs, just over the next page.
But other adventures had intervened. Prize-day, at school, had
come upon him as suddenly as a thunderstorm—the ominous
hushed gathering of the entire school into one large room, the
tense air of expectancy, the solemn speeches, all had reduced
him to a state of acute terror. There was something unintelli-
gible and sinister about it. He had, from first to last, a peculiar
physical sensation that something threatened him, and here and
there, in the interminable vague speeches, a word seemed to
have eyes and to stare at him. His prescience had been correct—
abruptly his name had been called, he had walked unsteadily
amid applause to the teacher's desk, had received a small black
pasteboard box; and then had cowered in his chair again, with
the blood in his temples beating like gongs. When it was over,
he had literally run away—he didn't stop till he reached the
park. There, among the tombstones (the park had once been a
graveyard) and trumpet-vines, he sat on the grass and opened
the box. He was dazzled. The medal was of gold, and rested on
a tiny blue satin cushion. His name was engraved on it—yes,
actually cut into the gold; he felt the incisions with his fingernail. It was an experience not wholly to be comprehended. He
put the box down in the grass and detached himself from it, lay

full length, resting his chin on his wrist, and stared first at a tombstone and then at the small gold object, as if to discover the relation between them. Humming-birds, tombstones, trumpet-vines, and a gold medal. Amazing. He unpinned the medal from its cushion, put the box in his pocket, and walked slowly homeward, carrying the small, live, gleaming thing between fingers and thumb as if it were a bee. This was an experience to be carefully concealed from mother and father. Possibly he would tell Mary and John. . . . Unfortunately, he met his father as he was going in the door, and was thereafter drowned, for a day, in a glory without significance. He felt ashamed, and put the medal away in a drawer, sternly forbidding Mary and John to look at it. Even so, he was horribly conscious of it—its presence there burned him unceasingly. Nothing afforded escape from it, not even sitting under the peach tree and whittling a boat.

ii. The oddest thing was the way these and other adventures of the week all seemed to unite, as if they were merely aspects of the same thing. Everywhere lurked that extraordinary hint of the enigma and its shining solution. On Tuesday morning, when it was pouring with rain, and he and Mary and John were conducting gigantic military operations in the back hall, with hundreds of paper soldiers, tents, cannon, battleships, and forts, suddenly through the tall open window, a goldfinch flew in from the rain, beat wildly against a pane of glass, darted several times to and fro above their heads, and finally, finding the open window, flashed out. It flew to the peach tree, rested there for a moment, and then over the outhouse and away. He saw it rising and falling in the rain. This was beautiful—it was like the vision in the infernal city, like the medal in the grass. He found it impossible to go on with the Battle of Gettysburg and abandoned it to Mary and John, who instantly started to quarrel. Escape was necessary, and he went into his own room, shut the door, lay on his bed, and began thinking about Caroline Lee.

John Lee had taken him there to see his new air-gun and a bag of BB shot. The strange house was dim and exciting. A long winding dark staircase went up from near the front door, a clock was striking in a far room, a small beautiful statue of a lady, slightly pinkish, and looking as if it had been dug out of the earth, stood on a table. The wallpaper beside the staircase was rough and hairy. Upstairs, in the playroom, they found Caroline, sitting on the floor with a picture book. She was learning to read, pointing at the words with her finger. He was struck by the fact that, although she was extraordinarily strange and beautiful, John Lee did not seem to be aware of it and treated her as if she were quite an ordinary sort of person. This gave him courage, and after the air-gun had been examined, and the bag of BB shot emptied of its gleaming heavy contents and then luxuriously refilled, he told her some of the words she couldn't make out. "And what's this?" she had said—he could still hear her say it, quite clearly. She was thin, smaller than himself, with dark hair and large pale eyes, and her forehead and hands looked curiously transparent. He particularly noticed her hands when she brought her five-dollar goldpiece to show him, opening a little jewel box which had in it also a necklace of yellow beads from Egypt and a pink shell from Tybee Beach. She gave him the goldpiece to look at, and while he was looking at it put the beads round her neck. "Now, I'm an Egyptian!" she said, and laughed shyly, running her fingers to and fro over the smooth beads. A fearful temptation came upon him. He coveted the goldpiece, and thought that it would be easy to steal it. He shut his hand over it and it was gone. If it had been John's, he might have done so, but, as it was, he opened his hand again and put the goldpiece back in the box. Afterwards, he stayed for a long while, talking with John and Caroline. The house was mysterious and rich, and he hadn't at all wanted to go out of it, or back to his own humdrum existence. Besides, he liked to hear Caroline talking.

But although he had afterwards for many days wanted to go back to that house, to explore further its dim rich mysteriousness, and had thought about it a great deal, John hadn't again suggested a visit, and he himself had felt a curious reluctance about raising the subject. It had been, apparently, a vision that was not to be repeated, an incursion into a world that was so beautiful and strange that one was permitted of it only the briefest of glimpses. He had, almost, to reassure himself that the house was really there, and for that reason he made rather a point of walking home from school with John Lee. Yes, the house was there—he saw John climb the stone steps and open the huge green door. There was never a sign of Caroline, however, nor any mention of her; until one day he heard from another boy that she was ill with scarlet fever, and observed that John had stayed away from school. The news didn't startle or frighten him. On the contrary, it seemed just the sort of romantic privilege in which such fortunate people would indulge. He felt a certain delicacy about approaching the house, however, to see if the red quarantine sign had been affixed by the door, and carefully avoided Gordon Square on his way home from school. Should he write her a letter or send her a present of marbles? For neither action did there seem to be sufficient warrant. But he found it impossible to do nothing, and later in the afternoon, by a very circuitous route which took him past the county jail—where he was thrilled by actually seeing a prisoner looking out between the gray iron bars—he slowly made his way to Gordon Square and from a safe distance, more or less hiding himself behind a palmetto tree, looked for a long while at the wonderful house, and saw, sure enough, the red sign.

Three days later he heard that Caroline Lee was dead. The news stunned him. Surely it could not be possible? He felt stifled, frightened, and incredulous. In a way, it was just what one would expect of Caroline, but none the less he felt outraged. How was it possible for anyone, whom one actually knew, to *die?* Particularly anyone so vividly and beautifully remembered! The indignity, the horror, of death obsessed him. *Had* she actually died? He went again to Gordon Square, not knowing precisely what it was that he expected to find, and saw something white hanging by the green door. But if, as it appeared, it was true that Caroline Lee, somewhere inside the house, lay dead, lay motionless, how did it happen that he, who was so profoundly concerned, had not at all been consulted, had not been invited to come and talk with her, and now found himself so utterly and hopelessly and forever excluded—from the house, as from her? This was a thing which he could not understand. As he walked home, pondering it, he thought of the five-dollar goldpiece. What would become of it? Probably John would get it, and, if so, he would steal it from him. . . . All the same, he was glad he hadn't taken it.

To this reflection he came back many times, as now once more with the Battle of Gettysburg raging in the next room. If he had actually taken it, what a horror it would have been! As it was, the fact that he had resisted the temptation, restored the goldpiece to the box, seemed to have been a tribute to Caroline's beauty and strangeness. Yes, for nobody else would he have made the refusal—nobody on earth. But, for her, it had been quite simple, a momentary pang quickly lost in the pleasure of hearing her voice, watching her pale hands twisting the yellow beads, and helping her with her reading. "And what's this?" she had said, and "Now I'm an Egyptian!" . . . What was death that could put an end to a clear voice saying such things? . . . Mystery was once more about him, the same mystery that had shone in the vision of the infernal city. There was something beautiful which he could not understand. He had felt it while he was lying in the grass among the tombstones, looking at the medal; he had felt it when the goldfinch darted in from the rain and then out again. All these things seemed in some curious way to fit together.

III.   The same night, after he had gone to bed, this feeling of enormous and complicated mystery came upon him again with oppressive weight. He lay still, looking from his pillow through the tall window at the moonlight on the white outhouse wall, and again it seemed to him that the explanation for everything was extraordinarily near at hand if he could only find it. The mystery was like the finest of films, like the moonlight on the white wall. Surely, beneath it, there was something solid and simple. He heard someone walk across the yard, with steps that seemed astoundingly far apart and slow. The steps ceased, a door creaked. Then there was a cough. It was old Selena, the Negro cook, going out for wood. He heard the sticks being piled up, then the creak of the door again, and again the slow steps on the hard baked ground of the yard, æons apart. How did the peach tree look in the moonlight? Would its leaves be dark, or shiny? And the chinaberry tree? He thought of the two trees standing there motionless in the moonlight, and at last felt that he must get out of bed and look at them. But when he had reached the hall, he heard his mother's voice from downstairs, and he went and lay on the old sofa in the hall, listening. Could he have heard aright? His mother had just called his father "Boy!" Amazing!

"It's two parties *every* week, and sometimes three or four, that's excessive. You know it is."

"Darling, I *must* have *some* recreation!"

His father laughed in a peculiar angry way that he had never heard before—as strange, indeed, as his mother's tone had been.

"Recreation's all right," he said, "but you're neglecting your family. If it goes on, I'll have another child—that's all."

He got off the sofa and went softly down the stairs to the turn of the railing. He peered over the banisters with infinite caution, and what he saw filled him with horror. His mother was sitting on his father's knee, with her arms about his neck. She was kissing him. How awful! . . . He couldn't look at it. What on earth, he wondered as he climbed back into bed, was it all about? There was something curious in the way they were talking, something not at all like fathers and mothers, but more like children, though he couldn't in the least understand it. At the same time, it was offensive.

He began to make up a conversation with Caroline Lee. She

was sitting under the peach tree with him, reading her book. What beautiful hands she had! They were transparent, somehow, like her forehead, and her dark hair and large pale eyes delighted him. Perhaps she *was* an Egyptian!

"It must be nice to live in your house," he said.

"Yes, it's very nice. And you haven't seen half of it, either."

"No, I haven't. I'd like to see it all. I liked the hairy wallpaper and the pink statue of the lady on the table. Are there any others like it?"

"Oh, yes, lots and lots! In the secret room downstairs, where you heard the silver clock striking, there are fifty other statues, all more beautiful than that one, and a collection of clocks of every kind."

"Is your father very rich?"

"Yes, he's richer than anybody. He has a special carved ivory box to keep his collars in."

"What does it feel like to die—were you sorry?"

"Very sorry! But it's really quite easy—you just hold your breath and shut your eyes."

"Oh!"

"And when you're lying there, after you've died, you're really just pretending. You keep very still, and you have your eyes *almost* shut, but really you know everything! You watch the people and listen to them."

"But don't you want to talk to them, or get out of bed, or out of your coffin?"

"Well, yes, at first you do—but it's nicer than being alive."

"Why?"

"Oh, I don't know! You understand everything so easily!"

"How nice that must be!"

"It is."

"But after they've shut you up in a coffin and sung songs over you and carried you to Bonaventure and buried you in the ground, and you're down there in the dark with all that earth above you—isn't that horrible?"

"Oh, no! . . . As soon as nobody is looking, when they've all

gone home to tea, you just get up and walk away. You climb
out of the earth just as easily as you'd climb out of bed."

"That's how you're here now, I suppose."

"Of course!"

"Well, it's very nice."

"It's lovely. . . . Don't I look just as well as ever?"

"Yes, you do."

There was a pause, and then Caroline said:

"I know you wanted to steal my goldpiece—I was awfully glad
when you put it back. If you had asked me for it, I'd have given
it to you."

"I like you very much, Caroline. Can I come to Bonaventure
and play with you?"

"I'm afraid not. You'd have to come in the dark."

"But I could bring a lantern."

"Yes, you could do that."

. . . It seemed to him that they were no longer sitting under
the peach tree, but walking along the white shell-road to Bonaventure. He held the lantern up beside a chinquapin tree, and
Caroline reached up with her pale, small hands and picked two
chinquapins. Then they crossed the little bridge, walking carefully between the rails on the sleepers. Mossy trees were all
about them; the moss, in long festoons, hung lower and lower,
and thicker and thicker, and the wind made a soft, seething
sound as it sought a way through the gray ancient forest.

        IV.   It had been his intention to explore, the
next morning, the vault under the mulberry tree in the park—
his friend Harry had mentioned that it was open, and that one
could go down very dusty steps and see, on the dark floor, a few
rotted boards and a bone or two. At breakfast he enlisted Mary
and John for the expedition; but then there were unexpected
developments. His father and mother had abruptly decided that
the whole family would spend the day at Tybee Beach. This
was festive and magnificent beyond belief. The kitchen became

a turmoil. Selena ran to and fro with sugar sandwiches, pots of deviled ham, cookies, hard-boiled eggs, and a hundred other things; piles of beautiful sandwiches were exquisitely folded up in shining, clean napkins, and the wicker basket was elaborately packed. John and Mary decided to take their pails with them, and stamped up and downstairs, banging the pails with the shovels. He himself was a little uncertain what to take. He stood by his desk wondering. He would like to take Poe's tales, but that was out of the question, for he wasn't supposed to have the book at all. Marbles, also, were dismissed as unsuitable. He finally took his gold medal out of its drawer and put it in his pocket. He would keep it a secret, of course.

All the way to the station he was conscious of the medal burning in his pocket. He closed his fingers over it, and again felt it to be a live thing, as if it were buzzing, beating invisible wings. Would his fingers have a waxy smell, as they did after they'd been holding a June bug, or tying a thread to one of its legs? . . . Father carried the basket, Mary and John clanked their pails, everybody was talking and laughing. They climbed into the funny, undignified little train, which almost immediately was lurching over the wide, green marshes, rattling over red-iron bridges enormously complicated with girders and trusses. Great excitement when they passed the gray stone fort, Fort Pulaski. They'd seen it once from the river, when they were on the steamer going to the cotton islands. His father leaned down beside Mary to tell her about Fort Pulaski, just as a cloud shadow, crossing it, made it somber. How nice his father's smile was! He had never noticed it before. It made him feel warm and shy. He looked out at the interminable green marshes, the flying clouds of rice-birds, the channels of red water lined with red mud, and listened intently to the strange complex rhythm of the wheels on the rails and the prolonged melancholy wail of the whistle. How curious it all was! His mother was sitting opposite him, very quiet, her gray eyes turned absently toward the window. She wasn't looking at things—she was thinking. If she had been looking at things, her eyes would have moved to and fro, as Mary's were doing.

"Mother," he said, "did you bring our bathing suits?"

"Yes, dear."

The train was rounding a curve and slowing down. They had suddenly left the marshes and were among low sand dunes covered with tall grass. He saw a man, very red-faced, just staggering over the top of one of the dunes and waving a stick. . . . It was hot. They filed slowly off the train and one by one jumped down into the burning sand. How strange it was to walk in! They laughed and shrieked, feeling themselves helpless, ran and jumped, straddled up the steep root-laced sides of dunes and slid down again in slow, warm avalanches of lazy sand. Mother and father, picking their way between the dunes, walked slowly ahead, carrying the basket between them—his father pointed at something. The sunlight came down heavily like sheets of solid brass and they could feel the heat of the sand on their cheeks. Then at last they came out on the enormous white dazzling beach with its millions of shells, it black-and-white-striped lighthouse, and the long, long sea, indolently blue, spreading out slow, soft lines of foam, and making an interminable rushing murmur like trees in a wind.

He felt instantly a desire, in all this space and light, to run for miles and miles. His mother and father sat under a striped parasol. Mary and John, now barefooted, had begun laborious and intense operations in the sand at the water's edge, making occasional sallies into the sliding water. He began walking away along the beach close to the waves, keeping his eye out for any particularly beautiful shell, and taking great care not to step on jellyfish. Suppose a school of flying fish, such as he had seen from the ship, should swim in close to the beach and then, by mistake, fly straight up onto the sand? How delightful that would be! It would be almost as exciting as finding buried treasure, a rotten chest full of goldpieces and seaweed and sand. He had often dreamt of thrusting his hand into such a sea-chest and feeling the small, hard, beautiful coins mixed with sand and weed. Some people said that Captain Kidd had buried treasure on Tybee Beach. Perhaps he'd better walk a little closer to the dunes, where it was certainly more likely that treasure would have been hidden. . . . He climbed a hot dune, taking hold of the feathery grass, scraping his bare legs on the coarse leaves, and filling his shoes with warm sand. The dune was scooped at the top like a volcano, the hollow all ringed with tall, whistling grass, a natural hiding place, snug and secret. He lay down, made excessively smooth a hand's breadth of sand, then took the medal out of his pocket and placed it there. It blazed beautifully. Was it as nice as the five-dollar goldpiece would have been? He liked especially the tiny links of the little gold chains by which the shield hung from the pin-bar. If only Caroline could see it! Perhaps if he stayed here, hidden from the family, and waited till they had gone back home, Caroline would somehow know where he was and come to him as soon as it was dark. He wasn't quite sure what would be the shortest way from Bonaventure, but Caroline would know—certainly. Then they would spend the night here, talking. He would exchange his medal for the five-dollar goldpiece, and perhaps she would bring, folded in a square of silk, the little pink statue. . . . Thus equipped, their house would be perfect. . . . He would tell her about the goldfinch interrupting the Battle of Gettysburg.

v.   The chief event of the afternoon was the burial of his father, who had on his bathing suit. He and Mary and John all excitedly labored at this. When they had got one leg covered, the other would suddenly burst hairily out, or an arm would shatter its mold, and his father would laugh uproariously. Finally they had him wholly buried, all except his head, in a beautiful smooth mound. On top of this they put the two pails, a lot of pink shells in a row, like the buttons of a coat, and a collection of seaweeds. Mother, lying under her parasol, laughed lazily, deliciously. For the first time during the day she seemed to be really happy. She began pelting small shells at father, laughing in an odd, delightful, teasing way, as if she was a girl, and father pretended to be furious. How exactly like a new grave he looked! It was singularly as Caroline had described it, for there he was all alive in it, and talking, and able to get up whenever he liked. Mary and John, seeing mother throw shells, and hearing her teasing laughter, and father's comic rage, became suddenly excited. They began throwing things wildly—shells, handfuls of seaweed, and at last sand. At this, father suddenly leapt out of his tomb, terrifying them, scattered his grave clothes in every direction, and galloped gloriously down the beach into the sea. The upturned brown soles of his feet followed him casually into a long, curling green wave, and then his head came up shaking like a dog's and blowing water, and his strong white arms flashed slowly over and over in the sunlight as he swam far out. How magnificent! . . . He would like to be able to do that, to swim out and out and out, with a sea-gull flying close beside him, talking.

Later, when they had changed into their clothes again in the salty-smelling wooden bathhouse, they had supper on the veranda of the huge hotel. A band played, the colored waiters bowed and grinned. The sky turned pink, and began to dim; the sea darkened, making a far sorrowful sound; and twilight deepened slowly, slowly into night. The moon, which had looked like a white thin shell in the afternoon, turned now to the brightest silver, and he thought, as they walked silently toward the train, of which they could see the long row of yellow windows, that the beach and dunes looked more beautiful by moonlight than by sunlight. . . . How mysterious the flooded marshes looked, too, with the cold moon above them! They reminded him of something, he couldn't remember what. . . . Mary and John fell asleep in the train; his father and mother were silent. Someone in the car ahead was playing a concertina, and the plaintive sound mingled curiously with the clacking of the rails, the rattle of bridges, the long, lugubrious cry of the whistle. Hoo-o! Hoo-o! Where was it they were going—was it to anything so simple as home, the familiar house, the two familiar trees, or were they, rather, speeding like a fiery comet toward the world's edge, to plunge out into the unknown and fall down and down forever?

No, certainly it was not to the familiar. . . . Everything was changed and ghostly. The long street, in the moonlight, was like a deep river, at the bottom of which they walked, making scattered, thin sounds on the stones, and listening intently to the whisperings of elms and palmettos. And their house, when at last they stopped before it, how strange it was! The moonlight, falling through the two tall swaying oaks, cast a moving pattern of shadow and light all over its face. Slow swirls and spirals of black and silver, dizzy gallops, quiet pools of light abruptly shattered, all silently followed the swishing of leaves against the moon. It was like a vine of moonlight, which suddenly grew all over the house, smothering everything with its multitudinous swift leaves and tendrils of pale silver, and then as suddenly faded out. He stared up at this while his father fitted the key into the lock, feeling the ghostly vine grow strangely over his face and hands. Was it in this, at last, that he would find the explanation of all that bewildered him? Caroline, no doubt, would understand it; she was a sort of moonlight herself. He went slowly up the stairs. But as he took the medal and a small pink shell out of his pocket, and put them on his desk, he realized at last that Caroline was dead.

THE FISH SUPPER

Faulkner looked out of the office window. It had stopped raining, and evidently was going to clear off, after all. A watery light was breaking through the rapid clouds, which were themselves of a softer texture, and the church spire in Wellington, three miles away, suddenly caught a pale beam of sunlight and glistened evanescently. Best and surest sign of all, old Sandy was out on the lawn with his motor lawn-mower. Faulkner watched him stoop over the machine, heard it begin to sputter, and then the old man climbed into the seat and began his slow onslaught on the dandelions. . . .

"It looks," said Ulrich, behind him, "as if we'd have our party, after all. And, believe me, I'd like a bottle of nice cold beer after a day like this."

Faulkner continued to look out of the window, feeling the stubble on his chin. Now that his wife had left him, he was no longer so careful about shaving every day. Her letter lay unanswered on his desk.

"Yes, I guess so," he said.

He could feel Ulrich waiting, deprecatingly as always, for some further assurance of interest; he even felt sure that Ulrich was holding some sort of document in his hand, turning it nervously; but he was damned if he'd make any further effort to be agreeable. He waited, watching Sandy's slow progress—it was as if he were sweeping the lawn of dandelions with a huge carpet-sweeper. When he got to the wire fence at the end of the company's grounds he turned the machine and began coming back. A pair of robins had already arrived to search the freshly cut grass for food.

"Well," said Ulrich, shifting his feet, "I'll drop in for you at five, if that's all right."

"Sure. Do that."

The apologetic footsteps moved away, the door closed, and—thank God—he was alone again. The clouds seemed to be in a great hurry—it was almost as if they really had somewhere to go. Somewhere to go. It would be nice to have somewhere to go. Something better, anyway, than this accursed factory, stuck down here in the country, miles from anywhere. He couldn't exactly blame Barbara for not wanting to live here. But then, where you got work you had to take it. If she had been everything that a wife ought to be—! But what, exactly, ought a wife to be?

He sat down at his desk, picked up the letter, opened it, and began, for the twentieth time in three days, to read it again. The phrases, in Barbara's babyish handwriting, had now become almost meaningless. "I am, of course, awfully sorry" (why did the word "awfully" always annoy him?) "that it all had to end like this"—"terribly disappointed in you"—"but of course you have always considered your own interests rather than mine"—"no sort of life there for the children"—"so I think it will be better for all concerned"—and so on, to the end, with its casual "Goodbye, Luke, and I really hope you'll be happy." Good God, what did she expect of a husband? He had been unhappy ever since that time when she fell in love with Paul, but he had, for the sake of the family, tried his best to conceal it. When his income had finally proved insufficient he had found this job here in the country, reorganizing a dilapidated factory; had given up his life in New York, which meant so much to him; had endeavored to endure a life of solitude, hoping that sooner or later she would come to join him; and, now, this was his reward. Of course, he had never been much of a success; in fact, to make lots of money had never been one of his ambitions. Why couldn't they have been happy as they were? Why was it so necessary that the children should be sent to boarding schools and dancing schools, and live on Riverside Drive or in a swell suburb—why was it so necessary that they should meet only the "best" people, and all that kind of folderol? That sort of thing didn't mean happiness. If the children couldn't have the same advantages *they* had had—schools and colleges and such—that was unfortunate, but it wasn't fatal, was it? . . . But now the axe had fallen.

He tried once more to find a suitable tone for his reply. He put his elbows on the desk and began rubbing his forehead with a sort of painful violence which was somehow a great relief to him. He was tempted to be bitter, to be unbridled, but a kind of sporting instinct forbade that; there was so much else that he wanted to say; in fact, he wanted, in a sense, to write her a love-letter, a loveletter which also would tell her in horribly brutal sentences what he really thought of her. But the whole thing was too complicated. How could you sum up in one letter all your feelings about ten years of married life? All the tendernesses, the secret symbols, the extraordinary elaborate and profound and—yes—*vascular* dual consciousness which their conjoined experience had given them? All the regrets, the anguishes, the ecstasies, the memories, the precious emblems of shared pleasure—no, it was impossible. It would all have to be left out. There was no kind of shorthand which could express it. It was as if the moss, torn from the wall, should try to tell you, with the raw surface, *what the wall had been like.* . . .

He could say *that,* of course; and the idea pleasing him, he took up his pen and drew a sheet of typewriter paper toward him and wrote on it "My darling." But the impulse ran out, died—or, more precisely, withered in the presence of his anger. It was no good. He would have to take refuge in a merely formal letter, a glazed official style, something inhuman and abstract. Polite, uncircumstantial, with perhaps just a suggestion of bitterness and more than a suggestion of affection, affection curbed. And just the same, it was ridiculous that at such a crisis of one's life one couldn't, simply couldn't, say what one really meant, and say it richly. If only Barbara had *understood* all this! If only she had seen—underneath his helplessness and his indifference to the conventional—his desperate loyalty and essential gentleness! . . . How absurd. This was tantamount to asking destiny, implacable destiny, to be one's mother; it was like trying to pillow one's head on a meteor.

He was still struggling with the problem, still remembering this and that and the other—their visit to Jackson Falls, the time when Betty had fallen into the river, the winter when Paul had taken to calling on Barbara every afternoon, Paul's habit of kissing her hand, her curious indifference to cleanliness in the house, the odd trace of exhibitionism which always showed in her in Paul's presence—when the door opened and Ulrich came in. He remembered, then, with a start, that the whistle had already blown; he had half noticed it at the time. He jumped up, crumpling the sheet of paper.

"Five o'clock, eh?" he said.

"My wife's waiting in the car," said Ulrich, tapping the edge of the desk with a rolled-up newspaper. He always carried a rolled-up newspaper. "And she says Miss Houston will meet us over there in Wellington."

II.   It was to be a fish supper, in a little secret restaurant which Ulrich had discovered: a place where they gave you very good fish, and also very good beer, smuggled across the lake from Canada. Ulrich prided himself on possessing little secrets of this sort. It was as if he felt some queer kind of inferiority, and sought to make up for it by knowing all sorts of out-of-the-way odds and ends. He always knew, for example, just which of the standard brands of cigarette contained, at the moment, the purest and best tobacco, and which of them were capitalizing their success by recourse to cheaper materials. He knew a buyer of tweeds in Buffalo, and could get his suits for a third of what it cost anyone else. And it went without saying that if there was a new place at which you could get something to drink he would know about it. Faulkner really disliked the man; he felt sure that Ulrich wanted to get something out of him. Was it merely a sort of social thing? a desire to be on friendly, not to say intimate, terms with the manager, whom he perhaps also suspected of being "superior"? His manner was always uneasily ingratiating; he smiled too much.

And his wife bore out this impression, as Faulkner immediately discovered when they joined her in the car. All the way to Wellington, while Ulrich drove, Mrs. Ulrich, a plump fair-haired little woman, who shut up her blue eyes when she laughed, did her best to captivate him and impress him. She was playing the "great lady," evidently under the impression that Faulkner moved in some social sphere of impossible grandeur—the world of marble halls and terraces with urns, which, in America, at any rate, exists only in the movies. She had cultivated a broad "a," and used it with devastating effect; except when, now and then, she used it where she shouldn't.

Faulkner was patient with her, replied to her lofty inanities, gave her a cigarette, and prayed that this Miss Houston (whoever she was) would be more interesting, more honest, and less on the make.

"Who is this Miss Houston?" he asked.

Mrs. Ulrich arched her eyebrows, and then immediately afterwards, for no discoverable reason, narrowed her eyes at him enigmatically.

"Ah," she said, "she's a woman of mystery."

Faulkner felt that he was expected to smile in reply to this challenge, and obediently did so, but without much conviction; at the same time, suddenly, feeling extraordinarily angry with this fool of a female. He saw the whole thing—all the months of scheming that had gone to this party, in order that she might let it be known in local society that she was an intimate friend of the manager, Mr. Luke Faulkner. Revolting. All the more revolting, and also pathetic, not to say tragic, when one knew—as he did—how silly and unfounded was this legend of his social splendor.

The conversation lagged. Mrs. Ulrich could think of nothing further to say, at the moment, and sat back, ladylike, holding her cigarette between two stiff fingers; and Faulkner watched the flight of wet trees past the car, and the fence-rails from which raindrops still hung, bright with the evening light. A sense of unreality came over him; he realized how little he knew these two people, and how little he liked them; he hated the back of Ulrich's head, and the little dark point of hair which hung over his collar; he disliked the silver vase beside the window, with its artificial bachelor's-buttons; he loathed Ulrich's habit of humming popular airs. And to be riding in a closed car, an expensive car, a car more expensive than he himself had ever had or wanted to have—to be riding in this, with two such commonplace people, and at a time when he particularly wanted to be alone . . . the thing was so incredible as to seem ludicrous. It was, in fact, so fantastic that the thought crossed his mind that the adventure might be amusing. Why not simply throw oneself into it, sink to this queer level, bathe in this strangeness? Might it not be in a way refreshing, invigorating? Suppose, for example, he were to make love to this pudgy and overscented female absurdity who sat beside him, bumping against him when the car bumped; what would happen? It might, at any rate, end this little campaign for social conquest.

III.   The "secret" restaurant turned out to be a kind of little yacht club, or boathouse, mounted on stilts over the lake. It looked like the sort of place that would sell you bait and rent you a dirty fishy-smelling boat. The dining room, however, was rather charming: a long, low-ceilinged room, windowed on three sides, with an uneven floor. They found a table at the far end, overlooking the lake, and sat down; and Faulkner remarked to Miss Houston that it was very like being on a ship. He could feel the whole thing moving.

"Wait till you've had two or three of their dry Martinis," said Ulrich, "and you'll think it's moving, all right!"

Miss Houston was a disapointment, as far as mystery was concerned; she was a nice enough girl of twenty-four or -five, dark, with level gray eyes, somewhat awkward and mannerless. Faulkner gathered that she had only recently been "taken up" by Mrs. Ulrich, and that they didn't know each other particularly well. It came out that she was a teacher of singing in Albany. It was evident that Mrs. Ulrich had romanticized her. Still, she was a pleasant enough creature, and knew Bach from Beethoven; and within a few minutes of the introduction she and Faulkner had formed a sort of alliance against the Ulrichs. Faulkner felt that if they should want to they could make the Ulrichs very uncomfortable.

"You studied music in Paris?" he said.

"No, in London. I was there for two years."

"Lucky woman! I had two months there, in a college vacation once, and I think it was the most exciting two months of my life. I had a room in Gray's Inn."

"In Gray's Inn! How simply delicious! . . . I lived in Lamb's Conduit Street—don't you love the names they give their streets? —and I often used to walk through the Inn."

Mrs. Ulrich, smiling a little constrainedly, turned to see if the cocktails were coming. The waiter was just arriving, with a double round, as ordered. Faulkner felt that she was glad of the interruption.

"Well, here's looking at us," said Ulrich.

The cocktails were as good as Ulrich had said; they drank two apiece, and then ordered a third, and after that came the beer and the fish. A phonograph squealed "The Cat's Whiskers" at the far end of the room, and two girls went down the gangway to a canoe by the float, fussed over some cushions, and paddled off on the lake. The water was like glass—pale pink with the reflected light of a waning sunset. One of the girls trailed her bare arm in the water.

Mrs. Ulrich was flushed and excited, and determined to make conversation with Faulkner; she was aggressive about it, challenging, and Faulkner began to be annoyed.

"My husband says you come from New York," she said. "Don't you find it dull here in the country after living in New York?"

"Oh, it might be worse," said Faulkner.

"I'm sure you don't really mean that."

"Why shouldn't I?"

Mrs. Ulrich straightened her mouth to a thin line.

"How can you? . . . After all the luxuries and excitements you've been used to in New York! Goodness—there are times when *I* think I shall go mad."

"Oh. You come from New York too?"

"Well, no, but I've been there a good deal; and I'm very fond of it. I've always tried to make a point of going down at least twice a year. I have a great many friends there, you see."

Mrs. Ulrich seemed a little confused as she said this, and looked uneasily at her husband and then quickly away again. Something in her behavior suggested to Faulkner that she was lying. But why should she take the trouble to lie about so trifling a thing?

"You probably know the city a good deal better than I do, then," he said. "It's always the occasional visitor who takes the cream off it, you know."

"Some people have all the luck," sighed Miss Houston. "I've been to New York just twice in my life—when I sailed to Europe and when I came back."

"Don't you think Fifth Avenue is simply wonderful? . . ." Mrs. Ulrich disregarded Miss Houston's interpolation, and addressed herself again to Faulkner. "And Broadway at night, with all those wonderful lights, and the crowds, and always the chance that you'll see a gang murder, or a girl being enticed by the White Slavers! It's so romantic, don't you think? I never can get enough of it."

Ulrich looked at his wife, cleared his throat somewhat loudly, and then dropped his eyes. He seemed embarrassed.

"And the shops! My goodness! I always want to buy everything. And the theaters! ... Well, the truth is I really regard myself as a New Yorker, nowadays, I've been there so much, and know it all so well."

Faulkner was polite.

"Where do you usually stay?" he said.

"Oh, I've tried a good many of the hotels"—her tone was a little vague—"but I guess I've been more to the Belmont than to any of the others. Or is it the Biltmore? I never can keep those names straight, they're so much alike, you know. I guess it's the Belmont. Yes, it's the Belmont."

"Let's see; the Belmont." Faulkner frowned a little, reflecting. "I'm afraid I don't just remember where that is. It's pretty far downtown, isn't it? Near the Square?"

"Well, it's not easy to describe, but I think so, yes. *Quite* near the Square. But of course it's very centrally situated, and very comfortable. Expensive, you know—but very good."

"Washington Square?"

"Yes, Washington Square. *That* was it, of course."

Miss Houston looked perplexed.

"Oh, but I thought—" she began to say.

Mrs. Ulrich interrupted her rapidly. She dropped her hand on Miss Houston's and gave it an affectionate squeeze.

"My dear, you really ought to cultivate the habit of going down there for your shopping! There's nothing else like it. I don't believe London is in it with New York. ... Do you think so, Mr. Faulkner? The buildings are so wonderful!"

Miss Houston glanced anxiously at Faulkner.

"Architecturally," he said, "some of them are very fine. I've always particularly liked Gimbels', with that tower of pink stone and the golden turret—especially at night. And its position is so commanding, too, there by Central Park. Don't you think so?"

"Beautiful," sighed Mrs. Ulrich. "Simply beautiful."

"Though just why they should have put the Museum right bang beside it, so overshadowed by it, I can't imagine. Don't you think it was a mistake?"

Mrs. Ulrich nodded rapidly.

"*Great* mistake," she said. "Not that I was ever one to care much about museums! . . . Me for the bright lights, and Coney Island! I'm afraid I'm rather a flibbertygibbet. Ralph always says so, don't you, Ralph?"

Ulrich smiled obediently.

"Did you ever take the tunnel over to Staten Island?" asked Faulkner.

"Let me see . . ." Mrs. Ulrich deliberated, tilting her head to one side. "Yes, I think I did—in fact, several times." She nodded rapidly again, remembering. "Oh, yes. In fact, I think I can say that I know my way about the city as well as anybody."

"What about another round of cocktails?" suggested Ulrich. "Any bidders? We might as well get tight."

There was a pause in the conversation while the cocktails were brought; and Faulkner began to feel a little drunk, just drunk enough to be reckless. He stretched out his legs under the table, and smiled.

"You know," he said, looking genially at Mrs. Ulrich, "I suspect you've never been to New York in your life."

Mrs. Ulrich turned scarlet.

"Why, what *do* you mean! . . . I guess you're kidding me!" She gave a little laugh. "Haven't I been telling you all this time that I'm a regular New Yorker?"

There was a silence. Faulkner half turned toward the lake and looked through the screen at the darkening water. He saw a canoe a little way off with a rosy Japanese lantern in it.

"Your details are singularly inaccurate," he said.

"I *beg* your pardon, Mr. Faulkner, but I'm afraid I don't know what you're talking about. . . . Ralph, don't you think it's time we were starting back? . . ."

Ulrich looked at his watch.

"What's the rush?" he said.

"That Staten Island tunnel"—said Faulkner—"doesn't exist, for example."

Mrs. Ulrich glared at him, flushing again; she tried to look him firmly in the eyes.

"I'm afraid you're mistaken," she said. "And aren't you rather rude?"

"And Gimbels' is not pink, and has no golden turret, and isn't in Central Park," he went on, implacably, feeling as if he had a knife in his hand. "Nor is the Hotel Belmont in Washington Square; it's by the Grand Central Station, on 42d Street."

Mrs. Ulrich jumped to her feet.

"Give me my cape," she said.

She refrained from looking at Faulkner; she turned her back, and began to walk out of the room, while Ulrich paid the bill. Miss Houston blew her nose. There was a distressing moment when nobody could think of anything to say. Then they all got up and moved toward the door.

Mrs. Ulrich had already got into the car; she was crying, and when her husband and the two others came up she turned her face away. Ulrich and Miss Houston got into the car, but Faulkner stood by the door with his hat in his hand.

"I'm sorry, Mrs. Ulrich," he said. "I've been worried and out of sorts, and the temptation was too much for me. . . . Forgive me, and don't do it again. . . . If you don't mind, Ulrich, I'll stay behind and get myself another drink. Too nice an evening to be going home yet awhile. . . . Good night, Miss Houston."

Ulrich smiled guiltily, made a feeble and meaningless gesture with one hand from the wheel of the car, and Faulkner walked back toward the restaurant. As he opened the door he heard the car moving off.

He went back to the same table, sat down, and ordered another cocktail. It was now perfectly dark. The canoe with the lantern had glided away to a distance, faint voices came over the lake, a night-hawk was mewing somewhere in the upper darkness. He put his elbows on the table and began again rubbing his forehead with cruelly violent hands. Everything was meaningless, mad, ridiculous. Those two poor fools—that nice harmless girl—the cocktails, the canoes, the evening—and his wife's unanswered letter. What on earth could he say to her? He took between thumb and forefinger the stem of the cocktail glass which the waiter had brought him, and revolved it to and fro. He began to imagine the letter. "My darling—this world is insane, ridiculous, mad, full of fools. When I revolve this cocktail glass the glass moves but the liquid remains still; and the olive stirs only faintly, like some weed at the bottom of the sea when a current wafts it. Someone is singing on the lake. I can hear the plop of a paddle. I am an old idiot, a failure, a blundering creature who means well. I love you much more than I thought I did. I shall have to hire a car to get back to the factory from here. I was cruel to Mrs. Ulrich—because I want to be cruel to you, and to myself. But I am no worse than anyone else—I am a harmless fellow, likable, amiable, and I want to have my life. Why did you fall in love with Paul? Why did you stand there by the door in your bathing suit, letting the raincoat momentarily slip from your shoulders in order that he might see you? I knew that you were thrilling to his presence, conscious of him with your whole being, and I was deeply hurt; I felt as if the world had fallen away from beneath my feet. And now I am lost."

Laboriously, he took out a cigarette and lighted it. The match fell to the floor still blazing, and he trod out the flame with an uncertain foot, taking a cruel pleasure in an unnecessary repetition of the treading. He had at the same time an impulse to laugh; but the laugh remained—as he himself phrased it, in continuation of the letter—a "cerebral giggle, which twice contracts the diaphragm."

I LOVE YOU VERY DEARLY

M_y darling, you'll be surprised to hear from me, to see an envelope addressed to you in your father's indecipherable, rheumatic handwriting—and perhaps it will surprise you to see that it comes from Paris. You probably thought you were at last through with Pauper after that revolting scene last year. But you know the old saying about the bad penny. You can't keep a bad man down. The truth is that I love you far too much to let you go out of my life like that, for no *good* reason at all. Even if we did quarrel, and even if it became obvious that we couldn't get on, you and Jim and I, and even if I *am* a Chinese egg (you know, the Chinese bury the eggs to let them ripen), that doesn't, I hope, prevent me from taking a deep and lasting interest in you and yours. I know only too well my faults; I never was any sort of a person to live with. Your poor mother found that out before we had been married two years—she always used to say that I was the kind that never ought to have married at all. The truth is, I belong to that unhappy and ridiculous type of human being that has an artistic temperament without having any talent. I am as selfish as a guinea pig and as immoral; there's no use denying it; I guess there isn't a worse father in the world. I made all your lives a perpetual torment, with my eternal fussi-

ness about meals and food and neatness, and my irascible out-
bursts about nothing at all. There is a sort of cruelty in me that
I never was able to control. If there was a horrible smell of fry-
ing fish in the house, I simply *had* to break out with some violent
profane remark about it. I even felt that you used to have smelts
just to provoke the usual reaction—though I knew perfectly well
that you did it for the sake of economy. That was how that last
scene started. I was sure, somehow (with the obsessive fear of the
maniac), that you had invited Warren to the house just because
you knew how I hated and loathed and despised him. I argued
with myself about it all that night, for I couldn't sleep a wink,
and though I could see perfectly clearly the other side of the
question—I mean, that he was a friend of yours, that you liked
him, and that you had a perfect right, in your own house, to invite him to dinner—nevertheless I was somehow secretly sure that
you were simply doing it to annoy me, and perhaps to drive me
out. I tried to smother this idea, and to behave myself, but it was
no good. If I didn't burst out about it in my usual manner, with
a "Jesus Christ!" or two, then I knew that I would revenge myself on you and Jim in subtler ways and more prolongedly; so I
decided to burst out. I knew I was wrong, and yet I did it. And
when I had done it, nothing on earth would have made me *admit*
that I was wrong.

Oh, well, I suppose there's no use in digging all this up. I don't
want you to think that I'm trying to apologize with the idea of
having you invite me to come back. I know as well as you do
that it wouldn't work. I just want you to realize that I blame
myself for it, not you. I also realize that we were fools ever to
think that we could live together, the three of us. When the children are grown up and married, it's time for the parents to fade
out of the picture—good old platitude. I thought when I went
away that I could never be happy again—it seemed to me there
was nothing left for me but to crawl off to a dark corner and
rot. It's no joke, beginning your life over again when you're sixty!
I felt beaten, there was nowhere I wanted to go, *nothing* I wanted
to do. I don't know how it was I got the idea of coming abroad;

but it was the thing that saved me. The little income I have (from the block of Union Pacific which I kept) just suffices to keep me going, provided I live modestly. I have got a flat here, in a slummy corner of the city, and—this will surprise you—taken to painting! I found that I had to have something to do. When I was just out of college, before you were born or thought of, I used to have vague ambitions of that kind. Well, I bought myself a *full* equipment of brushes, palettes, canvases, tubes of paint, and started in. And I'm enjoying myself hugely. I know perfectly well I'm mediocre; but I've discovered that I can, after a fashion, paint. So now I spend my days, when it isn't too dark, with a gaudy palette on my thumb, approved style, painting my little German model, Gretchen, or still-lives *à la* Van Gogh. I haven't yet imitated his pair of deserted and disastrous boots, or his famous yellow chair, but I don't doubt I will, before I get through. I know all the galleries like a connoisseur, go sometimes, when I'm flush, to the Opera, or to the Comique. In fact, I'm deliberately turning myself into one of those resigned and eccentric old failures, who wear shabby coats but pride themselves on their neat gloves and brilliant sticks, who haunt all the second-rate pensions of Europe, and who follow the seasons back and forth from Cairo to Scheveningen, arriving everywhere punctually with the blossoming of the cherry. As if one were a migratory bird—a swallow or a cuckoo. And I can truly say that I'm happier than I've ever been in all my life.

My dear Winky—my motive for writing you is a double one. In the first place, I wanted to let you know where I was, and what I was doing, and that I was *alive*; I wanted to make amends, if I could, for the abrupt and mannerless way in which I disappeared from Philadelphia without letting you hear a word of where I was going. For all you knew, I might have drowned myself in the Wissahickon. After I had told you at lunch that you were barbarians, and that it was impossible for a civilized being to live with you, and you had burst into tears, and when Muffet came in and saw this extraordinary scene going on, I went out, at first with the idea that I would of course come back. But the more I thought about it, the more I felt that it was impossible. I was ashamed to face you, and at the same time I was angry. So I telephoned Margaret to pack up my things and send them to the station for me; and I asked her to say nothing about it, assuring her that I was attending to that myself. I waited at the station, and as soon as my trunk and bags came, I started off to New York. That was horrible of me—but it's probably the kind of thing you have by this time learned to expect of your father. When you were little, I used to be cross with you for no reason, sometimes I slapped you or was harsh with you over some absurd trifle which you wouldn't at all understand. I would be nice to you one day, go for a walk with you, and tell you fairy stories by the hour, and the next day I would be morose and avoid you as if you were a little nuisance. You learnt to regard me as the most undependable being in the whole world, one who obeyed only one law, the law of his own egoistic nature. Like your brother and your mother, you learnt that if affairs went badly with me at the insurance office, you would be punished for it; and that if I had a headache, or hadn't slept well, the day would be ruined for the entire family. So in all likelihood you merely thought, when I vanished so unceremoniously, and without a word, that it was just the sort of thing the old crab *would* do. All the same, I want to tell you and Jim how sorry I am about it. In fact, I want to make a sort of final confession and apology. I regret almost everything in my whole career. I am ashamed of myself, most of all ashamed of the way in which I treated your mother. God knows I made a hash of *her* life.

Perhaps you'll think all this is maudlin nonsense, and in bad taste, or that I've been drinking. As a matter of fact, I have— Gretchen brought in a bottle of wine for our supper, and before that I had visited the *estaminet* at the corner; but I assure you this makes no difference, or only to this extent, that I can speak freely what it has long been on my mind to say. I've wanted to get *all* this off my chest, to square accounts with you. The chances are a hundred to one we'll never see each other again; I don't expect ever to come back to America; and I don't think you will want to see me if you should ever come to Europe. I think, in fact, that it will be better all around if we *don't* meet. There would be no use in it. For this reason, I want to take my leave of you with a kind of admission of my shortcomings; at least, I want you to know that I completely realize them. My life as a husband and father was a horrible failure, and the best thing for all concerned is that I should simply drop out of your lives. I am starting over again, on a humbler scale. I am starting off, I mean, with a frank admission that I'm a misfit, a second-rater, and one whose only excuse for living—well, I thought when I began that sentence that there was some excuse, but upon my soul I can't think of any! Is the fact that Gretchen loves me an excuse? God knows; perhaps. It is at any rate a reason why you will not want to come and see me if you ever *do* come to Paris. That is what I mean when I say that I am starting life over again on a different plane. Not that I mean to end my days in the gutter. But you will gather that my way of life is not that of Germantown.

My other motive for writing, darling Pops, is harder for me to speak of. It's partly because of it that I begin as I do, with this kind of degrading and dismal confession. I want you to know that I am not preaching to you as if I were myself any sort of angel. For once, I don't want you to think of me as a scolding father, or one who denies you the things you want, but as a good friend, who can advise you dispassionately. I am talking, you see, about this Warren affair. At the time of our quarrel, when I left, I didn't know in the least the real significance of it; I don't want you to think that. It is only in the last few months that I have heard what it was all about. I needn't tell you from whom I heard it, except that it wasn't Jim. Jim hasn't said a word to me, hasn't written me a line. It was someone else who wrote me, and who simply said that she thought that I, as your nearest relative, ought to know about it.

She was in the next room to yours at the Imperial, in Atlantic City, when you went there with Warren. She saw you first walking along the boardwalk—you and Warren—but luckily, as it

turned out, neither of you saw her. At this time she naturally
wasn't suspecting anything, and assumed of course that Jim was
with you, too. Then the same evening she opened her bedroom
door to go down to dinner, and saw you and Warren just coming
out of the next room. The poor lady didn't know *what* to do
then—she was afraid of embarrassing you—(and herself)—if she
went down to the dining room; so finally she ordered her dinner
sent up. And early the next morning she moved to another hotel.
You see, these things can't be concealed. It's absolutely no use.
I've found that out many times. Somebody will always see you;
it may be a good friend who won't gossip (like this lady, who
hasn't told a soul except myself) or it may be, and more likely,
one of those good upright souls who believe in virtue, but who
practice it in the singular way of inflicting the ultimate social
cruelty on those who are too strong or too weak to be enslaved
by the conventions. These people make me sick—they are hypo-
crites—at the bottom of their souls they would *love* to be wicked
themselves—they are frequently the ones who adore telling
smutty stories in mixed company, while at the same time they
disapprove of any *work of art* which is frank in the least—and
they get a kind of upside-down sexual pleasure in trampling,
socially, on anyone who actually *lives* his unorthodoxy. . . . They
are worms, despicable, but unfortunately you can't leave them
out of account. If X, this lady, saw you, it's possible that some
snooping Y did also, and will lose no time in spreading the exciting and delightful news in Germantown and Philadelphia. . . .

My dear child—I was terribly sorry to hear all this. You know
there is nothing Victorian about me, and that if I urge you to
take one course of action rather than another, it will not be because of conventional morals or scruples. The course of my own
life is sufficient comment on that! My advice to you is, of course,
to give this thing up, at once and completely; not, however, because there is anything wrong in it, but simply because it's in-
expedient. It's the long run that counts, and in the long run it
cannot possibly turn out happily. We may as well face the fact
that the human animal is fickle, faithless, has a roving appetite

(as regards love) and when he is tied down by marriage is always wanting to break out of the cage and go exploring. As far as the male is concerned, that is obvious enough. But I don't think it is sufficiently realized that the female is just as subject to these wandering appetites, these desires that are, so to speak, merely of the moment, or of the season. She has them, just as much as he has. She sees a man and is attracted to him—he has certain qualities which her husband lacks, and she is prone to leap to the hasty conclusion that this is, after all, the man she was all the while looking for. Well, maybe he is, but more likely he's not. Suppose she gives up her husband, her home, her place in society, her children (I won't sentimentally stress this point, but I can speak from experience when I say that to lose the regard of one's children is the worst thing that can befall one) and goes flying after this exquisite Lothario. What will happen then? The chances are at least even that before the year is out she will discover that it was just one of these momentary cravings, a whim, or even—at most—a passion; and that she will wish she had never given way to it. She will also find that *other* such desires will occur from time to time. Will she give way to these, too? No, my dearest little Winky, this won't do. Stability, as she will find too late, is the only basis on which a woman can be happy. She is not fitted by nature for a wandering life. You may just now believe passionately that life without Warren is inconceivable. But don't allow that belief to run off with you. Your real future, your only happy future, is the certain one, the one you have already launched yourself on. Make up your mind about this. Try to accept this as a kind of law, and make up your mind that these wandering appetites are going to occur to you from time to time, that they will make you momentarily unhappy, but that they can be overcome or forgotten, or temporized with, and that above all the thing for you to hang on to is your delightful home with Jim and dear little Muffet. These are the substantial things of your life—your capital, so to speak. Jim is a good fellow. I know you have had your troubles with him—there's no marriage worth the name that hasn't troubles. Of course, after one has been married seven years, one is no longer in love as one was at the outset. That isn't human nature. The first ecstasy dwindles off in a year, or even in a few months. And then the arrival of the first child changes and flattens the tone of the whole business. After that, you're *married*. It's no longer a mere love affair, and it's folly to try, as some people do, to pretend that it is. You just settle down to a mutual give-and-take, a deliberate tolerance and understanding. It's my idea that if it were possible, each of the partners ought then to be free to have a little *passade* or two, if that should seem advisable. I can easily imagine two people so deeply fond of each other, so used to each other, so desirous of each other's happiness, that they would say, 'Now, look here—I know you're a little bit in love with X or Y—go ahead, but *be careful*, don't allow gossip to start about you. Get this thing off your mind, or heart, and don't worry. I'll be just as fond of you when it's over, and I hope you'll tell me as much about it as you feel like telling.' Why not? There doesn't seem to me to be anything ridiculous or impossible in that. Human nature seems to me to be capable of it; it's only that we've been brought up with fantastic ideas about the nature of loyalty and its purpose. Loyalty isn't just a matter of keeping one's physical appetites for one person alone; it isn't even a matter of keeping one's emotional appetites for one person alone; it's a deeper and simpler thing than that. It's a desire to keep the marriage going simply as the only makeshift arrangement that will most probably promote the eventual and permanent happiness of all concerned.

Of course, I may be talking through my hat. Nobody can know better than I do how impossible it is to judge a situation like this from the outside. The intangibles, in a marital relationship, are as shadowy as they are numberless. I know only too well how, just by a step-by-step process, two excellent people can gradually reach a point where life together seems to them insupportable, and for extraordinarily little reason. They may find, one day, all of a sudden, that as a result of these tiny accretions, they hate each other. Perhaps you and Jim have reached such a point;

though I must say that when I lived with you I saw no sign of it. You always seemed cheerful enough; and if you didn't seem to have a lot to say to each other, that didn't necessarily mean much. After all, you can't go on talking to the same person for a lifetime with the same gusto that you shared during your courtship! But I don't think too much importance should be attached to this. Go about a little more, take a few holidays separately, and the chances are it will take care of itself. . . . On the other hand, if you *have* got to a point where you really hate each other, or where you really hate Jim (for I gather that Jim doesn't want you to go), then my urgent notice to you, Blinks, is to go slow, take lots of time, and think it over for at least a year before you do anything revolutionary. Whatever you do, don't be headlong. You may regret it all your life.

This sounds pretty preacherish. It's like those times when you used to argue with me about the use of going to school, of learning this and that and the other, and I used to take you by the hand and walk you along the river with me and scold and cajole you out of your sulks. I can remember one of those walks vividly. You were about sixteen, and you were all of a sudden terribly bored with everything—school, your home, your friends, Germantown. You wanted to be allowed to go to New York and go to work. Do you remember? Some friend of yours—Alice Whipple, I believe—had just gone there and wrote you what a fine time she was having, being perfectly independent. You were sick of restraint, you wanted to break out and start a life of your own. I can remember sitting by the water with you, somewhere, and arguing, and how by degrees we found that we had stopped arguing and instead were having a silly game of throwing pebbles into the water; and then both of us suddenly realized what a good time we were having, and how much we cared for each other. You got up and flung your arms around me and began kissing me as if it were the first time, almost as if we were lovers. I felt for you suddenly as I used to feel when you were three or four, when you used to call yourself my 'lap-bird' because you were so fond of sitting on my lap. My dear Winky——

That's all I'm going to say. I want you to be happy; and all this nonsense, and this blather of confession of my own worthlessness, will be excused maybe if it helps you out.

I'm staying here for another month, and then G. and I will go to Bruges for the summer. G. hasn't been well, and the change will do her good. She has an old friend there whom she is anxious to see—a former schoolteacher. G. will stay with her, and I shall put up at a pension. Then, at the end of the summer, we'll come back here, d.v., and struggle through another Parisian winter, floods and all. . . .

Give Muffet a "scratchy" kiss from me, and my best to Jim. Goodbye, and drop a line, sometime, to your dilapidated father,

HOWARD BOND.

I love you very dearly.

THE DARK CITY

His greatest pleasure in life came always at dusk. Its prelude was the reading of the evening paper in the train that took him out of the city. By long association the very unfolding of the grimy ink-smelling sheets was part of the ritual; his dark eyes dilated, he felt himself begin to "grin," the staggering load of business detail, under which he had struggled all day in the office, was instantly forgotten. He read rapidly, devoured with rapacious eyes column after column—New York, London, Paris, Lisbon—wars, revolutions, bargains in umbrellas, exhibitions of water-colors. This consumed three-quarters of the journey. After that he watched the procession of houses, walls, trees, reeling past in the mellow slant light, and began already to feel his garden about him. He observed the flight of the train unconsciously, and it was almost automatically, at the unrealized sight of a certain group of trees, oddly leaning away from each other, like a group of ballet dancers expressing an extravagance of horror, that he rose and approached the door.

The sense of escape was instant. Sky and earth generously took him, the train fled shrieking into the vague bright infinity of afternoon. The last faint wail of it, as it plunged into a tunnel, always seemed to him to curl about his head like a white tentacle, too weak to be taken seriously. Then, in the abrupt silence, he began climbing the long hill that led to his house. He walked swiftly, blowing tattered blue clouds of smoke over his shoulders, revolving in his mind the items of news amusing enough to be reported to Hilda; such as that Miss Green, the stenographer, who had for some time been manifesting a disposition to flirt with him, today, just after closing, when everybody else had gone out, had come to him, blushing, and asked him to fasten the sleeve of her dress. A delicious scene! He smiled about the stem of his pipe, but exchanged his smile for a laugh when, looking in through a gap in his neighbor's hedge, he found himself staring into the depraved eyes of a goat. This would add itself to the episode of Miss Green, for these eyes were precisely hers. He turned the corner and saw his house before him, riding on the hill like a small ship on a long green wave. The three children were playing a wild game of croquet, shrieking. Louder sounds arose at his appearance, and as he strode across the lawn they danced about him chattering and quarreling.

"Daddy, Martha won't play in her turn, and I say——"

"Marjorie takes the heavy mallet——"

The chorus rose shrill about him, but he laughed and went into the house, shouting only:

"Out of the way! I'm in a hurry! The beans are dying, the tomatoes are clamoring for me, the peas are holding out their hands!"

"Daddy says the beans are dying. Isn't he silly!"

"Let's get to the garden before daddy does."

As he closed the door he heard the shrieks trailing off round the corner of the house, diminuendo. He hung up coat and hat with a rapid gesture and hurried to the kitchen. Hilda, stirring the cocoa with a long spoon, looked round at him laconically.

"Chocolate!" he shouted, and pulled a cake of chocolate out of his pocket. He was astonished, he rolled his eyes, for it appeared to have been sat upon—"in the train." Hilda shrieked with laughter. He thrust it into her apron pocket and fled up the stairs to change.

He could not find his old flannel trousers. Not in the cup-board—not in the bureau. He surrendered to an impulse to comic rage. "Not under the bed!" he cried. He thrust his head out of the window that overlooked the garden and addressed his children.

"Martha! bring my trousers here this instant!"

He drew in his head again from the shower of replies that flew up at him like missiles and going to the door roared down to his wife.

"I've lost my trousers!"

Then he found them in the closet behind the door, and, laughing, put them on.

II.   He ran out of the side door, under the wisteria-covered trellis, and down the slippery stone steps to the vegetable garden.

"Here comes daddy, now," shrilled to him from Martha.

He lighted his pipe, shutting his left eye, and stood in pro-found meditation before the orderly, dignified, and extraordi-narily vigorous rows of beans. They were in blossom—bees were tumbling the delicate lilac-pink little hoods. Clouds of fragrance came up from them. The crickets were begining to tune up for the evening. The sun was poised above the black water tower on the far hill.

Martha and Marjorie began giggling mysteriously behind the lilacs.

"My hoe!" he wailed.

The hoe was thrust out from behind the lilacs.

"If anybody should drive up in a scarlet taxi," he said to Martha, accepting the hoe, "and inform you that your soul is free, don't believe him. Tell him he's a liar. Point me out to him as a symbol of the abject slavery that all life is. Say that I'm a miserable thrall to wife, children, and beans—particularly beans. I spend my days on my knees before my beans."

"I'll do nothing of the sort," said Martha.

He held his hoe under his arm and walked solemnly among the beans. The two girls followed him.

"Here's a caterpillar, daddy!"

"Kill him!"

"Here's another—a funny green one with red sparkles on his back. Oh, look at him!"

"Don't look at him! Kill him."

"He squirts out like green toothpaste."

"Don't, Martha!" he cried, pained. "Don't say such things! Spare your neurotic father."

He shrank visibly and strode off to the corner where his peas were planted and started methodically hoeing the rows, turning the rich loam up about the pale stalks. Now and again a pebble clinked, he stooped and threw it off into the meadow. Mary, the youngest, came to the top of the steps and cried. Martha and Marjorie went to her, and he forgot them. The rising and falling of the hoe-blade, shiny with much polishing in the brown soil, hypnotized him, and his thoughts fell into a sort of rhythm, came and went without his interference. "Ridiculous!" he thought, "that this solemn singular biped, whom other bipeds for convenience call Andrew, should stand here with a stick and scratch the skin of this aged planet. What does he expect to get for it? It pleases the aged planet. She stretches herself in the twilight, purrs like an old cat, and expresses her pleasure in the odd and useful effluvium we call peas. And this biped wears clothes. Think of it! He wears clothes; things made out of plant-fiber and sheep's wool, cunningly and hideously made to fit his arms and legs. He has in his pocket—a small pouch made in these singular garments—a watch, a small, shiny round object in which he has reduced to feeble but regular iambics the majestic motions of the sun, earth, and stars. He takes it out and looks at it with an air of comprehension and puts it back again. Why doesn't he laugh at himself?" . . . He chuckled. . . . "This object tells him that he has time for two more rows before dinner. Clink, clink. Damn these pebbles. My antediluvian anthropoid ape of an ancestor had to walk round them, they were so huge. He sat on them, cracked nuts against them, chattered with his family. He had no watch, and his trousers grew like grass. . . . Thank the lord, they've become pebbles."

He sighed, and for a moment rested his chin on the hoe-handle, peering out toward the tree-encircled swamp. The hylas were beginning to jingle their elfin bells. A red-winged blackbird sailed in the last sunlight from one apple tree to another.

"All a vicious circle—and all fascinating. Utterly preposterous and futile, but fascinating."

He dropped the hoe and trundled the wheelbarrow to the edge of the strawberry bed.

"Why can't you stay where you're put?" he said. "Why do you grow all over the place like this?"

With a trowel he began digging up the runners and placing them on the wheelbarrow. It delighted him to part the soft cool soil with his fingers, to thrust them sensitively among the finely filamented roots. The delicate snap, subterranean, of rootlets gave him a delicious pang. "Blood flows—but it's all for the best; in the best of all possible worlds. Yield to me, strawberries, and you shall bear. I am the resurrection and the life." When he had a sufficient pile of plants, he trundled the wheelbarrow to the new bed, exquisitely prepared, rich, warm, inviting. With the hoe he made a series of holes, and then, stooping, thrust the hairy roots back into the earth, pressing the soil tenderly about them. Then he rose, stretched his back, and lighted his pipe, shutting his left eye, and enshrining the flame, which danced, in the hollow of his stained hands. The cloud of smoke went up like incense.

"Water!" he cried. "Water! Water!"

Martha appeared, after a moment, bringing the watering pot. She held it in front of her with both hands.

"Quick, Martha, before they die. Their tongues are turning black."

"Silly!" Martha replied.

The earth about each plant was darkened with the tilted water, and the soiled leaves and stems were brightened.

"Listen, daddy! they're smacking their lips."

"They are pale, they have their eyes shut, they are reaching desperately down into the darkness for something to hold on to. They grope and tickle at atoms of soil, they shrink away from pebbles, they sigh and relax."

"When the dew falls, they'll sing."

"Ha, ha! What fools we are."

He flung the hoe across the wheelbarrow and started wheeling it toward the toolhouse.

"Bring the watering pot!"

Martha ran after him and put it in the wheelbarrow.

"That's right—add to my burden—never do anything that you can make somebody else do."

Martha giggled, in response, and skipped toward the house. When she reached the stone steps she put her feet close together and with dark seriousness hopped up step after step in that manner. He watched her and smiled.

"O Lord, Lord," he said, "what a circus we are."

He trundled the bumping wheelbarrow and whistled. The red sun, enormous in the slight haze, was gashing itself cruelly on a black pine tree. The hylas, by now, had burst into full shrill-sweet chorus in the swamp, and of the birds all but a few scraping grackles were still. "Peace—peace—peace," sang the hylas, a thousand at once. Silver bells, frailer than thimbles, ringing under a still and infinite sea of ether. . . . "Peace—peace," he murmured. Then he dropped the wheelbarrow in horror, and put his hands to his ears. "The enemy!" he cried. "Martha! hurry! Martha!" This time Martha seemed to be out of earshot, so he was obliged to circumvent the enemy with great caution. The enemy was a toad who sat, by preference, near the toolhouse door: obese, sage, and wrinkled like a Chinese god. "Toad that under cold stone." Marvelous compulsion of rhythm! . . . He thrust the wheelbarrow into the cool pleasant-smelling darkness of the toolhouse, and walked toward the kitchen door, which just at that moment Hilda opened.

"Hurry up," she said. Her voice had a delicious mildness in

the still air and added curiously to his already overwhelming sense of luxury. He had, for a moment, an extraordinarily satisfying sense of space.

III.   He lifted his eyes from the pudding to the Hokusai print over the mantel.

"Think of it with shame! We sit here again grossly feeding our insatiable bellies, while Fujiyama, there, thrusts his copper-colored cone into a cobalt sky among whipped-cream clouds! Pilgrims, in the dusk, toil up his sides with staves. Pilgrims like ants. They struggle upwards in the darkness for pure love of beauty."

"I don't like bread pudding," ejaculated Mary solemnly. "It's beany."

Martha and Marjorie joined in a silvery cascade of giggles.

"Where *did* she get that awful word!" said Hilda.

"Tom says it, mother."

"Well, for goodness' sake, forget it."

Mary stared gravely about the table, spoon in mouth, and then, removing the spoon, repeated, "It's beany."

He groaned, folding his napkin.

"What an awful affliction a family is. Why did we marry, Hilda? Life is a trap."

"Mrs. Ferguson called this afternoon and presented me with a basket of green strawberries. I'm afraid she thought I wasn't very appreciative. I hate to be interrupted when I'm sewing. Why under the sun does she pick them before they're ripe?"

"That's a nice way to treat a neighbor who gives you a present! . . . You *are* an ungrateful creature."

Hilda was languid.

"Well, I didn't ask her for them."

Her eyes gleamed with a slow provocative amusement.

"They're beany," said Mary.

He rolled his eyes at Mary:

"Our kids are too much with us. Bib and spoon,
Feeding and spanking, we lay waste our powers!"

They all pushed back their chairs, laughing, and a moment later, as he lighted his cigar, he heard from the music room Hilda's violin begin with tremulous thin notes, oddly analogous to the sound of her voice when she sang, playing Bach to a me-thodical loud piano accompaniment by Martha. Melancholy came like a blue wave out of the dusk, lifted him, and broke slowly and deliciously over him. He stood for a moment, made motion-less by the exquisite, intricate melody, stared, as if seeking with his eyes for the meaning of the silvery algebra of sound, and then went out.

The sun had set, darkness was at hand. He walked to the top of the stone steps and looked across the shallow valley toward the fading hill and the black water tower. The trees on the crest, sharply silhouetted against a last band of pale light, looked like marching men. Lights winked at the base of the hill. And now, as hill and water tower and trees became obscure, he began to see once more the dim phantasmal outlines of the dark city, the city submerged under the infinite sea, the city not inhabited by mortals. Immense, sinister, and black, old and cold as the moon, were the walls that surrounded it. No gate gave entrance to it. Of a paler stone were the houses upon houses, tiers upon tiers of shadowy towers, which surmounted the walls. Not a light was to be seen in it, not a motion; it was still. He stared and stared at it, following with strained eyes the faint lines which might in-dicate its unlighted streets, seeking in vain, as always, to discover in the walls of it any sign of any window. It grew darker, it faded, a profound and vast secret, an inscrutable mystery.

"She is older than the rocks," he murmured.

He turned away and walked over the lawn in the darkness, listening to the hylas, who seemed now to be saturating the hushed night with sound. "Peace—peace—peace—" they sang. *Pax vobiscum.* He gathered the croquet mallets and leaned them against the elm tree, swearing when he tripped over an unseen wicket. This done, he walked down the pale road, blowing clouds of smoke above him with uplifted face, and luxuriated in the sight of the dark tops of trees motionless against the stars. A soft skipping sound in the leaves at the road's edge made him jump. He laughed to himself. . . . "He had no watch, and his trousers grew like grass. . . ." He took out his watch and peered closely at it. The children were in bed, and Hilda was waiting for a game of chess. He walked back with his hands deep in his pockets. Pawn to King-four.

"Hilda! wake up!"

Hilda opened her candid eyes without astonishment and sat up over the chessboard, on which the tiny men were already arranged.

"Goodness! how you scared me. What took you so long? I've been dreaming about Bluebeard."

"Bluebeard! Good heavens. I hope he didn't look like me."

"He did—remarkably!"

"A *nice* thing to say to your husband. . . . Move! Hurry up! . . . I'm going to capture your King. Queens die young and fair."

He smoked his pipe. Hilda played morosely. Delicious she was when she was half asleep like this! She leaned her head on one hand, her elbow on the table. . . . When she had been checkmated, at the end of half an hour, she sank back wearily in her chair. She looked at him intently for a moment and began to smile.

"And how about the dark city tonight?" she asked. He took slow puffs at his pipe and stared meditatively at the ceiling.

"Ah—the dark city, Hilda! the city submerged under an infinite sea, the city not inhabited by mortals! . . . It was there again —would you believe it? . . . It was there. . . . I went out to the stone steps, smoking my cigar, while you played Bach. I hardly dared to look—I watched the hill out of the corner of my eyes, and pretended to be listening to the music. . . . And suddenly, at the right moment of dusk, just after the street-lamps had winked along the base of the hill, I saw it. The hill that we see there in the daylight with its water tower and marching trees,

its green sloping fields and brook that flashes in the sun, is unreal, an illusion, the thinnest of disguises—a cloak of green velvet
which the dark city throws over itself at the coming of the first
ray of light. . . . I saw it distinctly. Immense, smooth, and black,
old and cold as the moon, are the walls that surround it. No gate
gives entrance to it. Of a paler stone are the houses, tiers upon
tiers of shadowy towers that surmount those sepulchral walls. No
motion was perceptible there—no light gleamed there—no sound,
no whisper rose from it. I thought: perhaps it is a city of the
dead. The walls of it have no windows, and its inhabitants must
be blind. . . . And then I seemed to see it more closely, in a twilight which appeared to be its own, and this closer perception
gave way, in turn, to a vision. For first I saw that all the walls
of it are moist, dripping, slippery, as if it were bathed in a death-
like dew; and then I saw its people. Its people are maggots—
maggots of perhaps the size of human children; their heads are
small and wedge-shaped, and glow with a faint bluish light.
Masses of them swarm within those walls. Masses of them pour
through the streets, glisten on the buttresses and parapets. They
are intelligent. What horrible feast is it that nightly they cele-
brate there in silence? On what carrion do they feed? It is the
universe that they devour; and they build above it, as they devour it, their dark city like a hollow tomb. . . . Extraordinary
that this city, which seen from here at dusk has so supernatural
a beauty, should hide at the core so vile a secret. . . ."

Hilda stared at him.

"Really, Andrew, I think you're going mad."

"Going? I'm gone! My brain is maggoty."

They laughed, and rattled the chessmen into their wooden
box. Then they began locking the doors and windows for the
night.

LIFE ISN'T A SHORT STORY

The short-story writer had run out of ideas; he had used them all; he was feeling as empty as a bathtub and as blue as an oyster. He stirred his coffee without gusto and looked at his newspaper without reading it, only noting (but with a lackluster eye) that Prohibition was finally dead. He was having his breakfast at one of those white-tiled restaurants which are so symbolic of America—with an air of carbolic purity at the entrance, but steamy purlieus at the rear which imagination trembles to investigate. His breakfast was always the same: two two-minute eggs, a little glass of chilled tomato juice, dry toast, and coffee. The only change, this morning, lay in the fact that he was having these simple things in a new place—it was a somewhat humbler restaurant than the one he usually entered at eight-thirty. He had looked in through the window appraisingly, and had a little hesitantly entered. But the ritual turned out to be exactly the same as at the others—a ticket at the entrance, where the cashier sat behind a glass case which was filled with cigarettes, chewing gum, and silver-papered cakes of chocolate; a tray at the counter; the precise intonation of *"Two twos, with."* The only difference, in fact, was that the china was of a pale smoke-blue, a soft and dim blue which, had it been green, would have been pistachio. This gave his coffee a new appearance.

He sat at the marble-topped table near the window, and looked out at the crowded square. A light soft drizzle was falling on the morning rush of cars, wagons, pedestrians, newsboys; before the window bobbed a continuous procession of men and women; and he watched them over the half-seen headlines of his newspaper. A middle-aged woman, walking quickly, her umbrella pulled low over her head, so that the whiteness of her profile was sharp and immediate against the purple shadow. She vanished past the range of his vision before he had had time to see her properly—and for a moment after she had gone he went on thinking about her. She might do for the physical model of his story; but she wasn't fat enough, nor was she blonde, and for some obscure reason he had decided that the heroine must be fat and blonde. Just the same, she was real, she had come from somewhere and was going somewhere, and she was doing it with obvious concentration and energy. The rhythm of her gait was unusually pronounced, each shoulder swayed slightly but emphatically sideways, as if in a series of quick and aggressive but cheerful greetings—the effect, if not quite graceful, was individual and charming. He stopped thinking about her, and recovered his powers of observation, just in time to see a gray Irish face, middle-aged, hook-nosed, under a dirty felt hat, a hand quickly removing the pipe from the mouth, and the lips pouting to eject a long bright arc of spit, which fell heavily out of sight, the pipe then replaced. Such a quantity of spit he could not have imagined—his mouth felt dry at the mere thought of it. Where had it been stored and for how long? and with increasing pleasure, or increasing annoyance? The act itself had been unmistakably a pleasure, and had probably had its origins in pride; one could imagine him having competed, as a boy, in spitting through a knot-hole in a fence. He had trained himself, all his life, in the power of retention; his mouth had become a kind of reservoir.

II.   But the "story" came back to him. It had waked him up as a feeling of obscure weight at the back of his head or on the back of his tongue; it had seemed also to be in one corner of the shadowy ceiling above the bookcase, like a cobweb to be removed with a long brush. He had lain in bed looking at it, now and then turning his head to right or left on the pillow as if precisely to turn it away from the idea. It might be Elmira, it might be Akron, it might be Fitchburg—it was a small provincial city, at any rate, the sort of small town that looks its most characteristic in a brick-red postcard of hard straight streets and ugly red houses. But she wouldn't be living in one of these—she would be living in an apartment house of shabby stucco, and the entrance would be through a door of grained varnish and plate glass. It would have an air of jaded superiority. And as for her apartment itself, on the second floor, with a little curly brass number on the door——

The idea had first occurred to him in the lobby of the Orpheum. He had paused to light a cigarette in the passage that led past the lounge, where parrots squawked in cages, and canaries trilled, and goldfish swam in an ornate aquarium, at the bottom of which, dimly seen through the heavy green water, was a kind of crumbling Gothic castle. He was standing there, looking at this, when the two groups of people had suddenly encountered each other with such hearty and heavy surprise. He had caught merely the phrases *"as I live and breathe!"* and *"in the flesh!"* The two men and the two women he had scarcely looked at—the phrases themselves had so immediately assumed an extraordinary importance. They would both, he at once saw, make good titles—it was only later that he had seen that they both had the same meaning. They both simply meant—*alive.*

Alive. And that was the difference between life, as one conceived it in a story, and life as it was, for example, in the restaurant in which he was sitting, or in the noisy square at which he was looking. As I live and breathe—I am standing here living and breathing, you are standing there living and breathing, and it's a surprise and a delight to both of us. In the flesh, too— death hasn't yet stripped our bones, or the crematory tried out our fats. We haven't seen each other for a long while, we didn't know whether we were dead or not, but here we are.

At the same time, there was the awful commonplaceness of the two phrases, the cheapness of them, the vulgarity—they were as old as the hills, and as worn; æons of weather and æons of handshake lay upon them; one witnessed, in the mere hearing of them, innumerable surprised greetings, innumerable mutual congratulations on the mere fact of being still alive. The human race seemed to extend itself backwards through them, in time, as along a road—if one pursued the thought one came eventually to a vision of two small apes peering at each other round the cheeks of a cocoanut and making a startled noise that sounded like *"yoicks!"* Or else, one simply saw, in the void, one star passing another, with no vocal interchange at all, nothing but a mutual exacerbation of heat. . . . It was very puzzling.

He stirred his coffee, wondered if he had sweetened it, reassured himself by tasting it. Yes. But in this very commonplaceness lay perhaps the idea, he had begun to see, as he lay in bed in the morning, watching the rain: and as he wondered about the large blonde lady in Fitchburg, he had begun to see that Gladys (for that was her name) was just the sort of hopelessly vulgar and commonplace person who would pride herself on her superiority in such matters. She would dislike such phrases, they would disgust her. After the first two or three years of her marriage to Sidney, when the romance had worn off and the glamor had fallen like a mask from his lean Yankee trader's face, when the sense of time had begun to be obtrusive, and the deadly round of the merely quotidian had replaced the era of faint orchids and bright bracelets and expensive theater tickets, it was then that she became conscious of certain tedious phrases he was in the habit of using. There was no concealing the fact any longer that they really came of separate and different worlds; Sidney had had little more than a high-school education, he had no "culture," he had never read a book in his life. He had walked straight from school into his father's hardware shop. What there was to know about **cutlery**, tools, grass seed, lawn mowers, washing machines, wire nails, white lead paint, and sandpaper, he knew. He was a loyal Elk, a shrewd and honest business man, a man of no vices (unless one counted as a vice a kind of Hoosier aridity) and few pleasures. Occasionally he went to the bowling alleys, a pastime which she had always considered a little vulgar; he enjoyed a good hockey match; he liked a good thriller in the talkies (one of the few tastes they actually shared); and now and then he wanted to sit in the front row at a musical comedy. On these occasions, there was a definite sparkle or gleam about him, a lighting up of his sharp gray eyes, which reminded her of the Sidney to whom she had become engaged. This both puzzled and annoyed her; she felt, as she looked at him, a vague wave of jealousy and hatred. It must have been this gleam which, when focused intently on herself, had misled her into thinking him something that he wasn't and never would be.

III. *As I live and breathe.*

The story might even be called that.

A horse and wagon drew up at the curbstone outside the window. On the side of the wagon was inscribed, "Acme Towel Supply Company." Of course; it was one of those companies which supply towels and napkins and dishcloths to hotels and restaurants. The driver had jumped down, dropping his reins, and was opening the little pair of shabby wooden doors at the back of the wagon. The brown horse, his head down, his eyes invisible behind blinkers, stood perfectly still, as if deep in thought. His back and sides were shiny with rain, the worn harness dripped, now and then he twitched his shoulder muscles, as if in a slight shiver. Why did towel-supply companies always deliver towels in horse-drawn wagons? It was one of the minor mysteries; a queer sort of survival, for which one saw no possible reason. Beyond the wagon and the horse, the traffic was beginning to move forward again in response to a shrill bird-call from the policeman's whistle. A man in a black slicker had come close to the window and was reading the "specials" which were placarded in cinnamon-colored paper on the glass. When this had been done, he peered into the restaurant between two squares of paper; the quick sharp eyes looked straight at him and then past him and were as quickly gone. This meeting of his eyes had very likely prevented him from coming in; it was precisely such unexpected encounters with one's own image, as seen in the returned glance of another, that changed the course of one's life. And the restaurant had perhaps lost the sale of a couple of doughnuts and a "cup of coffee, half cream."

The way to get at Gladys's character, perhaps, was through her environment, the kind of place she lived in, her street, her apartment, her rooms. First of all, the stucco apartment house, the glass door, on which the name "Saguenay" was written obliquely in large gilt script, with a flourish of broad gilt underneath. Inside the door, a flight of shallow stairs, made of imitation marble, superficially clean, but deeply ingrained with dirt. Her apartment, now that she lived alone, was small, of course—it consisted of a bedroom, a sitting room, a bathroom, and a kitchenette. One's immediate feeling, on entering the sitting room from the varnished hallway, was that the occupant must be a silly woman. It was plushy, it was perfumed, there was a bead curtain trembling between the sitting room and the kitchenette, at either side of the lace-curtained window hung a golden-wired birdcage, in which rustled a canary, and on the window-sill was a large bowl of goldfish. The ornaments were very ornamental and very numerous; the mantel groaned with souvenirs and photographs; the pictures were uniformly senti-mental—several were religious. It was clear that she doted, simply doted, on birds and flowers—talked baby-talk to the canaries and the goldfish, even to the azalea, and always of course in that offensive, little, high-pitched fat-woman's coo. She would come in to them in the morning, wearing a pink flannel wrapper, brushing her hair, and would talk to them or wag a coy finger at them. And how's my sweet little dicky bird this morning? and have they slept well and been good in the night? and have they kept their little eyes shut tight to keep out the naughty bogey-man? And then at once she would forget them entirely, begin singing softly, walk with her head tilted on one side to the bathroom to turn on the bath, return to the kitchen to filch a cookie from the bread-box, and then go languidly to the front door for the milk and the newspaper.

The newspaper was the *Christian Science Monitor;* she took it, not because she was a Scientist, though she had an open mind, but because it was so "cultured." She liked to read about books and music and foreign affairs, and it frequently gave her ideas for little talks to the Women's Club. She had talked about the dole in England, and its distressing effect on the morals of the young men, and she had made a sensation by saying that she thought one should not too hastily condemn the nudist cult in Germany. Everyone knew that the human body craved sunlight, that the ultra-violet rays, or was it the infra-red, were most beneficial, so the idea was at least a healthy one, wasn't it? And the beautiful purity of Greek life was surely an answer to those who thought the human body in itself impure. It raised the whole question of what was purity, anyway! Everyone knew that purity was in the heart, in the attitude, and not really in the body. She thought the idea of playing croquet in the nude, queer as it might seem to us in Fitchburg, most interesting. One ought to think less about the body and more about the mind.

iv.   The towel-supply man seemed to have disappeared; perhaps he was getting a cup of coffee at the Waldorf next door. Or making a round of several of the adjacent restaurants all at once. The horse waited patiently, was absolutely still, didn't even stamp a foot. He looked as if he were thinking about the rain. Or perhaps, dismayed by the senseless noise of all the traffic about him, he was simply thinking about his stall, wherever it was. Or more likely, not thinking anything at all. He just stood.

To her friends, of course, and to her sister Emma (who was

her chief reason for living in Fitchburg) she posed as a woman with a broken heart, a woman tragically disillusioned, a beautiful romantic who had found that love was dust and ashes and that men were—well, creatures of a lower order. It was all very sad, very pitiful. One ought to have foreseen it, perhaps, or one ought not to have been born so sensitive, but there it was. If you had a soul, if you had perceptions, and loved beautiful things, and if you fell in love while you were still inexperienced and trusting, while you still looked at a world of violets through violet eyes, this was what happened. You gave your heart to someone who didn't deserve it. But what man ever *did* deserve it? Only the poets, perhaps, or the composers, Chopin for instance, those rare creatures, half angel and half man (or was it half bird?), who had great and deep and tender souls. And how many such men could one find in Massachusetts? It was all so impossible, it was all so dreadful. Everyone knew that in America the women were infinitely more refined and sensitive than the men, you had only to look about you. What man ever wanted to talk about poetry with you, or listen to an evening of the Preludes, or to a lecture about the love affair of George Sand and Alfred de Musset? They wouldn't know what you meant; they wanted to go to the bowling alley or talk about the stock market; or else to sit in the front row of the Follies and look at the legs. They were vulgar, they had no imaginations. And she remembered that time at Emma's when Sidney had got so angry and gone on so in that common and vulgar way and made such a scene—whenever she thought of it she got hot all over. Absolutely, it was the most vulgar scene! And done deliberately, too, just because he was so jealous about their having a refined conversation. And when she tried to stop him talking about it, he just went on, getting stubborner and stubborner, and all simply to make her feel ashamed. As if any of them had wanted to hear about those cheap drinking parties of his in Ohio. And that dreadful word, burgoo, that was it, which they had all laughed at, and tried to shame him out of, why what do you mean, burgoo, why Sidney what are you talking about, who ever heard such a word as *burgoo, burgoo!* And even that hadn't been enough, he got red and angry and went on saying it, burgoo, what's wrong with burgoo, of course there is such a word, and damned fine parties they were, too, and if they only had burgoos in Massachusetts life here would be a damned sight better. The idea! It served him right that she got mad and jumped up and said what she did. If you can't talk politely like a gentleman, or let others talk, then I think you had better leave those who will. Why don't you go back to your hardware shop, or back to Ohio, it doesn't seem this is the right environment for you. Or *anywhere* where you can have your precious burgoo.

But of course that was only one incident among so many, it was happening all the time; anybody could see that Sidney was not the man to ever appreciate her. What she always said was that nobody outside a marriage could ever possibly have any *real* idea of the things that went on there, could they. It was just impossible for them even to conceive of it. All those little things that you wouldn't think of—like Sidney's always leaving the dirty lather and little black hairs in the wash-basin after he shaved. Or the way he never noticed when she had on a new hat or ever said anything nice about the meals she got for him, just simply not noticing anything at all. That was a part of it, but much more was his simply not ever being able to talk to her, or to take any interest in intellectual things. And his vulgarity, the commonness of his speech, his manners! Every time she introduced him to somebody he would put his head down and take that ridiculous little confidential step toward them and say, "What was the name? I didn't get the name?" The idea! And if you told him about it he got mad. And as for the number of times every day that he said "as I live and breathe"——!

v.   It had begun to rain harder. The sound of it rushed through the opening door as a small man, very dark, a Syrian perhaps, came in shaking his sodden hat so that the drops fell in a curve on the floor. A bright spray was dancing on the roof of the towel wagon, and a heavy stream fell splattering from one corner of an awning. People had begun to run, to scurry, in one's and two's and three's, exactly like one of those movies of the Russian Revolution, when invisible machine guns were turned on the crowds. One would not be surprised to see them fall down, or crawl away on their bellies.

Or to see the whole square emptied of human beings in the twinkling of an eye. Nor would one be surprised to see a lightning flash, either, for it had suddenly become astonishingly dark —the whole dismal scene had that ominous look which seems to wait, in a melodrama, for a peal of thunder. The light was sulphur-colored; it was terrifying; and he watched with fascination all the little windshield wipers wagging agitatedly on the fronts of cars—it gave one the feeling that the poor things were actually frightened, and were breathing faster. As for the horse, he stood unmoving, unmoved. His head was down, and he seemed to be studying with an extraordinary concentration the torrent of muddy water which rushed past his feet. Perhaps he was enjoying it; perhaps he even liked to feel all that tropic weight of rain on his back, experiencing in it a renewal of contact with the real, the elemental. Or perhaps he merely enjoyed standing still. Or perhaps he simply *was*.

But the question arose, ought one now to switch the point of view in the story, and do something more about Sidney? What about Sidney? Where on earth was Sidney all this while? and doing what? Presumably, running his hardware shop—and presumably again in Boston—but this was a little meager, one wanted to know something more than that. One ought to give him a special sort of appearance—a pencil behind his ear, a tuft of white hair over his sallow forehead, sharply pointed brown shoes. Perhaps he was something of a dandy, with a vivid corner of striped handkerchief pointing from his breast pocket; and perhaps he was by no means such a dull fellow as Gladys thought. But this *would* involve a shift in point of view, which was a mistake; it was no doubt better to stick to Gladys, in Fitchburg, and to see Sidney wholly as *she* saw him, to think of him only as *she* thought of him. She would almost certainly, from time to time (self-absorbed as she was, and vain, and vulgar, and with her silly small-town pretensions to culture), she would almost certainly, nevertheless, give him credit for a few virtues. He was generous: he had offered her a divorce, as soon as he knew how she felt about it; and he had behaved like a lamb, really, if she did say so, like a lamb, about the separation. He had done everything he could think of to make it easier for her.

In fact, one thing you *could* say for Sidney was, that he was generous—generous to a fault. She often thought of that. She always thought of it especially on the first of the month, when the check for the separation allowance turned up, as punctually as the calendar—sometimes he even sent her something extra. On these days, when she bustled to the bank with the check tucked into her glove to deposit it and pay the rent, she always felt so secure and happy that she had a very special state of mind about Sidney, something that was almost affection. Of course, it couldn't *be* affection, but it was *like* it—and it was just that feeling, with perhaps the loneliness which had upset her to begin with, which had misled her at last into writing him. It was easy enough now, as she had so often said to Emma, to see what had made her do it; she was sorry for him; but it only went to show how right she had been in the whole idea.

Just the same, it had been natural enough to write to him in that affectionate and grateful way; and when he had answered by so pathetically asking her to let him come to see her she had certainly thought it might be worth trying; even Emma had thought so; perhaps they would find after all that the differences between them were superficial; they could patch things up, maybe she would go back to Boston to live wih him. The idea actually excited her—she remembered how she had found herself looking forward to having him come. Emma had offered to put him up for the night, so as to prevent embarrassment. And the thought of having him see her new apartment for the first time, with the canaries and the goldfish and the oriental rugs, and the Encyclopædia Britannica, had given her a very funny feeling, almost like being unfaithful. The day before he came she could hardly sit still. She kept walking to and fro round the apartment, moving the rugs and the chairs, and patting the cushions—and all the time wondering if two years would have changed him much, and what they would say. Naturally, she hadn't held out any real hope to him in her letter, she had only told him she would be willing to talk with him, that was all. He had no right to expect anything else, she had made that clear. However, there was no sense in not being friendly about these things, was there? Even if you were separated you could behave like a civilized human being; Emma agreed with her about that. It was the only decent thing to do. But when the day came, and when finally that afternoon she heard him breeze into Emma's front hall, stamping his feet, and went out to meet him, and saw him wearing the wing collar and the stringy little white tie, and the rubbers, and his little gray eyes shining behind the glasses with the cord, and when the very first thing he said was, just as if nothing at all had ever happened, "Well, as I live and breathe, if it isn't Gladys!"—and then stood there, not knowing whether to kiss her or shake hands—it was just a misdeal, that was all, just another misdeal.

The whole thing went down, smack, like a house of cards. She could hardly bring herself to shake hands with him, or look at him—she suddenly wanted to cry. She rushed into Emma's room and stayed there on the bed for an hour, crying—Emma kept running in and saying for God's sake pull yourself together, at least go out and talk to him for a while, he's hurt, you can't treat him like this; the poor man doesn't know whether he's going or coming; come on now, Gladys, and be a good sport. He's sitting on the sofa in there with his head down like a horse, not knowing what to say; you simply can't treat him like that. The least you can do is go out and tell him you're sorry and that it was a mistake, and that he'd better not stay, or take him round to your apartment and talk it over with him quietly and then send him back to Boston. Come on now.

But of course she couldn't do it—she couldn't even go with

him to the station. Emma went with him, and told him on the platform while they were waiting for the train that it was no use, it had all been a terrible mistake, and she was sorry, they were both sorry, Gladys sent word that she was very sorry. And afterwards, she had said it was so pathetic seeing him with his brand-new suitcase there beside him on the platform, his suitcase which he hadn't even opened, just taking it back to Boston where he came from. . . . When the train finally came, he almost forgot his suitcase; she thought he would have liked to leave it behind.

The towel-supply man came running back with a basket, flung it into the wagon, banged the dripping doors shut, and then jumped nimbly up to his seat, unhooking the reins. Automatically, but as if still deep in thought, the horse leaned slowly forward, lowered his head a little, and began to move. A long day was still ahead of him, a day of crowded and noisy streets, streets full of surprises and terrors and rain, muddy uneven cobbles and greasy smooth asphalt. The wagon and the man would be always there behind him; an incalculable sequence of accidents and adventures was before him. What did he think about, as he plodded from one dirty restaurant to another, one hotel to another, carrying towels? Probably nothing at all; certainly no such sentimental thing as a green meadow, nor anything so ridiculous as a story about living and breathing. It was enough, even if one was a slave, to live and breathe. For life, after all, isn't a short story.

THE NIGHT BEFORE PROHIBITION

When Walter Coolidge Swift woke up in his room at the Adams House he could see at once from the darkness of the morning that it was snowing, or about to snow. Turning over in bed, he saw the large flakes gliding down against the sooty wall of the court, outside the window, far apart and peaceful and leisurely; and immediately a sensation of relaxation and luxury overcame him. He smiled, clasped his hands under his head, half closed his eyes, and gave himself up to reminiscence. It was odd, the way this always happened —not the snow, of course, but the way that every time he came to the Adams House, on his semi-annual visits from New Hampshire, this same mood arose in him. No sooner would he be awake, in the morning, than he would begin thinking about the good old days when he lived in Boston—about the bars he had loved—Frank Locke's, the Holland House, Jacot's, the Nip, the Bell-in-Hand—about the theaters, the burlesque shows, the prize-fights, the ball-games—and then at the end, always, he would think, and most of all, about Eunice. Why was it that this never happened to him at home? He supposed it must be because he was always busy—busy at the office, busy with his wife, Daisy, and the children, busy at the Club. There was never any time for sentimental reminiscences. And besides, he had really settled down when they moved to Nashua—all that gay life had stopped as suddenly as if it had been cut off with a knife. With no theaters to speak of, no bars at all, and no boon companions, he had found himself with no longer much motive for dissipation, and in the twinkling of an eye his whole mode of life had changed.

Natural enough, no doubt—natural enough; but just as natural, too, when he came to Boston, to think delightedly of that other life, eight years ago, and all its pleasures. The old crowd was gone. Scarcely a soul was left that he knew, or much wanted to see: even the newspapers had changed. And the old *Record* office, that battered disorderly firetrap, where he had spent so many free hours, and helped Mike at midnight with his reviews of the latest musical comedy—that too was vanished, and with it every man and woman whom he had known there. The Negress elevator girl with red hair—Bill Farley, the sports writer, who had spanked the Follies girl in the lobby of the Lenox, and who had later died of consumption—the Virgin Queen, with the enormous breasts, who had edited the household page —where were they now? Where was gallant little Mary, who nightly picked her husband, Hal, out of the gutter beside Frank Locke's, and did his work for him in addition to her own? Nice people, nice people, and quite possibly dead. . . . And where, above all, was Eunice?

It still struck him as odd that he had made so little effort to keep in touch with her. Of course, he had fallen in love with Daisy, and then he had moved away—but even so, it had shown little foresight, and little knowledge of human nature or of himself. He might have known that he would eventually want to see her again—even if he couldn't have known that he was more than half in love with her. That was almost the strangest part of it: that he could have lived with her for three years without realizing the depth and beauty of their feeling for each other. Somehow, the affair had just seemed gay, and good; its note had been one of light-heartedness; the evenings had come and gone as so much mere amusement. It seemed to him that they had always been laughing—yes, from the very beginning, from the first moment of their meeting, when, in the Park Street Subway, reaching hastily for a strap, he had by accident taken her hand firmly and completely in his own. That had made her laugh—he had heard her laugh before he had heard her speak. She hadn't moved her hand from the strap, which she had held before him—she had merely turned and laughed, looking up at him with astonished amusement. And then, before he had been able to pull himself together, she had said, "My goodness—! You surprised me." He remembered vividly, still, how she had blushed, and with what enormous courage he had left his hand where it was. . . . And after that they had gone—where was it? —to a dirty Chinese restaurant, for tea. And then had had dinner together, at the Avery. She had explained how it happened —she would never have done such a thing if she hadn't had three cocktails at lunch. Never. And they mustn't, of course, meet again—she would walk with him along the Esplanade, he could see her to her door in Newbury Street, where she lived in a nurses' home, and that would be the end. The end! It had been the beginning of the happiest three years of his life, and perhaps of hers. They had dawdled and argued along the Esplanade—it was a fragrant night in June—sat on one bench after another, as he persuaded her to delay, and hadn't reached her door till midnight. What a torrent of farcical nonsense they had talked! And now he couldn't recall a single word of it—not a single word. Nothing but the sound of her voice, the sound of her laugh.

But the next afternoon—ah, that was another matter. In that absurd little bow-windowed room at the nurses' home, sitting side by side on the stiff cretonned sofa, while outside the open window the gardener was clipping the ivy. That gardener had been their best friend. His persistent presence there at the windows—moving from one window to another, slowly adjusting his ladder to a new position, solemnly climbing, solemnly clipping, and now and then of course glancing into the room—this had acted as a terrific restraint upon them both. Just at the moment when they most wanted to talk, to explore each other's minds, they had been compelled to be shy, and to speak in monosyllables, and to gaze. And, good Lord, how they had gazed! They had gazed and smiled, and smiled and gazed, and waited—and the waiting had made it all the more inevitable. How soon would the gardener be finished? How soon? When he wasn't looking, they had grimaced at him; but he must have stayed for a solid hour. It was getting on for sunset—the light was low and level and rich; and he remembered how it had shown him for the first time the beauty of her hair, a deep chestnut with an underglow of copper. But when the gardener had actually gone, and the clippers were quiet, and it was at last possible for them to talk— why then, strangely enough, they hadn't wanted to talk at all —they had merely wanted to kiss. And so they had kissed. And at once Boston had put on a rainbow, and the world was changed.

But now, when he tried to summon up particular moments— days—hours—weeks—it was astonishing how hard it was to get hold of anything specific, any speech, or gesture, or event. They had dined together so often, during that first phase, at the same hotels, that all those delicious dinners now seemed exactly alike, with the same bands, the same Benedictines and coffee (she had claimed that Benedictine made one passionate, and having confessed this had giggled) the same gaudy girls singing "M-i-s-s-i-s-s-i-p-p-i." Their meetings in the lobby seemed always to have been the same, at the same hour, by the same palm tree or brass spittoon. Gradually this new adventure had changed from the unknown to the known, had become a delicious ritual, a new and rich complex of habits. He had spent fewer and fewer evenings with Mike and Bill, had got out of the habit of going to ball-games and prize-fights, and instead had allowed his life to be wholly absorbed in his preoccupation with Eunice. The first three months had had a special charm—before they had begun to live together, and while there had still been an element of mystery. That odd nurses' home, for example—the pathetic little old bundle who was matron of it, Mrs. Burgess, from New

Bedford—and the nurses, Miss McKittrick, Miss Lamb, and Eunice's roommate Miss Orr—what a singular adventure it had seemed to him, all at once, to be plunged into an environment so strange to him, but so complete in itself! And slowly, as night after night they had dined together and then returned to the little bow-windowed sitting room, always with a formal greeting to Mrs. Burgess, he had possessed himself of that quiet and organized life which was as peaceful as the life of a nunnery, but by no means always as virtuous. Eunice had loved to gossip about her sister nurses. There was always some new little breeze of scandal coming up, and he smiled as he remembered the look of delighted mischievousness with which she would preface the telling of it. She would put her handkerchief to her mouth, and hold it there as if to repress the quite irrepressible little laugh, and then blush. And out the story would come. There had been, for instance, the nocturnal invasion of the "Tech" boys from next door—the adjacent building had been a private dormitory for Technology undergraduates. The two buildings were exactly alike, and from the back of each, at the third story, extended a flat roof on which it was pleasant to sit and smoke on summer evenings: one simply stepped out of the window of Miss McKittrick's room. The two roofs were divided by a low brick wall, only, and it was while Miss McKittrick and Miss Lamb were sitting there on cushions one night, in their "kims," that suddenly two impudent young faces had appeared over the wall. This had led to a series of gin-parties, now on one side of the wall and now on the other, which poor Mrs. Burgess had somehow never discovered. In fact, the two boys had once come into the bedroom, and Miss McKittrick had only just managed to shoo them out before the Doctor came. . . .

The Doctor was Miss McKittrick's fiancé—or so she had said. She had begun by being his "special"—he always called her in on special cases. Then they had taken a motor trip together, and another, and the nurses had understood quite well what was going on, and had envied her. He gave her a sealskin coat, and a Pierce-Arrow. It had gone on like this for two years, and then she learned that he was to be married to someone else, and had a nervous breakdown. She threatened him with a breach-of-promise suit, but was persuaded not to proceed with it; instead, she accepted from him Liberty Bonds to the value of $10,000, an action of which Eunice tartly disapproved. She, like the others, had always admired the Doctor, who was considered one of the best surgeons in Boston. And they had all thought him very generous.

Then there had been Miss Orr, Eunice's queer solitary room-mate, who read Keats and Shelley, but who also periodically developed a passion for "smut" books—at which times, for three or four days, she would do nothing but drink gin, and read all night; Eunice once or twice had to take her cases for her. As for Eunice herself, he hadn't been able, at first, to make out just how seriously she took her profession. She had a small income of her own, it appeared, and she took cases only often enough to keep from being bored, and then, if possible, only by the day; though now and then there had been exceptions. She had once or twice acted as nurse-companion to a rich old bird of sixty-five who took her with him to Hot Springs for a month or two in the winter. She claimed to have known him for a long while. Perhaps she had—for certainly Eunice was the most honest woman he had ever met; but at the time this had made him a little jealous, and a little suspicious. Was it possible—? No, it wasn't possible. She had liked the old fellow, liked his sister, too, he had paid her well, and it had of course given her a change.

It was against this background, which contained so much that was unfamiliar and titillating to the imagination, that their intimacy had developed. They had agreed that they would not fall in love, nor marry, nor do any such foolish thing—they would merely have a good time, and become very fond of each other. Eunice didn't want to marry, anyway, and he himself was too poor to marry, and had at the time poor prospects. Perhaps he had understated his prospects?—yes, perhaps he had. Why? It had been a part of his misunderstanding of the whole situation, a failure to assay his feelings for Eunice at their true value. They have a light and charming affair, if Eunice would permit become such, and let it go at that. But would Eunice permit it? He remembered a month of doubt, and indeed almost despair, about this, as the first autumn came on—a period when he had begun to drink rather heavily, feeling that the strain was becoming too great. For a week he had avoided Eunice, not even calling her on the telephone. Then, suddenly, when he paid her a surprise visit one evening, after dining at the Club, she had astonished him by inviting him to come up to her room. She had never before told him that this was allowed; evidently the fact that she had kept him in ignorance of this official permission had simply been a part of her defense. And then, of course —oh, Lord, oh, Lord. What a delirium, what a delirium!

And all, too, in a room which couldn't be locked! The key had been lost. There was always the chance, the remote chance, that one of the other nurses might suddenly walk in, or Mrs. Burgess—someone to whom she might not have had time to give a warning beforehand. Once, in fact, this had actually happened. Miss McKittrick, who had been out all day, and who had come home late, had charged in while they were on the couch together. It had been very funny—he had sat up abruptly and tried to hide his shoeless feet under the edge of the couch. They had tried in an instant to look very respectable and innocent, but not with much success; they could see that by the gleam in Miss McKittrick's eye, and the polite but amused smile with which she had then hastily vanished. And oddly enough, Eunice had seemed to be enormously pleased by the episode. Perhaps she felt—yes, perhaps she had then felt an equality, at last, with the others. Not with Miss Orr, who had never had a lover, being too shy, but with the others. Yes, that must have been it. That must have been it. She had known that now Miss McKittrick would tell the others, and that they would all look upon her in a new light. She had now joined the nunnery in earnest.

The first winter had been the nicest. As he looked back on it now, it seemed one long madness of laughter. For some reason, he had been able to amuse Eunice as he had never been able to amuse anyone else. Why was that? The simplest things narrated to her—his habit of forgetting things, his proneness to social blunders, his shyness at the telephone, his ineptitudes in making love, to her and to her predecessors (about whom he was able to be quite frank with her)—all these things she seemed to find endlessly entertaining. Partly, no doubt, because he had from the outset been able to talk so easily to her, so unrestrainedly. She had taken him into a new world, one less conventional than his own, freer, brighter, more honest. He had been able for the first time to shed all sorts of absurd Puritan inhibitions into which he had been born, and to experience an honest delight in complete honesty. The sensual and even the smutty had for the first time taken a place in the world, and an honorable place; and with his discovery of this had come an extraordinary sense of increased unity and power. He had walked on air. He had seemed to be a foot taller. In the presence of his friends, he had felt an integrity and clearness which at once had given him an enormous advantage; they too had felt it without quite knowing why. . . . But why had he been able to talk so freely and well with Eunice? So much more freely than, for example, with Daisy?

Partly, perhaps, because he had felt an intellectual and social superiority; though God knew he attached little importance to either. Just the same, it might have been that. He could relax, with her, as with no one else. She was always receptive, too, glad to see him, eager to be amused; she never reproached him if he absented himself for longer than usual, nor asked him why he hadn't come sooner, or where he had been; never wrote him, nor called him on the telephone; just waited for him to reappear; and when at last he called Back Bay 21307 was at once just as gayly responsive as ever. "Hello?" "Hello!" "Is that Mrs. Charles the Second?" "Oh no, I'm afraid you've got the wrong number. This is nobody *you* know." "Oh yes, it is!" "Well, your voice *is* familiar—" and then the little laugh, quenched in the little handkerchief, and in fifteen minutes she would be meeting him at the door, and they would climb the shabby carpeted stairs to the third-floor room. And there the pale oak desk, the oil painting of a sunset on a river, the clothes closet in which the gin bottle was kept among hat-boxes on the shelf, the low couch with a Paisley shawl spread over it and an ornamental calendar on the wall just above it, and Miss Orr's couch just opposite, pushed against the screen by the fireplace, and the toy monkey hung from the gas bracket, and the ugly upholstered chairs—these things were still a surprisingly real part of his life. He had been happy, in that room—happier than he would ever be again. If only he had known enough to know it! But how could he have guessed that merely to sit there with Eunice, listening to Miss McKittrick and Miss Orr talking and laughing slyly in the next room, would at last be remembered as something extraordinarily haunting and lovely? If only now he could recover those voices, or, for that matter, those talks with Eunice! Three years of it, and all he could recall was the look of the room, the chairs, the calendar, the view from the window toward the church at night with lamplight on the snow, the walk from the Club through slush and ice at eight o'clock, the departure punctually at ten-fifteen, when all guests were firmly expelled. Sometimes, in good weather, Eunice had strolled down with him to the river, and they had sat on the Esplanade, watching the lighted trains go over the salt-box bridge like dotted glowworms. At other times, when they had dined out, and when perhaps Miss Orr was ill, and they had been unable to go to the room, they had dawdled over dinner till late, and perhaps got a little tight, and then wandered along Commonwealth Avenue to the Public Gardens. And once, when they were both *very* tight—but what a scene! What a scene! They had crept up the narrow alley behind Newbury Street and into the little yard behind the house, and there under the ailanthus tree had surrendered to such a delirium as he had never known before or since. The full moon was above them, there were lights in Miss McKittrick's room, at any moment somebody might look out and see them or hear them. And after that, in Commonwealth Avenue, where the reviewing stands had just been built for the Liberty Parade—he groaned with delight when he thought of it. It had been sheer madness. Not a soul was in sight—it was after midnight. The lamplight came greenly through the leaves on the elm trees, the gaunt reviewing stands screened them on either side. . . . And then the whispered good-night at the door, and he walked to the Waldorf for his cornflakes and cream and coffee, and so home to the Fenway and to bed. . . .

Withdrawing himself again from the past to his room in the Adams House, he watched the large snowflakes fall heavily and slowly along the soot-blackened walls outside his window. It must be after eight. But the past was too delicious, too powerful for him, and again he plunged into his stream of recollection. What a magic thing was memory, and in a way, how painful! Here one could lie on a winter's morning, in the Adams House, and re-live a Spring long ago; look out of a hotel window, and at the same moment think of a sweetheart who was perhaps—dead. But could she possibly be dead? No. After all, it was now only two years since he had discovered, by the merest accident, where she lived, and that she was married—only two years since he had written her that carefully guarded note, signed Ethel Swift, asking her to meet him; that note to which she had replied only, on a postcard, "No!" Well, she was quite right, quite right. Suppose she had a jealous husband? Suppose her husband had, to begin with, been suspicious of her past? And no doubt he was; Eunice had spoken of him years ago, she had even then, from time to time, gone yachting with him at Gloucester. Tompkins—Thorwald Tompkins. Curious name. Why the Thorwald? Norwegian blood somewhere, probably. And of course Tompkins must have known about himself, just as he had known about Tompkins. He remembered that time, when, calling her by telephone from the Public Library pay-station, he had, by some queer accident, been connected with the Newbury Street telephone while Eunice was talking with Tompkins. It had given him rather a turn, to hear her laughing at another man's jokes, being natural and amusing with him, treating him as if he were an intimate! And to hear poor Tompkins urging, urging her to meet him that evening to dance, and Eunice evading skillfully, since she more than half expected a visit from *him*—it had been this that had reassured him, and prevented him from being furiously jealous. How amused Eunice had been when, ten minutes later, he had quoted that whole telephone conversation to her, verbatim! She had thought him a wizard, a necromancer, a fiend. He had teased her about it all evening. And she had been so obviously glad to see him, and not Tompkins. . . .

What sort of life did she have with Tompkins? Was she happy, he wondered? . . . But before that, long before that, Daisy had intervened. Ah! Yes. Daisy. Suddenly this new adventure, this new wonder, this new delight, and on a different social plane—it was all so absurd, so false! Merely because she came of a good family, and belonged to Sewing Circles and things, and had been to college, and was totally and blindly innocent—and grasping— good God. And by degrees he had gone to see Eunice less and less often. From every night it had dropped to every other night, from every other night to twice a week, once a week, once in two weeks—it had been shameful, and he had felt terribly ashamed. He had thought it was the best thing to do. What else was there to do? Could he tell her that he had fallen in love with another girl? That he wanted to marry? Hardly. It had been very awk- ward, and he had begun to feel dishonest. But then he had remem- bered all that they had said at the beginning, their agreement to make the affair a light and bondless one, their mutual assur- ance that whatever else they did they would never be so absurd as to fall in love, and had felt a little better about it. Eunice was a good egg. She wouldn't mind, when he finally told her—of course she wouldn't. She had never liked his spending money on her—wouldn't accept presents—made no claims—had even, once, said that if ever anything went wrong, and they had a child, she would simply disappear. Disappear. He would never hear from her again. She knew, she said, what a struggle he was having, and the last thing she wanted to do was to put any sort of extra burden on him. If such a thing were to happen, she would take the entire responsibility herself. She would go quietly away, have the child in some remote part of the country, see that it was properly adopted—or even adopt it herself—and never again communicate with him in any way. . . .

And when he did, finally, tell her—what a brick she had been! She merely put her handkerchief to her mouth, laughed, and said that she had guessed it for months. He remembered that she had got a little tighter than usual—and she had asked him a great many questions about Daisy. Natural enough. And he had told her everything there was to tell, and with what an enormous sense of relief! The confession had done him good. Was she tall? short? blonde? brunette? younger than herself? intellectual? . . . He described his first meeting with her, at a tea party, in detail; Eunice was fascinated. She had wanted to know all about the tea —who gave it, where it was, how many people were there, what was served. Was there dancing? Yes, there was dancing. It had been a sort of bazaar, as a matter of fact, with a fortune-telling booth, and he had had his fortune told by a pseudo-gypsy. She told him that he would have ten children and die at thirty-five, in complete bankruptcy. All his ten children would be girls. "A harem of your own," Eunice had said.

And then she had astonished him, when they were about to rise from the table, by saying that he was not to come home with her. It was finished. She would have dinner with him, if he liked, from time to time, but the rest of it was finished. Once more, then, they had walked along the Esplanade, talking, arguing, sitting on benches, rising to walk on again; but this time, when they arrived at Newbury Street, the door was barred. She was gay, amusing, even frivolous about it, but she was adamant. There was just a moment, when he had tried to push her ahead of him into the hall through the open door, when she showed for a fraction of a second a flash of anger; gone as soon as seen. They had stared at each other, stood, his hand on her blue taffeta wrist, smiled—and then he had come away. Dear Eunice—how perfectly right she had been. So right, and he himself had been so convinced of it, that for months he hadn't seen her at all; not, in fact, until after he had married, and returned from his honeymoon in Bermuda, and moved to an apartment in Cambridge.

Several months passed, and one day, when he was walking with Daisy along Tremont Street, he saw Eunice in the distance. He had felt a curious confusion in himself, a something not right, a loss of balance—what was it? And at once had begun planning to see her again, as soon as Daisy should have gone off to the country for the summer.

And this had happened the day before Prohibition went into effect. As soon as he had seen Daisy off on her train for Burlington, he had called up Eunice. "Hello?" "Hello!" "Is this Mrs. Charles the Second?" "No, I'm afraid you've got the wrong number. This is nobody *you* know." "Oh yes, it is!" "Well, I admit your voice *is* familiar! . . ." And then the little laugh, perfectly unchanged, with which he could visualize the handkerchief, and an agreement to meet for dinner at the Avery—with the proviso that she would have to return home immediately *after* dinner.

But in this, unfortunately or fortunately, Eunice had left out of account the fact that it was the night before Prohibition. For that matter, so had he. It was only when he stopped at the Raleigh for a Lone Tree cocktail, on his way to the Avery, that he had first realized that it would be a wild night. It had been almost impossible to get into the bar. Everybody was already drunk, fighting drunk. Tin horns were being blown in the streets as if for a holiday. It would be no sort of occasion for Eunice to be knocking around by herself, and he regretted that he hadn't arranged to call for her in Newbury Street. There was nothing to be done about it, now, however, so he went quickly to the Avery, and Eunice turned up unharmed, but excited. This had been rather a good thing—it diverted attention from what might otherwise have been a rather embarrassing meeting. As it was, the public fever communicated itself to them, and they drank twice as much as usual, and both of them became quite recklessly cheerful. They were glad to see each other; frankly and delightedly so. And Eunice was wonderful—simply wonderful. She wanted to know, without the slightest hesitation, whether the honeymoon had been a success. Had it been a success? Well, it had been a moderate success, a *moderate* success. But these voyages to Bermuda!—he could remember just how he had said that, shaking his head. And Eunice had at once been hugely amused, and everything had begun to go as if there had never been an interruption. They had drunk each other's healths in champagne, and then more champagne, while the band played, saying "For the last time!" "For the last time!" and looking at each other—ah—with as deep an affection as ever. Strange! Why hadn't he seen that at the time? Anyway, he hadn't. But what he had, at the time, seen, was that Eunice was in a state in which she was easily persuadable. If he put her into a taxi and took her to Cambridge, to his own apartment, without telling her where he was going——

And this, after the coffee and the Benedictines, he did. They both swayed a little as they crossed the floor, pushing through streams of late arrivals who also themselves swayed, and delicious it had been to feel once more the small delightful warmth of Eunice, now so strange and remote, after this long interval become so unfamiliar, moving against his arm and side. She too had felt this, and when they were seated in the taxi, and the taxi had turned, snarling with increasing speed, toward Scollay Square and Cambridge, they had again once more fallen into each other's arms, as if it were the most natural thing in the world, which it was. As they crossed the salt-box bridge, at which they had so often looked at night from a bench on the Esplanade, a momentary misgiving had crossed his mind—was it right to take Eunice to his wife's apartment? Was it right? But this had passed like a cloud, and in no time at all they were there. They climbed the stairs, opened the door, turned on the lights—got out the gin and the ice and the glasses—and then, of course, he had had to show Eunice round the apartment.

That had been very singular—very singular. What a queer, dark, unhappy delight, holding her glass in her hand, she had taken in seeing the home of her supplanter! Every nook and cranny. The clothes, the linen, the china, the rugs, the furniture, the photographs of Daisy which stood on the dressing table —the broom with which he had killed the mouse in the bath-tub, the stove under which the fire had broken out—she had to see it all. She seemed unable to see enough. Was there anything else? Nothing more? Nothing more at all? And then, after a while, the delirium in the dark room, the divine delirium—the profound simple happiness at being together again, after all these months, and in spite of the shadow of Daisy—or perhaps even more because of it. Would there ever again be such an hour in his life?

Possibly not. And yet, there had been something wrong with it. In spite of the sharp edge given to their delight by the fact that they were using Daisy's apartment and that Eunice was secretly and wickedly, as it were, usurping Daisy's place, a delight of which they had both been acutely conscious at the time, and in spite too of the feeling of revelry which it was impossible not to share with the public frenzy—for the streets were full of yodeling men and women—nevertheless, as they lay together, the queer shadow had come between them. Was it, after all, simply Daisy? Or was it simply that time had somehow sundered them? For suddenly he had begun, after the first raptures were over, to feel detached, remote, alone with himself; his gestures, even his voice, had gradually become more and more self-conscious; the impulse to make love to her seemed to have come to an end. He had lain there and stared at the dark ceiling, awkwardly and almost ashamedly aware of his hand that rested on her shoulder—afraid to caress her, lest the caress seem forced and false, and equally afraid to remove his hand, lest Eunice perceive the change. But she had perceived it, he knew now—as quickly as he had; she too had become strained and strange. A silence had fallen, during which they listened to the sound of running feet outside, drunken shouts, the noise of someone falling heavily, a caterwaul of falsetto laughter. And then by tacit consent they had begun to talk of—not themselves, not of this odd change, which would have been the wise and brave thing to do, but of any trifle, any straw of topic at which they could clutch, as if desperate to conceal their calamity. He remembered, at this point, suddenly realizing that he wanted her to go. He wanted to be alone. If she would go quickly, and if also perhaps she could show, ever so slightly and faintly, but courageously, that she was hurt, why then something might even yet be salvaged. He would be touched, his conscience would be moved, and through this circuit his feeling for her would be renewed. He wanted her to go, moreover, by herself—to have to accompany her all the way to Boston, at this hour, on such a night, with the prospect of a long and hideous return journey, would, he felt sure, be the final destruction of the delicately balanced thing. If, on the other hand, she were to *offer* to go alone, then again his feeling might be renewed, and he would perhaps actually *want* to go with her. . . .

But she had made no such suggestion; no doubt she was a little frightened; she had seen the situation—partially at any rate—and simply hadn't known how to deal with it. So they had lain together, increasingly silent, increasingly conscious of the dark turmoil of doubt and apathy which had arisen between them, until he had at last himself told her that it was very late. Extraordinary, extraordinary ending to what had promised to be so joyful a night! There was really no reason why she shouldn't stay with him till morning. But he wanted desperately to be alone. And so they had risen and turned on the lights; and Eunice had rearranged her hair, using Daisy's mirror; and he had said, a little lamely, that as he was fearfully tired he hoped she wouldn't mind if he merely saw her to the Square, and there put her on a Massachusetts Avenue car. . . . Good Lord! It had been scandalous. And on that, of all nights! Harvard Square was a bedlam. And the last car, the owl-car, when it appeared, was packed with the dregs of humanity, all drunk, all singing. And into this horrible crowd he had permitted Eunice to go alone. And the only woman in the car. . . .

He groaned as he thought of it; he could never think of it without closing his eyes. Astonishing that a mere internal necessity should have compelled him to do such a thing! And not very flattering. And yet, there it was, one of those freaks of psychology. He had had to do it, just as afterwards he had had to wait nearly two years before he felt again a genuine impulse to see her. It hadn't been that his feeling for her had really changed

—not at all. If anything, his feeling for her had been steadily and surely deepening all these years, and was perhaps deeper now than it had ever been. No, it was some subtle pang of conscience, some shadow of Daisy, some vague distaste for duplicity, which had dictated the whole fiasco, and brought to an end the loveliest relationship with a human being which he had ever known. And when, finally, he had tried to get hold of her once more—but again with a misgiving that the same fiasco would recur—it was to learn from Miss McKittrick that Eunice was married. Miss McKittrick had been distinctly hostile and hadn't in the least tried to conceal it. What was it, precisely, that she had said? He couldn't remember; but certainly she had conveyed to him, unmistakably, that he had made Eunice very unhappy, and had practically driven her into marriage with a man about whom she cared nothing at all. Miss McKittrick had remained standing during the brief interview, making it plain that she didn't want to talk with him. And so he had left the door of the Newbury Street house for the last time. He had walked almost automatically to the Waldorf, for a bowl of cornflakes and cream, as if somehow for the completion of a ritual, and as he sat there and stared at the ugly mosaic floor he had begun to know his misery, his misery which had never left him, and which perhaps would never leave him. He *must* see her—he *must* see her. He must, somehow, explain the whole horrible thing to her! But it was impossible. . . . And when, later still, he had written to her, she had merely said, "No!"

Well, it was time to get up, time for breakfast, and still snowing, and time for work. And later in the day—well, he would walk through Newbury Street; and look up at the three windows which had once belonged to Eunice.

Just as he allowed himself to sink gloomily into the deep brown leather chair by the fireplace, reflecting, "Here I am again, confound it—why do I come here?" —she came swishing into the room, rising, as she always did, curiously high on her toes. She was smiling delightedly, almost voraciously; the silver scarf suited enchantingly her pale Botticelli face.

"How nice of you to come, Harry!" she said.

"How nice of you to ask me, Gertrude!"

"*Nice* of me? . . . Not a bit of it. Self-indulgent."

"Well——!"

"Well."

She sat down, crossing her knees self-consciously; self-consciously she allowed the scarf to slip halfway down her arms. It was curious, the way she had of looking at him: as if she would like to eat him—curious and disturbing. She reminded him of the wolf grandmother in "Little Red Riding Hood." She was always smiling at him in this odd, greedy manner—showing her sharp, faultless teeth, her eyes incredibly and hungrily bright. It was her way—wasn't it?—of letting him know that she took an interest, a deep interest, in him. And why on earth shouldn't she, as the widow of his best friend?

"Well," she again repeated, "and have you seen May lately?" She gave him this time a slower smile, a smile just a little restrained; a smile, as it were, of friendly inquisition. As he hesitated, in the face of this abrupt attack (an attack which was familiar between them, and which she had expected and desired), she added, with obvious insincerity, an insincerity which was candidly conscious: "Not that I want to pry into your personal affairs!"

"Oh, not in the least. . . . I saw her last night."

"Where? At her apartment?"

"How sly you are! . . . Yes, after dinner. We dined at the Raleigh, and had a dance or two. Good Lord, how I hate these fox-trots! . . . Then went back and played the phonograph. She had some new Beethoven. . . . *Lovely* stuff."

"*Was* it?"

She lowered her lids at him—it was her basilisk expression. As he met it, tentatively smiling, he experienced a glow of pleasure. What a relief it was to sink comfortably into this intimacy! to submit to this searching, and yet somehow so reassuring, invasion! He knew this was only the beginning, and that she would go on. She would spare nothing. She was determined to get at the bottom of things. She would drag out every detail. And this was precisely what he wanted her to do—it was precisely for this that he felt a delighted apprehension.

"And I suppose," she continued, "she told you about our lunch together? For of course she tells you everything."

"Not everything, no. But she did mention it. . . . As a matter of fact, she was rather guarded about it. You didn't hurt her feelings in some way—did you?"

There was a pause. The fire gave a muffled sap-explosion, a soft explosion muffled in ashes; and they looked at each other for rather a long time with eyes fixedly and unwaveringly friendly. She smiled again, she smiled still, and began drawing the sheer bright scarf to and fro across her shoulders, slowly and luxuriatingly. She was devilish attractive; but decidedly less attractive than devilish. Or was this to do her an injustice? For she was honest—oh, yes, she was appallingly honest; always so brutally outspoken, and so keenly interested in his welfare.

"If I did, I didn't mean to," she murmured, letting her eyes drop. "Or *did* I mean to? . . . Perhaps I did, Harry."

"I thought perhaps you did. . . . Why did you want to?"

"Why? . . . I don't know. Women *do* these things, you know."

"You don't like her."

Hesitating, she threw back her fair head against her clasped hands.

"I like her," she said slowly, and with an air of deliberation, "but I find it so hard to make out who she *is*, Harry. I wish she weren't so reserved with me. She never tells me *anything*. Not a blessed thing. Heaven knows I've tried hard enough to make a friend of her—haven't I?—but I always feel that she's keeping me at a distance, playing a sort of game with me. I never feel that she's natural with me. Never."

He took out a cigarette, smoothed it between his fingers, and lit it.

"I see," he said. "And what was it you said that could have hurt her?"

"What was it? . . . Oh, I don't know, I suppose it was what I said about her way of *laughing*. I said I thought it was too *controlled*—that if she weren't just playing the part of a polite and innocent young lady she would let herself go. You *know* it's not natural, Harry. And she seemed to think that was my insidious way of accusing her of hypocrisy."

"Which it was."

"Well—was it? . . . Perhaps it was."

"Of course it was. . . . Confound it, Gertrude—what did you want to do that for? You know she's horribly sensitive. And I don't see how you think *that* kind of thing will make her like you!"

He felt himself frowning as he looked at her. She was swinging her crossed knee. She was looking back at him honestly—oh, so very honestly—her long green eyes so wide open with candor—and yet, as he always did, he couldn't help feeling that she was very deep. She was kind to him, she was forever thinking of his interests, first and foremost; and yet, just the same——

"It was just a moment of exasperation, that was all. . . . Hang it, Harry! It infuriates me to think that she's playing that sort of game with *you*. You're too nice, and too guileless, to have that sort of thing done to you."

Smiling—smiling—smiling. That serpentine Botticelli smile, which had something timid in it, and something wistful, but also something intensely cruel.

"Don't you worry about me."

"But I do worry about you! Why shouldn't I worry about you? . . . Good Lord! If I didn't, who would? . . . I'm perfectly sure *May* doesn't."

She emphasized this bitter remark by getting up; moving, with that funny long stride of hers (which was somehow so much too long for her length of leg), to the fireplace. She took a cigarette from the filigree silver box on the mantelpiece and lifted it to her mouth. But then she changed her mind and flung the cigarette violently into the fire.

"Hang it," she said, "what do I want a cigarette for? . . . *I* don't want a cigarette."

She stood with one slipper on the fender, staring downward into the flames. It was odd, the effect she produced upon him: a tangle of obscure feelings in conflict. There were moments, he was sure, when he thoroughly detested her. She had the restlessness of a caged animal—feline, and voluptuous, and merciless. She wanted to protect him, did she, from that "designing" May? But she also, patently, wanted to devour him. Designing May! Good heavens! Think of considering poor May, poor ingenuous May, designing! Could anything be more utterly fantastic? He saw May as he had seen her the night before. She had been angelic—simply angelic. The way she had of looking up at him as if from the very bottom of her soul—while her exquisitely sensitive and gentle face wavered to one side and downward under the earnestness of his own gaze! No, he had never in his life met anyone who loved so simply and deeply and all-surrenderingly, or with so little *arrière pensée*. She was as transparent as a child, and as helpless. She gave one her heart as innocently as a child might give one a flower. Gertrude could, and would, torture her unrelentingly. Gertrude would riddle her—Gertrude would tear her to pieces—with that special gleaming cruelty which the sophisticated reserve for the unsophisticated. And none the less, as usual, he felt himself to be powerfully and richly attracted and stimulated by Gertrude—by her fierceness, her intensity, the stealthy, wolflike eagerness which animated her every movement. He watched her, and was fascinated. If he gave her the least chance, wouldn't she simply gobble him up, physically and spiritually? Or was he, perhaps, mistaken—and was all this merely a surface appearance, a manner without meaning?

"No, I can't make it out," he said, sighing. He relaxed, with a warm feeling of comfort, and happiness, as if a kind of spell, luxurious and narcotic, were being exerted over him. "She isn't at all what you think she is—if you really *do* think she is. . . . She's as simple as a—primrose. And in spite of her self-centeredness, she is fundamentally unselfish in her love of me. I'm convinced of that."

"My *dear* Harry! . . . You know *nothing* about women."

"Don't I?"

"*A primrose! . . .*"

She laughed gently, insinuatingly, lingeringly, derisively, as she looked downward at him from the mantelpiece. She was delighted, and her frank delight charmed him. How she ate up that unfortunate, that highly unfortunate, primrose! She was murderous; but he couldn't help feeling that she had made something truly exquisite of murder—as instinctive and graceful as a lyric.

"A primrose!" she repeated gaily. "But, of course, I see what you mean. You *are* sweet, Harry. But your beautiful tenderness deserved something better. She has, I know, an engaging naïveté of appearance and manner. But surely you aren't so innocent as to suppose that it isn't practiced? Are you?"

"Yes and no. Of course, what one calls a manner is always, to some extent, practiced. But if you mean she is insincere with me, no. She is perfectly sincere. Good heavens, Gertrude, have I got to tell you again that she's in love with me—frightfully in love—as I am with her? One can't fake love, you know. And what on earth would she *want* to fake it for—assuming that she could?"

"That's easy enough. She wants your money. She wants your prestige. She wants your social position—such as it is. She'd give her eye-*teeth* to be married to you, whether she loved you or not."

How sharply she pronounced the word "teeth," and with what a brightening and widening of her incomparable eyes! Really, she ought to be in a zoo. She reminded him of that leopard he had seen the other day, when he had gone with his two little nieces to the Bronx. He had sat there, in his cage, so immobile, so powerful, so still, so burning with energy in his spotted brightness; and then, without the smallest change of expression, he had uttered that indescribably far-away and ethereal little cry of nostalgic yearning, his slit eyes fixed mournfully on Alison. Good heavens—it had curdled his blood! For all its smallness and faintness and gentleness, it had been a sound of magnificent power, a prayer of supernal depth and force. Wasn't Gertrude's magic of exactly the same sort? It was in everything she did. She was not beautiful, precisely—she was too abrupt, too forceful, too sharp, for that. Despite her grace, and the undeniable witch-charm of her face, her intensity gave her whole bearing an odd angularity and feverishness. He even felt, occasionally, that she might some day, all of a sudden, go quite mad. Stiff, stark, staring mad. Lycanthropy? For certainly it wouldn't surprise one to hear her howl like a wolf. And this animal madness in her spirit was a part of, if not the very base of, her extraordinary power to fascinate. One followed her queer evolutions as if hypnotized. If she entered a room, one looked at no one else. If she left a room, one felt as if one's reason for being there had gone.

"I wish I could make you *see* her properly," he mourned, stretching out his legs toward the fire.

"Go ahead! . . . Try."

"But what's the use? You seem determined—for whatever reason—*not* to see her."

"Not in the least. I'd *like* to believe you—I'd like nothing better."

"Women will never, never, *never* do justice to those members of their own sex who attract men in the perfectly natural way that May does. Of course she attracts men—and of course she knows it. How could she help it? Can the crocus help it if the sparrow wants to tear her to pieces? It's not a trick or a falsity in her. She's as naturally affectionate, and as guileless in her affections, and as undiscriminating, I might add, as a child of six. And one can see, with a little divination, that she has been painfully hurt, over and over again, by this habit of hers of wearing her heart on her sleeve. She gives her soul away forty times a day, just out of sheer generosity, just because she has such a *capacity* for love; and she is rewarded by a suspicious world with jeers and mud. That's always the way it is. The counterfeit makes its way. And the genuine is spat upon."

"How tactful you are to me!"

"Aren't I!"

"I distrust, profoundly, that madonna type. Really, my dear Harry, it's too easy."

"*You* couldn't do it!"

"No, thank God, and I don't want to. I'd rather be honest."

They were silent, and in the pause the black marble clock on the mantel struck the half-hour. Gertrude's face had become smooth and enigmatic. Abstractedly, she gazed down at her gray-slippered foot, turning it this way and that to make the diamonded buckle sparkle in the firelight. What was she thinking about? What was she feeling? What waxen puppets was she melting in the powerful heat of her imagination? He waited for her next move with an anticipation which was as pleased as it was blind. One never knew where Gertrude would come up next. But one always felt sure that when she came up she would come up with the sharp knife in her mouth and the fresh pearl in her hand.

"I have the feeling that she wouldn't even be above blackmail. Or a breach-of-promise suit. I hope you don't write her incriminating letters!"

"Oh, *damn!*"

"But go ahead with your charming portrait, your pretty Greuze portrait. I'll really do my best to be credulous."

"My dear Gertrude, if you could have seen her in that wood, last week, looking for Mayflowers under the dead leaves! . . ."

It was hopeless, perfectly hopeless, in the light of that baleful smile! He wanted to shut his eyes. It was like trying to sleep under a spotlight. Was there no refuge for poor May? . . . For it had been enchanting—enchanting. He had never expected again, in this life, to encounter a human spirit of such simplicity and gaiety and radiant innocence. That moment, now forever immortal in his memory, when he had found a nest of blossom among the brown pine-needles, and she had come galloping—positively galloping—toward him, with a dead oak branch in her hand! And the pure ecstasy of her young delight as she stared at the flowers, bending over and putting one hand lightly on his arm!

Gertrude collapsed into her chair, helpless with amusement; giving herself up to her laughter, she made him feel suddenly ashamed of that remembered delight.

"Oh—oh—oh—oh!" she cried.

"Well!"

"The shy arbutus! . . . Forgive me, Harry, but that's too funny. How old *are* you?"

He flung his cigarette at the back-log and grinned.

"I knew it was no use," he grumbled amiably. "I can't make you see her, and it's no use trying."

"Well—I can see this much. You *are* in love with her. Or you couldn't possibly be such a fool. But it's precisely when you're in love that you need to keep your wits about you. Or the wits of your friends. . . . You mustn't marry her, Harry."

"Well—I don't know."

"*No!* . . . It would be ruinous."

"Would it? How can you be so sure?"

"You think, I suppose, that life would be insupportable without her."

"An agony that I can't bear to think of. And to think that some other man——!"

"I know the feeling. I've been in love myself."

"It's pretty bad."

"Of course it is. Every time. But that doesn't prove anything. Not a single thing. That sort of agony is largely imagination. . . . Do you *really* think you'll marry her?"

"Well—I haven't exactly asked her to. But I shouldn't wonder if I would."

It was queer—he felt, and quite definitely, that he had said this to her as if challengingly, as if to see how she would react to it—as if, almost, he hoped to force her to some spectacular action. He smiled lazily to himself, his eyes glazed by the firelight.

She jumped up again, electric, her scarf slipping to the floor.

"Let's have some sherry!" she said. "Would you like to get it?—in the dining room. You know where it is."

"Good idea."

He stopped to pick up her scarf, accidentally touching her silken instep as he did so. She stood unmoving. Funny—he had the impression that she was shivering. Cold? . . . Excitement? . . . He wondered, idly, as he crossed the library to fetch the sherry decanter; and he came back with the tray, still wondering, but wondering with a pleasant confusedness. He began humming a theme from Opus 115.

"You know, those late Beethoven things are wonderful—wonderful." He put down the tray and removed the stopper from the decanter. "The purity of the absolute. For pure and continuous ecstasy——"

"Purity! . . . You seem to have purity on the brain. . . . Thanks, Harry."

"Here's looking at you. . . . Old times."

"Old times."

They sipped at the lightly held glasses and smiled.

"I wish," she then said, in a tone that struck him as new and a little forced—as if, in fact, she were nerving herself to some-thing—"that you'd do me a favor."

"You bet."

"If I thought there was any way in which *I* could save you, Harry—any way at all—I'd do it. Anything. And if ever you feel yourself on the brink of proposing to her—or if anything goes wrong—I mean, if she should let you down in any way, or not turn out what you thought—well, then, I wish you'd propose to me. Propose to me first. . . . Come to Bermuda with me. That's what I mean."

She drew her feet beneath her, in the chair, and smiled at him brightly but nervously.

"Heavens, Gertrude, how you do astonish me!"

"Do I? . . . I've always, in a funny sort of way, been in love with you, you know."

"Well—since you mention it—I've had my moments with *you*."

"'Was one of them two years ago in Portsmouth? . . .'"

"How did you know?"

"Do you think a woman doesn't guess these things? . . . I not only knew but I also knew that you knew that I knew."

"Well, I'll be damned!"

He sighed, he smiled foolishly, and for the moment he felt that he didn't quite dare to meet her eyes. He remembered that ride in Tommy's old Packard, and how she had so obviously leaned her shoulder against him; and afterwards, when they were look-ing at the etchings in the Palfrey House, how she had kept de-taching him from the others, calling to him to come and look at this or that picture, and standing, as he did so, so very close to him. The temptation had been very sharp, very exciting; but nevertheless he had run away from it, precipitately, the next day.

"You do alarm me," he added weakly. "And, in this age of withering candor, I don't see why I shouldn't admit that the idea is frightfully nice. But it hardly seems quite fair to May."

"Oh, bother May! . . . May can perfectly well look after her-self—don't you worry about May. . . . What I'm thinking of is what is fair to *you*."

"How angelic of you!"

"Not a bit. It's selfish of me. Deeply. Why not be perfectly frank about these things? I don't believe in muddling along with a lot of misunderstandings and misconceptions. . . . It's unfair to May; but what I feel is that it's only by that kind of treachery to May that you can ever escape from her. I don't say you *would* escape from her—but you might. And for your own sake you *should*. . . . Quite incidentally, of course, you'd make *me* very happy."

"If it weren't for May, it would make me very happy too. But you won't mind my saying that this May thing is very different. I'm in love with her in an extraordinary way—a way that I can't find any adequate symbol for. . . . Call it the shy arbutus, if you like."

"Oh, damn you and your shy arbutus!"

She sprang up, flung her scarf angrily into the chair, and went swiftly across the room to the desk. She put down her sherry glass beside the brass candlestick (made in the likeness of a griffin), revolved it once or twice between thumb and finger, and then picked it up again, turning back toward the fireplace. He twisted himself about in his chair so as to watch her. She stood looking at him, with her fair head flung back and the glass held before her. She was looking at him in an extraordinary manner —as if, in some remote, chemical way, she were assaying him, wondering which catalyzer to try next. Melodrama? Tenderness? Persuasion? Aloofness? . . . She hesitated. He felt sure, for an instant, that she was going to come and perch herself on the arm of his chair, and perhaps even put her arm round his neck. And he wasn't sure that he would so very much mind it. Mightn't it—even—be the beginning of the end? The notion both horrified and pleased him. Perhaps this was exactly what he had hoped for? It would be very easy—in these circumstances—to forget May. It was positively as if she were being drawn away from him. Gertrude would kiss him; and the kiss would be a spider's kiss; it would numb him into forgetfulness. She would wrap him up in the soft silk of oblivion, paralyze him with the narcotic, insidious poison of her love. And May—what would May be to him then? Nothing. The faintest and farthest off of recollected whispers; a sigh, or the bursting of a bubble, worlds away. Once he had betrayed her, he would be free of her. Good Lord—how horrible! . . . The whole thing became suddenly, with a profound shock, a reality again.

She came back toward him, tentatively, with slow steps, slow and long and lagging, as if, catlike, she were feeling the rug with her claws. She held her head a little on one side and her eyes were narrowed with a kind of doubting affection. When she stood close to his chair she thrust the fingers of her right hand quickly into his hair, gave it a gentle pull, and then, as quickly withdrawing, went to the fender. He smiled at her during this action, but she gave him no smile in answer.

"Shall we turn on the radio"—she said lightly—"and have a little jazz?"

"If you like. . . . No—let's not. This is too interesting."

"Interesting! . . . Ho, ho!"

"Well, it is, Gertrude."

"So, I dare say, is—hell."

"Oh, come now—it isn't as bad as that."

"But what further is there to say? It's finished."

"But is it?"

"That, my dear, dear Harry, is for you to say; and you've as good as said so, haven't you? You've been awfully nice about it."

He felt a little awkward—he felt that in a way she was taking an unfair advantage of him. And yet he couldn't see exactly how. He sat up straight in his chair, with his hands on his knees, frowning and smiling.

"If you could only *like* May!" he murmured. "If you could only see in her what I see in her—her amazing spiritual beauty! Then, I'm sure——"

"Give me some more sherry, Harry—I'm cold. And my scarf."

"Why, you're shivering!"

"Yes, I'm shivering. And my aged teeth are chattering. And

my pulse is both high and erratic. Is there anything else I can do for you?"

She smiled at him bitterly and coldly as he picked up the silver scarf from the chair; but the smile became really challenging as he held up the scarf for her turning shoulder. It became brilliant. It became beautiful. He allowed his hands to rest on her shoulders and looked at her intently, feeling for her a sudden wave of tenderness and pity, and of something else as well.

"The sherry!" she said, mocking.

"All right—I'll get it."

"Well—*get* it."

He inclined his face and gave her a quick kiss—and then another—at which she made no protest and no retreat; and then turned away, dropping his hands.

"And now let's have some jazz," she cried, as he filled her glass from the decanter. "I feel like dancing. . . ."

"The devil you do!" he said.

She emptied her glass, and turned her back to put it on the mantelpiece. She did this quite simply, without any sort of self-consciousness; there was nothing histrionic in the gesture; it was the entire naturalness of the action that made it, somehow, heart-breaking. And instantly he moved to her and touched her arm, just above the elbow, with his hand. She began trembling when she felt his touch, but she did not turn. And as he felt her trembling it was as if, also, he felt in himself the tiny beginning tremor of a great disaster. He was going to embrace her —he was going to give himself up. And May, stooping for arbutus in the wood, became remote, was swept off into the ultimate, into the infinite, into the forgotten. May was at last definitely lost—May was dead. He experienced a pang, as of some small spring broken in his heart, painful but obscure; the dropping of a single white petal; and that—for the moment— was all.

For the moment! . . . He hesitated, looking down at the

copper-gold convolutions of Gertrude's hair, and at the fair round neck still so beautifully young. He had the queer feeling that this hair and this neck were expectant. They were waiting, waiting consciously, to be touched. They were waiting for him to perform this act of treachery, they were offering to reward him for it, to reward him with oblivion. But was that oblivion going to be perfect? *Would* May be forgotten? *Could* May be forgotten? . . . Good God—how horrible! He closed his eyes to the chaos and terror of the future; to the spiritual deaths of himself and May; the betrayal and the agony. . . . And then he felt himself beginning to smile; while with his finger and thumb, he gently tweaked a tiny golden watch-spring of hair which curled against the nape of the white neck.

A MAN ALONE AT LUNCH

 Four-tined the silver-plated fork, and the glass-covered table, and the folded paper napkin, crinkled and fresh and flimsy, and a small saucer containing seven prunes of doubtful purple, and the small paper cup, with fluted sides and flanged edge, heavy with its little burden of water, and already beginning to be soggy and sodden like a little bladder; and then the larger dish, oval in shape, of heavy lusterless ware, with its remnant of four slivers of dull-fried potato. . . . Trays clanged, trays clashed, a butter dish chirruped falling to the mosaic floor of imitation marble, and at the counter, where the listless crowd waited, the ritual of repeated orders punctuated his thought: spaghetti special, and then farther off, *spaghetti special;* fried scallops medium, and then again *fried scallops medium;* ham and, and then again, *ham and.* . . . The lunch would be forty cents. Breakfast had been twenty. Dinner would be about sixty. A dollar and twenty cents a day; eight dollars and forty cents a week. Hell to be poor. And this week, the electric-light bill to pay; not very much, probably not more than half a dollar. Laundry, a dollar and five cents; he hadn't sent any pajamas. Ready tomorrow. And his shoes, resoled, ready on Friday. That would be an unexpected three dollars;

but it wouldn't happen often. God. And then the doctor's bill, which was imminent. If only he had had the courage to say he was hard up, or to ask for a delay. Damn. Hard to do, though. Osgood would have been surprised, maybe a little incredulous. For there had never been any hint of poverty before. . . . "Would you mind if I take a few months in paying your bill, Doctor Osgood? I'm a little hard up. . . ." While he was lying on the examination table, belly downward, he had thought of saying it; with his chin on his folded arms. But instead he had just looked out of the window at the sunlit house-front opposite. An old lady was putting a pot of ferns in a window; probably had been watering them. Almost all the houses in that neighborhood were inhabited by doctors. . . . "Now if you'll just push downward, Mr. Metcalf—and then relax—" Pleasantly embarrassing to have the girl assistant there. . . . "Take a look at this, Miss Paul—you see there's a little discharge there? Very slight. The kind of thing that might easily, for a long time, escape attention. . . ." Spaghetti special—that's three to come. *Spaghetti special—three on.* . . . And now an operation. Good God. How was it to be managed? Borrow from Bill. No. From Harry. From Cousin Lucy. No. Too humiliating. And just at this time, too, when Elizabeth was——

He shifted in his chair, to ease the pain, and then leaned forward on his elbows. Prune pits contained prussic acid, did they? like peach pits and apricots? Bitter. If only one could buy prussic acid. Instantaneous. That story of the dog, head and tail guillotined simultaneously, and traces of the acid discovered in the tip of the tail. Just a spasm, a single thrash, and it was all over. Or gas—but nowadays gas was hard to find. What was the use of living, when one had begun to reach the age of incipient decrepitude, when the machine was beginning to break down? In innumerable ways, too. Eyesight failing. Teeth decaying. One long unceasing warfare against this slow, remorseless encroachment of piecemeal death. No energy for the facing of all the problems. Tired even in the morning; having to lean against the washbowl while he shaved. And only a spurious and temporary feeling of well-being after the cold bath. God. How did people do it? What made them want to go on? Success, perhaps; if one were successful, made lots of money, had a car, could go to all the shows, live comfortably, happily, travel about the world whenever one liked—marry the girl one loved—make *her* happy—live over again in the lives of one's children. . . . Sunlight and beds of tulips in the spring. Gay voices, or voices that were just *assured*. The even tenor of their ways. Or like the other night at the Rankins', when he had helped Jim carry the radio across the lawn in the moonlight, and Sibyl had danced in the moonlight beside them, while the absurd machine went on pouring out music. Uncanny. And the deep masculine voice suddenly coming out of it; as if it were a coffin, and the corpse had suddenly come to life and sat up between them, speaking. It was like that. What had Sibyl and Jim done to deserve happiness? Nothing. And there they were, with everything they wanted. Two charming children, and a lovely house, and maids, and a car, lots of friends, music every night; opera cloaks and evening dress; and Taormina as familiar as Yonkers. Lucky devils—he had felt a deep deep pang of misery. A poor acquaintance, shabby, haunting the fringe of their life, apologetic for his presence; and having always to be considered. They didn't ask him to come along on their motor trips because they knew he couldn't afford it. God. And he was always so tired when he went there, in the evening, that he was dull. They were beginning to feel it. He couldn't go so often; they were insensibly and inevitably drifting apart. Sibyl looked at him pityingly. As if to say, "Poor Jerry—what's the use? why don't you give it up? . . ." He would have to, sooner or later. Sink to a lower level, haunt the byways, keep himself out of sight. Hell to be poor. The cuffs of his trousers were worn out, he had dreamed about them, his collars were all beginning to look shabby, his neckties were all old and stained, the Chinese laundry had lost one of his handkerchiefs. And now Jenkins was giving him less work to do, just when he needed it most, just when Elizabeth——

How lovely, lovely she had looked, as she came toward him

through the falling snow under her red umbrella, with the pale rosy light over her half-veiled face! "Shame on you, Jerry!" she had said—"Where are your galoshes?" He was ashamed to tell her that they were worn out and that he couldn't afford a new pair. How lovely she had looked! He would always remember that. Everything had gone just right that morning. It all went to show how much luck there was in such things, how much a mere series of tiny accidents can mold one's destiny. A rainy day, after a long unbroken chain of days of sunshine, and everything has a new quality; a new background is provided, and one's beloved has a new beauty. Or you misread comically a sign in a drugstore window, as you walk to meet her, and that's something delicious to tell her about. "Endearments" for "Enlargements"! And there had been Basil's letter to tell her about, and the meeting with the old perpetual-motion crank in the waiting station, and the funny dream about the cats. All these things were accidents—they might not have happened at all—and their love would have been just so much the poorer. Might not love fade away entirely, but for just such surprises provided by destiny? Best of all had been the miracle of the snow, and her astonishing newness under the red umbrella. Good Lord, how lovely she had looked: the red umbrella under the softly falling windless snow, her soundless approach through the deep virginal whiteness of it on the sidewalk, and the rosy light on her enchanting face, her face which, he had felt, must be cool to the touch! Ecstasy. The whole thing had deepened at a breath, the wonder had become more wonderful, the exquisite silence about them had become infinitely suggestive. How was it possible to see such happiness before one, and yet be balked in one's effort to grasp it? . . . Drop two on, sang the voice at the counter; then another voice, farther off, intoned it again, *drop two on*. And now just when Schmidt reappeared, with that hypocritical dark power of his, that curious half-hypnotic power of his over her soul, which so enslaved and weakened her—just when she needed him most, when he would have to fight for her as he had never fought before, to liberate her from this sinister and horrible shadow in her past life—just now, to have all this. . . . God. He was a weakling. He was a failure, unable to make money, unable to pay off that debt of hers, unable to open vistas for her of the alluring kind that Schmidt could open, unable even to come forward as a healthy man, ready at least to make a fight of it. She would slip back, slip away from him, succumb once again to Schmidt's cheap melodramatics and hypocritical violences, his passionate energy, his wealth. The whole terrible thing would happen over again. What was it that had given the thing so frightful a hold upon her? The sense of guilt, the fact that they had both of them been conscience-torn—if one could really believe that Schmidt had *had* any conscience about it? The fact that the whole dark passion had been so shot with agonies—with violent separations, wrenchings apart, when their religious scruples had come uppermost—and with reunions, when the separations had become unbearable, no less violent? Was it the sense of sin that made the thing so ineradicably and appallingly moving for her? Was it truly possible for her ever to love again, to love *innocently,* with anything like such a complete and terrible surrender of her soul? . . . Schmidt. Schmidt. Schmidt. Schmidt. . . . Her whole consciousness was inundated with him. She dreamed about him nightly. She was afraid of him—deeply afraid of him. She hated him—she said she hated him—but wasn't this hate merely a temporarily dislocated passion for him, a passion from which she could never escape? That monstrous hypocritical image was stamped, burned, scorched into her soul. She *was* Schmidt; she was his creation. He had taken sovereign command of her; soul and body. She spoke with his accent, she thought as he had taught her to think, she still wore the clothes which he had selected for her— his watch, his ring, his earrings. It was impossible for her to loose herself from him; everything about her, every visible trace of her conscious life, even this environment, was associated with him. The hotels where they had gone for week-ends. The restaurants where they had dined together. Thursdays, when he had always driven in to town to meet her. Thursday would always be a clandestine day for her; it would always, world without end, seem sinister and passionate to her. And that street, and that boarding house, where she had lived for two years, and where for two years he had come secretly to see her . . . that too was perpetually in her consciousness, with everything that had happened there, all the endearments, the caresses, the terrible intimacies which were both guilty and divine. All this was in her mind, scarcely as yet overlaid at all; and when she kissed him, Jerry, it poisoned the kiss for both of them, engulfed them both in its dreadful hypnotic shadow, sundering them with a feeling of hopelessness and impotence, as if they could never, through that shadow, touch one another's hands and hearts. God. And now, just as they *were* beginning to be happy, to find some sort of gaiety of approach, here was Schmidt come back again, and here was this operation to be gone through, and his job slipping away from him. . . . God. God. God. God.

To get away. . . . To get away. . . . To run, to fly, to take a fast train, to be whirled off with the speed of thought, farther than the Horn, farther than dream could compass. To be a dead leaf, dashed out into space, among the constellations—beyond the Pole Star and the Bear, beyond the uttermost sun, into the freezing Nothing of Nescience. *Our Father, Which art in Heaven, hallowed be Thy* . . . In Ronda, for example. If they could only get to Ronda, the two of them, with enough money to live there. Far, far away. In that little blue-plastered villa on the mountain slope below the town, surrounded by olive orchards and orchards of peaches and almond orchards and the white-blossoming cherries. And the river winding across the *vega,* dashing down among boulders toward the chasm, the sonorous deep gorge of virgin rock, with its caves and cold springs, and the kestrels sailing, brown-winged, from ledge to ledge, and the wild pigeons nesting among the prickly pear. In that blue-walled villa, with the red pan-tiled roof, and the tall grass coming to the door, and dwarf poppies among the olive trees, and quicksilver lizards darting in and out of the tangles of vetch. Elizabeth and himself sitting in the sparse shade of an olive

tree, reading together, talking, or simply musing—all these anguishes forgotten, all of it engulfed soundlessly and tracelessly
in the past. . . . *Thy Kingdom come, Thy will be done* . . . And
the goats with bells, going up the rocky slope toward the walled
cemetery, and the donkeys with bells filing down the rubble
path to the mill in the gorge, their baskets heavy with wheat,
the small boy running after them with an olive switch, shouting
bur-r-r-r-o, and flinging a fragment of Moorish masonry to
turn the leader from left to right. . . . *As it is in Heaven. Give
us, this day* . . . Everywhere, on every side, that inviolable and
infinite stillness, the mountain stillness, desolate stillness of
water and living rock, stillness in which bells could be heard for
miles, across the valley, and the harsh caterwauling of the pea-
cocks from the pine-hidden hill beyond the river, and the cry of
the pair of great eagles that circled at evening from edge to edge
of the gaunt amphitheater of the stony valley. In this stillness
they would find peace; among the sharp aromatic smells of the
mountain herbs they would find comfort; strolling up the rocky
slope at dusk to enter the little town and walk in the idle
crowds that filled the white-walled streets. And then a café, the
marble-topped table, coffee and *aguardiente,* the little liqueur
glasses standing in puddled saucers, the tasseled bottles, the
enameled mirrors with their absurd pictures of the gypsy Cor-
dobesita. . . . And the lottery-ticket sellers, the patient old
women with charming smiles, holding out their strips of lottery
tickets. . . . *For Thine is the Kingdom, and the Power, and the
Glory, forever and ever. Amen.* . . .

Spanish omelette, sang the voice at the counter, and farther
off the other voice intoned a fainter *Spanish omelette,* and the
busboy flung the coarse dishes harshly upon a tray. Forty cents.
Ten cents for carfare, and ten for a new pair of shoelaces. He
must arrange to have his mail forwarded to the hospital. Telephone Elizabeth. . . . And find out, by means of a guarded question, whether she had yet seen Schmidt.

Margaret O'Brien dreamed that she woke up late—the alarm clock on the table by her bed said eight o'clock—she couldn't account for it, and jumped out of bed in a panic. The Converses expected breakfast at eight-thirty. She flew down to the kitchen, without stopping to put up her hair or wash her face, and rushed to the stove. It was out. The grate was full of half-burned coal and ashes, cold, and she dumped out the whole thing; a cloud of dust filled the air, and she began to cough. Then she found that the kindling box was empty, and that she would have to go down to the cellar and get some. She stuffed newspapers into the grate, flung her hair over her left shoulder, and went to the door which led down to the cellar. It was locked or stuck. She pulled at the knob, wrestled with it, shook it violently; and just at that moment she heard Mrs. Converse's voice in the distance, calling her: *"Margaret!—Margaret!—Margaret!"* The bell began ringing furiously and prolongedly in the indicator over the sink, and she turned around and saw all the little arrows jumping at once. Someone —perhaps Mr. Converse—was running down the front stairs, running and singing. The voice trailed off forlornly, with the sinister effect of a train whistle. A door slammed—Mr. Converse had gone off without waiting for his breakfast—and she woke up.

Sweet hour, what a dream! She rubbed her hand across her forehead, looked up, and saw something unfamiliar over her head; it was the upper bunk of the stateroom, with long leaded slats of wood to support the mattress. Then there was a rack with a life-belt in it. Of course; she was on a steamship, going to Ireland. How funny! She relaxed, smiled, turned her head on the hard little pillow, and looked across to the other bunk; and there was Katy looking back at her and grinning. The ship gave a long, slow lurch, and the hooked door rattled twice on its brass hook. She put her hand quickly to her mouth.

"Gosh, what a dream I had!" she said. "I'm going to get out of this, or I'll be sick."

"Me, too," said Katy. "You could cut the air with a knife."

"What time is it, I wonder?"

Katy slid a bare leg out from under the bedclothes.

"I don't know," she said. "I heard a gong, but I don't know if it was the first or the second."

II.   It was a lovely day, and the ocean was beautiful. It was much smoother than they had expected it to be, too—a lazy blue swell with fish-scale sparkles on it. A sailing ship went by on the south, with very white sails, and tiny rowboats hung up on the decks, and one hanging over the stern. They could see a little man running along the deck and then hauling up a bunch of flags, some kind of signal. It was the kind of day when it is warm, almost hot, in the sun, but cold in the shade. They walked round and round the decks, after eating some oranges, and wished there was something to do. At eleven o'clock the band began playing in the lounge, and they went in for a cup of beef-tea. The room was crowded, and children were falling over people's legs. Some women were playing cards at a table. The deck-steward went round with a tray of beef-tea cups and crackers.

While they were drinking their beef-tea they saw him again—

the gentleman who had the room next to theirs; he just looked into the lounge for a minute, with a book under his arm, and then went out again. He was the nicest man on the ship: so re-fined-looking, so much of a gentleman, with a queer, graceful, easy way of walking and such nice blue eyes. He reminded Margaret a little of Mr. Converse, but he was younger; he couldn't have been more than thirty. She thought it would be nice to talk to him, but she supposed he wouldn't come near her. He had been keeping aloof from everyone, all the way over, reading most of the time, or walking alone on the deck with that book under his arm, and never wearing a hat.

"I'd like to talk to that man," she said, putting down the cup under her chair.

"Well, why don't you?" said Katy. "I guess he wouldn't bite you."

"He looks like Mr. Converse; I guess he's shy."

"I don't see what's the matter with Pat, if you want to talk to somebody."

"Oh, Pat's all right. . . ."

Pat, however, was in the steerage, and when Margaret wanted to talk to him they had to go down the companionway to the forward deck. It was all right, but it did seem a pity, when you were in the second cabin, to be spending so much time down in the steerage. And Katy had taken up with old man Diehl, the in-ventor, who was in the second cabin. He was after her all the time to play cards or walk on the deck or sit and talk in the smoking room. It was all right for Katy, but not much fun for Margaret. She couldn't always be tagging along with them, and she didn't like to feel that Mr. Diehl was paying for her glass of Guinness every time they had a drink.

A crowd of people rushed out to the decks, and others went to the windows, pointing; so they went out too, to see what the excitement was about. It was only another steamer coming from the opposite direction, with black smoke pouring out of its smokestacks. They walked along to the place where they played shovelboard, but some kids had it; so then they didn't know what to do. They looked down at the steerage deck, and there were Pat and the girls having a dance. Pat was playing his concertina. His black curly hair was blowing in the wind, and he looked up and saw them. He jerked his head backward as a signal to them to come down, so they did. They danced for a while, and one of the girls passed round a box of candy.

"I guess you think you're too good for us," said Pat, grinning.

"No, we don't," Margaret said. "But they don't like to have us going up and down these stairs. It's against the rules of the ship."

"Ah, tell it to the marines," said Pat.

He shut up his eyes and began playing "The Wearing of the Green," beating time with his foot on the deck.

"I hear Katy has a swell sweetheart," one of the girls said.

They talked about old man Diehl, and how he always carried around the blueprints of his inventions with him, and showed them all the time to everybody in the smoking room. Katy said she liked his voice; such a deep rumble, it carried all over the dining room—you could hear it above everything else, even the music. And it wasn't that he was talking loudly, either. He seemed to have lots of money. His daughter was with him, very pretty, but with a bad heart. She was kind of stuck-up, and wouldn't have anything to do with Katy, and was always dragging the old man out of the smoking room on one excuse or another. But she looked very pretty at the dance in that orchid dress.

"I guess he made a lot of money out of those inventions," said Katy.

"What did he invent?" one of the girls asked.

"One of those amusement things they have at Coney Island," said Katy.

Just then the whistle blew for noon, deafening everybody, and the steerage passengers had their dinner at noon, so they began going away. Pat strapped up his concertina and ran his hand through his hair.

"So long," he said. "Give us a look again, when you haven't got any swell company."

He dived down the dark little companionway, and they were left alone.

As they went up the stairs Margaret said that Pat gave her a headache. He made her tired. He made her sick.

III.   At lunch there was something of a treat. A special table had been put on the little platform where the band usually played—the piano had been pushed back—and a swell party was being given there. It was, in fact, the wedding breakfast, after a mock wedding which had taken place in the dining saloon just before lunch. They had come in just as it was over and old Mr. Diehl was in the act of kissing the bride, who was Mr. Carter dressed up in a girl's dress. The bridegroom was Miss Diehl dressed in a man's tuxedo. They all sat, eight people, at the round table on the platform, and they had several bottles of wine. Miss Diehl was wearing a white yachting cap to keep up her hair, which was pulled up to look like a man's.

"Your friend is there," said Katy, giving Margaret a nudge with her elbow.

And, sure enough, he was. He was sitting at the opposite side, next to Mr. Carter, and he looked as if he weren't enjoying himself at all. He kept sipping his wine and smiling in an uneasy sort of way, as if he were very much embarrassed. Most of the time he was looking down at the dishes before him. The rest of the party were making a lot of noise, talking and laughing and making jokes and slapping each other on the back. Then Mr. Diehl made a speech, toward the end, and the bridegroom got up and proposed a toast. Several toasts were drunk and speeches made, and they tried to get the nice man to get up and speak, but he blushed and resisted and sat still, though Mr. Carter tried to push him out of his chair.

"He's awful good-looking," said Margaret.

"Suit yourself," said Katy. "To my idea, he's too quiet-seeming."

"I wish he'd look at me once."

"Well, if you keep on staring at him like you are, he will, and then he'll be scared to death."

All the same, she felt as if she couldn't keep her eyes off him, she didn't know why; there was something very appealing about his face. His blue eyes were very kind and wise-looking, and he had a way of smiling to himself all the time as if he were having all sorts of humorous thoughts. She felt that he was very superior to all those other people, but he was too nice to show it. In fact, he was superior to everyone else on the ship. There was something important about him.

And then, all of a sudden—she didn't know just how it happened—he was looking at her. There were two tables in between, and lots of other people he might have looked at, and a branch of a palm tree that almost got in the way, but in spite of all these obstacles there could be no doubt about it: he was looking straight at her. A sort of shock went through her, and she felt herself blushing. But she kept her nerve, and looked back at him without in the least changing her expression, which she knew had been one of frank admiration. In fact, she felt her eyes widening a little, and a special kind of brightness going into them. And the strangest thing of all was the way he met this: he looked quickly away, but only for a moment; and then he looked right back again, while with one hand he fiddled with his glass of water. He looked at her almost as if he had suddenly recognized her, though of course they had never met before. His eyes brightened, in fact, in exactly the same way that hers had done; they brightened and widened, and he seemed to be unable to look away again. So they looked at each other for about two or three minutes like this, as if they were the only two people in the whole room. It was almost as if they were signaling to each other. Then Mr. Carter apparently said something to him, and he turned his head away.

"Well, he looked at me," she said to Katy, "and something happened."

"What do you mean, something happened?"

"I don't know, but it gave me a funny feeling. I think he likes me the same way I like him."

"Don't be too sure," said Katy. "Anyway, he isn't looking at you now."

"No, I know he isn't; but he was, just the same. It was a long look, and I felt all over as if I was melting."

"I guess what you need is some air," said Katy, "or else both of you'll have to be locked up."

IV.   They roamed the decks again after lunch, and sat for a while in the sun parlor at the back, in wicker chairs, watching the stern of the ship swoop up and down in quarter-circles against the sea, which seemed to be coming right up over the ship but never did; and for a while the old deckhand, a sailor with a nice white beard, stood with his pail in his hand and talked to them about the "old country." He also told them about a hawk that had been blown on to the ship. It was exhausted, he said. It had probably been chasing some other bird and followed it out to sea, and then didn't know how to get back. It stayed on one of the masts for a while, and they put out food for it, and then the next day they found it on the bow, huddled up against an iron thwart. It fought when they came near it, and it wouldn't eat, so they decided they'd better kill it. Finally, one of the sailors threw his hat over it and jumped on it, and killed it.

"Oh, what a shame!" said Margaret. "I think that's a shame."

The old sailor grinned, half embarrassed.

"We get hardened to it," he said. "There's always birds like that coming aboard, you know, and they never live. Those little yellowbirds, for instance. You can feed them, but they die just the same, and you might as well heave 'em overboard and be done with it. They get so tame, or scared maybe, that they'll come hoppin' right in here amongst these chairs."

After a while he went away, carrying his sponge in one hand and his pail in the other, walking very slowly, as if there was lots of time. Katy opened her magazine and began reading. Every now and then she turned a page, but she hadn't turned many when Margaret noticed that she was fast asleep. The twins went by, with their short skirts blowing way up round their skinny little legs, and then came Mr. Carter and Miss Diehl, in their proper clothes again. They brought the peg and began playing quoits. They were having a good time—just as they were going to throw the quoit the ship would give a slant and the quoit would go wild. They would laugh and stagger about. The noise finally waked up Katy. She yawned and stretched, and wanted as usual to know what time it was. The sky was clouding up and the wind seemed colder, so they decided to go and sit in the lounge. Margaret wanted to be doing something, but she didn't know what there was they could do.

"What are you so restless for?" said Katy.

"I'm not restless; only I get so sick of just sitting round and watching the water go by."

"Well, it *is* kind of monotonous, at that," said Katy.

They took a look down at the steerage deck, but there was nobody there, probably because it was getting chilly. In the steerage you got all the wind.

What she really wanted was to see the nice man again, but she couldn't exactly go looking for him. She hoped he would be in the lounge, and when she saw that he wasn't she thought of suggesting to Katy that they go to the smoking room, but she didn't quite have the nerve to do it. Instead they settled down in a corner and listened to the music and had their tea and watched the people and yawned. Margaret felt unhappy. It wasn't only because she wanted to see him; it was just as much because she was bored with being on a ship. Every day was like Sunday. After a while you got tired of walking round the decks and sitting here and sitting there and drinking tea or beef-tea and going to the dining saloon for another meal that was just like the last. The stewards were all the time trying to flirt with them, too.

All the same, she didn't see how it could just end there, after a look like that—it didn't seem natural at all. But would he do anything about it? Most probably he was too shy. He might even be so shy that he would try to keep out of her way. Or he might think that she was trying to kidnap him or something. She thought of that look again, and felt herself blushing just the way she did at the time. If any look had a meaning, that look did. There was no getting away from that.

"I'll be back in a minute," she said, suddenly jumping up.

She walked quickly out of the lounge without knowing at all where she was going—she just felt that she had to be doing something, going somewhere, anything but just sitting still. She felt excited, too, as she pushed open the door that led out to the deck—it had been shut for the night—and launched herself out into the wind. It was just getting dark. The water was black, with patches of moving white, and seemed to be sliding past the ship much faster than it did in the daytime. She walked briskly round the deck, keeping an eye out for other pedestrians, but there was nobody about. She tried the other two decks, but they too were deserted. Then she stood hesitating. After all, she didn't have the least idea of what to say to him if she met him—or whether she would find any excuse for it, or way of doing it. In fact, she wasn't sure that that was what she wanted. She just wanted to see him. Perhaps he was in the smoking room. She turned and went down a companionway to the lower deck again, and then round the sun parlor to the smoking room. She went in and stood near the door, as if she just wanted to look round for someone, and surveyed the whole room. Old man Diehl was standing by the bar with Mr. Carter and two other men; he seemed to be a little drunk. They were telling smutty stories. The bar-steward saw her and warned them, and they lowered their voices. Two other men were sitting in armchairs facing the artificial fire; neither of them was the man she was looking for. And there was no one else in the room. She returned to the sun parlor, which looked very forlorn with its deserted wicker chairs under electric lights, facing the darkness and emptiness of the sea, and sat down. Suddenly she felt defeated and miserable. She didn't want to see Katy or anybody—she didn't want to go down to dinner. She would excuse herself with a headache and go to bed. . . .

         v.   At lunch the next day she said she was going to speak to him if she died for it. She would ask him to join them in a game of whist. They could get old man Diehl to make the fourth, in case he accepted. Katy was skeptical but resigned.

"Anybody'd think you were in love with him," she said.

Margaret laughed and blushed.

"Oh, no," she said. "But I'd like to talk to him just the same. After lunch I'm going to find him if I have to comb the whole ship. He must be somewhere."

They had seen him only once in the morning—as usual he was walking the deck for his half-hour's constitutional. He passed them several times, and looked at them with interest but without speaking. Margaret said she thought he wanted to speak but was too bashful. He had that everlasting blue book under his arm, and his fair hair was all on end with the wind. Then he had disappeared again.

After lunch, accordingly, they went straight to the lounge and got a table, and Katy spoke to Mr. Diehl. Mr. Diehl said he would be in the smoking room and they could find him there any time in case they wanted a game. Katy got the cards and sat down at the table, and Margaret started off to make her search; and just at that very minute he came in and sat down at the other side of the room and opened his book. She didn't know whether he had seen them or not.

She walked right up to him, smiling, and stood in front of him and looked down at him.

"Would you care to join us in a game of whist?" she said.

He closed his book and looked up.

"Oh, it's you, is it?" he said, smiling.

She gave a laugh.

"Yes, it's me, large as life and twice as natural!"

He stood up, tucking the book under his arm.

"As a matter of fact," he said, "I never played whist in my life. Is it anything like bridge?"

"I don't know, but I guess if you can play bridge you can play whist."

They stood very close to each other, swaying with the ship, and again they found themselves looking into each other's eyes as they had done the day before at lunch. Margaret almost regretted that they had planned the whist game for it was now obvious that otherwise she could have him all to herself.

"All right," he said, again smiling, "if you can stand it I can."

She led him over to the table and introduced him to Katy. He said his name was Camp. Katy got up and went in pursuit of Mr. Diehl, and they sat down.

"You'd better be my partner," she said, "and then I can show you as we go along."

She took the chair opposite his and began shuffling the cards, at the same time looking at him. A feeling of extraordinary happiness came over her—she had never in her life felt so happy, or so much as if her whole happiness was in her eyes. And the queer thing was that she somehow knew that he was in the same state of mind.

"What do you do with yourself all the time?" she asked. "You hardly ever seem to be anywhere round."

"Most of the time I've been in the smoking room playing chess," he said. "But I've also been working a good deal in my stateroom. I've got some work that has to be finished before we get to Liverpool. And there's only two more days."

Margaret felt a sharp pain in her breast.

"I get off at Queenstown," she said. "Tomorrow night."

"*Do* you?"

He accented the first word, and looked at her with a curious helplessness. They both dropped their eyes and became silent.

At that moment Katy brought Mr. Diehl and introduced him, and the game began. Margaret and Katy explained how it went to Mr. Camp, with a good deal of laughter. Mr. Diehl gave Mr. Camp a cigar.

"What's your line of business, Mr. Camp?" he said.

Mr. Camp said that he was an architect. He was going over to superintend the construction of a new office building that an American firm was putting up in London. Margaret felt a thrill. She slid her right foot forward under the table, so that the toe of her slipper touched something. Then Mr. Camp, after a moment, caught her foot between his two feet and squeezed it firmly, and they looked at each other and smiled.

VI.   At four o'clock the deck-steward brought them tea, and Mr. Diehl began telling them in his deep voice, with a slight German accent, how he had come to America at the age of sixteen and worked in railroad repair shops. He said he was sixty-eight years old and strong as an ox, and he looked it. He told Mr. Camp about his Whirligig Car, at Coney Island, and how he got the idea for it in his work on trucks in the railroad yards. Now it had made him a fortune, and he was going over to Blackpool and Southport to put them in there.

Margaret couldn't listen. She was impatient. She wanted to go off alone with Mr. Camp. She pressed his foot hard, under the table, and smiled at him. But he didn't take the hint, or couldn't think what to do. It was Katy who saved the day. She got up and suggested that they all take a stroll—it was a lovely warm day and a shame to be indoors. Besides, the lounge was getting stuffy.

"Come on, then, Katy!" said Mr. Diehl.

He jumped up and gave her his arm with mock gallantry—

the sort of thing he was always doing—and they started off.

"Shall we walk too—or shall we stay here?" said Mr. Camp.

"Whatever you like," said Margaret.

"I feel terribly separated from you, without your foot," he said, laughing. "But I suppose we ought to get a breath of air."

They climbed up to the top deck and began walking to and fro. He didn't offer to take her arm, but walked rather distantly beside her. At first they couldn't think of much to say—they talked about the whist game and Mr. Diehl, but not as if they were really interested in these things. Margaret felt as if she wouldn't be able to think straight till she took his arm, so after a few turns on the deck she did so.

"That's better," she said simply.

"Much!"

"Tell me," she said, "if I hadn't spoken to you, would you ever have spoken to me?"

"That's what I came into the lounge for," he answered. "Ever since lunch yesterday I've been wondering what on earth to do about it. I'm kind of shy, and these things don't come natural to me. But I thought, if I went into the lounge, some kind of opportunity might occur. That's what I was there for. But I was terribly relieved when *you* started it off."

"You must think I'm very bold."

"Good Lord, no! You had a little more courage than I did, that's all."

They talked then about Ireland, and she told him that she was going back to visit her mother for the summer. She was a cook, she said, and her employer, Mr. Converse, who was very nice, had given her three months off and paid her passage to Queenstown. She had been in Brooklyn for ten years. She was twenty-five. He asked her if she was married, and she said no.

"I am," he said.

She felt again that pain in her breast.

"I thought you were," she said, looking intently at him.

He wanted to know why she thought so, and they stood and leaned against the railing, with their shoulders touching and their faces very close. His eyes, she noticed, were even bluer than the sea. She couldn't tell him why she thought so, exactly—it was just something about him.

"A woman can almost always tell when a man's married," she said. "But I'm glad you told me, all the same."

"I believe in being honest, especially at a time like this."

"How do you mean, at a time like this?"

He gave her a queer look—the corners of his mouth were twisting a little, as if he were under a strain, but there was a twinkle in his eyes.

"You know what I mean," he said.

"No, honest, I don't!"

"Well, you certainly ought to," he said. He turned around and put his arms on the railing and stared down at the water. "I mean the way we feel about each other."

She held her breath. He had said it so nicely and so quietly, and without even trying to hold her hand.

"How do you know we do!" she said, smiling.

He smiled back at her.

"All right—let's see you look me in the eye and tell me that we don't!"

She looked away from him, sobering.

"We oughtn't to be talking like this," she answered. "What about your wife? You know it isn't right."

"Of course it isn't . . . Or is it? . . . I don't know."

"What does your religion tell you?" she said.

"I haven't got any."

"Well, I have. I'm a Catholic."

"Do you go to confession?"

"Sure, I do."

They were silent. She was half-sorry she had rebuked him, and half-glad. But he had to know how she felt, even if it hurt her to tell him. She didn't want him to get any false ideas. After a minute, as he didn't say anything, but just went on staring at the water, she turned and looked at him. He was resting his chin on his hands.

"Would you like to walk some more?" she asked, almost timidly.

They walked round and round the deck, while slowly the sunset behind them faded and the sky darkened. He said that he always thought the sea sounded louder at night, and she stopped to listen to it, to see if it was true. She said she couldn't see any difference, or any reason why there should be any. They talked about Katy and Mr. Diehl. Miss Diehl, she said, was likely to die most any time—she had a very bad heart. But she insisted on doing everything just as if there wasn't anything the matter with her. Everybody at the dance had been scared that she would just drop down on the floor all of a sudden. Her face had got very white.

"Let's go down and find Katy," she suggested.

They went down the ladder to the lower deck and found them sitting in the sun parlor, holding hands.

"Is *that* what you're doing!" said Margaret.

Mr. Diehl gave his deep rumble of a laugh. "I've got a pretty nice little girl," he said, patting Katy's shoulder.

Margaret and Mr. Camp sat down at the other side of the veranda. He pulled his chair up close to hers and she dropped her hand on her knee, where he couldn't help seeing it. He put his own on top of it after a moment, and they just sat still without saying anything for a long while. He stroked her thumb with one of his fingers, to and fro, and the smooth hollow between the thumb and forefinger, and she felt as if she were being hypnotized. Once in a while he would slip his finger up her sleeve and touch the inner side of her wrist. And once in a while, as if accidentally, he would stroke her knee. She knew he wouldn't try to kiss her.

"My stateroom is next door to yours," he said, after a time. "If you should want me for anything in the night, don't hesitate to come in."

There was a pause.

"I don't think there's anything I'd want," she answered. "Unless one of us was to be sick, or something like that."

"Well, if there's anything at all," he said.

She tried to withdraw her hand, but he held on to it. She gave up struggling and allowed it to remain in his. She felt unhappy again.

"I always try to think the best of people," she said. "I'm sure you didn't mean anything wrong by that."

He didn't reply, but instead, after a pause, put his other hand on her forearm and gave it a squeeze.

"You're awfully nice, Margaret," he said. "If I were free, I'd like to marry you."

She shut her eyes, and didn't know whether to believe him or not.

VII.   After dinner she had a good cry in her bunk, while Katy sat and talked to her, and from time to time wet the washcloth to put on her eyes. The ship was making a terrible noise, blowing off steam, which was a good thing, as it prevented the neighbors from hearing her. Two of the bedroom stewards were hanging round in the corridor outside. Now and then she could hear them laughing. Katy sat on the camp-chair and argued with her.

"You just put him out of your mind," she said.

"But I can't. You think it's easy, Katy, but it isn't."

"I told you how it would be from the beginning, Peg, and you wouldn't listen to me. He doesn't care anything for you—don't kid yourself. He isn't our kind at all. You know how it is with that kind of man. He may soft-soap you, but really he looks down on us, and if he met us anywhere at home he wouldn't even speak to us."

Margaret moved her head from side to side on the pillow—back and forth, back and forth.

"No," she said, "he isn't like that. He's in love with me. He doesn't despise me because I'm a cook."

"Don't kid yourself. He might think so right now, when there's nobody else for him to fool with, but that's all there is to it. What's the use getting all upset about it, anyway, with him a married man!"

Margaret blew her nose and sat up.

"It's awful hot in here," she said.

"I tell you what, you need a little excitement to take your mind off this business. Let's get a glass of stout and then go down and have a bit of a dance with Pat and the girls."

Margaret was helpless, apathetic. She didn't care one way or the other, and she was too tired to resist. She bathed her eyes in the wash-basin, rubbed her cheeks with the towel, and tidied up her hair. Maybe Katy was right—maybe he really didn't care for her at all. He shouldn't have said that about her coming to his stateroom; though, of course, men's views were so different about those things.

She felt better after the glass of stout, and they went down the dark companionway to the steerage deck—the whole crowd was out there in the moonlight, Pat with his concertina, another boy with his mouth organ. Two of the men were whirling a skipping rope, and the girls were taking turns in seeing how fast they could skip and how long they could keep it up. A lot of people were sitting along the canvas-covered hatch. Katy had a try at it, and the very first thing the rope caught her skirt and lifted it way up so that her knickers showed, and everybody laughed. Katy didn't mind at all. She laughed as much as anybody did. She was a good sport. There was an English girl, about eighteen, who was the best at it—she would take a running start into the rope and put her hands on her hips and jump as if she was possessed. They couldn't down her at all, and everybody clapped her when finally one of the men dropped his end of the rope.

Pat tuned up on his concertina and they began to dance. A tall young fellow named Jim, who was a carpenter, asked Margaret to dance with him, and before she had time to make up her mind about it he had grabbed her and she was dancing with him and having a good time. They had a fox-trot first, and after that there was a jig, and in the middle of this, just when she had bumped into Katy and they were both laughing, she happened to look up at the second-cabin deck, and there was Mr. Camp, looking down. She waved her hand at him.

"Come on down!" she shouted to him.

He shook his head and smiled; Mr. Carter was standing with him. Jim yanked her hand and whirled her round, and when she looked up again he was gone.

VIII.   They spent the morning in packing, and getting their landing cards, and writing letters. He wasn't at breakfast when they were, and she took Katy's advice and kept out of his way. At lunch she avoided looking in his direction—she knew he was there, and Katy said he kept looking toward her, but she wouldn't look back. She guessed Katy was right. If he had really cared, he would have come down and danced with them. He was probably a snob, just as Katy said he was. After lunch she went back to the stateroom, and didn't go out till she heard they were sailing along close to the coast of Ireland; so she went up on deck. There was a crowd all along the railing, and she and Katy wedged themselves in and stared at the cliffs and green slopes and watched the little steam trawlers wallowing up and down in what looked like a smooth sea. A tremendous lot of sea-gulls were flying over the ship, swooping down to the water for the swill that was flung overboard, and all of them mewing like cats. The idea of landing at Queenstown was beginning to be exciting. Her mother and uncle would probably come in from Tralee to meet her, and she supposed they would all spend the night in some hotel in Queenstown.

When they went in for their last tea she rather hoped that Mr. Camp would turn up, but he didn't. By this time, most likely, he saw that she was avoiding him, and was keeping himself out of her track. Maybe his feelings were hurt. She was restless, unhappy, excited, and, try as she would, she couldn't stop thinking about him. She gulped down her two cups of tea as if she were in a hurry; but then she couldn't find anything to be in a hurry for. Her trunk was packed, her bag was all strapped and labeled, there was nothing to do. The orchestra came in and began playing. The sound of the music made her feel like crying. Katy said she was going to see if there was a night train out of Queenstown for the north. She got down a timetable from the shelves and looked at it, but couldn't make head or tail of it. Then two of the ladies at their table came with menus on which they were getting all their acquaintances to sign their names. She and Katy signed their names and said goodbye, in case they shouldn't meet again, for it wasn't certain whether they would have supper on board or not. The rumor was that they would get into Queenstown harbor about six o'clock, in which case the Queenstown passengers would have to wait and have their supper in Queenstown.

It was after dark when finally the ship swung into the harbor. They felt the engine stopping, and ran out on deck. They could see the lights all round them, and a long row of especially bright ones; there was the hotel, and another ship waiting a little way off—waiting, as they were, for the tenders to come out. Everything seemed very still, now that the engines were stopped; it was almost as if something was wrong with the ship,—unnatural. Everybody seemed to talk in lower voices. The harbor water was quieter than the ocean; it just lapped a little against the side of the ship, and there was a long narrow rowboat which had come out and was lying against the bow with two men in it, one of them giving an occasional flourish with a long oar. A light was played on them from the ship, so that they stood out very clear against the blackness of the water. Then at last they saw the tenders coming out, and they decided they had better go down and see about their things.

It was just after they had tipped the steward, and he had gone off with the trunks, and just when they heard the tender coming alongside, that Mr. Camp suddenly came to their stateroom door.

"I've just dropped in to say goodbye," he said, putting his hand against one side of the doorway.

Katy saw how it was, and said she had to go out for a minute, leaving them alone. Mr. Camp stepped in then, and shut the door behind him. He put out his hand and she took it, and they shook hands for a minute, feeling embarrassed.

"Goodbye, Margaret," he said.

"Goodbye, Mr. Camp."

"I've been hunting for you all day," he said. "Why did you hide yourself from me?"

"I thought it was better," she said.

She felt the tears coming into her eyes and was ashamed. He suddenly put his arms around her and kissed her. She tried to turn her face away from him, and he just kissed her cheek two or three times, lightly. His arms were holding her very hard. Then he kissed her once on the mouth.

"You musn't," she said. "You're a married man."

They looked at each other for what seemed like a long while, and then they heard someone coming to the door and he let her go. Katy and the steward were there. It was time to go. Mr. Diehl came running up too, and she hurriedly put on her hat and coat. Mr. Diehl took Katy's bag from the steward, and Mr. Camp picked up hers from the camp-chair.

They followed the other passengers and stewards with bags along the corridor, went through the first-cabin dining saloon, and then came out on to a deck where an iron door had been swung open and the gangway made fast. There was a great crowd there, and two officers standing at the top of the gangway taking the landing cards. Mr. Diehl gave Katy her handbag and tried to kiss her, right there before everybody, and she gave a screech and tried to run, but he caught her and kissed her. Then she started down the steep gangway under the bright lights. Mr. Camp handed Margaret her bag and shook hands with her again.

"Here's my address," he said. "Write me a letter some time, if you feel like it."

He gave her a slip of paper, and she tucked it under her glove.

"Goodbye," she said.

"Goodbye."

She turned and went gingerly down the gangway, taking short steps. When she got to the deck of the tender she didn't look for Katy, but walked right to the stern of the boat, where there was a semicircular bench, and put down her bag, and then stood and looked up at the ship. It seemed enormous, and at first she couldn't make out where the second-cabin decks were at all. The band was playing somewhere above her, in the night, and the decks were lined with people waving handkerchiefs. They were shouting, too. She ran her eyes to and fro over the crowds, looking for Mr. Camp, but she couldn't find him, anywhere. Maybe he wouldn't come. Then the gangway was hauled down, the bells rang, and the tender began chugging.

Just at that minute she finally saw him. He had got a little open space of railing all to himself, and was leaning way out, waving his arm. She felt as if her heart was going to break, and threw him three long kisses, and he threw three long kisses back. The steamship whistle began blowing, the tender drew away very fast, but she could still see him waving his arm. Then she couldn't see any more, because the tears came into her eyes, and she sat down and waited for Katy to come, and turned her head away from the ship and wished she were dead.

A couple of years ago I saw in the "agony column" of *The Times* a very curious advertisement. There are always curious things in that column—I have always been fascinated by that odd little company of forlorn people who so desperately and publicly wear their hearts on their sleeves for daws to peck at. Some of them appear there over and over again—the person who signs himself, or herself, "C.," for example: who regularly every three months or so inserts the message *"Tout passe, l'amitié reste."* What singular and heartbreaking devotion does that brief legend convey? Does it ever reach the adored being for whom it is intended, I wonder? Does he ever see it, does he ever reply? Has he simply abandoned her? Were they sundered by some devastating tragedy which can never be healed? And will she go on till she dies, loosing these lovely flame-colored arrows into an utterly unresponsive void? ...

I never tire of reflecting on these things; but the advertisement of which I have just spoken was of a different sort altogether. This was signed "Journalist," and merely said: "Your obituary? Well written, reviewed by yourself, and satisfaction thus insured." My first response to this oddity was mere amusement. How extraordinarily ingenious of this journalist! It seemed to me that he had perhaps found a gold-mine—I could well imagine that he would be inundated with orders for glowing eulogies. And what an astonishing method of making a living—by arranging flowers, as it were, for the about-to-be-dead! That again was fascinating—for it made me wonder what sort of bird this journalist might be. Something wrong wih him, no doubt—a kind of sadist, a gloomy creature who perhaps reveled rather unhealthily in the mortuary; even, perhaps, a necrophile. Or was he, on the other hand, perfectly indifferent and detached about it, a mere hack-writer who had, by elimination, arrived at a rather clever idea? . . . But from these speculations I went on to others, and among them the question—to me a highly interesting one—of what, exactly, one would want put into one's own obituary. What would this be? Would one want just the usual sort of thing—the "he was born," "he lived in Rome," "he was a well-known connoisseur of the arts, and a patron of painting," "conspicuous in the diplomatic society of three countries," "a brilliant amateur archæologist," "died intestate" sort of thing? . . . Or would one prefer to have one's personal qualities touched on—with perhaps a kindly reference to one's unfailing generosity, one's warmth of heart, and one's extraordinary equableness of disposition? . . .

By neither alternative did it seem to me that my "satisfaction could be insured." Neither for those who knew me, nor for those who did not, could any such perfunctory *eulogium* be in the least evocative. In what respect would these be any better than the barest of tombstone engravings, with its "born" and "died" and "he was a devoted father"? Mr. X. or Mr. Z., reading of me that I was an amateur archæologist and a kind old fellow, a retired diplomatic secretary, would form no picture of me, receive from such bare bones of statement not the faintest impression of what I might call the "essence" of my life; not the faintest. But if not these, what then? And it occurred to me suddenly that the best, and perhaps the only, way of leaving behind one a record of one's life which might be, for a world of strangers, revelatory, was that of relating some single episode of one's history; some single, and if possible central, episode in whose small prism all the colors and lights of one's soul might be seen. Seen just for a flash, and then gone. Apprehended, vividly, and then forgotten—if one ever *does* forget such things. And from this, I proceeded to a speculation as to just which one, of all the innumerable events of a well-filled life, I would choose as revelatory. My meeting with my wife at a ball in Calcutta, for example? Some incident of our unhappy life together —perhaps our quarrel in Venice, at the Lido? The effect of her suicide upon me, her drowning in the Mediterranean—the news of which came to me, while I was dining at the Reform Club, from the P. & O. Company? . . . I considered all of these, only to reject them. Possibly I rejected them—to some extent, anyway— simply because they were essentially painful. I don't know. Anyway, whatever the reasons, I did reject them, and at last found myself contemplating my odd little adventure with Reine Wilson, the novelist. Just why I fastened upon this, it would be hard to say. It was not an adventure at all; it was hardly even an episode. It was really nothing but the barest of encounters, as I see it now, or as any *third* person would see it. If I compare it with my protracted love affair with Mrs. M., for example, or even with my very brief infatuation with Hilda K., it appears to be a mere nothing, a mere fragrance.

A mere fragrance! . . . Yes, it was that; and it is for that reason, I see now, that it is so precious to me. Volatile and swift as it was, it somehow caught into itself all the scanty poetry of my life. If I may be pardoned for appearing a little bit "romantic" about myself, I might say that it was as if I were a tree, and had, in this one instance, put forth a single blossom, a blossom of unique beauty, perhaps a sort of "sport," which, unlike my other blossoms, bore no fruit, but excelled all the others in beauty and sweetness. That sounds, in the prosaic statement, rather affected, I am afraid; but it is as nearly a literal statement of the truth as I can find.

It happened when I was a young man, about four years after I had married. I was already unhappy and restless. I wasn't wholly aware of this—I had, at all events, no conscious desire, as yet, to go in search of adventure. All the same, it is obvious to me now that I was, *unconsciously,* in search of some sort of escape or excitement. I went about a good deal—and I went about alone. My own tastes being mildly literary, and my wife's not, I made rather a specialty of literary teas and "squashes," and had soon made a considerable number of acquaintances among the younger writers who lived in London at that time. Among these was a group of young folk who ran a small monthly magazine called *The Banner*—a magazine which, like many other such things, ran a brilliant but sporadic course for a year or two and then went bankrupt. My friend Estlin first told me about this, and called my attention to the work of Reine Wilson, whose first novel was coming out serially in *The Banner,* and whose husband was assistant editor of it. I read the first two chapters of "Scherzo," and I was simply transported by it. It seemed to me the most exquisite prose I had ever read—extraordinarily alive, extraordinarily poetic, and exquisitely feminine. It was the prose of a woman who was, as it were, all sensibility—of a soul that was all a tremulous awareness. Could one have—I asked Estlin—so ethereally delicate a consciousness, a consciousness so easily wounded, and *live?* And he horrified me by replying "No," and by telling me that Reine Wilson was—to all intents—dying. She had a bad heart, and had been definitely "given up." She might die at any minute. And she ought, by rights, to be dead already.

This shocked me, and also made me very curious; and when Estlin asked me, one day, to come to lunch with himself and the Wilsons, I needed no urging. We were to meet them at a little French place in Wardour Street—long since gone, I regret to say —and on our way thither we stopped at a pub for a glass of sherry. It was there that, by way of preface to the encounter, Estlin told me that there was something "queer" in the Wilson situation.

"Queer?" I said.

"Yes, queer. Nobody can make it out. You see, they lived together before they married—when they were both writing for *The Times*. For about three years. But then, all of a sudden, they married; and the minute they were properly married—presto!—they separated. She took a flat in Hampstead—and he took one in Bloomsbury. Once a week, they held a reception together at her flat—and they still do. But so far as anyone knows, they've never lived together from that day to this. He doesn't seem to be in love with anyone else—and neither does she. They are perfectly friendly—even affectionate. But they live apart. And she always refers to him simply as 'Wilson.' She even *calls* him Wilson. Damned funny."

I agreed with him, and I pondered. Was it—I asked—because she had a bad heart? too much of a strain for her? . . . Estlin thought not; though he wasn't sure. He even thought that the bad heart had developed *after* the separation. He shook his head over it, and said, "Rum!" and we went to meet them. He added, inconsequentially, that he thought she would like me.

She did like me—and I liked her. At first sight. I find it difficult to describe the impression she made upon me—I think I was first struck by the astonishing frailty of her appearance, an other-world fragility, almost a *transparent* spiritual quality, as if she were already a disembodied soul. She was seated at a small table, behind a pot of ferns, which half concealed her face. Her brown eyes, under a straight bang of black hair, were round as a doll's, and as intense.

"Isn't it like meeting in a *jungle?*" she said. She made the tiniest of gestures toward the fern; and I was struck by the restraint with which she did this, and by the odd way in which her voice, though pitched very low, and very carefully controlled, nevertheless contrived to reveal a burning intensity of spirit such as I have never elsewhere encountered. There was something gingerly about her self-control; and also something profoundly terrifying. It seemed to me that I had never met anyone whose hold on life was so terribly *conscious*. It was as if she held it—this small, burning jewel—quite literally in her hands; as if she felt that at any instant it might escape her; or as if she felt that, if it didn't escape, it might, if not firmly held, simply burn itself away in its own sheer aliveness. And to sit with her, to watch the intense restraint of all her gestures and expressions, and above all to listen to the feverish controlledness with which she spoke, was at once to share in this curious attitude toward life. Insensibly, one became an invalid. One felt that the flame of life was burning low—and burning low for *everyone*—but burning with all the more beauty and pure excellence for that; and one entered into a strange and secret conspiracy to guard that precious flame with all one's power.

II.   I had little opportunity, during that luncheon-party, for any "private" talk with Reine; the conversation was general. Not only that, but it was, as was to be expected, pretty literary, and I, perforce, took an inconspicuous part in it. Wilson struck me as a rather opinionated person, rather loud-voiced, rather sprawling, and I felt myself somewhat affronted by the excessiveness of his "Oxford manner." In fact, I disliked him, and thought him rather a fool. How on earth—I wondered—had he managed to attract so exquisite a creature as his wife? What on earth had she seen in him? . . . For there was something coarse in him, and also, I felt sure, something dishonest. He seemed to me hypocritical. He seemed to me to be merely *posing* as a literary man. And I thought that his loud enthusiasms were the effort of the insincere to make an impression, to carry conviction. Was it possible that Reine didn't see through this? Or was it possible—and this idea really excited me—that she *did* see through him, and that it was for this reason that they had separated? . . .

I found myself setting myself in a kind of opposition to him: not by anything so obvious as contradiction, but, simply, by being very quiet. I quite definitely exaggerated my usual quietness and restraint of speech, endeavoring at the same time to make it very pungent and concise; simply because I felt that this was what she wanted and needed. And she rewarded me by being, in our few interchanges, extraordinarily nice to me. I remember, when Wilson had been declaiming against the enormous emptiness of Henry James, and his total lack of human significance, that I waited for a pause and then said, very gently, that I could not agree: that James seemed to me the most consummate analyst of the influence of character upon character, particularly in situations of a profound moral obliquity, that there had ever been. Reine looked at me, on this, as if I had been a kind of revelation to her; her eyes positively brimmed with light and joy.

"*Isn't* he?" she whispered. She leaned forward, intently, with her small pointed chin resting upon her clasped hands; and then added: "No one else—*no* one—has made such beauty, and such *intricate* beauty, out of the iridescence of moral decay!" . . .

I don't remember what I said in reply to this—I am not sure that I said anything; but I do remember that I felt, at this moment, as if an accolade had been bestowed upon me. It was as if, abruptly, Reine and I were alone together—as if her husband, "Wilson," and my friend young Estlin, had somehow evaporated. I think I blushed; for I was conscious that suddenly she was looking at me in an extraordinary penetrating way—appraisingly, but also with unmistakable delight. We had discovered a bond—or *she* had discovered one—and we were going to be friends. Obviously. A subtle something-or-other at once took place between us, and it was as much "settled" as if we had said it in so many words. And when we got up to separate, after the lunch, it was almost as a matter of course that she invited me to come to tea with her on the following Sunday. She was, in fact, deliciously firm about it—as if she were determined to stand no nonsense. It was to me she turned and not to Estlin (Estlin was much amused), and it was to me she first put out her hand.

"You *will* come to tea, won't you? Next Sunday? And bring Mr. Estlin with you? . . ."

I murmured that I would be delighted—we smiled—and then, taking Wilson's arm for support (my heart ached when I saw this), she turned and went slowly out through the glass doors to Wardour Street.

Estlin was smiling to himself, and shaking his head.

"You're a terrible fellow," he said—"a terrible fellow!"

"Me?" I said. "Why?"

I knew perfectly well why, of course—but it pleased me to have Estlin say that I had made an unusual impression on Reine Wilson.

"And you may not know it," he added, "but she's damned hard to please. *Damned* hard to please. In fact, a good deal of an intellectual snob, and excessively cruel to those she dislikes. You just wait! . . . If she catches you admiring the wrong thing——!"

I laughed, a little discomfited—for I had already foreseen for myself that possibility. How could I, an amateur, keep it up? It was all very well to make one lucky shot about Henry James— but sooner or later I was bound to give myself away as, simply, not of her kin. . . . Or *was* I? . . . For I admit I was vain enough to hope that I might really be enough of a person, fine and rich and subtle enough, to attract her. How much was I presuming in hoping this? She had liked me—she had been excited by that remark—we had certainly *met* each other in a rather extraordinary way, of which she had shown herself to be thrillingly conscious. And I was myself, I must confess, very much excited by all this. She was, in every respect, the most remarkable woman I had ever met. I do not know how to explain this—for it was not that she had *said*, at lunch, anything especially remarkable; it was, rather, what she *was*, and *how* she said things. Her burning intensity of spirit, the sheer naked honesty with which she felt things, and the wonderful and terrible way in which she could appear so vividly and joyfully, and yet so precariously, alive—all this, together with her charming small oddity of appearance, the doll-like seriousness of face and doll-like eyes, combined to make a picture which was not merely enchanting. It was, for me, terribly disturbing. I was going to fall in love with her—and I was going to fall hard and deep.

Going to. I use the phrase advisedly. For there is always, in these affairs, a point at which one can say that one is *going* to fall in love, but has not yet done so; a point at which one feels the powerful and seductive fascination of this other personality, feels drawn to it almost irresistibly, and knows that *unless* one resists one is going to be enslaved. Nevertheless, it *is,* at this point, still possible to resist. One can turn one's back on the Siren, turn one's ship away from Circe's Isle, sail away—if one only has a little courage and good sense. Good sense? No. *That* phrase, I am afraid, has crept down to me from the Victorians. What I would prefer to call it now, in my own case, is coward-ice. Or, if you like, caution. Or again, respect for the conven-tions. For I am sure that is what it was. . . . During the five days which intervened between the luncheon party and my engage-ment for tea, I did a lot of thinking about this. I knew perfectly well that if I were to let myself go, I could fall in love. But did I want to fall in love? And suppose I did. Quite apart from my own domestic complications—and the situation with my wife was already quite sufficiently unpleasant—what good would it do me? For I was desperately, horribly, miserably sure of one thing and one thing only: that Reine Wilson would not fall in love with me. Or if she did, that she would fall out again in double-quick time. And there, hung up for the crows to peck at, I would be. . . .

I thought about this—and thought and thought. But I didn't —as the hours crept toward Sunday—find any solution. Of course, I would go to tea—there was no question about that. So much rope I would grant myself, and no more. No harm could come of that—or at any rate, no greater harm than was done already. One is ingenious, when one is falling in love, at finding good excuses for meeting with one's beloved. Yes, I would go to tea— and *then* I would make up my mind as to the future. A good deal would depend on what happened at tea. If I should dis-grace myself—if she were to find me out—or, as was only too likely, if she simply found me uninteresting, a nice young fel-low, no doubt, with an idea or two, but not at all on *The Ban-*

ner level—well, that would be the end of it. But if, on the other hand, our mutual attraction should deepen—if, somehow, by hook or by crook, I should manage to keep up the deception— or even, actually, to prove a sufficient match for her—what then? . . . What would happen to us? . . . What about my wife? . . . What about that detestable "Wilson"? . . . And, above all, what about her bad heart? . . .

III.   The new number of *The Banner* came out on Saturday, and it contained of course another installment of "Scherzo." I read this—and it seemed to me even more delightful and more obviously a work of first-rate genius, than the chapters which had gone before. It was in this installment that the description of the picnic occurred. This entranced me. Never, it seemed to me, had an *al fresco* party been so beautifully done in prose. The gaiety, the coltish rompings of the young girls, that marvelously described wood, and the cries of the children in it, playing hide-and-seek—the solemn conversation of the two little boys who had discovered a dead vole, and were wondering how most magnificently to dispose of it—the arrival of Grandma Celia with the basket—and, above all, Underhill's dream. It seemed to me a stroke of the finest genius to have poor Underhill, at that crisis of his life, dragged into such a party—frisked about, romped over, made to tell stories and to light fires; and then, when he sneaked away and found a clearing in the gorse and slept, having that marvelous dream—! The dream was so vivid and so terrifying that I felt as if I had dreamt it myself. It was I who had been in that cottage during the thunderstorm—it was I who tried vainly to shut the rattling windows and doors against the torrents of rain and hail, hoping to protect those mysterious "other people"— and it was I who finally, disheartened, despairing, had set out to climb the black mountain valley toward the storm. And the description of that Alpine valley, with its swishing pines and firs, and the terrible white cloud which hung at the upper end of it!

My blood froze as I moved toward that cloud and saw the death-lightning which shot from it unceasingly. It hung there portentously; like death itself. And I, who had at first moved toward it as if voluntarily, now felt myself being drawn off the ground and into the air—I floated at first a foot or two off the path and then a little higher—I was on a level with the tops of the trees, and every second drawing nearer to the dense white cloud—I could see, at last, that it was a magnificent cold arch of greenish ice, impenetrable and hostile—its cold vapor blew upon me—and then came a final flash and I knew that I was already dead. . . . It was superb, it was annihilating. And only the most daring of genius would have presumed to expand a mere dream, in the midst of a realistic narrative, to such proportions, and to concentrate in it all the agony and tragedy of a torn soul.

I was still in a fever of excitement about this when I was shown into Reine Wilson's sitting room by a young woman who seemed to combine the functions of housekeeper and trained nurse. Reine rose to greet me, rose slowly and weakly and with conscious effort, and then, having given me her hand, was assisted by the young woman to her chair by the tea-table. The young woman brought in the teapot and the hot scones, and then withdrew. I had seated myself on a couch by the open window. A double-red thorn tree was in blossom in the small garden, and its fragrance filled the room.

"I've just been reading"—I said—in a voice that I am afraid shook a little—"your new installment of 'Scherzo.' I think it's perfectly entrancing."

Reine looked at me, I thought, with a trace of hostility—I was certain that my approach had been too blunt.

"Oh, *do* you?" she said. And then immediately added, with a kind of careful lightness: "One lump or two, Mr. Grant? . . . Is this too weak for you?"

I stood up and moved to the tea-table for my cup of tea, and for the hot scone which she offered me; and suddenly I felt horribly shy. I had ruined myself at the outset—I had rushed in too fast and too far. I ought to have known her better. I ought to have known that I must leave the lead to her, and follow up the controlled reticence of manner with which I had made such a success at the luncheon party. A violent outbreak like that—! With a creature so exquisitely sensitive!—I felt clumsy and coarse and miserably ashamed. And I sank on to the couch again very much humiliated and very conscious of my hands and feet.

But Reine to my astonishment had mercy on me.

"I'm *so* glad you liked it!" she said. And she said it with such an air of relief, and with a voice so rich in delight, that I felt a shock of returning confidence as vivid and intense as, a moment since, its departure had been. And I had an instant and heavenly conviction that I could now throw all caution to the winds. She looked at me with wide-open eyes—it was almost as if she looked at me with wide-open soul. We had, abruptly, "met" again; and we had met more intimately than before. It was strange, at that moment, how everything seemed to be conspiring to make this mutual recognition complete; the long room lined with bookcases; the high mantel of cream-colored wood and the pale Dutch tiles which surrounded the fireplace; the worn Khelim rug which stretched between us, and the open window, which it seemed not improbable that the thorn tree itself had opened, in order that its fragrance and the London spring might come in to us—all these details were vividly and conspiratorially present to me, as if they were indeed a part of the exquisite mingling of our personalities at that poised instant of time. Was not I myself this room, this rug, that mantel, the tea-table spread with tea-things, and the inquisitive thorn tree? Was not I myself Reine Wilson, entertaining a strange young man in whom I felt a subtle and bewildering and intoxicating attraction? Destiny was in this—æons of patient evolution and change, wars and disasters and ages of darkness, the sand-like siftings of laws and stars, had all worked for the fulfillment of this ultimate minute, this perfect flowering of two meeting minds. I could not be mistaken in my belief that it was the same for her as for me. With the deep tremor in my own soul, I could feel the tremor in hers. If it were not true, she could not possibly be holding her teacup as she did, or frowning slightly as she did, or withholding, as she deliciously did, the smile of delighted confession which I knew she was near to giving me.

"You know"—I then added—"I think that dream is marvelous —simply marvelous."

"*Do* you!" she cried. "But how lovely! You *really* liked it? You didn't think there was too much of it? . . ."

She leaned toward me with the eagerness of a schoolgirl, her eyes wide with intensity.

"Too much of it! Heavens, no. I was never so enthralled by anything in my life."

"But do you *mean* it? . . . Why, you know, Wilson wanted me to 'cut' it. He said it was far, far too long. And everybody on *The Banner* has said so. . . . But *you* think it's all right? . . ."

"It's much more than all right. It couldn't possibly be anything but what it is. It seems to me to be the very *soul* of the thing—the center and source of light. It had to be that, hadn't it? . . . I mean, a glowing symbol for the whole thing. For Underhill's Gethsemane. . . ."

She looked at me, after this, for a long moment, and then she drew in her breath very slowly and deeply, subtly relaxing.

"Heavens!" she said—"you *are* a miracle."

"Am I?"

"You know you are. I hadn't *dared* to suppose that anyone would see what I intended by that. Or would like it, even if they did. . . . Isn't it extraordinary!"

She gave an odd light little laugh, not without a trace of bitterness, and then, with a smile still charmingly lighting her small face, gazed downward abstractedly at the Khelim rug. I knew what she meant by "extraordinary"—she meant that it was extraordinary that two minds should find each other as swiftly and easily as ours did. I knew also that she would not want the strangeness of this, and its beauty, too explicitly noted. For that would be to spoil it.

"Yes," I sighed, "it is. . . . Can I steal another scone?"

"Do! . . . Have one of the underneath ones—they're hotter!"

I took one, and returned to the couch. The room had suddenly darkened—it had clouded up—and a momentary patter of drops on the leaves of the thorn tree sounded in the silence, as if it were inside the room.

"Rain!" I said. . . . "I love it! Don't you?"

"You mean the sound of it? . . ."

"No—everything. The sound, yes, but also the light—rain has always had for me, ever since I can remember, a special sort of *magic*. On rainy days I experience a special kind of delicious melancholy—a melancholy that is happy, if that means anything to you. I brood, my imagination is set free, I am restless and depressed, and yet at the same time it is as if something inside me wanted to sing. . . . Don't I sound like a sentimental idiot?"

"Oh!" she said, "how *nice* of you!"

She rose, very gingerly, and coming to the end of the couch rested her two hands on the blue-canvas arm, one hand on top of the other. As she looked out through the window at the thorn tree, watching the small leaves curtsey and genuflect to the raindrops, and then spring up again released, I felt as if I were going to tremble. I found myself thinking about her heart again—she looked so astonishingly frail. How could so frail a body, a body so ethereally and transparently slight, contain a spirit so vivid? One felt that with the slightest flutter the bright bird might escape and be gone.

"Yes," she said, in almost a whisper, as if to herself, "it is beautiful . . . beautiful. It does make one want to sing. And how the thrushes adore it!"

"I remember"—I said—"how once, when I was a small boy, I went bathing in the sea on a darkish day. While I was swimming, it began to rain. I was at first astonished—almost frightened. The water was smooth—there was no sound of waves—and all about me arose a delicate and delicious *seething*, the low sound of raindrops on the sea. It was a ghostly and whispering sound—there was something sinister in it, and also something divinely soothing. I lay on my back and floated, letting the drops fall on my face while I looked up at the clouds—and then I swam very softly, so as to be able to listen. I don't believe I was ever happier in my life. It was as if I had gone into another world. . . . And then, when I went ashore, I remember how I *ran* to the bathing hut, for fear of getting wet! . . ."

"Of course!" she cried. "Of course you would! . . ."

She sank down on the couch, facing me. And then she went on: "You've given me back something I had forgotten. . . . It must have been when I was eleven or twelve. It was raining very hard—it was pouring—and when I went down to the library to practice at the piano the room was dark, with that kind of morning darkness that engulfs one. The French windows were open on to the garden, but the curtains hung perfectly still, for there was no wind, no current of air. One of those heavy, straight rains, on a quiet day—a rain as solid and serried as rain in a Japanese print. . . . I went into the room and closed the door behind me—and it seemed to me, so massive and insistent was the sound of the rain from the garden, with all its multitudinous patter and spatter, that the room itself was full of rain. The sounds were the sound of water, the light was the light of water—it was as if I were a fish in a darkened aquarium. I stood still for a long while, just drinking it in and staring out at the drenched garden, where all the trees and shrubs were bowed down under the unrelenting downpour. Not long before, I had seen somewhere some photographs greatly enlarged, of raindrops falling into the water; and now, as I went to the open French windows, I watched the large bright eave-drops splashing into the puddles on the brick terrace, and I was enchanted to see that *my* drops were exactly like those. They made the most exquisite little silvery waterspouts and umbrellas and toadstools, and all with such a heavenly clucking and chuckling and chirruping. The bubbles winked and were gone—is there anything so evanescent as a rain-bubble?—and other bubbles came, sliding a fraction of an inch to right or left before they burst. . . . I had a strange feeling, then, as I turned to go to the piano—I felt as if I belonged to the rain, or as if I were the rain itself. I had a sensation in my throat that was like sadness, but was also ecstatic—something like your desire to sing. I looked at the glossy black grand piano—and that too had a watery look, like a dark pool gleaming under a heavy overhang of foliage. And when I sat down on the cool piano-stool, and touched timidly my fingers to the keys, the keys too were cold, and it was as if I were dipping my hands into the clearest of rain-water. . . . Is it any wonder that the music sounded to me like the drops pattering and spattering in the garden? I was delighted to the point of obsession with this idea. I played a little sonata through three times, luxuriating in its arpeggios and runs, which I took pianissimo, and feeling as if I were helping the rain to rain. . . . Good heavens! If I had only known the Handel Water-Music Suite! The illusion would have been perfect. . . ."

"It's so perfect for me," I said, "that I am tempted to look at your hands to see if they are still wet."

We smiled at each other, then, our eyes meeting with a shyness that was not altogether a shyness; and after a moment, by a common impulse, turned to look out at the red-blossomed tree, from which arose a soft irregular patter. We were silent for a long while. In fact, I think we sat there in complete silence till the nurse-companion came back again for the tea-things; and I remember noticing everything, every minutest detail, in the small brick-walled garden. A laburnum tree at the farther end with long pendulous blossoms, of so bright a yellow that it gave one the illusion of sunlight against the dark wall. And a row of lupins along a flagged path, with a bright eye of water in every one of the dark hand-shaped leaves. . . . These things are still vivid in my memory. But what we said to each other after that I cannot recall. I don't think we said very much. We felt, I think, that we had already said all that was essential. I do remember Reine's saying that "Wilson" had gone off somewhere to play cricket; and also she said something about a dismal female tea-party to which she had gone in Earl's Court the day before. But that, I think, was all; and not long afterward I rose and came away.

IV.   I never saw her again. In the first place, I funked it—I was afraid that I couldn't keep it up. The thing was so exquisite as it stood, so perfect—and besides, what could I do? It seemed to me that almost anything, after that, would be an anticlimax. If I were to go again, there might be someone else there—we should have to be stiff and distant with each other—or we wouldn't be able to talk to each other at all. Wilson might be there, with his loud fake enthusiasms and his horrible Oxford manner and his sprawling tweed legs. . . .

At bottom, however, it was a kind of terror that kept me away. I was in love with her, and I had more than a hope that she was very nearly in love with me. But hadn't we already had the finest of it? The thing, as it stood, was all bloom and fragrance; and mightn't it be only too appallingly easy, by some unguarded shaking of the tree, to destroy the whole rare miracle? . . . Wouldn't I—to use a less poetic image—let the cat out of the bag, if I were to go again? And then there was her bad heart, and the fact that we were both, alas, married. The complications and miseries, if we *did* allow the meeting to go further, might well be fatal to both of us.

Even so, I am not sure that I wouldn't have gone, had not fate in the guise of the Foreign Office intervened. I was sent, only a few weeks later, to Rome, where my duties kept me for a year and a half. It was while I was there that "Scherzo" came out in book-form. Estlin sent me a copy—and I at once sat down and wrote a letter to Reine, a brief one, telling her again of the incomparable delight it gave me. It was a month or more before I heard from her—and then came a short note from Seville. It was rather cool, rather cryptic, distinctly guarded. She thanked me formally, she was glad I liked the dream so much, she felt, as I did, that the ending was perhaps a shade "tricky," of a "surprise" sort which didn't quite "go" with the tone of the rest. That was all. But there was also a postscript at the bottom of the page which seemed to me to be in a handwriting a little less controlled—as if she had hesitated about adding it, and had then, impulsively, dashed it in at the last minute. This was simply: "I always think of you as the man who loves rain." . . . That was all.

It was only a few weeks after this, when, opening *The Times* in a small café in the Via Tritoni, I was shocked to see her name in the column of death announcements. "Suddenly, at Paris, on the 18th of March." . . . Suddenly, at Paris, on the 18th of March! . . . I sat and stared stupidly at the announcement, leaving untouched on the little table before me my *granita di cafe con pana*. . . . Reine Wilson was dead—Reine was dead. That little girl who had stood in the dark room by the French windows, her sleeve brushing the stirless curtains, watching the rain—who had dipped her hands through the clearest rain-water to the white piano keys—and seen the little umbrellas of silver—was dead. I got up and walked out blindly into the bright street. Without knowing how I got there, I found myself presently in the Borghese Gardens. There was a little pond, in which a great number of ducks were sailing to and fro, gabbling and quacking, and children were throwing bread into the water. I sat down on a bench under a Judas-tree—it was in blossom, and the path under it was littered with purple. An Italian mother slapped the hand of her small boy who was crying, and said harshly, *"Piangi! . . . Piangi! . . ."* Cry! Cry! . . . And I too felt like weeping, but I shed no tears. Reine Wilson the novelist was still alive; but Reine Wilson the dark-haired little girl with whom I had fallen in love was dead, and it seemed to me that I too was dead.

A CONVERSATION

_____

The English lecturer, when he visited New Haven, Connecticut, was put up for the night at a certain club, the name of which need not be mentioned. After his lecture he managed to escape from several putative hosts, excusing himself on the ground of fatigue, and crept back to the club. He was tired of lecturing and tired of travel and tired of seeing new people and of trying to be polite to fools. He looked forward with an almost insane joy to the prospect of a night of rest. He had never been so sleepy in his life. Those American sleeping-cars! . . . Good Lord.

Unfortunately, his room communicated with the adjoining room by a door—locked, of course, and with a small table pushed against it—and no sooner had he crawled into bed than he discovered that sounds, through this door, were distressingly audible. There was first a shuffling of feet in the corridor outside, and then the voices began. There were two of them.

"Well _now_—if you'll look on the shelf in that closet, I think you'll find another glass."

"So there is."

"This is the best whisky I ever drank, but it might be worse. Old Royal. Ever hear of it on the other side?"

"Never."

"It's evidently been in the water. Soaked. They say they drop them off, you know, with buoys to mark them. The *label* looks all right. But what makes *me* suspicious is the cork. Just look at that! No self-respecting cork ought to come out like that. Perfectly good cork—stamped with the name——"

"Oh, I guess they tamper with them all right. Probably carry along an extra supply of corks, and put them in again after they mix it with water."

"Very likely. Here's looking at you."

"How."

A pause, and the Englishman tried to bury both his ears in the pillow.

"Damned good, all the same. Has the real smoky flavor. Usquebaugh. The real peat-bog flavor."

"It might be worse—it might be worse."

"And no smell of wood-alcohol, either."

"You know, I find the *bottles* are a great problem. Of course, everybody drinks—but I don't quite like to leave the empty bottles round for the servants to carry off."

"Like the problem of razor blades. What do *you* do with your used blades? My friend Edgett, in London, saves his up for a year, and then makes a neat package of them, takes them down to the middle of Waterloo Bridge, and drops them into the Thames."

"Ha, ha. I do better than that. I save mine and drop them off an Atlantic liner. But unfortunately, lately, I don't go abroad often enough."

"You might make a special trip, periodically."

"A little bit expensive."

"Phew! It's damned hot in here—must be eighty."

A pause, while a window was opened. The bells of a church, or the college, were heard striking the quarter-hour: *ding dong dang doom.* And a self-starter began its rhythmic skirling, like a dinosaur trying to be sick. *Ngu-ngu-ngu-ngu-ngu*——

"You know, to go back to that business—if the college gets wind of it, it might lose you your job."

"Good Lord. Do you think so?"

"Of course I do. They're pretty shy about that sort of thing. You ought to be more careful about being seen with her. Anyway, till the divorce is granted."

"Well, you do astonish me. What's wrong with her? She looks perfectly respectable."

"Oh, she may *look* perfectly respectable."

"Damn it, she *is* perfectly respectable."

"Hm, I'm not so sure, I'm not so sure."

"Why, of course she is! What's eating you?"

"Well, from what T. J. said to me over the telephone the other day, I'm not so sure. He didn't seem to think so."

"T. J. can eat my shirt. He makes me sick. That's all he knows about it. You know, he was pretty keenly interested in her himself, last year."

"That may be. But he found out quite a lot about her. And from what he said over the telephone, that's why he dropped her."

"She dropped *him*. That what's happened. And he's sore."

"Well——"

A pause, and the Englishman tried covering his head with the sheet, was stifled, and uncovered himself again.

"He's jealous. And he needn't try to pretend that he's just trying to protect me from a viper. Damn him and his hypocrisy and his paltry little Fine Arts anyway."

"He admitted to me that he's been engaged to her."

"Oh, he did!"

"Yes, he did. They were engaged for three months. Did she tell you that?"

"Well, she said they were pretty intimate."

"Oh . . . And he said that as he knew we were cousins, and didn't exactly like to approach *you* about it, he felt that he ought to talk to *me* about it. You know, he put detectives on her."

"The devil he did!"

"Yes. And right off, he discovered that while she was playing with him, and ostensibly in love with him, she was also playing with three or four other men. It might have been harmlessly— but just the same she was pretty intimate with them. Going off on long rides with them to joy-houses in the country, going to dances, expensive parties, and so forth. And she never told him a word about them. Pretended she was doing some important work for Morrison. He met her twice with that chap—what's his name?—the newspaper man Read. He asked her point-blank about that, and she said: 'Oh, he was just an old friend.' She insisted there was nothing in it, but just the same he was treating her to thirty-dollar dinners and that sort of thing. She admitted that, and also going off, two years ago, on a tour in his Packard, with him and some other people. She said that there was a female cousin of his along. Also she said that he wasn't at all interested in women—not *that* way. That may sound all right to you, but it sounds fishy to me."

"T. J. is a jealous fool, and that's one of the reasons she dropped him. If he couldn't trust her any better than that, he got what was coming to him. . . . Good God, getting detectives! The dirty spy!"

"Not at all. He said he hadn't been engaged to her a week before he caught her in a lie."

"*All* women lie."

"No—they don't. And here *you* are. Did she tell you she'd been engaged to T. J.? I don't believe she's trustworthy. There can't be so much smoke without fire. And as for Read, you know as well as I do that no man hangs around a woman for years and spends a lot of money on her if he isn't interested in *that* way, as she so tactfully put it. There ain't no such animals."

"Well, I'll admit that sort of thing does disquiet me a little about her."

"By gosh, it ought to!"

"All the same, I prefer to put another interpretation on it.

She just likes a good time, that's all.—Good Lord, there's no harm in that."

"None at all, if *that* was the whole story."

"She's modern, that's all. You can't expect a self-supporting woman, in this day and age, to cloister herself like a nun."

"Certainly not. There's no question of that. But T. J. says she's been really promiscuous. And this pose of inexperience on her part is all a fake. When T. J. got engaged to her, he thought he was the first man she had ever kissed. But he discovered his mistake soon enough!"

"He's more of a fool than I thought he was. . . ."

"May be, may be. He said he got a shock when he discovered, under all that screen of innocence, how damned proficient she was. It began leaking out in lots of little ways."

"Such as? You mean to say he told you all this over the *telephone?*"

"No, not all of it. . . ."

"Such as?"

"Oh, you know the sort of thing. At first she pretended to be awfully shy and inexpert—but then, at moments, she would forget herself, and say or do things that made it sufficiently plain that she had been there before. Lots of things; and of the most tell-tale kind. I don't need to describe them to you. She would be betrayed into doing them by her forgetfulness, and then she would break off, suddenly, and pretend to be terribly ashamed."

"Oh."

"And then she'd be histrionic about them, and ask herself and him what on earth could have made her do such a thing! . . . Have another drink?"

"Thanks—plenty. . . ."

. . . A pause. The bells were heard striking the half hour. *Ding dong dang doom: doom dang ding dong.* It was like the sound of a question-mark, left one suspended. The Englishman said "damn!" and turned on his right side.

"He said he wouldn't have minded so much, or been so deeply hurt, if she had only been honest with him. But she tried to conceal all this. And consequently he began feeling that there must be a *lot* to conceal. *You* know how that sort of thing works."

"Yes. But just the same I think he was wrong."

"That may be."

"He's just naturally suspicious and jealous, that's all."

"Of course, that's what she tells *you*. Naturally. But he investigated her and found out a good deal. Got hold of some friend of hers who was on the outs with her."

"Oh, *did* he."

"Yes. And he found out that her affairs had been innumerable. One man after another for ten years. Some of them for a short while, and some of them for longer. All sorts and kinds, too—she seems to have had no discrimination at all. Any sort of man, so long as he made love to her. There was a wealthy ice-manufacturer in New York, an Italian police-sergeant, an officer in the Coast Guard, a college boy from Arkansas—she had pretty heavy love-affairs with all of these."

"You mean she was *engaged* to them?"

"Oh, no. Who bothers to be engaged nowadays? I thought you were so modern."

"Well, I'm damned!"

"And a string of others, including Read, who still hangs on, I believe. T. J. had it out with her. There was a terrible scene: at the beginning she wept and said she was innocent, but at the end she was swearing and throwing things on the floor. All that delightful gentleness of hers, that you talk so much about, went to the winds. She admitted everything, and told him to go to hell."

"The *damned* liar!"

"But why should he take the trouble to lie?"

"I don't know, but he's lying."

"No, he isn't. Here, have another drop?"

"No, thanks."

There was a pause, the clink of a tumbler, and the sound as of a waste-paper basket kicked over.

"You might as well open your eyes. I daresay she's a nice enough girl, but you'd better disabuse yourself of the notion that she's a saint. Of course, that needn't make any difference to you. Even supposing that she *is,* as T. J. says, terribly man-handled——"

"*Damn*ation. It's impossible! . . ."

"Even supposing she is, it may be that it's only because she's played in bad luck. She may, each time, have been sincerely in love, and sincerely in hope of marrying. That's quite possible, though it doesn't seem likely. But T. J. thinks she is really, by nature, promiscuous. She basks in the admiration of men, she must have men around her, and he thinks she will be like that all her life. I don't know anything about her, of course— I'm merely telling you what T. J. said."

"Very *kind* of you."

"Look here, Paul—"

"I know—I beg your pardon. It really *is* kind of you. But you know I'm in love with her, and this sort of thing is painful."

"Of course it is. I'm sorry."

A pause. The Englishman listened. The pause lengthened itself.

"I admit, this shakes me a good deal. To tell the truth, I've been having the same experience with her myself, I mean——"

"Well? . . ."

"About her proficiency. It's been coming out, little by little, in just the way you described. And it hurts me horribly—horribly. If you knew what it is to be in love with someone you can't quite trust! . . . But I'm *sure* she's all right—I'm sure of it."

"Well, if you're sure of that, then you're all right."

"Man-handled! . . . Good God!"

"Don't be depressed by it. I daresay she's all right. If you're in love with her——"

"But I thought she was so completely *innocent!* That's what's so horrible. And I think she *is,* fundamentally. After all, what can it matter, if I'm in love with her?"

"But are you sure you're in love with the right image? I mean the true one?"

"I prefer to think that the woman I'm in love with is the real woman. That's what T. J. missed—that's what he *would* miss. I mean, her central idealism, her essential holiness. Yes, that's what it is. She has a kind of holiness about her that it's impossible to describe. And by God, I'll marry her. And to hell with T. J. and all his damned detectives."

"Well, if you're sure of that, you're all right. Let's change the subject . . ."

"We might as well—this doesn't get us anywhere . . . Let's talk about something else."

"Have a night-cap. *In vino sanitas.*"

"Thanks—plenty."

"Water?"

"No . . . My God, my God, if only I didn't——"

"What?"

"It's no use. *In vino sanitas* . . . Anything to be unconscious!"

A pause. The Englishman counted sheep. Two-four-six-eight-twenty-two at a time-two at a time-two at a time-wool in the hedge-gaps—wool on the hawthorn twigs—wool on the gorse——

"I hear Peter is back to try again. Poor devil! He certainly sticks at it."

"Poor devil."

"Poor devil."

The bells were heard striking the third quarter: *Ding dong dang doom: doom dang ding dong: ding dang dong doom:* and again a question-mark was left in the air.

NO, NO, GO NOT TO LETHE

This literary fellow, who was, as a matter of fact, only *half* literary—his real occupation being that of a teacher of English composition at the college—was named Samuel Pierce Babcock; but he always signed his name S. Pierce Babcock, and managed to have his friends call him Pierce. He disliked the name Samuel, which always seemed to him effeminate, and which in addition had been the name of his father's brother, whom he had detested. Besides, if one had to have a trade name, for literary purposes (and he was perpetually sending out poems, articles, and stories to the magazines), he thought S. Pierce Babcock was much more distinguished than (say) Samuel Babcock. And he rather liked the "social" air of S. Pierce Babcock. He had even thought of dropping the Samuel altogether; but to tell the truth he was prevented by the thought of the formalities he might have to undergo in order to change his signature at the bank.

He lived in a boarding-house in the charming little country town, in Massachusetts, which contained the aforesaid college (the name of which we had better not mention); he had no living relatives; he was a bachelor, aged thirty-two; he knew himself to be rather charming—one of those fortunate young men who unite the virtues of athlete and philosopher; and he prided himself on his complete independence, both socially and intellectually. He picked his acquaintances carefully, kept them carefully at a distance, used them, pumped them, gave himself to them quite liberally up to a certain point, but when that point had been reached became as inscrutable as the Sphinx. He had never yet encountered a human being who was worthy of his ultimate confidence; to no one had he, as yet, ever made full confession, poured from the heart. He had, moreover, an idea that to confess oneself too readily, or too freely, was, *ipso facto,* to weaken oneself. Not only was it a shameful kind of self-indulgence, unworthy of a mature being; it was also a definite and horrible draining of one's spiritual excellence, one's *virtue.* And by virtue he meant a sort of magic.

For this reason, therefore, and because he wanted to maintain this excellence intact for his literary purposes (and likewise for his nocturnal explorations of the truth—a very serious occupation with him) he kept his personal relationships at a decent minimum. His contacts at the college he managed very skillfully. He was tactful, friendly, on occasion he could be quite sufficiently convivial; he prided himself somewhat on his ability (a real one) to be all things to all men; and at the end of his second year of teaching he was, if not exactly popular, at any rate well liked. He could spend an evening with cheerful cocktail drinkers and get slightly tight; he could dine with a pair of middle-aged professors and discuss Grimm's law; or play a game of billiards with the manager and quarterback of the football team; or even, if necessary, attend a tea at the president's house, where he made himself agreeable to the president's wife. But if he did all these things easily, he did not do them often; and he never encouraged these acquaintances to seek him out. He became known by degrees as something of a mystery. He was respected, looked up to, and he was well aware of this; he knew that people pointed him out as that "brilliant young Babcock"; but he was determined to allow

no liberties to be taken. His life—his precious and secret life—
was to remain inviolably and wonderfully his own.

Just what he wanted to do with this, or make of it, he could
not precisely have said. It was something as yet unformulable:
it changed its shape from day to day and night to night like a
cloud; at times it seemed extraordinarily near and immediate,
as close and intimate as the sparrow on the window-sill; as
definite as a yellow willow twig, which the rain had darkened;
but at other times it was as elusive as one of those chance fra-
grances which awaken in one's memory, for a flash, some poign-
ant forgotten scene of which the poignance is all that one can
recall. Nevertheless, the seeking of this thing was his business.
He went deep into his soul for it, as if it were a cavern or mine
and himself a miner. Whenever he picked up in his reading,
or in his daily life, any sort of clue to the mystery, no matter
how slight, he was at once eager to try it out; and down at once
he would go into himself with this little lantern in his hand;
and up again, after awhile, he would come, defeated, but none
the less refreshed and none the less convinced that some day,
at last, he would discover the real thing. He was developing, in
fact, a keen and insatiable curiosity about every minutest facet
of life. Nothing escaped him. His pleasure in merely standing
at his window and looking along the street of the country town,
and watching (himself unobserved) the comings and goings of
his acquaintances, their little absurd manipulations of each
other, and the effect of wind or weather on them, the rain on
their hats, the wind blowing their skirts, the scarf that had to
be removed from the cheek—all these things gave him an
astonishing sense of wonder. In such things as these the secret
was not far off: in these, and in the fact that he *understood*
them. When he saw the professor of biochemistry making
exactly the gesture, with his elbow, which he had foreseen, he
experienced a definite intimation of immortality, and permitted himself (standing in his window) a self-conscious crow
of pleasure. And this, too, he immediately understood, and
did not despise. For there was nothing despicable.

And on the plane of personal relationships this business of exploration was perfectly inexhaustible. Here, indeed, was the real world: a vista of miracles as vast and interminable as the steppes and tundras of Asia, the prolific human jungles of India and China; a universe of star-fields; a soundable space which was all depth and height and fecundity. Each human creature with whom he came into contact, no matter how grazingly, was a marvel to be apprehended. He flattered himself that his tactilism was becoming an instrument of surpassing delicacy and divination: frequently, with one look, he penetrated to secrets of a personality which that personality itself might spend a lifetime in misunderstanding. And when opportunity afforded for a longer and more careful scrutiny, as with his pupils and his colleagues, he cherished with the nicest care his gradual peeling of layer after layer from the unsuspecting soul. It gave him a special ecstasy, in such cases, if, while thus reaching to the very ore-seams of another's soul, he could maintain his own soul's silence unbroken. An overwhelming sense of power came over him when he saw that soul's defenses going down, one by one, under the minute blows of his searching and surgical curiosity. Gradually, day after day, he moved closer to the frightened center of that being; he drove it in, as mowers in a field, moving always nearer to the field's middle, drive in the rabbit or the fox; until at length came the instant when the poor creature bolted; and for him, the onlooker, this was the moment of the miracle.

II. As might be imagined, his boarding-house was an admirable source of entertainment for him, and within a year of his arrival he had discovered everything transacted within it which was of the smallest interest. In this, of course, he had to exercise a fine discretion; it would never do to permit to any of these people the seeking of an intimacy. But as a matter of fact there had been no great difficulty about this. There was something in him—it was probably the keenness of his mind, his unsleeping critical faculty—which could always be counted on to keep these simpler folk at a comfortable distance. Mrs. Holt, his landlady, was unobtrusive and businesslike; Mandell, an instructor in history, and rather a pedagogue, who at first had been somewhat inclined (being lonely) to drop in of an evening for a smoke, had been tactfully impressed with the fact that the evening was sacred to the Muse; Wright, a terrible bore, with large teeth and large ears, who worked in the local bank, had given him up on discovering in him faint traces of socialism and pacifism; and the old couple who had the room opposite his own, the Brownlees, were decently self-absorbed. What there was to know about these good people he knew. Together they constituted for him, as time went on, a kind of unified organism: he always thought of them as belonging to each other and to him and to the house. Their toothbrushes hung in the bathroom, he knew their slippers, their bathrobes, their neckties, their breakfast habits, the names of their correspondents, their views on life. Now and then there was a minor altercation, as when one or another of them used the bath too indecently long; or a breeze of jealousy or competition would momentarily set them a-shaking; and these outcroppings and cross-currents he noted with delight. But for the most part they were miracles of expectedness: they seldom any longer surprised him; and the sense of joy he extracted from living with them, which was still very real, was largely derived from the queer feeling he had of being, in a sense, the house's *consciousness.* He carried the whole thing in his mind. When he lay in his bed, of a spring evening, looking out of his window at the locust tree, he felt, between the house full of human beings and himself, an almost physical identity. He could hear Mrs. Brownlee coughing, as usual, and old Brownlee thumping his shoes off, and Wright singing in the bathroom, and Mrs. Holt talking, at the back door, to the cat. Mandell was inaudible: he would be sitting, of course, at his hideous golden-oak roll-top desk, with a green visor on his noble brow, his shirt-sleeves rolled up, a very masculine array of pipes scattered around him (he was one of those pedagogues who affect the minor masculine characteristics, just to prove to themselves that they are men) and a drop-lamp focused glaringly on an opened book. His room was stuffy, and always smelt a little of sweat. . . . And the back door was shut, Mrs. Holt's footsteps mounted the carpeted stairs, she said a good-night to Wright, whom she encountered, the Brownlees got laboriously into bed, or Brownlee put his head out of the window and said it was a fine night, and the house came to rest; coming to rest, to all intents and purposes, in the brain of S. Pierce Babcock.

III.   In May, the Brownlees went away to California, with every intention of staying there till one or both of them died. Their departure was as casual as their arrival had been: no fuss was made about it. They had their breakfast as usual, without the slightest deviation of habit, said their goodbyes unexcitedly, and at lunch were gone. Mrs. Holt took the occasion to give the room a thorough housecleaning, and Babcock in turn took the occasion to inspect it: he had thought it might be preferable to his own. He walked in after dinner on the same evening, lighted the gas, and examined it. It had two windows, being a corner room; that was its chief advantage; but in other respects he didn't especially like it. The wallpaper was an affair of roses on trellises, the chest of drawers was painted a bright blue, and over the large old-fashioned wooden bed hung a steel engraving of Botticelli's "Birth of Venus."

Babcock's motive for making this careful inspection was, in truth, a double one. His intention of transferring to this room was not very serious; but it had occurred to him that here, for his study of the next occupant, was material which he could not afford to ignore. Not that there was anything of importance about the room itself, or anything remarkable in it: but simply because, such at it was, it was destined in the nature of things to be the outer shell of whatever queer individual should next occupy it. This was a fact which *was* important; and in making the room's acquaintance he felt that he was already, in advance, stealing under the barriers of that unknown individual. Here was the vast varnished bed he would sleep in: he would look out of the front window at the locust tree: he would place his hair-brushes on this blue chest of drawers: his neckties would hang from this mirror, his handkerchiefs would make themselves at home in this top drawer (from which Mrs. Holt had not removed the traces of talcum powder): and every morning on waking he would see Venus standing above him on her scallop shell. Babcock smiled a kind of cerebral smile of satisfaction as he foresaw all this. He felt like an inspired interloper. When he returned to his own room, and his table littered with papers, he was several steps nearer to the Thing-in-itself.

He had not foreseen, however, the delicious extra turn of the screw which fortune was to give to his pleasure. This was the arrival and installation, in the prepared room, of a rather charming young woman, Miss Mary Anthony, who came from Burlington, Vermont. She appeared one day at lunch, was introduced, and gave every promise (Babcock thought) of becoming an unusually interesting member of the community. She was about twenty-four; rather pale and intellectual in appearance; with a fine forehead, very white, and fine gray eyes—of which the pupils were remarkably large and dark, and, in a curious way, frightened; she was shy, but smiled easily; tall and graceful; and she had not bobbed her hair. She had taken a secretarial position in the bursar's office, and she was, it soon appeared, a college woman herself.

Babcock was surprisingly excited by all this. This was indeed a find, a prize specimen. He was not above a normal interest in the opposite sex—far from it. He was quite willing to expose himself unscathed, his independence unimpaired. He had never had a love affair, and for some peculiar reason did not especially desire one; but his relations with women were easy and pleasant, and always aroused his curiosity to an unusual degree. He wanted extremely to know what they felt, how they lived, what they thought, what sort of clothes they wore. And

no such first-rate opportunity as this had ever presented itself
to him. This charming young creature was simply delivered
into his hands; and her shyness, her apparent fugitiveness—
something a little suggestive in her of one doomed by some
sort of tension to celibacy—particularly sharpened the prospect of his pleasure.

Not only this, but also he could not help noticing at once
that he had, in the present situation, an extraordinary advantage. This was the fact that he alone, of the boarding-house
community, was capable of arousing in Miss Anthony a recipro-
cal interest. Wright bored her immediately; and poor Mandell,
who was as unimaginative and humorless as he was sexless,
simply did not exist for her. She was nice to him, as indeed she
was to everyone, but that was all.

It was for Babcock that she reserved what vibrance of response
she was capable of: if, in the first few days of her stay, he had
suspected this—during that period in which he was making
the preliminary explorations—he was soon to become convinced of it. He could talk to her (if he chose) of the things
that interested her: of Verlaine and Rimbaud and Gauguin:
of James and Dostoevsky and Havelock Ellis. In fact, her interests were if anything too perilously like his own, and he
discovered in this at the outset a sense of power over her of
which he would have to be sparing, lest she tend to become
something of a nuisance to him. It would never do to rush it.
The thing must be managed with care and precision, she must
be alternately stimulated and repressed; and if she showed
signs of coming forward too much, or of desiring to make, of
the acquaintance, more than he himself wanted to make of it,
he would have to be coldly indifferent to her.

This he managed with great skill for the first three months
of her stay. Clearly he had baffled her. She did not know what
to make of him. He was so charming to her at breakfast, or
lunch, or dinner; now and then he would really let himself go,
and talk to her freely (or so it seemed); and then again, of a
sudden, he would become exceedingly remote, reply to her in

amiable monosyllables, allow her questions to fall unanswered,
or even, on occasion, avoid her altogether by absenting himself from the boarding-house table for days at a time. If he
encountered her in the street he did not, as she obviously expected, pause to say something to her, but gave her merely the
stiffest of bows. He could see, at such times, how puzzled, or
even hurt, she was, and how she would hurry past him more
fugitive than ever. She would lower her head and check her
delicious smile and try to pretend that she had not meant to
be quite so friendly. But it was apparent enough that she was
deeply hurt and chagrined.

IV.   In August he went to the White Moun-
tains for a month. He had made his plans for this some time
before. Even if he had not planned the expedition, however,
he would now have decided on such a move: for he could see,
or, to be more precise, he could *feel* that his affair (to give it
the name) with Miss Mary Anthony was reaching an acute stage.
She was clearly fascinated by him. He could not be mistaken
about this: his whole consciousness had, by degrees, devoted
itself to this one problem. It was the most interesting thing
that was happening to him at the moment—literature and
philosophy had gone by the board. Gently, slowly, delicately,
insidiously, he had wormed his way through her guard; his
awareness had surrounded her completely; he saw himself as
a kind of psychological octopus; a vampire; taking no *personal*
interest in her, never for a moment allowing an atom of his
own feelings to become involved, he had nevertheless attached
himself to her with an exhausting completeness, and had, for
her, assumed an exhausting importance. He had made not the
slightest move toward the putting of the acquaintance on a
basis of friendship. He had never once invited her to take a
walk with him, or to go to the local movie with him—he had
never given her an opportunity to see him except, casually,
at the table. Lunch or breakfast or dinner over, he always rose

immediately and withdrew. To her tentative smiles, in the hallway or on the stairs, he replied with a smile as formal and elusive
as he could make it. . . .

Just the same, he had made himself indispensable to her.
He had only to come and seat himself opposite her at the
table to feel the slight shock that went through her whole
being. She became alert, she stiffened, her shyness was magni-
fied, even the little gestures with which she ate her food became
self-conscious. Studiously, she would attempt to make her conversation as general as possible, avoiding (when she could) any
appearance whatever of talking rather to him than to the others.
But of course she did not for a moment deceive him. He knew
that she was living for him alone, and living exorbitantly for
him. Not only this: he also knew that she knew that *he* knew
this. And by degrees, thus, a very queer relationship had sprung
up between them. Wright and Mrs. Holt and Mandell and old
Miss Fairfield (who had recently moved into the attic room)
saw nothing of this. They all accepted the acquaintance between
them as of the ordinary boarding-house kind—polite, amiable,
uninsistent; an affair of the table and nothing more; and if
they perhaps now and then resented a shade the fact that Miss
Anthony and himself occasionally took the conversation into
intellectual fields, or Parnassian pastures, where they themselves could not comfortably follow, they nevertheless attached
no importance to this.

Babcock, however, did. The pressure, he felt, was becoming
acute. Miss Anthony had made no overt move, but he had from
time to time an uneasy feeling that at any moment she might
do so: she had waited, hopefully, not to say expectantly, for *him*
to make some such move—and as he had not given a single sign
of the required sort, he was increasingly certain that she con-
templated some such sign herself. What form would this take?
He was not sure: but he greatly enjoyed thinking about it; at
the same time fearing that it might be a nuisance.

For this reason he decided that his month's absence would be a good thing. He went off to Jackson and forgot her. Not wholly: there were days when (to tell the truth) he could not effectively banish her from his mind. She was there, like a color or stain on his consciousness, and he was forcibly reminded of the important part she was playing in his emotional life. Toward the end of his stay in the mountains this became increasingly insistent, and his energetic expeditions to Crawford Notch and Franconia, and his three ascents of Mount Washington, followed by a night in the Madison hut, did little to mitigate his odd feeling as of being in a hurry. Why should he be in a hurry? No reason at all. She meant nothing to him, nothing whatever. Or rather, she was of interest to him only as the experiment is of interest to the chemist. He was curious to see what was going to happen, and that was all. Why not admit this? He admitted it and breathed a sigh of relief, and decided to take the afternoon train back to Massachusetts.

He arrived, as it happened, too late for dinner, and accordingly his first meeting with her had to be postponed till the day following. He could see that she was in her room: there was a light there, and the light was visible in the crack beneath the door. Moreover, he knew that she had heard his arrival. He shut the door (opposite hers) rather loudly, when he came in; and not very long after this he heard *her* door cautiously but squeakingly open and then shut again. And fifteen minutes later this performance was repeated, and the door this time was *left* open. He approached his own door quietly and listened; but there wasn't a sound.

Her little maneuver was, of course, quite obvious. He smiled to himself, fingering his lips, and began to luxuriate in the thing. There she was—he knew—sitting in the wicker rocking-chair, or perhaps standing at the blue chest of drawers pretending to tidy her hair; and she was waiting, desperately waiting, to see what *he* would do. She was deliberately exposing herself, deliberately inviting him to make—not the first move, since she herself had already made this—but the second. The door, he imagined, was half-open: she would not be quite so overt, or bold, as to open it wide; partly, no doubt, for fear Mrs. Holt might see it, or Mandell. Her heart was beating violently. In all probability, she hardly knew, in her confusion of emotions, what she was doing. If she was standing she would sit down and pretend to read a book. . . . And as he went over in his mind all these delicious possibilities, or probabilities, he began to wonder, amusedly, what might be the best step for him to take. Should he ignore the affair entirely? Perhaps that would be too cruel? It would be painful for her, it might even make her angry; which would have unpleasant consequences for him at breakfast. Besides, it would in a sense be an avoidance of a *modus operandi* more definitely and courageously creative. And again, he recognized quite clearly in himself a genuine desire to see her and be seen by her. But how best could this be done? . . .

He walked to his window and looked out at the summer evening. It was just growing dark: the street-lights were lit: a star or two was visible in the sky. It would be pleasant, for example, to go for a short walk: out to the bridge and back: which would involve an interval of twenty minutes, or less: so that presumably she would remain, for the interval, as she was, with the door open; making an excuse of the fact that the evening was warm, and that she desired through her room a current of air. But if he were to undertake this, then the second question became urgent and subtle; should he, or should he not, pause, as he went out, to speak to her? . . . This demanded a careful calculation. The meeting must be as casual as possible. And in view of her terrific state of tension—which he could positively feel, like a vibration in the air—it might be exceedingly difficult to manage it. Would she, for example—as seemed more than likely—presume, after the month's interval, that the tone of their encounter should be cordial, or even *intimate?* It might well be that she would instinctively try to press this advantage, and shift the balance between them, well, sharply toward a confessed state (on her part, at least) of "being in love." Could he trust himself to handle such a situation as this? With just the right mixture of friendliness and aloofness?

He decided that he could; and accordingly, taking his hat from the peg, he stood again beside the door for an instant and listened. There was still not a sound. Evidently she was not moving about—she must, as he had surmised, be reading or pretending to read; and in this case she would not immediately see him when he opened his door. He opened it quickly and stepped out.

What he saw astonished him, and took him completely off his guard. For she too was standing in her doorway—like him, with her hand on the knob—and with an unmistakable air of having stood there, in a kind of paralysis, for many minutes. Not only had she been waiting for him: she had actually, he realized, been on the point of coming to *see* him. Her whole attitude was alert and intense, as if she too had been listening; and when she saw him she started and was horribly embarrassed, as he was himself.

"Oh—" he said, going quickly toward her—"how do you do!"

"How do you do!"

She relinquished the doorknob and held out her hand, which was cold. At the same time she gave a curious little laugh and a shy nod of her head, looking a little to one side and downward. The gesture was oddly attractive, and suddenly made him sorry for her.

"You're still here, I see."

"Yes, I'm still here."

"And as for me, I've come back, like the prodigal son, or the bad penny."

"Did you enjoy the mountains? . . ."

"Very much."

He smiled at her, and she smiled back, biting her lip. With her hand, which she had at first dropped a little awkwardly to her side, she again grasped the doorknob, turning it slightly to and fro.

"I heard you come in," she said, twisting sideways toward her room, as if in sudden access of shyness, "and I was wondering whether to come and say hello."

"Oh." Babcock swung his hat, meaninglessly. "As a matter of fact, I was just wondering the same thing—I mean, whether *I* would come and say hello."

"Were you?"

She said this without any particular emphasis: though for a fraction of a second he wondered whether her intention might be ironic.

"Yes. . . . I was just going out for a little stroll."

"I see. . . . You won't come in?"

"Well"—he hesitated smiling—"wouldn't you like to come *out* for a little?" He hadn't wanted to say this; it sounded a shade unconvincing; so he hastened to add—"After that ghastly train ride, I'd like to stretch my legs! . . ."

"Yes, I'd like to. I'll get my hat."

"Good. I'll be waiting downstairs."

He went down the stairs, suddenly feeling rather frightened. The whole thing had gone wrong, appallingly wrong. What was going to happen now? *Anything* might happen. He walked nervously to and fro in the hallway, put on his hat and took it off again, stared at the Landseer stag over the hatrack, looked with unseeing eyes at the pile of dusty letters on the table. He could hear her moving quickly in her room—gayly, joyfully. Somehow, she had been too much for him. Was it that she had outwitted him—or was it simply that life itself was outwitting him, for once proving too subtly incalculable? Was she aware of what she was doing? No, he didn't think so. It was simply that all of a sudden this business had fallen upon him with a stupendous force which he had not in the least foreseen. Good God—the thing might really be dangerous. It would have to be controlled at once. They would have to get back to the casual note and immediately: there wasn't a minute to lose. But could it be done? And here was this walk, a thing he had never done before! How could he possibly counteract the effect, the obvious implications, of that? The step was already taken: there was no undoing it. And it was utterly impossible, now, to be rude about it, to treat her coldly—wasn't it? The break in the logic would be too extreme. And impossible, also, to be explicit about it—to say, abruptly, "Look here—I don't want you to misunderstand my motives in this . . . I'm not falling in love with you. Not in the least. And you had better not think so. . . ." No, this couldn't be done. It was out of the question. And the more hurriedly he thought, or tried to think, of expedients, the more genuinely terrified and confused he became. . . .

v. He noticed that she was flushed, when she came down the stairs toward him; and this did nothing to mitigate his uneasiness. She was excited, tremulous, and her excitement at once transmitted itself to him. He opened the screen door for her with an unexpectedly awkward gesture, a little strained—a confession of embarrassment which was very unusual with him, and which it gave him no pleasure to recognize.

"I thought—" he said, in a tone which he endeavored to make as light as possible, and at the same time somewhat cool— "we might go to the old bridge. I haven't seen it for a whole month!"

"Five weeks, isn't it?" she said.

"Yes—I believe it is."

For a few minutes they walked in silence. He stole a glance at her as they passed under a street-light, and saw that she was frowning.

"I suppose," he said, "it's been pretty quiet here. Did you get away at all?"

"Quiet!" She lifted her face and gave a charming little laugh, quite without bitterness. "It's been like a tomb. Literally like a tomb. Or a mausoleum—which sounds even deader. No, I didn't get away. My people are all abroad. . . . And, really, there were times——"

She broke off and made a shy, quick gesture with one hand, as if the thing transcended speech.

He saw what answer was expected of him; but also saw that there was no way of avoiding it.

"Times when *what*—" he said somewhat brusquely.

She paused, as if getting her breath, and then said:

"When I really thought I'd go melancholy mad. Have you ever been lonely?"

"Lonely! I should say so. But to tell the truth I rather like it."

"Then I don't believe you know what it is."

"Don't I! As a matter of fact, I've *practiced* loneliness all my life. I believe in it."

"Oh!"

An uneasiness had come between them—as if, psychologically speaking, they had fallen out of step. He had deliberately failed to follow her lead, or to allow *her* to follow it; and they were both aware of this. Babcock felt a kind of momentary relief. Perhaps, after all, it wasn't going to be so bad—he was keeping her at a distance. At the same time, he felt horribly conscience-stricken. He stole another glance at her—it was just as they turned the corner of the road into Langham Street, which led to the bridge—and saw that she was definitely unhappy. She had again lowered her chin into the orange scarf at her throat, and with her left hand was lifting a part of the scarf against her cheek. There was something extraordinarily pathetic about the gesture.

"Yes, you may not believe it, but I like it."

"*I* don't," she said; and then on a lower tone, as if half to herself, she added: "Perhaps I've had too much of it. . . . Here, for example, in this funny little town—! . . . I don't know what I would have done, without *you*."

"Me!" Babcock's laugh was somewhat hollow.

"Yes. Those *dreadful* people at the boarding-house! They'd have driven me mad."

They had come to the bridge: at the middle of it they stopped, by tacit agreement, and rested their elbows on the hand-rail looking down at the black water. Everything was extraordinarily still. The water itself made scarcely a chuckle, the willow leaves which trailed in it were stirless, a faraway train whistle, with its mournful cry, only deepened the nocturnal peace. And suddenly it seemed to Babcock that all these things—the bridge, the river, the night, the willow trees, the profound silence—were in a subtle and terrifying way driving himself and this girl together. With a start he realized that his elbow was touching hers: and instantly he moved his arm.

"But those dreadful people—" he said deliberately and coolly —"as a matter of fact have been my chief source of entertainment. I have a passion for studying the human being at close range—it's a habit worth cultivating. If you can do it without allowing them to infringe on you——"

She turned her head and looked at him rather intently.

"You mean to say——!"

"What?"

She averted her face from him quickly, almost angrily.

"Are you as heartless as all that? Heaven knows I don't *like* them! But I don't think I could do that. . . . Just what do you mean?"

"Just exactly that. . . . I like to *surround* them, so to speak, with my awareness. I like to know just what they're doing and thinking, every minute of the day. And usually, after they've been there for a month or two, I flatter myself that I do . . ."

"I see."

"Will you smoke?"

"No, thank you."

Babcock struck a match. The bright flame danced before his face, and he was aware that the girl took the opportunity to look at him rather sharply.

"Well, then," she said, "I suppose you've made no exception of *me*."

"No."

"How funny! How very funny! And I suppose you know *all* about me?"

"Well—I dare say I know a good deal. . . . I've enjoyed think-ing about you——"

"Thank you——!"

"Wondering what you were up to—what you thought when you woke in the morning and looked up at the Botticelli 'Venus,' for example—or your blue chest of drawers—oh, all those little odds and ends that make up our lives—so many of them too complex for explicit expression. A kind of divination."

"And all, I suppose, without the slightest feeling for me."

"Well—why *should* I have?"

"And I, meanwhile, have been—in love with you! Isn't it absurd?"

She turned and gave him a queer smile.

"I knew you were," he said quietly. "That was one of the things that most interested me. . . . To tell the truth, I was deliberately experimenting with you. Why shouldn't I be frank with you?"

"Why, indeed, since *I've* been so frank with you!"

"Exactly."

Leaning over the hand-rail he tapped his cigarette, and the hot ash fell with a faint *psst* into the dark water. He smiled secretly thinking of the really unparalleled uniqueness of the situation: smiling also because he now at least felt that he had it perfectly under control. His self-consciousness was leaving him. He turned toward her more easily, urbanely. But just as he was about to speak, the girl began laughing—and laughing with such a queer recklessness that for a moment he feared she might be becoming hysterical. She stopped, however, as abruptly as she had begun.

"That really is very funny," she said. "To think of your pacing to and fro in your little room, meditating on the comings and goings of so utterly unimportant a person as me! Did you *really* wonder what I thought about in the morning, when I looked up at the Botticelli 'Venus'? or in just which one of my drawers I kept my knickers? or how often I indulged in deli-cious thoughts of Mr. S. Pierce Babcock?"

"I really did!"

Babcock tried to give to this statement an air of scientific detachment; but he was aware that it hadn't quite come off.

"Well, go on and tell me some more. This simply fascinates me. Just how, for example, did you think this experiment would end?"

"You'd really like to know?"

"Of course. . . . You see, I'm not quite the sensitive plant you thought I was."

A tremor in her voice just faintly belied this assertion: or was it simply that she was angry? But Babcock decided to be ruthless, and to end the thing once and for all.

"All right, I will. . . . Do you know the story about Dostoevsky, and the girl he had been in love with, who lived in the room next to his? He was tired of her; he began to hate her; he ignored her, let her starve; he knew, by a sort of divination—the sort I was just now speaking of—that she was in despair, and about to kill herself; and finally, one night, he actually listened to her in the process of hanging herself. He heard the chair drag across the bare floor to the gas-fixture: he heard a silence and then the sound of the chair falling over: and he stood perfectly still, giving her plenty of time to die. . . . A very pretty story. . . . Well, I wasn't quite so ambitious! But I wanted to see just what you *would* do. I knew you wouldn't kill yourself—as somebody remarked in 'Hedda Gabler,' 'people don't do such things.' But I wondered whether my mere presence, combined with my total indifference to you, might not drive you away. And in any case, I wanted to *see* . . . That's all.

There was a pause, during which they both stared down at the moving water. Babcock felt oddly excited: he found that he was breathing a little quickly. Before he had time to wonder why, the girl patted him twice on the shoulder, reassuringly.

"Well, don't worry," she said. "I'm not going to drown myself or hang myself—'No, no, go not to Lethe!' To be perfectly frank with *you*, in my turn, I don't quite think you're worth it. Don't you *really* think you're one of the most revolting people you've ever met, and one of the unhappiest, and *the* blindest? But I'm sorry for you."

"Thank you!"

"And now I think, if you don't mind, I'll go back to my Botticelli 'Venus' and my blue chest of drawers: to give you the pleasure of wondering what I think about before I fall asleep —which I assure you I shall do without waste of time. . . . Good night!"

Before Babcock could say a word in answer, she had gone: the night had swallowed her up. He stared into the darkness, feeling very foolish. Good Lord—what an extraordinary thing! To run after her would be absurd—he would have to give her a sufficient start. He waited, therefore, flung his cigarette into the river, walked to the other side of the bridge and back, listened to a freight train in the distance, panting rhythmically as it tried to get under way, then lighted another cigarette and began slowly to take his way homeward. And what would happen now? She had admitted that she loved him. Had her love suddenly turned to hate? Would she cry herself to sleep? No, it was most unlikely. She was probably smiling ironically. She was despising him. Perhaps even she was planning—

The thought made him stop dead: his heart began to beat violently: he felt himself beginning to perspire. Good God— suppose, now, she was to *reverse* the roles—and make a remorseless study of *him?* She already had the whip hand, for he had told her everything. He was at her mercy—absolutely at her mercy. If now she were to keep *him* at a distance—make *him* the *corpus vile* of a prolonged experiment—watch his comings and goings—freeze him and scrutinize him—could he endure it? Would *he* have to go? . . .

He let himself in through the screen door, went softly up the stairs—resisting, with a queer pang, the impulse to listen, to see if she might be crying—and crawled into bed. For a long while he was unable to sleep.

VI.   The next morning he went to Boston— for no particular reason, except that he wanted time in which to collect himself, to try to analyze the extraordinary emotional confusion which had suddenly beset him. He did not see her before he left. He merely informed Mrs. Holt that he would be gone for a week, on business. In a sense, this was tantamount to an admission of defeat; but, also, he thought, it might conceivably be a good tactical move.

But Boston, he found, did little to help him. He could take no interest in his favorite pictures at the Art Museum; the movies bored him; his friends were out of town; it was hot and dusty, and his hotel room was not too comfortable. He was troubled with insomnia, also, and even began to wonder whether he might be ill. When Friday came he was glad, not to say eager, to pack his suitcase and go home.

A surprise awaited him: Miss Anthony had gone. Her room was empty—the door was open, and he saw at a glance that all her things had been removed. The Botticelli Venus smiled down at a bed which had been stripped: one of the drawers in the blue chest was half open, and on entering he saw that it was empty. A broken match-box lay on the table, and on it a crumpled cigarette stub.

At once an appalling feeling of desolation came over him. His heart contracted. He knocked at Mrs. Holt's door and asked whether Miss Anthony had gone away for a holiday, trying to disguise his agitation.

"A holiday? No, Mr. Babcock, she's gone abroad. She gave up her position suddenly, and went to join her family."

"Did she say for how long? or leave an address?"

"I think it was to be for a year at least. She didn't leave any address—I think she left it maybe at the post office."

"I see . . ."

That night, Babcock wrote to her and told her that he loved her. And two months later he received a picture post-card— of a particularly fiendish gargoyle on the cathedral at Amiens —which bore the words: "No, no, go not to Lethe."

PURE AS THE DRIVEN SNOW

Bill Massingham, who was still called, in his second year at college, "Messy," a nickname first given him at school for various reasons, walked furtively up the ill-lighted alley which led to the stage door of the Majestic Theatre. His coat collar was turned up, the brim of his hat was pulled down, his handsome but extremely weak and sensual face looked frightened. He had a habit of blinking his pale blue eyes when he was nervous, and he did this now, as he passed several loiterers on his way to the theater door. He always, on these occasions, came a little late, so that most of the chorus girls would have made their assignations and gone away. He was afraid of being seen by one of his classmates, or even by a professor: one never could be too sure.

Still blinking, and adjusting his pince-nez with one hand, he stopped at the door and peered into the dark entry. At first he thought it was deserted, and that Bella might have left. But suddenly there was a little squeal, she launched herself out of her hiding-place behind the door, her arms were round his neck, and his hat had fallen into the snow.

"For God's sake," he said, angry and alarmed, "be careful! Somebody might see us."

The girl, who was a Cuban, kicked his shin smartly, so that he gave a little cry of pain. Then she snapped her fingers. She looked hard at him and said:

"I don't care if the president of your college is out there, and your darling damn fool father, too."

Messy stopped, picked up his hat, brushed the snow from it. His face had flushed. Apparently she was in one of her reckless moods, and he became uneasy.

"Damn you," he said, "look what you've done to my hat! Gent's best hattings, too."

"To hell with your hat."

"You shouldn't talk about my father like that."

"To hell with your father."

"All right—if that's the way you're going to talk to me you can do all the talking yourself."

He began to walk away, lifting his chin, and instantly she caught his arm and clung to him, drawing her small dark face upward toward his.

"Darling!" she said. "Kiss me!"

"No."

"Oh, but darling, kiss Bella!"

"I will when you've apologized."

"Oh, for God's sake, are you going to preach again tonight?" She flung her arm away from his with a violent gesture, and stamped one of her galoshes in the light snow.

He stopped where he was and smiled at her, weakly.

"Haven't you any respect for me?" he said. "Come on, Bella, be a good girl!" He put out his hand, took her arm, and they embraced, quickly, furtively, Messy watching with one detached eye to see if anyone was coming. Then they walked swiftly, laughing, to the end of the alley, crossed the street, and went into the dining room of the Klondyke Hotel, where Bella was staying. They got a table at the edge of the floor, by the gilt railing, ordered oysters and White Rock, and in another minute were dancing. They danced in silence, Messy gazing downward into Bella's eyes with an extraordinary sleepy catlike sensuous-ness feeling, with his arms and knees and thighs, every subtle insinuation of her body. Their faces were close together and never moved. Now and then Bella closed her eyes, only to open them a moment later with a more effective look of adoration. Messy could feel that she was deliberately pressing her breasts against him, and this excited him, but also alarmed him a little. He glanced quickly round the room, to see if there was anybody he knew. He saw no familiar faces.

Returning to the table, Messy held the glasses under the tablecloth and poured rye whisky into them from his curved silver flask. They had several drinks, several dances, more drinks, and Bella's eyes began to be bloodshot. They were half-closed, amorous, her lips were parted, and she leaned forward on the table. Under the table, their knees were interlocked; and once, putting his hand down, he touched the cool skin above her rolled stockings. At once he blinked and smiled.

"Bad boy!" she said, wagging a finger.

"Bad girl! Aren't you ever going to learn to be modest?"

She blew a long breath of cigarette smoke, and then leaned back in her chair as if to examine him with further perspective. Her dark face was tilted backward, a little theatrically. She looked a little sullen and a little sleepy.

"How long is this going on?" she said. There was something cold and witheringly real in her tone—not the usual lightness. Messy put himself on his guard.

"What do you mean?"

"You know what I mean."

"I don't."

"You do—liar!"

"I don't . . . I suppose as long as the show is here and you are here—a month more?"

"You know that isn't what I mean."

"Well, what *do* you mean?"

She extinguished her cigarette angrily in a saucer. Then she leaned toward him on the table again.

"I can't stand it," she said. "I've told you before."

Messy licked his dry lips.

"Don't be silly, Bella—have we got to go all over that again?"

"Not if I know it, we don't! I'm sick of your damned pious goodness and preaching. You and your parson popper! You both make me sick."

"You can't talk about my father like that."

"All right, go to hell then."

"Go to hell yourself."

"Billy darling! . . . Come upstairs—come up to my room."

Messy's heart was beating with terrifying violence. He tried to keep from blinking, while he stared desirously at the half-drunken and pretty little face, which so frankly implored him.

"How could I do that?" he said. He took a drink of water.

"It's easy. I'll go up by the elevator—you follow up the stairs. The door's unlocked, and you walk in. There's never anybody there in the hall—if there is, it doesn't make any difference. . . . Will you?"

After a pause he said:

"Just this once."

He remained at the table to pay the bill, and then, with assumed nonchalance, which successfully concealed a tremor, crossed the worn marble lobby and began climbing the red-plush stairs. He could hardly breathe. The image ahead of him was too paralyzing. This wasn't right. He had wanted to avoid it. He had hoped to keep the relationship on a different sort of plane, somehow—that he and Bella could be just pals. Of course, in a way, he wanted to do this—as he was never tired of telling Fred and Butch, she was a "hot tamale and no mistake." There were times when she drove him almost crazy, when he couldn't sleep all night. Once or twice he had almost given in to it—but always at the last minute the thought of his mother and father and sisters had "saved" him.

When he got to the door of Number 218 he paused for a second to get his breath. Too much smoking. Then he opened the door and walked in.

He stood still.

Bella was lying on the bed.

"Do you know what time it is?" he said, looking at his wrist-watch. "It's almost two o'clock. I've got an English examination tomorrow."

She reached up a hand and turned off the light. In the darkness he could hear her moving.

"Billy—come here."

"No."

"Come here, you hypocrite! I'm going to teach you how to kiss."

Messy could see the light from the street through the window —the rest of the room was in darkness. He groped his way forward, touched the foot of the bed, dropped his hat and coat, and in another second felt Bella's warm arms around him. She gave a cry, and began kissing his face all over—his forehead, his eyes, his nose, his cheeks, his ears. She ran her hands through his hair, pulling it fiercely.

"My darling!" she kept saying. "Darling! darling! darling!"

Messy was profoundly moved—he had never in his life experienced anything like this. It touched him, there was something pathetic in it, something childlike, but also it was wildly exciting, and he felt himself being swept away. He closed his eyes and surrendered to it, and it seemed to him, as he kissed Bella's delicious soft throat, that she was going to have a sort of convulsion. She began to rock from side to side, rhythmically, and to moan; she began to nip his cheek with her teeth, with a kind of quick light fierceness; she seemed incapable of lying still. And then suddenly she had reached up and turned on the light, and almost with the same gesture had ripped her blouse off, so that it had fallen down about her hips.

Messy stared at her: he was now sitting on the edge of the bed. She was beautiful: she looked at him with such an expression as he had never seen before. He thought her breasts the loveliest things he had ever seen in his life. Then he reached for his pince-nez, and put them on, blinking.

"You are beautiful," he whispered.

"Love me."

"Bella—"

"What?" Her voice made scarcely a sound.

"It wouldn't be fair. We mustn't. Listen."

"What?"

A drawn, an agonized and suspicious look had come across Bella's face—she was staring at him almost as if she were being hypnotized. She drew back from him a little, and shivered.

"We can't only think of ourselves. It wouldn't be right. You know it wouldn't. There are others to think of. I know you make fun of my father—you think because he's a preacher he's a fool—but he's a good man. I know I'm weak, but I am trying to live up to his ideals, and my mother's ideals. My mother is a perfect saint. You've seen her picture. Do you know she's stone deaf? And I've never heard a word of complaint from her— never a word of complaint. She's a good woman, Bella. And my little sisters, Daisy and Gwen—I keep all their pictures on my dressing-table. They are innocent, all of them, the way we ought to be. And what good would it do us? It's just the flesh, just an appetite—there's no more in it than that—we'd be no happier, would we. . . ?"

Bella's lips had parted, but she said nothing.

"We wouldn't be any happier. We'd feel degraded. We'd feel ashamed, afterward, and dirty in our minds. And how could I ever look my little sisters in the face, or my mother? Bella—" he reached out his hand and laid it softly on her knee—"let's be brave. Will you? . . . Say you will. It will make our love deeper than ever."

Two tears had sprung from Bella's eyes, and were starting irregularly down her cheeks. She began to sob, at first softly, then more loudly, putting her face down on her arms. Messy patted her shoulder, afraid that somebody might hear them.

"Bella!" he said. "Bella!"

"Yes." The voice was choked and faint.

"I'll tell you what we'll do. Have you ever seen a sunrise? Have you ever seen the milkman bring the bottles? . . . We'll go out and walk along the river and watch the sunrise. That's what we need. . . . Will you? . . . Come along now!"

He went on talking to her, quietly, gently, tenderly—he could feel that he was impressing her. He told her about his home life, about the morning prayers, when each member of the family knelt before a chair, about his mother's patience and sweetness, and all their belief in him. If they knew he went out with chorus girls it would break their hearts. How could they know, as he did, that Bella was an exception? But he knew it, and she did; they both knew that their relation was a beautiful one, and pure. Wasn't that true? He stroked her knee with his hand, this time not withdrawing it from the warm flesh. By degrees Bella's sobbing diminished. She leaned her little face against his shoulder, and seemed, for a while, to be asleep. Her breathing became slower and more regular, now and then she gave a little sigh. Messy pulled the silked blouse up about her, with a feeling of infinite goodness, and put his arms around her. Poor little girl, he thought, poor little thing.

They both slept. And early in the morning, when they had waked, and she had washed her face, they stole separately out of the hotel, and were walking across the dark Gardens toward the frozen river. The sky was beginning to grow light, with a tint of faint coral, and everything was perfectly still. They walked arm in arm, holding very closely to each other, their footsteps echoing sharply over the frozen and crusted snow; and Messy thought how wonderful life was, how deep. how strange, and how beautiful its promise for the future.

ALL, ALL WASTED

It was one of those lovely spring afternoons when she resented bitterly, in spite of her strict Presbyterian upbringing, the economic necessity which compelled her to coop herself up in this stuffy little schoolroom. She sighed, and looked out through the open windows at the sky, which had that melting softness of hue that comes only in April. Outside, in the eaves and on the roofs, and in the budding trees, she could hear the bubbling and squeaking of the absurd starlings—so human and so comical. Good heavens! If one were only as free as the starlings! If only one's father weren't a mere country parson, with no money, and no influential friends, and no society to provide for his daughters! Why must it be like this? . . . Of course, it would be better in the autumn, when she escaped from all this and got away to college at last—then she would have some freedom, would meet new and interesting people and have a life of her own. But even then, how could she manage on the tiny allowance which was all that her poor father could afford? Even with the scholarship that she was almost sure to get—?

The little bell in the school cupola began ringing, and the rows of little girls made a great bustle of putting away books and papers. Thank goodness—it was over. Over till tomorrow, anyway! She rose and pushed back her chair and gave the signal for the girls to stand and form in line. What was Violet Masters blushing for, looking so ridiculously self-conscious? Oh well, she couldn't be bothered to try to find out. She gave another signal, and they filed past, becoming noisier as they drew near the door that led into the hall and street. The sound of their shouts and laughter came in through the windows, and the clattering of their shoes on the cobbles. They too were relieved —just as much as she was. It was absurd, this everlasting business of schooling, of preparing—and preparing for what? What good did Latin do them, or the binomial theorem? Would it help them to roast a joint or darn their husband's corduroy breeches? Or to keep their brats from falling into the river or getting enlarged tonsils?

She frowned, pulling on her worn gloves, gathered up the bundle of Latin exercises that she would have to correct in the evening, and moved toward the door. It was only then that she permitted herself to think of that—to think of the delicious thing that all afternoon had underlain her every consciousness. Yes: the distinguished visitor—her father's old friend, Mr. Waite, the novelist—would already have arrived at the house, where he was going to spend the night. He would be there now, sitting in the small library, while Mother was getting the tea. Or perhaps in the back yard, under the lilac tree. Or playing the piano. To think, after all these years during which there had been no visitors at all, of having anyone so famous come to see them! And wouldn't he be surprised at finding her— Mary—so grown up, and so—well, why not admit it?—interest-ing? She blushed with pleasure at this thought. She could im-agine clearly how astonished he would look, how his blue eyes would light up, and how he would smile as he held out his hand. He would be too polite to say anything about it, of course—he would contrive to say it merely in the way he took her hand. But none the less he would be impressed. He would at once see that this was someone to whom he could talk freely, to whom he could open his heart. She could see just how it would be. He would at first be perhaps a little shy with her—at finding, as it were, a new "person" in the family to be dealt with. And then, instead of simply spending all his time with Father, as he used to do years ago, he would manifest a disposition to loiter in the room with her. Perhaps he would ask her about her music. "Well, Mary, and how is the music? . . ." And she would play the "Sonata Appassionata" for him—first lighting the candles on the piano. And he, standing behind her, would turn the pages. . . .

Heavens, what a lovely day—what a lovely, lovely day. Those little white cirrus clouds swimming like fishes beside that frail wafer of a moon—and the warm light on the red roofs of the little town—and the air filled, simply saturated, with the voices of birds. Every chimney-pot had its happy starling, every starling was tilting up his beak and puffing out his throat and whistling; the gardens were filled to bursting with the rich loud songs of thrushes; and here and there, high up in the sky, were twos and threes of rooks, flapping lazily to some mysterious rendezvous in the Marsh. Heavens—heavens—heavens—heavens. How could one possibly contain all this magic and loveliness? How could one? It was really too much—one's heart felt as if it would break, just for sheer happiness. If only one could burst into bloom, like a tree—like a young hawthorn blossoming for the first time! How delicious, to feel the flowers breaking out of one's hands and arms, covering one's breast, crowding and clouding before one's eyes, so that one could no longer see, become blind and drunk with one's own fragrance and beauty! Was there any joy in life that was comparable to that? Of course there was, or one wouldn't imagine it. It would be exactly like that—exactly like that . . .

She was deliciously conscious of her grace as she ran up the four steps to the door and fitted the key into the lock. She would say "hello," and then dash upstairs and change—but no, there was nobody in the library, nobody at all. Perhaps they were going to have tea in the garden. Yes, it must be that. She

stood still in the hall for a moment, and listened: and sure
enough, she could hear Milly's loud infantile laughter coming
from the direction of the garden, and then a bumble of men's
voices. Why would Milly laugh in that disagreeable and vulgar
way? And they all encouraged her in it, too—it was disgraceful. She must be spoken to about it. It was really just a desire
to show off—she did it to attract attention. And Father humored
her far too much. In fact, she was being spoiled. . . . Well,
she would change first—it was perhaps better, for her hands
were rather grubby. And this old suit, too—it would be much
better to have on her green silk, and the cream-colored stockings, and the morocco slippers. And of course the scarlet sash. . . .
She flung the papers on her bed, and then her coat and skirt,
and kicked off her slippers. The voices came with startling
clearness from the garden—and also other voices from farther
away, perhaps from the Leightons' garden. And—yes—there
was Mr. Waite's nice deep murmur, and Father laughing in
that funny half-silent way he had. Should she go to the window
and take a peek? No—they might see her, and that would be
dreadful. How lovely! What a luxury! To have such a charming
and distinguished visitor, and already to hear him talking in the
garden, and to eavesdrop in this delicious and secret way!
To share in his presence in this manner, and yet remain
hidden! It was like having some precious thing that no one
knew about. She poured water from the jug into the basin,
and dashed it against her cheeks and eyes: and it was as if,
instantaneously, a grimy cobweb of sums and declensions and
syntaxes had been washed away from her soul. Exquisite relief!
To feel like a muddied daffodil washed clean by the rain!
Could anything, anything, be nicer? Her face still dripping,
she snatched the towel and gave her cheeks a hard rub, to bring
up the color, and then dashed to the chest of drawers and took
out her lovely cream-colored silk stockings. How refined and
ladylike they felt, after these woolen things! How much lighter
she was, and how much nimbler! And now the green silk frock,
with its broad scarlet sash: she dropped it over her shoulders,

shook her head free, and began smiling as she looped the four little braid frogs. To go into this, after that wretched old suit, was like coming out of a chrysalis.

She ran down the stairs, and then, as she approached the door that gave on to the garden, slowed her steps and became suddenly sedate. She must be dignified—to let him see at once that she had grown up—but not too dignified: one arm dropped at her side, and the other hand caught, idly, in the broad loop of her sash. Then perhaps she would raise one hand to shade her eyes. . . . Unfortunately, as she stepped out into the garden she saw that her carefully prepared entrance had not been perceived. Father and Mr. Waite had their backs turned, Mother was in the act of pouring a cup of tea, and Milly was leaning against Mr. Waite's shoulder, apparently looking at something on his knee. A book. Well! No matter—she would just go up to them quietly. Quietly and gently, as suited her nature.

"Just in time," said Mother. "Mary dear, would you mind getting some more hot water? . . . But first you can say how-do-you-do to Mr. Waite."

How infuriating! As if she were a little girl in a pinafore! She felt herself flushing; and surprisingly enough, as Mr. Waite turned his head, and half made as if to rise, but didn't succeed, she directed a part of her annoyance at him; and instead of shaking hands with him, as she had thought to do, gave him rather a stiff little nod. Well! If that was the way things were going to be! If they were going to be so casual and distant about it, she could be casual and distant herself. Certainly. Why not? She would let them see that she was no longer a baby like Milly. Good heavens! She took the hot-water jug from the wicker teatable; nonchalantly and disdainfully; tilted up the metal lid, as if to make quite sure that it was, as reported, empty; and sauntered back to the house, swinging it at her side. Damn. If only Milly hadn't been snuggling against him like that, pretending to take an interest in that accursed book— and it was notorious that at ordinary times she never could be got to look at a book—or if the chairs had all been faced the other way—how damnable that destiny had such a way of hanging by trivial and disgusting trifles like that! It was really too monstrous. . . . She filled the jug from the kettle, and banged the kettle back on the gas ring, resentfully. She would take her time. Why should she put herself out for people who paid no attention to her? There was no reason at all: none whatever. She peered into the cracked mirror that balanced on the pipes over the kitchen sink, and then glanced out through the window. The book had been put aside; and Mr. Waite, uncrossing his brown tweed knees, was leaning forward to take a slice of bread-and-butter. Father, clasping his hands behind his head, was looking up at the sky and laughing. They had already forgotten about her completely. Just as if she had never been. . . .

"Of course Milly does!"

"Of course Milly does what?" answered Mary, depositing the jug on the table, and then sinking into a deck-chair.

Mr. Waite gave her rather an odd shamefaced look—as if a little surprised. Had her tone been too sharp?

"Expect a present. . . . Suppose you were to look in my pockets, Milly? Eh?"

He beamed at Milly with what was—yes, really!—a fatuously benign expression. The heavy uncle. Oh these damned patronizing adoptive uncles, with their portly benefactions! Milly laughed with quite unnecessary violence and darted a hand first into the right pocket and then into the left. After this second invasion she gave a shout of delight and drew out a small white box.

"Oh!" she cried. "Chocolates!" And then, tearing at the wrapper, "and they're hard centers! Oh, how lovely!"

She danced absurdly, waving the box in the air.

"Very nice of Mr. Waite, I'm sure," Mary murmured, dropping a lump of sugar in her tea. "Sweets to the sweet, and all that sort of thing."

Again too sharp. But in the flurry that attended the passing of the chocolates, perhaps it hadn't been too much noticed.

"And how's my friend Meg?" cried Mr. Waite with exaggerated gaiety, holding up a chocolate almond.

"Who? Meg she was a gypsy?" said Mother. "But hadn't you heard?"

"Heard? No—has anything happened to her?"

"It was dreadful," cooed Mother, with a smile which seemed to luxuriate in the dreadfulness. "She was found dead in Covey's barn, by some boys, just a fortnight ago. Covered with straw. She had apparently been dead for some time. And do you know—"

"Agnes!"

"Well, it is too horrible. But Milly's heard it already—so why shouldn't Mr. Waite?"

"Mother! Really!" said Mary.

But Mother, smiling mischievously, was not to be stopped.

"The rats had been at her!" said Mother, triumphantly. "Just think of it. The poor old thing—she had just gone in there and died alone."

"Good gracious!" said Mr. Waite.

"Really, Mother, you're a perfect savage."

"Well, I am sorry to hear that," said Mr. Waite.

"She was such a picturesque figure, too. And what will the local police worry about, with old Meg gone? They seemed to spend most of their time moving her on. . . . Do you remember the time we met her down by the pig-farm with her shoes in her hand? She was funny!"

Mother gave a sigh, her attention already wandering elsewhere; Father got up to return his cup to the tray; and the conversation dropped. Was this the best a novelist could do in the way of talk? And the best her family could do in the way of entertaining him? It was disgraceful—truly disgraceful. She rose with her teacup—Mr. Waite might have offered to take it from her—and moved lightly to the table.

"More, Mary?"

"No, thank you, Mother. . . ."

There was a long silence, during which a dozen starlings could be heard, practicing their boyish whistles, and Mrs. Leighton's voice in the next garden, giving instructions to a gardener. "No, I think the lupins had better go here," she was saying. "If the slugs will permit." If the slugs will permit! How silly. Why can't people be natural? Why must they always be showing off, trying to say facetious things, even to gardeners? If the slugs will permit!

"Well, Frank, I've got a letter to write, if you'll excuse me."

"And I must do my dishes. Will you stay in the garden? . . . If garden it can be called. Though I must say that lilac is really lovely. Last year it really almost broke under its weight of bloom!"

"It's a charming spot," said Mr. Waite. "I'll stay here and gobble up Milly's hard centers."

He gave Milly a roguish look through his glasses—oh so consciously roguish—and began filling a filthy old briar pipe.

"I'll let you have just three!" Milly leaned against his knee, in a scandalously abandoned way, with the open box in her outstretched hand. And what made it worse—oh, infinitely worse—was the fact that Mr. Waite seemed to enjoy it. He put his arm around her, hugged her benevolently, and then ran his fingers through her black frizzy hair.

"In exchange for that," he smiled, "I'll let you light my pipe. Do you know how to light a pipe for an old gentleman? Eh?"

"Of course I do! Where are your matches?"

Briskly, with the coquettish air of an all-conquering female, she put down her chocolates and began searching his waistcoat pockets for the box of matches; and finding them, struck a match, wrinkling her nose. He gave several rapid puffs, and the blue clouds of smoke rose in the still air. Her gray eyes admired him—she adored him. Then, laughing, she flung away the match as if it might have been a noxious beetle. It blazed for a moment in the tall grass and went out.

Phweeeeee—phweeeee—whistled a starling on the Leightons'

highest chimney-pot. The warm slant sunlight of evening touched him to brilliance; he was seraphically illuminated and idiotically happy. Up the scale went his self-conscious whistle, till it became a mere silvery mouse-tail-tip of sound, and then down it slid again, to end in a series of ecstatic chattering bubbles. The Leightons' cat—a meager hollow-flanked tortoise-shell—paused in its prowl along the wall-top, and looked up at the feathery thing with a profound yearning. . . . So it was all going to end like this. There was to be nothing but this. All her preparations had been for just this. She was to be defrauded of her happiness by Milly. Could anything be more monstrous? Of course she could perhaps find some little excuse for sending Milly indoors—tell her it was time for her to do her "prep," or some such thing—and thus manage to be left alone for a little with Mr. Waite. But, after all, was it worth the trouble? No. Not in the very least. If he could make so little effort to be agreeable, why should she? One had one's pride. If one was ignored in this fashion, simply ignored—! And there was so much that they might have talked about! So many enchanting things! All of life, all of life. . . .

"I'm sorry—I'm afraid I'll have to go and correct some papers," she said, rising. "I've got some beastly Latin exercises to look through."

She brushed a strand of hair back from her forehead, and gazed, as if absent-mindedly, at the cat, which was emitting a silent miaow in the direction of the starling.

"Oh," said Mr. Waite. "How dreary. And on an afternoon like this!"

"Beggars can't be choosers, Mr. Waite. . . . Perhaps, if you like, Milly will take you for a little walk. . . ."

Heroic self-sacrifice! . . . A deep pang opened in her heart as she glided slowly toward the house. Wasted, all wasted. She ought to go and help Mother with the dishes—Mother would be expecting it—but she was hanged if she would. No. . . . She climbed the stairs to her room, and shut the door with an infinite gentleness. She had an impulse to rip off her sash savagely, and kick her slippers across the room, but instead she picked up the little pile of Latin exercises and sat down at her table. An oblong of rich tawny sunlight lay on the wall beside her, and she could hear Father moving a chair in the library. The starling whistled again, frightfully pleased with himself, and Milly laughed. Why were things like this? Why? . . . She opened Elspeth Homard's paper, which was covered, simply covered, with ink-blots, and tried to focus her attention upon it.

Sunt rerum lacrima. Sunt rerum lacrima. . . . And suddenly a large tear fell on Elspeth Homard's paper, right on the word *"mensa."*

THE MOMENT

My friend Ward Hamerton and old Miss Thingumabob (he always referred to her thus) had been sent to Italy by some museum or other to examine and catalogue and describe and photograph certain Etruscan ruins and relics. I don't know exactly where these things were, or what they were, or whether they were worth the trouble. All I do know is that Hamerton found it a great trial. He did the photography—Miss Thingumabob did the rest. They traveled furiously from one part of Italy to another, riding all day in trains, trying to keep down their expenses, putting up at cheap and obscure hotels. Hamerton was bored to death. He hated it. He disliked photography—God knows how he happened to have got so singular a job. And Miss Thingumabob was by no means an ideal companion. She was about twice his age— white-haired, distinguished-looking, ultra-refined, horribly intellectual. After a hard day's work of travel and photography, running from museum to museum and ruin to ruin, she would be prepared, and eager, at dinner, to discuss the descent of Van Gogh from Cimabue, or the moral implications in the later novels of Henry James. Hamerton would reply in monosyllables, drinking the wine of the country in great quantity.

She was awfully nice—he kept saying to me—awfully nice; but she was a holy terror. And the worst of it was that he couldn't, in decency, abandon her. He couldn't run off by himself and have a good time; he had to be a gentleman. If Hamerton had been more dashing, more adventurous—but then there would have been no point to this humble story. Hamerton was nothing of the sort. He was shy, finicky, something of a highbrow; and if he nourished in his bosom a secret desire to be something of a Don Juan, he kept it a very dark secret. At any rate, from Miss Thingumabob.

He did nourish such an ambition—but alas, the whirlwind of official duties and the constant and zealous companionship of his aged Egeria made it hopeless. He encountered a charming creature in a train coming from Rome to Naples—perfectly ravishing. But although he did manage to engage her in talk, what could it possibly amount to, under the bright maternal eye of Miss Thingumabob? She too had taken part in the conversation: and of course that had been the end of it. The talk had at once taken an official and "tourist" turn. The subtle something-or-other, which had been on the point of being born, had been slain outright. The ravishing creature had withdrawn to her Baedeker again. And Hamerton cursed.

That was only one of several such incidents. After a series of them, he positively hated the sight of ravishing creatures: an obvious enough case of sour grapes. If a lovely young thing asked him the way to the Coliseum, or the baths of Caracalla, he was downright rude to her; and at the discovery of a bevy of beautiful girls who were dining at the next table to his and Miss Thingumabob's in the hotel, he would become as morose as a hypochondriac. He would listen in torment to the delicious voices, the charming and fatuous conversation, the amusing attempts to speak Italian with the bored old waiter, who vastly preferred to conduct the meal in English; and then, when the agony became no longer endurable, he would plead a headache to old Miss Thingumabob and retire to his room. His trip to Italy was being ruined. Absolutely ruined.

He bore it, nevertheless, with fortitude; and he was careful (he insisted) to remain scrupulously polite to his extraordinary companion. What else, indeed, *could* he do? Duty was duty, the work had to be done, but he was not the sort that sulks. He was unhappy, but he behaved like a perfect gentleman. Day after day, therefore, they rushed from place to place, cataloguing and photographing; and he simply tried to forget that this was, after all, Italy, attempting to see it as simply a corner of his blessed museum. And he comforted himself with the thought that some day, at last, it would come to an end.

It did: but not before it had culminated, for Hamerton, in what he termed a "moment." He had a singular theory about moments—he believed that one's life consisted of at most half a dozen moments of supreme experience, or perhaps not even as many as that. There might be nothing to show for these moments—they might be simply an instant of acute awareness, or of misery, or of exaltation. You never knew when they were coming, or whether you would have the courage to seize them by the tail as they flew. A great deal depended on this matter of courage. Hamerton said that it was a source of perpetual anxiety to him that he was rather timid about these things. Several such crises had come and gone, and he had remained supine before them—paralyzed, hypnotized, fascinated, but unable to act or to feel with sufficient speed and self-forgetfulness. The chief requisite was a complete and glorious recklessness, a sublime willingness to risk one's whole life, one's sanity, one's everything; and all for the very dubious pleasure of being able to say, afterward, that you *had* so jeopardized yourself. He told me of one such moment which had occurred when he had just reached the ripe age of ten. He was enthralled, at that time, by the sea and by ships. He used to haunt the wharves of the New England seaport town in which he lived, keeping, in a notebook, a list of the names of all the ships he encountered. One day he talked with the captain of a coal barge, and asked whether small boys like himself ever got a chance to go to sea. The captain surprised him by saying that if he would bring with him half a dozen books and fifteen or twenty old magazines (the captain seems to have been something of a reader) he could come aboard and sail to Norfolk, Virginia. Hamerton was electrified. He spent the night in a fever, selected six books, tied up a bundle of old magazines (which he found in the attic), and felt that he was already as good as at sea. But somehow or other he never went near that particular wharf till the barge had gone. And the moment was irretrievably lost.

That was the kind of thing he meant; and his singular trip to Italy was destined, for all its unpromising beginning, to provide him with a really first-rate example—a brilliant and unique specimen. It happened in Rome. He and Miss Thingumabob used Rome as a kind of "support"—they would dash away from it to some obscure hilltown, where they had heard rumors of some priceless item hidden away in a church crypt, and then, having tracked down this phoenix of Etruscan beauty, or discovered it to be a myth, they would dash back again. They always stayed at the same hotel, a small one in the Piazza Barberini, which had the great advantage of being cheap. They had been to it a half dozen times, in all; and on the eve of their final departure from Italy they returned to it once more. On this particular occasion they had come from Assisi, and the return journey had been brightened and blighted for Hamerton, in about equal proportions, by the fact that the train was filled, simply filled, with beautiful English girls. There were about fifteen of them, and they were all entrancing—very free-and-easy, smoking cigarettes, sophisticated, charmingly dressed. They literally swarmed over the train, chattering like sparrows. Hamerton had gone to sleep, finally, in sheer self-defense. With old Miss Thingumabob sitting opposite him, bolt upright, mercilessly eager to assimilate every detail of Italian life as revealed in the sliding landscape (and terrifyingly intelligent about it), he couldn't bear to look at them.

Imagine his delight and horror, therefore, when he discovered, on arriving at the Hotel Concordia, that the fifteen beautiful English girls, every one of them, had preceded him.

There they were, swarming around the bewildered old *concierge*, quarreling with three or four taxi drivers, darting in and out of the portico—they had simply taken possession of the poor old Concordia. It was exactly, he said, as if a flock of Brazilian parakeets, or birds of Paradise, vociferous of tongue and hued like the rainbow, should suddenly take possession of a bare little tree in the Public Gardens of Boston, Massachusetts; just as brilliant, and just as surprising. The Concordia was at once changed for him. It became a place of more than tropic beauty and luxury—it glowed, it sang, it vibrated, it positively rocked, with color and light. The bare corridors, with their coconut-fiber mats and potted palm trees, had formerly seemed dreary to him; but now they were full of mystery and wonder; overtones hummed in them, perfumes raced through them; and he wouldn't have been in the least surprised if the gray walls had suddenly blossomed. The hotel had acquired a soul.

For the first time since the arrival in Italy, he was ridiculously happy. He sang as he washed in the little washbowl which was all that his room afforded; it was the same room that he had once before, but now he felt an outburst of deep affection for it. He looked out into the dark courtyard at the back, surrounded by tenements with high balconies, and saw the camellia tree standing there in the moonlight. There it was, in bloom, and there, as usual, were the innumerable cats who used its shadow for their nocturnal assignations. How he had hated those cats! But now, he almost loved them. An indefinable magic, emanating from the fifteen English girls, had touched and altered everything. He put on a clean shirt and the most splendid of his neckties, and sauntered down to the dining room, feeling exalted and powerful, like Jason approaching the golden fleece.

But alas, everything went wrong. Miss Thingumabob had forestalled him; she had already arrived, and she had already taken a table; she was sitting there, dressed in decent black, like the Sibyl herself; and worst of all, the Brazilian parakeets had been assigned to the long table at the extreme opposite end of the long room. There was absolutely nothing to be done about it—he groaned to himself and sat down; and for once he allowed his feelings to overcome his manners. He was unable to say a word. Miss Thingumabob tried one topic after another, with her usual unconquerable brightness, but to all of them he was wearily unreceptive. The Coliseum by moonlight, she suggested? No, he was too tired. A concert at the Augusteo? Heaven forbid; he was sick of these Italian audiences, and their childish habit of booing and hissing and jumping up on their seats. He never wanted to see another Italian as long as he lived. A café in the Piazza di Venezia, with perhaps a *cassata ala Siciliana?* Miss Thingumabob obviously played what she thought was a trump card in this, for she knew his passion for *cassatas;* but even to this he turned a deaf ear. He wanted his parakeets—he wanted to sit near them and see them, he wanted to listen to their delicious gossiping chatter, to see them come and go in the lounge, reading guidebooks and magazines, pulling the bright silk scarfs over their shoulders, smoking their English cigarettes, and glancing eagerly about them with their beautiful English-blue eyes. That was all he wanted—and he wanted to be able to do it alone. He wanted to be rid of Miss Thingumabob. He urged her, therefore, to go along to the Augusteo—she could take a cab, and it would be quite simple and quite safe. Perfectly. He found himself becoming really oratorical on the subject, in the hope of making it obvious to Miss Thingumabob that he wanted, for once, to be by himself. Perhaps, if she realized this, she would be offended, and go to her room. But he had no luck. She merely sighed and smiled and gave him up; realized, with excessive reasonableness and good nature, that he must, after so hard a day, be very tired; it would indeed be better for both of them to spend a quiet evening in the library, talking things over.

And they did so. They marched unswervingly through the lounge—where the parakeets were already chattering and preening and splashing their bright colors about them—and settled grimly in the deserted library. Poor Hamerton had never been

so miserable in his life: he wanted to die. Miss Thingumabob
got out her notebook and went over all the details of the work
at Assisi, pitilessly. Items were checked off, accounts were balanced, the expense list was verified for the fifth time, with
emendations and queries (Miss Thingumabob had a terrific
sense of honor with regard to the expense account), and when
ten o'clock came Hamerton was in a state of suppressed fury.
He yawned frankly and said he was going to bed, if she would
forgive him. She forgave him sweetly, and off he went. He
sneaked into the lounge, but alas, the birds had flown. The
room was empty, barren, dead. The ashtrays were littered with
cigarette-ends, the air smelt faintly of Turkish tobacco, but
otherwise as if the stale room had never known any such seraphic
visitation. Defeated, Hamerton crept off to bed. A last despairing hope that he might at least encounter one or two of the
parakeets on his way upstairs, or passing through the winding
corridors which led to his room, was frustrated. He didn't meet
a soul, or hear a sound. He paused outside his door, with his
hand on the knob, as if waiting for some blinding apocalypse,
but no apocalypse was vouchsafed. The Hotel Concordia had
resumed its natural deadness.

He undressed slowly, with many excursions to the open window to survey the camellia tree and the Roman cats—looked
longingly at the Roman moon, resting his hands on the stone
sill—listened resignedly to the fragments of Italian conversation
which came to him from the adjacent balconies. But now, the
subtle flavor of these things was again lost. The magic had departed. The cats were cats; the courtyard was a smelly dank
hole, none too clean; the loud conversations of the Italians were
a nuisance. He crawled into bed, closed his eyes, and fell asleep.

Almost at once, it seemed, he was awakened. He was wide
awake, but at first could discover no reason for it. Something
had happened, he knew, but he was not aware what it was.
Was it a knock on his door? . . . Had someone called his name
or spoken to him? . . . Or was it merely the usual crying of
cats? . . . He lay and listened, with his head raised from the

pillow, and then the sound was repeated: it was a distinct knock on the wall beside his bed. It sounded startlingly near; and then he remembered that when he had occupied this room before he had noticed this peculiarity. The wall which partitioned this room from the next was extremely thin, and the bed in the next room rested against the wall at exactly the same point as his own. He had been able to hear the nocturnal twistings and turnings of his fellow-sleeper with extraordinary distinctness, a distinctness which at the time he had thought distressing. But now, a sudden and deliriously exciting idea burst into blossom in his mind with something of the beautiful violence of that mythical aloe which blooms only once in a hundred years, and then with a clap of thunder. Suppose this should be one of the fifteen? Good heavens. He went over in his mind as many of the other guests as he could recall—but there was practically nobody else in the hotel. Nobody. The chances were at least ten to one in his favor. At the mere thought, he broke into a miraculous perspiration and began to tremble. The knock had not sounded like an accident: not in the least. But perhaps it would be as well to make certain. He lay there, propped up on one elbow, scarcely breathing, and waited to see if it would be repeated. And almost at once, it was. There was a tap, and then a pause, and then another tap. And then the midnight silence was resumed, a silence only broken up by the distant wail of a cat.

Immediately, Hamerton became a being transformed. His lethargy was gone, his wits were sharpened to a point almost excruciatingly incandescent, a divine fury of excitement possessed him. His heart began beating so violently that it shook the bed. He nerved himself, listened a moment, as if indeed he expected to hear the breathing of his mysterious tête-à-tête, who lay so near to him and who was nevertheless unknown—and then, lifting his hand, gave an answering knock—just one deliberate knock, neither too soft nor too loud: a knock that *might* be an accident (in case it should turn out that he had been mistaken in his assumption) but that would, on the other hand, be considered an unmistakable reply, if his assumption should turn out to have been correct.

The assumption was correct. The reply came without hesitation—*three* knocks this time—and Hamerton, exulting, knocked three times in answer. There could now no longer be the slightest question, on either side, of the fact that a deliberate, and marvelous, and profoundly exciting conversation was in progress. Confessedly, they had become Pyramus and Thisbe. Hamerton moved as close to the wall as he could get: he was determined to miss nothing. He wanted to hear every sound— every rustle, every whisper—even, if possible, the creature's breathing. If she should murmur something, for instance, or give a little cough—? It would be horrible to ignore an overture of that sort. He pressed himself against the wall, therefore, with a zeal that was almost amorous, as if the wall itself were the body of his beloved, and then lay perfectly still, in an agony of suspense. Would she continue this extraordinary conversation? Or would she drop it at this point, having already sufficiently amused herself with it? Perhaps she was merely teasing him, merely pulling his leg. On the other hand, it was just as possible that she had been overcome by timidity, at this point —on discovering that her vis-à-vis was, if anything, too eagerly responsive. And then again, it was possible that she now felt that the initiative, for a moment, should pass to him. It was perhaps *his* turn to commit himself. . . .

He waited another moment, accordingly, during which a church clock struck one, and it seemed as if all the cats in Rome yowled in despondent unison; and then, trembling, he raised his hand, poised it, and gave one loud thump on the wall with his knuckles. There was a perceptible pause and then the answer came: this time the knock was rather a gentle one, rather remote; as if the lady had decided that she might have appeared a little too forward, and had wished to be more modest. As if, indeed, she were saying "Oh, well,—perhaps, after all—" or "This is really rather silly of us, don't you think?— and we'd far better be going to sleep." Hamerton was immediately aware of all these implications. He concluded that he must himself, at this point, mitigate his eagerness. He controlled himself, counted fifty, and then gave a tap even more fugitive and half-hearted than hers had been—a tap in which he contrived to say: "I too am a modest violet. Did you think I would wish to be a nuisance to you? Heaven forbid!"

He had no doubt that the reply to this would be instantly and urgently reassuring: but in this he was mistaken. His beloved proved herself more femininely subtle, at this juncture, than he had given her credit for being. She made him wait. A minute went by—two minutes—three—and then four. An appalling chasm of silence opened in the night. There wasn't a sound, not a ghost of a sound. Hamerton felt himself growing old, white-haired, tottering to the grave. Should he repeat his summons? Did she mean by this that he ought to assume a masculine role, be importunate, confess frankly and uncontrolledly his passionate eagerness? Was she going to sleep—or had she *already,* bored, fallen asleep? . . . His thoughts raced in a panic, and he resolved to be really bold. He smote the wall three times with gusto, and then held his breath. No answer. He began to sweat with mortification: a feeling of genuine and profound embarrassment came over him. He had been a fool—an idiot—a blithering idiot. Good Lord. How she must be laughing at him. She had been leading him on, all this while, and now she was going to ignore him, hard-heartedly and implacably. It was even possible—wasn't it?—that he had imagined the whole thing. Her first knock had been an accident. It was only upon hearing his serious reply to it that she had taken the thing up, and then only with the idea of humiliating him. He relaxed a little and very gingerly allowed himself to fall away from his tense position against the wall. He too would pretend that his participation in the exchange had been accidental. He would give a casual and meaningless thump or two, as if it were merely the natural collision of one who was restless in his sleep, and then withdraw entirely. . . .

It was while he was calculating what ought to be the precise weight and nature of this blow—calculating it as much with the contracted muscles of his raised forearm as with his mind, and just as he had reached the conclusion that the blow, for best effect, should be a *grazing* one—that a reply came which was as witty as it was startling. It was a rendering into a series of sharp taps, sharply rhythmed, of a familiar whistle-call: rat-atat-tat: tat-tat: *tat;* with a magnificent emphasis on the last syllable, magnificent and at the same time deliciously interrogative. Instantly, Hamerton became burningly alive again. He flung himself against the wall as if he were positively going to embrace it, and gave, with alternating hands, a double tattoo of the same kind. He even, he said, pressed his face against the cold plaster in his eagerness to be as near as possible to this subtle being. That she was subtle and witty and charming, there could now be no doubt: he could see plainly just what sort of creature she must be. Rather sharp, rather cruel, a good deal of a tease, decidedly a flirt, but also just as obviously a woman of extraordinary charm and depth. She was, in fact, everything that he desired. The whole course of the conversation proved that—with its delicious mixture of advance and retreat, of the candid and the ironic. She was more than a match for him. And the cunning cruelty with which she had pretended that the whole thing was a joke, or an accident, and that she had dropped it—all so beautifully calculated to sharpen their mutual pleasure when the interchange was renewed! This was a stroke of genius.

It was nothing, however, to what was to come. For if the interchange had been delicious up to this point, it now became a thing of transcendent wonder, a thing of poetry and genius all compact. They began conversing, through this extraordinary medium, with a rapidity and (on his side, at least) a virtuosity, which had no parallel in Hamerton's existence. Stubborn assertions were followed by satirical queries; satirical queries led to gay denials; gay denials gave way to joyous duets of sheer lyricism, the lyricism of the skylark. If the palm of the hand asked a question, the knuckles gave emphatic answer. The fingertips interpolated a sly objection, the elbow truculently insisted, the fingernails etherealized the object and made of it the most delicate of innuendoes. Pauses now and then prolonged themselves until they became agonies, in order that the ensuing dialogue might all the more take to itself the hue of the ecstatic. And with what abandon after such a pause, they threw themselves against the dividing wall! Hamerton was simply beside himself with joy. He said he would not have believed it possible that a human being could display such an inventive genius in the medium of pure rhythm, or in the shadings of the loud and soft: it was the most exquisite music he had ever heard. Without a word spoken, without a whisper, these two creatures exchanged the profoundest secrets of their souls, sounded the deepest and brightest abyss of human knowledge, met angelically, with poised wings, in an ether of pure communion.

It was when she reached, finally, an ultimate perfection of communication, by *clawing* frantically at the wall, as if in frankest desire to dig her way through, that Hamerton awoke, with a sudden and sharp sense of reality, to the fact that one of his "moments" was before him. What else, indeed? There it was, staring him in the face: the most brilliant moment of his life. Incredible that he should only now have perceived it! But he perceived it; and at once was paralyzed with all it meant. For what did it mean—what *could* it mean—but that he must now definitely and courageously and unreservedly go forward? To allow the thing merely to end like this would be tantamount to disastrous retreat. It was clearly impossible. Everything— every discoverable sign-post in the whole universe—pointed the other way. Forward into the unknown—forward into the untrodden. For him, as for Faust, there was no alternative.

Hamerton admitted to me that it took courage; but, for once, he had it. There was a bad moment, an instant's agony of hesitation, when the thing seemed madly reckless, possibly ruinous; his whole career might conceivably be wrecked by it; the shape of the possible catastrophe hung huge before him. To act or not to act: there was the question. But the question was no sooner formulated than decided. He sprang out of bed, slid his feet into his slippers, went to his door, opened it, listened intently for a second or two, and finding the hallway deserted, he stepped forth. He proceeded without further hesitation to the door of the next room. His heart was beating painfully—he was in the most terrible funk he had ever known—but destiny now had him fairly in her grasp. He raised a trembling hand and knocked.

There was no answer; but he heard, within the room, the creak of the bed; and then slow footsteps—footsteps that sounded frightened and reluctant—came toward him, the key was turned in the lock, the door most cautiously opened. And Hamerton faced the most stupendous surprise of his life.

A young man—a German young man, clad in a grotesque old-fashioned night-shirt—stood before him, very obviously shivering with fright. They stared at each other—"goggle-eyed" (as Hamerton put it) with astonishment. And while they stared, caught in this extraordinary predicament, alone together in a hostile and inscrutable world, Hamerton found himself, all of a sudden, feeling very superior and extremely angry.

"Were you knocking on my wall?" he said, belligerently.

"*Wie?*" said the German.

"I said, were you knocking on my wall?" Hamerton's voice rose to a higher note, and he gave with his hand in the air a quick knock at an imaginary wall.

The frightened German youth shook his head, his eyes wide open and appalled.

"*Ich verstehe nicht,*" he said stupidly.

Hamerton stared at him furious. There seemed to be nothing to do or say. Should he slap the fellow's face, knock him down? He desired to do something like this, something really outrageous; but the suitable action didn't occur to him. He merely stared, therefore, with concentrated contempt for any such worm; at the same time, in the back of his mind, feeling that the whole thing was extraordinarily funny, but that he wouldn't for the world admit it. They continued to stare at each other; the grotesque scene protracted itself timelessly. And then, turning on his heel, "Oh, Hell," he said, and stalked with extravagant dignity back to his room.

And the moment was over.

THE WOMAN-HATER

It was half past ten on a night in May, and the three medical students had just been through their notes in histology for the third time. The windows were open, and a sound of dripping could be heard on the stone window-ledge; the desultory drip, gradually slowing, that succeeds a spring shower. One of the men lay face down on a couch, his face pillowed sideways on his bare arms. His eyes were shut. The other two sat in fumed-oak Morris chairs, with their legs stretched out before them, and smoked cigarettes. Empty glasses stood on the floor beside them. They had taken off their coats.

"Well, what do you say, Bill? How about it?"

"I guess it's stopped raining."

"Sure, it ain't gonna rine no more. . . . Let's go."

Bill, retying his loosened necktie, got up and went to the window. He rested his freckled hands on the sill and leaned out.

"Yes—it's stopped, all right. And the stars are coming out. . . ." He turned around, looked down at the man on the couch, and idly dislodged a cushion from the couch-arm, so that it fell on the sleeper's face. "And, by God! I couldn't learn another symptom if I was paid a million dollars for it. Wake up, Pete."

Pete lay unmoving. "Leave me alone," he murmured.

"Oh, come on, Pete. It'll do you good. You need a little excitement to get the adrenals working."

"No," said Pete. And then with violence: "NO!"

"What time did you tell her we'd meet her, Dil?"

Dil got up and stretched, eyeing his reflection in the mirror over the mantelpiece. He smoothed his sleek hair with his hands, with something of an air of vanity. He was dark and handsome.

"I said we'd be at the stage-door at twenty of eleven. . . . What do you say about another little drink? . . . Say, Pete, what's the matter with you, anyway? Why don't you come and meet her? She's a peach. She's a creamer. She isn't any ordinary chorus girl, you know."

"Women don't interest me," said Pete.

"There he goes again," said Bill. "What's the use?"

"You're both of you damn fools," said Pete. "Just spending your money for nothing. What does she care about you? All she wants is food and somebody to dance with. She just uses you to kill time. She's probably got a couple of husbands in New York."

"You're crazy," said Dil mildly.

He went into a bedroom, and came back with his coat.

"Come on," he said.

"All right," said Bill. "Wait till I get my coat. Sure you won't come, Pete?"

"No, I'm going to bed. And for the love of Pete don't be so damned noisy when you come back. Last night I thought somebody was being murdered."

The two men put on their hats, without comment, and went out. Dil carried a malacca stick with a silver band around it. They went down the stairs in silence, and emerging into the spring night turned to the left.

"It's funny about Pete," said Dil. "I wonder what's the matter with him."

Bill ruminated.

"He was always that way," he said. "That was the way he was all through college."

"Didn't he ever have a girl?"

"Never a girl. Never would go to a dance or anything. You know, it isn't that he's shy, or anything like that. He came into my room once, by accident, when I was giving a tea. And he got along perfectly all right. In fact, my sister was crazy about him. She tried like the devil to get hold of him again. Even called him up on the phone to ask him to dinner. I was there when he answered it. And he just kind of drawled back at her, kidding her along. He just kept saying, 'No, I guess not, thanks,' till she got tired. Gee! she was mad. He didn't bother to give any excuse. Just refused point-blank."

"Maybe he just needs to be waked up."

"Maybe he does. . . ."

They turned to the left again, entering a main thoroughfare, which was crowded and brightly lighted. They passed a lunchroom, and then the portals of a stone church. A lot of sodden confetti was scattered on the wet sidewalk.

"He's right about one thing," said Dil. "This business costs a lot of money. I'm getting kind of low."

"By gosh, *that's* true."

"But then, it's worth it."

"Sure. There was a picture of her in *Theatre Magazine* last week. It said she was considered the most beautiful woman on the musical-comedy stage."

"Everybody runs after her. I wonder why it is she's taken such a fancy to us. I guess maybe she meets so few men who are decent to her. You know how it is."

"Well she seems to like us, all right. Anyway, she likes *you*."

"I'm not so sure about that. But she's pretty keen on you, Bill. I could tell it last night by the way she looked at you."

"Oh, go on."

"When she was dancing with you. I had an idea I'd better go

home and leave you alone together. But then I thought you might be embarrassed."

Bill gave a flattered and uneasy little laugh.

"That's just the way I felt about you," he said. "I guess maybe she's pretty fond of us both, really. It must be a kind of a relief to a woman like that to feel sure that a man isn't all the time trying to take advantage of her. She feels safe with us."

Dil hung his stick over the crook of his arm.

"You don't suppose she gets bored with us, do you?" he said. "I was wondering last night whether she just thought of us as kids. It was when she was talking about that week-end party she went to at the painter's on Long Island. It sounded pretty gay—almost fast."

Bill pondered. The lights of the theater-canopy were just ahead of them. The people were beginning to come out, and the line of cars was forming. "Why should she?" he said. "After all, we're as old as she is. And we aren't either of us fools. . . . Of course a girl like Mae is bound to run into some fast parties. She has to be a good sport. But that doesn't prove anything against her. And you've only got to look at Mae to see that she's nice. And the way she's all the time telegraphing and telephoning to her mother."

Dil sighed.

"Absolutely," he said. "Right turn."

They greeted the doorman at the stage-door with the dignified knowingness of men of the world, and informed him that Miss Melville was expecting them. Dil tapped the ferrule of his stick against the door-jamb. They waited in silence, and other men were waiting also, with their coat-collars turned up. They looked like conspirators. Two chorus girls came out, two men stepped forward quickly and bowed, taxis came and went.

"She's coming now," said Ollie, the doorman.

"Hello, boys!" she cried. "I didn't see you out in front tonight."

"No, we had to sweat for an exam," said Bill.

She stood on the step, drawing the fur collar against her

lovely chin. She smiled amiably at each of them in turn, and they smiled back at her.

"You look fine," said Dil.

"Don't waste time flattering me," she said, "let's get a taxi."

They got a taxi and piled into it and drove to the Shawmut. The hotel lobby was crowded, and so was the grill-room, but they found a booth. The band was playing a fox-trot and people were dancing in the railed-off center of the floor. A lot of the tables had toy balloons tethered to them, and some of the couples carried balloons with them as they danced.

"Same old crowd," said Mae. "There's grandpa and his cutie. He's got a new pair of spats."

"Would you like a little fox-trot?" said Dil.

"I don't mind a little one. Let's go."

Bill ordered the supper while they danced. Dil was talking to Mae, and she seemed to be listening with great amusement. They took a few turns and came back.

"I've been telling Mae about Pete," said Bill.

"He sounds too fascinating," said Mae. "Tell me some more about him. Does he live with you?"

"Sure, he lives with us," said Dil. "Regular old crab. Got the best head in the class."

"He's a real woman-hater. Won't have a thing to do with them. My sister tried to get him to come to a dinner-dance once, and he turned her down flat."

"What does he say about women?" said Mae. She leaned forward on her elbows. Her eyes were very bright. Then she took out a little mirror and began titivating her eyelashes and nose with a tiny finger-tip. She smoothed the powder round her nostrils.

"Oh, he just says 'women don't interest me.'"

"Well, I'd like a drink," said Mae.

"I've got a flask," said Dil, "and there's some White Rock coming."

"Is my nose all right?"

She snapped shut the lid of the little box and looked brightly from one to the other. Then she opened it again and, tilting her head to make sure that her hair was not disarrayed, she patted a golden wave or two lightly with the palm of her hand.

"Perfect," said Bill.

"Absolutely perfect," said Dil.

The music stopped, the couples drifted back to their booths with trailing and bobbing balloons, and in the distressing silence the waiter opened the White Rock. As soon as he had gone away Dil took out his flask and poured from it into the three glasses. The saxophone began again. Mae subtly swayed her shoulders, narrowing her eyes a little.

"Mm—what I *mean!*" she said, lifting her glass.

"Well, here's to poor old Pete," said Dil.

"Oh, yes, tell me some more about Pete. Is he good-looking?"

"He's red-haired and blue-eyed," said Bill. "Red curly hair. He's not what you'd call handsome exactly—do you think so, Dil?—but he's awfully *nice*-looking. He's terribly innocent."

"This is a nice drink," said Mae. "I needed it badly. Gosh, it was hot in that dressing-room! I thought I would die. I thought I would faint or something. I tell you what, boys, I'm going to bed early tonight."

"Oh, don't say that. The night's still young."

"I'm going to bed at one o'clock on the dot. You see if I don't. Just the same, I'd like to do something exciting, if I weren't so tired."

"Are you feeling tired? This drink will fix you up. We were feeling pretty shot ourselves. We've been working since three this afternoon. But I'm feeling a lot better already. All you need is a little jazz."

"What would you like to do, Mae?" asked Dil. "How about riding out to the Bell-in-Hand and having a dance? Some of the fellows are going to be out there."

Mae considered, her pretty head on one side. She watched the couples dance by, watching with a sort of melancholy, bored expression. She rested her chin on knitted fingers.

"I want to do something *exciting*," she said. "Gosh, how I hate this sleepy town."

"Oh, it's not so bad," said Bill.

"Sleepy Hollow," said Dil.

"What else does Pete say about women, Dil? I bet some girl turned him down. That's the way it usually is."

"No, nothing like that. It's just the way he is. He's a real woman-hater. We tried to make him come and meet you, but he wouldn't. He said women didn't interest him."

Mae smiled at Dil in a queer sleepy sort of way. Her eyes were very blue and very deep.

"He didn't want to meet me?" she said.

"It would have been the same with anybody," Bill said, a little anxiously. "He never goes out anywhere. Never goes to a show."

"What's he doing now?"

"Now? This minute? Probably gone to bed."

"Well, let's go and wake him up."

Dil laughed. Bill poured out the rest of the White Rock. The glasses were empty.

"By gosh, that would be amusing," said Dil. "I wonder what old Pete would do if we came in and woke him."

"Throw a fit or something," said Bill.

"I'd like to meet a real woman-hater. I've never met one. Does he bite and scratch?"

Dil smoothed his black hair; he was very urbane.

"Oh, no. He's very polite. But the only things that interest him are surgery and hunting. He went big-game hunting in Africa just after he got out of college. Shot a couple of lions, and nearly got killed by a lioness."

"My, my, just think of that. Where was this—in California?"

They laughed, and drank.

"No movie stuff," said Dil. "Honest-to-God Africa. He's got the gun to prove it."

"Well, now, isn't he the little hero," said Mae primly. "Let's go and wake him up and talk to him. I'd like to talk to him. We can go there, can't we?"

"Sure, we can go there."

"That's a swell idea," said Bill. "By gosh, it'll be fun to see Pete in a situation like that! By gosh, I wonder what he'll do. It wouldn't surprise me if he shot you or jumped out of the window."

"No; do you know what I think he'll do? He'll just take one look at Mae and go to sleep again. That's what he'll do. He'll open one eye like a sick hen and then shut it again and tell us to go to hell."

"What will you bet? I'll bet I can make him like me," said Mae. "I'll bet you a dinner. Give me a cigarette, that's a good boy."

"All right, I'll bet you can't."

"Come on, then, let's go."

"Wait till I pay the bill. You go ahead and get a taxi."

Mae and Bill got up and moved through the returning dancers, and a moment later Dil followed them. They walked down the steps from the lobby under the lighted glass canopy and got into a scarlet taxi. The stars were out. Mae sat between them and held their arms, and laughed.

"This is great," she said.

"It's only just around the corner," Bill murmured. "Here it is."

"What—already? We could have walked."

"Well, you'll have walk enough going up the stairs."

"All right, you'll have to push me."

They put their hands against the small of her back and pushed her, all three of them laughing. Bill took out his key and opened the door. The apartment was dark, and he felt along the wall and switched on the light. Everything was exactly as they had left it—the glasses still on the floor, the window open, and the cushion just where Pete had flung it. A purple galleon was embroidered on the cushion, and there was a rip at one corner.

"He's gone to bed," said Dil. "Just what I said."

"Where does he sleep? In here?"

Mae went to one of the bedroom doors, on tiptoe.

"No, here."

"Let me see him. . . . You leave this to me!"

She flung off her cape and went to the door. Bill reached his hand in and turned on the light. Pete was asleep. His head was twisted a little to one side, and his left arm lay outside the blanket, across his breast. His lips were lightly closed, and his face had the soft and relaxed look of one who sleeps deeply.

"Isn't he *darling!*" Mae whispered. "Sh-h-h!"

She removed her slippers and went to the bed, where for a moment she leaned over the sleeping figure.

"Hello, Pete!" she said softly.

Pete didn't stir. His breath was perfectly even. Mae knelt on the bed, stretched herself out beside him, very gently, and put her arm across him. She leaned her face above his, by degrees allowing him to feel more and more of her weight. Then she inclined her head and gave him a kiss. As she withdrew her face, smiling deliciously, Pete opened his eyes. He didn't move—his face didn't change expression. He looked up at the smiling and beautiful face that hung over him, very much as if he thought he might still be dreaming. Then he put his arm around her shoulders and drew her down to him, without saying a word.

Bill and Dil retreated. Bill sank down on the couch, and Dil went to the window. They both felt a little hurt.

"Well, I'll be damned!" said Dil.

"Can you beat it?"

"So that's the end of poor old Pete."

Bill went to the door and looked in. Mae was sitting on the edge of the bed, smiling still, and Pete was staring up at her, entranced, as if his visitant were a sort of archangel. Neither of them said anything.

"The drinks are on us," said Bill, "any time you're ready. Come on, Mae, and let the great man get some clothes on."

Mae jumped up and laughed.

"So that's that," she said. "Put on a record, someone, and let's dance. Don't look so gloomy, Bill! . . ."

"By gosh, that was too easy."

"I like him," said Mae. "He's a darling! Why didn't you tell me he was such a darling?"

"Oh, yes, he's a darling, all right," said Dil.

There was a silence, a little awkward, during which Pete got up and shut his door. They could hear him moving around at a great rate, getting dressed. Bill put on a record and wound the phonograph. His eyes met Dil's, and they both looked away, They were both wishing that it hadn't happened. Then the fox-trot began whining, Bill snapped his fingers, and Dill took Mae in his arms, grinning, and started to dance.

THE PROFESSOR'S ESCAPE

When Professor—his colleagues called him Tubby—Milliken emerged from the waiting room of the North Station, after seeing his wife and little daughter off on the evening train for Portland, he found that the rain was beginning, gradually, to change to snow. A few large flakes were falling, soft and white and—yes!—heavy-bellied; they clung to his furry sleeve without melting; and he felt that this change, and the sight of hats and coats already beginning to be spangled with snow, after a dark day of rain, accorded subtly with his mood. He sighed, and set off to climb the hill to his rooms, thinking how pleasant it would be, for once, to have an evening all to himself. It was all of six years since such a thing had happened. Not since the time when Molly had gone to Hartford for the funeral! And that had been only for two nights. And now—a whole week of unrestricted freedom. It was too good to be true. He would be able to read—if he liked—all evening. Or (surreptitious delight!) solve chess problems uninterrupted; or even (the thought of this was not so unmixedly delicious) make some notes for his lecture on guild socialism. . . . But no—there would be time enough for that. Wouldn't something a little more festive be in order? He might, for example, accept Mrs. Trask's (his landlady's) many times repeated invitation to join the usual poker-party. Molly had always vetoed this idea—and of course she was perfectly right. It wouldn't do to become embroiled with those queer and some-what vulgar people—that fat Doctor Something-or-other and the publicity man who wore the loud checked suit. And besides, Mrs. Trask was such a terrible gossip and liar. . . . Nevertheless —the notion was not unattractive. Mrs. Trask was a rather fine old tragedy queen—and not so very old, either. Not over forty-five—or perhaps fifty. Fond of port wine, and with a florid countenance to match. And such fine bold black eyes! And such an air as of a duchess—*temporarily* reduced to the low business of keeping a boarding-house! . . . And her parties—as he passed her door on the stairs—always sounded so gay.

He sighed again, and inserted his key in the lock. It stuck, as it always did, but after a moment's struggle he managed to open the door. And there before him, sitting by the marble-topped table, was Fred, hat in hand, his galoshes unfastened, his little blue eyes (in which wit and innocence was so felicitously fused) beaming through thick spectacles.

"You're coming to dinner with me," he said. "Mrs. Trask tells me you're a bachelor."

"You bet I will! . . . I was wondering what the devil to do with myself. I *ought* to be making some notes for a lecture—"

"Lecture be damned. Do you know what night this is?"

"No. What night is it?"

"*Saturday* night. And Bill Caffrey is meeting us at Jacot's. Come on! We'll discuss Freud and drink Château Yquem."

"Yum yum," said the Professor. "Only, if you don't mind, I think it will be a nice fat bottle of Beaune."

"The nearer the Beaune, the sweeter the meat," said Fred, rising lazily. "Let's go."

"Fie!"

The two men went out, linking arms, and descended the steep street to the Common. The paths and grass were already sprinkled with white—the snow, a stage snow, was falling perfectly straight through the windless air. Looking up at a tall elm, beside which hung a purple arc-light like a snowdrop, the Professor saw that the fork of the tree was white, and that the bare twigs were beginning to be feathered. He suddenly felt happy. Life was like this—a dark day of rain, the gloom and nostalgia of a departure, the sensation of release and escape, and then a soft curtain of snow. And Fred—the unexpected and delightful arrival of Fred, and the void evening suddenly filled with light and joy. Fred flopping along beside him with open galoshes, and his toes turned in, and his shrewd face downcast in amused meditation.

"Yes," he murmured, "I'm a bachelor—and it feels kind of nice to be a bachelor again."

"Ah, you married men! . . . It must be nice to break out of the cage now and then. And sow—as somebody said—your wild oats in a windowbox. . . . What do you say—shall we have a Hop Toad?"

"A Hop Toad? . . . What on earth are you talking about!"

"My dear Tubby! You *are* married!"

Fred turned his delicious sly smile toward the Professor, and then without explanation led the way into the Touraine Hotel and down the worn marble stairs into the smaller grill-room—the men's grill-room. Holding up one finger, he ordered two Hop Toads.

"You must wait," he said. "You'll wonder how you managed to *live* without a Hop Toad."

He smiled mysteriously into the far corner of the room, which was almost empty.

"I take it a Hop Toad is a kind of intoxicating drink," said the Professor. "Not *too* intoxicating, I hope."

"It's very, very subtle—not to say insidious."

"Two Hop Toads," said the waiter.

"Here's looking at you," said Fred, raising the wide glass and then lowering it to his smile, which was that of an Etruscan Dionysus. The Professor lifted his glass by the clear stem, beamed happily at the frothed pink liquid, and sipped. Then he sipped again, and rapidly smacked appreciative lips, throwing back his head.

"You do that like a hen," said Fred.

"It tastes like a sunset!"

"No—no—that's where you're all wrong. It's an Aurora Borealis."

"Not at all—it's the grenadine I refer to—the grenadine gives it a kind of glow—if you know what I mean—I'll compromise with you by calling it an Alpenglow."

"That's better. That's not so bad. Because it's *cold,* you know —but it has a fire in it like the light in a moonstone.

"Yes. I feel it. By gosh, it's good. There's an enormous cabbage rose opening in my belly—with deep, crimson petals."

"Yes, it certainly gets you forrader," sighed Fred. "Bill will be furious when he hears we've been having Hop Toads. It was his discovery. By the same token, we ought to move. Bill will be waiting."

They rose, they climbed the stairs, they pushed through the glass revolving doors, they crossed the white street, and descended the match-strewn stairs into Jacot's. It was another such room as they had just left, with a bar in one corner. Most of the tables were marble-topped and bare; but one or two were covered with tablecloths, and at one of these Bill Caffrey was sitting, with his chin sunk in his hands. He watched their approach without change of expression.

"Hail," he said.

"Hail," said Fred.

"Hail."

"We've been having Hop Toads," said Fred.

"Confound it! Why didn't *I* think of that? . . . My imagination couldn't get any farther than a Lone Tree."

"Tubby's a bachelor."

"Ah, indeed."

"His wife's gone away—left him flat."

"Do tell."

"And so he's breaking out; going to get riotously drunk, like the time when he slept in the ash barrel."

"Nothing of the sort. Just because I suggested a modest bottle of Burgundy——"

He beamed, he felt himself beaming, as he left the sentence hanging in air; Fred and Bill grinned sympathetically; and all three gave themselves to the business of ordering. Freshwater-fattened oysters from Poppennessett. Mock turtle soup. Filet mignon with mushrooms and fried egg-plant. Ice-cream—pistachio—and coffee. And two bottles of Beaune. Yes, sir, and again, yes, sir, said the waiter; making solemn notes, as if for a ritual; and in the pauses could be heard the bartender, who was cracking ice with the handle of a chisel. The bloated Poppennessett. The watery bivalve. And the imprisoned sunlight of the Beaune. Musing of these delights, already in his thought so vivid and intense, the Professor again felt suddenly and inexplicably happy. Life was like this—the gloominess of a huge sooty railway station on a winter's night, the forlorn clanging of locomotive bells, the scurrying of sodden commuters, and then this marvelous translation to another world. A world of soiled mosaic floors, bottles of scarlet-capped Burgundy, brass spittoons (florid survival of a barbarous age), and the magnificent bar, with its baroque richness of gilt and mirrors, and its shelves of many-colored bottles, upheld by brown dryads of carved wood. What luxury! What comfort! What freedom! And the joy of sitting with cynical Fred and the impassive, morosely subtle Bill.

"You know," said Bill, "I really like English oysters better than American ones."

"Oh, come," said Fred.

"Yes. And the Dutch, too. They have a more frankly *marine* taste—seaweedy and salt, like those slippery blistered kelpy things that you pop with your fingernails. These great things— good Lord, you might as well be biting bags full of water."

"Anglomania," said the Professor.

"Yes. And have you noticed his tweed suit?" murmured Fred. "Oh! And that reminds me."

The waiter put down the soup and poured the Burgundy. They lifted the thin goblets, all three, sniffed appreciatively, and simultaneously drank.

"That reminds you of what," said Bill, somberly.

"Tubby! We must get him to tell his story."

"What story?"

"The one on the ship. Coming back last winter."

"By George, yes!" said the Professor. "Let's have it, Bill."

Bill permitted himself the tiniest of guarded smiles, then again tasted his Burgundy. He frowned at his soup. Perplexed and pleased, and a little embarrassed also.

"No," he said. "I really couldn't. Not at the point of the gun, like this. Maybe some other time."

Fred smiled—slowly and charmingly.

"Isn't he skillful? This is his way of beating up our interest."

"Not at all. I'd just as lief tell it—but the trouble is, you're both of you in the wrong state of mind for it."

"How come?" said the Professor.

"Because you're both expecting something—well, scandalous. This isn't that sort of thing at all."

"No?"

"No. . . . There are plenty of episodes of this kind, as you know, that delight one just because they are scandalous and strange. Like that tale Frisky Speare told us, of his exploit on the train to New York. All amusing enough, too. But this isn't like that—and I'm not like that either."

"Ho ho," said Fred, dryly."

"Ho ho," said Bill. "I'm not. I'm neither polygamous nor promiscuous, and I'm not the sort that women throw themselves at. That's one thing that made this thing surprising. The other thing that made something—to my mind—extraordinarily lovely of it, was its spiritual intensity."

The Professor crunched a small slippery mushroom, wiped his lips, and drank a full rich mouthful of Burgundy. Spiritual in-

tensity. Just the kind of thing Bill *would* be going in for. Just
the kind of guard—defense—he *would* erect about his indiscre-
tions. Honest? Dishonest? Honest! One had only to look at his
compressed lips, downturned with melancholy, and the level
serious gray eyes, to recognize in Bill the contemplative stillness
of spirit which would, precisely, make a distinction of this kind.
One could imagine him, in the very midst of the most sordid of
adventures, sitting perfectly quiet, thus, in the act of extracting
its spiritual beauty. And then rising, hat in hand, and departing,
with this beauty among his permanent possessions.

"It sounds all the better," said the Professor.

"It *was* all the better. . . . I should preface the story by saying
that on the ship with me, when we sailed from Cherbourg, were
a New York newspaper man whom I knew slightly, a friend of
his, and a young graduate student who worked with me three
years ago. I ran into them *after* the adventure had started, and
their presence—they were always sitting in the smoking room—
gave a queer and delightful contrapuntal quality to the adventure itself. If I'd run into them *before* the adventure started, the
adventure would probably never have happened at all. For in
that case I'd have arranged to sit at their table the first night,
and I wouldn't have met Lovely."

"*Lovely?*" Fred's voice was just faintly ironical.

"Lovely. That's what I called her. I never called her anything
else; in fact, for several days I didn't know her name."

He paused, stared down at the tablecloth, shifted a spoon
beside his plate, and raised his half-filled glass.

"She and her mother sat at my table on the first night, you
see, before the regular places had been assigned. I was there first
—and then she came, a little bit flustered, and sat down opposite. I'd seen her half an hour before on the deck—just a glimpse
—but enough to see that she was one of the loveliest beings my
eyes had ever fallen upon. An astonishingly beautiful girl, about
twenty-five."

"Of course," murmured Fred.

"Don't be *snooty*. She was. And the minute—the *minute*—

she looked at me, across the table, I could see that something extraordinary was going to happen. Her eyes had that astonished brilliance that only happens when one recognizes—as one does only once or twice in a lifetime—what the newspapers used to call a soul-mate. I was electrified. I'm not used to being looked at in that fashion. I'm a sober God-fearing old citizen, as you both know, not at all given to flirtation—but the minute she looked at me like that I began to feel subtly transfigured myself. I felt my own eyes opening wider, and a light in my face to which I'm not in the least accustomed."

"The light that never was," said the Professor.

"And lies and lies," said Fred.

"Certainly. . . . Not that I fell in love. I didn't. I knew I wouldn't. There was no question of that. I was destined, in a sense, to play an entirely passive part, and I knew that from the beginning. It was she who supplied the energy for the scene— it was she who started the thing going and kept it going—for the good and sufficient reason that she had fallen in love with *me*. Could I refuse to play that passive part which was indicated? Could I do anything but acquiesce?"

Fred gave a little groan.

"Don't be a boob," he said.

"I was and am a boob. I was never so completely helpless, powerless, in all my life. Not that I wanted very much to be anything else. I was fascinated. Like the sparrow by the anaconda. I just sat and chattered, and shivered my paralyzed wings. I had no desire to run—she was far too beautiful for that—but I confess I was damned scared. For one thing, there was her nice old mother, with smooth white hair and kind eyes and knitting and everything. She hadn't noticed a thing—but wouldn't she be sure to? For another thing, Lovely was wearing a wedding-ring."

"Married!"

"Married. . . . That gave me pause. It suggested a good many rather disquieting things."

He broke off and meditated, with a tiny retrospective smile.

"Well, get on with the story," said the Professor. "Don't keep us in suspense."

"She asked me if I played bridge. I said I did. So after dinner we had a three-handed game, in the library, till about nine o'clock. All very polite and a little formal. She'd been over to Paris, visiting her sister, who had married a Frenchman, and was on her way back to her husband in Trenton. Her husband was a manufacturer, and wealthy, I gathered. Then at nine o'clock, she said she thought she'd like some fresh air—so I suggested a turn around the deck. Mother said good night and went down to turn in, and Lovely and I went out and walked for an hour. Somehow or other, I couldn't say a thing. I suppose because I was too uncomfortably aware of the extent to which I agitated her. But anyway, it wasn't necessary; she talked a blue streak. All about Paris—the trip over—her sister—her mother—her husband—her shopping. Everything. A complete nonstop outpouring: as if she were trying to talk against time. Or rather, as if she were afraid of what might happen if she *stopped* talking. And meanwhile, she kept a fast hold of my arm with her hand, occasionally tightening her grip with an almost spasmodic intensity, and leaning her shoulder against me with obvious delight as we rounded the corners. As for me, I just shivered—for it was a coldish evening—and said yes or no or is that so or well-well or anything at all that was sufficiently monosyllabic—for it was clear enough that *she* wanted to do all the talking. In fact, I had the feeling that the poor child had never, before that night with me, in all her life, had a *chance* to talk. For some reason, the mere sight of me had released her. . . . Pour and pass, Fred.

"Well. That was the first night. As we separated, she again looked at me with that same brilliantly astonished look, as if I might be some sort of divine revelation, and quite unnecessarily shook my hand. I did my best to play up, of course—not unwillingly. Good heavens! It isn't every day in my life that a beautiful young woman pays me that sort of compliment. We looked hard and deep at each other, smiling protractedly and deliciously, and arranged for another game of bridge in the morning. And then I went into the smoking room and found Peters and Marks and the other chap and chewed the rag with them for half an hour, and so to bed.

"Next morning we had the game of bridge—all very polite and formal, just as before. Mother suspected nothing. She was just as nice and sweet and innocent as she could be. As for Lovely, I had the feeling that she hardly dared to look at me. After an hour or so of bridge, we went out for a walk, abandoning Mother; but we'd scarcely got outside when she said that she had suddenly remembered that she had something she wanted to show to me: an Egyptian thing. So she ducked below and came back in a few minutes with a curious terracotta bas-relief of an Egyptian head—a woman's head—young, beautiful, and with the eyes closed in sleep. And yet not as if altogether asleep, either—there was a kind of drowsy and voluptuous consciousness in the face, and one felt, as it were, a tremor in the closed eyelids—as if, perhaps they were closed merely for the duration of a kiss. Anyway, that was what I felt when I looked at it—perhaps partly because I could see that it was something of this sort that *she* felt. She was so obviously thrilled by it! Thrilled and mystified. I took the thing in my hands and stared at it—and then, prompted by all the subtle intangibles of that extraordinary situation, I achieved what I haven't the slightest doubt was a stroke of genius: I told her that this was the face of the Egyptian goddess of love—I made up on the spur of the moment a fantastic name for her—and then solemnly, holding the thing between my two palms, I raised the beautiful somnolent mouth to mine and kissed it. . . ."

"Well, I'll be jiggered," said Fred. "And you a married man with eight children."

There was a pause. The waiter put down three ice-cream

plates, each bearing a little green Fujiyama of pistachio ice. Detachedly, with a slight frown of preoccupation, Bill decapitated the apex of the smooth cone. The Professor watched him, smiling. It was a good story—it was going to be a good story— and the Burgundy was warming his heart. And to think that Bill Caffrey was a lecturer in economics!

"Yes, that was a stroke of genius. I could see it at once. Just exactly the right thing, the one and only thing, for me to do. She believed me—she believed in the utter sincerity of my gesture. That will give you an idea of the sort of creature she was—rapturously and incorrigibly romantic, starved for love, and utterly, utterly, utterly unsophisticated. Perhaps you can guess from that, too, how I felt about it. Half fascinated and half terrified. I was simply being taken off my feet by the force of her passion for me. My own feelings—almost nil. That's a *slight* exaggeration, but you see what I mean. I knew then, as I handed Smet-Smet, or Rert-Rert, or whatever the thing's name was, back to her—when I saw the really idolatrous expression that shone in her eyes—that she had abdicated entirely, and that heart, soul, and body she was mine. And I knew also that it was too late for me to try to run—vigorous as the impulse was."

"Oh, come," said Fred.

"Vigorous—but, I admit, ambiguous. . . . And it must be admitted, further, that I *didn't* run. At least, not very much nor very fast nor very far. I escaped from her shortly afterward, and didn't see her again till the evening. She came out of one of the main doors to the deck just as I was going in. And I was so delighted to see her, in that unexpected manner, and she looked so extraordinarily beautiful in a black satin dress, open at the throat, with a Spanish shawl over her shoulders, that I was surprised into addressing her as Lovely. Explain that how you will. I swear I had no wish, *of my own,* to make love to her. Yet I then and there, and from that minute on, found myself doing it. I did it like a sleepwalker—automatically. My conscience simply went to sleep. My family ceased to have any reality whatsoever. I didn't give them so much as a thought. Her attraction to me was so profound and so powerful that I was completely polarized by it."

"Polarized! . . . You *do* find nice apologies for things," said the Professor. "Polarized!"

"That was precisely it. I was as incapable of independent action as a magnetized watch. From that time, I behaved *to* her, and to her alone; no matter where I was or what I was doing. When I played bridge with the boys in the smoking room, it was all I could do to tell a king from a two-spot."

"Well, well, well," said Fred. "But let's have a little less theory and a little more narrative."

"No—that's where you're wrong; for the exquisite beauty of this episode is entirely in the incidents and overtones. . . . However, if you're getting impatient for the *dénouement,* I'll cut it short for you."

"For heaven's sake *don't,*" said the Professor.

The three men sat silent for a moment, all three of them faintly smiling, as if in a queer kind of communion of spirit. The waiter removed the ice-cream plates and deposited coffee-cups and a silver pot of coffee. Cigarettes. Afterward, perhaps, a little syrupy glass of green Chartreuse. Fred poured the coffee, and Bill struck a match. Might they not—thought the Professor —adjourn afterward to the Parthenon, for Turkish coffee? But no, it would be too late. Already after nine. And already as delightful an evening as it could be. This story—how it opened like a flower! Bill's odd and secret life, opening like a flower. Life was like this—the emptiness and sharp nostalgia of a departure, and then an unexpected and beautiful story. From the North Station, on a winter's eve, to Smet-Smet, whose eyes were closed for a kiss. . . . But wasn't Smet-Smet the hippopotamus goddess? . . . The Professor felt himself frowning; but, thanks to the warm burden of Burgundy, frowning with an amiable remoteness. He blew the ash from his cigarette—phhhh.

"That night, after the bridge-game, the adventure took a swift step forward, I knew it would—I knew it couldn't be long de-ferred. We went out and climbed up to the boat-deck—B Deck. It was dark there, there were no lights, and not a soul in sight. The night was surprisingly warm—I suppose we must have been getting into the Gulf Stream. We went to the forward end of the deck, where we could get a wide view over the bridge and bow to the black sea, and stood there for five minutes without a word. Her hand was under my arm. And then, just naturally, without any preliminaries of excitement, we kissed."

"Ah!" said Fred. "I knew it. . . . I notice these spiritual adventures always end in a kiss."

"You needn't be so superior about it—I was quite conscious of that ironic fact, even in the act of kissing. I thought to myself —'Now, Bill it's all over with you; you've now definitely let yourself in for it.' And in a way I was very unhappy about it. I foresaw all the wretched complications, the evasions, the concealments, the necessities for furtiveness and secrecy, and the inevitableness—or is it inevitability?—with which this furtiveness must poison the relation between us. I also foresaw the awful physiological or biological or psychological determinism which, in such a situation, carries one forward a little farther with each meeting, until disaster is reached. There is something magnificent and horrible in that. Relentless Nature. She has no pity on us. Once you give in to her at all, in the smallest particular, you're a gone goose. There can never be any backward step. You begin by merely gazing, then you touch hands—ah, that exquisite first touch!—and then you embrace and kiss, and then you kiss more passionately, and the next time more passionately still—there is no breaking that spell except by flight. And there we were on a ship, where no flight was possible. . . .

"Everything, of this sort, was implied in that first rather shy and fugitive kiss. And what was not implied she immediately went on to *say*. She said that she had fallen in love with me the minute she saw me: she had begun to tremble violently, and had wanted to come right up to me, there on the deck, and speak, but had not dared. She had then quite deliberately waited till I had taken my seat in the dining saloon, in order that she might seat herself at the same table. Astounding. And then she said, when we began to talk, my voice—just think of it, my *voice!*—put the finishing touch on it. She said her reason simply forsook her. And when, in the morning, I lifted Smet-Smet to my lips and kissed adoringly the beautiful terracotta mouth, it appears that I had put an enchantment on her that would never, *never* be broken. She knew then, once and for all, that the thing was fatal.

"Of course, I replied in kind. I said all sorts of absurd and frantic things. I told her—what was true enough—that I had never in my life seen anyone so beautiful, and that I, too, in the same way, had been completely swept off my feet. Isn't it extraordinary, the madness that comes over one on these occasions? I held her in my arms and stared into her eyes and said 'Lovely! Lovely! Lovely' over and over again. And nevertheless, I was thinking to myself 'I must get out of this,' and wondering how soon I could decently make my escape. And the very fact that I was aware of this duplicity, of this horrible treason, made me redouble the ardor of my embrace and the ecstasy of my speech. I had allowed her to assume that I was as much in love with her as she was with me; and in the face of this, and of the really appalling intensity with which she loved me, I saw nothing for it but to surrender unconditionally, at the same time hoping that the good ship *Imperator* would break all records and reach New York at least three days before she was due."

"Zeus and Atropos!" murmured the Professor. "Now if it had been Fred, he'd have been wishing that it was a World Cruise."

"You bet," said Fred. "Shall we proceed to whisky and soda? . . . Let's have a whisky and soda."

He signaled the waiter and gave the order. Bill unrolled a long oilskin tobacco-pouch and began filling his charred and battered pipe.

"However," he resumed, "we weren't so far sunk that we could ignore the practical social difficulties that lay ahead of us. And so the disagreeable element of secrecy was introduced at once. I explained that I had friends on the ship, and that I would therefore have to be very careful; she, on her part, added that of course there was her mother to be considered. We couldn't simply surrender ourselves to this—*passion*—and blindly ignore all consequences. We would have to plan a kind of cold-blooded campaign of discretion and secrecy, not to say deception. So it was arranged that we should have three hours a day; one in the morning, one in the afternoon (when her mother always took a rest), and one in the evening after the bridge-game and before I joined my three friends in the smoking room. In this way, we thought, we could probably keep the thing as inconspicuous and normal as the usual sort of ship-acquaintance, and avoid anything in the nature of gossip. This was unpleasant, and gave me a bad moment of panic—if only because, in this illicit way, it took our affair for granted, and gave it a twisted kind of legality. I was now in the position of an accepted lover, but without in the least being in love. I, who had never in my life been unfaithful to my wife, and never desired to be, and I didn't even now desire to be, was being railroaded into a clandestine liaison of really grandiose proportions. . . . Here's how."

"How," said Fred.

"How," said the Professor.

Ruminating, they sipped their whiskies. The bartender was shaking cocktails for two college boys who leaned with careful nonchalance, in wet raincoats, against the bar. The snow, one of them was saying, had turned to rain.

"That touches the spot," said the Professor. He put down his glass and smiled. He felt extraordinarily good-natured. "Lovely! Lovely! Lovely!" . . . Bill's phrase, in Bill's suave and intense and—yes—*gauzy* voice, ran in his head hypnotically.

"To resume. I'll cut the thing short—for of course you can imagine the next few stages well enough for yourselves. Nothing much happened in the morning and afternoon of the third day —but in the evening, when we climbed up to the boat-deck again, things began to happen pretty fast. She was in a frenzy— had an idea that I had been cold to her all day—accused me of

avoiding her, not looking at her—and so forth. Naturally, I
denied this, and took the easiest way of doing so—I embraced
her ardently and kissed her, swearing that if I had appeared to
avoid meeting her eyes it was only because I was so afraid of
giving myself away in public. She hugged me, she kissed my
hands, she ran her fingers up inside my coat sleeves, and then,
beginning to cry, she told me about her husband. . . . It appears
that he was a typical American businessman—successful, energetic, cold, *hard-boiled*, as the saying is. She had been married
to him for five years—he was twelve years older than she—and
for the first year or so she had been more or less happy. But
then she began to discover their temperamental differences.
She was passionately in love, and he was not. She was romantic,
and he was not. She wanted adventure, color, excitement,
parties, music, poetry, art—you know the sort of things: a kind
of American Emma Bovary; and he, alas, became every minute
more absorbed in his business life, a mere walking ledger. What
relaxation he sought was in his club or on the golf-links, and
always alone. In a nut-shell, he was indifferent to her because
he was sexless. Nothing new in the situation, of course—we
read about it every other day in the divorce cases. But it astounded me, as it still astounds me, that *anyone* could have
married such a being as she was and remain indifferent. She
said he had no tact, no understanding, whatever: *gave* her
things, of the kind that money could buy, and gave generously,
but never gave himself. A perfunctory kiss at breakfast, and
another when he came home from the office. And there had
been no children. . . .

"*Quae cum ita sint*, she was unconsciously ripe for such a
misadventure as befell her with me. She thought me romantic-
looking; and I had then only to kiss Smet-Smet, and murmur to
her how nice it would be if we could fly away together to
Tahiti or Karnak, and she was certain that in me she had found
her great lover, her ideal. In fact, she said so. That I was myself
married—I had fortunately mentioned this at the outset—
didn't affect her in the least. No matter what happened, she

said, she would now and henceforth be happy all her life, by virtue of this memory. She now knew—so she said—what it was to love and be loved. Just think of it! She had extracted all this from a few clandestine embraces on B Deck and the paltry half-dozen romantic phrases which I had managed to recall from my reading of soupy love-stories in the cheaper magazines. If that isn't an irony, what is? I was horribly ashamed of myself—I've never in all my days felt so miserably cheap and dishonest. A perfect cad. And yet, when I looked back over the affair I couldn't, to save my neck, see any point at which I could decently, or mercifully—yes, mercifully—have behaved otherwise than as I did . . . Good God!"

He paused, removed his pipe from his mouth, stared at the ashes in it as if a little surprised, struck a match absent-mindedly, without using it blew it out, and then resumed.

"Yes. . . . That's how it was. . . . And you can imagine exactly how it affected me. I exerted myself, on the one hand, to make love to her more passionately; and on the other hand, I had my eye perpetually on my watch, or my ear on the ship's bells, so as to reduce our meetings to a minimum. I worked my three acquaintances for all they were worth—told her that they were already a little suspicious, and that I would have to be a good deal more careful. Pretended also that I had some very important work to do—reading for lectures, et cetera. She took it like a lamb, believed me without question. And—heavens!—how astonishing it was, to go down from that dark upper deck, where we stood for an hour under the stars, absolutely immobile with passionate absorption in each other, in that blind state of panic when the whole universe seems to flow into one's soul—to go down alone from this to the smoking room and hear Peters saying, in his lazy drawl, 'Well, according to Einstein—' or Marks telling the other chap the theoretical value in tricks of each card in a bridge-game. That, in addition to my own singular detachment—call it dishonest if you like—gave the thing an exotic unreality, a nostalgic remoteness, of an unmatchable loveliness. I experienced a profound feeling of gratitude that such an adventure should have befallen the least romantic of men: and I was terrified, with the genuine sacred terror, when I wondered what the future might hold in store for me.

"I remarked, earlier, on the inevitable step-by-step progression of such affairs, from the less to the more intense, and this was no exception. With each night, as we approached nearer to America and the American winter, the weather grew colder—but nothing could daunt us. On the last night, when we climbed up for our farewell meeting, it was actually snowing. We had our heavy coats on—and there we stood, being literally drifted under, while the ship plunged and corkscrewed in a gigantic sea. It was marvelous—as if the elements themselves were conspiring with us to give our *Liebestod* a touch of grandiosity. No—grandeur! For it was *that*. Certainly, with Lovely, it had become a grand passion. I admit that I'd never had any idea what terrific force a passion could have. It she could have torn me limb from limb, as the Bacchantes tore—who was it? I've forgotten his name—she'd have done so. As it was, she kissed me with a kiss that was more like flame, lambent flame, than I could have conceived it to be: restless, rapid, devouring. She even opened my waistcoat, and slid her hand in against my heart; and we stood there, motionless in the blizzard for all the world like a pair of stanchions or davits, and apparently as lifeless.

"What happened then is the thing that gives its whole point to the story—if it has a point at all—and it's essential that you should see it in the right way. If you regard the thing as merely a tidbit of scandal, and hope for a climax of the approved smoking-room style, you'll be disappointed, and you'll miss what is to my mind the real beauty and pathos, or rather tragedy, of the actual event. I need hardly say that when we finally groped our way down below again, shaking the snow off our hats and coats, we were in no mood to separate. It was late—eleven-thirty—for one hour had stretched to two; and when we stood in the corridor to say good night we found ourselves alone, in a ship which to all intents and purposes had gone to sleep. We said good night: I had my hand on her wrist:

and then, once more surrendering to an impulse that seemed to come from her rather than from myself, I asked her to come to my room. The question seemed to hang there for a long while, portentously reverberating, catastrophically reverberating, while we stared at each other: and then, shutting her eyes as if in an agony, she said '*no.*' I didn't urge her. I merely added that I would wait for her—that I would expect her in three minutes —told her how to find my stateroom—and that I would leave the door ajar. With this, I turned my back and departed. She stood there, unmoving.

"In three minutes, she came into my room. When I embraced her, and told her how happy she had made me, I felt that she was trembling—trembling violently. She was in a queer passive trancelike state; and while I kissed her, she kept her dark eyes wide open, as if she were desperately looking for something, something unresolved or unresolvable. And then, gently detaching herself from me, and leaning her back against the door, she said the most completely surprising and most completely terrifying thing that was ever said to me. 'I am yours—' she said—'irrevocably and utterly yours. I must stay here with you, if you like. But I must tell you that if I do this, then I shall never, never, *never,* as long as I live, let you go. I'll follow you everywhere—I'll follow you to the ends of the earth. Your wife won't matter to me, nor my husband, nor social scandal, nor anything: I will sacrifice everything to be near you, and I'll never give you up, so help me God. I've got to tell you that. And then you can decide whether you want me to stay. . . .'

"Well! . . . To say that I was frightened doesn't begin to suggest to you what I felt. In a second—a *second*—my spurious (perhaps not wholly spurious) passion for her had vanished. I stared at her as if at a total stranger who had somehow blundered into my stateroom; and I felt incredibly foolish and false. What on earth could I do? . . . Nothing. Absolutely nothing! If I'd been of more heroic mold, or anything at all of a Don Juan (which Heaven knows I'm not), I suppose I'd have made the final grand gesture and taken, unflinching, the final risk. But being a mere timid married man, unquestionably loyal and decidedly less than *moyen sensuel*, I was, to be quite frank, in a horrible funk, and could find nothing to do but look silly. I must have looked *damned* silly. But I did manage, after a moment, to pull myself together—and I said, with as much gravity as I could muster, that so great a sacrifice, on her part, was out of the question, and that of course any such permanent relation between us could not for a minute be considered. She gave me a queer, long, hard look, at that, with her hand on the doorknob—rather uncomfortably, as if she had suddenly seen *me* for the first time—and then said a flurried little goodbye, gave me her hand, and was gone. . . . And I never spoke with her again."

Fred took off his spectacles and stared.

"Well, I'll be—*sunk*," he said.

"Sunk isn't the word," murmured the Professor. "I never heard such an outrageous anticlimax in all my life. You mean to say——"

Words failed him. He felt himself to be visibly speechless. So far—so agonizingly far—in pursuit of an *ignis fatuus*! To Karnak and back for a grain of sand! He finished his whisky at a gulp.

"Well, Bill," he added, rising, "I congratulate you on your firm moral stand. It was splendid. Worthy of the best traditions of the college. Anyway, it's a blamed good story, and now I've got to go home."

"It's a hum-dinger," said Fred. "Did it really happen like that?"

"Absolutely, word for word."

"Well, it's a hum-dinger."

The waiter being summoned, they paid the bill, put on their coats and galoshes, and climbed the worn stairs. The Professor felt himself to be a little unsteady on his feet, but perfectly clear-headed—perfectly. And he visualized the final scene in the stateroom with astonishing distinctness. There were certain details, however, about which he wished Bill had been a little more specific. Had they, or had they not, actually——

He was interrupted in this sly speculation by Fred's asking him if he would like to ride in a taxi as far as Charles Street.

"Yes," he said, and stepped in beside Fred, waving a hand to Bill, who was remaining behind.

"Good night!"

"Good night!"

They were off, and in three minutes had stopped at the corner of Charles and Beacon streets. It was snowing again, as he plodded up the hill—large soft flakes. Well, well—well, well! To think of a thing like that! Now if such a thing would only happen to him——

He inserted his key in the lock, and it stuck again. It wouldn't go in any farther, or come out, or turn. Damn. He wrestled with it—he tugged at it—it was no use. Backing away into the street, he surveyed the front of the house to see if there were any lights. None. The servants, of course, had gone to bed. No light in Mrs. Trask's room, either. Damn again. A hundred purple damns. He rang the bell, and nothing happened. Not a sound of a footstep. He rang again, prolongedly, and heard the bell trilling remotely in the distance, with the lost and melodramatic sound of a stage-bell. And the—joy!—the light in the hallway brightened, and the door opened. It was Mrs. Trask herself, clutching an ample black silk dressing-gown about her throat.

"I'm sorry," he said—"my key has gone and got stuck. I think it must be defective. I'm afraid it will have to stay there."

He pointed to the guilty key, smiling. Mrs. Trask smiled, too —he had the idea that she was smiling suggestively. Thinking him drunk, perhaps—because of the key? Or was it merely that she liked him? . . .

"I know it looks suspicious!" He gave a little laugh.

"*Very* suspicious!"

"But I assure you it stuck earlier in the evening as well!"

"Oh, *did* it?"

"Yes, it did."

Mrs. Trask smiled again, as if waiting for something—of course, she was waiting for him to precede her upstairs. What an idiot he was!

"I'm sorry," he said again, in a heartfelt tone, and then added, "good night, Mrs. Trask."

"Good night, Mr. Milliken."

Irony? . . . No. . . .

And then, as he stood before his mirror, a brilliant thought occurred to him—a positive illumination. Of course! She was attracted to him! Any fool could see that! If he were to go downstairs again, and knock quietly at her door—very, very quietly——

No sooner said than done. He knotted the cord of his bathrobe about his middle, opened his door, and listened. Nobody stirring—the hall was dark. He crept out, descended the stairs softly—his heart beating with absurd violence—and on the landing beside Mrs. Trask's door paused to listen again. Not a sound—Mrs. Trask must have gone back to bed. He lifted one knuckle, poised it fatally, and knocked—once, twice.

"Who's that?"

Mrs. Trask's voice sounded muffled, a little frightened. To his dismay, the Professor found that his own voice had unaccountably failed him. He stood and waited, in abject and appalling silence.

"Is that you, Mr. Milliken?"

Ridiculous! He *must* do something. He summoned up his waning courage.

"Yes, it's I, Mrs. Trask."

"Are you ill? . . . Did you want something?"

Another portentous silence—a positive abyss. The hallway reeled. But wasn't this, thank heaven, an opportunity for escape?

"Yes, I am. . . . Have you any brandy, Mrs. Trask?"

"I'm sorry—" came the muffled voice—"I haven't . . . I'd get up, but I've just had an attack of vertigo myself——"

"Oh, don't bother, please . . . I just thought if you had any brandy——"

He turned in an agony of humiliation and shame, and confronted the stairs. Ruined! He had all but ruined himself. Good Lord, what would Molly say when she heard of this! They would have to move. At once. . . . He stood as if paralyzed, clutching the post of the stair-rail. And then, for no valid reason, he twice struck his forehead against the post, and went quietly back to his room.

THE ORANGE MOTH

A hot, sticky August evening. Almost six o'clock. The freckled young man, whose name was Cooke, had his watch before him on the table where he was writing. His sleeves were rolled up, showing thin freckled arms with sparse blond hairs, and he had taken off his collar, which lay on the top of the bookcase. He looked down through the tall open window into Twenty-third Street and saw, across the way, the latticed saloon door perpetually swinging. A man in his shirt-sleeves, carrying his pale alpaca coat over his left arm, fanned his red face with a panama. He said something to the woman, then disappeared through the swinging door. A girl came out carrying a tin pail brimful of beer—"rushing the growler." A dingy terrier briskly trotted round the corner, trotting obliquely, carrying its hindquarters well to starboard. He peered under the swinging door, with one paw lifted, and the cat, crouched on the brown steps next door, began to arch her back. Then a green-and-white street car, crowded, cut off his vision, and Cooke again regarded, somewhat wearily, his manuscript. He was using yellow paper—he had bought a thick block of it in a Ninth Avenue shop, hoping that yellow would make him more prolific. But it didn't seem particularly

to help him. At the top of the page "Beauty" was written, and
twice underscored. Below it was one long paragraph, disordered
with cancellations and interpolations. He completed the sentence: "but to stare at Beauty, to attempt to track it down, to
set snares for it, to turn a powerful glare of consciousness upon
it, is almost inevitably to frighten it away. Beauty is the chimera
which exists only in imagination. It is the mirage, born of
drought, which the more it is approached, the more it dissolves.
It is the gold and purple Phoenix which is reborn only out of
ashes. . . ." No, this wouldn't do at all. He crossed it all out,
peevishly. This, as he had only just finished learning at college,
was a mere purple passage. He wanted something purple, certainly, but not this frayed and mothy purple as of the old
stage-robes of the player King. Something like "the eastern
conduits ran with wine": that was what he wanted. He opened
De Quincey again—it had been helping him, or discouraging
him, all afternoon—and read a page, opened to at random;
while he read, he kept pulling at his shirt, which was soaked
through with perspiration, to detach it from his body. Damned
discouraging—he would never capture the secret of that style.
. . . Perhaps it would be better if he tried red ink, like Flodden,
who had the next room, and whom he could hear moving on
his bed. . . . Or should he go back to blank-books? . . . He
opened his latest blank-book, where an uncompleted poem
ended with the lines:

> "Like Erisichthon, by a sad mischance,
> Gnawest thou at thine own enfeebled limbs?"

Well, by God, that was pretty good! He would go on with it:
the glamour of life was renewed in him by something connected
with those lines: twilight, soft music, women's faces—white
under arc-lamps. He felt melancholy. After all, it was wonderful,
living in a dirty boarding-house in the great city. He thought
of the girl he had seen at Child's in Madison Square the day
before: she wore a lavender-colored soft dress and a wide straw

hat. After lunch he had followed her irresolutely as far as Brentano's. Then he had gone into Brentano's—to read all the foreign magazines. He looked everywhere for clues to beauty, to some short-cut by which he could learn to write as he wanted to—with power and subtlety and magnificence. But what he wrote was always commonplace.

The six o'clock whistles began to blow. The tom-tom downstairs in the basement, where the dark dining room was, began its soft swelling clamor, ending in a brazen crash. He heard Billington, in the room over his head, push back his chair which screeched on the bare floor, and take several soft steps. Flodden's bed began creaking agitatedly. The iron gate in the front yard clanged, and looking down he saw Mr. Ezra D. Ramsden, the detective (sour-faced idiot), walking up the path. He was carrying a paper package under his arm, and looking at the red headlines of a newspaper: the creaking of his shoes was audible and the basement door rang automatically as he went in. . . . Two fingernails ticked the door, and Flodden entered, his white Hapsburg face grinning, his bad teeth showing, and black gums.

"Alas," he cried, "what boots it with incessant care: to strictly meditate the thankless muse? . . . Were it not better done, as others booze, to sport with Phyllis at the Palisades?"

"The Palisades tonight? Too damned hot."

"Out in the vestry, too damned hot," sang Flodden. He shuffled to the window in his red carpet slippers, and spat neatly to the path below. "It's too hot for anything but cold baths and naps. That's what I've been doing all afternoon, one after another. When I wasn't in the bath, Mother Ramsden was; when Mrs. Ramsden wasn't, I was; and vice versa and et cetera *ad infinitum*. And when I wasn't either soaking or sleeping, I read the *Lake*, as being the coolest book I could think of. . . . Certainly the coolest of Moore's! Ha, Ha."

"Papa Ramsden is back from the Wild West with his disguise under his arm."

"More likely it's a touching little gift for the missus. Sister

Susie, being in hopes, read the works of Marie Stopes. Now she's in a sad condition because she read the wrong edition."

"How delightful! Where do you pick up these engaging trifles, Flod!"

"Solicit not thy thought with matters hid: leave them to Flod. I wonder if the mail's come. I'm expecting a check for a thousand dollars from the *Smart Set*. If it's come I'll treat you to a dinner at the free lunch over the way."

"What have you sold to the *Smart Set*?"

"The usual cynical little triangle story. I turn them out by recipe. Take one sweet, tired, gingham wife in a Long Island village: one successful climbing husband, who wants to build him more stately mansions, O my soul, but finds his wife still feeding the chickens—come, chick, come, chick! add one deep-dyed chorus girl recuperating in the country from housemaid's knee. Stir till thick. Separate them. Sprinkle with Belasco sauce. And there you are. . . . I cut all the descriptive passages out of the newspapers. Much easier than trying to grasp the contemporary style myself."

He knocked out his pipe on the window-sill, humming. While Cooke was fastening his collar, Billington came in.

"I say, where are we going to hog it, tonight? . . . Shall we go to that new Chinese place in Sixth Avenue? . . . No, let's go to Keen's. . . . No, Schwartz's would be better—pig's knuckles and cold beer. No, I feel like something *really subtle*. What about Leveroni's and a lobster? . . ."

He beamed, leaning on a massive walking-stick almost as long as himself: pirouetted around it, excited.

"One at a time, Steel-trap!"

"I don't feel like eating at all," said Cooke, jerking his striped tie.

"Cooky's romantic," laughed Flodden. "Waitah! Waitah! Bring me, please, the underdone uvula of a bat—and waitah, one moment, please—I'll have just a half-portion, please, just a half-portion."

"Dry up, Flod! You make me sick."

"Well, if we're going out in serious quest of food, I'll have to take off my beautiful slippers."

"Go barefoot, Flod," said Billington, his black eyes glittering. "Wrap a sheet around you and carry a lily."

"Tush," said Flodden, and disappeared into the hall.

II.   On the way downtown, Cooke said little to his two companions, feeling that they irritated him. They were older than he. They were fairly successful hack-writers, knew the ropes, talked esoterically of the editors they knew. Certainly, they fascinated him. He liked living with them. But why the devil did they chatter so incessantly? How could they keep up, as they did, their clever patter? There seemed to be nothing serious in them—they were always laughing and smirking. Cooke, from the window of the elevated train, stared out, peered into all the house-windows. All those lives, in there! Secret, rich, mysterious. He liked to see the people moving there, inside, folding newspapers, taking pots from stoves, turning back bed covers, reaching up arms to light the gas. He liked the heavy Jewesses leaning out into the evening, apathetic, their massive breasts spread out on the cool stone, their faces like the faces of oxen. The street swarmed with children; children ragged and noisy. The vast multiplicity thrilled him and made him melancholy. There it was, so close to him, so immediate, yet he could do nothing with it! Some poison in his brain turned it all to dullness, to mud—no, worse than that, to a kind of lifeless simulacrum, a mechanical formula—as soon as he tried to touch it. Why was it? Oh, God, if he could only get hold of beauty! It was so simple a thing—this tawny evening light flung slantwise from the west through dirty streets—streets of wholesale warehouses strewn with broken crates and straw—ash cans and blown papers.

"Ah, Paree!!" Flodden exclaimed, as he stepped off the iron

stairs and tapped the sidewalk with his malacca stick. Billington was laughing.

"No, seriously, Flod! How did you do it? You aren't beautiful, you know."

"Cookie, he says I'm not beautiful. . . . A thing of duty is a boy for ever. That's the secret of my success."

Billington took Cooke's arm.

"He won't tell me how he got his gallery of mistresses in Paris. You know, those photos in his room. *'Votre Petite Amie, Dolorine.'* 'To my dear little cabbage, with all my heart, from Goo Goo.' And so forth."

"Never-never!" cried Flodden. "Betray the little darlings? *Grossly* indelicate."

They all laughed.

"All the same, Flod, I believe you bought the whole collection—of pictures, I mean—for a franc."

"Half a franc. There was nothing indecent in them, so they went cheap."

In the dark French restaurant, with its bare polished tables, its winy smell, and rows and rows of bottles and great casks, bottles tiered all the way to the ceiling, Flodden chuckled.

"My dear Bill, my poor Bill, I understand you perfectly, and sympathize with you deeply. Yes, you lack that something, that *je ne sais quoi*, which brings the bird to your hand. If you really want to know how I did it, it was like this. When I wanted a mistress, I went into the Magazin du Louvre, or the House of a Thousand Shirts, pretending to seek a hat for Madame— Madame Flodden. The hat girls are usually very pretty. Flirtations. Discreet innuendoes. Flattery. And there"—he snapped his fingers—"it was."

Anchovies—crabmeat salad—Amer Picon—how romantic! thought Cooke. He was excited by the conversation between Billington and Flodden, but was ashamed to ask questions. He would have liked to know everything about it—everything. How unbearably hot it was in here. Electric fans whirled their colored ribbons of paper. Did Flod really do that? The photos on Flod's bureau had agitated him—soiled and scented trophies of six months in Paris. Flod was lucky. Once or twice he had talked seriously about Dolorine, who had lived with him on Montmartre. They had been on a picnic together to some place near Paris where there were houses in trees. They sat in a sidewalk café drinking beer under a chestnut tree which was in bloom. Dolorine had a sad sensual face, was pale, had a habit of putting her elbows on the table and resting her chin on her hands. *"Monsieur,"* she said, *"monsieur, monsieur."* How astonishing to climb the dark tenement stairs at night with Dolorine, a French girl. Dolorine struck a match, lit the gas, and squealed. Ah! those devils! they have forgotten my milk. Oh, Toto! Your poor coffee! You will have no coffee. She squealed again, when Toto—Flod—kissed her, tipping her hat to one side and getting a feather in his eye. The bed was by the window.

Billington was talking excitedly, as he always did, his eyes sparkling and darting about, never resting anywhere for long. "It's perfectly true—I do lack something, I do. I don't know what it is—I don't really! I'm shy, but just the same women stimulate me simply extraordinarily, and I can talk to them— oh, infinitely better than I can with men. And yet I don't make the slightest impression on them! Not the slightest. Now this afternoon I went to see Celia Daggert—you know, the miniature painter. She lives on Sixty-second Street. She attracts me very much, and I should like immensely to make her fall in love with me—in which case I'd fall in love with her. Well. This afternoon she had a *terrific* effect on me—absolutely terrific. She has a quick mind—she has a kind of tired prettiness, if you know what I mean. And really, she intoxicated me. I never talked so brilliantly before in my life. I talked like a genius— like a genius! I showered epigrams—I was a chandelier-tree, showering crystal. I was *conscious* of my power—I used it up to the last notch—I was like a magician, making strange and beautiful things come out of words. I was so excited that I couldn't sit still. I stood in the middle of the floor and talked to her. Really, I'm not exaggerating at all—I'm quite detached about it. And Celia was amazed—and that was the end of it. Now how do you explain it? It's most tiresome."

"Wasting your sweetness on the desert air," said Cooke. "I think it's a mistake—you probably frightened her. I think what women like best is to have you confide in them."

Flodden slapped the table.

"Oh, Cookie, you're so nice and young! Ha, ha! What do you confide in them, Cookie? Come, now, tell us. Can't you just *hear* him, Bill, confiding in a sort of throaty, hesitating voice, you know, with his dear face turned a little away, sadly—'Nellie, if you only knew how unhappy I am!—but there! I mustn't bore you by talking about myself.' "

"The foul fiend fly away with you," growled Cooke, blushing, "and pick your pox-pit bones."

Flodden's remark hurt him and made him angry; he was silent; but he reflected that it was for just this sort of remark that he most cherished Flodden. His utter recklessness of other people's feelings and, so often, the sharpness of his perceptions! Just the sort of sharpness he himself lacked. Arrows dipped in dragon's blood. It was curious, just the same, that Flodden didn't write any better—all his ability was on the surface. Dull, facetious little pot-boilers. The humor of the comic strips. He sipped his Amer Picon.

"You haven't had your bat's uvula," said Flodden. "Waitah!" he cried, but not too loud. Then a thought struck him. "By George! I forgot to tell you, Cookie, you have an admirer—a great man admires you. Not a woman, I regret to say—no stage queen. But old man Butler, the portrait painter. I was talking with him at the Petit Pas the other night. 'Who was the boy,' he said, 'in Bill's room the other day—with the honest blue eyes? A lovely face! And of an innocence inconceivable.' He wants to meet you again—he wants you to sit for him. . . . Look at him blush! By God, he *is* innocent."

When they had finished their dinner they strolled down to

the Battery. Flodden, swinging his stick, walked ahead, singing, as if he had forgotten them. At the water's edge they sat, dangling their feet. They took their coats off, sat in silence watching the Staten Island ferries. Lights rippled on the water, and a faint east wind cooled their faces.

III.   Cooke liked to feel the strong draught blowing through the subway express, with its rubbery underground smell. A gale in a cellar. Escaped newspapers floated like ghosts from car to car, crashed against the doors, wrapped themselves round people's legs, flapped, wheeled, spread themselves out flat. Bill was talking about some poet he knew and his prowess as a swimmer. Flagrant plagiarism from Byron and Swinburne. "Powerful! I never saw anything like it. He beats the waves with tremendous, imperious arms. Yodles in the water, wallows there like a monster, like a leviathan! By God, it's wonderful to watch him. We went to Midland Beach. He absolutely *subjugates* the sea. . . . And when he comes out, hairy and immense, he runs up the sand, dances, sings, stamps, exults like a god!"

Flodden laughed.

"All the same, his poetry is rotten. Just what you'd expect, too—he wallows like a monster in a sea of spurious ecstasy— yodles a froth of evaporated cream."

Twenty-third Street, dark, was still far from quiet. A long freight train clanked slowly, red-lighted, along Death Avenue. A street car, nearly empty, brilliantly lighted, rattled under the elevated. In the arc-lighted yard, under the mangy ailanthus tree, the detective and his wife sat, silent, watching the cat sharpen its claws against the smooth bark. "Hot night," said Ezra D. Ramsden.

In the stifling room, Cooke dipped his pen and held it over the yellow page. Out of all this, out of all this, wasn't it possible to catch a single thing? He took a new blank-book from the shelf and opened the fair unspotted page. Perhaps that would be better. But it was no use—all he could think of was Flodden saying "of an innocence inconceivable," and "honest blue eyes." De Quincey didn't help him—neither did Pater. He was a failure. He'd give it up—he'd get a job. After meditating for a long while he undressed and went to bed, drawing over himself a single sheet. He heard the Ramsdens murmuring in the yard. "Well, I tell you, things like vegetables are cheaper there, but that's all." Presently he slept. He dreamed that an orange-colored moth flew heavily in through the window, and settled with wide velvet wings on the opened page of the blank-book. The orange wings covered the two pages completely. He sprang up, shut the book, and the beautiful thing was caught. When he opened the book, he found that the pages were soft orange moth-wings; and incredibly fine, indecipherable, in purple, a poem of extraordinary beauty was written there.

THE NECKTIE

"Oh, Henry, darling! My smelling salts! *Will* you be so kind?"

There it was again—that eternal headache. How did she endure it? How did she ever endure it? Her life was one long martyrdom to headaches. Headaches and jealousy. Henry jumped up and took down the small handbag from the rack. The train swayed, and in taking an involuntary step to balance himself, he trod on Charlotte's foot. She gave a faint scream—a faint middle-aged scream.

"Oh!" she wailed. "Henry!"

"My poor little Charlotte! My poor Charlotte! Is it very bad? There it is. Now you shut your eyes and try to take a nice little nap until we get to Paris. There's a whole hour. Shut your eyes, dear! . . . That's right!"

Charlotte took a deep breath at the green bottle, and a look of ineffable relief came over her suffering face. She relaxed in her corner, gave a little comfortable wriggle, and then, with an adoring look at Henry, allowed her quivering eyelids to close. Poor Charlotte! Poor, poor Charlotte! It would be a good thing if she could have a little sleep—otherwise the first night in Paris was sure to be too much for her. Far too exciting. And especially as she had been looking forward to it for so long. She would be sure to go to bed right after dinner—or was this one of the nights when she would go before, and have a tray sent up? Very likely. Weeeeeee—weeeeee—said the train. Absurdly small voices, these European trains had—like children, compared with American trains. American trains with their hoarse, coarse, lugubrious nocturnal moans. He tried to look out of the window, to see what they were passing, but it was too dark. A cluster of lights whisked by, very close, and a single light farther off, more slowly. Was it a tunnel they were coming to? No, a bridge. Rattle rattle rattle, a hollow nostalgic clatter, the voice of the void. A gully of some sort, or a small river. These European rivers were so absurdly small and neat. No—too dark to see a thing. All he could see was the reflection of his own face—his round spectacles, his round chin, his thin middle-aged hair parted in the middle. Funny ineffectual face he had, so young too for forty-five. Pity he kept so young-looking, while poor Charlotte was aging so fast. Too bad, too bad. That was what made her so jealous, of course—that, and the fact that he was so—that he was so—very attractive to women. Why was it that women liked him? It was a mystery. He had never understood it. Of course, he always dressed well—always. The high collar —and stand-up collars were so rare nowadays that they gave one a distinguished look—the black cord running to his glasses, the rich tie, the well-cut suit. But it was more than that. Too bad, too bad. And here was Paris! Here they were, almost at Paris! He must, he positively must, have a party, a celebration of some kind. If Charlotte, poor little Charlotte didn't feel up to it, why then he would go out alone. After dinner he would go out. Just for a prowl, a drink or two, and to see the gay crowds. Perhaps one of those sidewalk cafés he had heard so much about. Or even the Folies Bergères. How exciting, how delightful it would be! And what a good thing he had polished up his French! It had certainly proved perfectly adequate at the *douane*. That official had been very polite to him—very polite. And all these signs in the train were so ridiculously easy to read! *Ne pas se pencher au dehors,* for instance. Even if it weren't also given in English that would be childishly simple. *Signal d'alarme,* too—really, all one needed was a little intelligence, so many of the French words were exactly like the English ones. And this, of course, was the season for bock. Was it *un* bock or *une* bock? Oh, well, it didn't matter, so long as one made oneself understood. And these Frenchmen did most of their talking with their hands anyway—conversation was a form of physical exercise. You said bock, and then drew one hand upward from the other, indicating in the air a nice tall cold glass with an amber fluid in it. The very smile with which you said it was probably enough to suggest what it was that you wanted. Said he with a bockish smile, or smiling bockily.

Wheeeee—wheeeeee—said the train again. More lights sliding past, whole thick constellations of them, triangles, oblongs, circles and squares, Cassiopeia, the Pleiades, and Charles' Wagon. They must be getting close to Paris—closer than they thought. Perhaps they were almost there. Perhaps he ought to wake up poor Charlotte. No, let the poor child sleep. How pathetic she looked, snuggled up there in the corner with the blue cape over her knees and the green bottle getting ready to slip from her pale little hand. Here she was, almost at Paris, and still suffering, while he—while he—made his plans for a nice little party. Too bad, too bad. Was it Montmartre that one went to? Well, he would just go out and walk around, and if he got lost he could always take one of those taxis you were always hearing about. *Hotel Angleterre, s'il vous plaît.* Or was it *d'Angleterre?* No matter. *Avenue Victoria. Châtelet.* The train gave a jerk, a series of jerks, and began stopping. Henry sprang up, electrified. No, it was going on again. Suburban stations. He sat down, sighed, then reached across and gently, gently, removed the green bottle from poor Charlotte's sleeping hand. Even in her sleep she seemed to be grateful to him. And what for? For his perpetual sympathy and kindness? But could he do less for one who suffered so, one whom he loved so? Too bad, too bad. . . .

Nevertheless, it was a fact that she had aged very fast, while he—
ah, it was most unfair, most unfair. Just a little prowl, a drink
of bock, to see the foreign crowds and the Parisian lights. Just
that, or perhaps—if poor Charlotte felt up to it, of course, they
would go together and sit in a café and have a coffee. *Garçon!
Deux cafés au lait, deux.* How was it possible to begrudge her
that simple pleasure? He removed the stopper, the little green
coronet, and sniffed, once, twice, three times; the green flame
licked a corner at the very back of his brain. Whoof! . . . like a
little snake. Strange, how the odor seemed to tickle the very
medulla oblongata and to permeate one's whole consciousness.
And think of having to do that all the time, day after day, year
after year, till one was—

They were in the station, they were really stopping. He must
have fallen asleep himself.

"Charlotte! Charlotte!"

Charlotte opened bewildered and adoring eyes. Pandemon-
ium. Cape, steamer-rug, umbrellas, and three bags. He was
holding up six fingers to the porter who slung the bags one by
one on his strap. Then they were in the taxi, a garishly lighted
stone-paved square, they were passing sidewalk cafés, and green
trees imprisoned in cages. He took Charlotte's hand in his and
patted it.

"Darling! How do you feel?"

"Oh, I'm so sorry, Henry dear, to spoil it all for you! . . . I'll
have to go to bed. . . . Will you forgive me?"

"Of course I'll forgive you."

Oh! The hotel was too gorgeous, far too gorgeous. A brilliantly illuminated glass canopy, officials in green uniforms,
more officials in dress suits, obsequious porters, and a haughty
young woman at the desk who gave them their keys. Two adjoining rooms, but they regretted that there was no adjoining
bath. If there had been more warning . . . Madame would like
to see the menu? Certainly. The tray would be sent up at
once. A little *vol-au-vent* and some coffee. For two? No, mon-

sieur would come down to dinner. The dining room was just there, and he would find a table reserved. Oh, damn—he would have to dress for it. Far too gorgeous, far far too gorgeous.

However, the dinner passed off well enough. Eight-forty-five. It would now only take a jiffy to change back into ordinary clothes. Was poor Charlotte asleep? . . . He tiptoed to the door and opened it softly. Dark, and not a sound. The four-poster bed pale in the gloom, and slotted light coming through the French blinds, which swayed a little in the air that came from the Seine. Tap-tap went the blinds, and he closed the door again. Just as well he had changed in the dark—the light through the transom might have waked her. Where had he put his hat? On the bed, of course. An umbrella? No, the stars were out. A warm starlit evening in Paris, an evening in May. He began humming to himself—

> *"On a warm day in the spring*
> *Auntie sent me marketing;*
> *Birds were twittering, tra-la-la . . .*
> *Gaily twittering—"*

So this was Paris. And all these crowds in the street were French, and all these lights were the lights of Paris. Too bad poor Charlotte wasn't with him to share in the excitement. And there was the Châtelet theater, with a huge sign announcing the Ballet Russe. Too bad, too bad. He turned away from the river, and came to a broad boulevard—what could it be? Ah— the rue de Rivoli. He had heard of that, often. A famous street, a street known all over the world. To walk along the rue de Rivoli was almost *ipso facto* to become a distinguished person. Everybody looked well-dressed, especially the women— French women certainly knew how to dress. Charming hats! Delicious shoes! And they seemed to walk with such gaiety and *joie de vivre!* He fancied that one or two of them just faintly smiled at him—just faintly, but flatteringly. He too was well-dressed, a distinguished person—probably they recognized him to be a foreigner, an American, and very likely they were thinking him some very famous or wealthy man, or a diplomat. He straightened himself a little, and walked with a joyful *insouciance*—that was the word, *insouciance*. And here, just at the right moment was a café. He would have coffee.

"*Café noir*," he said, holding up one finger. And then, when it had been brought, "*Combien?*"

All very simple and nice, though it couldn't say very much for the coffee. But what next? A bus was stopping by the kerb and without the slightest hesitation he jumped on and went inside. He seated himself, and found that the bus would take him to the Etoile. Nothing could be better. The fare paid, he turned to look out at the crowded sidewalk, also regarding for a second his own reflection. Heavens! Good Lord! He had on no necktie! What could have—how could he—he remembered laying it out—it was changing in the dark that had done it! Was it possible? Yes—there was the stand-up collar, but no tie. A naked white expanse, which, even in the dim reflection afforded by the bus window, looked extremely silly. No—he mustn't put up his hand to feel it—that would draw attention to the disaster. How awful, how incredibly awful and humiliating! And what was he to do? Not even an overcoat he could put on! It was like one of those dreams in which you find yourself at a tea-party with no clothes on, and on the point of shaking hands with a duchess! All very well in a dream, but in real life! Not so funny. Shops? No. The shops were all closed at this hour. No wonder all those people had smiled at him. Flatteringly, indeed! No such luck. And that girl across the aisle was looking at him now. Good lord, how simply frightful. Impossible to stay here—he must get off, dive into a side street, preferably a dark and shabby one, and get time for reflection.

He did so, first turning up his coat lapels, and clutching them together against his throat. The conductor looked at him, astonished, frankly and physically astonished. These French had no reticences at all. Perhaps, if he kept his hand up like this, they would merely think that he had a sore throat. He walked toward the river again, along a street none too dark, and at the corner came to another café. A drink would do no harm. And there was a table behind a lattice, where he would be partially screened. Good idea. He sat down and lifted a finger toward the waiter.

"Whisky," he said.

"Large or small?" said the waiter.

"You speak English?" said Henry.

"*Un peu.*"

"A large, a very large one," said Henry.

Here was a ray of hope. Perhaps, if he explained his predicament the waiter would make some brilliant suggestion. But if not—then what on earth was he to do? Go back to the hotel? Heavens, no. Every one would see it, and they would think— and the very first night he was there, too! Impossible to get in through that garish entrance, with all those uniformed Frenchmen standing about doing nothing, without being detected; clearly impossible. Something else would have to be improvised. One of them would probably have the cheek to come right up to him and speak about it. *Pardon,* he would say, but *monsieur* has neglected his necktie. Or something like that. And then a sly smirk. . . . Good lord.

"Whisky," said the waiter.

This was the moment—but suddenly he felt shy about it. Better wait till after the next drink. But no, the longer it was left, the more difficult it was to explain. He lifted his finger again at the retreating waiter. What a blessing that he spoke English.

"A moment, waiter," he said. "Perhaps you could be so kind as to tell me where I could get a necktie."

"*Pardon?*" said the waiter.

"I have forgotten a necktie," said Henry, feeling somewhat foolish.

"*Monsieur* has forgotten something? A coffee?"

"No, a necktie! Do you understand? A necktie!"

Henry turned down his coat lapels and revealed his shame. The waiter's hand at once made an intelligent gesture in the air.

"Ah! he cried, delighted, "*monsieur* has lost his cravat! He left it behind him, perhaps—when?" He ogled Henry with an offensively knowing look. Exactly. Just what these Frenchmen *would* suppose. It became more and more obvious that it would be impossible to go back to the Angleterre until he had somehow possessed himself of a tie. He felt weary, and drank his whisky at one gulp.

"No, no, you don't understand. I was changing my clothes after dinner at my hotel and forgot to put on a necktie. Do you know where I could get one? I would be much obliged. . . ."

"*Monsieur* would like a cravat? Wait!" He dashed off to attend to a very fat Frenchman who had seated himself at a table. In a moment he was back again, skimming like a swallow. He wore a look of concentrated intelligence and held up one finger.

"If *monsieur* will wait five minutes," he said, "I can get him a cravat. Very *chic*. A little black butterfly—*comme ça*." He described two small wings in the air above Henry's empty glass. "It is mine, but *monsieur* is welcome, if he will be so kind."

"Thank you! I should be most grateful. . . . And another whisky, please."

What a relief! Poof! The strain had been on the point of becoming quite unbearable. Now he would be able to resume his joyful excursion. The hotel again seemed a friendly place, and he felt a positive affection for the burly door-porter, as if he would like to shake him by the hand. The haughty girl at the desk also: a nice girl, very accommodating. Very very nice indeed, and rather handsome, if her eyes weren't quite so protruding. Too bad, too bad. Ah—here he was, bringing the whisky in one hand and the tie—good lord, how frightful! one of those! One of those little machine-made things that hooked on to the stud! One of those abominations!

"Voilà, monsieur! Very *chic, n'est-ce pas?"* He held it off a little way, turning it admiringly. It was infinitesimal, not more than an inch and a half across, and on one wing was a spot.

"A little spot," said the waiter, apologetically, "but it will see *monsieur* safely home. As you Americans say, any port in a storm! Ha! ha!"

He proffered the revolting insect, holding it exquisitely between thumb and finger—there was nothing to do but accept it.

"Thank you, thanks ever so much," said Henry sadly. And now he would have to put it on! "Have you a mirror?"

"Inside, *monsieur.*"

Horror upon horror—with an ordinary collar it would not have been quite so bad; but with a stand-up collar it was appallingly plain to an observer that it was a made-up tie, for there were no strings. It perched on the stud with the detached air of a fly which had just alighted. How absurd! How odious! It gave him the look of a cheap comedian. Looking at himself in the mirror, through the white enamel letters which said "Amer Picon," he suddenly felt sick—positively sick. Life had again became as black as the black hole of Calcutta.

"Very nice," he murmured, "very nice. . . . I am most grateful to you."

The waiter appeared slightly chagrined—he would perhaps have enjoyed seeing a little more enthusiasm than Henry at the moment could muster.

"It is very becoming," he said.

"Oh, very," said Henry, returning gloomily to his whisky. Very becoming. But becoming what? He drank his whisky morosely, paying no attention to the crowds that flowed past. Good heavens, to think of having his first night in Paris spoiled like this. And how on earth was he to manage his return to the Angleterre? It was now worse than ever. Walk into that grand lobby, under all those lights, with this absurd little clown's necktie on? He would rather be killed: rather be killed. And on the other hand, if he stayed out late enough to escape the attentions of all save the door-porter what would Charlotte think? She would be sure to wake—she always woke when it was inconvenient for her to do so. She would look at him in that mournful way, as if she were crying in her heart of hearts, and then lie awake all night. Poor little Charlotte! A martyrdom to jealousy, and so absolutely without cause. The visit to Paris would be spoiled for her; she would always suspect him of having spent the evening in the darkest of iniquity. . . .

Well, there was no use in staying *here*, anyway—he could hardly ask the waiter for *another* tie. Of course, he was less exposed here; but then he couldn't just go on sitting all night. It was already ten o'clock as it was. Charlotte might be waking at any time and looking at her watch and then coming to his room to see if he had come back. Henry! are you here? Henry? . . . No Henry. No Henry for a long while yet, either. Better wander down to the river and then perhaps across to the other side—that was the Latin Quarter, and there perhaps they were more used to seeing middle-aged gentlemen who wore peculiar neckties. There would also be other cafés, where he might again try his luck. . . . A pity, too, when it was such a lovely spring night, so ideal for his first sight of the gay night-life of Paris. Good gracious, how disgusting it all was, a trifle like this upsetting everything. It was like a shabby little episode on the vaudeville stage, with himself as the ridiculous victim, laughed at by everyone. Well, at least he could turn up his coat collar again, though even that didn't really conceal this poisonous little monstrosity. . . . No—there was a girl giggling at him this very minute! The strumpet! As for finding some *nice* girl and having a drink or two—quite innocently—before going home, that was now out of the question. Or almost. And he had rather looked forward to some such little adventure as that—just a little conversation—so interesting to see how life is lived in a foreign city. One of these midinettes you were always hearing about, so gay and carefree, so unselfish and warm-hearted! But no, it was impossible to look anyone in the eye, as long as he had on a tie like this. The brand of Cain, or the mark of the beast, or something.

He crossed the bridge. Ah, yes—there were the quayside bookstalls. How romantic to be sure. Oh, for a stall that sold neckties! He wandered on disconsolately, entered a wider street, a boulevard, and came then to some gardens, very pretty, with lights among green leaves of trees. Were these the Luxembourg Gardens? Very pretty, very pretty, and what a place for making love, as all these young people had discovered. My, my, that soldier and his girl. He began humming again

"On a warm day in the spring—"

but stopped at once. Impossible to be light-hearted. If it were only his carfare he wanted, that would be quite simple—he could beg, simply beg, till he found someone who believed his story. But beg for a necktie, at this hour! Could anything be more preposterous? He sat on a bench under a tree, shaded from a lamp, and pondered darkly on his singular misfortune. The sort of thing which one could not possibly have foreseen— who could have imagined it? Such misery to arise from a cause so very slight? *"Oui oui oui oui!"* cried a man's voice, and *"Non non non non!"* cried a girl's in answer, laughing. Well, *that* was easy to understand. That was indeed a kind of Esperanto. He rose again, and in a dark spot under an avenue of trees, suddenly plucked off the nefarious little tie and flung it away into the night. At least be rid of that, and start afresh. Somebody would find it tomorrow and wonder. As for him self—

The cellar café looked attractive—the sort of place you saw in movies, with Apaches dancing wildly. But there were no Apaches, and in fact no customers at all. Oh, yes, a girl at the counter on a high stool, drinking coffee. He had thought at first she was one of the staff, but he saw now that she had on a kind of tam-o'-shanter.

"Whisky," he said to the sleepy waiter, holding up one finger.

"Whisky," the waiter repeated sadly, and hobbled away behind the counter, shuffling his red carpet slippers on the stone floor. A martyr to his feet. Too bad, too bad. At the word "whisky" the girl lifted her coffee-glass from the counter and turned around. Dark excited eyes, very large, very dark. Very pretty indeed, and quite young. French, of course. Why so excited? Was she drunk? No, no. You never could tell with these French, they always looked so excited even when sober. Besides, she was drinking coffee. She tilted her glass and drank, eyeing him over the rim. My goodness—that was a dangerous look; the kind of look that wrecks empires. Ah! she had turned away again. Perhaps she had seen that he had no necktie. Confound. *Slip-slap—slip-slap*—came the old sleepy waiter, hobbling in his carpet slippers, with trouser-legs, much too long, lying in laps on his insteps. Advancing with a series of painful jerks, his activity seemed tremendous; but his progress was slow.

"Whisky," he said, putting down the glass, and almost at the same moment the girl at the counter turned and spoke.

"*Un café, garçon,*" she said.

"*Oui, mademoiselle.*"

Those dark eyes again! Too marvelous! And looking with such—with such—demoralizing good humor—into his own! He raised his glass toward her and smiled. She smiled in answer; and then, when he beckoned, she slid down from her stool and came toward him with slow steps. Black satin slippers with silver buckles. A broad scarlet sash, from which a streamer fell at one side. He rose, put out his hand, bowed elegantly, and was on the point of saying "*Bon jour*" (which hardly seemed appropriate) when she, smiling delightfully (and a little shyly) exclaimed—

"Hello, American!"

Well, now! What was one to say to that?

"You knew I was American? You speak English?"

She shrugged her shoulders extravangantly and sat down. She looked at him with her dark good-natured eyes, she looked down at the table, from which she picked up a dead match, and then again looked humorously at him, this time obliquely.

"Not much," she said. "A little. I can read."

She clasped her slender hands under her chin.

"You will permit me to pay for your coffee, *mademoiselle?*"

"If you like."

"Would you care for a glass of wine? or an Amer Picon?"

"No—I do not drink. Coffee only. *Merci.*"

"Coffee is bad for you. How can you sleep?"

"Sleep! I sleep all day. Till two—three—in afternoon!"

"No!"

"Oui oui!"

Slip-slap the waiter again, bearing coffee, and Henry paid for it. The waiter beamed upon them and murmured his thanks. How nice of him not to be surprised. How very nice of him, and how nice everything was—sitting in Paris, in this Apache place, with such a charming girl, and all so innocent too! It was delightful, an experience to remember all one's life. But suddenly he remembered his necktie. Ah—he would tell her about it. It would amuse her.

"I am in trouble," he said, smiling, "very serious trouble."

"You are in trouble?"

She smiled doubtfully, seeing that he smiled, but at the mention of trouble her dark eyes (magnificent!) had grown even darker with a beautiful swiftness of sympathy.

"You are in trouble, great trouble? It would be good to speak of it?"

"Great, great trouble. . . . I have forgotten to put on a neck-tie."

"You have forgotten to—?"

"Put on a necktie—a cravat."

He raised his hand to his naked collar, parting his coat lapels. She opened her eyes very wide, very wide, and they grew intensely bright, as if whole chandeliers had been lighted in them.

"Oh!" she cried. "How droll! *Monsieur* has forgotten to wear a cravat!"

"Exactly—a cravat!"

She began to laugh, with a soft dovelike sound, leaning forward on the table. She put her hand on top of his, just for a second, quick as a wing.

"Oh, how droll!" she cried. "How funny it makes you look!"

"But it is serious! I can't go back to my hotel!"

"Comment?"

She didn't at once fathom this.

"I can't go back to my hotel. . . . What would they think? It is very, very serious!"

"Serious? Ah! . . ." She stared at him, sobering, her eyes resuming their natural look of melancholy good-humor. She still smiled a little, however. "You are married, perhaps," she then added.

"Yes, married. And what would the *concierge* think?"

"Ah, I see. It is very serious. Life and death. You will be disgrace."

"Disgrace! You bet I will."

Her eyes twinkled with delicious malice, and she was on the point of laughing again, but instead she picked up the dead match and touched with it the edge of his sleeve.

"No," she said, "I will save you. If you will be so kind and give me one more coffee."

"You will save me!" His heart gave a great bound of joy. "Waiter! *Garçon! Un café! Et whisky!* . . . But how?"

She waved the match before him, mysterious.

"You will see," she said. "I suprise you! Ha ha! How funny you are!"

She gave a wriggle of delight, shaking her dark head. Was she laughing at him? But no, it was sympathetically. She tittered, and took a sip of coffee, and tittered again. Henry shook his finger at her sternly.

"You are making fun of me!" he said. "Now, now!"

"Non, non, but it is so droll! . . . and I will save you from this disgrace—this—how you say *épouvantable?"*

"Frightful?"

"—this frightful disgrace! You must thank me. Yes, you must!"

"Thank you! I should say I would! . . . But how are you going to save me?"

"You have finish your whisky? All right. You go, and wait outside, not far. In a minute I come too. It is not good to see me go out with you. *Comprenez?* I stay and finish my *café.*"

What a delicious turn of fortune! And such a nice girl! Still, it was high time that *something* turned up, and time he was back at the hotel. What must poor Charlotte be thinking? Heavens! He walked fifty yards away from the café, and then turned and walked slowly back. Twenty minutes past eleven. Too late— far too late. Otherwise he might ask her to come out to supper with him somewhere, or to a dance-hall—what fun that would be! But no. This necktie business must be settled, and he must hurry back. Damnation. Life was always like this. Just as something nice and interesting occurred, destiny must intervene with some pressing engagement or responsibility which could not be ignored. Or else the event occurred when, as in this case, you were not in a proper state of mind for it—obsessed with something else. Too bad, too bad. And how thrilled Charlotte would be when she heard about it! But no—on second thought, she had better not hear about it. Goodness no—she would become insanely jealous, and wouldn't believe a word of it! One of her mute reproachful spells, a four days' headache, tears falling drop by drop in her secret romantic heart of hearts, and then a protracted and exhausting reconciliation. Poor, poor Charlotte—life was so hard for her; and the least he could do was to try and make it a little more bearable. . . . Ah! There she was! Coming with a little skip of joy, like a chamois! How young she looked, too! Not a day over twenty-five!

"Here I come!" she cried, taking his arm affectionately. "My room is over there—behind that corner. You can climb?"

"Climb?"

"Stairs? . . . Five stairs—one, two, three, four, five—poof!"

"Well, I think I might!"

"Come then! I go first. It is dark, a little."

They had crossed a moonlit stone-paved court and entered a

cavelike doorway, and were climbing the gas-lighted stone stairs.
The last flight was completely dark, and she disappeared ahead
of him, her slippers going *pat-pat* on the dusty stone. He was
trying to feel his way along the wall when a match spurted, the
gas went *puff*, and he was flooded with light from her open door.
She was standing there, with a finger on her lips; and when he
had entered the low attic room, with sloping walls, she closed
the door behind him.

"My friend below asleep," she said. "You like my room? Nice,
eh?"

"Delightful! Geraniums, too."

"And nice curtains, and a nice bed?"

"Charming!"

"Ah, you are frightful! You don't look, you don't like it,
and you think only of your cravat! Egoist!"

"No no!"

"*Oui oui!* But see—I have pity on you. Look now."

She pulled out the top drawer of a chest of drawers, clutching
him by the sleeve. "Look!"

Well! You could have knocked him down with a feather!
Astounding! The drawer was *filled* with neckties! Every kind!
Striped, plain, diamonded, knitted—two dozen at the very
least! It was like Christmas—he could feel the eyes fairly popping out of his head.

"Choose one," she said, thrusting her hand among ties as one
might dip among goldfish in an aquarium. "You like this
one?"

She held up a heavy blue satin, luxuriously thick.

"Ah!" he cried, "a beauty! It's beautiful. May I have it? You
will let me buy it from you?"

"Buy it?" She looked blankly at him. "Buy it?"

He held the tie in his hand. She turned her shoulder against
the drawer and slowly pushed it shut. Taking off her tam-o'-
shanter, she flung it angrily on the bed. Then, leaning against
the drawer, she looked at him with narrowing eyes, standing
perfectly still.

"Oh," she said, looking at him with an extraordinary in tensity of detachment. "You would like to buy it."

"Why, of course! Why not?"

"Certainly *not!*" she cried, stamping her foot. "You can put it on and go! I *give* it to you."

"Oh!" he stammered, suddenly perplexed. "What have I——'

"Put it on and go! *Quick!*"

"I beg your pardon!" he cried. "I didn't mean——"

"Here! Give it to me."

She snatched the tie, whisked it round his collar, tied it swiftly, tucked the ends under his waistcoat, and then went lightly to the door and threw it open. She pointed dramatically down the stairs. As he hesitated, she gave him a little push. She was smiling: ironically, cynically, with an infinite contempt.

"You will not permit me to see you again?"

"Good night!"

"*Mademoiselle,* forgive me! And let me thank you!"

"Good night!"

"You will not even shake hands with me?"

"Good night!"

Implacable, she began slowly shutting the door. In the narrowing crack of light he descended, keeping close to the wall, which smelt of damp white-wash. His heart was beating with uncomfortable violence. . . . Well! . . . Well! . . . Who could have foreseen—who could have guessed—that it would be like that! He had offended her! She had expected—had she expected him to—make love to her? No, no. It was just that he had been— had been—*too greedy!* Seeing all those ties in that drawer! . . . Oh, oh, oh. And it had been so nice talking to her, and perhaps he would have asked her to come out to supper with him—

He stood still in the court for a moment, still breathing a little fast. The moon was shining. The light from her attic room gashed across a tiled roof opposite, and a shadow moved in the gash of light. . . . Well! He had his necktie. And it would really have been too late, anyway. Perhaps it was just as well. . . . Too bad, too bad.

O HOW SHE LAUGHED!

It was a minor episode in my life—happened when I was taking my examinations for college—and I will tell it briefly.

My family—which consisted of my father, my mother, and my brother Phil—had just moved to a rather shabby little boarding-house in Oxford Street. It was one of our recurring periods of poverty: the "old man" was always impractical; just as we had really got our heads once more above water he would buy a lot of worthless securities, and down we would go again, from a house to a flat, from a flat to a boarding-house. Phil and I never understood these remarkable alternations of fortune: but I suppose my mother did—poor thing—well enough. Anyway, when my father died, a few years ago, we found that he had accumulated, during his life, a good-sized trunkful of beautifully engraved and embossed securities which weren't worth a penny. There were enough of them to paper the walls of a house, and they would have looked very well.

Neither my father nor mother were particularly "social," and it was therefore all the more surprising that, in the Oxford Street lodgings, they should so suddenly have made friends of the Lyntons. We all sat at one long table, of course, like a

Last Supper—and some sort of acquaintance with the other boarders was inevitable; but we had survived many such exposures, before, without making any friends. The Lyntons, however, seemed from the outset to amuse my father (who was rather a shy man) inordinately. I think my mother was not so convinced—for she was a queer, bitter sort of frustrated "high-brow," and very critical—but even she, for once, unbent a little. In a very short time, an extraordinary intimacy had sprung up between the Lyntons and the Beebes which, if it involved my mother and father more than Phil and myself, nevertheless involved us too.

In fact, almost the first thing I remember about the life at Oxford Street was going to a circus with the Lyntons—a party so incredibly gay and frivolous that Phil and I, who were more accustomed to seeing the old people play cribbage, or now and then, in a wild moment, poker (the chips being broken matches, the stakes nil), were absolutely staggered. And Mrs. Lynton was the life of the party. Mr. Lynton was a good laugher—a very good laugher. His foxy eyes would close themselves up into watery slits, his beautifully pointed Vandyke beard would prod at his necktie, he would wriggle to and fro and emit far-off falsetto cries, and become quite helpless—especially when it was Mrs. Lynton who had provided the cause.

But Mrs. Lynton was better still. O how she laughed! She laughed at the elephants, she laughed at the kangaroos, she laughed at the monkeys, at the clowns—she had only to roll her brown horse-chestnut eyes at Mr. Lynton, and he too collapsed almost into the sawdust—even my father succumbed, and my staid intellectual mother. It was only Phil and myself who got rather tired of this surprising and sudden and motiveless gayety. Eventually we struck rather a false note in the party by adopting (in taciturn unison) a stubborn silence. . . . The older people thought we were prigs.

And that circus lasted us for days. No meal passed without three or four hilarious passages devoted to it. A mere word sufficed to set them off.

"And *do* you remember that little monkey with the pink behind?" Mrs. Lynton would say, and it would all begin over again.

"And the kangaroo skipping softly in and out under that little door!"

"And the smells! the smells! the smells!"

"And the way that clown would spit into the bottle!"

Whereupon Mr. Lynton would shut up his eyes and bury his little brown beard in his chest, and Mrs. Lynton would become extraordinarily girlish, and my poor father would become positively foolish. And Phil and I, exchanging covert sorrows, would decide to be glum, if only for the preservation of decency.

Apparently, the Lyntons were as poor as we were. Mr. Lynton was an architect, with an office of his own, but no business. Mrs. Lynton was an artist, with a little studio in Joy Street, to which she went every day, always bringing back with her a new sunset or landscape. I thought her pictures were terrible, and never was in the least surprised that she couldn't sell them. So far as I know, she never *did* sell them—not one. But every night when she returned to Oxford Street, there would be a new canvas under her arm; and every night, just before dinner, we all had to file into the Lyntons' room, where the new masterpiece would be tilted on a chair, or on the carefully propped pillows of the bed, and with an air of mystery and secrecy we would have to put our heads on one side and say, "Wonderful! Marvelous! That effect of shadow among the trees! The delicious sense of distance! . . . Was it an actual scene somewhere? Oh, done from a note? from memory? It's beautiful!" And I could feel my father uneasily wondering whether the Lyntons expected him to buy it, and how much it would cost, and groping for phrases about painting (of which he didn't know a thing), and then we would have a cup of fruit punch, and go down to dinner.

Both my father and mother thought Mrs. Lynton was captivating—simply captivating! My father perhaps a little more

than my mother. Now and then it seemed to me I detected a
note of faint scepticism on the part of my mother. "Isn't she
charming? ridiculous?" my father would say, "she's like a
child. She's never grown up. . . ."

Which was perfectly true. She was nothing if not playful.
Playful was her middle name. She had more facial tricks than I
ever remember to have seen in a single creature. She rolled
those great conscious eyes to every point in the compass—arched
her careful eyebrows singly or together, blushed at will—to
give a touch of girlish modesty to some outrageous statement—
pouted, frowned, or looked hurt like a spanked baby—and all
with an air of entire assurance. She assumed that she was the
best be-all and end-all of existence. Not that she wasn't pretty!
—she was. Her small face was really quite charming. But that
she should so perpetually consider it necessary to behave like a
girl of ten, and take it for granted that everyone would be enslaved to her, as her husband was—this increasingly infuriated
both Phil and myself. It was evident that she thought herself
a great artist, and that her husband thought so, too.

But did he?

One night after dinner Phil burst into my room, where I
was pegging away at a problem in specific gravity, and said,
with a scared face—

"Come upstairs, boy. Say, they're having the hell of a row!"

"Who?"

"The laughing hyenas."

We sprinted up the stairs and listened. Phil's room adjoined
the Lyntons'. Sure enough, I could hear Mrs. Lynton—not
laughing, for once—but actually crying. I was astounded. I was
embarrassed. She was crying hysterically, and trying to talk at
the same time, her voice rising and falling with extraordinary
fluctuations and breaks and changes.

"No—no—no—no—" she said, "go away from me, don't
touch me! you've broken my spirit! I'll never paint again! I
hate you, go away, go away!" And then more sobs, and unin-
telligible murmurs, and then Mr. Lynton's voice, quite sur-

prisingly harsh and loud—as if he suddenly turned, as it were, "at bay"—

"Shut up! . . . I'm tired of having to treat you like a child! Why in God's name don't you grow up? Stop being a damned kitten!"

"I'm *not* a kitten. You know it's just my nature!"

"Nature? it isn't *human* nature!"

We could hear Mr. Lynton's footsteps pacing the floor, to and fro, to and fro, and it was as if we could actually see him, with his hands in his pockets, and his beard pressed firmly down on his necktie.

"Why are you so cruel to me? You know I only try to be happy!"

"Idiot! . . . You're driving me mad. Your happiness is just plain selfishness, that's what it is! What in *hell* do you ever think of but yourself? Not *me* certainly. All I exist for is to appreciate you. I have to be amused by you. Good God, I've had to flirt with you publicly for fifteen years, and I'm sick of it. Your whole life has just been one long promiscuous flirtation with the whole damned Western Hemisphere! . . . What kind of a life is that for *me*?"

"You're a brute, that's what you are; you're a sadist! You don't love me any more, that's what it is! And you want to stop me from painting! And you want to get rid of me!"

There was a silence, as if both of them were standing still. Then abruptly the door slammed, and we heard steps rushing down the stairs. In a moment Mrs. Lynton began to sob, more loudly than ever; and Phil and I crept back to my room to discuss this amazing turn of events. Words failed us. The event stupefied us. We decided that all was not well in Denmark, and let it go at that.

And the very next night—as if nothing at all had happened —we were all invited to go to Mrs. Lynton's studio in Joy Street for a Patriot's Day party.

At dinner, the Lyntons were as hilarious as ever. Mrs. Lynton was bubbling over with her comic misadventures in the preparations for the celebration—Chinese lanterns had caught fire, a beer bottle had exploded frothily over the fireplace, two of the eggs had been bad, and had smelled like Roman catacombs, mice had eaten half the sardines, and so on, and so on. She rolled her brown eyes, grimaced, was arch and moody by turns, became almost tearful as she told us of the sardines—poor little things—and my father and Mr. Lynton fairly crowed with delight. Phil and I looked at her with renewed wonder.

And the whole party went off in that fashion. Never was a studio so consciously arty. There were no chairs at all—only black cusions on a scarlet floor—and we had to squat round the hearth and toast marshmallows at the wood-fire (though it was a very warm night) and another lantern blazed up, and the sardines (what remained of them) were rancid—but everything was made into one huge, uproarious, continuous joke. Paintings were stacked everywhere; and it seemed to me that a little —perhaps commercial?—pressure was being put upon my poor ignorant father to look at every one of them. In fact, we all had to look at them. They were stood for us in every conceivable light: autumn trees, violet sunsets, marshes in moonlight, haystacks on Cape Cod, cranberry bogs, wharfs, dories hauling up nets—water-colors, oils, crayons, every damned kind of picture that I ever heard of. And all of them atrocious. We went through the vocabulary of praise till it was worn to a fiber. "Wonderful! Marvelous! . . . Did you do this one recently? . . . It seems to me your sense of color has deepened. . . . And that aerial perspective, that effect of fog!" Though I myself ventured only a few scared words, my throat began to feel as parched as if I'd been ten days on a desert. And all the while Mrs. Lynton was coquettish and playful, laughed girlishly, wrung her hands, was so pleased with everything—wasn't it a sweet little studio? A sweet view over the river and the bridge? And what a lark to have to sit on the floor like Indians! And to eat rotten little fishes! . . .

It was then that the shock, the terrible shock, of pure hard reality occurred, and from the most unexpected quarter.

My mother was looking at a painting of a sandy beach, with grass-covered dunes and lobster-pots, all done in a purple light that never was, thank God, on land or sea.

"But isn't that a little gem?" said Mr. Lynton. "Isn't it a *marvel?*"

"I particularly like the sand," crowed Mrs. Lynton. "And do you know why it's so good, so sandlike?"

"Just feel it, Mrs. Beebe," said Mr. Lynton, positively purring through his beard, "it even *feels* like sand!"

My mother felt of the beach, sceptically.

"Now, doesn't it?" cried Mrs. Lynton. "And do you know why?"

"No," said my mother, a little coldly, and drawing back from the easel. "Why?" Her voice was curiously flat.

"Because I mixed sand with the paint!"

This was a dramatic moment: we were expected to be impressed. It was, as it were, the very last word an æstheticism. The Lyntons glowed at us. They waited with delighted eagerness for our praise, our astonishment. But instead my mother became all at once quite acid.

"I'm afraid," she said, "I think that's just sentimental nonsense. Do you want to scratch matches on it?"

It was as if a torpedo had been exploded in the room. Mr. Lynton walked toward the window and blew his nose. My father looked sheepish. And in an instant the whole party had obviously come to an end—the gayety seemed false, the studio looked tawdry, we all felt poor and miserable, there was nothing to say. We drank the bad coffee, which Mrs. Lynton presently brought us, vainly endeavored to make her talk or laugh again, and then, a little later, went home.

That was the end of the curious intimacy between the Lyntons and the Beebes. A week later, the Lyntons moved away from Oxford Street. And six months later, we learned from the *Herald* one morning that Mrs. Lynton had died of pneumonia. I believe a note of condolence was written, and was never answered—and we never saw Mr. Lynton again.

WEST END

It was five o'clock, dark, and beginning to drizzle. I crossed Oxford Street by the Marble Arch, wondering what to do—for I had no raincoat—and my eye fell on the signboards of a small cinema theater. There was an early Chaplin film—"The Pawnshop"—and I could think of no better way of passing an hour; so without hesitation I approached the woven-wire *guichet*, pushed a shilling and two coppers through the little pigeonhole, received a metal ticket in exchange, and walked into the dark theater. A color-film was on the screen—and a string quartet, with a tinny piano, was playing, or trying to play, the "Unfinished Symphony." I sank into the seat illuminated by the usher's electric torch, lit a cigarette, and watched a procession of muleteers descending a rocky gorge. It was somewhere in Spain. The rocks were red, glaucous prickly-pears leaned above them, the donkeys picked their way down a winding pathway, with wagging bells. The riders, sitting astride the little beasts, and wearing wide-brimmed hats, looked enormous by comparison. They came to a ford—the water was beautifully green. The donkeys plunged in with no sign of alarm save that they put back their ears; and then, floundering out on the farther bank, among broken rocks and poppies, wound in single file through an orchard of cherry trees, which were in bloom. The colors were excellent—the trees looked as if they were foaming. I stretched out my legs, relaxed, and began watching the film with that dazed and hypnotized fascination with which one always watches an ever-changing motion. As one follows the flowing of a stream, with its innumerable sparkles and fluctuations of shadow and gleam, so I followed this soundless cataract of adventure in Andalusia. London, and February in London, and my engagement for the evening with the Proctors, became remote and unreal.

It was after half an hour or so of this state of abstraction that I became aware of the woman who sat on my left. I had felt a sort of stealthy pressure from her—very much as if she were trying to pick my pocket; and on looking down sharply to see what she was doing, I found that she had dropped her right hand over the arm of the chair, allowing it to rest against my side. I looked quickly then at her face, which, in the dim light, I could see to be that of a woman middle-aged. She knew that I was observing her, but she made no effort to withdraw her hand. Instead, after a moment, she leaned more closely toward me, so that her elbow pressed hard against mine. At the same moment, also, with the least perceptible motion of her face and eyes, she stole a quick glance at me, simultaneously giving a discreet little middle-aged cough.

My first feeling was one of cynical amusement. I withdrew, as gently and inoffensively as I could; and then it occurred to me that this was rather heartless. Besides, I was curious. So without more ado, I took out my cigarette case and offered her a cigarette. She accepted it with a quietly said "Thank you," I lighted it for her, she slipped her arm through mine, and we began a desultory conversation about the film. She didn't like Chaplin—she thought he was vulgar; but she liked Harold Lloyd. She was very fond of Theda Bara, and of the vampire type of film in general. She told me that Theda Bara had been born on an oasis in the Sahara Desert. She thought she had a marvelously beautiful mouth, and that she looked as if she were very passionate. I countered by saying that my own favorite movie-actress was Mary Pickford. At this point, Charlie was taking the alarm clock to pieces on the counter of the pawnshop. I laughed, and she gave me a look of tolerant disdain.

"How *can* you see anything funny in it," she said.

I replied that I thought he was simply delicious.

Her answer to this was a disquieting squeeze of my arm. It became apparent that she was going to make love to me. The idea was not in the least attractive—it struck me as grotesque. For an instant, I felt trapped; a kind of amused panic seized me; I wondered how on earth I was going to get out of the situation. I had cruelly misled the poor thing—it would be impossible for me simply to get up and walk away. I thought rapidly, and then suggested that we go out and have tea, or a drink.

"Don't you want to stay here?" she said.

"No, I'm thirsty. And I've seen this picture before."

She hesitated, as if disappointed.

"All right," she said. "I've had my tea, but I wouldn't mind having a glass of port."

She rose, clasping the feather boa round her neck, and we went down the aisle to the emergency-exit at the left of the stage. Pushing through the heavy plush curtains, we found ourselves in a bare stone corridor. It was here that I had my first good look at her. She was a woman of about fifty—small, shabby, pathetic, fadedly genteel. When they were new, her brown satin dress and tweed coat must have been "good"; but now they looked weather-beaten. Her shoes were scarred and down at the heel; her stockings (which passed for white) were mud-spattered; the feather boa had moulted about half of its feathers.

I took in all this as I held the door open for her; and I found myself smiling at her in an effort to conceal my real feelings. I was terribly afraid that she would guess my attitude—that she would be hurt. Would she imagine—and justly—that I was somewhat chagrined at finding myself in such company? I smiled, therefore, to encourage her; and I must admit that I smiled also because there was something in her face and in her tired blue eyes which moved me to sympathy. It was a dilapidated face—red where it should have been white, and white where it should have been red—but for all its dilapidation it was a face not without charm, and must once have been pretty. Pretty, but weak. Charming, but destined for defeat. Life had been too much for her; and she had become (I could see at a glance) one of that countless army of semi-respectable women who frequent, after nightfall, the "family bar". . . . She smiled back at me, affectionately, taking my arm; and we scuttled round the corner to the King's Head. It was raining hard. The idea of sitting in a warm pub, and drinking port, was not unpleasant.

There was a small green baize table in one corner of the private bar—an aspidistra plant stood on it (in a horribly ornate sham-majolica pot) and an empty glass ringed with the brown froth of stout. I removed the glass, and brought in its place two large ports.

"This is the kind of night," I said, "when port tastes good. Even port from the wood. Any port in a storm."

"Don't you like port from the wood?"

"Not as a rule—it's too sweet."

"Oh, I *like* it sweet," she said.

She took off her black gloves and lifted the glass to her lips.

"The port they have here is good," she added. "I often come here. Whenever I go to that cinema, I come here afterward."

"And do you go often to the cinema?" I asked.

"Oh, yes—three or four times a week."

"You mean you go and see the same pictures over again? . . . How on earth do you stand it!"

She gave a little embarrassed laugh—the kind of laugh that must, when she was younger, have been accompanied by a blush—and looked down at the table, turning the stem of the glass between her fingers.

"I don't go there for pleasure," she said.

"Oh—I see."

There was an awkward pause. I tasted my port.

"What's the use pretending?" she then went on. "You can see what I am, and I'm not ashamed of it, either. You've got to live, somehow, and I suppose there are worse ways."

I murmured that I supposed there were, but that it must have taken a great deal of courage. To this she demurred.

"Courage? Oh, no. Not now. At the beginning, yes, but not now. I'm a hardened old sinner. . . ."

II.   She unclasped the feather boa from her neck and flung it rather sharply into the empty chair beside her—like a gesture of defiance. At the same time she gave me a quick little grimace of a smile, which was intended to be arch. The corners of her mouth at once, however, drooped into their natural expression of gentle petulance; and I found myself smiling back at her a little too long. She then took a rouge-stick from her handbag and began touching her lips with it.

"Not that it does any good," she said, looking up at my slyly. "The port will wash it off. . . . How old do you think I am?"

I guessed, as flatteringly as I could, after submitting her to a friendly inquisition of inspection; and she told me that she was fifty-three. On my expressing my disingenuous surprise, she added that she was married and had a boy of fifteen. I was impressed.

"Somehow, you don't look like a mother," I said.

"Don't I? . . . I'm a good mother, just the same, if I do say it as shouldn't."

I asked her if her husband and boy lived with her. She said that the boy did, but not her husband. He had been a bad egg from the beginning. He was in the army—and it was when he was sent out to India that the trouble had started. His idea was that he would send for them after a while, but he had never done so. He wrote to her very seldom, and sent her very little money. She supposed he was having love affairs with "brown girls," and spending it all on them. Anyway, she began to be hard up. And she didn't know where he was.

"Of course, I may say it was a relief to both of us," she said. "He was always drinking when he was home, and betting on the horses. It wasn't much of a life. . . ." She gave her empty glass a little insinuating push toward me, with two fingers. "Get me another, will you—like a good boy?"

I took her glass and had it refilled at the bar. As I sat down again, I said something about the problem of "separation" in marriage—the way it leads to alienation. She looked at me cynically, or with a look that was intended to be cynical: but the narrowed lids, which were red at the edges, and the wandering blue eyes, failed to convey the desired effect. The attempt at a pose of refined cynicism was pathetic.

"Nothing of that," she said. "I was as glad to be shut of him as he was to be shut of me. As a husband, he was a fair washout."

"So now you and the boy live together," I said. "I should think that would make complications."

She shook her head, doubtfully; and then went into a kind of abstraction. She gazed over the table at the sawdust-sprinkled floor, sucking in her lower lip. The port was beginning to flush her faded cheeks, and to give her (I could see) that kind of bemused feeling of well-being in which one becomes totally indifferent to one's surroundings. She was remembering something, and wondering whether she was too bored to talk about it. Perhaps, also, she was remembering how often before she had thus talked about her life to strangers. But what did it matter? It didn't matter at all. It wasn't of any consequence. You lived indifferently, and you talked about it indifferently. Either way, the thing was hopeless, but also rather amusing. You might as well talk as not.

She began talking again, therefore, with her eyes still oddly fixed. She talked as if I were an accident, a mere nonentity. The complications had existed, she said, only at the beginning

—and then the boy was too young to know what it was all about. Nowadays, it was different. But there had been some funny things at the beginning. She gave a chuckle, and looked at me appraisingly—as if she wanted me to ask her what these funny things had been. I smiled, and she smiled back. We exchanged, as it were, an unspoken agreement about the excessively odd things that life will do. Life was, indeed, riotously funny. The idea brightened in her eyes, and she began to laugh.

"You'd never guess," she said, "what started me off."

I admitted the hopelessness of this. It occurred to me to begin improvising, extravagantly, on this theme, but I was afraid it would fall flat, or throw her off. So I merely shook my head and admitted it again.

"It was seeing all those West End tarts," she said.

"What?"

She repeated the remark, paused, laughed, and then elaborated it. It was when she was feeling very blue, she said. No money coming from Mac—her husband—and no other way of getting any. It was costing more to live, too, with the boy growing up. Saving on gas and food didn't do any good. She'd always been a bit of a fool—couldn't even mend a frock properly—couldn't fancy herself going into "the service." But she had to do something. And one night, when she was wandering round in Piccadilly Circus, seeing all those West End tarts in their satin slippers, the idea had occurred to her. She had been in the habit, she said, of haunting Piccadilly Circus—she liked to see the crowds, and she had nothing else to do in the evening. She couldn't go on reading the newspapers all day, could she? I admitted, cheerfully enough, that she couldn't. So she took to haunting the region of Piccadilly Circus. And she was infuriated by seeing the West End tarts. They were having such a good time—they were so well-dressed—they always had somewhere to go and something to do. They went to the best restaurants, and rode in taxis. It was seeing all this that put the idea in her head.

"It came to me all of a sudden," she said. "I just stood still and said to myself, why shouldn't I be a West End tart? . . . And I couldn't think of any reason why I shouldn't."

She put her head on one side, and looked at me distantly. The pause was rhetorical—she wanted me to appreciate the immensity of this decision. It had been astonishing—she seemed to say—but also it had been entirely natural. Nothing in the world could have been *more* natural. The only wonder was that she hadn't thought of it before. Nothing (said the tilt of her head) could have been so obvious. . . .

"So that was that," I said, with perhaps a trace of heartless flippancy.

She was annoyed, but annoyed only fleetingly: nettled. I wasn't to think it was as easy as that. Not at all. It might have been easy to make the decision—to act upon it was another matter.

"I couldn't think how to go about it," she said.

"Naturally," I replied.

She added that if you'd been brought up a lady, it wasn't so easy. How could she begin? She tried to pick up men in the streets, but it was no good. They were always the wrong sort of men, and they looked so horrible staring at her from under their hats. At the crucial moment, she always got frightened and walked on. She would hold her breath, and if she heard them coming after her, she would run. I was asked to imagine what it must have been like. I imagined it, and lighted another cigarette for her. It was as if together we watched her nocturnal maneuvers in Shaftesbury Avenue and Regent Street, her pauses in dark doorways, her uncertain hoverings at the corners.

"It wasn't any good," she said. "I decided it wasn't my line. I had to think of something else."

She narrowed her eyes at me, partly to screen them from the cigarette smoke, partly in an effort to assume the appearance of a person very wise and very resigned. I assumed the same pose, and said that she ought to have known that she was not the kind of woman for that sort of thing—she was obviously far too refined. She nodded, acquiescing.

"I decided to try the Café Bonaparte. You know the Bonaparte?"

I told her that I knew it only too well.

"You know what it's like, then," she said. "I didn't—except from hearing about it. But I was told that it would be very easy there. So one night I went."

She indulged in a sour little retrospective smile, the corners of her mouth sharply turned down. Then she looked off toward the dark window of the bar, on which the rain was beating.

"The question was what to do with the boy. You see? I couldn't leave him at home all evening alone. So I took him along with me."

"To the Bonaparte?"

She gave me a withering look, and then shook her head wearily: I had been very stupid.

"Certainly *not*," she said. "I took him to a cinema in Leicester Square and told him to wait there till I came for him. Then I had a drink and went to the Bonaparte by myself."

She began to laugh. It was very funny—the whole thing was hysterically funny. To think that she had been so frightened, by anything so simple! This amused her intensely. She went in, she said, trembling like a rabbit—absolutely trembling like a rabbit. The crowds, the smoke, the mirrors—the whole thing dazzled her. She had no idea what she was doing. She walked in as fast as she could and sat down in the first empty seat she came to. And then, right off, she saw a sign which said that ladies without escort were not admitted. Imagine. A waiter was rushing toward her, and she was on the point of running out again in a panic, when a man sat down opposite her and said good evening. Just like that: she nodded at me for emphasis. He asked her to have a drink with him and she accepted. Then he invited her to dine with him. He was very nice—a clean type of man, she could see that at a glance. But when he asked her to dine with him, she didn't know quite what to do. . . . She asked me if I saw the difficulty of the situation, and I said that I did.

"I couldn't leave the boy there all evening without his dinner, could I. . . ."

"Of course not."

So she told the man all about it. He asked her questions, and got more and more interested. She could see that he was surprised: of course, that was natural enough. But he was damned nice about it. And he said, when he heard the whole story, that that settled it—they would go and get the boy and all three have dinner together. He paid for the drinks, and they went round the corner to the cinema theater, where she got the boy; and then the three of them went to a Spanish restaurant for dinner. It was the first real dinner, she said, they'd had for a long time. A big bottle of wine, fried eggs with bananas, some Spanish sweets for the boy—they both ate themselves almost sick. And the whole thing was so funny, when she stopped to think about it. She and the Major—he was a major —both said that at the time. They couldn't get over it. They laughed and laughed. . . . And the Major kept patting the boy on the head and calling him Cupido. After that, he always called him Cupido. The boy and the Major took to each other at sight, you might say. . . .

The *really* funny thing, however, came later: it was when it came time for them to go home.

"It was when we were in the taxi, and the boy kept going off to sleep, that it first came to me. . . ."

The trouble was that there was only the one bed, where she and the boy always slept together. She couldn't think how they were going to manage. When they got to the flat in Bayswater, she showed the Major how it was. Just the two rooms, and the one bed, and the boy so sleepy that he couldn't stand up. . . . Had I ever heard of a situation like that?

I admitted that I hadn't.

"So what did you do?" I asked.

She didn't answer me at once—she wanted to be sure, first of all, that I savored the situation to the full. She cocked her head on one side again, breathed smoke out through haughty nostrils, and surveyed me with amused cynicism. The point was too good: it must not be hurried over. Situations like that, she seemed to imply, didn't occur too often in life, and should be relished for all they were worth.

"The Major settled it," she then said. "We put the boy to bed and waited. When he was asleep, we picked him up and carried him into the sitting room and put him on the floor. And later on we carried him back again. . . . While we were waiting for him to fall asleep we just talked."

She smiled at me, with an air of modest pride and triumph, and I smiled back. Tacitly, thus, we agreed that life was a really extraordinary business. You could never tell what tricks it would play. She and the Major and Cupido, there in the little flat together, and for that astonishing purpose—could I ask for a queerer thing than that, or one that did her greater credit? It was really unparalleled—really unique. . . .

III.   After that, it had been comparatively plain sailing. The Major continued to look after them, and she and Cupido had lived in what you might call luxury. They had everything they wanted. Holidays two or three times a year at the seaside, good clothes, good food. The Major was very fond of Cupido, and talked of putting him into a school. Two or three times a week he came and dined with them, or took them to the theater. Everything went along beautifully; she was happy for the first time in her life. But then all of a sudden, out of clear sky, Mac came walking in. Just strolled in to tea, with a bag full of crumpets, as if he'd never been away. She cried all night, wondering what to do. The next day it all came out by accident—it was when Mac said something about where they were going to dine that evening. Cupido piped up with "But Mummy, tonight, don't you remember, we're having dinner with the Major." "Major? What Major?" said Mac; and the whole thing came out, then and there. There was hell to pay. It was the end of Mac, however—he kicked things around a bit, and then put on his tunic and went. It was the last she ever saw of him, and a good riddance, too.

"I was properly fed up with him," she said.

I said that I didn't blame her, and got up to replenish the glasses. Then I asked her about the Major. Had he sent the boy to school? He sounded to me like a good fellow.

She gave a flaccid little laugh, brief and bitter.

"What do you suppose?" she said. "No, he didn't."

This, apparently, had been too much to expect. But she bore him no grudge—quite the contrary. He had continued to stand by them for three and a half years after that, which wasn't so bad.

"Especially," she added, "considering that I wasn't as young as I used to be. I was getting on. My looks were going. And when I finally lost them, I lost the Major. He just went off to France and never came back. Wrote me a lovely letter, and enclosed a draft for a hundred pounds. He didn't try to make excuses: that wasn't his way, ever. He just said 'My dear, our affair has run its course.' That was all. I couldn't blame him. I cried my eyes out, and I didn't know really what to do with myself at first, as if I was lost, but I didn't blame him."

"I suppose it's what you have to expect," I said.

"It's what *women* have to expect," she answered.

"Well, it's a man-made world, and no mistake—what did you do then?"

She shrugged her shoulders, relaxed, sighed, seemed suddenly to become a great deal older.

"I did the only thing I could do. I went back to the Bonaparte."

"Oh?"

"I made the hundred pounds last as long as I could, first—but when it was getting low, I saw that I'd better do something. So I went back. But it was too late."

I failed to catch her meaning, and she rather wearily explained. She was too old, that was all—the men paid no attention to her. Evening after evening she would sit in the

Bonaparte, drinking coffees, only to come away alone. To begin with she had been too proud to give up; refused to admit the truth. But then it dawned on her. Her clothes were giving out —she had to find something else—so she hit on the cinema. She began to haunt the cheaper cinemas, and found that she could just make a living out of it. She would approach men— preferably the older ones—as she had approached me. She had two or three "regulars" whom she saw every few days. They gave her half a crown, and sometimes a drink or two afterward. It was, in fact, one of her regulars—an old man—whom she had been waiting for this afternoon, at the Elite Palace, when *I* had come along. So that was that.

"What an extraordinary thing!" I said.

She didn't seem to think so. It was like everything else.

"What can you expect?" she said.

I suddenly remembered the Proctors, and the distance from Marble Arch to St. John's Wood; and I looked at my watch.

"The only thing is," she went on, "if I should happen to be ill. What would I do? . . . For instance, one day last autumn I slipped on those greasy cobbles in Covent Garden and hurt my ankle. I fainted among the cabbages and cauliflowers and when I came to I was in the ambulance. They took me to the hospital and gave me ether. I had such a funny dream when I went under—I was stuck in a long red sewer-pipe, with one doctor putting his head in one end and another at the other, and both of them bellowing at me to come out. Suppose it had been something serious? As it was, I was only laid up for a fortnight, and it happened I had enough money. The boy went shopping, and I could hobble round enough to cook. But suppose I'd got a broken leg. . . . My God! . . ."

She gave an amused, rather maternal, chuckle.

"It would be awkward," I admitted.

There was a pause, and then I said that I would have to be going. She flushed, looked a little scared, cleared her throat.

"You couldn't spare me half a crown, could you?" she said.

"I think I'll stop here and have a sandwich."

I took out a ten-shilling note and gave it to her. She thanked me.

"Goodbye," I said, shaking her hand, "and the best of luck."

She half stood up, and then sank back into her chair, smiling confusedly.

"If you're ever in the Elite Palace again—" she said.

"Right-o."

I pushed open the glass door and went out. It was still raining. A clock was striking the half hour. I walked to Oxford Street, hailed a taxi, and started off to St. John's Wood.

Ann and Jim would already be mixing the cocktails. Poppy would be playing the piano, and the host of kittens would be charging from end to end of the long corridor under the rain-sounding skylight. I would tell them about it—I would tell them what life was really like. Would they believe me? Yes, they would be fascinated. It was just the sort of thing to tell at dinner—it would start the party off admirably. And then there would be a discussion. I could hear Jim saying "But is life that, or is it this—the four of us sitting here and talking about it?" Poppy would be bored, as usual, and Ann would be furious. Jim would offer us a choice of vermouth or beer. We would drink, talk, listen to music, wonder whether a little more garlic ought to have been injected in the lamb. Poppy would tell us about X's, the painter's, latest rout. And meanwhile, the West End lady, having finished her sandwich and perhaps her fourth glass of port, would be returning to the Elite Palace.

"Don't be melancholy, darling, I'm sure it will all come out all right."

"But how often have I got to tell you that I'm *not* melancholy? I'm not melancholy at all. I'm afraid you're old-fashioned. You just think I *ought* to be melancholy!"

"It's all these subterfuges, all this concealment. The way you had to go to the hospital under an assumed name. And signing a false name to the birth certificate. And now living here in this one-horse town! Good lord."

She smiled at him, as if affectionately amused by his despair, took his arm, and they walked slowly, very slowly, up the little hill in the park. He kept his head lowered, as if thinking, and when he didn't respond to a repeated tug at his elbow, she brought her face so close to his that her forehead touched the rim of his hat.

"Besides," she said, "you're forgetting that the whole idea was mine. Wasn't it?"

"Oh, I know, but that has nothing to do with it. There's so much I want to do for you and Bibs, and can't. You oughtn't to be living here, buried away like this, and especially as I can

only get here so seldom. No. And all the time I have the funniest
feeling——"

"What?"

"Well, it makes me laugh sometimes. But I keep feeling that
you and Bibs ought to be living with the rest of us."

"*That's* a bright idea. Your wife would be so glad, wouldn't
she?"

"Gosh, yes. Just the same, if you ever saw the other kids——"
He stopped suddenly, and grinned at her.

"*That* would be all right. But suppose *she* saw *Bibs!* She'd
know it in a flash."

They resumed the walk, very slowly, they passed under a
maple tree, scarlet leaves had fallen on the path from the scarlet
mass above them, and the sweet smoke came up to them from
a smudge fire at the bottom of the hill. The delicious melancholy held them still for a moment. They stood under the tree
and said nothing.

"That's for instance why it would be, I suppose, dangerous
for you to live in New York. God knows New York's large
enough, but if you ever *did* meet——"

"It's got to be postponed."

"And that's the sort of thing that makes me sick. This everlasting secrecy. Hole in corner."

"I told you in the beginning that I knew all about that and
was prepared for it. Didn't I? And that I assumed full responsibility. It's my funeral, not yours."

"That's exactly what I'm afraid of, Enn——"

"Oh, I didn't mean *that!*"

"It's bound to be, at least in some respects. It isn't good for
you. You haven't met a soul here. The minute you meet people,
they'd begin to smell a rat. Mrs. Doane suspects already—I
could see it this morning when I met her here with Bibs."

"Well, what did she do, did she bite you, or give you a dirty
look?"

He didn't answer. He disengaged his arm, took out a cigarette and lit it; then flung the smoking match into a red privet bush. He was frowning. He thought how odd it was that Enn could take the whole situation so calmly. He was even tempted to believe that she was somehow lacking—but lacking in what, he found it difficult to say. Morals? But there could be no question of that—the moral issue had never arisen, there was no such thing. If it was anything, it was something like delicacy. Or was it merely that she was sensible—more sensible than any woman he had ever met.

"O God, Enn, there are so many things. That awful dingy apartment of yours. And the neighbors watching you."

She took his arm again, and shook him, and laughed, her long gray eyes narrowing provocatively.

"Is that all? Is there something more?"

"Heaps. What about Bibs?"

"How do you mean, what about Bibs?"

"Well, she's four. She notices things. She knows when I spend the night there. That would be all right, if only—"

"What?"

"She knew I was her father."

She drew a deep sigh, looked away from him, said nothing. Then she pulled him closer, with her hand under his arm—so closely and so tenderly that to walk thus together, with their knees touching and disengaging, arm against arm and side against side, became difficult, and slow, and self-conscious, a delicious and awkward intimacy.

If I could only go on like this, if only it could always be like this. Their bodies seemed to be saying it, but their faces and minds were averted. He felt extraordinarily touched. It was tragic, it was beautiful.

"I sometimes wonder if you really feel it, Enn."

"Don't be a goose."

"But really, I do."

"You silly boy, we've been over it so often, haven't we? You must reconcile yourself that Bibs is mine. Not yours, mine. You agreed to that. I wanted her, not you."

"Oh, I know all that. It's a good theory."

They had come to the bench at the top of the hill. Below them the little river, with birches along the nearer margin, turned out of sight under the dilapidated wooden bridge. He remembered how they had come here before Bibs was born—he remembered the last time of all, when she had wanted to come up to see the sunset, and he had tried in vain to dissuade her, and they had climbed up so slowly, and she had turned so white. What was it she had said, something very funny. A quotation from somebody. Oh, yes—"O to be oviparous, now that spring is here."

"Do you think Mrs. Doane is a good influence, Enn?"

She had sat down on the bench, her hands flat on the green wood, the fingers spread out fanwise.

"Of course. She's as good as gold. She adores Bibs."

"I know. But I don't like the slang."

"Oh, don't worry about the slang. Good heavens, if that was all!"

"What do you mean?"

"It's when I go down to New York to see you; when I'm away —all those weeks. When I come back, Bibs likes Mrs. Doane better than she does me. She always says she wants to stay with Boo. You know she calls her Boo."

He stood facing her, his head a little on one side, his cigarette lightly held between two fingers.

"And do you think that's good? Do you think it's so good?"

"Of course I don't think it's good. But what can we do? *Somebody's* got to look after her when I go away."

"But why not be sensible and give up your job, and let *me* swing it?"

Alternately, she slapped her hands on the bench, in a queer and mountingly mischievous rhythm, then clapped them together before her, wrung them at him, and laughed.

"The possessive male!"

"Possessive nonsense! It's simply a question of what's best

for you and Bibs. This sort of thing is no good. It's sure to hurt you both."

She was still smiling, but as he watched her intently, her expression gradually became one of quizzical scrutiny. She looked up at him sidelong, as if making a careful appraisal.

"Are you sure you're being quite straight about this? You love Bibs and want her. You love me and want me. You don't want to be independent. Do you?"

He turned his back and took a few steps toward the edge of the grass slope. At the bottom of the hill he could see a man emptying a basket of dead leaves on the smudge fire: the bright flames shot up for a moment into the basket as if licking away the last few morsels of the year. What Enn said was, of course, perfectly true. Or partly true. But that didn't really change it —not at all. He watched the man walk slowly along the path and drop the basket into a wheelbarrow. Yes, partly true—he did want to have them, to keep them. And why not? It seemed ridiculous that he shouldn't. They were—they ought to be—a part of his life.

Enn's voice floated toward him lightly—it gave him oddly, before he turned, the feeling that she was watching him very closely, very affectionately.

"Don't be melancholy, darling! It will all come out all right!"

She was laughing at him, laughing at her use of his own words.

"Curse you, Enn—you never can be serious for five minutes on end." He said this as he walked back to the bench: he sat down beside her and dropped his hat on the grass. "What's going to happen to her when she goes to school—when she finds that other children have fathers, when they ask her who her father was? I suppose you'll have to tell her some damned fairy story about it. And then what about me? As she gets older, and sees me around—what's she going to think? She's no fool —believe me, she'll put two and two together and make it sex! And a hell of a lot of good that will do her. She'll end by hating me."

"Darling!"

He suddenly felt sorry for himself, he felt hurt and angry and stubborn, he wanted to be urged or comforted, and this feeling was only accentuated when she dropped her hand on his knee and lightly pinched him.

"No, Enn, it's no use."

"But darling! you forget there is such a thing as *time*. Lots can happen, lots *will* happen. All this is only a phase. When the time comes, I'll go to New York and get a job there. I'll adopt Bibs—she'll take my name, and it will be easy enough later to explain to her that I took her from an orphanage, or that nobody knew who her parents were. You'll see, it will be quite simple."

She said this unhurriedly, almost as if with no attempt to persuade—the effect upon him was to make him feel that she was, as always, overwhelmingly reasonable.

"Well, what about me—when she's older, she's sure to suspect. What about that?"

"I know, my dear. But there are other things to consider. It might be that you wouldn't any longer—be coming to see me. We might decide—for Bib's sake—that it would be better if we separated. You might decide to give us up. Or fall in love with someone else. Or even, just decide to be a devoted father to your *own* children. After all, you *have* got them, and you do love them. It isn't as if you had nothing else. Or as if you need to begrudge me Bibs. Is it?"

"O good Lord."

"We might as well be practical about it."

"Practical!"

He took out his leather cigarette case, tapped a fresh cigarette repeatedly on the back of it, and lit it from the stub. Then with his forefinger he touched her hand, which still lay on his knee. She was smiling at him, but her eyes were grave, and he gave her a quick smile in answer.

"You ought to have been a lawyer, Enn. You're the most

devilishly and unmitigatedly reasonable being I ever met. If I didn't know better, I'd say you had no heart."

"But you do know better, don't you. . . . I'm sorry you've got to go back tonight."

"So am I."

They were both silent; a curious mutual awareness of peace came upon them, they watched the smoke from the smudge fire, which the breeze was idly sculpturing into a long blue curve over the river, over the tops of the birches. A policeman had stopped to talk to the man with the wheelbarrow. The sun was beginning to be low—he took out his watch. Four o'clock.

"Four o'clock. What time did you say—"

"I told her to bring Bibs here at half-past three. She must be late."

"She *is* late."

"Well, she probably won't be *very* late, because she has to go somewhere, she said, at half-past four. She was just to bring Bibs and go. Perhaps if we walk back—or would you rather stay here?"

"Let's walk."

They walked in silence, with linked arms, and as they turned the shoulder of the little hill, and saw the park below them, and Bibs running up the narrow path toward them, he began to feel for the first time the full force of what Enn had just been saying—(as usual)—with such extraordinary calm. Separation! Yes. It had been hanging over them for a long time, he had always known that sooner or later the shadow would begin to become substance; it was inevitable—or was it?—and now at last it had been spoken of. Very likely she had foreseen it from the outset—it was like her to foresee things, to plan things— she had known that sooner or later they must separate, and she had quite calmly decided to have Bibs, if only as an insurance against a bankruptcy which might otherwise have been complete. Yes. That was it. And now, as a consequence of the foresight itself, and as a consequence of Bibs, the separation, which she had merely foreseen as a possibility, was gradually becoming a necessity: Bibs, whom she had decided to have as a protection, must now be protected: cause had led to effect, and now effect was leading to cause. It was this—and he knew somehow that the same thoughts were in her mind, the same feelings —it was this that made her now tighten her hold on his arm, now as Bibs came running toward them, with her blue leggings and blue beret and a wilted stalk of blue chicory in her hand, tightly held. This—she was saying—is what you are losing, a part of yourself, which you must lose. And Bibs, who seems to be running straight toward you, chattering and laughing to herself, making up one of her absurd and delicious stories, will not stop here, or greet you, but will pass by and go on, you will never see her again.

"And did you see the Christmas trees, all the Christmas trees, Mummy? They said how-do. I said how-do to them and they said how-do to me."

"But you haven't said how-do to Boyar."

"Will you give Boyar a big kiss?"

"No. Did you see the how-do trees, Boyar?"

"Yes, I saw the how-do trees."

When Mrs. Doane had gone, they counted the Christmas trees, and said how-do to them, and he took off his hat and shook one of them by the hand.

"And Boo says their fathers were little teeny tiny tiny *tiny* seeds, no bigger than—no bigger than a—"

"What?"

"No bigger than a *pumpkin!* An old gray pumpkin man with gray teeth and gray ears!"

"Did Boo say that?"

"Yes, Boo said that."

"And who was *your* father, Bibs? Was he a pumpkin man too?"

"Tell Boyar, blueberry."

The "secret" expression came over her face: she stood still, she held the chicory flower before her, and gazed at it, smiling at her delicious and secret idea.

"No, he wasn't a pumpkin man. He was a—he was a—he was a—"

She began to squeal with delight, she was planning a joke, a surprise. And at once she announced triumphantly:

"He was a June-bug!"

"A June-bug! Are you sure? Why Bibs!"

"Yes, he was a June-bug. And he flew and he flew and he flew and he flew and he flew!"

Conrad Aiken was born in Savannah, Georgia, on August 5, 1889. He was graduated from Harvard in the famous class of 1911 (among his contemporaries in Cambridge were Walter Lippmann, John Reed, and T. S. Eliot). Mr. Aiken's first book, *Earth Triumphant,* a volume of poetry, appeared in 1914. Since then he has published nearly forty books—poetry, short stories, novels, criticism, drama, autobiography—and has also compiled several anthologies. Mr. Aiken was a contributing editor to the old *Dial,* London correspondent of *The New Yorker* (under the pseudonym Samuel Jeake, Jr.), and a teacher of English at Harvard where one of his students was Nathan Pusey, later President of the University. Many honors have come his way: the Chair of Poetry at the Library of Congress, a Pulitzer Prize, the National Book Award, the Bollingen Prize, a Guggenheim Fellowship. His work appears in numerous anthologies and textbooks.

Mr. Aiken's *Collected Poems* were published in 1953. His best known novels are *Blue Voyage, Great Circle,* and *King Coffin.* An autobiography, *Ushant,* was published in 1952, and a collection of his criticism, *A Reviewer's ABC,* appeared in 1958.

Mr. Aiken is the father of three children. He and his wife, Mary, now divide their time between two homes, in Brewster, Massachusetts, and in Manhattan.